CW00670950

Captain W.E. Johns

This edition first published in 2010 by

Prion
An imprint of the
Carlton Publishing Group,
20 Mortimer Street,
London W1T 3JW

King of the Commandos First published in 1943
Gimlet Goes Again First published in 1944
Gimlet Comes Home First published in 1946
Gimlet Mops Up First published in 1947

Copyright © W. E. Johns (Publications) Ltd.

All rights reserved.

This book is sold subject to the condition that it may not be reproduced, stored in a retrieval
system or transmitted in any form or by any means, electronic, mechanical, photocopying
recording or otherwise without
the publisher's prior consent.

A catalogue record for this book is available from the British Library

ISBN 978-1-85375-768-6

Illustrations by:
King of the Commandos and *Gimlet Mops Up* – Walter Foster
Gimlet Goes Again – Studio Stead
Gimlet Comes Home – Dylan Roberts

Typeset by e-type, Liverpool
Printed in Thailand

1 3 5 7 9 10 8 6 4 2

Contents

Introduction

Gimlet? Now there's a strange name. What on earth is a 'gimlet'? And why would Captain W.E. Johns, creator of Biggles, one of the most successful boys' adventure story heroes of all time, choose to name one of his characters Gimlet?

It sounds like it could be a pet that one of Tolkien's Hobbits would keep at home in 'The Shires'. You can just imagine Frodo Baggins sitting laughing with his friends Sam, Pippin and Merry, feeding acorns to their tame gimlet. But that doesn't seem right. W.E. Johns' Gimlet is no adorable pet. He is a ruthless warrior who kills without compunction – and he is anything but tame.

'Gimlet' also hints at industrial connotations, as though it might be a small but vital part of some monstrous machine tool, probably the bit that keeps breaking and dropping off. In fact, although it's not a huge industrial asset nowadays, a gimlet really is a workman's tool. It is a kind of drill bit with a wooden cross handle that is used for boring holes in wood. It looks a little like an old-fashioned corkscrew that you would use for opening a bottle of wine. Now we're getting a little warmer with our guessing game. A gimlet is no imaginary, soft, fluffy pet but a sharp instrument of cold steel. That sounds much more like a fighting man.

The penetrating quality of the gimlet tool inspired the use of the phrase to 'stare with gimlet eyes', a 'gimlet-eyed' look being a steely gaze that truly penetrated any defences that the object of the gaze might have deployed, seeing through any disguise or subterfuge. That's a lot more like W.E. Johns' Gimlet. He was the sort of chap who could immediately tell whether someone was being straight with him and he was direct enough not to shy away from delivering a penetrating stare while deciding whether another chap was made of the right stuff. You could almost believe that the phrase, 'gimlet-eyed stare', was invented with our Gimlet in mind.

W.E. Johns was definitely aware of the hand-held-drill meaning of his hero's name, referring to the gimlet tool in a letter he wrote to promote the Gimlet series. The letter appeared in W.E. Johns' books and was addressed 'to every boy who reads this book'. In the letter Johns warned his readers that the tough commando's 'methods are not always as gentlemanly as Biggles" and says that he is still in action, this being long after the end of the Second World War, 'not regularly, but from time to time when something unusual crops up, some nut that cannot be opened by normal diplomatic nutcrackers. Gimlet usually manages to bore a hole in it.'

Now we're getting a good deal closer to finding out where this weird name came from, but there are still another couple of pieces to slot into the puzzle because a gimlet is not merely a boring tool (no pun intended), it is also an alcoholic cocktail. To make a gimlet you mix a measure of gin with a drop of lime and a dash of soda. Like all cocktails, of course, there are variations on the recipe. Some would replace the gin with vodka, serve it over ice or insist that it is shaken, not stirred, like James Bond's vodka martini. While he preferred his own precisely defined vodka cocktail concoction, James Bond would have known all about the gimlet. He was, after all Commander Bond of the Royal Naval Volunteer Reserve, and the gimlet was a drink invented for officers of the Royal Navy. In an attempt to persuade his fellow officers to take lime juice (which contains an abundance of vitamin C) in order to ward off the debilitating disease, scurvy (which stems from a lack of vitamin C), the gimlet was invented by ship's surgeon Sir Thomas Gimlette. Sir Thomas joined the Royal Navy in 1879 and served until 1913 when he retired as Surgeon General, having enjoyed a successful naval career as well as giving his name to a cocktail for the wardroom.

So the Royal Navy may also have leant a hand in inspiring Gimlet's unusual name, even though the navy was the one branch of the armed forces in which Gimlet did not serve. He certainly wasn't like Commander Bond, although Gimlet may have been one of Bond creator Ian Fleming's many inspirations. W.E. Johns' all-action hero appeared in ten books and one short story collection. The first Gimlet adventure, *King of the*

Commandos, was published during the Second World War in 1943 while the final book, *Gimlet Takes A Job*, appeared in 1954, just a few months after Ian Fleming's Bond was brought to life in his first book, *Casino Royale*.

Now that we are close to the root of his nickname, which Johns maintains in the letter to his readers was coined for Gimlet by the men who served under him, perhaps we should take a look at from where the idea for such a character emerged. Captain Lorrington King, D.S.O., M.C. and Bar came from a long line of military heroes. We learn from the Gimlet books that both his father and his grandfather had been awarded the Victoria Cross, his father earning his VC in the First World War and his grandfather being awarded his for heroism during the Boer War. The King family had a distinguished heritage, Gimlet living on a country estate at Lorrington Hall in Devon and, in *Gimlet Comes Home*, inheriting another estate, Strathcarglas, in Scotland. If any further proof were required of Gimlet's aristocratic ancestry then it comes with the fact that he served as an officer in a guards regiment before the Second World War. Only those from society's top drawer had the privilege of being selected to become guards' officers.

When war broke out, however, Gimlet decided he wanted to fight not on the ground but in the air. He trained as a fighter pilot and flew in the Battle of Britain. He shot down two enemy aircraft on one sortie, having taken off still dressed in his tennis kit and was later lucky to survive a mid-air collision with another German. He went on to form his own commando unit that became known as 'King's Kittens' after their wildcat insignia. You might think that W.E. Johns went a little off track with his new character at this point, but if you find it a bit hard to believe that an aristocratic former guards officer would be given command of an elite outfit of special forces raiders, then you don't need to look far to find a precedent. Former Scots Guards officer Simon Fraser, 15th Lord Lovat, led commando raids on the Lofoten Islands in Norway, on targets on the French coast that earned him the Military Cross and took No 4 Commando to Dieppe as its Commanding Officer, achieving his objectives and earning the Distinguished Service Order, despite the fact that the raid itself was a catastrophe. On D-Day in 1944, Lord Lovat waded ashore with his men, accompanied by his personal piper Bill Millin, who played his bagpipes as Lovat led his unit towards the enemy. Meanwhile, another Scots Guards officer, Lord Lovat's cousin David Stirling, had broken off his training to climb Mount Everest in order to lend his weight to the war effort by forming another elite unit, the SAS.

W.E. Johns could not, however, make King's Kittens like any real commando unit. The real commandos' training methods and the specialist equipment that they used were highly secret when Gimlet's first adventure, *King of the Commandos*, was published in 1943. Johns' had to rely on his own military training to make the stories as realistic as possible.

William Earl Johns, having trained as a surveyor, was working as a sanitary inspector in Norfolk when, with war looming, he first joined the Territorial Army in 1913. When war broke out in 1914, his regiment was based in Britain while still in training, but by the autumn of 1915 he found himself on the SS *Olympic*, sister ship to the ill-fated *Titanic*, heading for Gallipoli. He saw action in the trenches in the Dardanelles before being shipped out to Suez and retrained as a machine gunner to be sent to fight in Greece.

While recovering from a bout of malaria in 1917, Johns applied to join the Royal Flying Corps and was accepted, being sent home to learn to fly at the School of Military Aeronautics at Reading. Like so many budding pilots at that time, Johns had his fair share of crashes and near misses, such was the inadequacy of the training aircraft available, but he survived to qualify as a pilot. He was then sent to Marske-by-the-Sea where the Commanding Officer of the air base was Major Champion, still bearing his old army Royal Flying Corps rank despite the new Royal Air Force having now been established. Major Champion was affectionately nicknamed 'Gimlet'. Clearly, that was a name that was going to stick in Johns' memory.

Johns was soon in action in France as a bomber pilot with 55 Squadron, flying the two-man De Havilland DH 4 biplane. He took part in numerous raids but always made it home until one sortie in September 1918 saw Johns and his observer fall foul of a formation of enemy fighters. Their wood-and-fabric bomber was riddled with machine gun rounds from the German aircraft, forcing Johns to crash land in a field. His observer had been killed during the air battle and Johns, wounded in the leg, was taken prisoner. He spent the next two months attempting to escape, never managing to evade re-capture for more than a few days, until the war came to an end in November 1918. Johns' arrival home in December was a shock to his wife and young son as he had been listed as missing and presumed dead!

Having no wish to return to civilian life, Johns tenaciously clung on to his RAF commission through the swingeing post-war cutbacks, working as a flying instructor and later as a recruitment officer. He famously turned down an applicant named John Hume Ross who wanted to enlist as an Aircraftman, not knowing that the man was actually Lieutenant Colonel Thomas Edward Lawrence – Lawrence of Arabia. Lawrence did ultimately manage to join the RAF.

Johns was to remain in the air force until 1928, by which time he was also writing and had begun to produce illustrations, mainly of aircraft, which was to provide him with a new career when he eventually left the RAF. The illustrations Johns had supplied to various magazines led to him writing articles about flying and eventually to becoming the editor of *Popular Flying* magazine. It was in this publication that James Bigglesworth, created by Johns in a short story for the first issue of the magazine, first appeared in an adventure called 'The White Fokker'. In 1932, Johns' Biggles short stories were assembled in a collection called *The Camels Are Coming*, the first in a series that would run to almost 100 books over a period of 35 years.

By the time the Second World War began in 1939, Johns was, at the age of 46, too old for military service as a pilot, but he found he had another role to play. So many young men who applied to become pilots with the RAF claimed that they had done so because they were inspired by Johns' *Biggles* adventures, that the Air Ministry suggested Johns might encourage recruitment to the W.A.A.F. – the Women's Auxiliary Air Force – by writing a series of adventures based around a female central character. No sooner said than done – Flight Officer Joan Worralson, 'Worrals' to her friends, first appeared in *Worrals of the W.A.A.F.* in 1941. The intrepid adventuress was to star in a further ten books up to 1950.

So, if Biggles helped to encourage recruitment to the RAF, and Worrals did the same for the W.A.A.F., why shouldn't Johns create an army hero as well? The War Office thought it was a great idea, giving Johns every encouragement to develop a character that would do for the army what

Biggles had done for the RAF. Paper was in short supply during the war years, forcing some magazines and newspapers to suspend publication and limiting the number of books that were published. Some priority was, however, given to books that could be distributed for the entertainment of British troops around the world. Such books were integral to the propaganda drive, uplifting stories of British heroes triumphing in the face of seemingly insurmountable odds, designed to help raise the morale not only of our armed forces, but also of those at home. The first of the Gimlet books were to become part of that propaganda effort, although such was the popularity of the character that his adventures continued long after the war was over.

At last we seem to have got to the bottom of it. A gimlet is not some kind of cute pet from a fantasy realm, or a small psiart that's dropped off a machine in a factory. It is a sharp, steel tool; a bold, discomforting look in the eyes; a toff's cocktail invented for naval officers; the nickname of one of W.E. Johns' commanding officers and, for all those reasons, the nickname that Johns' gave to his wartime army recruitment and propaganda hero, Captain Lorrington King.

A letter to every boy who reads this book

A MAN YOU SHOULD KNOW

Have you met Captain Lorrington King, D.S.O., one time leader of the hard-smiting commando unit known to the three services as King's Kittens? You may remember him better by the significant nickname coined for him by his Kittens – Gimlet, because in the stories of his wartime exploits Biggles more than once played a part by taking him and his lads to the objective, or collecting them after the job in hand had been buttoned up. Gimlet's trusted assistants were, you may recall, a Cockney corporal named "Copper" Collson; the taciturn French Canadian, "Trapper" Troublay, and "Cub" Peters, who ran away from school to look for his father at Dunkirk, was left behind at the evacuation, and with some French boys founded a gang called "the Grey Fleas of the North" to nibble the skin of the enemy when he was trying to rest.

Gimlet is still on the job – not regularly, but from time to time when something unusual crops up, some nut that cannot be opened by normal diplomatic nutcrackers. Gimlet usually manages to bore a hole in it. So if you haven't met him keep an eye open. He's around in the bookshops. His adventures have been told in the following books: – KING OF THE COMMANDOS, GIMLET COMES HOME, GIMLET GOES AGAIN, GIMLET MOPS UP, GIMLET'S ORIENTAL QUEST, GIMLET LENDS A HAND.

A word of warning. His methods are not always as gentlemanly as Biggles'. When things get rough he's apt to get tough. Which is why, of course, he was given a bunch of wildcats to command. After all, kid gloves are about as useful to a commando on his job as roller skates would be to a steeplejack.

Yours Aeronautically,

W.E. Johns

KING OF THE COMMANDOS

CHAPTER ONE

A Strange Encounter

Night had drawn its black-out curtain across the coast of Northern France; but like most black-out curtains it was not perfect; from time to time a crescent moon peered mistily through lowering clouds which, as sullen and menacing as the Nazi invaders who had set their heel upon the land, marched in endless procession across the dome of heaven. The dim light fell on a bleak, deserted foreshore, and close at hand, the uneasy waters of the English Channel.

From the summit of a low dune, lying deep in the coarse grass that softened its outline, Corporal Collson regarded the scene without emotion – Corporal Albert Edward Collson, to give him his full name.

Not that anyone called him Albert – at any rate, not in the Special Service Troop of the Combined Operations unit, No. 9 Commando, of which he was a member.

In that small band of hard-hitting warriors, sometimes known as King's 'Kittens', he was invariably known as 'Copper', due to the fact that he had once been a member of the Metropolitan Police. He bore no resemblance whatever to a kitten. It happened that the shoulder cypher chosen for No. 9 Commando was a wildcat.

This, with that whimsical humour which is never far distant from British fighting men, had been interpreted by other commando units as a kitten. Captain Lorrington King happened to be the commanding officer – whence the title, King's Kittens.

As we have remarked, Copper Collson had nothing in common with a kitten. His six feet two inches of bone and muscle, which had twice enabled him to win the City Heavyweight Championship, would, he had decided, be better employed in smiting the enemy who had bombed his Wapping home, than in directing London's traffic. In this he was undoubtedly correct, for apart from his sometimes startling strength, he had other qualifications for the work on which he was now engaged.

He made no secret of the fact that he had been brought up, to use his own expression, 'rough.' He did not mention, however, that his father had died when he was a boy, leaving him with the responsibility of supporting an invalid mother. That he had got on sufficiently well to gain admittance to the River Police was due more to shrewd Cockney alertness than education.

Another detail he did not mention was that, prior to joining the police, an uncle had given him an intensive course of instruction in petty crime, with the result that he could pick anything, from locks to pockets. But when this same uncle had made a slip that resulted in his being sent to prison for five years, young Albert had the wit to perceive that as a means of gaining a livelihood, crime had such definite disadvantages that he abandoned it forthwith – not that he had started on it seriously.

From errand boy he had worked his way up the ladder until at last he found himself in a blue uniform, this being the immediate limit of his ambition. In this capacity, his early training in crooks and their methods stood him in good stead.

As a commando, combined with his waterfront experience and knowledge of small craft, it was even more useful.

For the rest, his methods were direct and simple. Like all true Londoners he loved his London, and his transference to one of the first commando units followed swiftly upon the blitzing of the City, when his home, like many others, had disappeared in a cloud of dust and rubble. His mother had survived, but true to type had refused to leave London, and now occupied a room in the house of a friendly neighbour.

'I want to get my hands on the blokes who done this to London,' he had told his superintendent grimly, when he had applied for transfer.

The superintendent had smiled, and let him go. And in due course Copper had got his huge hands on 'some of the blokes who had knocked his house about', not once, but several times. On these occasions there was definitely nothing kittenish about him.

At the moment he was lying among the dunes that fringed the coast of Northern France with a Sten gun snuggled against his side. He had been lying there for an hour, which, in his opinion, was too long, and he made a remark to this effect to his one companion.

'*Ma foi*! You've said it,' was the impatient reply, in a curious foreign accent tinged with American drawl. 'I tink something goes wrong with Gimlet this time.'

And in case it should be thought strange that a British commando should speak with a foreign accent it must be explained that Private 'Trapper' Troublay was not, from the point of view of breeding, entirely English. He was, in fact, a French Canadian, a lean, dapper product of the great backwoods, wherein he had spent ten of his early years of life as a trapper and prospector. Hence his nickname, Trapper.

Having spent most of his time hunting in the wilds, often in the company of Indians, it followed naturally that he should have exceptional sight and hearing; that he should be a deadly shot; and when it came to stalking, he could move with no more noise than the moon passing across the heavens. All these were very useful accomplishments for a commando.

Copper and Trapper were more than ordinary comrades. They had first met at the training centre, but it was not until the raid on Glamfjord Power Station, in Norway, that they had hooked up in the arrangement known in the Commandos as 'me and my pal'; wherein two men make a pact to stand by each other through thick and thin. They had been through the carnage at Dieppe together, as well as in several smaller raids, when Trapper's knowledge of French had come in useful.

Trapper's French accent, which became more pronounced under the stress of excitement, had at first worried Copper somewhat, because, as he often declared, he hadn't much time for foreigners.

Copper had also looked with sceptical amusement at a small piece of private equipment which Trapper carried on his forays in enemy country – but only until he perceived how useful it could be. This was a weapon, a weapon one would hardly expect to find in a war of high-velocity firearms. It was, in fact, a bow and arrow – quite a small one. Its advantage, a great advantage on commando work, was that it made no noise beyond a faint *phung* when an arrow was released. Trapper's skill with this deadly toy was uncanny. Yet this again was not remarkable, as he had explained, for on more than one occasion when his stores and ammunition had run out in the back of beyond, he had sometimes had to live on this simple weapon for weeks at a stretch.

At first, the C.O. too had smiled tolerantly at this unorthodox addition to standard equipment, but neither he, nor Copper, smiled any longer. When it became necessary to dispose of a Nazi sentry in silence, a sentry who could not be approached without risk of starting an alarm because he was standing in the open, the whisper would go along the line for Trapper. Trapper would take a little arrow from the slim quiver that hung over his right hip. *Phung*! Usually the sentry died without knowing what had struck him.

For ordinary operations Trapper relied on two heavy service revolvers strapped low on his thighs, and, for close work, an Indian, horn-handled, skinning knife, which he could wield, and throw, with fearful dexterity – again the result of long practice. He had once killed a bear that had got him in its clutches with that same knife: and if, as he said with simple logic, it would kill a grisly, it would almost certainly kill a Nazi. Before it had died, the bear had slashed open his face, leaving a scar that he would carry for the rest of his days as a reminder of that grim encounter. The scar could not now be seen, for Trapper's face, like that of his companion, was blackened for night work, commando fashion. White faces are apt to show up even on a dark night.

Copper picked his teeth reflectively with a stalk of grass. 'Gimlet's a long while,' he muttered for the tenth time. 'I hope he ain't bit off more than he can chew single-handed. It must be getting near dawn.'

Trapper grunted – another habit he had acquired from his Indian friends. Then he stiffened, crouching even lower in the grass. '*Enfin*! Someone comes,' he breathed.

Copper had heard nothing, but after hitching the Sten gun forward to cover a deserted road that wound a serpentine course through the dunes, he, too, sank lower into the grass. Silence settled over the scene, a melancholy silence broken only by the gentle sighing of the breeze through the harsh herbage, and the fretting of little wavelets on the beach.

But presently there came another sound; a swift patter of running footsteps; soft, furtive footsteps, as if the runner ran on bare feet.

'That ain't the Skipper,' whispered Copper.

Trapper did not answer. All that could be seen of him, even of his face, were the whites of his eyes and the flash of white teeth under a wisp of black moustache. His right hand moved slowly to the butt of the revolver that lay flat against his thigh.

The runner soon came into view. A slim figure topped a slight rise in the ground about twenty paces distant, and then stopped, looking to right and left with the jerky movements of a startled fawn.

Copper relaxed with a hiss of disappointment. His finger slackened on the trigger of his gun. 'It's only a kid,' he muttered. 'What the devil's he doing here at this time of night?'

The boy, for that much was obvious, spoke in a tense, urgent voice – strangely enough, in English. 'Commandos! Where are you?' he said in a hoarse whisper. 'They've got one of your men. Where are you?'

Trapper slithered away through the grass like a snake, and with no more noise than one. Copper waited for a few seconds and then rose up, huge in the uncertain light.

The boy sprang back with a strangled cry of alarm, which was hardly to be wondered at, for the sudden appearance of the black-faced apparition so near at hand, out of the very ground, as it seemed, would have frightened anyone. Another shadow rose, silently, this time behind the boy, who only stopped when his back came into contact with the hard muzzle of Trapper's revolver.

'Don't shoot, I'm a friend,' said the boy hastily. 'I've brought information.'

Copper advanced. 'All right. You won't be hurt as long as you behave yourself,' he said coldly. 'Who are you and where have you come from?'

'I'm English,' was the quick reply. 'What does it matter where I've come from? You'd better listen to me if you want to save your friend.'

'What's your name?' snapped Copper.

'Peters.'

'What are you doing here?'

'Scouting.'

'And you swam the Channel to get here, I suppose?' suggested Copper sarcastically.

'Listen,' said the boy crisply. 'Half a mile down the road there is a hut.'

'What of it?' demanded Copper suspiciously. His manner was still uncompromising.

'After you came ashore, the three of you—'

'Half a mo,' interrupted Copper. 'Who said there was three of us?'

'I did,' was the curt reply. 'I watched you land.'

Copper frowned. 'So you did, did you? Go on.'

'Two stayed here, and the other went on to the hut,' resumed the boy. 'The hut looks like a radiolocation station, but it isn't. It's a fake. It's a trap to catch raiding commandos. There were Nazis inside, waiting. The man who went along has been captured. The Germans have telephoned for a car to take him away, and for reinforcements to round you up.'

'*Zut!*' growled Trapper.

Copper drew a deep breath. 'You know a lot for a youngster. How did you get hold of all this?'

'I make it my business to know,' answered the boy shortly. 'Having been here for over two years I know a lot more about what goes on than you do.'

'Two years!' gasped Copper. 'Doing what?'

'Sabotaging the enemy,' was the astonishing reply.

'*What!*' Copper's voice was pitched high with incredulity.

'If you stand here talking much longer you'll find yourself in shackles,' declared the boy impatiently. 'If you want to rescue your pal, you'd better be quick about it. If you don't, I'll push off, and leave you to work it out for yourselves.'

'Strike me purple!' choked Copper. 'Who do you think you're bossing about?'

'I reckon you're a couple of loose kittens,' was the casual reply.

Copper sucked in his breath. 'You know a sight too much, my young cockalorum. How many Jerries are there in that hut?'

'Ten, with two sentries outside.'

Trapper chuckled. '*Psst! De l'audace!*'

The boy shrugged his shoulders, and answered coolly in the same language. '*Que faire?*'

'Talk English,' snarled Copper.

'All right,' agreed the boy. 'I'll give it to you straight. I'm not going to stand here talking any longer – it's too dangerous. There's ten thousand francs waiting for the man who turns me into the Germans. That's how badly they want me.'

'For doing what?' asked Copper in a dazed voice.

'Pulling up railway lines, cutting telephone wires, fusing electric circuits, setting fire to dumps – and that sort of thing,' was the calm rejoiner. 'It's my guess that you're Gimlet King's outfit. Oh yes, we know all about Gimlet – so do the Nazis. They've got you all taped through their spies, even to your names. You've led 'em a fine old dance up and down the coast, but if ever they get hold of you they'll skin you alive. With my own ears I heard *Generaloberst* Gunther – he's in charge of this area – promise to drown every Kitten that fell into his hands. That was after you bumped off his garrison in the Luvelle lighthouse. If daylight finds you here you won't have a hope.'

Now, all that the boy had said about the Kittens, the hut, and the Luvelle raid was true, for which reason Copper was not a little shaken. Security training warned him to beware, but common sense told him that this astonishing youngster knew what he was talking about. His leader, Gimlet King, had gone forward to reconnoitre the hut, a supposed radiolocation station, with a view to blowing it up. He had been gone for so long that the boy's story concerning his capture sounded feasible.

'The man who has been captured was Gimlet himself,' he said slowly. 'Do you know how it happened?'

'Yes, I saw the whole thing,' was the frank reply. 'I was watching the hut with *Le Renard*—'

'With what?' broke in Copper.

'*Le Renard*. Renard is French for fox. He's one of the gang. We never use our own names, but call ourselves after animals, so that we can't give each other away. I'm The Cub.'

'I see,' said Copper.

'I was watching the hut from a safe distance with The Fox, when *Le Faucon* – that's Falcon, in French – ran up to say that three commandos were landing from a motor canoe. Two remained to guard the road and the other was walking through the dunes. I should have warned him, but

I was too late. The Nazis weren't inside the hut. They were lying in a ring outside. They let the commando go through. When he went into the hut they closed in from all sides. He hadn't a chance. The Rat had got the telephone tapped further back, and he reported to me that a message had gone through saying that a British commando, who wouldn't give his name, had been taken prisoner. I thought I'd better let you know what has happened.'

'Okay, Cub, you did quite right,' replied Copper. 'That was smart work.'

'Are you going to try a rescue?'

'Sure. Sure we are,' put in Trapper. 'Either we all go home together or none of us go. That's our rule.'

'That's what I thought,' remarked The Cub.

'Will you show us the best way to the hut?' asked Copper.

'Of course.'

'Just one thing, though,' went on Copper. 'If this is a trick, you'll be the first to get what comes out of the muzzle of this gun. I'll fill you so full of holes you'll drop apart.'

'Save your bullets for the Nazis,' advised Cub calmly.

'If we run into a bunch of Jerries, you keep out o' trouble,' warned Copper.

The Cub laughed softly. 'This way, and go quietly,' he said.

Followed by the two commandos he struck off through the sombre dunes.

CHAPTER TWO

How Cub Peters Went to War

The Cub's amusement at Copper's well-meant advice to keep out of trouble was natural, for in more than two years there had scarcely been a moment when he was not in peril. Trouble and danger had long ago ceased to mean anything to him, for, strange though it may seem, one soon becomes accustomed to having Old Man Death for a companion. And this is how it had all come about.

When France had collapsed before the overwhelming surge of Nazi Panzers, and the abandoned British troops had fallen back upon Dunkirk, Nigel Norman Peters – to give The Cub his proper name – then in his fifteenth year, had been engaged in the tiresome occupation of writing lines in the fourth-form classroom of Brendall's School, this being the punishment awarded for a bird's-nesting expedition on the Essex marshes, on which occasion he had broken bounds by a considerable margin. To tell the truth, at that fateful moment of history, when the news reached him he was not so much concerned with the British army, which he confidently assumed would be able to take care of itself, as a particular member of it – his father, Colonel Lionel Peters, D.S.O., of the Buffs, and, incidentally, his only living relation. Nigel thought the world of his father.

When report reached the school that every craft, large and small, moored along the Essex coast, had put to sea in the desperate hope of bringing home the outnumbered troops, excitement ran high. This soared to a new high level when it became known that two masters with sailing experience had gone out in a leaky wherry to join in the stupendous task. But excitement came near to hysteria when the word flashed round that three prefects had slipped off in a dinghy.

This was all hands to the pump with a vengeance, and more than any normal healthy boy could be expected to watch from a distance. At least, so Nigel decided, and with his lines unfinished he had joined in the throng surging towards the creek where, so rumour asserted, battle-stained troops were being disembarked from the miscellaneous craft that had brought them home. Naturally, he was actuated chiefly by the hope of seeing his father.

In this he was disappointed, but he did find a soldier of his father's regiment, who declared that the colonel, when last seen, was lying wounded on the bomb-torn beach of Dunkirk.

Something like panic swept over Nigel at this disagreeable news, and he decided there and then that something would have to be done about it. If nobody else could find a means of bringing his father home, then it was up to him to do it. He formed the opinion, somewhat hastily – and quite wrongly, of course – that his father would be pleased to see him on the bloodstained battlefield.

This line of thought was perhaps natural, but as a serious proposition rescue was hardly practicable. Unfortunately, as it transpired, at that juncture Nigel was not in the least concerned as to whether his scheme was practical or not. He was concerned only with one thing, and that was how to get to Dunkirk. The means was at hand. A small pleasure launch, with several significant holes in its funnel, manned by three unshaven long-shoremen, was just casting off for its third trip, and almost before he had realised what he was doing Nigel had jumped aboard and stowed himself beneath the splintered superstructure. Dusk was closing in and nobody saw him go.

That was the end of his career at the famous public school, although at the time he was blissfully unaware of it.

Not only did his spectacular plan fail, but never for a moment did it look like succeeding; for as the launch backed in towards the now thin-ning lines of waiting troops, a bomb fell alongside and threw it clean out of the water.

Just what happened after that not even Nigel could say for certain. After swimming for a while he somehow found himself on the beach, very wet, very cold, and more than a little scared.

In particular he was scared about what would happen when he got back to school, for so far it had not dawned upon him that he might not get back. This thought came later, when, after a fruitless search for his father, the beach was suddenly swept by bullets and a number of German soldiers appeared. Real German soldiers they were, in coal-scuttle helmets just like he had seen on the films.

He could hardly believe it. He decided that he was dreaming. But when the hideous truth was no longer in doubt, that he was alone on a stricken battlefield with a mob of victorious Nazis, terror took him by the throat and he ran as he had never run before, not even on last sports day, when Smith minor had beaten him by a yard in the junior sprint.

Where he had gone, what he had done, and how he had survived those first few dreadful days he himself hardly knew. It was all a nightmare. Without shoes, for he had kicked them off while swimming in the sea, his clothes in rags, hungry, tired and miserable, he had wandered about like a lost dog, living on such scraps of discarded food as he was able to find. Quite often he ran into parties of Germans, but they took no notice of him, and he soon became accustomed to the grey uniforms. All he thought about at this period was, of course, how to get home. But no more ships came, and as he could not swim the Channel, he at length perceived that he was marooned upon a hostile shore as effectively as if he had been cast away on an atoll in the middle of the Pacific.

It was about a month later that he had met Louis Morelle, a French boy who had once lived in Dunkirk, now in ruins.

They had discovered each other in a bomb-blasted church in which they had passed the night. It turned out later that Louis was nearly seventeen, but at the time he affected juvenile garments to avoid being made to work by the Nazis. A curious comradeship had developed, and together they had made their way down the coast, without any particular object in view, collecting other waifs and strays like themselves, until at length there were a dozen of them hiding in the woods behind Le Havre.

At first they had lived like animals, content to keep out of sight, but as time went on some sort of order had emerged. Louis, who had the instinct of a town rat for danger, by reason of his age became the leader; and food forays, from being haphazard affairs, became cunningly organized pillaging expeditions on the Nazi storehouses. From this, growing bolder, they came to inflicting damage on enemy property whenever and wherever it could be found.

Louis had been an apprentice motor mechanic, and it was but a short step from making military vehicles unserviceable to jamming the breechblocks of cannon.

By the end of a year the gang had become a small, well-organized, highly mobile force, intensely loyal, with its spies in every town and village, and its headquarters deep in the Forest of Caen. Lacking imagination, apparently it never occurred to the Nazis that the dirty little ragamuffins who hung about their camps under the pretence of looking for scraps, but really to listen to their conversations, could be the thorns in their sides. Incidentally, it was in this way, from the Germans themselves, that the gang first learned about the commandos, and their astute leader, known to his men as 'Gimlet.' No German could move without it being known at the gang's headquarters. An intricate system of signals had been arranged – a broken branch, a feather, a sprig of broom, the cry of a sea-bird ... all these had meanings. The enemy soon knew that an organization of some sort was at work, but although they stormed and blustered, and occasionally shot hostages, they could never discover what it was.

The local French people knew what was afoot, of course, but the Nazis learned nothing from them.

As time went on more ambitious projects were planned by the gang, which now styled itself, somewhat ingloriously Nigel thought, *Les Poux Gris du Nord*, which being translated means, The Grey Fleas of the North. Louis thought of the name, because, as he explained, they were like fleas, always irritating the Nazis without being caught. Trains unaccountably ran off their rails; oil and petrol dumps caught fire; bridges collapsed; trees fell across the roads, blocking them and tearing down telegraph wires, interrupting communications. German troops fell sick as a result of poisonous herbs finding their way into the canteen soup. Nazis officers walking home at night fell into manholes from which the covers had been removed. In short, sabotage was rife, and all this was the work of a score of urchins, so dirty and so ragged that they would have disgraced a city slum.

Names, being dangerous, were forgotten, and each member of the gang was identified by the name of an animal, a bird, reptile or insect – The Fox, The Wolf, The Snake, The Owl, The Grasshopper, for example.

Nigel, now sixteen, was The Cub. He had learned a lot in the two years he had been adrift in France. He spoke French and German as well as he spoke English, and he knew every hole and corner, every coppice, every back street, from Calais to Cherbourg. He had travelled far, exploring prison and internment camps in the hope of learning something about his father, but in vain. He had even planned a raid into Germany itself, for not to know whether his father was dead or alive was a pain from which he was never free.

Aware that there was just a chance that his father had been carried to England, he often looked long and thoughtfully across the grey-green waters of the Channel towards his homeland, but so far no reasonable chance of getting across had presented itself. Apart from which he was loath to leave his comrades.

Needless to say, two years of hard living and desperate enterprises had left their stamp upon his face, which was thin, and set in rather hard lines; but his nerves were like steel, and he moved with a self-assurance beyond his years. He had looked upon death too often to have any fear of it; which was why he had laughed when Copper had suggested that he should keep out of trouble – he, who under his threadbare breeches carried a small arsenal of lethal weapons filched from the Germans. He smiled again as he strode on through the dunes, wondering what the two commandos would think if they knew the truth about him.

Sometimes stopping to listen, keeping always below the skyline, he walked on for some ten minutes, and then, dropping to his knees, wormed his way to the top of a low dune. The hut was at once in plain view, appearing as a black oblong shadow about forty paces distant. It might have been an empty cowshed. Not a crack of light showed. All was silent. Far away a sea-bird uttered its mournful cry, thrice repeated.

Cub indicated the building with a jerk of his thumb. 'There it is,' he breathed. 'You've no time to lose. The Nazi car has already crossed the bridge of St Jean.'

'How do you know that?' demanded Copper.

'A little bird told me,' answered Cub. 'You can take my word for it. What's your plan?'

'We'll rush the place,' decided Copper, who was always in favour of straightforward methods.

'If bullets start flying, your officer will probably stop one,' Cub pointed out evenly. 'Why not get the sentries first? There's one of them now, just come round the corner.'

Copper threw a puzzled glance at this astonishing boy who, in circumstances calculated to strain the nerves of a war-toughened veteran, could think and behave with such nonchalance. Then he looked back at the hut, and, a few paces from it, the dark silhouette of the German sentry who, with a rifle in the crook of his arm, had halted, and now stood gazing out to sea. He nudged Trapper. 'Knock him off, chum,' he ordered.

'*Bon ça. Tout simplement.*'

It was now Cub's turn to be surprised. He watched in amazement as Trapper rose to a kneeling position and fitted an arrow to his bow. *Phung*! sang the cord.

The German gasped, staggered a few paces, and then fell with a heavy thud.

A voice spoke, in German. It said: 'What's the matter, Karl? Did you see something?' With the voice, the second sentry appeared in the open, from the end of the hut where evidently he had been standing.

Cub had been watching Trapper, fascinated by the spectacle of a modern warrior using a bow and arrow, so he had not seen Copper disappear. When he looked round he had gone. 'Where is he?' he whispered to Trapper.

'Wait, my chicken,' was the soft reply. '*Voilà!*'

The German sentry had by this time seen his companion on the ground. Foolishly, or perhaps unthinkingly, he ran to him, and stooped to see what was the matter. As he did so another figure appeared. For a few seconds the two merged, like a piece of statuary. Then they broke apart. One sagged to the ground.

'*Beaucoup bon*,' murmured Trapper. 'Copper break his neck, I think. He does not know his own strength, that one. You stay here, my infant. *Sacré nom*! Here comes the car.'

The dimmed headlights of a car had appeared on the road. Trapper ran forward to the hut, drawing his guns, and Cub, forgetting or ignoring the injunction to remain where he was, followed him.

'Here's the car – let's clean this place up,' greeted Copper, in a natural voice. 'Out of the way, youngster.'

Hitching his Sten gun forward Copper walked up to the door, and putting his foot against it sent it crashing inwards with one tremendous shove. 'Flat, Skipper!' he roared, as light blazed through the open doorway.

Cub caught a fleeting glimpse of a group of German soldiers, and a slim figure in commando battledress dropping to the floor like a coat slipping from a peg. Then several things happened at once, with a good deal of noise. The Sten gun streamed flame. The light went out. There were shots, shouts and groans. Unseen things smashed and crashed. Splinters flew in clouds. A German blundered out through the open door. Trapper's revolver blazed from his hip and the German appeared to dive into the sand. Another figure emerged on all-fours.

'Steady with that gun,' said a calm voice, as the figure rose erect. 'Give them the fruit and we'll be going.'

Trapper took an egg-shaped object from his pocket, raised it to his teeth, flung it into the hut and backed quickly away. An instant later there came an explosion that nearly shattered Cub's eardrums. As the sound died away he heard Copper's voice say, 'You okay, sir?'

'Yes, I'm okay,' came the reply. 'We'll make straight for the beach.'

As the party began to retire, the same voice asked, 'Who's this boy?'

'English, sir. Wandering without fixed abode,' answered Copper. 'He told us the Jerries had grabbed you.'

'Good. Bring him along.'

'But—' protested Cub, for whom things were moving rather fast.

'You 'eard what the Skipper said,' snarled Copper. 'Keep going.'

Contrary to Cub's expectations the retreat was quite orderly. He noted that the leader walked with a slight limp. A good deal of noise was coming from the direction of the hut, but the commandos appeared to take no notice. They went on along the beach until they came to a low cliff, from the shadow of which a small craft was lifted and carried to the water. An engine came to life, and a propeller thrashed the sea into foam.

'Get aboard, boy,' ordered the officer.

'But—' began Cub.

Copper cut him short. 'You 'eard what he said,' he snarled. 'Get aboard.'

Cub got aboard. Having been up all night he was really too tired to argue. Besides, searchlights were sweeping the dunes, and voices were calling on all sides. The little craft moved out across the dark water.

'Same course as usual,' said the officer.

'Aye-aye, sir,' answered Copper.

Thus did Cub come home. Not that he was aware of it, for he was fast asleep in the bottom of the boat when its keel grated on a south-coast beach.

CHAPTER THREE

Cub Makes His Choice

When Cub awoke it was broad daylight. Observing that he was in a room – an unusual event – he was up in a flash, gazing wonderingly at his surroundings. Then he saw two men in commando uniform and remembered all that had happened. They looked quite different now. One, whom he judged to be Copper, was a tall, fresh-complexioned, loose-limbed giant in the early twenties; the other, who looked a trifle older, was a swarthy, dark-eyed, black-haired man with a mere wisp of moustache, equally black. A scar, stretching from the left ear to the chin, disfigured what otherwise would have been a handsome face. Both were smiling at him.

'What-ho, chum,' greeted Copper. 'How goes it?'

'Hello,' answered Cub. 'Have I been asleep long? What's the time?'

'Half-past three, as near as makes no difference,' replied Copper.

Cub was aghast. 'Good Lord! Have I been asleep all that time?'

'Dead to the world, *mon petit*,' declared Trapper, who was feathering an arrow with meticulous care.

'I must be going,' asserted Cub.

'What's the hurry?' inquired Copper.

Cub hesitated, trying to grasp the fact that he was in England.

'How about a cup of Rosy Lee?' suggested Copper.

'Cup of what?'

'Rosy Lee – that's a cup o' tea down our way. There's some grub going too, but that'll have to wait. Gimlet's waiting to see you. Got a couple o' brass-hats with him, an' all.'

Cub looked interested. 'I've heard about this Gimlet,' he said slowly. 'The Jerries talk about him. Why do you call him that?'

'Well, some say one thing and some say another,' answered Copper. 'Some say it's because he goes straight through anything he meets; others say it's on account of his eyes. They sort o' bore right into you. You'll get what I mean when you see 'im. But don't worry; his bark's worse than his bite – unless he happens to be barking at a Jerry.'

'Had he got a wooden leg, or something?' asked Cub. 'I noticed he walks with a limp.'

Copper looked horrified. 'Strike me pink! Don't ever let him 'ear you say that, chum. He's sort o' touchy about that leg. He got it smashed when he was in the Air Force – collided with a Jerry, they say, during the Battle o' Britain. But he kids himself that no one notices it. All the same, he's a pukker sarb – as they say in India. Owns a castle, he does, down in Devon. Used to be a regular Guards officer, but 'e couldn't get enough action out o' that, so he gets himself seconded to an Air Force squadron for a bit. He used ter fly before the war, they say. Playing tennis, he was, one day, when the alert goes. Up he went just as he was, in white flannels, and bags a brace with a left and right. I tell you, chum, he's hot stuff, is our Gimlet. He can ride anything that moves on legs, wheels or wings. His father was a V.C. in the last war; so was 'is grandad, in the Boer War. Like them, he's got red hair – maybe that has something to do with it. When you see his hair begin ter curl on top – that's the time ter watch yer step. Am I right, Trapper?'

'Are you right? *I'll* say you're right,' confirmed Trapper.

'He talks a bit la-de-da, but don't let that kid you,' went on Copper. 'Bit of a dandy, too, in 'is way. I'll bet he wouldn't come down if his house was on fire till his slacks had a crease in 'em. One day, in a sortie, he gets a spot o' blood on his shoulder. Disgusting, he ses ter me. How perfectly disgusting. Made me wipe it off with me 'ankerchief, 'e did. Never gets excited, 'e doesn't. On a sticky job he's as cold-blooded as a fish, and the worse things are the chillier 'e gets; but in action – blimey! He's like a panther what's been fed on quicksilver. They must 'ave mended that game leg of his with a steel spring. He'd walk the wandering Jew himself off his pins. Am I right, Trapper?'

'Are you right? *I'll* say you're right,' agreed Trapper.

'We reckon they put pistons in 'is arms at the same time they mended 'is leg,' continued Copper. 'When 'e goes all quiet is the time to look out. I see him talk to a runaway horse once, and I'll take my oath that horse stopped like it was paralysed. Oh, he's a one all right. Not that any other sort would be much good at the head of the Kittens, mind you. These Kittens 'ave claws, and some of 'em ain't particular who they scratch – but they don't scratch Gimlet. No blooming fear. Not on your sweet life. I only ever see one man give 'im lip. I won't tell you what happened – no names no pack drill. For weeks afterwards that Kitten went white ter the gills every time Gimlet's eyes dropped on 'im. Take my tip, don't you ever answer back; and when he says Tally-ho, start runnin'. Am I right, Trapper?'

Trapper clicked his tongue. '*I'll* say you're right.' he agreed. 'He's halfway between a bull moose and the Wizard of Oz. They say he was born in a pink suit, spit-the bullets, with a gun in one hand and a grenade in the other. He threw the grenade at his nurse because she wouldn't give him a stick of dynamite to chew. *Tiens*! That's what they say, and it may be true.'

'No, you've got it wrong,' argued Copper. 'It was a detonator 'e asked for, and when the nurse wouldn't give it to 'im he reached up for an ancestral battle-axe and swiped 'er over the boko with it.'

Trapper shrugged. 'What does it matter? You will both be swiped with a battle-axe if you keep him waiting.'

'That's right,' agreed Copper. 'We'd better put a jerk in it.'

'I heard you call him Skipper – does that mean he's a captain?' inquired Cub.

'He's acting major now, but his substantive rank is still captain, so we still call 'im Skipper,' Copper explained. 'Between ourselves, me and Trapper usually call 'im Lorry, since we heard the Duke of Marlingham call 'im that. On the mole at St Nazaire it was, with everything blazing and bangin' like somebody had taken the lid off hell. The duke – 'e was in the Navy – climbs up out o' the sea with burning oil runnin' down his pants. "Why, hello, Lorry old man," he says, all casual, like we was at a blinkin' garden party. "How's the huntin'?" sez 'e. S'welp me, that's what 'e said, as true as I stand 'ere, without a word of a lie. Am I right, Trapper?'

Trapper showed his white teeth. '*I'll* say you're right.'

'We didn't know then that Gimlet's first name was Lorrington – Captain Lorrington King, D.S.O., M.C. and Bar, of Lorrington Castle, Devon.

That's 'is name and address. But I reckon it wouldn't do fer 'im ter hear us calling 'im Lorry. Let's go and see 'im.'

First impressions are often misleading, and Cub was conscious of a feeling of disappointment when he was marched into the orderly room, and, really for the first time, set eyes on the man whose reputation he had learned from the enemy. For here was no elderly ferocious-looking martinet such as he had visualised, but a slim, good-looking young man of medium height, with a quiet, unassuming, almost gentle manner. He might have been twenty-five – certainly not more. His hair, close cropped, was a fair auburn rather than red; but it was his eyes, when they were turned on him, that held Cub's attention. In fact, they almost gave him a shock. They were blue, the brightest, most startling blue that he had ever seen. It was not a soft blue, but rather had the hard gleam of burnished steel in sunlight. And that was not all. They seemed, in a disconcerting manner, to bore right through·Cub's eyes into his brain, as if they·would read what he was thinking; and Cub realised there and then that it would be futile to try to deceive him, let alone lie to him. With him, one on either side, sat two elderly officers of senior rank, one in naval uniform.

When King spoke, Cub was again aware of a feeling of disappointment. The voice did not line up with Gimlet's reputation. It was soft, well-modulated, with a pronounced what is known as Oxford accent – in fact, the sort of voice that is sometimes ridiculed on the screen.

'Pull up a chair, laddie,' said King quietly. Then, glancing at Copper, he added, 'All right, Corporal, you had better stay.'

A chair was placed in front of the desk and Cub sat on it.

'Tell me,' began King in an easy manner, 'what were you doing in France?'

'Secret-service work and sabotage mostly, sir,' answered Cub.

King smiled faintly. It was clear that he did not take Cub's assertion seriously. 'Did you have any success?' he inquired.

'Well, I haven't done badly sir, I think,' replied Cub. 'I've helped to derail five trains, including the one that fell into the river at Dinan. That was when Dorsmann of the Gestapo was drowned. We knew he was on it. I blew up the big dump at Trouville, and with some friends set fire to the oil storage depot at St Brieux. Of course, these things are fairly easy when you know the location of the German camps, the position of the guards, and their orders.'

King's smile faded. 'Good God!' he said in a startled voice. 'Did *you* do that?'

'Yes, sir.'

'How did you come to start in this business?' asked King curiously.

'In the first place I went to France to try to find my father, Colonel Peters of the Buffs, who I heard was lying wounded on the beach at Dunkirk. I couldn't find him, though. A bomb sank my boat, and I was left behind after the evacuation.'

King glanced at his companions, and then leaned forward. 'Go on,' he said softly. 'Tell us the whole story.'

In dead silence Cub recounted the full tale of his adventures. All eyes were on his face. No one spoke until he had finished, and even then silence persisted for a full minute.

King took a cigarette from a gold case and tapped it on the back of his hand. 'That,' he remarked, 'beats anything I ever heard. You've actually been in France over two years?'

'Yes, sir.'

'Tell me, Nigel—'

'Cub, if you don't mind, sir,' interrupted Cub. 'It's better to avoid proper names from the start, in case of accidents.'

'You're right, by thunder. I only wish everyone over here was as careful,' said King, deadly serious. 'You've learned absolutely nothing about your father?'

'Nothing, sir, although I hung around a good many prison and internment camps, including a secret one I found in a castle down on the Loire, at Chateaudun. The War Office may like to know that there are several senior officers and diplomats down there, some of whom, I believe, have been reported dead.' Cub named some of them. 'I was unable to ascertain the actual purpose of this camp,' he added.

'Are you telling me that these officers you have named are alive?' cried King, moved for once from his easy manner.

'They were a month ago – I saw them through the wire,' asserted Cub.

King drew a deep breath. 'This is interesting – very interesting indeed.

We'll have another talk about it when I've reported the matter to the Higher Authority. Meanwhile, I'll ask the War Office if they have any information about your father. What are your plans now?'

'I'd like to be put back in France the next time you go across, sir,' requested Cub.

King raised his eyebrows. 'Do you mean that – seriously? Haven't you been in danger long enough?'

'You wouldn't suggest that I abandon my comrades?' said Cub reproachfully. 'They'll wonder what's happened to me. They're probably hunting high and low for me at this very minute. Besides, Tyke would miss me. He's our dog. He's only a mongrel, but what he doesn't know isn't worth knowing. A Nazi booted him once, and he's never forgotten it. Moreover, I'm carrying information in my head which the gang may need. We never put anything on paper – it's safer not to. Of course,' went on Cub quickly, as an idea struck him, 'if I went back, if you like I could meet you somewhere, any time, and tell you what Jerry is up to – act as a guide perhaps? I know my way about.'

'By gad!' breathed King. 'That certainly is an idea. But why stay in France? I take it you could make contact with the – er – Fleas, whenever you wanted to?'

'Of course.'

'Then surely they could collect the information and you could act as a link between us – that is, between the Commandos and the gang?'

'He's a bit young for that sort of thing, isn't he?' put in the naval officer.

'I don't see that age has much to do with it, sir,' returned Cub sharply. 'After all, I've been at this game, right under the noses of the Nazis, without getting caught, for more than two years, so I think I can claim to know something about it. I've friends everywhere, loyal French people of all ages, ready to help me, and that's an organization even the Commandos haven't got. I'd say my age was an advantage, and that goes for all the Grey Fleas. Had we been older we could never have got away with the things we've done. Why, I've even cleaned a German general's boots – and nearly cut through the laces at the same time, so that they broke when he was on parade. What full-grown man could do that?'

'Marvellous. Absolutely marvellous,' chuckled King. 'I think we'd better put you in the Commandos as a special enlistment.'

Cub shook his head. 'That's very kind of you, but I'd rather stay with the gang. But there's no reason why I shouldn't be attached to your Commando, to the Kittens, as a sort of liaison scout. I should be safer in these rags than in a uniform. That wouldn't prevent me from putting on decent clothes, and having a bath occasionally, if I was over here, as no doubt I should be, sometimes.'

King considered Cub thoughtfully. 'We shall have to think about this,' he decided. 'You run off now and get some food. The corporal will fix you up. For the moment, at any rate, you can regard yourself as on our strength. That's all for the present.'

Cub rose. 'Thank you, sir. How long will it be before I can get back to France, do you think? You see, if the gang thinks the Nazis have bumped me off, they're liable to do something desperate.'

'You'll be back pretty soon, I fancy,' answered King drily. 'In fact, I'll see to it that you are.'

There was a new respect in Copper's voice when they got outside, and walked across the parade ground to the old house that was used as a mess.

'You're a coughdrop,' he remarked. 'That tale o' yours fair took the blinkin' biscuit, particularly the bit about cuttin' the general's bootlaces. It'll tickle Trapper to death when I tell 'im.'

'You and Trapper aren't the only Kittens left alive, by any chance?' queried Cub.

'No bloomin' fear,' declared Copper warmly. 'Only it happens – keep this ter yourself – that me and Trapper are Gimlet's right-hand men. We act as sort of pathfinders fer the others, for which reason we go our own sweet way, if you get what I mean? Once in a while we do a little sortie on our own, like last night, fer instance. Me and Trapper share quarters where we can talk things over; there's bags of room for another bunk, so you can muck in with us if you like, till you know what you're goin' ter do.'

'Thanks, that'll suit me fine,' agreed Cub, who was already attracted to these two genuine if unusual men.

'Then let's go and swipe some grub before the hogs get their feet in the trough,' suggested Copper. He glanced at the Cub's bare feet. 'Would you like me ter scrounge a pair of shoes for you?'

'After two years without them I reckon leather would rub my feet, thanks all the same,' declined Cub. He grinned. 'Besides, the soles of my feet don't wear out – shoes do.'

Copper laughed, so loudly that for a moment Cub was startled. 'Blimey! you certainly are a one for knowing all the answers,' he averred. Then, becoming serious, 'Remind me of a kid I used ter know down the Old Kent Road, you do. Smart kid 'e was, too – poor little blighter.'

Cub looked up. 'Why poor? Did something happen to him?'

'Yeah,' returned Copper grimly. 'Something happened to 'im. Volunteer fire messenger, 'e was, in the blitz. One night 'e never came back. I helped dig 'im out. The same night, it was, my Ma had our roof on top of 'er.'

Cub noticed that the big Cockney's hands were opening and shutting, and he understood, then, why the Nazi sentry outside the hut had died so quickly.

During the next twenty-four hours he came to know more about the Commandos, particularly his new-found friends. They showed him the armoury, and the gun pits, and demonstrated some of the weapons.

'I reckon they'd be a bit too heavy for me,' said Cub regretfully. 'But I get on pretty well with this,' he went on, putting his hand inside his ragged shorts and displaying a small Mauser automatic. 'It's only a thirty-eight,' he continued, putting three shots in quick succession through the bull's-eye, 'but it hits pretty hard.'

Copper stared. 'Strike a light!' he gasped. 'Where did you learn to do that?'

'In France – there's plenty to practise on.'

Copper glanced at Trapper, who was smiling approval. 'He don't need no one ter take care of him,' he asserted. 'Next thing we know he'll be taking care of us.'

Trapper clicked his tongue. '*Mot de Cambronne*! I guess you're right.'

Late that afternoon Cub's presence was again requested at the orderly room. After one glance at King's face his heart sank.

'Yes, I'm afraid it's bad news,' said Gimlet. 'The War Office has no information about your father beyond the fact that it is known he was seriously wounded in the rear-guard action. What happened to him after that no one knows. The beach was bombed incessantly, and a lot of our fellows are simply on the missing list. Occasionally one turns up, but not often. It's always better to face facts, Cub, and although it may hurt, I wouldn't set too much hope on seeing your father again. If he died – well, he died like a soldier, and that being so he'd expect you to take it on the chin. I'm sorry.' Gimlet held out his hand.

Cub took it. 'That's all right, sir,' he said in a steady voice. 'It's just one more grudge I have against the Nazis.'

'Good,' replied King briskly. 'Now let's get down to business. The Higher Command has decided to exploit to the full the information you possess, but as you are British, and under age, they don't like the idea of your wandering about loose in France. They suggest that you return to school and resume your studies where you left off.'

Cub's jaw sagged. 'To *school*!' he cried incredulously. 'To go back to prep – Euclid, Latin verbs, and all that sort of rot, after what I've been doing!'

Gimlet's blue eyes twinkled. 'There's an alternative,' he admitted. 'If you prefer, you may stay on the strength of this unit for such duties as I may decide – purely as a volunteer, of course. You would come under me for discipline, and draw pay and rations like any other commando.'

Cub drew a deep breath. 'That's better,' he agreed vehemently.

Gimlet looked stern. 'Don't get the idea that you're going to run wild with a Tommy gun. You're still a bit young for that sort of thing. But as a guide, your knowledge of the country should be invaluable.'

'I understand, sir,' said Cub. 'When do we start?'

The corners of Gimlet's mouth twitched. 'Don't be in such a devil of a hurry. I haven't decided yet just what we're going to do. Headquarters are anxious to know just what dirty work is going on at Chateaudun, so we may run down there and have a look round.'

'I could think of a dozen things we could do right away,' exclaimed Cub eagerly. 'In the Grey Fleas we were always rather stumped for equip-ment—'

'One thing at a time,' broke in King. 'You must realise that as we commandos work, the great difficulty is getting to and from the objective

– that is, the enemy coast – without being spotted. U-boats are always on the prowl and enemy reconnaissance aircraft are always on the lookout for small craft in the Channel. It isn't so much the danger of being caught on the open sea in daylight, although it would probably be a bad business if we were; but should that happen, the element of surprise, which is vital to the success of a sortie, has gone. It is useless to go on after being spotted. Sometimes, of course, we bale out of aircraft over the objective, and arrange to be picked up somewhere on the coast by the Navy after the job's done. But that isn't always possible; in nine cases out of ten it means a sea voyage at the finish. In short, getting to and fro is the most tricky part of a raid.'

'I didn't think of that,' confessed Cub. His face brightened. 'Why keep going to and fro? We could cut out a lot of that by mucking in with the Fleas in the Forest of Caen, and operating from there. In that way we might do several jobs at one crossing, so to speak. In my experience the Nazis haven't much imagination. Because, after a raid, you have always departed by sea, that's where they'd look for us. It wouldn't occur to them that we might have dodged inland. In any case, sir, you really ought to meet The Fleas, so that if anything happened to me you would still have scouts on the other side.'

Gimlet stared. 'There's something in that, by gad! That *is* a new idea. But wouldn't that be throwing a load of danger on The Fleas?'

'They'd love it,' declared Cub. 'But without me you'd never find them. We don't fight the Nazi search parties because that would put the whole forest under suspicion. We just fade away – unless, as has happened once or twice, we show the Nazis the way through the forest, taking care to keep away from those parts we don't want them to see.'

Gimlet nodded approval. 'Nice work.'

'There's one thing you ought to know, sir,' remarked Cub. '*Generaloberst* Gunther, who is in charge of the coast defences, is a proper Nazi. He's shot scores of French hostages, and he's sworn to drown any Kittens who fall into his hands. But his adjutant, *Hauptmunn* von Roth, is even worse. He's the devil himself in uniform. Old men, women and children – it makes no difference to von Roth when he gets his hands on them.'

King's eyes looked frosty. 'I'll remember it,' he said softly. 'That's all for the moment. I'll put a scheme forward. Report at my quarters at seven o'clock this evening and we'll go into it. Copper and Trapper will be there.'

Cub raised his eyebrows. 'Do you always call them that, sir?'

Gimlet smiled. 'Not always – certainly not on the parade ground. But in the sort of work we do, when we're on the other side of the Channel – well, badges of rank, social position, rates of pay, and that sort of thing don't matter very much. We're comrades then, and that's all that matters.'

Cub nodded. 'I understand, sir. I'll try to live up to that standard.'

'That's the spirit,' murmured Gimlet.

Cub departed to find his comrades.

CHAPTER FOUR

Under the Greenwood Tree

If Cub thought that twenty-four hours would see him back in France, he was mistaken. He learned that commandos do not rush to and fro across the Channel at a moment's notice. He was informed that a plan, a plan embracing the most minute details and covering every possible contingency, is prepared before the first move is made, and this takes time. Four days and nights were to elapse before he again set foot on the coast of Normandy.

The hour was midnight, and the moon not yet risen, when he guided a small, flat-bottomed, blunt-nosed landing craft into a tiny cove of his own recommendation.

In the boat were Gimlet King, and his two new friends, Copper and Trapper, for the expedition was in the nature of a private enterprise, no more than a scouting sortie with the primary object of making contact with the Grey Fleas and establishing a dump of useful equipment at their forest hide-out. This equipment, comprising guns, grenades, demolition charges, ammunition and tinned food had presented a problem, for it made a heavy load.

To avoid the danger and difficulty of carrying it across nine miles of hostile country to the forest retreat – for the forest stretches away to the south of the town of Caen, which is only a matter of five or six miles from the coast – the services of the R.A.F. branch of Combined Operations had been called in.

At 3.0 a.m.* a low-flying Hurricane fighter-bomber was to drop by

---

* Actually, the Commandos use the 24-hour clock, but for the purposes of this narrative normal times will be more readily understood.

parachute two containers, with the equipment packed inside, in a stretch of uncultivated country fringing the forest, a spot selected by Cub, and marked by him on an aerial photograph of the district taken expressly for this purpose. Nothing was left to chance.

There had been a suggestion that they themselves might land by parachute, but after careful consideration Gimlet had opposed this for a number of reasons.

Firstly, they would be left without any means of getting back unless an assignation was made with another aircraft, or a marine craft sent in by the naval branch. This would necessitate a definite appointment which might be difficult to keep. At all events, such an appointment would set a time limit on their raid, and in view of the indefinite nature of the sortie, which might last for some days. Gimlet was loath to tie his hands, so to speak.

Another reason was, Gimlet was anxious to have sight of the country between the coast and the rendezvous, particularly the cove, which Cub had asserted was ideal for their purpose. It was, in fact, the cove used by The Fleas when they wished to have access to the sea, for which reason, although the Nazis were unaware of it, a passage had been made through the barbed wire; and land mines – the bugbear of a raiding force – had been removed. As a matter of detail The Fleas had watched these mines being laid, so as they knew just where they were their removal had presented no great difficulty. The mines had been transported to the forest for use against the Nazis at some future date should a suitable opportunity present itself.

Having arrived in the cove, the boat, which obviously could not be left on the beach through the hours of daylight, was disposed of by the simple expedient of filling it with rocks until it sank – this in shallow water close to a low cliff. When the boat was again required it would only be necessary to remove the rocks, when air-filled floatation chambers would bring it to the surface.

The immediate objective was the spot where the Hurricane was to jettison the equipment. If nothing unforeseen occurred to hold them up they would be there when it arrived – for thus it had been planned – in which case, to remove the last possibility of error, they were to flash a signal from a torch showing a green light. This rendezvous was two miles from the old hunting lodge used by The Fleas as their headquarters, where the equipment was to be hidden.

This lodge, Cub had told them, was rather worse than a ruin. In places the walls, all overgrown with ivy, were still standing, but for the most part it was no more than an area strewn with blocks of stone, in a tangle of briars, nettles, and similar wild vegetation. But – this was the point – beneath the ruin there was a range of cellars, the entrance to which, hard to find at the best of times, had been made doubly secure from discovery by blocks of weed-covered masonry. As the ruin was far away from any beaten track it was well suited to their purpose.

Legend attributed the original building to William the Conqueror who, prior to the conquest of Britain, resided in his palace at Caen. As his great passion was hunting – witness the New Forest which he established in Britain – it seems likely enough that he hunted regularly in the Forest of Caen, and that being so, it is reasonable to suppose that the legend of the hunting lodge rested on a foundation of fact. At any rate, it was at Caen that William mustered his knights for the invasion of England, and to Cub it seemed right and proper that the process should now be reversed. Should the spirit of William linger in the vicinity, he must, Cub thought, regard the matter with approval, for William, while a gallant warrior, was not above a spot of trickery when it suited his purpose.

With the boat disposed of, Cub took the lead, and moving forward with confidence guided the party through the wire to the coastal road where a cautious reconnaissance was made. This precaution was an obvious one, and it was as well that it was taken, for a minute later a German cyclist patrol appeared. The Nazi troops passed the commandos all unaware that within ten yards two Sten guns were trained on them. They were allowed to pass on this occasion because the business of the commandos was not with them.

As soon as the Nazis had disappeared into the night the advance was resumed, with Cub, still acting as guide, avoiding roads and habitations. His intimate knowledge of the country was at once revealed. Without such a guide progress must have been slow; as it was, they marched with such assurance that the party arrived at the objective with a quarter of an hour to spare, which enabled them to rest and refresh themselves from their haversacks. It was a bleak, lonely spot, undulating, occupied chiefly by gorse and bracken, with an occasional birch or holly, with the forest looming dark in the background. Several times during the march Cub had halted to listen, and uttered the harsh, honking cry of a wild goose. He did so again now, and on this occasion the cry was answered from a distance by the screech of a nighthawk, a double screech, twice repeated.

'Good,' said Cub approvingly. 'That's Falcon. He'll pass word on to the others that I'm back. They'll be here in no time. We ought to hear Fox yapping pretty soon.' But although they listened, and although the forest seemed suddenly to have developed a wealth of wild life, there was no yap of a fox.

At two minutes to three, searchlights in the direction of the coast, and a sparkle of distant flak, heralded the approach of the Hurricane. Very soon it announced its own arrival with a drone that quickly became a roar. Gimlet flashed the signal, whereupon the aircraft bellowed overhead, unseen, and passed on into the darkness. In the silence that followed, two thuds, at no great distance, could be plainly heard. The party ran towards the spot and found the two containers, with their dark-coloured parachutes spread over the ground near them.

While the parachutes were being folded, a dog of the lurcher type dashed up and greeted Cub with those unrestrained manifestations of joy with which a dog displays its affection. Cub fondled it while it kept a watchful, suspicious eye on the others.

The screech of a nighthawk came again, close now. Cub honked, and a moment later a small figure in ragged overalls, capped with a beret dragged down over one ear, loomed up. It stopped abruptly, and then disappeared in a flash, presumably when it caught sight of men in the party. Cub called, whereupon the lad reappeared, and running up to Cub kissed him on both cheeks.

'They – er – the French, do that sort of thing,' explained Cub uncomfortably. To Falcon he said, 'It's all right. These are friends, British commandos.'

Upon this, addressing Cub, using his hands as well as his lips, Falcon broke into a veritable torrent of speech, words pouring from his lips so fast that Gimlet, who spoke French well, and Trapper, whose accent was somewhat different, found it hard to keep pace. By the time Falcon had finished speaking six more Fleas had arrived on the scene.

'What's the trouble?' asked Copper shrewdly.

Cub raised his hands for silence and then turned to the commandos. 'I don't know how much of that you were able to follow, so I had better explain. There has been a tragedy. The Nazis have captured The Fox, our leader. Apparently it happened the night I left France. The Fox, in his anxiety to find me, made the mistake of getting too near the hut. He was caught in the cordon the Nazis threw round the place, and *Hauptmann* von Roth, who is no fool, guessed he had some hand in the matter. To make matters worse, Fox was caught with his weapons on him. He was put in the *gendarmerie*, which of course has been taken over by the Nazis, and in the morning was hauled up before *Generaloberst* Gunther. The Fox refused to speak, but the French people are in a state about it, naturally, because it's on occasions like this that Von Roth goes mad and shoots people – perfectly innocent people. Some of the French people want The Fox to speak, to save a massacre; some, regardless of consequences, want him to remain dumb. At times like this, when the citizens get at logger-heads with each other, it's hard to know what to do for the best. But the ghastly thing is, at eight o'clock tomorrow morning The Fox is to be publicly flogged, in Caen, to make him open his mouth. If he refuses he will be shot.'

For a moment silence reigned.

'And where is this nauseating spectacle to take place?' asked Gimlet quietly.

'In the Place de la République, which is in front of the Hôtel de Ville, where Gunther has his headquarters. The *gendarmerie* is close by, in the next square – the Place de la Préfecture. But excuse me while I tell the others who you are. They don't understand.'

In a profound hush Cub made the necessary explanations. It was evident that The Fleas were not a little impressed by the new arrivals, but their satisfaction, and their joy at seeing Cub again, whom they had given up for lost, was largely offset by the impending fate of their leader.

'It looks as if we shall have to take a hand in this affair in the Place de la République,' said Gimlet. 'But for a start, let us get this stuff stowed away in a safe place. Good thing we've got it. Looks as if we shall need it. Lead on, Cub.'

There were now plenty of willing hands to carry the containers, which were picked up. The party then entered the timber, following what Cub stated was an old boar path, for these animals still lingered on in the most inaccessible parts of the forest.

Half an hour's walk through a jungle of undergrowth, above which rose the spreading arms of ancient oaks, brought the party to its objective – the ivy-clad walls and fallen stones that were all that remained of the Conqueror's hunting lodge.

In a cellar beneath, a candle stuck in a bottle threw a flickering yellow light on a scene that was a mixture of fantasy and drama. The actors were now able to see each other, and The Fleas looked at the commandos with the same curiosity as the British troops looked at the strange tribe that swarmed about them. The Grey Fleas of the North, while often unlike each other in appearance, varying in type from blonde Celts to swarthy Latins, had one characteristic in common.

On every face was an expression of earnest, almost fierce determination. Each was so deadly serious in his purpose that humour found no place in the assembly.

Gimlet sat on a container. Copper and Trapper sat on the other. Cub stood up, giving orders curtly, in charge of the gathering. On his instructions The Fleas formed themselves in a half circle and waited expectantly. All eyes were on Gimlet's face, for the word had gone round that this was the famous British commando leader.

Gimlet made a brief speech, congratulating The Fleas on their work. He then took a guide-book from his pocket and opened it at a plan of the town of Caen. He glanced at his watch. 'If The Fox is to be saved,' he said, speaking in French, 'we have no time to waste in idle chatter. Let us make a plan. I take it you all know your way about the town?'

There was a chorus of affirmation, which was only to be expected, for most of the boys had been born there, or close by.

'I shall need assistants,' said Gimlet. 'The work will be dangerous, but every Flea who volunteers to take part must be prepared to go through with it, come what may, for in an enterprise of this sort perfect timing is everything, and the success of the whole depends upon strict adherence to orders on the part of each member. Who will volunteer for the rescue?'

Every hand shot up.

Gimlet's blue eyes flashed round the semicircle of eager faces. '*Bon*,' said he. 'Now let us work out the plan.' He glanced at Cub. 'I take it that sentries have been posted?'

Cub looked pained. 'Sentries are *always* on duty, sir,' he said. 'No one, neither French nor German, can approach within two miles of this place without my being informed of it.'

'I beg your pardon,' said Gimlet. 'Let us start by making a rough model of the square, the Place de la République, which will be the scene of action.'

CHAPTER FIVE

Gimlet Signs His Name

When day dawned in the time-mellowed town of Caen, it dawned much as any other day since the Nazi occupation. Black-out blinds were drawn, and slatted shutters fell open, carelessly, reluctantly almost, as if the houses themselves saw little purpose in opening misery-dulled eyes to gaze once more upon their own dilapidations.

In the Place de la République a few starved-looking sparrows took up their customary positions on the eaves of the dingy shops that lined three sides of the square, and preened themselves without enthusiasm; for even they scarce knew where to look for their next meal in hungry France.

An occasional cart, drawn by a horse too skinny to eat, passed through, and one or two fishermen plodded heavily homeward from the direction of the Canal Maritime. Few of the shops had anything to sell, so for the most part they remained unopened. There was no bustling activity outside the Café Normandie, as there was in the almost-forgotten days of peace. The brisk aroma of fresh roasted coffee and baking bread was but a memory. The newspaper kiosk stood silent, abandoned, a little awry, as forlorn as a moorland milestone. Occasionally a heavy-booted Nazi patrol marched through the square, or a motor cyclist, with a clatter that seemed almost sacrilege, like shouting in a church, delivered despatches to General Gunther's headquarters in the Hôtel de Ville – which in France is what in England is called the town hall. In the intervals, an atmosphere of hopeless lethargy hung over all. The only permanent visitor to the square appeared to be a boy who took up a position, a somewhat precarious one, on a flat roof commanding a view of the Rue Auber, the little street that connects the Place de la République and the Place de la Préfecture with its adjacent

51

gendarmerie. Only a close observer would have noticed that this boy (if he noticed him at all) from time to time made seemingly meaningless gestures with his hands, as though he were an idiot.

At a quarter to eight, however, there came a sudden note of busy movement. Four Nazi soldiers, under an *Unteroffizier*, appeared from the direction of the *gendarmerie*, carrying between them three short scaffold poles. They marched to a position in the middle of the square, halted, and then, in a businesslike manner, arranged the three poles in the form of a tripod; that is to say, with the feet wide apart and the three tops forming an apex. In this position the poles were fastened with ropes. The soldiers then fell into line a short distance away and stood at ease.

There were still no curious spectators to see what all this was about, as might have been expected, but here and there the blind of a bedroom overlooking the square moved slightly, and a face peered furtively at the scene.

At five minutes to eight the boy on the roof made another of his imbecile signs, and a moment later, with a steady tramp – tramp – tramp, three squads of Nazi soldiers, twelve to a squad, rifles at the slope, marched into the Place and with admirable military precision formed up in line on three sides of the scaffolding, but some little distance from it, leaving the fourth side, facing the Hôtel de Ville, open. Rifles were 'ordered', and the troops stood 'at ease.'

On the stroke of eight came another sound of marching, followed by the appearance of another body of troops, six this time, in open order. By their side, a little apart, marched a sergeant, carrying at the slope a short-handled whip, the several tails of which hung far down his back. In the centre of this imposing procession, looking singularly out of place, a slim youth, his hands in his pockets, walked with jaunty step and defiant air. As the party marched across the square towards the scaffolding the youth began to sing, and the song he sang was the Marseillaise.

'*Stillschweigen!*' roared the sergeant.

The boy continued to sing. Indeed, he sang with greater enthusiasm, whereupon the sergeant broke into the ranks and struck him across the mouth. With blood running down his chin the boy continued to sing. He sang while his shirt was ripped off, and he was tied, spreadeagled, to the tripod. The sergeant took off his tunic, folded it carefully, laid it on the ground and rolled up his sleeves.

At this juncture there appeared on the steps of the Hôtel de Ville an officer, immaculate in a dove-grey uniform, a smart figure indeed, but somewhat spoilt by the fact that his field boots seemed to have been made for a larger man, for they sagged round the ankles. For a moment he paused to survey the scene. At a shout of command the assembled troops sprang to attention. The officer advanced towards the tripod, followed by a rather fat bespectacled soldier, carrying an open notebook. The youth continued to sing with fervour.

Apart from those described, the square was deserted. Even the boy on the roof had disappeared. But that is not to say that there were no spectators. As a matter of fact there were several, although none was visible.

From the front ground-floor room of old Marcel Boudrier's abandoned paint and wallpaper establishment, which had lately been partly gutted by fire, with his face just above the charred windowsill, Copper Collson regarded the scene with cold, hostile eyes.

'If I hadn't seen this with my own eyes, on my oath I wouldn't have believed it,' he said in a hoarse whisper. 'Forty perishing Nazis to whip one boy, s'welp me.' Apparently he spoke to Trapper Troublay, who crouched near him, also watching the scene; close at hand were Gimlet King and Cub.

'Don't talk!' snapped Gimlet, whose face was pale. 'Prepare for action. Trapper, take the fellow with the whip. Copper, you take the officer. Then get busy with the Sten gun. Wait for it!'

With a little sigh that held in it a note of affection Trapper snuggled a rifle to his shoulder. The sergeant's arm, whip in hand, was raised for the first stroke.

'Fire!' said Gimlet.

There came a crack more vicious than the whip could have made. Simultaneously Trapper's rifle gave a little jerk. The sergeant's whole body twitched spasmodically. And there he stood for a split second, his arm raised, while sparrows whirled upwards in alarm at the unexpected interruption; then he crashed headlong, the whip flying from his hand. Came another crack. This time the officer spun round in a manner scarcely human, and with his fall some sort of understanding of the situation seemed to dawn upon the troops. With a rising murmur of voices, looking wildly about them they broke ranks; but before the movement was properly begun the air was rent by the tearing snarl of a machine gun, and the shrill whine of bullets ricocheting from hard earth and cobblestones.

In the confined space of the square, with echoes crashing to and fro between the walls, the noise was considerable. Nazis fell. Some stumbled about, firing their rifles indiscriminately; some sank to their knees; others ran first one way and then another, not knowing what they were running from, or where they were running to, as it seemed. The line of men immediately in front of old Marcel Boudrier's shop, enfiladed, went down like a row of ninepins.

Gimlet raised a whistle to his lips, and its piercing blast cut across the pandemonium which had so devastatingly descended on the sleepy square. In response, as though the whistle were a piece of mechanism that had released them, a number of small round objects, that might have been miniature Rugby balls, appeared, bouncing across the gravel. They came from several places, from doorways, from alleys, and empty shops. At least one came spinning down from a roof, to strike a cobbled area with a crash, and bouncing high, explode in mid-air in a manner that can only be described as spectacular. Then came a swift succession of explosions, and on the instant the *Place* became filled with dense white smoke that rolled and surged as if it might have been a liquid. The scene was blotted out.

'Your innings, Cub,' said Gimlet, in a thin dry voice. 'Copper, plaster the door of the Hôtel de Ville. Trapper, put a squirt across the entrance to the Rue Auber to prevent fresh troops from coming up from the *gendarmerie*. You can use grenades, but be careful of the boys.'

Before Gimlet had finished speaking Cub was streaking across the square in the direction of the tripod, a knife in his hand. He disappeared into the smoke made by the smoke bombs. Within a minute he reappeared, running like a hare, with The Fox at his side.

As the two boys emerged from the smoke Gimlet again put the whistle to his lips and blew a number of short blasts – the prearranged dispersal signal.

'All right,' he said calmly. 'Let's go.' Then, seeing that tears were running down The Fox's face, he asked sharply, 'What's the matter – are you hurt?'

'*Non, m'sieur,*' answered The Fox. 'I was thinking of the people here, who will be blamed for this.'

'Ah,' breathed Gimlet. 'I see what you mean. In that case we'll let Gunther know who is responsible.'

Several pots of paint stood on a shelf, one with the lid off, and a brush in it. Gimlet took the brush, dripping with green paint, and walking out quickly to the derelict newspaper kiosk, in three swift sweeping strokes made a mark, in the rough shape of a gimlet, thus:

He tossed the brush aside and returned to the shop. 'Let's be going. Lead on, Cub.'

'It's all right, sir, The Grasshopper's there, I've seen him,' said Cub, as he led the way to the rear of the building where a back door opened into the Rue Jacques. There, a tired-looking horse was standing between the shafts of a ramshackle cart, in which lay a heap of old potato sacks. A small boy, with a pinched, freckled face, sat on the driver's seat.

'*Montez, messieurs,*' said he.

'*Du courage,*' muttered Trapper.

'*En avant,*' called Cub as the party got aboard and pulled the sacks over them.

The boy clicked his tongue. Iron-shod hooves clattered on the road; the horse moved forward, and on objurgations from the driver broke into a trot. The noise of shooting and shouting in the Place de la République died away.

The ride that followed, as rides go, was not a pleasant one. For one thing the cart stank of stale vegetables, if nothing worse, and was entirely destitute of such modern appliances as springs. Fortunately there was some improvement when the vehicle left the cobbled area of the town and ran on into the country over a gravel-surfaced road.

Presently a motor cycle came tearing along behind, and stopped with a screech of brakes.

'*Halte-là!*' shouted a voice.

The cart stopped. A question was asked, and The Grasshopper replied, in a level voice, that he had seen some men running across the Pont de la Courtonne towards the Canal Maritime, as if making for the sea. The motor cycle roared off and the cart continued on its way. After about twenty minutes it made a sharp turn and shortly afterwards came to a stop.

'*Descendez, messieurs*, if you please,' chirped The Grasshopper.

The occupants of the cart jumped down and found themselves in a farm-yard enclosed by barns. The farmer, who Cub said was The Grasshopper's father, looking rather anxious, received them. His anxiety was pardonable, for in occupied France there is only one punishment for harbouring refugees.

'At your service, *messieurs*. This way, if you please,' said the farmer, leading the way into a barn that was, or appeared to be, entirely filled with trusses of hay. But he pulled one aside, disclosing a cavity large enough to accommodate the party in comfort.

'It would be advisable to remain quiet,' said the farmer. 'I shall replace the truss of hay, so you should be secure. Presently I will bring you soup. Then you can sleep. Tonight, I should be glad if you would depart, because my nerves are not as good as they were, and should the Boches come searching, my fears might betray all of us.'

'We are deeply in your debt, *monsieur*,' said Gimlet. 'It shall not be forgotten.'

'I could do no less,' said the Frenchman simply, as he replaced the truss of hay in the hole and departed.

There were now in the party five persons, Gimlet, Copper, Trapper, Cub and The Fox, The Grasshopper having gone, as Cub averred, to put the horse away and watch the road for danger. 'It all went like clockwork,' he added.

'No reason why it shouldn't,' replied Gimlet. 'I hope the boys got clear after rolling in those smoke bombs.'

'By this time they will have vanished like mice in a cornfield,' declared

Cub. 'It is not the first time they have had to do it. In their own time, from different directions, they will return to the forest. In uniforms, that would not have been possible for you, but after dark it should be fairly easy. I'm afraid The Fox will no longer be able to appear in public, though.'

The Fox, who, although no worse for his imprisonment, seemed to be slightly stunned by his dramatic rescue, now recovered and stepped into the conversation. He expressed his joy at Cub's reappearance, and addressed the commandos in a manner not far short of reverence. When he learned that they had brought equipment with them, and intended staying in the country for a time, he broke down from sheer emotion and wept unrestrainedly.

Copper sniffed. 'Okay – okay,' he muttered impatiently. 'Cut it out.'

'Leave him alone, you big stiff,' interposed Cub. 'He'll be better when he's got his feelings off his chest. Don't worry, when it comes to action The Fox may be able to show you a thing or two.'

'Blimey, 'ark at 'im,' growled Copper, grinning.

The farmer's wife brought in a great pot of soup, and some cups. When the soup was finished the party stretched themselves out on the hay.

'Let's get some sleep while we can,' said Gimlet. 'After this morning's diversion we'll see about getting down to the work that brought us here. By the way, Cub, you might ask The Grasshopper to swab his cart out, in case we have to use it again. It's filthy, positively filthy.'

Cub smiled. 'Very good, sir,' he said.

Copper chuckled. 'But it was better than no cart at all,' he murmured softly. 'Am I right, Trapper?'

'Are you right?' grunted Trapper. '*I'll* say you're right.'

CHAPTER SIX

Sabotage De Luxe

Twilight was creeping in through the grimy barn window when Cub was awakened by the low murmur of voices, to find Gimlet, with a map on his knees, engaged in quiet but earnest conversation with Copper and Trapper. Missing the Fox, Cub asked where he was.

'No use asking us, chum,' said Copper. 'He was gone when we woke up.'

'Probably gone on the prowl to find out what's happening,' opined Cub. 'We needn't worry; the Fox lives up to his name – but unlike an ordinary fox he doesn't leave a scent.'

'Come over here, Cub,' ordered Gimlet. 'We were just having a look at the lie of the land between here and Chateaudun. The Government would like to know what's happening there, and why it is necessary to keep an internment camp under the hat, so to speak.'

'It's a fair step – about a hundred miles south of Dieppe and fifty miles west of Paris,' returned Cub. 'That means it's a good eighty miles from here. It took me about a week to get there, although, of course, I was in no hurry, and did a spot of scouting on the way.' Cub looked dubious. 'In uniforms, you'll only be able to travel after dark – the country isn't as lonely as all that, not even if we kept to the fields.'

'Yes, I realise that,' answered Gimlet, resuming his study of the map.

'We might ride down,' suggested Copper.

'Ride? In what?' demanded Cub.

'Borrow some bikes, or get a lift on a goods train, maybe.'

'We might get a bit nearer that way,' agreed Cub.

At this point of the conversation there was a rustle in the hay, and The

Fox, after the manner of his namesake, appeared. He carried a parcel. He stated – as Cub had predicted – that he had been to make contact with The Fleas, to find out what was happening. As he spoke, and Cub translated, the Fox's hands lent eloquent support to his words.

'The whole place is in an uproar,' he reported. 'Gunther is raging like a maniac, they say, since the gimlet sign was found on the kiosk.' The Fox chuckled. 'That was a touch, *mon commandant*.' Then he became serious. 'But this is no matter for laughing. When Gunther is in this mood he is capable of any devilment, and I am afraid for the people. They, too, are afraid. Into such a fury as this he flew when it was learned that Jacques Voudrier had escaped in his fishing smack to England, to join the Fighting French. That was an affair most unfortunate.'

'It sounds all right ter me,' said Copper.

'It was bad for the people Jacques left behind,' explained The Fox. 'Von Roth, as an example to others, as he said, shot Jacques' wife, his mother, and his two children, Jeanette and Paul. Had there been other relations, doubtless he would have shot them, too.'

Gimlet's eyes were on the Fox's face. There was a frosty gleam in them. 'One day I hope to have the pleasure of meeting this fellow von Roth,' he said softly.

'Pleasure?' greeted Cub.

'The pleasure on that occasion will, I trust, be entirely mine,' answered Gimlet, in a voice that was like cracking ice. 'Go on, Fox.'

'There are Boches everywhere, even in the forest,' resumed The Fox. 'The Fleas have gone into hiding, and it would be well for you to do so, *monsieur*, until things settle down. On the dunes there are many patrols, with Messerschmitts flying low, and the sea swarms with E-boats to make sure that this time the commandos do not get back. To approach the sea while things are like this would be madness, so I have brought some food from the store in case it is needed.'

'We were just talking of going the other way, towards Chateaudun,' said Cub. 'I am rather out of touch with things, but perhaps you know if a goods train goes south tonight?'

The Fox shrugged. 'I doubt it. I have just spoken with the Frog, whose father, as you know, works on the railway. Already an ammunition train, a goods train, and a loose engine are held up at Falaise junction, waiting for a troop train to go through.'

'What's that you say?' asked Gimlet sharply.

'A troop train is taking new U-boat crews to Cherbourg,' replied The Fox. 'Since the British bombing broke the bridge only one line operates, so much traffic is held up at Falaise, in a siding which the Germans have built there.'

'And an ammunition train is now waiting at Falaise?'

'*Oui, monsieur.*'

'How very interesting,' murmured Gimlet.

'Falaise is on our way to Chateaudun,' prompted Cub.

'So I see.' Gimlet was looking at his map. 'I seem to know this name, Falaise. Didn't something once happen there?'

'It was in a dungeon of the castle that King John had his nephew, Prince Arthur, murdered,' replied Cub. 'The *concierge* is a friend of ours, by the way, if ever you are in trouble.'

Gimlet nodded. 'If someone started this ammunition train, would it run down the line and meet the troop train?'

'Not exactly, but it could be done,' returned The Fox. '*Voilà.* This is the situation.' Using stalks of hay to demonstrate his meaning, he continued. 'We are a mile outside the town, you comprehend? Here is the main line, so. The troop train comes from the east, from Paris, although just where it is now I do not know. Here is the siding, with the ammunition train facing west, also the goods train. The loose engine waits between them. Here is the junction. This line that runs south to Argentan. It would only be necessary to switch the points at the western end of the siding to put the ammunition train on the main track – *comme ça.*' The Fox juggled with his pieces of hay.

'That, I suppose, would have to be done from the signal box?'

'Not necessarily,' put in Cub. 'The control cables run above ground. It is possible to pull on the cable at any place between the signal box and the points, to work the switch. We have wrecked several trains that way, in other places, haven't we, Fox?'

'But certainly. If it is desired that the points be switched, the Fleas will do it. I had such a plan in mind, until this affair in Caen. Now it is known that there are commandos in Normandy there may be guards – I do not know.'

'What about the drivers of these trains – are they French?' questioned Gimlet.

'*Non, monsieur*. The Boches no longer trust French drivers – at least, not with important war trains.'

'I see,' said Gimlet. 'We shall have to pay a call on this place, Falaise, I think. It's nearly dark, so we can soon be on the move. I take it, Cub, that you know the best way?'

'I know every inch of the ground,' declared Cub.

Gimlet turned to The Fox. 'And if we seize the engines, you, with The Fleas, will attend to the points?'

'With pleasure, *mon commandant*,' agreed The Fox readily. 'And afterwards?'

'Afterwards, you had better return to the forest, where we can find you should we need you again.'

'*Oui, mon commandant*.'

The final details of the plan were soon settled. The commandos were to give The Fox half an hour's start in order to get The Fleas together.

The gang would then spread out in the manner of a protective screen, and travelling cross-country move ahead of the commandos, to ascertain the position of enemy patrols, should there be any. On arrival at the Falaise siding the commandos would first dispose of the driver and fireman of the ammunition train. A whistle would announce that this had been done, upon which the train, driven by Gimlet, would move on to the main track. When the train stopped, The Fleas were to switch the points. The train would then be started in reverse, so that it would run backwards up the main line, and meet the troop train coming down.

Naturally, the commandos would jump off as soon as the train was started on its last trip. If possible, the goods train would also be switched to the main line, and sent along, driverless, to pile into the wreck. The Fleas would then return to the forest, and the commandos proceed on their way towards Chateaudun. This was the broad plan, but in the event it did not work out that way.

The Fox departed on his mission, and when half an hour had elapsed, the commandos rose.

Leaving the hay barn, they found The Grasshopper keeping watch outside. He reported that German patrols were constantly on the move; all roads were guarded, and travellers were being questioned. He was told to let his father know that the commandos were leaving, and to thank him for his hospitality. Then, under Cub's guidance, the party set off in single file across the sullen countryside. There was nothing to indicate that The Fleas were somewhere ahead, but about twenty minutes later The Fox, with Tyke at his heels, loomed up in the darkness and had a whispered conversation with Cub, after which he vanished as silently as he had appeared.

'There's a searchlight battery in the field ahead,' Cub told Gimlet. 'We shall have to make a detour, that's all.' Striking off at a tangent he strode on.

Time passed, and at length The Fox again appeared, to report that all was quiet at the siding, which was only a short distance ahead, but that an armed guard, comprising an *Unteroffizier* and three men, had been posted at the signal box.

'What are these troops doing?' asked Gimlet.

'One stands at the foot of the steps,' answered The Fox. 'The others are trying to make the telephone work.'

'Is it out of, order, then?'

'*Oui, monsieur*. It is out of order because we have cut the wires on both sides of the box,' answered The Fox calmly. 'That is always a good precaution.'

Gimlet turned to the commandos. 'I think we had better deal with these fellows first, otherwise they'll try to interfere when we start shunting the trains. Cub, tell The Fox to lead us to a position from which we can see the signal box.'

Cub passed the order, and the party again moved forward.

The signal box soon came into sight – a small frame building, as usual built high, and entered by a flight of wooden steps. It stood at the western end of the siding. From the top of the low embankment that occurred at this spot it was possible to see the sentry, and hear him, for he strolled up and down in the careless attitude of a man who feels that he is doing an unnecessary job. Within the building above him, dark shadows moved from time to time against a background of dim light.

The siding was also in plain view, with the trains standing in the positions The Fox had described, thus:

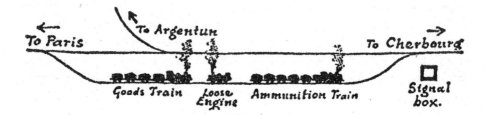

Smoke curled idly from the engines. From the locomotive of the ammunition train came a low hiss of escaping steam. The Fox reported that The Fleas were in position to work the switch. Gimlet ordered him to rejoin them, and stand by for the whistle, which might be some minutes, as they had first to deal with the Nazi guard. Obediently, The Fox faded away.

Gimlet touched Trapper on the arm. 'The light is tricky,' he whispered. 'Do you think you can get that sentry or shall we go down after him?'

Trapper unslung his bow. '*Ma foi*!' When I can't hit a man at thirty metres I will use my arrows for firewood.'

There were a few moments of tense, almost painful silence, while he fitted an arrow to his bow, and the sentry, all unconscious of his impending doom, began to sing a ribald song.

'Why, the silly swipe has been on the booze,' grunted Copper in a disgusted voice. 'A sentry who gets a skinful before going on duty deserves all 'e gets. Am I right, Trapper?'

'Name of a dog! *I'll* say you're right,' agreed Trapper. '*Regardez.*' He rose slowly to one knee. *Phung*! sang the bowstring.

The singing stopped abruptly. Almost before the sound had died away, Gimlet, gun in hand, was sliding down the bank. The others followed, although Cub observed that there was no need for haste. With an arrow projecting from his heart the sentry lay still and silent beside the line he had so unwisely guarded.

Gimlet threw a glance at the smoking engines, and then switched his eyes to the signal box. As he did so the door above opened and a voice shouted, in German, 'The wires must have been cut. There may be commandos about, so watch what you're doing, Rudolf.'

'*Ja*,' grunted Gimlet.

'I don't like it,' continued the voice above. 'I'm sending number fifty-six down to the siding in the town, to be on the safe side.'

'*Ja, ja*,' grunted Gimlet again.

The man above, presumably the *Unteroffizier*, re-entered the signal box, leaving the door open. A moment later there came the crash of a lever, and the harsh swish of a cable. Somewhere down the line a signal clanged.

For a second or two the commandos stood staring, uncertain as to what was happening, for to them the *Unteroffizier's* statement was vague; but when the engine of the ammunition train suddenly spurted steam and began to move, it became all too clear. The ammunition train was leaving, which at once threw the whole scheme out of gear.

Gimlet rapped out new orders to meet the situation. 'Trapper, don't let anybody out of that signal box,' he said tersely. To Copper he snapped, 'Come on,' and began running towards the ammunition train which by this time was rumbling slowly past them.

Not from the start was there any question of reaching the engine, which had already gone past and was now gathering speed. Indeed, Cub was convinced that it was too late to do anything, although he followed as a matter of course, not knowing what else to do.

From then on there was little time for thought, and his actions were prompted by those of his comrades. He saw Gimlet race for a moment beside the train and then make a flying leap at a truck. Copper did the same, dropping his Sten gun in the effort. The clatter of its fall was drowned in the noise made by the train.

In sheer desperation Cub grabbed at a passing buffer. Instantly he was dragged off his feet, and all but fell under the wheels, but he managed to hang on and drag himself up. Somehow he clambered to the top of a tarpaulin-covered truck, and there he lay, panting from exertion and excitement. He could see the others, dimly, just ahead, and wondered what they would do. His brain was in a whirl. To tell the truth, he was already repenting his haste.

It seemed that they had all bitten off more than they could handle, for the train was now travelling so fast that dismounting would be a perilous undertaking.

Then he saw Gimlet's slim figure rise up, and begin jumping from truck to truck towards the engine, swaying, and sometimes falling. Copper, looming huge in the darkness, did the same. Cub, realising that they did not know he was aboard. followed.

CHAPTER SEVEN

A Ride to Remember

Cub followed, not so much because he had any hope of taking part in what the others were going to do, as because he did not relish the idea of being left alone. He felt that anything might happen at any moment.

The trip down the train, necessitating as it did a jump from one truck to the next, together with the noise, the rush of wind, and the smoke and soot that swirled aft, was a nightmare. This was bad enough, but worse was to come, for while he was staggering on, to add to the horror, from out of the darkness overhead suddenly came a stream of living sparks of fire.

Even above the noise of the train came the roar of a low-flying aircraft, and he realised that the train was being shot up by a British intruder intent on making a sieve of the engine. Remembering that he was on a train loaded with ammunition, had there been the slightest hope of surviving the fall he would have jumped for his life; but the engine driver, apparently aware of his danger, had increased speed to something in the order of fifty miles an hour. Then, to cap all, from somewhere ahead of him, on the train, a pom-pom began spitting back at the aircraft. He recalled, vaguely, that French trains were being equipped with guns, with German crews, to answer the menace of British intruding aircraft.

It was in something like panic that he began to move forward again, in the hope, now a desperate hope, of getting in touch with the others, to let them know he was there. Tracer shells and bullets were still flying in a most terrifying manner.

Then, suddenly, the engine driver had had enough; or so it must be assumed, for the brakes, screaming in protest, were clapped on with such force that the train jolted violently, nearly throwing Cub overboard. As it was, he fell, and to save himself clung to the rope lashing the tarpaulin.

The train, bumping and jolting, but fast slowing down, plunged into a deep cutting, and at the same time the shooting stopped. At any rate, the aircraft disappeared. What happened to it Cub did not know. He never knew. At the time he was quite content that it should go.

Rising, he ran forward, and nearly trod on Gimlet and Copper before he saw them, for they were lying flat, firing their revolvers at point-blank range into the gun crew, of which only two members remained. They jumped off – or fell off, he was not sure which – leaving the pom-pom, which was mounted on an iron trolley.

'Strike me pink!' cried Copper when he saw Cub. 'Where did you spring from?'

'Same place as you,' answered Cub grimly, dropping beside him.

'You watch your step.' warned Gimlet, and then ran on towards the engine.

'He's crazy,' averred Cub.

'Don't you believe it, chum. He's having the time of his little life,' declared Copper. 'The fun hasn't started yet.'

'Fun!' snorted Cub, as he followed Copper in the wake of their leader.

They were just in time to see the end of the first chapter of the night's work. It was not without its humorous aspect. The engine driver, a very fat man, had already abandoned the footplate, and was sprinting down the line – a ludicrous spectacle. The fireman was made of sterner stuff. He made a terrific swipe at Gimlet with his long-handled shovel. Gimlet ducked, and the tool passed over his head with such force that its weight carried the man off his perch, so that he fell flat on his back beside the track. He was up in a flash, running for dear life.

'All right. Let him go,' said Gimlet, as he dropped lightly to the footplate. Then he laughed. 'By gad! We shall need a bath after this,' he remarked. Which was true enough, for they were all as black as chimney sweeps with the grime flung back from the funnel. 'Quite a trip, wasn't it?' he added cheerfully.

'Er – yes,' agreed Cub.

'We'd better get back to see what's happened to Trapper,' went on

Gimlet, and putting the engine in reverse he sent the train back up the track.

They had not gone far when sparks, and a reek of burning, sent Cub to the top of the tender. He let out a yell. 'The train's on fire! That plane must have set it alight. Let's get off.'

'Get off? Why?' demanded Gimlet.

'Well – er – the ammunition,' stammered Cub.

'Oh, that,' rejoined Gimlet carelessly. 'No jolly fear. I've been to too much trouble to get this train to throw it away. Besides, I don't feel like walking all the way back to the siding.'

'But the ammunition may go up,' argued Cub.

'It has to get hot, quite hot, you know, before it explodes,' said Gimlet evenly.

'We shall get quite hot, too, if it does go up,' growled Copper.

'What was that?' demanded Gimlet curtly.

'Nothin', sir.'

'Don't get in the habit of thinking aloud,' snapped Gimlet.

'No, sir,' assented Copper, nudging Cub.

The fire, fanned by the wind, grew quickly worse, so that the train appeared to thrust before it a miniature volcano. Cub, who by this time was really scared, fearing that the whole train would blow up at any moment, was more than a little relieved when the signal box came into sight. As Gimlet applied the brakes and slowed down, Trapper appeared, running beside the engine. He seemed to be excited about something.

'You're on fire!' he shouted.

'Did you suppose I hadn't noticed it?' inquired Gimlet sarcastically.

'But the train, the troop train, she comes!' yelled Trapper. 'Voilà!' He pointed up the track.

'By gad! That's lucky; just in time,' said Gimlet. 'Off you get, you fellows,' he ordered.

Cub and Copper needed no second invitation. They jumped to the ground. Gimlet started the engine, and standing on the step, called brightly, 'Two to Waterloo!' Then he, too, jumped off.

The train, with swiftly increasing speed, puffed on, tail first, towards the oncoming locomotive, the headlight of which could now be seen.

'We'd better get under cover, sir,' urged Copper, backing away.

'I think you're right,' agreed Gimlet. 'There's going to be a bang, quite a bang, in a minute. If there isn't, I shall be disappointed.' They hurried to the embankment. 'What happened at the signal box, Trapper?' he asked.

Trapper clicked his tongue. 'Those Nazis would try to come out,' he answered plaintively. 'So I tossed a grenade through the window to keep them amused.'

'And The Fleas?'

'*Les Poux*? They say they return to the forest, but I think they lie somewhere to watch.'

A minute later, about four hundred yards from the siding, the two trains came into collision. To Cub it sounded like the end of the world. First came the crash of the impact. It was followed instantly by a single explosion, and then a roar that rocked the earth. It lasted for nearly a minute, like a tremendous roll of thunder, and with it came a blast of air that flattened trees as though they had been tissue paper, and flung the signal box on its side. The heavens blazed with a lurid glare that made the landscape as light as noon. As the roar ended, and the glare began to fade, there came the clash and clatter of falling debris. These sinister sounds lasted for some time, and at the end were followed by an ominous silence. Above the scene of the explosion a mighty pillar of smoke coiled high against the starlit sky.

'That'll learn 'em,' remarked Copper approvingly.

'Quite a bang, wasn't it?' said Gimlet quietly. 'Spoilt the trains, I should say. Bit tough on the fellows in the trooper.'

'Not 'alf tough enough,' growled Copper. 'I don't forget what they done ter London, and, from all accounts, a lot of other places. They asked for it. Now they're getting a bellyful of it themselves I'll bet it ain't so funny, not by a long shot. Am I right, Trapper?'

Trapper hissed through his teeth, stroking his little moustache. 'Are you right, pal? *I'll* say you're right.'

Gimlet picked up a lump of chalk that had fallen from the embankment, and crossing to the signal box, made his mark, the gimlet. 'What about the goods train?' said he, and walked on down the line. 'We may as well finish the job.'

They found it abandoned, which in the circumstances was hardly surprising. What had become of the driver and his mate is open to conjecture, but it seems likely that they bolted when they saw that a collision was inevitable. The goods train stood as they had left it, with steam up.

'The line that runs to the east, you say, has its terminus at Cherbourg?' queried Gimlet.

'That's right, sir,' confirmed Cub.

'In that case, as the Nazis will be waiting for it, we may as well send it through,' decided Gimlet. 'It would be a shame to disappoint them. Pity we can't be there to see it arrive.' He made his mark on the side of the engine. Then, climbing into the cab, he took the train slowly to the main line. Then he opened the throttle and jumped down. The train, beyond all human control, rolled ponderously into the night.

'That should bend the old buffers a bit, when it gets to Cherbourg,' opined Copper. 'The funny thing is, when I was a kid, I hated playin' with trains.' He walked over and retrieved his Sten gun, returning as Gimlet rejoined the party.

Gimlet stopped suddenly. 'Hark!' he said. 'It sounds as though we've stirred things up a bit.' This was obviously true, for from several directions came the sound of motor traffic travelling at high speed.

The Fox dashed up. '*Départ, messieurs, tout suite*!' he cried. '*Les Boches* – they come.'

'Which way?' asked Gimlet calmly.

'From all directions,' answered The Fox urgently. 'They will come to the siding.'

'Yes, I quite think they will,' agreed Gimlet.

'*Regardez*! Here are some, coming down the line from Argentan.' The Fox pointed with a quivering finger.

'I think it's time we were moving off, if I may say so, sir,' suggested Copper tentatively.

'You're right – definitely right,' answered Gimlet. 'Did someone say that the line to Argentan is on the way to Chateaudun?'

'Yes, but you can't walk that way,' said Cub. 'There are troops coming up the line – I can see them.'

'Who said anything about walking?' inquired Gimlet. 'I always did hate walking, and I see no reason to walk when we can ride. We'll borrow the loose engine – it seems to be doing nothing. Fox, switch us to the main line, then over to the junction. Afterwards, make yourself scarce. *Au revoir*.'

'*Au revoir, mon commandant*.' The Fox dashed off.

'Take care of Tyke,' called Cub.

'*Oui*.'

The commandos boarded the loose engine which, like the goods train, had been abandoned. The first shunt took them to the main line, and the second, to the branch line, which curved away to the south.

'Tally-ho! Here we go,' said Gimlet, and sent the train puffing down the line. 'Give the boys a squirt as we go through them, Copper, just to show there are no hard feelings,' he suggested.

The Nazi troops, who were coming up the line at the double, flung themselves aside as the engine thundered towards them. Copper, leaning out of one side, sprayed the crouching figures with bullets from his Sten gun, while Trapper, from the other side, blazed away with two revolvers. It was all over in a moment. The engine, bathed in the lurid glow of its furnace, roared on into the night.

'This is a lot better than walking; yes, by gad!' asserted Gimlet.

'As long as we don't meet something coming the other way,' muttered Copper.

'Never thought of that,' admitted Gimlet. 'Still, if we do, we shan't know anything about it,' he added brightly. 'We *are* having fun.'

'Some of us are,' grunted Copper.

'What was that?' inquired Gimlet crisply.

'Nothin', sir.'

'I thought you spoke. By the way,' went on Gimlet, 'does anyone know exactly where this line ends?'

'For my part, I tink we go to Kingdom Come,' said Trapper anxiously. 'When we stop the loco, if we do not hit a station on the way, the Boches will know where we are.'

'Ha! That's where you're wrong, my comrade from the wide open spaces,' disputed Gimlet. 'When we leave the engine we shall send it on without us. Then the beastly Nazis will have to guess where we got off. Hello! Here's a station, by gad! No stopping for refreshments, I'm afraid.'

They roared through the station, catching a fleeting glimpse of figures running for their lives.

'What station was that, Cub?' asked Gimlet.

'That,' answered Cub, 'was Argentan. Aren't we going rather fast, sir?' he added anxiously.

'As fast as this old barrow will go,' answered Gimlet cheerfully.

Cub moistened his lips. Remembering the conversation in Copper's quarters, for the first time he began to wonder if Gimlet was really sane.

'What's the next station, Cub?' inquired Gimlet.

'Alençon. At this rate we shall be there in five or six minutes.'

'Do you know of a good hiding-place there?'

'Yes – the one I always use when I go south.'

'Splendid! What is it, exactly?'

'It's a barge, moored on the river Sarthe, an old one, but still serviceable when I last saw it,' explained Cub. 'It belonged to an old man named Jules Rochet, who ran it with his son and daughter. The old man was shot for some small offence, and the son was sent as a forced labourer to Germany. Marcelle, the daughter, still lives in the boat, which used to come up as far as Caen, where I first met her – but I don't think she works it any longer. There isn't anything for it to do. You can guess how much *she* loves the Nazis. She knows about The Fleas. In fact, she once hid some of us. She would have joined us, I think, but she stays on the river in case her brother should escape and get back.'

'Will she put us up, do you think?'

'Without a doubt – if the barge is there.'

'And does the river run on to the south?'

'Yes, more or less. It passes a fair distance west of Chateaudun, though.'

'That should suit us fine.'

'Yes, sir,' agreed Cub. 'But we're nearly there. If you're going to make for the barge you'd better start stopping.'

'In that case I'll turn off the juice,' answered Gimlet, suiting the action to the word. 'Tell me just where to stop.'

Cub leaned out and surveyed as much of the countryside as could be seen. 'Steady,' he called.

The brakes went on, and the engine thumped over an iron bridge.

'Stop her!' called Cub sharply.

Slowly, with many wheezes, the engine came to a stop.

'That's fine,' declared Cub. 'We're only about five minutes' walk from the river.'

'I'm sorry to part with this old barrel,' said Gimlet regretfully. 'Still, we shan't want her again, so we'll make her last trip something to remember. Off you get.' He waited until they were on the track before opening the throttle and joining them. The engine, gathering speed, puffed off into the night. As they watched it disappear Cub wondered where it would end its life. He never knew.

'This way,' he said.

They struck off across a field, and as Cub had promised, a walk of five minutes brought them to a broad stream. Another two minutes, at a bend, Cub stopped and pointed. 'There's the barge,' said he. 'Let's go and find if Marcelle is at home.'

At that moment the sound of a woman's voice, muffled, though pitched high in anger, came from the rivercraft.

'I should say she is at home,' murmured Gimlet drily. 'And I don't think she's alone.'

Walking forward, Cub's voice was tense when he answered, 'Just a minute. I'll see what goes on.' He crossed to the barge by a short plank, and rapped sharply on the cabin door.

There was a moment's pause. Then the door was thrown open and a figure appeared, framed in yellow candlelight. It was a German soldier, a burly man of about forty-five, with a truculent expression on a heavy, bloated face.

CHAPTER EIGHT

Death Comes Aboard

Whatever it may have been that Cub expected, it was not a Nazi trooper. He stared, and continued staring, for once at a loss for words.

'What do you want, *gamin*?' demanded the German harshly, in villainous French.

'I – er – want to see Mademoiselle Rochet,' answered Cub, recovering himself.

'You can't,' snarled the Nazi, and slammed the door in his face.

Cub looked over his shoulder at the others, who had dropped flat on the river bank. 'Did you – hear that?' he asked in a hoarse whisper. 'I think Marcelle is in trouble.'

'If there are Nazis there you can bet on it,' said Gimlet. 'Something tells me that we have arrived at an opportune moment, a most opportune moment, by gad! Stand aside, Cub. I'll deal with this.'

As Gimlet advanced to the companionway that gave access to the cabin, Cub stepped back. The two commandos took up positions on either side of the door.

Gimlet took out his revolver and with the butt knocked gently.

'*Donnerblitz!*' rasped a voice inside, and again the door was flung open. The same German appeared, his face flushed with anger. 'I said—' he began, and then stopped, his jaw sagging, and the flush fading from his face as his eyes fell on the slim figure in battle-dress: they stood out like those of a frog, with shock, fright, or astonishment, or maybe a combination of all three.

'You said – what?' inquired Gimlet, in a voice that had iron in it.

The Nazi began to back away, and Cub caught sight of another, sitting at a table with a bottle of wine and some playing cards in front of him.

'Where is Mademoiselle Rochet?' asked Gimlet, in a tone ominously quiet.

The German began to bluster, and the one inside, having had time to recover, or perhaps thinking he was unobserved, made a grab for a rifle that leaned against a bulkhead. His hand never reached it. Gimlet's revolver roared. The German stiffened convulsively, turned in his seat, and then, quite slowly, slid to the floor, where he lay still.

The original German made an equally fatal mistake. He seemed to lose his head. With a leap of surprising agility for one of his size, knocking Gimlet's arm aside he sprang past him to the companion steps and made a dash for the plank. He had no idea, of course, that anyone else was there. When Copper's gun crashed down on his head his legs collapsed under him and he fell into the water with a mighty splash. As the splash subsided a few bubbles came floating up, nothing else.

'Any more in there, Skipper?' asked Copper calmly.

'I don't think so,' answered Gimlet.

By this time Cub was in the cabin. 'Marcelle, where are you?' he cried.

'Here,' answered a voice beyond the cabin.

Cub crossed the floor and unlocked a door.

A girl, a pretty girl of about eighteen, looking dishevelled and bewildered, almost fell into the cabin. Her eyes went round with fear when she saw the soot-grimed commandos – which was not surprising.

'It's all right, Marcelle,' said Cub quickly. 'These are friends. What has happened? What were those Boches doing here?'

Marcelle steadied herself with a hand on the table. She gasped when she saw the dead man on the floor.

'Mother of God!' she breathed. 'You've killed him. You know what that means. We shall all be shot.'

'What were these men doing here?' insisted Cub.

Marcelle passed a hand wearily over her face. 'They came with orders to seize the barge,' she replied. 'The Nazis are taking all the barges, so I was not surprised. They came at eight o'clock, but they did not go. They searched the barge, and found a little wine which my father had hidden.

They stayed to drink it. When they began to get drunk I tried to run away, but they caught me and locked me in the galley.'

'You're not hurt?' questioned Gimlet.

'*Non, monsieur* – only this.' The girl turned her face so that a red bruise could be seen. 'This one did it.' She pointed to the man on the floor. 'He would try to kiss me, so I smacked his face. Then he struck me.'

'*Le diable*! I wish he was not dead, so that I could kill him again – slowly,' grated Trapper.

'You'd better get him out of the way,' commanded Gimlet. 'He isn't pretty to look at. I think the river is the best place.'

'*Psst!*' hissed Marcelle. 'Someone comes.' She ran to the top of the companion and looked out. She was back in a flash. '*Les Boches*,' she said breathlessly. 'A patrol is coming up the path. They can only be coming here.'

'How many?' asked Gimlet dispassionately.

'Ten – twelve – I do not know. Quickly – in here. I will talk to them.' She sped across the room and opened the galley door.

Gimlet inclined his head. 'Inside, everyone,' he said. 'Bring that stiff with you, Copper.'

'I shall stay and see Marcelle through with this,' declared Cub. 'She may need support.'

The commandos disappeared into the galley, taking the dead German with them. As the door closed, footsteps could be heard on the plank, and a moment later the head and shoulders of a German officer, a *Leutnant*, appeared at the top of the companion. For a second he stood, or rather, crouched, peering into the cabin. Then he came down. After a perfunctory glance at Cub he addressed Marcelle, speaking in French.

'There was a noise that sounded like a shot not long ago. It came from this direction. Did you hear it?'

'Yes, *Leutnant*,' answered Marcelle, with ingenuous frankness.

'Where was it?'

'It was not far away,' asserted Marcelle. 'My friend, here, heard it too.'

'You have seen nobody, then?'

'We stayed inside. Those are the orders, when there is shooting, as you know, *Leutnant*. It was not our business, and we have no desire to get into trouble.'

The officer picked up one of the playing cards. It was a German pack, quite unlike the French. 'What are those things doing here?'

'They belong to the soldiers, *Leutnant*.'

'What soldiers?'

'The two soldiers who were sent to inform me that the boat is required by the authorities.'

'Where are they?'

Marcelle shrugged. 'German soldiers do not tell people like me where they are going. Perhaps they were responsible for the shooting?'

The German raised his eyebrows. 'Whom would they shoot?'

Marcelle's native wit was now well into its stride. She made a little grimace. 'They might shoot each other.'

The officer frowned. 'Shoot each other! Why?'

Marcelle's eyes went to the wine bottle. 'They drank, and played cards. One tried to kiss me, and then they quarrelled. I was struck in the brawl – look.' She pointed to her bruised cheek.

'How long since you saw them?'

'Only a few minutes, *Leutnant*.'

'Zo! If they come back, you will tell them that *Leutnant* Zimmermann has been here, and orders them to return to camp.'

'*Oui, Herr Leutnant.*'

The officer's brow knitted. His eyes were on the floor. He bent and touched something. When he stood up, his fingers were red. 'This is blood,' he said in a hard voice.

'I told you, there was fighting here,' said Marcelle simply.

The officer threw a curious glance at Cub. 'Did you see this?'

'But no, *Herr Leutnant*. I only arrived a minute ago.'

'What are you doing out at this time of night?'

'I have no home. I sleep where I can.'

The German considered the scene for a moment and then turned to the steps. '*Bonsoir,*' he said abruptly.

'*Bonsoir, Herr Leutnant,*' said Marcelle and Cub together.

Footsteps thumped on the plank. An order was rapped out. Feet marched, retreating.

Cub glanced at Marcelle. 'You were magnificent,' he breathed.

'Pah!' sneered Marcelle. 'They are dolts, these Germans – animals.' She went to the head of the companion, looked out and returned. 'They have gone,' she announced, and crossing to the galley door threw it open. 'The swine have departed, *mon capitan*,' she told Gimlet. 'May I offer you a glass of wine?'

'Not at the moment, *mademoiselle*, thanks,' answered Gimlet. 'We have things to do.'

Acting on his instructions, Copper and Trapper between them carried the dead German to the deck. There was a splash, and they returned.

To Cub, Marcelle said: 'Now tell me. Why have you come here?'

'We needed a hiding-place.'

'And now what? The barge has been commandeered. In the morning the Germans will come, seeking the two soldiers. They may search the barge. It is not a place the most safe, *mon ami*.'

'Don't worry about us, *mademoiselle*,' put in Gimlet. 'We'll be on our way long before then.' He looked at his watch. 'It's just midnight,' he announced. 'It is unlikely that the Germans will come back before dawn – it may even be later. What are you going to do?'

'Me, I shall sink the barge so that the Boches can't have it, and then go to an uncle in Le Mans, who will hide me.' Marcelle started. '*Hélas*! An idea. We can go to Le Mans, which is on the river, in the barge.'

'I know the town pretty well,' stated Gimlet. 'I used to come over for the motor races, before the war. Jolly good fun.'

'It's a long way,' Cub pointed out. 'The river winds about.'

'By dawn, downstream, Charon, who is eating his head off in the field, will cover eighteen, perhaps twenty miles,' declared Marcelle.

'Charon is the horse,' explained Cub.

'You could all get some sleep then, as we travelled,' went on Marcelle, warming up to her idea. 'I will lead Charon down the tow-path.'

'It takes two people to handle the boat,' Cub pointed out. 'You know the river, so lead Charon, and I will take the tiller.'

'*Bon*. And when it gets light we will find a quiet spot to sink the barge,' said Marcelle.

Gimlet looked concerned. 'But the barge is your home. Is it necessary to destroy it?'

'The Germans will take it, anyway,' Marcelle pointed out. 'If I sink it the Germans may spend much time looking for it,' she argued, with shrewd logic. 'They will not know where to look for me, so they will not be able to ask awkward questions.'

Gimlet smiled. 'You have your wits, *mademoiselle*.'

'One needs wits, *mon brave*, to live in France, at such times as these.'

'You are sure your uncle in Le Mans will look after you?'

'After all of us, if you wish, *monsieur*. He was a soldier in the last war. Now he is a mechanician, although he keeps the shop of an ironmonger in the Place des Jacobins. Even so, I know he tries to think of a way to get to England, to carry on the fight.'

'Then we may be able to help him,' asserted Gimlet. 'If we should be parted, make your way to the Forest of Caen, and wait there with The Grey Fleas for our return.'

'*Entendu, monsieur*. Now, the sooner we are on our way the better.'

The matter being settled, she fetched the horse from the field, harnessed it, adjusted the tow-rope, and cast off.

'*Allez, mon vieux*,' she ordered.

The horse strained on the rope and the barge began to move. Cub went aft to the tiller. The commandos went below and closed the door.

The clumsy vehicle moved ponderously down the stream.

CHAPTER NINE

Down the River

Dawn found the barge still surging slowly down the river, through a typical, flat, pastoral landscape, which has so often been depicted by artists. Poplars, never far distant in northern France, broke the horizon at regular intervals. Bullrushes, and an occasional willow, lined the banks. Beyond, on either side, cows ruminated in fields of lush, dew-soaked grass. At one point an ancient windmill pointed a derelict arm to heaven. Crows sailed serenely across a sky of pale azure blue. It was a pleasant scene, a picture of peace. The war might have been a thousand miles away.

Breaking the placid water with its blunt bows the barge moved on with hardly a sound, leaving only a broad V of ripples to mark its passage. It was not one of those huge vessels common in the Thames Estuary. Compared with them it was small, as are most French barges, the size being governed by the speed at which some of the rivers flow – it would not be possible to tow a heavy craft against a fast-moving stream. Marcelle, bare-legged, a black beret hanging over her right ear, plodded steadily beside the horse. Cub leaned, half asleep, against the tiller.

A sudden splash brought him to his senses with a rush. It came from somewhere forward, and he darted to the side to ascertain the cause. His nerves relaxed when Gimlet's face appeared beside the barge. His body, looking strangely white in the pale light, and rather absurd, Cub thought, in blue silk trunks, floated by.

'Just having my tub,' called Gimlet cheerfully, as the vessel slid by. 'Get some of that disgusting soot off, by gad.' He allowed the barge to pass him, and then, overtaking it in a flashing crawl stroke, seized the rudder and climbed aboard. 'That's better,' he observed. 'I'll be with you in a minute.' Swinging the water off his arms he returned to the cabin.

Yawning, Cub returned to his leaning posture on the tiller.

Soon afterwards a whistle from Marcelle again brought him to the alert. Seeing nothing ahead, he looked back and observed a man overtaking them, a cyclist. He seemed to be one of the peasant class, dressed in his best clothes. A bulky parcel was tied on the back of the machine. With a casual '*Bonjour*' he overtook the barge and passed on.

Presently came two more men, of similar type, walking briskly. One carried a bundle and the other a suitcase. Not far behind marched yet a fourth man, again of similar type, with a bundle on his shoulder. As he drew level, moved to curiosity by this strange procession, Cub accosted him.

'*Bonjour, monsieur*,' he greeted. 'As it is not Sunday, where do you go so early, dressed in your best clothes?'

'To Le Mans,' was the answer.

'Is there a fête, or something?'

'There is no fête, but there is a meeting,' answered the man, with bitterness in his voice. 'Another hundred men have been called up from this district, and I, alas, am one of them.'

'Called up?' queried Cub, not understanding. 'For what? By whom?'

'By the Germans – who else? We go to Germany to work.'

'Why do you go?'

'Because,' returned the man in a hard voice, 'if I do not report this morning I shall be shot. The Nazis have promised, and this is one of the promises they do keep – may the devil seize their souls.'

'*Sacré nom*!' ejaculated Cub. 'Where is this meeting, and at what hour?'

'In the Place des Jacobins, at noon.'

'A hundred men, eh?'

'So it is said.'

'Which way do you travel?'

'First to Paris, then Germany. That's all I know. *Au revoir*.' The man strode on.

The cabin door opened and Gimlet's face appeared, his chin freshly shaven. 'Did I hear talking?' he questioned.

Cub replied that he did, and gave him the gist of the conversation.

Gimlet nodded. 'How far are we from Le Mans?'

'Seven miles, perhaps eight.'

Marcelle dropped back until she could join in the talk. 'I don't think it would be safe to go much farther,' she averred. 'There are people about.'

'They will see us more plainly if we get out and walk,' argued Gimlet.

'Not if we hide, *monsieur*.'

'Hide where?'

'There is a marsh just ahead.'

'I once caught cold lying in a marsh,' asserted Gimlet. 'For that reason I have detested marshes ever since. I would rather go to Le Mans.'

Marcelle looked startled. 'But your uniforms, *mon capitan* – they would be seen.'

Gimlet admitted that this was a possibility.

'But wait!' cried Marcelle. 'An idea! In the clothes of my brother it might be possible.'

Gimlet's eyes brightened. 'You have clothes? Men's clothes?'

'But certainly – the clothes of my father and my brother. They are not of the best quality, you understand—'

'So much the better,' declared Gimlet. 'Cub, you take over the horse, while Marcelle trots out the togs. Come aboard, *mademoiselle*.'

Copper's face appeared at the head of the companion. 'What's the idea, sir?' he asked suspiciously.

Gimlet looked sad. 'An unfortunate thing has happened,' said he. 'We have been called up by the Jerries, to work for them in their beastly country. We are due to report in the Place des Jacobins at ten o'clock.'

Copper shook his head. 'I might 'ave known something like this would 'appen,' he lamented.

'What's that?' asked Gimlet crisply.

'Nothing, sir.'

'This should be fun, quite good fun,' declared Gimlet, as he helped Marcelle aboard.

Marcelle was not long below. She went ashore laughing at some private joke. 'Oh, la-la, what types,' she remarked to Cub as she took over, and Cub agreed that the three commandos were, as she called them, types. Types described them aptly, he reflected.

After that, the first to appear was Gimlet. He wore three articles of clothing. A striped singlet, much faded; a pair of rust-red sailcloth trousers, rather too large for him, and a pair of dilapidated rope-soled sandals. Copper followed, in a grey sweater with a monogram worked over the heart, and dark blue pantaloons, full at the waist and small at the ankles. Trapper looked entirely native in one of those fantastic outfits the French affect when they wish the world to know that they are sportsmen. The main features were skimpy knickerbockers, and a check jacket decorated with an unnecessary number of trappings, of the same material, sewn on to it.

In reply to a question Copper told Cub that their uniforms, and the Sten gun, were below, in sacks.

Seeing them, Marcelle halted the horse and came back. 'We are three miles from Le Mans, *monsieur le capitan*,' she told Gimlet. 'I doubt if it is safe to proceed farther.'

'Why not?'

'The boat, *monsieur*. If a search is made by the river, as doubtless it will be, she will be observed. You forget that the barge has a name.'

'Ah! Of course. What is her name?'

'Jeanne d'Alençon.'

Gimlet thought for a moment. 'Have you any paint?'

'But yes, *monsieur*.'

'Fetch it, please.'

The barge was brought quietly to the bank, and in a few minutes, by the alteration of four letters, the Jeanne d'Alençon had become Jeanne d'Avignon. A handful of dust was sufficient to remove the impression of newness.

'Now,' said Gimlet, 'there is no need to sink the barge. Also, there will be no need for us to walk.'

Marcelle considered the matter seriously. 'It is a risk worth taking,' she decided. 'In the town, among the other barges, perhaps she will not be noticed.'

'There are other barges?'

'Many.'

'Where do you usually tie up?'

'At the Quai Louis Blanc.'

'Then let us go there.'

'As you wish, *monsieur.*'

Marcelle returned to the horse, and Cub to the tiller. Gimlet lolled on the deck house, and the two commandos disposed themselves in comfortable positions near Cub. The barge proceeded.

Just outside the town two German soldiers, accompanied by a French *gendarme*, appeared, walking briskly up the towing path. Watching them closely, Cub saw their eyes go to the name on the bows, and he did not need to be told what they sought. The search for the Jeanne d'Alençon was on.

The *gendarme* raised his hand. 'Hi, there!' he hailed. 'Have you passed the Jeanne d'Alençon?'

'No, *monsieur,*' answered Cub respectfully – and truthfully.

'What are all those men doing on your boat?' questioned the *gendarme.*

'They are workmen, on their way to report at the Place des Jacobins, *monsieur,*' answered Cub readily. 'They were walking, so I offered them a lift.'

The *gendarme* nodded approval. 'Very well. Proceed.'

'Thank you, *monsieur.*'

The barge moved on, and the search party continued up the towing path.

'Easy,' muttered Copper scornfully. 'What was that Frenchie doing with those Jerries, Cub?'

'I expect he is an agent of Vichy,' answered Cub.

'He ought ter 'ave his block knocked off,' growled Copper. 'Am I right, Trapper?'

Trapper spat into the river. '*I'll* say you're right,' he agreed.

Signs of unusual activity became apparent as the barge entered the town. Many people could be seen, mostly men carrying parcels or suitcases. Some were talking in little groups, with an occasional German soldier moving among them, breaking up the groups when they exceeded five or six. An unusual number of motor vehicles, mostly old lorries, which the French call camions, or camionettes, were also converging on the town.

Marcelle walked on and brought the horse to a stop at a stone quay where a number of other barges were already moored. Cub leaned on the tiller, and guided the slowly moving vessel to a vacant berth. Jumping ashore, he joined Marcelle in the short task of making fast. The commandos sat on the deck-house watching the scene.

Marcelle called to a swarthy, flashily-dressed young man who stood talking to a small party of idlers. The man looked round, started visibly, and then hurried towards the barge. The colour drained from his face, and he snatched nervous glances up and down the quay.

'Will you take Charon to your stable, as usual?

The man came up, obviously agitated. '*Mon Dieu*!' he almost hissed. 'Are you mad? What folly made you fall out with the Germans? Don't you know that the police are looking for your boat? Are you trying to get me into trouble? What about the money you owe me already?'

'I will pay you one day,' promised Marcelle.

'One day? If you can't pay, why should I risk my life? Why come here at all?'

Marcelle shrugged. 'Where would you have me go? A barge cannot fly, neither can it travel overland. Be calm. Take Charon and go, and forget what you have seen.'

Bertrand's eyes swept nervously over the barge. 'Who are these men?' he queried petulantly, his eyes narrowing with suspicion – or it may have been jealousy.

'Ah, I am glad you are at least able to recognise men when you see them, my worm,' answered Marcelle with bitter sarcasm. 'Ask no questions, and answer none. *Adieu*.'

Bertrand threw a last startled glance at the party, shrugged his shoulders and departed, leading the horse.

'That girl has got guts,' observed Copper soberly, if vulgarly. 'From what I can see of it, the women and kids in this country ought to wear the trousers.'

'She is magnificent,' agreed Trapper, his dark eyes glowing. 'She has nerves, that one.'

Marcelle turned to them. 'Let us go,' she said quietly. 'Fortunately the house of my uncle, Gaston Boulanger, is in the Place des Jacobins, towards which everyone is walking. If we are questioned, you are of the party going to Germany – you comprehend?'

'Lead on, *mademoiselle*,' answered Gimlet.

At this juncture a civilian, a middle-aged man in dark clothes, came walking along the quay. He stopped in front of the barge. 'What are you men doing?' he inquired curtly.

'Can't you see they are of the party going to Germany?' inquired Marcelle.

'What is in those sacks?'

'Tools, my donkey,' answered Marcelle tartly. 'What use is a mechanician without his tools?'

The man gave her a surly look and passed on.

Cub drew a deep breath of relief. He was wondering what would have happened had the man opened one of the sacks and found a Sten gun and a commando's uniform.

Marcelle made her way unconcernedly through the streets to the Place des Jacobins, which lies only a short distance from the river. No one took any notice of the little party, which, after all, was typical of several. The French were too concerned with their own affairs, and the German troops were busy directing the traffic, both human and vehicular – the latter mostly ramshackle camionettes from the country.

The square reached, Marcelle threaded a course through the assembly to the far side, and after another short walk stopped at a narrow street, where the corner was occupied by an unpretentious little shop in which a miscellaneous assortment of dusty hardware was displayed for sale. Confidently, she turned the handle of the door, and then drew back, throwing a swift glance over her shoulder. For the first time her face betrayed anxiety.

'Locked,' she said laconically. 'I don't understand. Let us try the side door.'

She turned into the narrow street and tried a door from which most of the paint had peeled. 'Locked,' she said again, and rapped urgently on a panel. There was no reply, so she knocked again, harder.

A woman put her head out of an upstairs window of the next house. 'Whom do you seek?' she called.

'Gaston Boulanger.'

'He has departed,' stated the woman bluntly.

'Departed?' faltered Marcelle. 'Where?'

'*A là bas!*' The woman pointed to the square. 'All mechanicians have been conscripted by the Nazis for work in German factories. Today he goes, *mademoiselle*. The shop is closed for the duration.'

'Thank you, *madame*,' answered Marcelle in a dull voice.

CHAPTER TEN

The Ironmonger of Le Mans

Marcelle quickly recovered her composure. 'This is an affair the most unfortunate,' she announced quietly.

'What about your aunt?' suggested Cub.

'She is dead.'

'The party for Germany does not leave until noon,' put in Gimlet. 'If you can find your uncle, all may yet be well. We cannot help you so we will remain here.' Gimlet sat on the doorstep.

'It is an idea,' admitted Marcelle, and hurried off into the square, where she could be seen looking urgently to left and right.

An uncomfortable interval of about ten minutes followed. A soldier looked at the little party more than once, and at last he called: 'What do you want there? Take your places in the square.'

Fortunately, very soon afterwards Marcelle returned, bringing with her a tubby little man whose face, decorated with an enormous pair of black moustaches, was a picture of concern. Arrived at the side door he took a key from his pocket, inserted it in the lock with a trembling hand, and opened the door. The others followed him in, when he again closed the door and locked it.

'What happens, Marcelle?' he asked in a voice tremulous with alarm. 'Name of a name! Is this a day to come visiting?'

'To be sure,' answered Marcelle calmly. 'We could not have chosen a better day. You do not wish to go to Germany, my uncle, do you?'

'Who are these?' Boulanger indicated the commandos with a sweep of his arm.

'Just friends,' answered Marcelle airily. 'But why do we stand here? Let us go up to the parlour, where we can talk in comfort.' Without waiting for a reply she led the way upstairs into a sitting-room that overlooked the square.

Monsieur Boulanger now asserted his authority. 'I asked you, who are these *apaches*? And what are you doing with them?' he demanded in no uncertain voice.

Marcelle shrugged. 'Since you must know, my uncle, they are British commandos,' she answered evenly.

Boulanger's face blanched. He stared stupidly, with beads of perspiration breaking out on his brow. 'Ten thousand devils!' he got out at last. Then he threw up his hands. 'This is the end,' he went on heavily. 'I might as well cut my throat. *Alors*! What is in those sacks?'

'Guns, my uncle. Only guns, and uniforms.'

The little ironmonger clapped his hands to his head. 'Guns,' he echoed. 'Did I hear you say guns, or has madness come upon me?'

Gimlet stepped into the conversation. 'Come, come, Monsieur Boulanger,' he said sadly. 'There was a time when your nerves were not so delicate.'

Boulanger stared hard at Gimlet. '*Mon Dieu*! I know this face,' he gasped.

'You should, you old road-hog,' returned Gimlet, smiling. 'Once, in the good old days, I chased you for forty miles in my Bentley. You were racing mechanic to Monsieur le Comte de Rozay, who had the big Lancia, if I remember?'

Boulanger's fat face broke into a smile. 'Monsieur King! But of course. Forgive me. It is these Germans – they deprive me of my wits.'

Gimlet frowned. 'You won that race because I had a puncture. A puncture is not an unusual thing, my old one. But two punctures, both with brand-new nails, at the same moment – that *is* unusual. I have often wondered how it happened that you passed over those nails without injury, and I did not.'

Boulanger looked disconcerted. 'You don't think that I—'

'No. No, no. I know you wouldn't do such a thing as to throw nails overboard,' said Gimlet slyly.

Marcelle joined in. '*Messieurs*, is this a time for the reminiscence, however pleasant?' she inquired plaintively. 'Let us speak of what is urgent.'

'Yes, yes, of course,' agreed Boulanger, who seemed more than willing to change the subject. 'Soon I must be going.'

'Do you want to go?' asked Gimlet.

'I would as soon visit the devil in hell,' declared Boulanger.

'Let us sit down,' suggested Gimlet.

They found seats, Gimlet drawing a chair forward so that he could see across the square. It presented an animated appearance. Conscripts, accompanied by their friends, or their women-folk, wandered about or stood in little groups, some talking, some weeping, in spite of the efforts of German troops, who did their utmost to muster them in some sort of order at the far side of the square. With the lorries they had more success, compelling the civilian drivers to form a line against the kerb immediately under the shop window. In some of these vehicles conscripts had already taken their places. At the head of the line stood a large open touring car, with a swastika pennant on the radiator cap, and behind it, a large mobile petrol tank, also decorated with the Nazi insignia.

'Tell me, Gaston, my old warrior, precisely what happens here,' requested Gimlet.

Boulanger explained. 'The camions are those that have been commandeered by the Nazis. They will go all the way to Germany and stay there, taking the conscripts with them – that is the usual thing. Each driver is provided with enough petrol to bring his lorry into the town, and no more. The Germans see to that, in case one should decide to make a bolt for it. Now, when there is no longer any risk of that, the tanks will be filled, ready for the journey across France. In the touring car will ride the escort, armed with rifles, to see that none escapes. Also, it sets the pace. Motor cyclists ride up and down the column.'

'But some of the lorries are already loaded with other things,' observed Gimlet.

'Ah yes. Those are of a convoy that has come up from the south. As you know, the Germans are taking everything. The barrels you see contain brandy, from Cognac. They say the Germans take it for the alcohol, to put in their aviation petrol. There is also, as you see, hay and straw that is needed by our own farmers. There is butter, too, and, in that green camion, candles from the big factory here. Now you will no longer wonder that France is being stripped bare.'

'It's a shame,' opined Gimlet softly.

Boulanger shrugged. 'We can do nothing about it.'

'That, my old grease-gun, is where you are wrong,' argued Gimlet. 'It seems to me that it would be a simple thing to prevent this convoy from reaching Germany. Consider, for example, how well the hay and straw would burn. And the brandy, and the candles.'

Boulanger did not take Gimlet seriously. 'It would be a fine thing to watch,' he admitted.

'It would be even better to depart while the diversion kept the Nazis busy,' declared Gimlet. 'I want to go to Chateaudun, which is some distance from here – nearly fifty miles, if I remember. Rather than walk all that way I would prefer to ride in a touring car.'

Boulanger stared. '*Monsieur* is not serious?'

'You would not have me walk all the way to Chateaudun?'

Again the colour drained from the Frenchman's face. 'Pardon me, but *monsieur* talks like a man who has either drunk too much wine, or has a beetle in his brain.'

'What purpose shall we serve by sitting here?' asked Gimlet. 'Is this spectacle so pleasing? No, I shall go to Chateaudun, where the scenery is better. And I shall ride. You, Monsieur Boulanger, may go to Germany if you wish, but you would serve France better by going to England.'

The little ironmonger drew himself up and struck his chest. 'I am ready to die for France, *monsieur*,' he said proudly. 'Give the orders.'

'It would be much better to go on living,' responded Gimlet. 'Pay attention, everyone. This is what we will do. The driver of the petrol lorry, fearing nothing, is eating his breakfast, I observe, on a table outside the café opposite. First, I shall throw the pipe-line in the gutter, and then turn on the petrol, which will run along under the line of camions. Cub, you will oblige me by finding a hammer in the shop below, and with it knock in the bungs of as many of those brandy casks as you can before you are discovered. This will happen when I give the signal raising my hand. At the same time, Gaston, you will take your place beside the driving seat of the touring car, ready to mount when the fire starts. That should not be difficult, because all eyes will be on the fire. Marcelle will go with you. Copper and Trapper will stand by the rear seat to deal with any unforeseen emergency that may arise. When I have lighted the petrol we shall all enter the car and drive away.'

'It is not possible,' declared Boulanger vehemently.

'Why not?' inquired Gimlet.

'Because such things are not done.'

'Oh, but they are,' replied Gimlet lightly. 'You don't know the Kittens. As soon as we are all in the car you will take the road to Chateaudun, driving not too fast until we are clear of the town, and all the time taking care not to hit a telegraph pole in your excitement.'

'The Nazis will telephone along the road,' asserted Boulanger.

'They will not, because I shall stop to cut the wires,' answered Gimlet.

'We shall be followed by motor cyclists and shot.'

'That we shall be pursued is certain, I admit,' went on Gimlet. 'A Bentley once pursued a Lancia. And what did the man in the Lancia do? Have you forgotten, my old cheat?'

Boulanger's sense of humour overcame his natural fear. He smiled. 'He sprinkled the road behind him with nice new nails.'

'At the time I was most displeased,' continued Gimlet. 'But now I perceive that there is a reason for all things. On that day you taught me a trick, one that we will now use to even better advantage against these unpleasant fellows in grey uniforms. Doubtless there are nails in the shop?'

'I have a very good stock of nails.'

'Could we fill two small sacks?'

'With ease.'

'Good. Copper and Trapper will carry the sacks to the back seat of the car, but the nails will not be used until they are required. Is there any food in the house, Gaston?'

'There is food here in my bag. The Germans have issued rations to last us to Germany.'

'Excellent. As we are not going to Germany we will eat it now,' declared Gimlet. 'We shall all work better on full stomachs.'

CHAPTER ELEVEN

On the Road to Chateaudun

There were moments during the next half hour when Cub had serious doubts as to whether what he saw was real or imaginary; when he asked himself, was this truly happening or was it all a dream? Here, in the heart of enemy-occupied country, within a few yards of a German convoy, practically surrounded by the hated grey uniforms, sitting by an open window were three British soldiers, eating black bread and sausage with no more concern than if they had been picnicking on Hampstead Heath. It took some believing. What added a final touch of fantasy was that none of the commandos made the slightest reference to the business, much less dwelt on the peril of their position.

Gimlet took the occasion to discuss with Trapper the prospects of trout fishing in Canada after the war. Copper contributed a story of how, from a police launch, he had once seen a shark in the Thames Estuary, a tale that ended lamely when he admitted that on close inspection the shark turned out to be a log.

Every now and then the little ironmonger would look from one to the other, shrug his shoulders and shake his head as if the whole thing was beyond him – as it probably was. Once, Marcelle burst out laughing, and on Cub's look of inquiry stated that the affair was 'droll.' Cub was by no means convinced that this was the right word.

When the food had been consumed Gimlet carefully brushed some crumbs from his clothes and announced that they might as well be moving on. 'I have a feeling,' he remarked, 'that this ought to be rather fun.'

Cub had doubts, but did not express them. He surveyed the square and saw that the situation was unchanged, except that the lorries were now lined up, and the conscripts marshalled in some sort of order on the far side of the *Place*.

Gimlet got up. 'Let's get the nails, Gaston, my old trench rat,' he suggested.

The commandos picked up the sacks containing their equipment and the party returned to the ground floor where, in the shop, Gaston found two small sacks, about the size of sandbags, into which he emptied several drawers containing nails of various sizes. With a twinkle in his eyes he held up a horse nail.

'Did you ever see anything like that before, *monsieur*?' he inquired.

'Yes,' answered Gimlet. 'I once drew two out of a perfectly good tyre – you old twister.'

'Monsieur le Comte had promised me a thousand francs if we won the race,' explained Gaston. 'And I am a poor man,' he added with a sigh.

'Add some of those nails to the others,' ordered Gimlet. 'They seem to do the job well.'

'That is what I thought,' observed Gaston naïvely.

For Cub he found a hammer suitable for knocking in the bungs of the brandy casks.

Gimlet opened the side door and glanced up and down the narrow street. 'All quiet,' said he. Then, addressing Gaston and Marcelle in particular, he enjoined them to keep their heads, no matter what happened. 'I mention this,' he concluded, 'because when the fun starts it should be fast and furious. You all know what you have to do.'

Copper spat on his hands. 'If my Ma could see me now she'd throw forty fits, s'welp me, she would.'

'Don't talk so much,' ordered Gimlet. 'I want no shooting unless it becomes imperative – you understand?'

'Yes, sir.'

'Good – let's go.'

Although he had been toughened by long association with danger, to Cub the events of the next few minutes were a whirl of excitement not far short of madness, although for reasons which will become apparent they were somewhat hazy.

The business started quietly enough. Without interference or question they went into the square where each took up his allotted station. Gimlet looked up and down to make sure they were all in position and then raised his right hand – the signal for operations to begin.

Cub at once climbed on the brandy truck beside which he had halted, and for the next minute or so was too taken up with his task to see how the others were getting on. Two smart blows on the first bung were sufficient to drive it in, the noise being hardly noticeable among the other noises filling the square. The brandy gushed out, soaking his legs and feet, and although he was unaware of it, upsetting his equilibrium. He was conscious of a reek of brandy as the volatile spirit began to evaporate in the warm sunshine, but it did not occur to him that this might affect his actions, that by smell alone he might become intoxicated. This, evidently, is what happened, although, as we have said, he was unaware of it, and saw nothing strange in his behaviour. The exhilaration that came over him he assumed to be the natural outcome of the excitement of the moment.

With a mighty swing he drove in another bung to such purpose that the spirit squirted into his eyes, causing him some pain which, far from having a sobering effect, spurred him to more ambitious efforts. In quick succession he drove in three more bungs, and looked round for another, laughing joyously as he did so. Gimlet was right. This was fun. Bang! In went another bung. There was now a noticeable recklessness in his manner as, almost overcome by the fumes, he went from cask to cask. In great good humour he drove in two more bungs, and then looked round, rather unsteadily, to see how the others were getting on.

Observing that Gimlet had worked his will on the petrol lorry, for its contents were now gushing down the gutter, he hailed him merrily. 'Nice work, Gimlet!' he shouted – in English.

Gimlet threw him a startled, penetrating stare, and dropping what he was doing made a dash for the brandy truck. Actually, his work was finished, and he was only waiting for Cub.

'Come off that,' he rasped.

Cub, taken aback by Gimlet's manner, attempted to obey with such alacrity that he fell, and might well have broken his neck had not Gimlet caught him.

'What have I done wrong?' he demanded indignantly.

'You're drunk, my pup,' snapped Gimlet, looking quickly up and down. 'My fault – I should have thought of it. Come on.'

Cub wiped his brow. 'Phew! It's hot.'

Gimlet grabbed him by the hand. 'It'll be hotter in a minute if we don't get out of this,' he said grimly. 'Run.'

Cub was promptly sick, which was hardly surprising, for the combined fumes of brandy and petrol were overpowering. But he felt better. 'Sorry,' he said apologetically.

'You disgusting brat,' grated Gimlet. 'Come on.'

Now it is not to be supposed that all this had occurred without notice being taken. One or two passers-by, fortunately French citizens, had halted to gaze at the curious scene, and then bolted incontinently, presumably for fear of being implicated. Someone far down the line of lorries was shouting something about petrol, and this may have served the commandos a good turn, for the attention of the crowd was attracted to that direction. Quite a number of men, both French and Germans, were staring at the lorries, not with any particular alarm, but in the bovine manner of a crowd that suspects something is wrong, but does not know what.

Only one German soldier, who turned out to be the driver of the touring car, apparently had a good idea of what was happening, for he began running towards his vehicle. The other Germans shouted orders, holding up their hands to control the conscripts, who were beginning to move uneasily. The Germans seemed to take the view that a riot was imminent. Gimlet, holding Cub by the hand, began to drag him towards the car, with Cub protesting that he could see no need for haste.

This was the situation when, with a terrific swoosh, the petrol took fire. In an instant the gutter, and the air above it, was filled with flame, a spectacle so terrifying that Cub was nearly sobered with shock. How the petrol caught fire, or who set fire to it, was never known for certain; but as far as the plan was concerned the explosion was premature. Copper afterwards asserted that the fire was started by a German officer who at the crucial moment arrived on the scene, and perhaps wishing to create an atmosphere of tranquillity, lit a cigarette, afterwards tossing the match in the gutter. If this were so, no man defeated his object more effectually. As the line of flame leapt up there was a murmur of voices that grew in volume like an oncoming tidal wave. It ended in a roar. Pandemonium followed; and only those who have seen a French crowd lose its collective head know the real meaning of the word. The parade broke up in disorder and the German troops were overwhelmed by the milling crowd.

Still dragging Cub, Gimlet ran on to the car. As they arrived, Cub had a brief but clear picture of Copper's huge fist catching the Nazi driver on the point of the jaw with such force that the German was lifted clean off the ground. Gaston and Marcelle, both looking rather pale, were already in their seats.

Copper and Trapper tossed their sacks into the rear of the car and climbed on to the back seat. Cub was staring fascinated at a pillar of flame that was leaping skyward from a straw-laden lorry when Gimlet picked him up by the scruff of the neck and the seat of his pants, and threw him on to Copper's lap. By the time Cub had scrambled to his feet the car was on the move. Gaston took the first turning out of the square and the atmosphere at once was calm and orderly, although from behind there still came a great noise of shouting.

Copper sniffed, and then stared suspiciously into Cub's face. He caught him by the front of his shirt. 'Why, you young swipe,' he growled. 'Who told you to swill the stuff?'

'It was the fumes.' Gimlet threw the words back over his shoulder. He had squeezed himself in between Marcelle and her uncle. 'He's not to blame; I should have guessed that would happen,' he added.

Cub, grinning foolishly, flopped down between Copper and Trapper. 'We're on our way – hic,' he hiccoughed.

Copper roared with laughter. 'Bad luck, kid,' he condoled.

The car glided on, unmolested, and after taking several turnings came out on a broad macadam highway.

'The road to Chateaudun,' announced Gaston, putting his foot down on the accelerator.

'Got your cutters handy, Trapper?' called Gimlet.

'Aye-aye, sir.'

'Stand by to cut the wires. Stop her, Gaston.'

The car came to a skidding stop. Trapper was out in a flash, running to the nearest telegraph pole. To Cub's spellbound admiration he went up it like a monkey. A dozen snips and the wires flopped. Trapper slid down the pole and ran back to the car.

'Pour the sauce,* my old periwinkle,' he told Gaston, and the car shot forward.

The little ironmonger, who by now had entered into the spirit of the adventure, broke into a torrent of words, but Gimlet told him curtly to watch what he was doing and look where he was going. This was necessary, because to lend emphasis to his words the old mechanic thought nothing of taking his hands off the wheel. The car tore on.

Some minutes passed without incident, and then, on one of those long stretches of road that make the Le Mans district an ideal race track, the first signs of pursuit appeared. Two motor cyclists, riding side by side at break-neck speed, swung into sight. They were followed by several other riders, strung out, and a powerful-looking car. It was soon evident that they would overtake the tourer.

'Let go the nails, Copper,' ordered Gimlet evenly. 'Don't waste them – use just enough to give the road a good sprinkling.'

Cub had now recovered sufficiently to take a normal interest in the proceedings. He thought they would be worth watching. He was right. They were. Copper hauled up a sack, no light weight, and resting the open end on the back of the car moved it from side to side to ensure that the whole road surface received an even share of nails.

There was no doubt as to when the leading motor cyclists reached the spot. Almost immediately one of them soared over his handlebars in the fashion of the young man on the flying trapeze, while the cycle, riderless, struck the verge, and after a high jump landed on its side in the middle of the road. The second motor cyclist, who had been slightly behind, managed to avoid it, but soon afterwards pulled in to the gutter, presumably with a normal flat tyre. Most of those following suffered similar fates, but a few got through. However, the second bag of nails stopped everything with the exception of one motor cycle and the car, which by something like a miracle had escaped disaster.

* A French idiom, meaning, Open the throttle.

'That guy must have solid tyres,' grunted Trapper. 'For the chap on the motor cycle it is going to be too bad, I tink. He would have done better to pick up a nail.' He opened his sack and took out his bow and an arrow.

'Wait till you see the whites of his eyes,' advised Copper.

'Hold the car straight, Gaston, *mon vieux*,' requested Trapper, and resting a knee on the back seat, took aim.

The motor cyclist, a brown-shirt trooper, was now close enough to consider shooting. He drew a revolver and raised it to the level of his shoulder. That was as far as he got. *Phung*! sang Trapper's bow. Where the arrow hit the man Cub could not see, but the motor cycle whirled to the side of the road where it struck a telegraph pole with a crash that made him wince.

'What-ho!' exclaimed Copper dispassionately. 'That'll learn 'im. My turn, chum. Leave the car to me.' He glanced at Gimlet, who was looking over his shoulder, for approval.

Gimlet nodded. 'Go ahead.'

Copper reached for his bag, took out the Sten gun and prepared for action, addressing the weapon in affectionate tones, as if it might have been a pet canary, as he did so. 'Come along, my little beauty. Never bin known ter miss, she ain't, and that's no lie,' he told Cub with deadly seriousness. 'Am I right, Trapper?'

'*Tiens*! *I'll* say you're right,' confirmed Trapper.

By this time the car was no more than sixty yards behind. It was loaded, overloaded in fact, with German soldiers. One, supported by others on either side of him, was standing up trying – not very successfully – to take aim with a rifle over the head of an officer who, with the driver, occupied the front seats.

'Look at 'im,' said Copper plaintively. 'What a hope he's got, tryin' ter shoot in that position; s'welp me, all he'll do if he ain't careful is push that officer's brains into his lap.'

The rifle blazed. The bullet went wide – at least, it did not come anywhere near the tourer.

'There you are,' sneered Copper. 'What did I tell yer? Not a hope.'

'Get on with it,' ordered Gimlet curtly. 'This is no time for fooling.'

Copper threw a shocked glance at Cub. 'Hear that?' he asked in a hoarse whisper. 'He thinks I'm fooling. Strike me pink! Them Jerries won't think I'm fooling, not on my oath they won't. I wish my old Ma could see this. You watch.'

Getting into a comfortable position on the back seat he trained the machine-gun on the overtaking car.

There was a brief pause. Then it spat – and kept on spitting.

The effect on the car was instantaneous, and, Cub thought, appalling. Steam and water spurted from the radiator. Stars appeared all over the windscreen. Glass flew. Splinters of wood and strips of metal leapt into the air. The troops fell into a confused heap, either to escape the hail of lead or because they had been hit. Then the car swerved sickeningly, tried to climb the bank, and overturned.

Copper lowered his gun. 'That'll stop them laughing in church, I reckon,' he observed calmly. 'Did that look like fooling, Cub, to you?'

'No,' answered Cub. 'Definitely no.'

Trapper put his bow away. 'Now we can sit back and enjoy the drive,' he remarked.

Gimlet turned to Cub. 'Change places with Marcelle.' he commanded. 'I want to talk to you about what we're going to do when we get to Chateaudun.'

'What we're going to do?' echoed Cub.

'I mean, where are we going to park the car?'

Cub shook his head. 'I hadn't thought of that,' he confessed.

CHAPTER TWELVE

Gunther Takes a Hand

In the front seat of the car they discussed the matter.

'I thought you had friends everywhere; haven't you any in Chateaudun?' asked Gimlet.

'No.'

'Where did you stay when you were there?'

'Father Edwinus – he's the *curé* of the Church of the Madeleine – let me sleep in the old chapel in the cemetery.'

'Did he know what you were up to?'

'He didn't ask me, and I didn't tell him, but I fancy he had a pretty shrewd idea. He's a true Frenchman, and I think we could trust him.'

'Thinking isn't enough at this game,' said Gimlet. 'One has to be sure. Is this chapel open?'

'Yes. It's very old, and no longer used. You couldn't park the car in it, though.'

'Can you think of any place where we can hide it? The point is, a car isn't a thing you can just throw away. If we merely abandon it the Nazis will find it, and they'll know we're in the district. We've got to dispose of it so that it won't be found, at least for some time.'

'There's the aerodrome,' said Cub slowly.

'What use is that?'

'It was a French military aerodrome, about two miles from Chateaudun on the Orleans road. It isn't used any longer. The buildings were only of the temporary sort, and they got knocked about pretty badly by German bombs before France fell. The planes were taken long ago. We could put the car in one of the empty sheds – it might be some time before it was found. Of course, things may have changed. It's over a month since I was here.'

'It sounds hopeful, anyway,' returned Gimlet. 'In the meantime, if we wanted a car urgently, we should know where to find one. It's worth trying.' Turning to Gaston he told him to drive straight on towards Orleans.

Actually, when the position was explained to him, Gaston did better. Knowing the country, he took a turning that by-passed the town of Chateaudun, and struck the Orleans road not far from the aerodrome. Studying the road anxiously, he remarked that the sooner they were out of the car the better. After what had happened it was probably the most dangerous vehicle in France. Every German in the country would be on the look-out for it.

To Cub's infinite relief, the aerodrome, when it came into sight, was as he had last seen it. Not a soul could be seen. The buildings stood derelict, forlorn, showing signs of the damage done by the German bombs. The grass was long, and had almost overgrown the short track that led to the hangars.

Gaston drove straight into a building that looked as though it might have been the station garage. The doors, if ever there had been any, had gone. Sparrows and starlings whirled out when the car drove in, confirming the impression that the place was deserted. Gaston ran on into a dim corner and stopped.

'I don't think we could have found a better place,' declared Gimlet, looking round. 'All the same, the sooner we ourselves are out of this the better. We've got to do some quick thinking. First of all, what about you, Gaston, and you, Marcelle? You can't continue with us. We're soldiers, but you're civilians, and to be found with us would settle your fate. Will you stay in France or would you like to go to England if it can be arranged? Either way, I can give you money.'

Without hesitation they voted for England.

'I think you're wise,' said Gimlet, taking a wad of money from his pocket and peeling off several thousand-franc notes, which he handed to them. 'As long as you keep clear of Le Mans there doesn't seem to be any reason why you shouldn't travel by train,' he remarked. 'Make for Caen by a roundabout route, and then hang about the forest until you make contact with the Fleas. I understand Marcelle knows some of them. If you don't actually stay with them, leave a message where we can get in touch with you. After that you'll have to wait for our return. I think that's about all.'

'Thank you, *monsieur*,' acknowledged Gaston, with tears of gratitude sparkling in his eyes. To Marcelle he said, 'We can catch a train from Chateaudun to Paris, and go from there to Caen.'

Marcelle pointed out, and Gimlet agreed, that after what had happened, Chateaudun might not be a healthy spot, and while it would be a longer walk, Orleans would be better. Gaston agreed.

The parting was brief, and rather embarrassing, for neither Marcelle nor Gaston really wanted to leave their friends. Indeed, they said so, but Gimlet was adamant. So they went, and with sympathetic understanding, wondering if they would ever see them again, the commandos watched the two lonely figures disappear up the dusty road towards Orleans.

'She's got pluck, that kid,' said Copper huskily.

'And brains,' added Trapper. '*Ma foi*! She would make a man a wife. I—'

Gimlet interrupted. 'This is hardly the moment to contemplate matrimony,' he said coldly. 'You'll have time to think about that when we get home. Let's get down to business. This is the position. Point one. As much as I dislike these disguises it would be silly to try to walk about France in British uniforms. Therefore, for the time being, we shall have to remain as we are. Point two. We've got to get nearer the town, where we can keep in touch with things. What about this chapel you spoke of, Cub?'

'I can guide you to it.'

'How far is it from the internment camp?'

'No distance at all.'

'Where exactly is the camp, by the way?'

'It's the castle.'

Gimlet raised his eyebrows. 'You mean the chateau itself?'

'Yes. Of course, there's barbed wire round it – it goes all round the grounds, which are not very large.'

'What sort of a place is this chateau?'

'It's enormous. Part of it's very old, and other parts not so old.'

'Have you ever been inside it?'

'Oh yes. I went all over it a long time ago, with the custodian, before it was an internment camp. I called to see him the last time I was down – that's how I discovered that the place had been turned into an internment camp. Before then it was uninhabited, some of it being more or less in ruins.'

'Can you give us a description of the place?'

Cub thought for a moment. 'It's too big for that, I'm afraid. We shall see it on the way to the chapel. In fact, if I remember rightly, it's possible to see the tower from the chapel. Chateaudun itself isn't a very big place, and the castle stands high, overlooking the river Loire. There's the usual open square in the middle of the town. A little street of old houses leads down a hill to what remains of the castle wall, where there is a gateway, and the cottage where the custodian used to live. It's the guardhouse now. That's all I can tell you – except that the castle was captured by the Germans in the war of 1870. They knocked the place about, using the chapel – I mean the chapel in the castle – as a stable for their horses.'

'Hm. That doesn't help us much,' muttered Gimlet. 'We'd better see what the guide book has to say about it.' Taking the book from his pocket he flicked through the pages. 'Here we are,' he added, and read aloud: '"Chateaudun. The castle. An interesting edifice dating from several epochs. The original fortress was erected in the tenth century, on the pointed cliffs above the Loire. The donjon, a huge round tower a hundred and fifty feet high on the left of the courtyard, was rebuilt in the twelfth century. The chapel was added in the fifteenth century. The view is imposing. For permission to enter apply to the custodian." That's all.' Gimlet closed the book. 'Let's go and have a look at the place. We shall be less noticeable if we break up the party. I'll go on ahead with Cub. Copper, you follow with Trapper. If anyone speaks to you, Trapper can answer.'

'Aye-aye, sir,' agreed Copper. 'What about our uniforms and gear?'

'Ah yes. I don't think we'd better try carrying sacks about with us – the Jerries are getting inquisitive. We'll leave them here, taking only the things we're likely to need – knives, pistols, wire cutters and our torches. We'll dump the sacks in the overgrown ditch beside the track that leads to the road. If it's reasonably possible we will return for them after dark.'

106

'Can I take my bow?' queried Trapper. 'It may be useful. If I unstring it, it can ride in the leg of my trousers.'

'All right,' agreed Gimlet. 'Any more questions?'

There were none, so the party set off, with Cub and Gimlet a hundred yards or so in advance of the others. There was nobody in sight. Even the country wore a hopeless, abandoned look, and Cub remarked that it appeared as if a blight had settled on the land.

'It has,' answered Gimlet grimly.

Occasionally they saw a man or woman working in the fields, but on the road itself traffic was negligible. This, of course, did not surprise any of them, for they knew that all transport had been seized by the Germans. The appearance of a motor-cyclist despatch rider gave them an uneasy moment, but he passed without a glance, as did the driver of a German military lorry. Just as they reached the town a formation of swastika-decorated bombers passed over, but the travellers paid little attention to them.

The chateau came into view in the near distance. 'There it is,' said Cub, pointing.

Gimlet studied it for a moment with thoughtful eyes, and then walked on.

A few minutes later, avoiding the square, whence came sounds suggesting a certain amount of activity, they arrived at the cemetery, a dreary area made no less so by rows of the usual ornate French tombs, on which the hand of time had left its mark. Most of them were half buried under a mantle of moss, ivy and rank undergrowth. In a corner, in the shadow of some sad-looking cypresses of great age, was the chapel, a small, grey-stone building of Gothic design, and like the rest, fast falling into ruin. This they entered through an arched portal fitted with a heavy, iron-studded door, and found themselves in what can best be described as a stone cell, some thirty feet long by fifteen wide. There was no furniture, not even a chair. Plaques of various shapes and sizes, bearing the names of persons long since dead and forgotten, decorated the walls. That was all.

Soon afterwards Trapper and Copper came in, and the door was closed.

'What tale do you suggest we tell, if anyone finds us here?' Gimlet asked Cub.

'We can say we are making our way south,' answered Cub. 'Many people from the north are doing that. Although a pass is really necessary, the Germans don't stop them because they want the Channel ports evacuated, in case of a British invasion. Many houses have been bombed, too, so people sleep where they can. No one thinks it odd to find people sleeping in any old building.'

As they settled themselves on the floor, for lack of seats, Gimlet remarked, 'The next question to arise will be food.'

'That isn't easy to find in France,' Cub pointed out.

'I know that,' replied Gimlet. 'Unfortunately, we can't do without it. We could always fall back on our iron rations, which will last us a couple of days, but I'd rather hang on to them for a real emergency – always bearing in mind that it may take us several days to get back to the stores at Caen.'

'Suppose I go and have a scrounge round the town?' suggested Cub. 'After all, I've been on the scrounge for a couple of years, so I know the ropes. I might pick up some news by listening to the people talking. There may have been changes made in the garrison. When I was last here there was a platoon of a Bavarian regiment quartered in the Hôtel de Ville. They provided the guard for the chateau. The commandant of the camp, by the way, is a Vichyite French general.'

'I think it would be a good idea if you had a look round,' assented Gimlet. 'Watch your step, though. The pursuit from Le Mans will probably have reached here by now. In fact, after this morning's dust-up the whole countryside is likely to be buzzing. It would be useful to know what direction the hunt is taking, so see if you can find out – but be careful.'

'I'll watch it,' promised Cub, and departed on his mission, thoroughly happy to be entrusted with work of such importance.

If he was conscious of danger he paid no heed to it. Accustomed by long association to German military uniforms, he took little notice of them, but in the light of what was to follow, it is to be feared that this may have been a case of familiarity breeding contempt.

Be that as it may, it was with more satisfaction than concern that he found the *Place* buzzing – to use Gimlet's expression – with Nazi activity, for this provided a harvest of useful information. With his hands in the pockets of his threadbare shorts he strolled along with the utmost confidence. No one paid the slightest attention to him – he would have been surprised had it been otherwise.

A slow stroll round the groups of soldiers soon revealed that Gimlet's surmise had been correct. The commandos had stirred things up. The talk was all of the affair at Le Mans, although reference was also made to the ammunition-train disaster at Falaise. He gathered it was thought that these were the work of the notorious Gimlet and a small party of his commandos, who were believed to be still in the country. The search of them was being pursued with energy, for the German Higher Command was extremely angry, and *Generaloberst* Gunther, and his adjutant, von Roth, under the lash of reprimand, were turning the country upside-down. Throughout Normandy and Brittany patrols were on the move. Bridges were guarded. All leave had been stopped.

The Germans talked freely, for the most part grumbling about the extra work all this involved, regardless of a conspicuous notice on the wall of the Hôtel de Ville that conversation should be guarded. No one appeared to notice the untidy youth who wandered about apparently without any object in view – which shows how disregard of official warnings may upset the plans of those who issue them.

Cub got a mild shock when an officer, a captain, walked over to him and accosted him.

'Here, you,' said the German roughly, speaking in French, 'how long have you been about?'

'Most of the morning, *Herr Hauptmann*,' answered Cub readily, and with respect.

'Have you seen a car go through here?'

'I have seen several cars, *Herr Hauptmann*.'

'Have you seen a grey car, open, with a flag on the bonnet?'

'A swastika flag?'

'Yes.'

'But yes, *Herr Hauptmann*.' Cub pretended to think. 'It must have been nearly an hour ago. I noticed it because it travelled very fast. In it there were ...' Cub puckered his forehead. 'Four or five men ... I'm not sure.'

'That's right,' declared the officer with some excitement. 'Which way did it go?'

'It took the road to Chartres, *Herr Hauptmann*.' Cub pointed to a road that led north-east. Orleans lay to the south-east.

'Are you sure?' cried the officer.

'I'm certain of it,' declared Cub.

The officer raised his hand and shouted to the driver of a car to join him. The car came over, and Cub got a real shock when the driver, after a good look at him, said in a curious voice, 'Didn't I see you in Le Mans this morning?'

'But no. That is not possible,' lied Cub fluently. He had long overcome any scruples about lying where Nazis were concerned, for they themselves, he had observed, were past-masters at it.

'That's queer,' said the German, looking puzzled. 'I could swear I saw you in Le Mans.'

Cub shrugged. 'But how could I get from Le Mans to Chateaudun already?'

For this shrewd question the German had no immediate answer. The distance was nearly fifty miles. Few French people were permitted to use motor transport – certainly not a ragamuffin like Cub. The Nazi could hardly be expected to guess that he had ridden in the wanted car. Still looking puzzled, however, he considered the mystery.

How this incident would have ended had there not been an interruption it is impossible to say; but at this juncture a new factor appeared on the scene, one that set Cub's brain racing, and, it must be admitted, turned his lips dry for the first time. A big car came roaring into the square, and there was an all-round stiffening to attention when it was observed that it carried no less a personage than *Generaloberst* Gunther, with his adjutant, *Hauptmann* von Roth. The officer responsible for Cub's interrogation saluted stiffly, and the car came to a stop beside him. Slowly, with imperial dignity, as if aware of the importance of their arrival, the occupants descended.

In appearance, *Generaloberst* Gunther was not that grotesque type of Nazi so often ridiculed by caricaturists. Nor was his stature imposing. On the contrary he was a smallish man, with a skin of a curious grey pallor. In civilian clothes, from a distance, he might have appeared harmless enough; the small, thin-lipped mouth might have appeared merely mean, and the pale eyes unusually large; but seen close there was something repellent, sinister, about him, an indefinable suggestion of evil, as there is about a snake, which even though it is not venomous makes the blood curdle.

His adjutant, von Roth, was a different type. He was heavily built, swarthy, and looked what he was – a typical Prussian bully. Power had simply made a savage of him. In his hand he carried a cane.

The general, ignoring Cub, addressed the officer. 'Any news, yet?' he demanded in a thin voice, a voice as sour as vinegar.

'Yes, sir,' answered the officer eagerly. 'This boy saw the car go through the town an hour ago. It took the Chartres road.'

'Then why the delay? Why have you done nothing about it?'

'We were considering if his evidence was reliable. There is a suggestion that the boy was in Le Mans this morning.'

The general glanced at Cub. 'Nonsense,' he said curtly. 'This boy lives at Caen.' His glance passed on.

Cub drew a deep breath of relief – but it was short lived. The general's glance switched back, his eyes clouding, as though he had only just grasped the significance of what he had said. 'If he lives at Caen, what is he doing here?' he muttered. 'I saw him in Caen quite recently.' Addressing Cub, he demanded peremptorily, 'How did you get here?'

'Except for an occasional lift, I walked, your highness,' replied Cub humbly, but without hesitation.

'Zo! Why did you come here?'

'I am on my way to Orleans, highness.'

'Why?'

'To visit relations there.'

'Ah! Without a permit, I suppose?'

Cub dropped his eyes. 'Yes, highness.'

'You know the regulations about travelling without a pass? Why did you do it?'

'Because …' Cub faltered for the first time, groping blindly for an excuse.

Von Roth's cane swished with vicious force against the back of his hand. 'Answer,' he snarled.

Cub cried out under the pain of the blow. Then his wits, sharpened by experience, came to his rescue.

'I was driven out of the town, *Generaloberst*,' he stammered.

'Driven out – by whom?'

'By a fellow—'

'What fellow? No lies, now.'

'You would not know him, general. A fellow by the name of Louis Morelle.' (This, it will be remembered, was the proper name of the Fox.)

The general stared. His jaw set. 'That gutter-rat! I know him. Why did you leave Caen on his account?'

'He beat me,' whimpered Cub.

'Why?'

'Because I would not do the things he wanted me to do.'

'What things?'

Cub's voice dropped to a whisper. He seemed to choke over the word, 'Sabotage.' This was not betraying the Fox, who had already been convicted on this charge.

'Ah!' The general drew a deep breath. His pale eyes flashed to von Roth and came back to Cub. 'So that was it? Morelle was arrested. Didn't you know that?'

'Yes, highness, but he escaped. It was then that I fled for my life, fearing that he would lay the blame for his arrest on me, and kill me with his knife. He is a bad one, this Morelle.'

The general's eyes narrowed. 'Do you know where this young devil hides?'

'No, highness. He vanishes – I don't know where.'

'But by returning to Caen, and pretending to work for him, you could find out, eh?'

'Perhaps,' answered Cub doubtfully, perceiving that he was getting into deep water.

'You could try.'

'Yes, highness,' admitted Cub. He could hardly say otherwise. Apart from which he was desperately anxious for this questioning to end before it occurred to the Nazis to search him. No story he could invent would avail him if he was found to be in possession of a German automatic. As it was he marvelled that the Germans should overlook a precaution so obvious, and he reasoned, probably correctly, that it was his age that saved

112

him, as it had before. An adult suspect would certainly have been searched. Nazi imagination evidently did not go so far as to suppose a boy would be equipped with German firearms.

'We'll talk about this later,' decided the general. He turned to the local officer. 'Keep your eyes on this boy. Don't let him go. After this Morelle business I wouldn't trust any of these little French swine. For the present you'd better put him in the castle.'

'*Ja, Generaloberst.*' The officer beckoned to some soldiers who were standing near and pointed to Cub. 'This boy is under arrest,' he said. 'Take him to the castle.'

CHAPTER THIRTEEN

The Man of God

Back in the chapel, with nothing to do, time hung heavily on the hands of the commandos, who were in no mood to settle down. As their future movements would depend largely on Cub's report they awaited his return with impatience.

'He's a long time,' remarked Gimlet, looking at his watch. And an hour later, 'What the deuce can he be up to? I hope he hasn't run into trouble.'

'If ever I saw a kid able ter take care of himself it's 'im,' opined Copper.

'All the same, it's time he was back,' said Gimlet, looking worried.

The afternoon wore on, and dragged slowly into evening. When twilight began to creep silently through the unglazed windows, and still Cub did not come, Trapper suggested that he made a reconnaissance in the hope of learning something, pointing out, with justification, that on account of his French extraction he was the most suitable one for the job.

'I'm afraid it's no use kidding ourselves any longer,' answered Gimlet. 'That boy's in trouble or he'd be back by now. All right, Trapper, see if you can find him.'

Trapper was on his way to the heavy door when he stopped suddenly. '*Ecoutez*!' he whispered, clipping the word and at the same time moving like lightning as footsteps, heavy purposeful footsteps, echoed in the stone-flagged portal. With his hand in his pocket he took up a position against the wall behind the door.

A moment later the big iron handle was turned from the outside. The door swung open, and a man stood on the threshold, a man in the sombre habit of a priest. He was rather past middle age, stout, yet with the dignity that portliness gives to those who are getting on in years. His face was hairless, and his skin as smooth as that of a child. For perhaps ten seconds he surveyed the scene before him in silence. Then, without haste, he closed the door and advanced into the room.

'What are you doing here, *messieurs?*' he inquired in even tones, speaking of course in French.

Gimlet hesitated for a moment before he replied. 'Are we compelled to answer that question, father?'

'No,' returned the priest quietly. 'You are not. To do so, however, would be a matter of courtesy. I was bound to ask.'

'Are you by any chance Father Edwinus?' said Gimlet.

The priest's eyebrows lifted. 'I am. Have we met before?'

Gimlet shook his head. 'No.'

'You are not French.' This was a statement rather than a question.

'No,' responded Gimlet again. 'In your own interest I suggest that you ask no more questions, but depart, forgetting what you have seen.'

The *curé*'s eyes, soft and sad, rested on Gimlet's face. 'It may be that I can be of service,' said he.

Gimlet considered the priest. How much did he know? It seemed likely, since he would hear the gossip in the town, that he had guessed who they were. Would it, he wondered, be advisable to take him into their confidence? It would be a risk, but not, he thought, a very great one. Unless he were a traitor, which was unlikely – particularly so since he had once helped Cub – he would be against the Nazis.

'It may be that you wonder how we knew your name, father,' went on Gimlet. 'I will tell you. Some time ago you befriended a boy, a boy of Caen, who was in these parts. It was he who told us of you, and this place.'

'You mean the English boy, he who calls himself Cub?' returned the priest imperturbably.

Gimlet stared. 'You knew he was English?'

'I guessed. Men of my age and experience are not easy to deceive, my son. It was to see if he had been here that I came.'

'What led you to think that he might have come back?'

'Something that I have just learned in the town.' The *curé* looked from one to the other. 'The boy's a friend of yours?'

'He's more even than that.'

'In that case, *messieurs*, you will be grieved to learn that he has been apprehended,' said the priest heavily. 'He is a prisoner in the chateau.'

Silence fell. It was broken by Gimlet. 'I was afraid something of the sort had happened. How did this come about?'

'I don't know the details. Did he come here with you – or you with him?'

'We were together. He was acting as our guide.'

'From which I judge that you, too, are British?'

'We are,' admitted Gimlet quietly. 'And if you are the man I judge you to be, we have nothing to fear on that account.'

'Thank you,' said the priest softly. 'On the contrary, *messieurs*. Under my cloth there still beats a French heart, and for that reason any service I can perform for you will be undertaken willingly.'

'You know the risks of concealing British troops?'

'Too well. But what is risk of life at a time like this?'

'Do you know who we are?'

'You must be, I think, the officer who is called Gimlet, for whom the Germans are seeking. As I came through the town a notice was being posted on the wall of the Hôtel de Ville, offering a reward of fifty thousand francs for your body, dead or alive.'

Gimlet smiled. 'Only fifty thousand? I trust they will have occasion to double that before very long. How did you guess?'

The priest shrugged. 'There cannot be so many British soldiers in this part of France. But now that we understand each other, tell me how I can be of service?'

'We shall need food, father, if it is procurable,' answered Gimlet. 'But there is no hurry. First, can you give us any more information about Cub?'

'I only know that he was questioned by the Germans, and that it was under the orders of *Generaloberst* Gunther that he was detained and sent to the chateau for safe custody.'

'Gunther! Is he here?'

'He was, but has, I think, gone on. Search is being made for you, for it is thought that you are still in France. You are far from safe here, but I know of no better place, so you may as well stay. Food is not easy to procure, but there is still a certain amount, in spite of the Nazis, for those who need it.' The priest glanced at the window. 'But the light fades. Soon it will be dark, and then it will be less dangerous to move about. I will endeavour to learn more about the fate of the boy.'

'Thank you, father. We shall not leave France, of course, without making every effort to save him – and others who I understand are confined in the chateau.'

'Was it on account of these others that you came to Chateaudun?' inquired the priest.

'Yes,' admitted Gimlet. 'The Allied Governments are anxious to know their names, and discover, if possible, why pretence was made by the Germans that these prisoners were dead – at least, that is what we were given to understand.'

'I can answer these questions for you,' said the priest. 'There are in the chateau twelve men – mostly French, but not all. There were more, but some have died as a result of the brutal treatment they received. Some of these men are diplomats, or government officials; others, military leaders; but in every case it is their misfortune that they possess information which the Nazis are anxious to obtain. Here, within those grey stone walls, they are subjected to torture, physical and mental, to make them speak. They are stubborn men, what you would call hard cases, men who have refused to yield even though they are in durance. Some, as I have told you, have died rather than betray their country. Since they were already presumed dead, their fate causes no concern.'

Gimlet's face was grim. 'In what part are the prisoners confined?'

'The Nazis, I regret to say, have turned the chapel into a dormitory, in which they are locked every night.'

'Is this hell-hole – saving your presence, father – under the jurisdiction of *Generaloberst* Gunther?'

'Yes, aided by his able assistant, *Hauptmann* von Roth, and a man of Vichy, who has sunk so low that he has sold his honour to the enemy. His name is Colonel Frey, an Alsatian – probably a man of German descent.'

'I shall remember the name,' said Gimlet slowly.

'The latest victim in the chateau is General Romortin, who, before the war, in the opinion of many, was France's military genius. For a long time he was a prisoner in Germany, and, doubtless to account for his disappearance, it was reported that he had died. This, like most Nazi stories, was untrue. He has been sent here for more drastic treatment. Unhappily for him, he knows where certain documents of great importance are hidden, including particulars of weapons that were being developed in France at the time of her collapse. If he does not know where the papers are the Germans believe he does, which as far as he is concerned comes to the same thing. The information, by any foul means they can think of, the Nazis will endeavour to wring from him. If you have a pencil I will give you the names of the others.'

Gimlet opened his notebook and jotted down the names as the priest dictated them.

'This information is of the greatest importance, father,' he said, as he closed the book. 'If I get back, your co-operation shall be made known to the leaders of the liberation, when it comes.'

'I ask no thanks,' said the *curé* simply. 'What I do is no more than any true Frenchman would do for our beloved France. Is it possible that your Government can help these unfortunates, *monsieur*? Retribution when the Nazis are driven out will be of no comfort to them if they are already dead, as it seems likely they will be.'

'Something shall be done,' replied Gimlet firmly. 'How did you learn all this?'

'That is a question I prefer not to answer,' returned Father Edwinus. 'I have sources of information. Does it matter where it comes from?'

'Not in the least,' answered Gimlet.

The priest, who had turned casually to the crumbling window, and the darkening scene beyond, suddenly stiffened in an attitude of intense interest. 'I see something,' he said sharply. 'Look! On the tower – a rag, it waves, as if in the hands of one who wishes to attract attention. A signal – yes. It must be. Alas! I cannot read military signals.'

By this time the others were at his side, staring at the top of the chateau's great cone-topped tower. What the priest had said was manifestly true. Someone was waving a piece of rag, jerking it to and fro in movements that were too regular to be accidental.

'It's Morse, s'welp me,' muttered Copper; and as they were signalled he began reading the letters aloud. 'Dash dot dash dot – C; dot dot dash – U; dash dot dot dot – B. It's him. It's Cub. Come ter think of it, he knows we can see the castle from here. He's trying to attract our attention. What's he saying?' He went on reading the signal. 'C-U-B … H-E-R-E.'

Gimlet jerked into action. 'We've got to stop him before someone else sees that,' he said tersely. 'Stand fast, I'll do it.' He dashed outside, and whipping out his handkerchief flagged the 'message received' sign. He followed this with the 'stop sending' signal, and added, 'wait, but watch.'

The distant rag obediently disappeared.

'That's something to work on, anyway,' remarked Gimlet, when he rejoined the others. 'How the deuce did he get to the top of that tower, I wonder?'

'He was in the upper compartment, waving through a loophole,' said the priest, whose placid calm had broken down under the excitement of the moment. 'That is a place most dangerous to approach, with great holes in the floor, through which the defenders once poured boiling oil on those below. I have seen it, and shudder even now to think of it.'

'How's it reached, this chamber?' demanded Gimlet.

'By a spiral staircase that winds, it seems, for ever upwards. It is just wide enough for a man to use his sword arm.'

'Is it possible to get close to that tower without actually entering the castle grounds, which I understand are surrounded by barbed wire?' asked Gimlet.

'It is possible to get within a reasonable distance,' rejoined Father Edwinus, after a moment's reflection. 'About four acres are enclosed, but there are places where the wire comes closer to the actual building than in others, because of the existence of some cottages on one side. It was decided that these cottages must be outside the wire, you understand. Nevertheless, they were evacuated, the reason given being their proximity to the chateau. No one is allowed to enter them under pain of death. The houses are locked, no doubt, but I have not been to see.'

'Would it be possible to speak to anyone in the tower from one of these cottages?'

'The tower is a hundred and fifty feet high, *monsieur*. It must be well over a hundred feet to the loophole. It would be possible to shout a message, but that would be heard by the sentries.'

'Ah! The sentries. Can you tell me about them?' queried Gimlet.

'There are perhaps twelve soldiers always on duty at the chateau, not counting the regular staff – the cooks, the waiters, and so on,' rejoined the priest. 'The gate-house at the *Porte d'Abas* is the guard post. Two sentries stand there, with those not on duty inside. Four sentries patrol the wire in regular beats, turning when they meet each other.'

'Inside or outside the wire?'

'Inside. And I must tell you that there are little bells on the top of the wire, so that if anyone tries to get over they would ring, and bring the sentries to the spot.'

'Is the wire very deep?'

'You could see it from the cottages because it passes the end of the gardens. There are, as it were, four fences, on which the wire is stretched taut, with loose wire between – perhaps five paces in all. Of course, in daylight none of the prisoners could approach the wire without being seen; at dusk they are locked within the chapel, as I told you.'

'I am not thinking about them getting out; I'm thinking about us getting in,' asserted Gimlet. 'I think we'd better go and survey the objective before attempting to make a plan. Will you, Father Edwinus, guide us to the cottages you spoke of? You could walk a little ahead of us so that if we were challenged you would not be implicated.'

'But certainly, *monsieur*. Is it your intention to go at once?'

'Immediately, otherwise it will be dark and we shall be unable to see anything. The moon does not rise until the early hours of the morning. Having seen the place we shall be in a better position to make a plan, although it is unlikely that we shall be able to put it in motion before the moon comes up.'

'But what about food? I can promise only bread and cheese, and salads from my garden.'

'We are in no case to be particular, father,' stated Gimlet. 'I would prefer to see the chateau while any light remains. For the moment, take us to the cottages. We will talk of food later, when a greater need for it arises.'

'As you wish, *monsieur*,' agreed Father Edwinus. 'I will go by a roundabout way, taking a path that is little used, so that we should not be seen. *Monsieur* will pardon me if I appear presumptuous, but you realise that if you are caught in those garments you will be shot as spies?'

'We should probably be shot anyway, if we were caught,' replied Gimlet. 'If it comes to that, I admit I would prefer to be shot in my uniform – but that, too, is a matter that can wait.'

'You intend to attempt a rescue?'

'Yes.'

'At once?'

'That is unlikely,' answered Gimlet. 'It may be better to wait until things are quiet, or we may need the light of the moon. We shall see.'

The priest gazed steadily at Gimlet. 'I fear you are attempting the impossible,' he said with a sigh. 'To enter the chateau gate without force of arms is not to be thought of, and even if you got in the grounds, you would need the wings of a bird to reach the chamber at the top of the tower. One shot will bring out the whole garrison.'

Gimlet smiled faintly. 'There may not be shooting, and we may not attempt to force the gate. For the rest, the business of commandos, reverend sir, is the attempting of the impossible, otherwise there would be no need for them. Our soldiers can quite well handle ordinary military enterprises. But come, let us go and reconnoitre this Nazi torture house.'

CHAPTER FOURTEEN

'Careless Talk Costs Lives'

Cub's ascent to the top of the donjon tower was mainly a matter of luck. At any rate, it was not premeditated at the outset, but was a development of a situation that arose.

On the way to the chateau, after his arrest in the *Place*, perceiving that his plight was desperate and likely to get worse rather than better, he considered seriously the chances of making a bolt for it. But the risks were too great; not only were his two guards armed with rifles which they would most certainly use, probably successfully, but there were a number of other Germans about who would stop him before he could get far. Such an attempt, if it failed, would be an admission of guilt that could only make matters much worse, for at present the attitude of his guards suggested that he was not so much a dangerous prisoner as a foolish or disobedient child who needed restraint.

In these circumstances he walked on, determined to wait for a more promising opportunity.

His great fear was still that he might be searched, but try as he would he could think of no way of disposing of his incriminating equipment. This exercised his mind all the way to the guardhouse, because he felt that while he was regarded as a child he still had a chance. The discovery of a loaded pistol on his person would put an end to that.

They went on through the medieval gate in the wall, where his name was taken and entered in a book by the sergeant of the guard. Naturally, he did not give his proper name, which would have betrayed his nationality. Instead, he chose one at random – Henri Blanc. It was at this stage that his ascent of the tower really began, for so harmless did his escort consider him – or so it seemed – that one of them stayed behind talking to the sergeant. Cub, therefore, went on with only one guard, whose manner was that of a nurse taking a child to church.

Passing under the noble façade they found themselves in the stone-flagged hall, from a corner of which the majestic stone stairway, the admiration of tourists before the war, leads to the upper part of the building. Here the escort's casual regard for his prisoner was again revealed.

'Wait,' he said. 'I report to the commandant. No doubt he will wish to see you.'

It may be that the Nazi, now that his prisoner was safely inside the barbed wire, ruled out of his mind any possibility of escape; if he did he is hardly to be blamed, for such an attempt appeared hopeless. At all events, leaving his charge standing in the hall, he walked on to a massive door at the far side of the vestibule.

Cub had no desire to see the commandant. Far from it. Not only would he ask automatically if the prison had been searched, but Cub's French, while almost perfect – certainly good enough to deceive a foreigner – might not get by a Frenchman.

Wherefore Cub looked about him swiftly for some place where he could at least hide his equipment. There was no place. The stone walls were devoid of even a shelf.

He looked at the stairway, then back at the Nazi, and saw that he was still facing the door, presumably waiting for permission to enter. In a flash, moving on tip-toe, Cub was on the bottom step. Then, hardly knowing what he was going to do, he was on his way up, glancing to right and left for a suitable place in which he could secrete the pistol. His knife, he thought, did not matter so much. Three steps were sufficient to take him out of sight of the hall. He heard the soldier call, 'Blanc!' which told him that he had been missed, but in the spirit of 'in for a penny, in for a pound', he held on his way.

To describe in detail his movements for the next few minutes, without making a long story, would necessitate some knowledge of the interior of the castle – which, as we know, Cub possessed.

The great stairway, known as the *Escalier d'Honneur*, sweeps round to the front of the building, overlooking the courtyard. This is repeated twice, mounting to the second and third floors, where access is obtained to the twin turrets. From the third floor a narrow corridor of some length leads off at right angles, and after traversing some awkward – not to say dangerous – angles, where the timber has rotted to such an extent that a false step might precipitate the visitor into the courtyard far below, it ends at the donjon, which is the oldest part of the building. In times of peace most visitors are content to accept the rest for granted, and retrace their steps, for the ascent to the top of the tower is a grimy as well as an arduous performance, and, moreover, it requires a steady head.

Cub had passed several places where he could well have concealed his pistol, but by this time he was inspired by a more ambitious project.

Up the narrow spiral staircase he went, sweeping aside cobwebs with his arms, and stepping over oblique holes, dropping sheer into space, left by the masons for the discharge of arrows, quicklime, boiling oil, and the like, as was customary in earlier forms of warfare. The staircase is so narrow as to permit the passage of only one person at a time, and it would be no exaggeration to say that it could be held by one determined man against an army – provided the defender did not have to eat or sleep. Cub was not thinking of anything so violent. He had just remembered that from the compartment in which the staircase ended it was possible to see the chapel.

He arrived in it hot, dusty and dishevelled, and not a little out of breath; but it was with a feeling of triumph that he gazed out of one of the four square apertures that serve as windows, gulping clean, cool air into his overworked lungs. He had a good look at the chapel. The commandos were not in sight, and he did not expect that they would be. Then he turned his attention to the chamber.

He was quite sure that he would be followed; or perhaps, since no one knew which way he had gone, it would be more correct to say that he knew the chamber would be examined in the search that would soon be ordered.

There could be no question of retreat. The only way down was the way he had come up – unless he took a flying leap on to the roof of the main building, some forty feet below.

What he needed now was a hiding-place, and that was something the chamber did not possess; or so it appeared at first glance, for the circular wall was as bare as the face of a cliff. On top of it was the massive wooden truss which supported the conical roof; and this was carried by two enormous beams, some eighteen inches square, fitted in the form of a cross with their ends built into the masonry.

Had it been necessary for him to reach these beams quickly it is unlikely that he would have been able to do so, for they were not less than eight feet above the floor. But as it happened he had plenty of time, and by prizing out some mortar from the wall with the point of his knife, he was able to make toe and finger holes deep enough to support his weight and elevate him to the timber. He gave it a trial before he was satisfied, and finding that the climb now presented no difficulty, he returned to the floor, and resting his elbows in a turret gazed upon the scene spread out before him.

The view, as the guide-book states, is imposing. On one side, far below, the little town of Chateaudun lies spread out like a model. Looking southward across the grey pile of buildings one sees the river Loire, rolling majestically in great curves towards the distant sea. On the other two sides magnificent panoramas of green fields and woods, heath and plough land, recede unendingly to the horizon. Cub was not interested in views or landscapes.

He returned to the window that overlooked the cemetery, and gazed longingly at the little building in which his friends reposed, unconscious of his fate. And as he watched he saw a man in a priest's habit walking swiftly through the tumbling tombs towards the chapel. Even at that distance the portly figure told him that it was Father Edwinus. What would happen when he found the commandos there?

With eager eyes he watched, hoping to get some indication of what was passing. But he saw nothing. The priest did not emerge, from which he could only hope that those within were engaged in profitable conversation.

During this time, from the courtyard, had come sounds, shouts and the banging of doors, which indicated clearly enough that the search for him was proceeding with vigour; but he paid no attention. This was only to be expected. But now a new sound sent him to the head of the spiral staircase. From far below came a murmur, a curious whispering noise, such as a receding wave makes on a shingle beach. He was in no doubt as to what caused it. Men – at least two men, since they were talking – were coming up the stairs.

Moving quietly, without undue haste, he mounted to one of the great beams, and gathering his rags round him to make sure that they did not overhang, stretched himself at full length and waited for what might befall.

He had not long to wait. The murmur gave way to a scraping of nail-studded boots. Then, panting, into the chamber came two German soldiers. From the top of the steps they made a quick survey of the compartment.

'He isn't here,' said one.

'I didn't expect he would be,' replied the other. 'How would he find his way up here? We've come up all those cursed steps for nothing. Let's get back.'

'No hurry,' returned the first speaker. 'The sergeant will only send us some-where else. We might as well have a breather. I'll have a draw at my pipe.'

'A lot of fuss about nothing, I reckon,' said his companion, 'all over a brat.'

'From something I've just heard, the general may have got the right idea when he ordered his arrest,' observed speaker number one, mysteriously. 'Fine view from up here.'

'Maybe that's why Frey is in such a sweat, wondering what the general's going to say when he learns that the boy has disappeared.'

'He can't have got away. The sergeant swears he didn't go through the gate, which means that he's still inside the wire. There are plenty of places where he could hide, in a pile this size. Sooner or later he'll have to give himself up for want of food, though, unless he falls off the roof – if that's where he is – and breaks his neck.' The speaker crossed the room, passing under Cub, and leaning in the window turret looked down on the roof of the main building. 'He doesn't seem to be there,' he remarked, returning to his companion.

'I shouldn't worry. The general is more taken up with this Englander they call Gimlet. I hear they're offering fifty thousand francs for him, dead or alive. If it's my luck to bring him in he'll be dead – no sense in taking chances, with all that money at stake. I should like to see him, just once, for about three seconds.'

As it happened, this wish was to be fulfilled, but the speaker was unaware of it. So was Cub, who, flat on his beam, was listening to this conversation with no small interest – wishing fervently, nevertheless, that the men would go.

'Well, let's be getting down,' ran on the man who had last spoken. 'I'm on duty tonight. I'd as soon be at the front. Nothing happens in a hole like this. Even the French are too scared to squeak. Come on, before the sergeant starts yelling for us.'

The other tapped out his pipe with thoughtful deliberation. 'You know, a thought has just struck me,' he remarked in a curious voice. 'I was talking to Hans Schneider, the despatch rider, just now. It looks as if they're going to catch this fellow Gimlet. The general is no fool. The reward did the trick – it usually does.'

'What have you heard?' inquired the other, in a low voice.

'Keep this to yourself,' replied his comrade, in that off-hand manner which some men affect when they know something important – or think they do. 'I shouldn't talk about it at all, really, but nobody is likely to over-hear us up here. But don't repeat it.'

In spite of his predicament Cub could hardly repress a smile. Here, indeed, was a classic example of how, in almost impossible circum-stances, information can reach the enemy. But his smile faded as the man continued.

'From what I can make out we've as good as got this fellow Gimlet. About an hour ago, after the reward notices were posted, a fellow turns up at headquarters, at Caen, and says he has information worth part of the reward. A gipsy horse dealer, of Le Mans, he said he was. He gave evidence that a barge belonging to a girl named Marcelle something or other came into the quay at Le Mans with some suspicious characters on board. The girl asked him to look after her horse. These men, he swears, were dressed in the clothes of the girl's father. Now, that fitted in with what was already known, because, the night before, the barge was up at Argentan. It had been commandeered, but the two men who went to take it over didn't come back. By dragging the river one of the bodies was found. The chap had been shot, and a forty-five British service bullet was found in him. So it looks as if Gimlet and his men went down the river in the barge. At any rate, this horse dealer, Bertrand Dacosta, says there were three men with the girl, and he gave a description of them. He thinks there was a boy with them, but he's not sure – he didn't pay much attention at the time. Anyway, if there was, he couldn't remember what he looked like. We know Gimlet came this way, and it just struck me that this brat the general picked up might be the same one. He comes from Caen, and that's where the trouble started.'

'*Donner*! That was pretty smart work. Our people must be wide awake.'

'More than you guess. What about this. They've spotted the girl already. Saw her, so Hans tells me, at Orleans station. Got a man with her, supposed to be her uncle, and it turns out that he's an absconding conscript from Le Mans.'

'They were arrested, I suppose?'

'Ha! That's what you'd do, no doubt. The general is smarter than that. Arrest them? No fear. Leave them alone, but watch them that's his plan.'

'He'd look silly if they gave him the slip after all.'

'Not much chance of that. They've taken tickets for Paris. They missed the morning train, so they've got a long wait. There isn't another till the night train which comes up from Narbonne. Gets to Paris about four in the morning.'

'But what's the idea of leaving them loose?'

'Fool! Don't you see these two must know this man Gimlet. It's ten to one they'll meet him somewhere. When they do – *phut*! We've got them all in one net.'

'Sounds too good to be true.'

'Hans told me – and he should know. But keep this to yourself. You know how these things leak out?'

'Don't worry about that. I can keep my mouth shut.'

'The joke is, it seems that this gipsy has been detained – to keep him from talking, so they say; but I expect the truth is, the general doesn't trust him a yard. But we'd better be getting back.'

To Cub's infinite relief the two men disappeared down the staircase. He waited until the footsteps had receded to a safe distance, and then sat up. His face was white, and his lips dry with shock. His hands, as he lowered himself to the floor, were trembling. Crossing to the window the Germans had just vacated he stared, at first with unseeing eyes, across the vista. His brain was reeling, and he found it difficult to think clearly. Snatches of the conversation he had overheard kept running through his mind like a scratched gramophone record repeating itself. It took him a little while to recover, but even then the position seemed so hopeless that he nearly gave way to despair. It was really anger, or rather, cold fury, that saved him. 'That gipsy rat,' he grated. 'The dirty traitor. The craven money-grubber.'

It was natural that he should look across to the chapel, now mellow in the glow of the setting sun. If only he could get in touch with Gimlet, he thought feverishly. If he could warn him, the position might yet be saved. But how? And then, as an obvious possibility occurred to him, he wondered why he had not thought of it before. His handkerchief was really too small for his purpose, so with a recklessness born of the gnawing anxiety that gripped his heart, he tore off the tail of his shirt and waved it through the loophole.

Nothing happened. He went on waving. Still nothing happened. For all he knew, he thought bitterly, the priest might have gone. They might all have gone, if it came to that. Still, he went on waving. There was nothing else he could do.

It was ten minutes that seemed like hours before his signal was answered, and when he saw Gimlet's handkerchief flutter he could have shouted with relief and joy. As he read Gimlet's curt order he realised at once the wisdom of it, and although he would have preferred to signal the terrible news he had just heard, regardless of consequences to himself, he withdrew to think the matter over, and wait, taking up a position from which he could keep an eye on the chapel.

Soon afterwards he saw the handkerchief flutter again, and made out the signal – not without difficulty, for dusk was closing in:

Leaving here. Watch cottages below you direction east. Message ends.

Cub moved to a new position, one that commanded a view of the cottages, and settled down to wait. Night came, and with it a melancholy silence that dragged like millstones on the feet of Time.

CHAPTER FIFTEEN

Gimlet Makes His Plan

During this period of early darkness the commandos moved from the chapel to the cottages, an operation that was carried out quietly, and with complete success.

Father Edwinus went first, taking the roundabout route he had advised. He walked slowly, with head bent as though in profound meditation, although in fact his eyes and ears and nerves were braced for the first sign of danger. The commandos followed, loafing rather than walking like men on a definite errand, with a fair interval between them. The arrangement was that they should keep within sight of each other. Should trouble develop, the others were to close up and take such action as the situation demanded. As it happened, nothing of the sort occurred, and the little party reached its objective without seeing a soul.

It turned out that the cottages referred to by the *padre* comprised a row of four tiny dilapidated dwellings, set on a slope, and terminating in an old tavern, also empty, in much the same condition. This inn, Gimlet found on close inspection, seemed to be larger than its position warranted, for it was built round a cobbled yard. That is to say, there was an opening in the middle large enough to permit the entrance of a vehicle into the yard, and the stables beyond – a not uncommon arrangement. The priest explained that in times gone by the inn had been a posting house, where travellers could ride in and change their horses.

Still under the *curé*'s guidance they returned to the top cottage, which was the one nearest to the chateau, and tried the door. Having ascertained that it was locked, access to the inside was quickly gained by the simple expedient of forcing a window – a task which Copper performed in silence.

Passing to the rear of the building the back door was opened from the inside, so that it was possible to survey the imposing pile beyond, although in the failing light little detail could be seen. Against the darkening sky the building looked enormous, with the donjon rising up like a mighty monument. For the first time the immensity of the ancient bulwark, or keep, to give it its proper name, could be really appreciated. The windows, or the apertures left in the masonry which served as such, could just be made out, a little darker than the rest. Nearer, the course of the barbed-wire fence could be followed, passing, as the priest had described, the end of the garden. The distance from the wire to the base of the tower was about thirty paces, and consisted of a flat, open, gravelled area, the home of a few sun-parched weeds.

All this Gimlet regarded for some time without speaking, but at last he put a question to Trapper.

'Could you,' he asked, pointing to the top of the great round tower, 'put an arrow through that window?'

Trapper looked dubious. 'It's a long shot, and the light is bad, but it might be done, although I would not swear to hit the mark first time. It would be easier after the moon comes up. It would be easier now if I could stand on the roof, there.' He pointed to the roof of the chateau proper, which ended in a high gable under the tower. 'There is plenty of good old ivy, so an ascent should be possible,' he added.

'If you miss,' returned Gimlet thoughtfully, 'the arrow will fall into the yard, perhaps with enough noise to attract a sentry.'

'And if he hits the mark the arrow might hit Cub in the face, if he happens to be looking out,' put in Copper shrewdly.

'I hadn't overlooked that,' said Gimlet. 'Before we begin operations I shall flash a message to Cub with the torch, telling him to stand clear. He will be waiting for a signal, no doubt. By standing well back in the house the light should not be seen by sentries. It will of course be necessary to cut a way through the wire.'

'Don't forget the bells,' murmured Copper.

'By working on the bottom strands we ought to be able to do the job without disturbing them. That will take time.' Gimlet's tone was still pensive.

'What's the general idea, sir, if I may ask?' inquired Copper.

'Well, in view of what the *padre* tells us, it's pretty obvious that we couldn't hope to get into the building through the front door without colliding with the guard. That would result in a good deal of noise, and noise is something we must avoid. Anything in the way of an alarm would bring the whole garrison down on us, and that would knock any attempt at rescue right on the head. My idea, therefore, is to join Cub in the Tower. If I can do that, not only should I gain admission without disturbing anybody, but Cub, who knows his way about the inside of the place, could guide me to the chapel, where the prisoners sleep.'

'Are you thinking of evacuating everyone out of that window?' asked Copper incredulously, pointing to the tower.

'That's it.'

'But how are you going to get up?'

'By means of a rope, I hope.' Gimlet turned to Father Edwinus, who stood listening to the conversation. 'Can you procure for us a rope – it would have to be a long one – and a ball of string?'

'May I ask for what purpose, *monsieur*?'

'The string will be fastened to an arrow, and the arrow will be shot through that window. To the string will be fastened the rope. Cub, by hauling on the string, will draw up the rope and make it fast.'

'I have string, but no rope long enough for that purpose,' said the priest regretfully.

'What about the church ropes – those you use to ring the bells?'

'*Pst*! Dolt that I am! But, of course. I did not think of that. You think of everything, *monsieur*.'

'Not everything, father,' said Gimlet, smiling. 'But we are trained to think of ways and means. If you will let us have the rope, I promise you shall have it back, so that you will not be incriminated in the affair – as you would be if the Germans found the rope and recognised it.'

'I will fetch it at once,' offered the priest. 'It will take a little while.'

'It will be long enough for our purpose?'

'Ample, *monsieur*. There are three ropes, and they can be joined together.'

'Then fetch them, *mon père*. There is no need for haste. Don't forget the string.'

'I will return as quickly as may be,' promised the priest, and departed forthwith.

Gimlet turned to the others. 'That settles that. Now then, if we get those chaps out we are going to be quite a party. There are several of them, and some, after ill usage by the Nazis, will be in no state for a forced march. Yet, once the job is done, the sooner we are away from this place, the better. In the car which we left at the aerodrome we could travel faster, and farther. I see no great difficulty in getting it. We shall have to wait for the rope, anyway. Also, I think it's time we got back into our uniforms. Not only would they make our attack a military operation, but they would convince the prisoners that we are genuine; otherwise they might not believe us, taking our intrusion as some sort of new trick by the Nazis. Copper, I want you to go to the aerodrome and fetch the car. Bring it here and park it in the courtyard of the inn, just below; no one will be likely to see it there. While you are away we'll make a start on the wire – it will take time to cut a clean gap.'

'Aye-aye, sir!' assented Copper. 'I shall feel more at home in khaki.'

'All right. Move off. Remember, I shall depend on the car.'

'You'll get it,' promised Copper cheerfully, and vanished into the darkness.

Gimlet turned to Trapper. 'Get the cutters out and let's see about this wire,' he ordered. 'You do the cutting, working only on the bottom strands. I'll draw it out as you cut, and put it out of the way. You can ignore the sentries. I'll watch for them. If I tap you on the foot, stop working and lie still. Two taps will mean you can carry on.'

'Okay, sir!' Trapper produced the powerful cutters, and making his way cautiously to the bottom of the garden, began work. Lying flat, he cut pieces out of the wire, methodically, with the dexterity of long practice. Gimlet knelt behind him in a position from which he could watch the fence in both directions, and taking the loose ends of wire as Trapper passed them to him, drew each piece clear, and disposed of it by tossing it into the next garden.

A few minutes later the first sentry made his appearance. He wore a greatcoat, for the air was chilly, and on his head a field service cap, not a steel helmet – a detail that was noted by Gimlet, who, seeing him coming, tapped Trapper's foot. They both lay flat, motionless, while the sentry sauntered by, his rifle at the slope.

A short distance below he met his half-section, had a few words with him, and then strolled back, passing within ten feet of where the commandos lay. As soon as he was at a safe distance the work was resumed.

This happened on and off for the next hour, by which time the gap was complete, and Father Edwinus had returned with the information that he had brought the rope, the string, and a small parcel of food.

Gimlet remarked that Copper was not yet back, but that there was no need to delay on that account. The stars were bright in the sky, and Trapper announced that these provided enough light to give him a reasonable chance of putting an arrow through the window at the top of the donjon.

'It would be easier from that roof,' he averred. 'To reach it, though, I guess I should make some noise in the ivy – and there are sentries. In any case, I do not like these sentries about,' he declared. 'They would be better out of the way.'

'I think you're right,' agreed Gimlet. 'We'd better dispose of them first. It will be safer that way. We'll knock the first one on the head as he passes; when his half-section walks along looking for him, we'll deal with him in the same way. According to Father Edwinus there are two more sentries on the far side. They may appear in due course, but we should be able to handle them. After that things should be nice and quiet – at any rate, until the new guard takes over. That should not be yet. I expect they're doing the usual four hours on and four off. We'll get the two sentries on this side for a start; then I'll signal to Cub to get his head out of the way and you can try your luck with an arrow. If you can't manage it from the ground, you'll have to get on the roof.' Gimlet turned to Father Edwinus. 'There is no need for you to stay any longer; to do so would be taking a needless risk. Things may go wrong. Thank you for all you have done. Maybe we'll meet again some day. No doubt you will hear in due course of our success or failure. The rope, when we have finished with it, we will leave in the kitchen of this cottage. You can collect it after we have gone.'

'If it is all the same to you, my son, I would prefer to see this business through,' answered the priest. 'At last I feel that I am doing something for

France. It would be better, too, I think, if I waited for the rope, and took it away with me.'

'As you wish,' concurred Gimlet. 'But,' he added grimly, 'for the next few minutes the work will be better suited for soldiers than for priests – you understand?'

'I comprehend perfectly, *monsieur*,' said Father Edwinus quietly. 'I understand also that this is total war, and that the Nazis started it. Someone said long ago that those who sought to live by the sword should perish by the sword. There was a time in the history of this castle that priests took an active part in the defence of their homeland. They did so in the war of 1870, when here at Chateaudun was fought a bitter battle by the people against the invading Prussians. In better times you can see a tablet in the *Place* commemorating the deeds of those brave souls. What those who were here before me could do, so I, under God's blessing, can also do. Proceed, my son, and take no account of me.'

Gimlet smiled faintly in the gloom. 'That's the spirit, father!' He glanced at Trapper. 'It's time Copper was back,' he said anxiously. 'I wonder what he's up to?'

It was, perhaps, a good thing for his peace of mind that he did not know what Copper was up to.

CHAPTER SIXTEEN

Copper Gets a Shock

It had been in no spirit of apprehension that Copper had set out for his objective. He did not expect there would be any trouble in fetching the car, for he was the fortunate possessor of one of those minds that never does expect trouble, and is both surprised and indignant when it is encountered.

It was no use, he often stated, trying to jump a fence before you came to it.

There were some among his comrades who put this attitude down to lack of imagination; and there may have been something in their contention. Be that as it may, there is no doubt that Copper's sanguine outlook was a useful attribute on such work as now occupied his attention. Such plans as he made were primitive in their simplicity. If he were challenged, he decided, it was going to be too bad for the man who challenged him; and if anyone tried to stop the car after he was in it, it was going to be too bad for him, too. Such was the extent of Copper's practical philosophy, as he walked boldly down the road, intent on reaching his objective in the shortest possible time.

Being alone, he disdained such undignified manoeuvres as crawling, or dodging from cover to cover, which always irritated him. After all, he had been a policeman, and London bobbies did not do that sort of thing. It went against the grain to do it now. Still, he was not wantonly reckless, and he did on one occasion, after a short tussle with his pride, stand behind a tree while some army lorries went by. He encountered one or two men on the road; they passed him with a nervous *bonsoir*, to which he grunted a reply that was not in any known language. Fortunately – fortu-

136

nately for them, that is – they were Frenchies, as Copper called them, so it did not matter.

As he approached the short drive that led from the Orleans road to the aerodrome, certain sounds, and one or two dim lights, caused him to suspect that something had happened on the landing-ground during the short time he had been away. Perceiving clearly that he would not discover just what this was by standing still, he walked on, his stride not shortening by an inch.

His predominant reaction was curiosity. What *could* have happened? he asked himself – without guessing the answer. It was dark, much too dark to see anything from a distance, so with a slight frown of annoyance lining his forehead he advanced for a closer inspection.

He nearly walked into a German sentry who was standing at the gateway. Luckily this sentry, being a hundred miles away – as he supposed – from any possible trouble was in much the same frame of mind as Copper. It is reasonable to assume that he took the belated pedestrian for a stray Frenchman making his way home. At any rate, his 'Wer da?' was spoken quite casually.

'Wer da?' is the German equivalent of the British 'Who goes there?' but Copper did not know that. He only knew that the speaker was a German, because he had learned to tell the difference between French and German. He was sure that the words spoken in the darkness were not French; therefore the man must be a German. As a matter of fact, by this simple logic he arrived at the truth. To be precise, the man was a member of the Luftwaffe, on gate duty.

With his hands rolling themselves into fists, Copper walked straight up to him. He could just see the rifle raised threateningly, but he guessed that the man would not shoot, because he had often been a sentry himself, and he knew that a man, any man, hesitates to fire his weapon until he is quite sure that such action is justified. One can get into serious trouble, for example, for shooting one's own officer, who might be returning home late after a night out. What the sentry thought we do not know, for if he made a decision at all it came too late to serve any useful purpose. His rifle was brushed aside, and Copper's great fist crashed like a battering ram into the middle of his face. Under such a blow the proverbial ox would have staggered, at least.

The sentry, who happened to be a little man, did more than that. His cap flew off as he was lifted from his feet and hurled with considerable force against the gate which he was supposed to be guarding. He slumped to the ground and lay still.

Copper leaned over him for a moment, gazing into the unconscious face; then he dragged the inert body to one side, tied the hands and feet with the man's own lanyard, and placed him carefully in the bottom of the hedge.

'Sorry, chum,' he said apologetically, 'but you asked fer it!'

It is not to be supposed from the foregoing that Copper was a fool. Far from it. He would not have been in the commandos if he were. He had already realised that if a sentry had been posted there must be an enemy unit of some sort in the vicinity; and what place could be more likely than the aerodrome? That this was so he soon verified by advancing a short distance, and then lying down to get a clear view of the skyline. What he saw brought his favourite expletive to his lips. 'Well, strike me pink!' he muttered, as he made out the silhouettes of a number of aircraft, so big that they were obviously bombers, lined up in front of the dilapidated hangars. 'Strike me pink!' he breathed again. 'That's awkward!'

But on further consideration he did not see that the presence of these machines should necessarily interfere with the carrying out of his orders, which were to get the car, and the sacks containing the uniforms. The sentry was disposed of – that was the main thing, he reasoned. If there were any more – well, they would have to be disposed of, too. This, he appreciated, would have to be done without noise, if possible; nevertheless before advancing towards the shed in which the car had been parked, he made sure that his revolver was handy.

The sight that confronted him when he reached the shed threw him for a moment into confusion. The garage was full of vehicles; not merely were a few cars parked in it; the building was literally packed with lorries of all shapes and sizes, to the number, he judged, of not less than thirty. And somewhere behind all these, presumably, was the car he had come to fetch.

He had a good look round to make sure that no Germans were about, and then, scratching his head in perplexity, considered his problem. One thing was at once clear. It was going to be a long time, a very long time, even if he were not interrupted, to move all these vehicles, one by one, in order to get to the car at the back. It would, he perceived, take more time than he could afford; apart from which, the Germans might come and ask him what he was doing. They might even object. What was the answer?

Copper could think of only one answer; and it was, in fact, the only practicable one. If he could not get to his own car, then he would have to take one of the lorries. As far as he knew, it would serve Gimlet's purpose equally well, except that a lorry was not as fast as a car. Yes, he decided, it would have to be a lorry. Nothing else for it.

Having reached this decision he returned to the sentry to make sure that the man was in no condition to cause trouble at an inconvenient moment.

The German was still unconscious, so, acting on the spur of the moment, he picked up his cap and put it on his head, remarking: 'You don't mind if I borrow your titfer,* chum?' This was no mere fooling. He knew that seated in a lorry little more than a man's head and shoulders can be seen by a person standing on the ground; the hat, while far from being a disguise, might serve a useful purpose if he were questioned – might, in fact, save him from being questioned, a contingency which, since he could speak neither French nor German, he preferred to avoid.

Leaving the sentry, he walked back down the track to the place where the sacks containing the uniforms and equipment had been dumped. It took only a moment to recover them, and pile them in a heap on the grass verge. This done, he returned to the garage and selecting a new-looking five-ton lorry, climbed into the seat and started the engine.

He frowned when a voice suddenly called something from the back of the building – the voice speaking, of course, in German. He had not known that anyone was there, nor even suspected it.

'I don't know what you're talking about!' he growled in English, and drove out, stopping when he came to the heap of sacks. He had just pitched them into the back of the lorry and was moving round to the front seat, when a German officer appeared, walking briskly up the track towards

---

* Army rhyming slang, derives from tit-for-tat – hat.

the camp. He stared hard at Copper, and, although he was unaware of it, he was never nearer to death than at that moment. With inspired presence of mind Copper saluted. The officer returned the salute in the perfunctory way officers usually return salutes, and walked on without stopping.

Copper gazed after the retreating figure. 'Strike me purple!' he muttered. 'That takes the blinkin' biscuit! Fancy me, saluting a perishing Jerry! Trapper won't 'alf laugh when I tell 'im about it – not 'alf he won't.' Climbing up into the seat, he continued on towards Chateaudun. Nothing happened – not that he supposed anything would happen. Why should it? he reasoned, naïvely.

He cruised quietly through the town, and without being challenged ran on down the hill past the cottages and brought the lorry to a stop in the courtyard of the inn, in accordance with orders. Walking to the top cottage, he found Gimlet waiting for him.

'You've been a long time,' accused Gimlet.

'Had a spot o' trouble,' answered Copper briefly.

'What happened?'

'There's some flying blokes moved in,' explained Copper. 'I couldn't get ter the car fer lorries, so I brought a lorry instead.'

'That'll do. Get the kit?'

'It's all here.'

'Good!' murmured Gimlet. 'We're all set? Let's get into our uniforms.'

'Aye-aye, sir,' agreed Copper.

CHAPTER SEVENTEEN

Dizzy Work in the Dark

Cub, in his lofty prison, was far from happy. It seemed a long while since he had received the signal from the chapel, and he could not imagine what his comrades were doing. He had lost all count of time. Naturally, having been warned to do so, he watched the cottages closely and unceasingly, but he saw nothing, except the vague shapes of the sentries patrolling the wire. Even these eventually failed to appear; at any rate, he saw them no more, although, curiously enough, he did not connect their disappearance with the commandos.

Then, at long last, he saw a light flash in what he took to be the kitchen of the nearest cottage. Actually, it was little more than a reflection on the window-panes, but it told him things were on the move, and he read the message eagerly, as letter by letter it was flashed in the Morse code.

Take cover. Stand by to receive arrow. Haul on string and make rope fast. Am coining up. Whistle if O.K.

Cub whistled softly, whereupon the light went out and was seen no more. With his heart beating fast he sat on the floor and waited. So taut were his nerves that he started when he heard a sharp *snick*, as if some object had struck near the window. It was followed almost at once by a faint clatter far below, and he guessed that Trapper had missed his mark. Twice more the same thing happened; then, with a whizz and a smack the arrow flew through the window to strike the wall on the far side, and fall with a thud.

It took him only a moment to find it, with the string attached. Crossing to the window, he began to haul in, hand over hand. Extra weight told him when the rope began its upward journey, and it needed all his strength to drag it in. Making it fast to one of the great beams that already had served

141

him so well, he again whistled softly. Instantly the rope creaked as it took the strain, and he peered down into the gloomy depths below to see if he could discern the climber.

What puzzled him was how Gimlet – assuming that it was Gimlet – hoped to climb the dizzy height, for as he knew well, climbing a rope is no easy matter.

Then he saw a figure already so close, and in such a position, that he gasped with astonishment and the most acute anxiety. It was not hanging vertically; instead, it stood out at an angle from the wall, feet in the ivy, head and shoulders in space. He understood, then, how the climb was being made. Gimlet was not climbing the rope in the literal sense of the word; he was, so to speak, walking up the wall, leaning back on the rope, using the gnarled ivy as footholds. Even so, Cub shuddered as he looked down the fearful height and contemplated the consequences of a slip, of one false step.

In a surprisingly short time Gimlet's head and shoulders appeared in the aperture, and Cub had another shock when he observed that he was in uniform. A brief final struggle, and Gimlet was inside, on the floor, breathing heavily.

'By gad!' he panted. 'That was a stiffish – climb. Are you – all right?'

'Right as rain, but I've some ghastly news,' answered Cub.

'Tell me while I'm getting my breath,' invited Gimlet.

'That rat of a fellow in Le Mans, Bertrand, whom Marcelle asked to mind her horse, was a Vichyite. He has betrayed us.' Cub repeated the gist of the conversation he had overheard between the two German soldiers.

'Not so good,' was all Gimlet had to say. 'One fine day that fellow will get what's coming to him.'

'But don't you realise, sir, that they'll capture Marcelle and her uncle, to say nothing of The Fleas, if Marcelle tries to make contact with them?'

'Of course I do, but that mustn't be allowed to happen,' returned Gimlet curtly.

'But Marcelle and Gaston will soon be on their way to Paris!' said Cub in a strained voice.

'So shall we, I hope,' replied Gimlet evenly.

'The Gestapo will meet the train.'

'Any reason why we shouldn't?' queried Gimlet, as he got up. 'But we've several things to do first.'

'You mean – you're thinking of going to Paris – in that uniform?' Cub was incredulous.

'Suppose we talk about that when the time comes?' suggested Gimlet. 'You know your way about this place, I understand?'

'Pretty well.'

'Good. I want you to show me the way to the chapel. That's where the prisoners are confined – or should be. I propose to bring them up here – or at any rate, those who are prepared to take their chance with us. They can go down the rope to Trapper, who is waiting at the bottom.'

'They'll have a job – getting down the rope.'

'Not such a job as I had to get up it, I'll warrant,' said Gimlet warmly. 'Lead on. By the way, have you still got your pistol?'

'Yes.'

'Then have it handy – you may need it. We're going through with this, whatever happens – understand?'

'Yes, sir.'

'Very well. Let's go. Don't make a noise.'

'There are some pretty bad places,' warned Cub.

'Tell me when we come to them. Go ahead.'

The descent of the spiral staircase in the dark was to Cub something of a nightmare. The steps seemed interminable. What Gimlet thought about it all he did not know, for he made no comment; nor did he make any remark as they traversed the upper passage, stepping over the holes in the floor.

After descending two more flights of stairs, slowly, and with infinite caution, Cub stopped. 'We're on the ground floor,' he whispered. 'You see the passage in front? If you turn to the left it takes you to the entrance hall. If you turn to the right it brings you to the chapel door. The door is on the left-hand side.'

'Good. I'll take the lead now.'

Moving noiselessly in his rubber-soled shoes, Gimlet went on in front towards the glow of light that illuminated the passage which Cub had indicated. Reaching it, he lay flat, and peered round the corner, looking both ways. He was back in a moment, on his feet, a finger on his lips.

'Sentry – outside the chapel door.' His lips did little more than frame the words.

With what interest Cub now watched Gimlet prepare for action can be better imagined than described. His heart was palpitating with such excitement as he had never known, the more because it had to be restrained. Yet it all seemed so simple – afterwards.

Gimlet loosened his dagger in its sheath and took his revolver in his right hand. Then, quite calmly, without any attempt at concealment, he turned the corner and strode towards the sentry, who was, Cub now saw, about six paces distant.

Gimlet had covered the distance before the sentry became aware of him. '*Hande hoch*!' ordered Gimlet crisply.

The German did not move. He stood, gaping foolishly, his eyes round, at first with wonder, then fear. He behaved like a man stricken by a sort of mental paralysis, and made no protest as Gimlet, with his gun in the man's stomach, took the rifle from his hands. Slowly the sentry obeyed Gimlet's order to put his hands up.

Cub could almost feel sorry for him. The shock must have been terrific, and most men, he reflected, suddenly confronted in the dead of night by the devil himself, as it were, would probably have behaved in the same way.

'The key,' said Gimlet tersely, still speaking in German.

Dumbly, the wretched man pointed to a key that hung on a nail beside the door.

'Open the door, Cub,' ordered Gimlet, and as Cub complied he pushed the sentry inside. 'Keep him covered,' went on Gimlet. 'If he makes one false move, or let's out one squeal, let him have it. We can't afford to be squeamish. It's unlikely that a shot in here would be heard outside, through these old walls. Always remember, what we are doing to him is nothing to what he'd do to us if he had the chance.'

By this time, from inside the room, which was of course in darkness, came exclamations of surprise and alarm. Gimlet closed the door.

'Is there a light in here?' he asked, speaking in French.

'Yes,' came a voice. 'The switch is by the door.'

'Is the room blacked out?'

'Yes.'

Gimlet switched on the light, and all was plain to see. Beds lined the walls. In them, men, mostly elderly men, were sitting up, facing the intruders.

Gimlet spoke again. 'Gentlemen,' he said, 'am I correct in supposing that you are all prisoners?'

There was a murmur of assent.

'Is General Romortin in here?'

'I am General Romortin,' said a tall, fine-looking old man, getting out of bed. 'What is the meaning of this?'

'I address myself to you, *monsieur le général*, as the senior officer present, although what I have to say applies to all,' stated Gimlet. 'My name is Captain King, commanding a unit of British Combined Operations. We have come here to effect your escape, and, if possible, take to England those who wish to go. Please make up your minds quickly because the matter is somewhat urgent.'

Dead silence greeted this pronouncement, which must have been startling to the hearers.

'Is there anyone here who does not wish to escape?' queried Gimlet.

There was a murmur of conversation. 'I speak for all,' said General Romortin. 'We wish to escape.'

'You will follow me?'

'With pleasure, *capitan*.'

'Is anyone ill?' inquired Gimlet. 'I ask because escape involves a descent by rope from the Donjon to the courtyard, where my men are waiting. The sentries have been disposed of, but it is not a trip for a sick man.'

'No man here is so ill that he would not seize this chance, even at the risk of his life,' answered the general. There was a chorus of confirmation.

'In that case will you please dress quickly, gentlemen. Minutes are precious.'

This request was not really necessary, because most of the prisoners were already dressing in feverish haste.

Gimlet turned to the German, who had now recovered sufficiently to grasp what was going on; but with Cub's pistol in the small of his back he made no attempt to move. Gimlet forced him to a bed, and having tied a blanket round his head lashed him to it – a task in which Cub took a hand. Gimlet then went to the door, where, as each one finished dressing, the prisoners assembled. When all were ready he spoke to them again.

'Gentlemen, I rely on your implicit obedience to my orders. He who fails in that will imperil the lives of all. Now follow the guide. No talking, please. You will be warned of the dangerous places.' Gimlet turned to Cub. 'Show the way,' he ordered. 'I shall guard the rear. The first to reach the tower will begin the descent immediately. Lead on.'

'This way, *messieurs*,' said Cub, and started off, followed by the prisoners in single file. Gimlet locked the door behind him, leaving the sentry inside.

Then began the return journey to the donjon, with Cub still not quite sure whether he was asleep or awake. He could hardly believe that so much could be achieved so quickly, and with so little noise. Every instinct in him urged him to run, to escape before their intrusion was discovered; but copying Gimlet's imperturbable manner, he held himself in hand. This, he thought vaguely, was discipline – or the result of it. How different, he reflected, were The Fleas' frantic, haphazard methods!

In ten minutes the main party was mustered in the chamber in which he had spent such a long vigil. The first officer was on his way down the rope. Gimlet stood guard at the head of the staircase.

'Don't forget, gentlemen; follow the instructions of the soldier whom you will find waiting at the bottom.'

The prisoners said nothing – or very little. They seemed to be stunned by the suddenness, the almost miraculous nature of the escape, savouring as it did more of medieval intrigue than modern military tactics. One by one they took the rope firmly in their hands, and disappeared from the window on the perilous descent, each one signalling by a tug on the rope when he reached the bottom. At last Gimlet and Cub remained.

'Down you go!' ordered Gimlet.

'What about you, sir?'

'I'm not coming this way.'

Cub started. 'Why not?'

'Because the rope must go down. To leave it would incriminate Father

Edwinus. Someone must stay to unfasten it. Copper and Trapper understand this. After giving those below time to get clear, I shall go down the staircase. I hope to be with you shortly. If I do not join you in fifteen minutes you will go without me. Copper knows what to do. By the way, stand clear when you get down or you may get the rope on your head.'

'But that means you'll have to go through the front—'

'You've got your orders!' snapped Gimlet.

'Yes, sir,' acknowledged Cub heavily, and taking the rope, crawled through the window and started down hand over hand. When he reached the bottom he gave a tug and stepped quickly away. Trapper was waiting. The rope came down with a swish. Trapper coiled it, and slung it over his shoulder.

'This way,' said he.

As they walked across the gravelled area, keeping sharp watch for danger, Trapper said, casually: 'We thought we'd lost you. What's the news?'

'The news is,' returned Cub, 'that rascally horse-dealer in Le Mans has, for a sum of money, told the Nazis about Marcelle bringing us down in her barge. Marcelle and Gaston have been spotted at Orleans, waiting for the Paris train. They are being watched by the Gestapo.'

Trapper stopped dead. His expression, usually cheerful, was suddenly grim. 'Is zat so?' he said slowly. '*Enfin*! Now let me tell you something, kid,' he went on, in a voice that was brittle with passion. 'If those swines lay a finger on that girl, one finger only, I'll – I'll—' Something seemed to stick in his throat. Then, recovering himself: 'This is no time for talking,' he said coldly. 'Keep going.'

Cub followed him to the wire, where Copper was waiting.

'Through the hole, kid,' said Trapper softly.

Cub crawled through the gap in the wire. It struck him that the cold-blooded efficiency of these men was almost past belief.

'I don't like going without Gimlet!' he muttered.

'Neither do we,' returned Copper. 'But when Gimlet gives orders, it's as well to obey them without arguing the toss. Am I right, Trapper?'

'Sure. Sure you're right,' answered Trapper in a dull voice, as though his thoughts were far away.

Copper glanced at him and nudged Cub. 'What's wrong with 'im?' he asked curiously.

'It's bad news, about Marcelle. The Gestapo are watching her,' replied Cub.

'Oh, blimey!' murmured Copper. 'If that's right, chum, Gawd 'elp any Jerries who get in 'is way after this. But come on.'

Followed by Cub he strode on, leaving Trapper standing by the gap in the wire, the Sten gun in the crook of his arm.

CHAPTER EIGHTEEN

Gimlet Goes Alone

From his elevated position, quietly smoking a cigarette, Gimlet watched those on the ground make a successful exit through the wire. Then, with the businesslike air of a man going to work. he dropped the cigarette on the floor, put his foot on it, and walking over to the staircase, began the descent. All was still quiet. The atmosphere within the thick old walls was that of a tomb.

Reaching the corridor on the ground floor, he glanced first in the direction of the chapel, and then turned to the left, towards the entrance hall, which he had never seen. Voices now came faintly to meet him, muffled, yet harsh, as though an argument was going on in some distant part of the building. But as he advanced, gun in hand, the voices reached him more clearly; and although he could make out that the language used was French, he was still unable to catch the actual words.

The hall, or one end of it, came into view, lighted – as he presently discovered – by a single electric bulb. Proceeding more slowly now, keeping close against the wall, he was able to survey the entire vestibule.

There was no one in it – he had fully expected a sentry. It was larger than he had imagined, but devoid of anything in the way of furniture. Floor, walls, and ceiling were of stone, bleak and grim, like a large prison cell. His eyes went to the massive double doors that opened on to the courtyard. They were shut.

A huge iron key projected from the lock, as though the door had been closed for the night, and for some reason opened again. In a moment his hand was on the latch.

Then he stopped, head half turned in a listening attitude, as from somewhere near at hand came a fresh outburst of voices, speaking in French. One was raised high as if in authority; another answered sullenly. The words reached him distinctly, and it was really on this account that he waited.

Said one, in guttural Teutonic French, stiff with anger: 'Fool! Don't you realise that I have made a special journey? The boy can't be far away. It is important that this fellow should see him at once. If he turns out to be the boy who travelled in the barge with those cut-throat Englanders, we should soon tear some useful information out of him. Why did you not report immediately that the boy had disappeared?'

'I did not want to cause a scene unnecessarily,' came another voice – this in fluent French although in a cringing tone. 'Naturally, I hoped the boy would turn up.'

'Imbecile!'

'It was not my fault!' went on the second voice. 'I tell you, I did not even see him. It was while his escort was reporting to me that he vanished. The escort was one of your men. Blame him – not me!'

'*Ach zo*! Well, we shall hear what the *Generaloberst* has to say about this when I get through to him. Already he is in no sweet temper. He has given me twelve hours to find this cursed commando captain. *Gott*! What would I not give to clap my eyes on him! The boy was a heaven-sent chance, and you—'

At this juncture a telephone-bell jangled.

'This will be Gunther,' went on the voice, with a threat in it. The bell cut out abruptly as the instrument was picked up. '*Ya – ya, Generaloberst*, this is *Hauptmann* von Roth. I regret to report that Colonel Frey has allowed the boy to escape.'

Now, all this time Gimlet had been standing by the door with his hand on the latch, looking over his shoulder at another door that stood ajar on the inner side of the hall. It was from the room beyond that the voices came. And as he listened his expression hardened. Curiosity was replaced by understanding, for he now had a pretty good idea of who was in the room, and what was going on. A dozen swift paces took him to the door, and he pushed it open, gently, a trifle more, so that he had a clear picture of the inside.

The room was furnished as an office. Papers were strewn on a heavy desk behind which stood a man with a French officer's tunic, unbuttoned, pulled on over pyjamas, as though he had been fetched from his bed. Standing in front of the desk, with the telephone in his hands, was a German officer who could only be von Roth. A little apart, looking ill at ease, was the man whom Gimlet had last seen on the quay at Le Mans, the man Marcelle had called Bertrand, the man who had betrayed her. Von Roth was talking volubly into the telephone, but Gimlet was no longer interested in the conversation even though his name was frequently mentioned. Besides, he had no time to waste.

He stepped into the room and closed the door behind him.

The movement must have been both seen and heard by those already there. All eyes switched to the door. After the first sharp intake of breath the only sound was *Generaloberst* Gunther's voice, harsh and distorted, coming over the telephone receiver. Staring, very slowly, blindly, von Roth put the instrument on the desk. There was a crash as it overturned, but the voice at the other end went on speaking, or rather, shouting.

Gimlet's face was expressionless. His eyes were hard and cold, like glacier ice.

'You know who I am?' he said quietly.

No one answered.

'Come, *Hauptmann* von Roth, surely a moment or two ago I heard you express a desire to meet me?' went on Gimlet, a suspicion of banter creeping into his voice. 'Well, here I am!'

Still no one spoke, or moved. Only the quisling colonel's tongue flicked nervously over his lips.

'Well, come on, what are you staring at?' Gimlet snapped the words. 'You've all got weapons. Use them. Or would you, von Roth, rather that my hands were tied behind my back, as were those of the civilians you murdered in Caen, and other places?'

The German found his voice. It was pitched high with incredulity. 'What are you doing here?' he asked. His eyes were still on Gimlet's face, as if it fascinated him.

'That is something you will soon learn,' answered Gimlet.

'What are you going to do?' muttered von Roth.

'I'm going to kill you, unless you can kill me first,' rejoined Gimlet evenly. 'None of you is fit to live – *stand still*!' Gimlet's gun switched like the head of a striking snake to cover the gipsy who, pale as death, had started to back away. 'I am going to count three,' went on Gimlet inexorably. 'On the word three, whether you move or not, I shall shoot.'

'This is murder!' blustered the Nazi. 'I demand to be treated as a prisoner, in accordance with the Rules of War.'

Gimlet's voice was soft and low. 'Murder,' he breathed. 'You talk of murder. That, admittedly, is something you know much about. You prattle glibly of the Rules of War. What do you know of the Rules of War? You ask for mercy. What do you know of mercy – you thug, you hell-hound? What mercy did you show those innocent hostages in the market-place at Caen? when in your foul fury you vented your spite on them because you could not catch a man who had slipped through your fingers. You slew them in cold blood.' Gimlet's voice quivered for a moment. 'And now,' he went on, with steel in his voice, 'you ask for honourable treatment. What do you know of honour? Get your gun, butcher, because I am going to count. One – two—'

The Nazi moved like lightning. His hand flew to his holster and he dived for cover behind the desk. He did not reach it. Gimlet's gun roared, flame streaking from the muzzle.

The German stopped as though he had collided with an invisible wall. His hands clawed at the desk, but the slipping fingers found no hold, and he crashed in a crumpled heap. For a second or two his heels beat a spasmodic tattoo on the floor. Then he lay still. Silence fell, a silence loaded with pale blue haze and the acrid reek of cordite.

Gimlet's eyes, frosty, relentless, found the gipsy.

'No!' gasped the man. 'No! In God's name!' His terror was pathetic, but it made no impression on the man who confronted him.

'So you call on God?' sneered Gimlet. 'Were you thinking of God when you betrayed a girl who has more courage in one finger than you have in the whole of your vile body? Yet you would have sent her to her death for a handful of Nazi-tarnished francs. You *Judas*. Now go and spend them in hell!'

The gipsy screamed, running like a hunted rat to the end of the room, seeking an exit where none existed. Again Gimlet's gun roared. The man sprawled across the floor, moaning. Presently he, too, lay still.

Gimlet turned to the Frenchman. 'Take off that tunic,' he ordered curtly.

'Take – off—?'

'Take it off, I said!' rasped Gimlet. 'It's the only decent thing about you. Too many brave men have died in that uniform for you to share the honour – you traitor – you cheat – you wolf that would gorge himself on the bodies of his comrades. Take it off!'

With hands that shook, his eyes on Gimlet's face, Frey took off the tunic and put it on the desk. Then, suddenly, he raised his hands above his head. 'You wouldn't shoot – you couldn't shoot a man with his hands up!' he faltered.

'Craven, too, like all traitors!' scoffed Gimlet. 'You have made many mistakes, Colonel, but this, your last, is the greatest of all. You are an enemy of my country and your own, and of all true Frenchmen. Doubtless you have a pistol handy. If you prefer not to use it, that is your affair; but if you could not live like a man, at least try to die like one.'

The quisling must have read his fate in the blue, scornful eyes, for with a speed born of despair he whipped open a drawer or the desk and snatched up an automatic.

Two shots came so close together that they sounded as one. Actually the colonel fired first, but he was in too great a hurry. The bullet struck the floor at Gimlet's feet and ricocheted with a shrill whine from floor to wall and from wall to ceiling. Gimlet did not move. The other staggered back a pace and fell into his chair, coughing. His eyes, glazed with horror, were still on Gimlet's face.

From the telephone came Gunther's voice, bellowing now, lending a macabre touch to the scene. Gimlet walked over, picked up the receiver, and spoke.

'Hello! *Generaloberst* Gunther? This is Captain King speaking. You know me better, I think, as Gimlet. Ah! You do know me? What am I doing here? Use your imagination, general. I can't stop to talk to you now. You heard shooting? Yes, there are some casualties. The chateau will need a new commandant, and you, *Generaloberst*, will need a new adjutant. Von

Roth has left your service to take up duties in an even more sulphurous headquarters where, I hope, you will presently join him. *Gute nacht, Generaloberst*!'

With a swift jerk Gimlet tore the 'phone cable out of the wall, took a last glance round the room, and walked out. Closing the door behind him, he stood for a moment or two, listening. He did not think that the sounds of the shots would be heard outside, through two stone walls, the outer one several feet thick; and it seemed that he was right, for no one came. All was quiet.

Walking on to the main entrance doors he opened one of them a little way and looked out. A sentry who was on duty, his rifle at the slope, jumped to attention, as if expecting an officer to emerge, having, apparently, seen the door open.

Gimlet spoke to him sharply in German, taking care to keep out of sight. 'Come here,' he said. 'There has been trouble in the office of the commandant.'

'*Jawohl*! I thought I heard something,' said the soldier, and marched into the hall. In the light he saw Gimlet at once. As his eyes took in the uniform from top to bottom it was evident that he knew what it was, for his mouth opened foolishly. But no sound came – probably because Gimlet's gun jabbed him in the stomach.

'Not a sound, if you wish to live,' said Gimlet softly. 'To the commandant's office – march.'

The soldier, who may have heard of the reputation of the commandos, obeyed. Gimlet followed and opened the door.

'Inside,' he said shortly. 'You will find something to interest you there,' he added. 'If you are wise you will think a little while before calling for help. You will be sorry if I come back.'

The German went in. He was an oldish man, a member of a Bavarian regiment, and looked more like a farmer than a soldier. At any rate, he had no stomach for a fight with the lean, business-like commando.

Gimlet locked the door behind him, and returning to the front entrance, looked out. The moon was just coming up, shedding a wan light over the courtyard. It was deserted, although voices of talking and laughing came from the guardhouse at the gate in the outer wall. Closing the door behind him, he locked it and put the key in his pocket; then, keeping close to the building, watching the guardhouse, he walked on until he was opposite the gap in the wire. Another glance to right and left and he crossed the open space swiftly.

'That you, Skipper?' came Trapper's voice, in a hoarse whisper.

'Yes.' Gimlet crawled through the wire and stood up. 'Everything all right?'

'Sure – but I'd just about given you up.'

'I had several things to do,' explained Gimlet.

'The party is in the lorry, only waiting for us to move off.'

'In that case we'll get cracking,' returned Gimlet. 'There's going to be quite a rumpus here presently.'

As they walked down the road to the inn, Trapper remarked: 'Cub tells me they've got the low-down on Marcelle. That double-crossing gipsy horse-dealer squealed. *Ma foi*! I'll have his scalp—'

'You're too late,' interrupted Gimlet. 'I've already had it. He was inside.'

Trapper stopped dead. '*Sacré nom*! How did he die?'

'I shot him.'

'Ah, that was too quick, sir!' muttered Trapper. 'You should have called me. There is an Indian trick I know for making people die slowly—'

'We're not Indians,' broke in Gimlet curtly.

'No,' agreed Trapper; 'there are times, though, when I think it is a pity.'

The lorry was waiting in the yard of the inn, Copper at the wheel.

Said Gimlet, looking at his watch: 'The time is one-thirty-five. I want to be in Paris, at the Quai d'Orsay Station, in time to meet the Orleans train. It's due at four. The distance is about eighty miles. Can you do it?'

'Easy, sir,' answered Copper cheerfully.

General Romortin's head appeared round the fabric cover of the lorry. 'Did I hear you say you were going to Paris, *capitan*?'

'Yes,' replied Gimlet. 'We have to pick up two friends there.'

'If you could stop at my house in the Bois de Boulogne I could pick up some papers that your Government would be glad to have – those the Germans were so anxious to obtain.'

'We will discuss it on the way, general,' returned Gimlet.

'Certainly, *monsieur*.'

'You cover the rear with the Sten gun,' Gimlet told Trapper, and climbed in beside Copper. 'All right – let her go,' he ordered. 'Good-bye, Father Edwinus, and a thousand thanks.'

The priest raised his hand. 'Farewell! God go with you.'

The engine purred, and the lorry swung out on to the open road.

CHAPTER NINETEEN

Paris

Cub saw little of the journey to Paris. He slept most of the way, for now there was an opportunity to relax, weariness came upon him, and he succumbed to it, as he was bound to, for sleep is something before which even the strongest must sooner or later fall. His dreams were punctuated by occasional incidents, but only two of them really brought him back to full consciousness. Three times – or it may have been four – the lorry stopped, and Trapper got out to cut the telegraph wires that followed the road. He could see his silhouette against the sky, clinging to the top of the post, in a manner reminiscent of 'a monkey on a stick', and heard the soft snick of the cutters as they bit through the wires with no more effort than if they had been made of thread. Then, monotonously, the lorry resumed its journey.

There was an incident of a different sort when a helmeted motor-cyclist came tearing along, passed them, and half-turning in his saddle, signalled to the driver to stop. Copper gave the wheel a vicious twist, causing the lorry to swerve sharply, so that it struck the motor-bike broadside-on and sent it crashing into the ditch. Without a backward glance Copper drove on.

'That'll learn 'im!' said he, dispassionately.

Trapper spat out of the back of the car. 'In future, I guess that guy will think twice before he tries to stop travellers on the road,' he remarked to Cub, without emotion.

'This is the maddest thing I have ever heard of,' declared Cub. 'You'll never get away with it. The whole country must be looking for us – and besides, how are we going to get all this bunch across the Channel?'

'I reckon Gimlet knows what he's doing,' returned Trapper, with calm assurance. 'You'll be surprised.'

'Nothing,' said Cub distinctly, 'would surprise me.' He dozed again.

The next incident was more serious – sufficiently alarming to awaken him thoroughly.

It happened between Maintenon and Rochefort where, at a bend, the road narrows as it swings under a railway arch. A red light appeared under the bridge. As the lorry approached other lights appeared, waving in what were obviously stop signals. Copper switched on the headlights, and their glare revealed a barrier comprising two planks, supported by what seemed to be a heap of sandbags on either side. A number of German soldiers stood in the road.

Cub heard Gimlet say to Copper: 'Step on it. We're not stopping.' Then, turning: 'Trapper, let me have that gun.'

As Trapper put the Sten gun into his hands the lorry leapt forward.

Cub did not see what happened – he only heard. Knowing what was likely to happen, he ducked instinctively, and covered his face with his hands. The French officer sitting next to him muttered an urgent prayer. There were shouts. The Sten gun spat in one long burst that only ended when, with a frightful crash, the front of the lorry struck the planks. The lorry jolted, swerved a trifle, and then went on.

Copper laughed. 'That'll learn 'em!' said he.

'Look what you're doing,' ordered Gimlet tersely.

'Aye-aye, sir.'

The Frenchman next to Cub rubbed his shoulders, and crossed himself fervently. 'Insane,' he murmured in a resigned voice.

'Sanity, *monsieur*, would not have brought us as far as this,' opined Cub.

'Better cut the wires again, Trapper,' said Gimlet.

The wires were cut and the lorry went on. Cub dozed again, but shook himself into some sort of wakefulness when he saw that they were running through the dingy, dreary suburbs of Paris.

Gimlet, who had been having a quiet conversation with General Romortin, looked at his watch. 'I think we can just do it,' he said. 'All right, Copper, I'll take over now. I know my way about.'

He and Copper changed seats, and the lorry went on to stop, at a sharp word from the general, against the kerb in front of a stylish house of some size. The general was out in a moment, and disappeared up the short drive. Inside five minutes he was back, carrying a portfolio under his arm. He climbed into his seat, and the lorry went on through dark, silent streets, deserted except for an occasional *gendarme*, who took no notice of the German military vehicle.

'Listen, everyone,' requested Gimlet. 'This is the general set-up. We are now going to the Quai d'Orsay Station, terminus of the Paris-Orleans railway. I shall park the lorry in a side street which you will presently see. Cub, I am going to detail you for the most vital task because you are the least likely to attract attention. You will go into the station and meet the Orleans train. If it's on time it should arrive in about five minutes. Make contact with Marcelle, but – this is important – do it without allowing it to be known to others who will also be there to meet her. They will most likely be civilians, members of the Gestapo, although there may be soldiers as well. You'll have to use your discretion. What you have to do is to induce Marcelle and Gaston to follow you. They will, of course, be followed in turn. You will then simply return to the street, and enter an alley which I will show you when we get to it. Leave the rest to us. Is that quite clear?'

'Perfectly clear, sir.'

'Here we are.' Gimlet cruised quietly across the broad thoroughfare in front of the station, and turning into a narrow street with tall, imposing houses on either side, brought the lorry to a stop a few yards past a passage that separated two blocks of houses. 'There's the alley,' he went on. 'When you come back walk into it – and keep walking. You saw the station as we turned in? Off you go – you haven't too much time.'

One of the Frenchmen questioned the wisdom of sending a boy on what was obviously a man's errand.

Gimlet reproved him sharply. 'You will oblige me by not questioning my decisions, *monsieur*.'

'*Pardon!*' murmured the officer.

Cub dismounted and walked back to the station, which he found lighted by a few dimmed lamps. There were some belated travellers about, mostly German soldiers going on or coming back from leave, judging by their kit-bags, with a sprinkling of French civilians; but compared with the bustle of normal times the station was strangely silent and empty. Somewhere an engine ejected steam with a hiss that sounded sinister in the gloom, and a regular clang of metal against metal proclaimed that a mechanic was testing the wheels of a train by striking them with a hammer.

Cub found a porter and asked at which platform the Orleans train came in.

'*Là-bas!*' The porter pointed.

Cub moved slowly towards the barrier, observing with satisfaction that few people were waiting there. There were five, to be precise. One was a ticket-collector, one was an elderly woman in widows' weeds, one was a French *gendarme*. These stood alone. The remaining two were together, talking in low tones. One was a brown-shirted trooper adorned with a swastika armlet; the other was a civilian, also a German. Cub knew that from the shape of his head and the cut of his clothes, but he strolled past to make sure. As he expected, they were talking in German. There, he guessed, were the men detailed to meet Marcelle and her uncle. They took no notice of him – did not, in fact, appear to see him; so he sauntered on to a vacant seat not far away and prepared to wait.

The train was six minutes late. Cub was glad when sudden activity, and a rumble, announced its arrival. Waiting for a late train is always tedious; in the circumstances he found it a strain on his nerves. Rising, he took up a position in front of the barrier, some ten yards or so from it.

There were more passengers than he expected; indeed, there was quite a crowd strung out along the platform, moving in procession towards the barrier, which now stood open with the ticket-collector by it. Some of the travellers carried luggage, and this gave Cub an idea – an excuse for being there in case he was being watched by unseen eyes; for he was well aware that the eyes of the Gestapo agents were everywhere. As the travellers passed him he touched his forehead with a plaintive, '*Service, monsieur – service, madame.* Shall I carry your baggage?' At the same time he moved up and down quickly in case someone accepted his offer – which was, of course, the last thing he wanted.

His nerves tingled when the *gendarme* shouted: 'Hey, there! What are you doing? Get off home. This is no place for you!'

'*Oui, monsieur.*' answered Cub respectfully, and backed away until the travellers were between him and the policeman.

Either by accident or design Marcelle and Gaston were among the last to appear. For a horrible moment Cub feared they were not on the train. Then his heart gave a bound when they came into view, walking arm in arm among the stragglers. He watched them as they came through the barrier and gave up their tickets, to be followed at a fair distance by the Gestapo agents. He braced himself, for the moment had come, the moment on which all depended, the most dangerous moment of all, he thought. He was afraid that when they saw him they would stop and speak, perhaps exclaim – a natural thing to do. This would at once place him under suspicion as an accomplice, so it was a thing to be avoided, if possible. However, the risk had to be taken.

Approaching, he touched his forehead and said loudly, 'Any luggage, *monsieur-dame?*' Adding in an urgent whisper: 'Keep walking, don't stop.'

Gaston faltered, with a half-strangled little exclamation of astonishment, but the quick-witted Marcelle grasped the situation instantly. Or, at least, she guessed, from Cub's presence there, and method of approach, that something was amiss.

'No baggage,' she said loudly, and kept on walking, dragging the dumbfounded Gaston with her.

Cub slouched along behind them – an insignificant figure. 'You are watched by the Gestapo,' he whispered. 'But fear nothing. Friends are near. Follow me when you see me in front of you. Behave naturally.'

'Hey, there!' shouted the *gendarme*. 'Get off home, you *gamin*. I've told you once!'

'Instantly, *monsieur!*' answered Cub, with alacrity, and pretended fright.

The command suited him very well, for it gave him an excuse to hurry. He even dared to run a little way, passing Marcelle. With a clear lead he walked on, hands in his pockets, whistling cheerfully. As he turned out of the station he glanced behind him and saw that Marcelle and Gaston were following, with the two Germans a little in the rear. He walked on, or rather, meandered, sometimes stopping to examine the contents of the wire baskets erected for the collection of waste-paper. Not only was this playing up to his character of a street-urchin, but it enabled him to see what was going on behind him. He could imagine how poor Gaston, hearing the footsteps behind, was feeling, but he himself was thoroughly enjoying the picture of two members of the hated Gestapo walking into a trap. He was only sorry that all France could not see it.

Reaching the main street he hesitated for a moment at the corner and then went on. Marcelle and Gaston had closed the distance somewhat, and he was a little alarmed to see that Gaston, in his nervousness, was hurrying. He walked on, past the lorry standing by the kerb, and halted again at the alley. He stared into it, but could see nothing. Silence reigned. But he whispered, 'They're coming!'

He waited until Marcelle and her uncle had almost reached him, and then went on down the alley. After a dozen paces he waited again, to make sure that they were following, and when he heard their footsteps turn in he said in a low voice, 'Keep walking.'

After that he was too far away to see exactly what happened. In any case, it was dark in the alley. But sounds told the story almost as well as sight. He heard the Germans turn in and heard them increase their pace. Then came a thud, gasps, a cry cut off short by a vicious smack, a groan, and the thump of a falling body. A brief silence. Then Copper's voice said, brightly: 'Okay, Cub. All over.'

Cub ran back to Marcelle and Gaston and clasped their hands. 'Congratulations, dear friends,' he said, smiling. 'You were superb!'

Gaston mopped his forehead with a large handkerchief. '*Mon Dieu*!' he breathed. 'The Gestapo – phew! What happens?'

'Bertrand betrayed you to the Nazis,' explained Cub quickly. 'You were seen at Orleans and put under Gestapo surveillance. But it's all right now.'

Gimlet came up. '*Bonsoir, mademoiselle. Bonsoir*, Gaston. Come along. This is no time to stand talking. We have a journey to make.'

Copper and Trapper were standing at the entrance to the alley. 'Nice work, kid,' said Trapper. '*Bonsoir, Marcelle*.'

'Where are the Boches?' said Cub, not seeing the bodies.

Copper inclined his head. 'They're all right – just having a nap in that doorway. Strike me pink! They must have thought a house had fallen down on them. Well, that'll learn 'em not ter follow folks on a dark night. I remember once, down the Old Kent Road—'

'We're in Paris – don't talk so much!' snapped Gimlet. 'Get aboard. I'll drive. Copper, you come in front with me. You'd better come too, Cub. I'm heading north-west, and you may help if I'm not sure of the road. Trapper, watch the rear and let me know at once if you see anything following us. Marcelle, Gaston, inside, please. We've a long way to go, and it's going to be a race against daylight.'

Within a minute the lorry was once more on the move, cruising through the war-stricken streets of the once-gay capital. It was soon out of the fashionable quarter, purring through the dingy northern suburbs.

'All we have to do now is to get home,' remarked Gimlet cheerfully.

'All?' queried Cub. 'I should say that will take some doing. The country was buzzing when we left Caen; by this time it must be in an absolute uproar.'

'France is a big place, quite a big place, you know, to search for an odd lorry,' returned Gimlet evenly. 'Besides,' he added meaningly, 'we happen to have friends in France as well as you, although we're not allowed to go near them except in case of dire emergency.'

Cub looked at Copper. 'You didn't tell me. Did you know about that?'

'Me? Well, I've heard rumours,' admitted Copper. 'But there's some things they don't tell poor blinkin' corporals!'

'Don't get a bee in your bonnet on that account,' adjured Gimlet. 'If the whole British Army knew Intelligence secrets, they wouldn't be secrets any longer. Naturally, we have our agents in the occupied countries; the Nazis know it, and they go to some trouble to find them; that's why, unless we are hard pressed, we keep clear of them. Were we alone I wouldn't consider going near one of our chaps, but in view of the size of the party, and the documents General Romortin is carrying, I think we are justified in calling on the Intelligence Branch of Combined Ops, for assistance.'

'Then we're not going back to Caen?' queried Cub.

'No.'

'What about the stuff we left in the forest?'

'That'll come in handy later on, no doubt. We needed a dump like that, to save us bringing over a big load every time. I'm quite happy to leave it there – I imagine The Fleas will look after it?'

By this time the lorry was running through open country at high speed.

Copper chuckled. 'It's a good thing my old Ma can't see me,' he remarked.

As the telegraph poles flashed by the feeling again came over Cub that this was not really happening; that it was a dream, a dream that had been going on for so long that he must soon awaken, to laugh at the absurd improbability of it all. He yawned, for he was still tired, and presently fell into a state midway between consciousness and sleep.

CHAPTER TWENTY

At the Sign of the Cheval Noir

Cub started and sat up. The lorry was still speeding through the night, although above the eastern horizon the stars had lost their brilliance.

'I've been asleep,' he said. 'What's the time?'

'Half-past five,' answered Gimlet.

Cub looked about him, and saw that the lorry was travelling on a second-class road over a vast undulating expanse of cultivated country, hedgeless fields forming a curious geometrical pattern that stretched away monotonously as far as he could see. Here and there a lonely poplar thrust its spire towards the sky. In the far distance, to the north-west, the direction in which the lorry was travelling, pale searchlight beams were scissoring the heavens into wedge-shaped sections.

'For a guess,' said Cub, 'I should say we are in the Département of Seine Inférieure.'

'Quite right,' confirmed Gimlet.

'Where are those searchlights?'

'On the coast – we're no great distance from the sea.'

'Dawn is on the way,' observed Cub anxiously. 'Have we much farther to go?'

'We're nearly there.'

'Thank goodness!' sighed Cub. 'We seem to have been rushing about for years.'

'Don't talk so much,' said Gimlet. 'Keep your eyes skinned for trouble – we may run into it at any moment.'

The lorry topped a slight rise, and then dropped down into a wide depression where at frequent intervals willows drooped, and tall reeds stood stiffly beside stagnant pools of water. A solitary house appeared ahead, with straggling outbuildings, looking drear and lonely in the wan moonlight. Presently Cub made it out to be one of those rambling old taverns that dot the bleak face of northern France, relics of not-so-long-ago when visitors to the Continent from England travelled to Paris by private coach, or by the public horse omnibus. He read the name on the dilapidated sign, and saw that it was the *Cheval Noir*, otherwise the Black Horse. The inn stood, he observed, at a cross-roads, surrounded by the eternal hedgeless fields. A glimmer of light escaping from a ground-floor window revealed that the tavern-keeper was already astir.

He was surprised when the lorry swung into the yard, for Gimlet had given no indication that this was their destination. Even before he could get down a door had opened, and a man came out. He was, Cub noted, typical of the district – untidy, unshaven, dirty shirt open at the throat, legs in faded blue, well-patched trousers. His feet were thrust into an old pair of carpet-slippers.

When this man spoke Cub had the shock of his life. So certain was he, so automatically had he assumed that the man was French, that he could hardly believe his ears when he addressed Gimlet in English that was not only faultless, but with an accent that said quite plainly, 'public school.'

'Hello, Lorry, you old buccaneer!' he greeted with a smile.

Gimlet jumped down. ''Morning, Freddie. You're up bright and early. Anyone would think you were expecting us.'

'Well, as a matter of fact, I was,' was the surprising rejoinder. 'I gather you've been having some fun? You've fairly set things alight this time.'

Gimlet's eyebrows went up. 'How did you know?'

The other's smile broadened. 'I should think the whole world knows by this time. I've just been listening to the radio – the Jerry private short-wave. It's positively hysterical. The whole country is up, laddie, thirsting for your blood. I couldn't think how you were going to get through the cordon along the coast, so it struck me you might roll up here.'

'I've got a big party to get over, and it's important that it should get through,' said Gimlet seriously. 'I'm sorry to inflict myself on you, Freddie old boy, but it seemed to me that our best chance was to come here and get you to put a signal over the air, asking for a 'plane. But the thing that has got me cheesed is what to do with this beastly lorry. It's probably the most badly wanted vehicle in Europe.'

'Don't worry about that,' answered Freddie calmly. 'I'll fix it.' He went to the tavern door and shouted, 'Charles!'

Charles appeared. He was a short, fat little man of about fifty, a French peasant – or so he appeared. Cub, who was beginning to distrust his eyes, was quite sure that he was English.

'We've got to get rid of this thing,' announced Freddie, pointing to the lorry. 'I think you'd better take it down to the swamp and turn it over in the lake. It should settle down nicely in the mud, and be out of sight in half an hour.'

'*Oui, monsieur.*'

So he *is* French! thought Cub helplessly.

'Better bring your party inside,' suggested Freddie. 'They could probably do with a bite of breakfast while you're waiting. Tell them not to leave anything lying about – in case we have visitors.'

Gimlet went to the back of the lorry. 'Come along, Marcelle,' he requested. 'Descend, gentlemen, please. Into the house.'

The party, a woebegone party after the long, anxious drive, got out and followed Freddie to the tavern. The man called Charles took charge of the vehicle. He backed it on to the road. Presently it disappeared over the brow of the hill and was seen no more.

The commandos followed the party into the tavern, and found everyone assembled in the huge old kitchen. Freddie closed the door.

'Better tell your boys to keep an eye on the roads,' he said casually.

Copper and Trapper took up positions at the windows, which commanded views of the roads.

'I'd better see about getting you an aircraft before I do anything else,' went on Freddie. 'It'll be broad daylight in half an hour. Pity there's no cloud about – a covered sky would have made things easier.'

'It'll have to be a big machine,' Gimlet pointed out.

'We'll give the number of passengers and leave that to them,' returned Freddie. 'They'll probably send a Liberator – we had one over last week to pick up a batch of refugees. If you're lucky you'll get Bigglesworth for a pilot. Good bloke.'

'You mean the chap they call Biggles?'

'That's right. His Squadron is doing co-operation work with us at the moment. Crazy crowd, but tough as they make 'em.'

While he was speaking, Freddie had crossed over to the big fireplace, and resting his hands against the chimney-beam put his weight on it. The beam, which looked as if it had been undisturbed for centuries, slid to one side, revealing a battery of dials and valves. He held up a hand for silence, put head-phones over his ears and manipulated the instrument. Lights glowed. A buzzer chattered.

Cub stared. He had guessed, vaguely, that this sort of thing must go on, but he never expected to see it. He glanced at Copper. Copper caught his eye and winked.

Freddie was a minute or two at the wireless transmitter. Cub could hear the buzzer zipping away, but he had no idea of the signals; not that he expected to understand them, aware that they would certainly be in code. At last the Intelligence Officer took the 'phones from his ears, switched off, and slid the beam back into place.

'Okay,' he said with a nod. 'A Liberator will be on its way in two minutes. It ought to be here in a quarter of an hour. The landing-field is only a short step from here, so you've nice time for a cup of coffee and a biscuit.'

'Top hole,' answered Gimlet. 'Personally, I could do with a bath, but a wash will have to suffice. The trouble about these jobs is, one gets so disgustingly filthy. Marcelle would probably like a wash and brush up, too.'

Freddie grinned. 'My accommodation isn't exactly *deluxe*,' said he. 'You'll find what there is at the end of the passage.'

What amazed Cub about all this was the casual way it was done. The two leaders, Gimlet and his friend the Intelligence Officer, might have been in a regimental dining-room, in England, for all the concern they showed. The French officers evidently thought this, too, judging from the way they looked at each other, with shrugs and blank expressions.

Very soon an aroma of coffee filled the air with warm fragrance. A plate of buttered ham rolls and a tin of biscuits appeared on the table. No one asked where these things had come from. Freddie just produced them. Coffee was served in a miscellaneous collection of cups, but no one minded that. The hot beverage put everyone in good heart.

In the middle of all this a motor-cycle patrol swept past the tavern. A car followed. A minute later an aircraft roared overhead, and Cub, thinking it must be the rescue 'plane arriving, hastened to the window. He was mistaken.

'Messerschmitt!' he exclaimed, with something like dismay in his voice.

Freddie poured more coffee.

'It's a Messerschmitt,' repeated Cub sharply, thinking that he could not have been understood.

'We heard you the first time,' stated Freddie drily. 'By the way, Lorry, old man, have you still got that grey mare with a rat tail and flea-bitten hocks – Seagull, I think her name was?'

'Yes, she's still in the paddock,' answered Gimlet, sipping his coffee.

'I'm expecting to go across for a spot of leave shortly. Can I borrow her for a few days?'

'With pleasure,' granted Gimlet. 'She needs exercise.'

'That mare jumps like a cat,' declared Freddie, a note of enthusiasm creeping into his voice for the first time.

'What I like best about her,' asserted Gimlet, lighting a cigarette, 'is the way she keeps her eyes open for rabbit holes in the park. She's never stumbled over one in her life.'

'Strike me perishin' purple!' growled Copper in Cub's ear. 'They're off. If they get set on horses, we're liable to be here for hours.'

The Frenchman who had spoken to Cub in the lorry shrugged his shoulders with an air of hopeless resignation. 'Insane!' he muttered fiercely.

Another motorised patrol raced down the road, an officer shouting orders.

'Things seem to be warming up a bit,' observed Freddie lightly. 'I think, Lorry, old boy, we'd better see about making a move.'

Gimlet looked at his watch. 'Another minute.'

Cub looked at the sky, now pallid with the near approach of day, and getting lighter every moment. He wondered if the rescue plane would get through. In his heart he doubted it.

'Finish up now, please,' said Gimlet. Then, turning to Freddie. 'This is your show, old boy. What's the programme?'

'It's very simple,' replied Freddie. 'I shall go out now and walk up to the top of the rise you can see on the right. From there I get a pretty good view all round. I shall take a hoe with me, for the look of the thing. While I hold it up it will mean that the road is clear. You will then come along. There's a bit of a bank beside the road – keep behind it. If I lower the hoe, go flat and stay flat until I raise it again. It will mean that something is about. For the moment stay where you are. I shan't raise the hoe till I see the Liberator coming. If Bigglesworth is at the stick its wheels will be about a foot from the ground – that's his usual technique. When the sky is clear like this he usually brings an umbrella with him.'

'Umbrella?' echoed Cub, in a puzzled voice. The expression was new to him.

'Escort,' muttered Copper.

'I'll move off now,' announced Freddie. 'Stand fast till you get the signal.' He went out, and presently could be seen making his way up the gentle slope to which he had referred, stopping occasionally to cut down a weed with his hoe.

Cub's heart came into his mouth when a motor cyclist, a storm trooper, appeared on the road, and pulling up as near to Freddie as he could get, shouted something.

Freddie strode over to him and touched his forehead. A brief conversation took place and the German roared on. Freddie resumed his walk, and was soon a conspicuous figure on the skyline, a distance of perhaps two hundred yards from the tavern. Almost at once he raised his hoe.

'That's it,' observed Gimlet. 'Off we go. Don't get in a bunch. I'll lead. Copper, you take the rear with the Sten gun.' With his eyes on Freddie all the time he led the way to the road, and then took a course parallel with it, keeping on the field side of the low bank.

Freddie's hoe came down.

'Flat!' ordered Gimlet crisply, and the party dropped prone.

A car roared by. They did not see it. Gimlet was watching Freddie. The hoe went up. 'Forward,' he ordered.

The party proceeded. Cub's heart was thumping with suppressed excitement. The thing was like a game – with death the penalty for the losers.

The party reached Freddie on the crest of the hill just as the plane arrived. There was nothing spectacular about its approach. It came gliding in with its wheels just clear of the ground, with no more fuss than if it had been landing on its base aerodrome. The wheels touched down, and the big machine rumbled on until it was in line with the spectators, when its brakes brought it to a stop.

'Clockwork,' said Copper. 'That's what it is – clockwork.' Whether he was referring to the aircraft, or to the whole episode, was not clear.

Freddie waved to the pilot, and got a wave back. 'It's Bigglesworth,' said he. 'I'll leave you to it now. I must get back to the pub in case I have customers. Cheerio!'

'Thanks, old boy,' said Gimlet without emotion.

'Don't mention it – pleasure, and all that,' returned Freddie. 'So-long. All the best.' He went off down the hill, hoe at the slope.

A second figure had appeared with the aircraft, standing at the open door. He was a youngish flying officer with a freckled face and ginger hair.

'Hi! Come on,' he called impatiently. 'We haven't got all day.'

Up to this time Cub had had eyes only for the aircraft. The clatter of its engines drowned all other sounds. But now, as the party moved forward, the air was suddenly filled with another noise, a shrill whine, rising swiftly to a fierce crescendo. With it appeared an aircraft, dropping like a meteor out of the blue. He recognised one of the latest Messerschmitts, and the muscles of his face went stiff with consternation. Even though the Messerschmitt was diving it seemed to be making an astonishing amount of noise, and Cub, lifting his eyes, saw the reason. The machine was not alone. Coming down vertically to intercept it was another, and behind, covering a wide area of sky, there were others. They were Typhoons. Then multiple machine guns snarled, punctuated with the heavier reports of cannon. Tracer flashed.

The Messerschmitt swerved, staggered, half pulled out of its dive and then went on again, its motor wailing like a lost soul. It did not stop. The wail ended abruptly as the aircraft struck the ground with a splintering, tearing, rending crash, that was like nothing so much as the fall of a giant tree. Pieces bowled over the ground, leaving a trail of flame. Cub, his mouth dry with horror, could not take his eyes from it. He heard Copper say, with a short laugh, 'That'll learn 'im.'

Then a fist smote him between the shoulder blades. 'Get in,' snarled a voice. 'What do you think this is, a circus?'

Cub looked into an angry face topped by ginger hair, and fell into the Liberator. The others were already aboard. The ginger-headed flying officer slammed the door and made a signal to the pilot, who was looking back into the cabin. The machine began to move.

'Make yourselves at home,' called the flying officer. 'We shan't be long, but you'd better hang on to something in case we have to take evasive action. There's a little opposition to our trip – as you may notice.' He went forward and joined the pilot. Gimlet did the same.

Cub sat on the floor. He began to understand dimly how it was that Britain had survived that dreadful year of the war when she stood alone, outnumbered in men, planes, tanks and guns. Men like these were responsible, men like Gimlet, Freddie, Bigglesworth, Copper … all of them. They did their jobs, and went on doing their jobs whatever happened, calmly – yes, that was the point – without losing their heads. It was not merely bravery, but downright thoroughness.

For the next ten minutes things were a trifle confused. The machine skimmed the ground, jumping over – or so it seemed – houses, trees, and other obstacles as they occurred in its path. Sometimes it swerved sickeningly. Two of the French officers were, in fact, sick. Once, with a vicious bang, a piece of something tore a hole in the side of the fuselage, and once another plane flashed past a cabin window so close that Cub flinched. There was no question of standing up to see what was going on outside.

Copper leaned over and shouted in Cub's ear, 'If my old Ma could see me now she'd throw a fit, s'welp me, she would, not 'alf she wouldn't.'

Cub found no difficulty in believing this, but he grinned – or tried to.

Trapper was sitting beside Marcelle; they were smiling at each other, apparently quite oblivious to what was going on.

Then, suddenly, the machine was flying steadily on even keel. The ginger-haired flying officer came back into the cabin.

'Mademoiselle and gentlemen,' he said. 'Welcome to England.' Then he added as an afterthought, with a smile. 'I hope you enjoyed your trip.'

Some of the party looked doubtful.

Copper clapped his great hands together. 'Now *that's* what I call a snappy crossing,' he declared.

There were several officers waiting on the aerodrome when the Liberator landed – Navy, Army, Air Force and Fighting French were represented. The latter at once took charge of their own people. Gimlet ordered the commandos to stand fast while he went over to speak to what he called the 'reception committee.'

Presently one of these officers, in army uniform, came across to Cub. 'I imagine you are Nigel Peters?' he said pleasantly.

Cub, wondering what was coming, said that he was.

'I have some news that should cheer you,' went on the officer. 'I'm from the War Office. We've just had word that your father, Colonel Peters of the Buffs, is in Spain. Apparently he was wounded and taken prisoner, but he escaped and made his way across the South of France to the Spanish frontier. It took him some time, which is why we lost track of him. Arrangements are being made to bring him home.'

Cub stood stiffly to attention. His expression did not change, although his eyes moistened suddenly with thankfulness.

'Thank you, sir,' he said.

The officer nodded with a smile and returned to where Gimlet was talking.

Copper nudged Cub in the ribs. 'That's the stuff,' he murmured. 'Congratulations, chum.'

Trapper smiled. '*Bon ça, mon ami,*' said he quietly.

A Waaf appeared and told them that the canteen was being opened for them.

Gimlet came over. 'All right, you fellows. You can fall out for half an hour. Then a car will take us back to the depot. I'm going off to have a tub. By the way, corporal. I notice you need a haircut. See to it.'

'Yes, sir.' Copper saluted as Gimlet went off with the officers.

'Did you hear that?' murmured Copper plaintively. 'Did he say, Thank you, my dear brave corporal? No! Did he say we've had a sticky trip? No! Did he say we was lucky ter be 'ome? No! All 'e thinks about is 'is perishin' tub. All he sez is, get yer 'air cut. Strike me all colours! But it's a bit 'ard. What say you? Am I right, Trapper?'

Trapper's white teeth flashed. 'Are you right? *I'll* say you're right,' he agreed sadly.

'Well,' said Copper in a resigned voice, 'we may as well go and get a bite of grub. Then I must drop a line to my old Ma.'

Arm in arm the comrades walked towards the canteen.

GIMLET GOES AGAIN

'Keep still and don't make a sound!'

CHAPTER ONE

A Patriot Dies For France

From the war-blinded soil of Northern France, like a radiant lance, a searchlight beam struck into the heart of the night: and by a million to one chance that must have astonished the operators it smote the aircraft at which it was directed, smote it fairly and squarely, so that the machine became at once a solitary firefly gleaming in the mighty vault of heaven.

This was unfortunate for Cub Peters. Extremely unfortunate. Besides which it was bad luck. The beam caught him half in and half out of the machine. A second earlier and he could have drawn back. A second later and he would have gone. As it was, it caught him – to use a service expression – on one leg, so that for two frantic seconds he knew not whether to hang on or let go, a problem which was not made easier by a temporary blindness caused by the glare. To say that in the end he jumped would not be strictly true. It would be more correct to say that the decision was made for him by his pilot, who took evading action. So Cub fell out, following into the void his leader, Captain Gimlet King, who had left the aircraft a second before the beam had flashed. For a fleeting instant, as Cub fell through the fierce white light, his parachute fluttering behind him like a wisp of smoke, he bore a curious resemblance to a comet. Then darkness engulfed him. But he knew that he must have been seen; knew, even while he was plunging earthward, that the Nazi anti-aircraft organization below would already be operating at full power to secure his arrest. It was a bad beginning.

He had not far to fall – a trifle more than a thousand feet; and when, a few seconds later, the earth loomed black and solid beneath him, his legs were already performing the action of running, to break his fall. One hand clutched the parachute release. Striking the ground he stumbled and fell; but he was up in a flash, and having discarded his harness, set off at a sprint for the nearest cover – a wide belt of timber that towered stark and black against the sky a hundred paces distant. Then a short sharp whistle with a peculiar trill in it, clear above the drone of the receding aircraft, made him swerve towards the sound. A moment later a figure came into view, running fast and crouching low. He recognized the slim form of his C.O. Another vague shape loomed suddenly behind it.

'Look out, sir!' shrilled Cub. 'Behind you!'

Gimlet jumped sideways like a cat, whirling round at the same time.

A rifle blazed and a bullet zipped.

Red flame spurted from Gimlet's side, low down. With it came the crash of a heavy service revolver. The pursuing figure stumbled and dived into the ground.

'Run for it,' said Gimlet curtly. 'You know where we are better than I do, so you lead. We seem to have dropped into the middle of something.'

'It was the searchlight. It caught me as I jumped,' asserted Cub as he started off.

'I saw it,' answered Gimlet shortly.

'I hope the Fleas are about. They would see what happened, and take defensive action,' said Cub.

After that there was no more talking. For a while, noises made by converging enemy troops – shouts, whistles, and the roar of high-powered transport – decided Cub's course for him. He turned frequently to avoid trouble. But at length, reaching a hedge, he followed it back to the wood. An owl was hooting somewhere along the fringe, and he headed towards the sound. A hundred yards and there came a furtive rustle in the out-thrust arm of a great oak.

Cub pulled up short, uttering a sharp yap.

'Straight on,' said a voice from the vague shadow overhead. 'The Fox waits at the end.'

Another quarter of a mile and the wood gave way to rough heath, broken by clumps of gorse and bramble. Cub yapped again.

A shadow separated itself from a mass of thorn not five paces distant. 'Cub,' breathed a voice, hoarse with urgency.

'Renard!'

'This way – *vivement*,' snapped the Fox. 'Name of a dog! Why must you jump into a hornets' nest?' He set off at a run towards a stand of timber that loomed darkly at no great distance. Halfway, and a wild boar squealed – or there came a sound like the squeal of a boar. Bushes rustled – it was hard to say where.

Instantly the Fox turned at right angles and dived flat into a fold of the rough ground. Plucking at Gimlet's sleeve, Cub followed. All lay still, trying to steady their breathing. Heavy footsteps approached, running; throats panted hoarsely with exertion; military accoutrements creaked, and a file of black shapes, appearing monstrous in the starlight, ran past.

'Nazis,' grated Fox. The instant the troops were out of sight he was on his feet again, running. Just short of the forest a night-hawk screeched three times.

'*Bon!*' said the Fox. 'That means there are no more Boches this side.'

Another figure appeared mysteriously beside the runners. He spoke in a low voice to the Fox, and again faded into the night.

Said Gimlet to Cub as they ran on, 'The Fleas have brought this business to a fine art.'

'They've had plenty of practice,' returned Cub briefly, as they neared the edge of the forest.

After walking a little way into the inky recesses of the trees the Fox stopped. 'Phew! What an affair! But now we can take our time, *mon capitaine*,' he announced. 'We were all ready for you in case you came. For two days and nights we have waited.'

'The signals were seen last night,' said Cub. 'We came as quickly as arrangements could be made. What's the trouble?'

'It would be better, *mon ami*, if we went to earth before we discuss that. It is a matter the most serious, and the story will take time.' The Fox set off at a steady pace, heading deeper and deeper into the forest, muttering an occasional warning, such as: 'Beware the fallen tree', or 'Attention to rabbit holes.'

Half an hour of this, with the undergrowth getting ever thicker, and the Fox halted before a shapeless mass which the others knew was ivy-covered masonry. For a full minute he stood still, listening intently.

Then he whistled softly. Instantly there came an answering whistle from the pile.

'All clear,' said Fox. 'Enter.' Walking up to the ruin he dragged aside a mass of leaves, and switching on a torch disclosed a flight of steps leading downward. The party descended, and after traversing a short corridor emerged in a vaulted chamber lighted by a candle stuck in a bottle. The dim light revealed half a dozen urchins seated on stones and boxes. They sprang up and saluted when they recognized the visitors.

Gimlet returned the salute. 'Sit down, everybody.' He himself found a seat on an empty case, glancing at his watch. 'Let us get down to business,' he suggested. 'We are all right for time, but we have none to waste.'

Gimlet found a seat on an empty case.

'What is the arrangement for getting back?' Fox asked Cub.

'Copper and Trapper are lying off-shore in a fast motorboat, waiting for our signal to be picked up. If they do not get it before dawn they will return to base and come back tomorrow night. Why did you ask?'

'Because you may not be going back so soon,' was the reply. 'Something has happened, something the most tragic.'

'Tell me about it,' invited Gimlet.

'First, *mon capitaine*, there is a question I am burning to ask you,' said the Fox. 'Come this way, please. Cub, come if you wish, but I warn you the spectacle is not of the best.'

The Fox led the way to the far end of the chamber, where a long object lay on the ground under a brown blanket. On the blanket lay a small tricolour, the flag of France, and this gave Cub a clue to what lay beneath, so that the shock was not so great as otherwise it might have been when the Fox lifted the blanket to reveal the body of a man.

A torch put a spotlight on the face of a man of about thirty years of age. The features were composed in death, but they were pathetically thin, and held an expression of weariness, as if the man had been subject to great strain for a long period of time. For the rest, it was quite an ordinary face – that of a typical middle-class Parisian, thought Cub, who had seen too much of death to be shocked. The only feature that could be called distinguishing was a slim black moustache turned down at the ends.

'Do you know this man, *mon capitaine?*' asked the Fox in a low voice.

'No,' answered Gimlet.

With reverent care the Fox replaced the blanket. 'That is all,' he said. 'Now he can be buried. I thought you had better see him first. Let us return to the others.'

Now in order that a better understanding of these sinister proceedings may be gained a few words of explanation become necessary. Following the events narrated in *King of the Commandos*, the commandos had made another sortie into Normandy, to re-establish contact with the Fleas, and to arrange a scheme whereby the organization, should it find itself in possession of important information, could get in touch with the commandos across the Channel. The arrangement was simple. Should the Fleas have vital information to transmit they were to flash the letter X, in the Morse code, thrice repeated, to British aircraft that operated nightly over that area. At home, Gimlet had arranged with the Higher Command that air crews should be warned to be on the look-out for such a signal. This plan was as fool-proof as could be devised. For five weeks nothing had happened. Then, the night before this story opens, more than one pilot had reported seeing the signal. An operation to make contact with the Fleas had at once been planned. Gimlet and Cub were to drop by parachute near the Fleas' headquarters in the Forest of Caen. A night landing by an aircraft at this spot being impracticable, Copper and Trapper were to stand by in a fast boat, watching the enemy coast for a pre-arranged signal that the parachutists were to send when they were ready to be picked up. All wore commando uniform, Gimlet insisting that as they were soldiers – at any rate, not officially secret agents – the sortie must be regarded as a military operation, at least in the first place. Should circumstances arise to make the wearing of uniforms suicidal, the matter could be reconsidered.

Everything had gone off as planned, except that, as already stated, by an unlucky chance a searchlight had picked up the operating aircraft at the very moment that Cub was leaving it. The enemy was therefore aware that at least one British parachutist was in the district, so that beyond all possible doubt an intensive search would follow. However, for the moment, in the heart of the forest, Cub felt reasonably safe. The difficulty of the return journey could be dealt with when the time came.

The Fox led the way back to the main chamber, and having reached it, invited Gimlet and Cub to make themselves comfortable while he told his story.

'Four days ago,' began the Fox, 'it was reported to me by the Grasshopper that a patriot had been found hiding in the barn near his house – the same barn in which the Grasshopper's father once allowed us to take refuge when we were running from the Nazis. The unfortunate man had been wounded. Actually, although we did not know it, he was dying. Before he died he told us certain things – told them slowly, you understand, and with difficulty, for he was in great pain. It seems that he had been pursued from Paris, and was overtaken, at night, near the place where he was found. In spite of his wound he evaded the Nazis, and crawling under the straw in the barn, escaped detection. When he was discovered by the Grasshopper's father he was in great distress, not only on account of his wound, but because of a mission he had undertaken but would not now be able to perform. The search for him was still going on, so we decided to bring him here where he would be safe. This was done, and we brought here a doctor whom we could trust; but there was little he could do. At great risk the doctor came, and helped us to remove the clothes so that he could make an operation. He took out a bullet, and having done all that was possible returned to Caen, leaving the wounded man in our hands. But all was in vain. He died, died for honour and country, which, *monsieur*, is as much as a man can do. It was here, with the sweat of death on his brow, that he told us what I shall now tell you; and you will perceive, *mon capitaine*, that the matter was of even greater importance than we supposed. This is what he told the Fleas as the life went slowly out of his eyes.

'His name was Jacques Catron, and he was of Paris, by trade a clerk. Yes, just a poor clerk; yet he was one of the original organizers, and the leader in his department of the French Underground Movement, which, as you know, is only waiting for the word from England for the right moment to strike. The Nazis know that too, and they have tried – so far in vain – to plant a traitor in the organization, to learn the names of everyone concerned. Also, they would like the Underground to strike before its proper time, for then all the members would betray themselves to no purpose. You comprehend, *monsieur*?'

'Perfectly,' answered Gimlet. 'Continue.'

'Jacques Catron was on a special mission for the Underground. He was a courier, and his work was perhaps the most dangerous of all. His present task was to make contact and keep in touch with the British agents in Normandy. It was the work of the British agents to get to London the information which he brought. *Alors*, Jacques carried no papers. Everything he knew he carried in his head. For more than a year he had done this work with great success. A week ago it became necessary for the Underground to transmit news of the first importance to England. Jacques volunteered for the job. Yet somehow, in spite of all the precautions, the Nazis learned of this. Not only did they know that a courier was going through to the coast, but they knew that Jacques Catron was the man. They *must* have known, or the things that have happened could not have happened. How do they learn these things? I do not know. Perhaps they had already been watching him. They watch everybody, the Gestapo. But what does it matter how they know? They knew, and Jacques was a doomed man.

'You would think that knowing Jacques to be a patriot they would have arrested him. But no. These Germans know more tricks than the devil himself. They let him start, hoping perhaps that he would betray some of his comrades *en route*. But we too have our spies, and Jacques was informed that he was being followed. And now this is the point, *mon capitaine*. He was followed so that when the moment came he could be seized, and another man, a Nazi spy, put in his place. Thus it would be the Nazi spy who arrived at the rendezvous to meet the British agent. No doubt the intention was that this Nazi should learn, or try to learn, what the British were doing. He would find out who the British agents were, and also the names of the French patriots who were communicating with them. In short, *monsieur*, the patriots and British Secret Service agents in France were to be wiped out together. At this moment there is a Nazi spy working between the French Underground and the British Secret Service.'

'But they did not catch Jacques,' Gimlet pointed out.

'No, but they saw him fall. They knew he was wounded. They knew he could not reach the rendezvous, so it would be safe for the spy to go there in his place.'

'Who is this spy – do you know?'

'*Non, monsieur.*'

'Is he a German or a renegade Frenchman?'

'We do not know, but he is probably of the Vichy French, the better to present himself as a patriot. Some of these Vichy rats are terrified now that they know the army of liberation is closing in on them.' The Fox spat.

'Did Jacques tell you the rendezvous?'

'Yes – the *Restaurant des Voyageurs*, at Caen. It is a cheap restaurant in the Rue Basse, just behind the Canal Maritime. Jacques, by skill and courage, had nearly reached Caen when he was overtaken by the enemy.'

'When was this appointment for?'

'Tonight.'

'At what hour?'

'Ten-thirty.'

'They will have finished eating by then. Will the restaurant still be open?'

'Yes. The tables will be cleared, but the regular customers will be there, playing cards, or dominoes, drinking a little wine perhaps, as is the way in France.'

Gimlet looked at his watch. 'It's just on nine already,' he muttered.

'We should have got in touch with you at once, but the weather was bad and there were no planes over,' explained the Fox. 'Not until last night could we send the signals.'

'They were seen, but it was too near dawn for us to do anything immediately,' put in Cub. 'So we came tonight, as soon as it was dark.'

'Tell me this,' said Gimlet, speaking to the Fox. 'What was the important information Jacques was so anxious to get to England?'

'I do not know, *monsieur*.'

'Jacques didn't tell you?'

'He was about to do so when he died. He struggled hard, but death overtook him.'

'Pity,' murmured Gimlet softly. 'It comes to this. If the Nazi plan succeeds, the whole French Underground movement may be exposed, and our agents on this side of the Channel rounded up and shot.'

'Of a certainty, *monsieur*.'

'We must stop that,' decided Gimlet. 'Let me think.' He lit a cigarette, and stared fixedly at the floor for two or three minutes before he resumed. 'There are two things we can do,' he said slowly. 'We can either try to catch this Nazi spy, or warn the British agent of his danger. Unfortunately there seems to be a big snag in each case. We have no means of recognizing either of them. Did Jacques Catron tell you, or did he know, what this Nazi spy looked like?'

'He may have known, but he did not tell me, *monsieur*. He died before we could discuss such details.'

'What about the British agent? How was Jacques to recognize him?'

'Here perhaps I can help you,' declared the Fox. 'Jacques did not know the man he was to meet, but he told me that the Englishman would be able to recognize *him* or would know him for the man he had come to meet.'

'How?'

'I do not know, *monsieur.*'

Gimlet frowned. 'That doesn't make sense to me. Jacques comes to Caen to meet a man he does not know. The man, presumably, has never seen him before, either. Both are taking their lives in their hands. If either makes a mistake the consequence might be fatal. How was this British agent to be *sure* that Jacques was his man? Was there a password?'

'Jacques did not mention one.'

'Was Jacques carrying a badge, a passport of some sort?'

'He told me he carried no papers. It was too dangerous. No man in France knows when he is going to be searched.'

'What was the point of Jacques telling you this? What did he expect you to do about it?'

'I told him the Fleas could get in touch with the British.'

'I see. That was the arrangement. You were to get in touch with us.'

'*Oui, monsieur.*'

'Nothing was said about you going to the *Restaurant des Voyageurs?*'

'*Non, monsieur.*'

'Why not, I wonder?'

'I would not know the Englishman, and he would not know me.'

'That brings us back to where we started from,' declared Gimlet. 'How was Jacques to be known, if there was no password, and he carried no papers?'

The Fox puckered his forehead. 'Now you speak of this I have a faint recollection that Jacques said something, just before he died, about a card of identity being given to him when he reached the restaurant. At the finish Jacques spoke with such difficulty and his mind wandered so much that it was not easy to follow him, *monsieur.*'

'If you got this right, it would seem that somebody in the restaurant would know Jacques. A member of the Underground, perhaps.'

The Fox shrugged. 'Perhaps. I am not a member of the official Underground.'

Gimlet bit his lip thoughtfully. 'It begins to look as if the men who sent Jacques on the trip had made arrangements about which he himself did not know.'

'It is possible,' agreed the Fox. 'I know that every scheme undertaken by patriots is surrounded by secret safety devices, and still more devices, to prevent a trail from leading back to headquarters should anything go wrong. Each man knows so much and no more, so that he could not betray his comrades even under torture. A man cannot tell what he does not know.'

Gimlet nodded. 'Well, I don't quite see how it is to be done, but we've got to try to prevent this meeting at the *Restaurant des Voyageurs* from taking place.'

Fox snapped his fingers. '*Zut*! An idea. I wonder if Georges Latroux could help us?'

'Who's he?'

'The proprietor of the restaurant.'

'Is he to be trusted?'

'Absolutely, *monsieur*. At least, he knows of the Fleas, yet has never reported us, although a big reward has been offered.'

'That's worth knowing, although I don't see that it helps us much,' averred Gimlet. 'I can't just walk up to Latroux and ask him questions. For obvious reasons he wouldn't tell me anything even if he was in the scheme. Another point is, after what has happened in Caen in the past, the town isn't exactly a healthy place for us. I suppose *Generaloberst* Gunther is still in charge?'

'Yes.'

'He'd recognize me if he saw me, if not you, sir,' observed Cub.

'In the dark it's unlikely that he would see us, even if he was about,' answered Gimlet. 'All the same, we can't go into the town in these uniforms. Fox, could you find plain clothes for us?'

'For Cub, yes, *mon capitaine*, because there are many Fleas of his size. But for you I have nothing, *monsieur*.'

'Then that settles it,' muttered Gimlet.

'Just a minute, sir. There is one way.' Cub was looking straight into Gimlet's face.

'What is it?'

Cub hesitated for a moment. 'I hardly like to suggest it, but Jacques Catron looked about your build. He won't need his clothes any more.'

Gimlet's eyes opened wide. 'Well thought of, Cub,' he said softly. 'As an idea, it isn't exactly a pretty proposition, but when we go for a ride with the devil driving we can't afford to be squeamish. You've hit on the answer. There's one other thing. What are we going to do about Copper and Trapper?'

'They'll go back to base when we don't show up.'

'That is the arrangement, but I'm wondering if we can't improve on that. One could go back and report what was happening. The Higher Command ought to know. The other might come here, and take charge of things while we're in the town.'

'The Fox could send the signal to bring them ashore, and when they arrived, explain the position,' suggested Cub. 'Trapper, who speaks French well enough to pass for a native, could come here. Copper could go home and report.'

Gimlet looked at the Fox. 'Do you think you could handle that – bearing in mind that the Nazis saw our plane, and will be on the alert?'

'But certainly, *monsieur*.'

'All right then. Consider it settled,' stated Gimlet, rising.

'Just what are we going to do, sir?' asked Cub.

'There's only one thing we *can* do,' answered Gimlet. 'We'll change our clothes, go into the town, and call at the restaurant to see how things are shaping. We'd better be moving.'

CHAPTER TWO

Restaurant des Voyageurs

At a few minutes before ten-thirty Gimlet and Cub entered the restaurant, and selecting a wall table that commanded a view of the door, sat down. To be more precise, they sat side by side on a fixed wooden seat which ran the length of the room, with their backs against the wall and a small table in front of them. From this position they could see the entire dining room – if such it could be called.

For a moment or two Cub's eyes remained on the door by which they had entered. He was not very comfortable, for he was by no means sure that they had not been followed. Outside, from the general military activity, it was evident that the hunt for the parachutists was going on with unabated zeal. Troops were everywhere, coming and going, on foot, on pedal cycles, on motor bikes and in cars. A number of curious spectators, civilians, were also in the streets, either to watch events or to ascertain what the fuss was about. This suited the two commandos, who turned the situation to advantage by keeping to the main thoroughfares, it being Gimlet's opinion that this was a safer method of approach than slinking through the side streets. This opinion was proved in practice; at any rate they reached the restaurant without hindrance, although the journey was not without its moments of anxiety.

Cub had discarded his uniform in favour of a miscellaneous set of garments that would take more time to describe than such a detail warrants. In an old jacket, knickerbockers, black stockings and rough shoes, he looked what he pretended to be – a nondescript youth of the lower middle class. Had he been alone he would have preferred to descend to the lowest class, but the attire of his companion called for something

On his head Gimlet wore a beret a trifle too small for him.

better. Too much of a contrast, it was decided, might look odd, if not suspicious. For Gimlet, in a dark striped suit of typical French cut, with the usual built-up shoulders, was almost smart. His shoes, which were of a sickly ochre tint, rather spoilt the effect. On his head he wore a beret a trifle too small for him. These garments, of course, had been the property of the dead patriot. Gimlet had no compunction about using them, asserting that Catron, were he in a position to do so, would enjoy the spectacle of his clothes carrying on the work which his murderers, as far as he, personally, was concerned, had terminated.

The *Restaurant des Voyageurs* was a sorry hole as eating places go. The room and its furniture were drab, drab with a sordidness that not even a garish wallpaper could dissipate. The lighting, either because the proprietor economized in electricity or because the black-out was defective, was bad, giving the place an atmosphere of gloomy melancholy. A heavy smell, in which rancid fat, stale vegetables, and sour wine were the most noticeable ingredients, did nothing to raise the general tone of the establishment. There were several tables, with a fair amount of space between them. They presented plain deal boards to the diners. Some, in addition to sundry receptacles containing condiments, carried dirty crocks. One corner of the room was occupied by a short counter, or bar; behind it rose shelf after shelf of bottles in astonishing variety. This, presumably, was for effect, for even from where he sat Cub could see that most of the bottles were empty. Such was the *Restaurant des Voyageurs*, and it was much as he expected. Similar places are to be found in the lower-class quarter of any town in France.

Yet, surprisingly, the restaurant was fairly well patronized – an implication, if not actual proof, that the food was tolerably good. No Frenchman goes twice to eat where the food is poor, either in quality or quantity.

There were present no fewer than fifteen persons: thirteen were customers; the other two, behind the bar, were apparently the proprietor and his wife. To the customers Cub now directed his attention, for one of them might be – indeed, should be – the British agent. They were arranged in this fashion: at one table were three elderly working-class Frenchmen; at any rate, they spoke French loudly and volubly, as two played at dominoes while the third watched and offered advice. Two fishermen, judging by their blue jerseys, also French, occupied another table. They talked in low tones with a carafe of wine between them. At another table were two tired-looking German sailors, smoking cigars. At another table three German soldiers were drinking beer and making a good deal of noise about it. A coarse, middle-aged man in blue overalls, and a slattern of a woman, sat at another table, somewhat apart, arguing. One man sat alone, reading a newspaper. He was short, fat, and heavily moustached; a peaked cap suggested that he was employed in a minor capacity by the local authority – a postman or a tram conductor, perhaps. These were the customers. To attend to their wants were the man and woman behind the bar. The man, in shirt-sleeves, was wiping glasses. He was a dark, pale, miserable-looking fellow, with furtive eyes and a jerky manner. He coughed almost incessantly, as if he suffered from some lung trouble. The woman, who was counting the money in the till, was a robust, capable type of female. Her movements were as assured as those of the man were hesitant.

This, then, was the scene that greeted the new arrivals; it took less time to survey than to describe.

'I don't see anybody like the man we're looking for,' murmured Cub, dropping naturally into French.

'I don't suppose he'll look anything like what either of us would expect,' returned Gimlet whimsically. 'The business of these secret service fellows is to look like what they are *not*, not what they are, otherwise they wouldn't last long.'

The woman behind the bar, who had made a thoughtful scrutiny of the new arrivals, spoke to the man in a low voice. He nodded, and flipping a piece of dirty rag over his arm in lieu of a napkin, came briskly to the table.

'*Monsieur?*' he queried, looking at Gimlet for his order.

Gimlet asked what there was to drink, and it turned out that there was little choice. He ordered a carafe of *vin ordinaire* and some water. This the man brought, and put on the table with two glasses. Even while he was doing this it struck Cub that his manner was not normal, although it was not easy to perceive exactly in what respect. It would create a false impression to say that there was anything remarkable about his manner; yet there was a certain stiffness, a slow deliberation, about his movements, and the way his dark eyes went from one customer to the other, that gave Cub a pang of uneasiness. With his back to the room, the man's final act, with a motion that was definitely surreptitious, was to take a folded piece of stiff paper from his napkin and lay it on the table. With one finger resting on it he looked Gimlet straight in the eyes. 'Voilà! *monsieur*,' he said softly, and departed.

Without examining it, for his eyes were on the other customers to observe if any were watching, Gimlet transferred the paper to his pocket. With his clean-cut features set in thoughtful lines he switched his glance to the retreating figure, watched it for a moment, and then looked back at Cub. 'Take it easy,' he breathed. 'More is going on here than there would seem.'

'What was that paper?' whispered Cub.

'I'll look at it in a minute. No hurry – sit still.'

At this juncture the door was thrown open – literally thrown open – and a man entered. Cub's heart missed a beat. It was a German *Unteroffizier*, a military policeman, as denoted by an armlet. His manner was in accord with his uniform.

'Stay where you are, everybody,' he ordered harshly, speaking first in French and then repeating the order in German. In the uncomfortable silence that followed he strode to the nearest table, which happened to be the one occupied by the two German sailors. 'Papers,' he demanded.

They were produced. The *Unteroffizier* scanned them and handed them back. 'Your shore leave expires in fifteen minutes. Get back to your ship,' he snapped.

Without a word the sailors got up, threw some coins on the table and went out.

The *Unteroffizier* went on to the table occupied by the solitary Frenchman. He held out a hand. 'Your card,' he said brusquely.

The Frenchman took a wallet from his breast pocket and produced his identity card.

'He's going all round,' said Cub softly, conscious of a fluttering sensation under his ribs, for neither he nor Gimlet carried papers of any sort. He braced himself for trouble.

As it happened their turn came last, by which time the rest of the clientele, except for three soldiers who had followed the sailors, had resumed their occupations in a manner very much subdued.

'Cards,' said the *Unteroffizier* in a peremptory voice.

Gimlet met his eyes and answered apologetically, in French. 'A thousand pardons, *monsieur*, but I left my *carte* in my working clothes. If you will excuse me for a moment I will fetch it.'

'But no, *monsieur*,' broke in a quiet but anxious voice. 'I am sure you are mistaken, for a few minutes ago I saw you drop your card and pointed it out to you. You put it in your pocket.' It was the proprietor who spoke. He had followed the *Unteroffizier* at a respectful distance.

The policeman glared at Gimlet. 'Is this your idea of a joke?'

'But no, *monsieur*,' answered Gimlet quickly. By this time he was feeling in his pocket, the one into which he had put the paper left on the table by the proprietor. He took it out and stared at it with a surprise that was not simulated, for it was an identity card. He breathed a sigh of relief.

'I'm very sorry,' he said contritely. 'I was afraid I had left it at home.'

The German snatched the card. Reading it, a furrow appeared between his eyes. 'What's this?' he growled. 'Why was your card not stamped last week? You know the orders.'

'I was ill, and it slipped my memory,' explained Gimlet in an abject voice.

The *Unteroffizier* kept the document. He looked at Cub.

'Where's *your* card?'

'It's in my other jacket, sir,' answered Cub meekly.

'So! Some of you people need a lesson,' grated the *Unteroffizier*. 'Come with me, both of you. We'll see what the *Herr Kommandant* has to say about this.'

'But—'

'You dare to argue with me?'

'No, *Herr Leutnant*.'

Gimlet stood up, and Cub, taking his cue, did the same.

They followed the *Unteroffizier* towards the door. Just as they reached it, it was opened from the outside and a man came in. Cub was too occupied with his own predicament to pay much attention to him, but he noted in passing that the newcomer was a civilian, a Frenchman of about thirty years of age, with a thin, pale face. On his upper lip he wore a thin, black moustache turned down at the ends. The fellow reminded him vaguely of somebody, but he could not remember who. Not that he tried very hard. His mind was concerned with other matters. The man went on into the dining room while they followed the *Unteroffizier* into the deserted street; or it appeared to be deserted. But before they had taken six paces two men, again civilians, stepped out of a doorway. A torch flashed in Cub's eyes.

'What's this?' said a voice sharply, speaking in German.

The *Unteroffizier* answered in the same language. 'Your authority, please?'

'Gestapo.'

'Pardon. I picked this pair up in that hole of a restaurant. I'm not satisfied with them, so I'm taking them to headquarters.'

'Are you acting under orders?'

'The street comes in my beat.'

'Very well. Pass on. Don't come back this way.'

'*Jawohl.*'

The little party moved on. Nobody spoke. The corner of the street reached, the way lay beside the Canal Maritime on the one side, and low-class shops on the other. Not a soul was in sight. About fifty yards were covered in silence. Then, suddenly, the *Unteroffizier* said 'Halt.' An automatic had appeared in his hand. He held it so that it could be seen. When his order was obeyed he went on quickly, tersely, speaking in French. 'Stand with your backs to the wall.' Then, addressing Gimlet, he continued in a voice that had iron in it. 'Tell me where you got those clothes. Speak quickly. No lies – unless you are in a hurry to die.'

For the first time a hazy suspicion of the truth penetrated Cub's racing faculties. He heard Gimlet say, 'They belonged to a friend of mine.'

'His name?'

'Jacques Catron.'

'Had you said any other name my answer would have been a bullet,' said the *Unteroffizier* coldly. 'Where is Catron?'

'He is dead.'

'How did he die?'

'He was shot by the Gestapo.'

'Ah!' There was a brief pause. 'What are you doing here, in his clothes?'

195

'Before he died he asked me to meet a friend with whom he had an assignation.'

'Where?'

'At the *Restaurant des Voyageurs*.'

'Do you know this friend?'

'No.'

'Does he know you?'

'No.'

'Then how could you recognize each other?'

'I hoped that by some chance it would be possible. It might be that Georges Latroux, the proprietor, would help. I was waiting when you came in.'

Cub listened to this conversation in puzzled amazement. The two men, he realized, were sparring, like boxers, both on their toes, each expecting the other to strike. One thing only was clear. The *Unteroffizier* was not what he pretended to be. Wondering what was coming next, he became aware that a development was imminent. Approaching from the direction in which they themselves had come, keeping close against the dingy shop fronts, were two figures, one large and one small; and from the sinister method of their advance it was evident that these were not ordinary pedestrians. Already confused by a confusing situation, Cub did not know what to make of them; but if, as it appeared, they were stalking the German policeman, nothing was to be gained by interfering. He knew that the *Unteroffizier* had not seen the furtive shadows creeping along the pavement, for his back was towards them; but of Gimlet he was not so sure.

Meanwhile the conversation had ended in a sort of stalemate. The atmosphere was tense. Each was suspicious of the other. Neither was prepared to say the final word that would either betray or reveal his true identity.

The drama closed swiftly. Without a sound, without even a patter of footsteps, the two figures loomed suddenly behind the man in German uniform. Cub recognized the Fox. With him was a man he certainly did not expect to see. It was Trapper. In his right hand, held by the muzzle, was a revolver.

Gimlet must have seen this, too, for his voice cut into the silence like the lash of a whip. He spoke in English. 'Hold hard, Trapper.'

The *Unteroffizier*, thus warned, spun round. As he did so Gimlet leapt forward and gripped him so that his arms were pinned to his sides. Trapper, too, jumped in and grabbed the hand holding the automatic. There was a brief struggle. Then a voice said, in English, 'For God's sake go easy. What the devil are you fellows playing at?'

The figures fell apart. 'I thought so,' said Gimlet. 'Are you the man Catron was to meet?'

'I am,' said the *Unteroffizier*.

'Then you're British?'

'Sounds like it, doesn't it? Who the deuce are you? I can't get you weighed up at all.'

'I'm Captain King, Ninth Troop Combined Ops – you may have heard of the Kittens?'

'Spare my days!' exclaimed the pseudo-German. 'So that's it. No wonder I was all at sea. I'm Intelligence – but how did you get into this?'

'I'll tell you in a minute,' answered Gimlet. He turned to Trapper, who was in ordinary battle dress. 'What in thunder are you doing here?'

'The Fox told me what was cooking, sir. He brought me along in case you needed help. We were watching the pub. When you came out we followed.'

'Are you out of your mind, walking about this town in uniform?'

'The Fox brought me through the back streets – they're pretty dark, sir.'

'What about Copper?'

'He's gone back to base to report, sir.'

Gimlet turned to the secret agent. 'We'd better not stand here. D'you know some place where we can talk?'

'Follow me,' was the quick response. 'We haven't far to go. Don't follow in a bunch – break the party up.'

'Go ahead,' invited Gimlet.

By this time, of course, the situation was clear. Cub realized that the appointment at the restaurant had been kept – by a German N.C.O. He remembered Gimlet's prediction that the British agent, when he came, would not look like anything they expected. He had been right. Not for an instant had Cub suspected the truth, and his respect for the men who did this sort of work went up with a bound.

The man in German uniform strode on, followed by the others, walking in pairs. He took a turning, skirted a churchyard, dived into a narrow alley, and after a few quick steps pulled up short before a little shop. A key clicked in a lock.

'Come in. Go straight ahead,' requested the agent.

They all went in. The door was closed. A match flared. The man in German uniform lighted a candle. 'This way,' he invited, and going through to the back of the house opened another door disclosing a flight of steps leading to a cellar. They went down. 'Make yourselves at home,' continued the secret service man. 'You'll find some empty casks and things to sit on.' He put the candle on a ledge. 'Now let's get this sorted out,' he suggested. 'Sorry I can't give you my name, for obvious reasons, but officially at home I'm known as Number Nine – Numero Neuf here. You can call me Numero, for short.'

'I've no proof of identity on me, naturally, but enough has been said, I think, to make it unnecessary,' returned Gimlet. 'You'll have to take me on chance. I'll tell you what I know, and why I went to the restaurant.' He gave a concise account of the night's work. 'I realize now that Latroux, the proprietor of the restaurant, must be in the game, but I wasn't to know that when I went in. In fact, I was completely in the dark. What I still don't understand is how Latroux, and you, knew that I was your man.'

'That suit you were wearing was your passport,' explained Numero with a faint smile. 'The material is cut so that the stripes on the lapels meet, forming a letter V. It isn't the sort of thing one would notice unless one was deliberately looking for it. The stripes on Latroux's dirty shirt meet in the same way. But never mind about that now. This is tragic news about Catron. My business here was to meet him. Incidentally, had he been in the restaurant I should have treated him just as I did you.'

'Was that fake identity card really unstamped?' asked Gimlet.

'No. I put on that act to get you outside. It may sound rather silly and melodramatic, but believe me, when you're working under the eyes of the Gestapo it's better to have too many precautions than too few.'

'Then you didn't know Catron by sight?'

'No. Couriers are changed constantly. The fewer the people who know each other the less chance there is of one giving the others away. Latroux knew a messenger was coming, so he was on the watch for a man with marked lapels. He tipped me the wink that you were the man as soon as I came in. The rest of the act was simply playing up to my part. That, too, was necessary. The town fairly stinks of Gestapo. When you failed to return the prearranged answers to my questions I knew that you were a phoney; at least, I knew that you weren't Catron – who should have come alone, anyway. I brought you outside to find out just who you were, and, if possible, what your game was. If I surprised you, you certainly surprised me. I didn't guess that I'd picked up a British commando – much less Gimlet King himself. Let's forget that now. Catron had vital information for me. Do you know what it was?'

'No. Catron didn't pass it on. Either he died before he could, or he daren't risk it.'

'Then it must be very important. This has got me worried. From what you tell me there is a German agent in the restaurant at this very moment, passing himself off as Catron. He must be the man who came in as we went out.'

'As a matter of fact he bore some slight resemblance to Catron,' put in Cub.

'Is that so? He must be the man, then. The Gestapo was outside, watching him, as you noticed. They've probably got a cordon round the place. Fortunately they let us through. The question is, what to do next. The position is serious, we needn't doubt that. If this fellow whom the Nazis have substituted for Catron manages to worm his way into the Underground, anything can happen. If the Underground cracks, the work of years will be wiped out in a flash. Thousands would die. Here in Caen alone there are hundreds of patriots whose lives are now in peril.'

'How about bumping off this phoney guy when he comes out, sir?' suggested Trapper.

Numero answered. 'It might be done, but the risk would be enormous. If he's a crooked Frenchman – and I expect he is – the Gestapo will have their eyes on him all the time. Moreover, if he was killed, the Nazis would probably shoot a hundred hostages tomorrow. No, we daren't risk that – not for the moment, anyway. The biggest tragedy of all is, we haven't got this information Catron was carrying in his head. To make it worse, the people who sent him will not know that he died before he could get in touch with me to pass it on.'

'Can't you make contact with them?' queried Gimlet.

'Given time, yes. But my orders are to return to England tonight. Never mind how I get there, but my people are waiting for me. If I'm not back by dawn it will be presumed that I have slipped up, and another man will be sent out.'

'To the restaurant?'

'Yes. As things are he'll walk into a trap. For that reason alone I must let my department know that the mission has failed. I can't go to England and Paris as well. Wait though! There may be a way. We could ...' Numero's eyes were on Gimlet's face.

'Go ahead.'

'How about you going to Paris? I could put you in touch with the Underground there.'

'Here, just a minute,' protested Gimlet. 'I'm a soldier, not an Intelligence agent.'

Numero smiled lugubriously. 'You'd have a job to convince the Nazis of that if they caught you in that rig-out. I'm not asking you to do any spying. I'm only asking you to act as a messenger. My suggestion was just an expedient to straighten things out. After all, it was this very job that brought you to France. Had Catron not been killed the Fleas would not have sent for you. Of course, if you'd rather not go, I should be the last man to blame you. This game isn't everyone's cup of tea.'

Gimlet moved uncomfortably. 'Fair enough. If you put it like that I can't very well refuse. If you think that the situation calls for such a measure I'm willing to try it. You can let the people at my headquarters know what's cooking. But what about papers – travel permit, railway ticket, and all that?'

'Oh, I can fix those. We've facilities here for that sort of thing.'

'All right, fix it.'

'Going alone?'

'No. I'll take this lad with me.' Gimlet indicated Cub. 'He's been on the loose in France for two years, so he's probably better at this sort of thing than I am. Trapper and the Fox can go to the forest and wait there for orders. I take it that as soon as I've reported to the Underground in Paris what has happened here I'm at liberty to go home?'

'Of course. But if you're going you've no time to lose. It's just on eleven, and the last train for Paris leaves at eleven-forty. It gets in – if it's on time – about five. It will still be dark.'

'Okay. Tell me what I do when I get to Paris.'

Numero spoke slowly and distinctly. 'Commit this to memory,' he cautioned. 'You will go to number 117, Rue de Lorraine, which is a little street behind the Opera. Number 117 is the workshop of a cabinet-maker named Pierre Sabonier. He repairs antique furniture. You will ask him what has become of Monsieur Rouge – that being the name by which the head of the Underground is known. He will answer that Monsieur Rouge has gone into the country, whereupon you will reply that you have urgent business with him. While this conversation is taking place you will hold in a casual manner the left lapel of your jacket, so that your thumb rests in the V. That's all – he'll do the rest; but for heaven's sake be careful. The Underground takes no chances. One slip and you'll be a dead man. When you have made contact you will report the fate of Catron. The next step will be for them to decide. They may send another messenger, or, if you are willing, and they know you are returning to England, they may ask you to bring the information across. Either way, you'd better get back across the Ditch as quickly as possible.'

'Will you come back to France after you've been home?'

'Probably, unless I get orders to the contrary. If I am in Caen, all being well you will find me here – but the less you use this place the better. If I'm not here, there will be someone else who will recognize you.'

Gimlet's eyes went up. 'Recognize me – how?'

Numero smiled. 'You have been covered by a gun ever since you came in here. You see, you *might* have been an enemy spy. Had you been one you would not have left here alive. The morning tide would have carried your body out to sea.'

Gimlet frowned. 'This is a murky business. I prefer to do my fighting in the open.'

'So do we all, my dear fellow, but unfortunately the choice of what we do is not always in our own hands – not in times like these. Somebody has to do the shady work. We don't get any V.C.s in our department, either. The only crosses we get are when things go wrong, and then they're wooden ones.'

'A cheerful look-out.'

Numero laughed quietly. 'You get used to it. Got a gun?'

'You bet I have.'

'All right. It's time we were moving. You'd better have some food before you go.' He went to the wall, knocked, and called, 'Oh, Marie!'

A section of the wall folded back and a woman came into the cellar. Cub gasped, for it was the woman he had last seen checking the till in the *Restaurant des Voyageurs*.

'This place backs on the restaurant,' explained Numero, observing his expression.

In the little room now disclosed two men were standing, revolvers in their hands. They did not speak. They did not smile. They gave no greeting, no signal. They just stood there, watching, and Cub began to understand the real meaning of the word Underground.

'Some food, Marie, please,' requested Numero. 'And tell Charles I want to see him about papers.'

'*Oui, monsieur, tout de suite,*' answered Marie.

CHAPTER THREE

Paris Express

At eleven thirty-five, with counterfeit documents in their pockets, Gimlet and Cub arrived at the *Gare de l'Ouest*, the main-line station and a regular halt for the fast trains running between Cherbourg and Paris. Numero had departed about his business. Trapper and the Fox had gone to the forest, there to await events.

Probably no place ever devised by man is more dismal, more depressing, than a blacked-out railway station on a wet night; and if the structure has been damaged, and most of the glass shattered by bombs, the general effect of desolation and woe is even more pronounced. Thus was the station at Caen – at least, so thought Cub, as with his chief he stood beside a heap of fallen masonry waiting for the Paris train to come in. From time to time strange noises punctuated a sullen silence, which in the intervals was broken by the steady drip of rain. Metal clanged on metal. Cables rasped and signals clashed in the unseen distance. Human shapes, ghoulish in the gloom, moved about their business. A porter trailed a clattering barrow along the platform.

'How long does this train wait in the station?' Gimlet asked him.

'Three minutes, *monsieur*,' was the answer, as the porter disappeared into the murk.

The train, like most war-time trains, was behind schedule. It was twenty minutes late – the longest twenty minutes in Cub's memory. But at length, with a heavy rumble, hissing and wheezing, a crimson glow casting fantastic shadows behind the footplate, the train rolled in. Simultaneously a few shaded lights were switched on, to make pools of sickly yellow light on the wet platform.

The coaches of French long-distance trains have only two pairs of doors, placed at either end. Gimlet walked quickly to the nearest, climbed in, and made his way along the corridor until he found an empty compartment. The train, Cub noted with satisfaction as he followed, was half empty. What passengers there were, were mostly German sailors, with a sprinkling of troops, presumably going home on leave.

Gimlet dropped into a corner seat facing the engine, and cautiously moving aside the black-out blind, peeped out. For a moment he was silent. Then he said, in a low voice: 'Take a look – be careful.'

Cub looked, and clicked his tongue to indicate that he understood. Standing within the circle of light cast by one of the overhead lamps were three men. One, a civilian, had his back towards them so that his face could not be seen. The other two Cub recognized instantly. One, in uniform, was no less a person than *Generaloberst* Gunther, commandant of the town. The other was the pale-faced man whom they had seen enter the *Restaurant des Voyageurs*, the man who they had good reason to suppose was the false Catron. The occasion now seemed to prove it. All three were engaged in earnest conversation.

Allowing the blind to fall back into place, Cub turned swiftly. 'We've still two minutes to go,' he said urgently. 'I'm going to find out what's going on.'

'Watch your step,' warned Gimlet.

In a moment Cub was in the corridor. A quick glance to left and right and he hastened to that end of the coach near which the three men were standing. There he left the train, not by the door which gave access to the platform, but by the one that faced it, overlooking the permanent way. Ducking under the buffers and couplings, he brought up in a crouching position against the low wall of the platform, from which he had hoped to hear distinctly all that was said; but steam was hissing from a leaky joint, and, while this did not entirely defeat his object, it made hearing difficult. Tense, he listened until the raucous voice of the guard called, '*En voiture, messieurs, en voiture!*'

The party on the platform broke up. The general stepped back, making it clear that he was not to travel. Cub dare not wait to watch what happened to the others, but ducking back to his door, mounted the train and returned to his compartment.

Gimlet's eyes asked a question.

'I couldn't hear everything, but Paleface is on his way to Paris,' announced Cub. 'I think the other civilian was a Gestapo man. I couldn't see him distinctly.'

'Is he on the train?'

'I don't know. He seemed to be giving Paleface some orders, and his job is to find out why Catron came to Caen. They know he was carrying information, and they're anxious to find out what it was. I don't think they realize that Catron is dead; in fact, I'm pretty sure of it, because the general said something about him being kept hidden by local partisans.'

'In other words, Paleface – as you call him – is going to Paris to try to worm his way into the Underground.'

'I imagine so.'

'How is he going to do that, I wonder?'

'But for the confounded steam hissing I might have heard. As it was, I could only hear enough to make me think that Paleface has been given information that should help him to make contact with certain people in Paris.'

The train started, and creaked slowly out of the station into the night.

'I wish I could have found out if that Gestapo man is aboard,' muttered Cub.

'If he and Paleface were going to travel together, there would seem to be no reason why they should discuss the thing on the platform,' remarked Gimlet. 'Of course, it may be that they are both on the train, but don't want to be seen together. Knowing the Gestapo, I should say it's likely that they would travel independently.'

Cub's eyes switched to the corridor as the sliding door was dragged aside. Framed in the opening was one of the men of whom they were speaking – Paleface. For a moment his eyes, cold and expressionless, rested on them. '*Pardon*,' he said, and withdrawing, went on down the corridor towards the rear of the train.

Cub looked at Gimlet, knowing that they were both thinking the same thing. 'Did he recognize us, do you think?'

Gimlet shook his head. 'I don't know. He only saw us for a moment in the restaurant, and may not actually have looked at us. Sooner or later we shall know if he *did* recognize us, no doubt – that is, if he is suspicious. He may not be. After all, nothing happened in the restaurant to connect us with Catron.'

'We were with the *Unteroffizier*, don't forget. By this time the Gestapo may have realized that he was a phoney.'

'Perhaps.'

'I'm inclined to think that he knew us, and is suspicious,' averred Cub.'

'Why?'

'Why else should he beg our pardon, and find another compartment? There was plenty of room in here.'

'Maybe, like us, he was looking for an empty compartment. He has as much reason for being alone as we have.'

Cub said no more, but for some time he watched the door anxiously. Nothing happened. The train roared on, its wheels churning a monotonous rhythm, with an occasional break as they crashed over points. Still no one came into the compartment. Eventually he dozed.

Without any idea of how long he had been asleep he was awakened by the scraping of the door as it was pushed aside. A man entered, a civilian, a middle-aged man wearing a dark overcoat over a dark suit, and a soft black hat on his head. He might have been a lawyer, or a professional man of some sort, thought Cub. Without taking the slightest notice of his fellow passengers the man took a corner seat, back to the engine – the same seat which, at the far end, was occupied by Cub, who was sitting facing Gimlet.

Cub noted that the train was getting up speed, as if it had slowed down. Looking at Gimlet, and speaking in French, he said, 'I've been asleep. Do you know where we are?'

'You were asleep for some time. We've just left Evreux,' was the answer.

'Then we ought to be in Paris in just over an hour.'

Gimlet nodded. His eyes were on the man in the corner, who had now opened a newspaper – a French paper – and started to read, holding the paper up so that it concealed his face. Cub assumed that he had boarded the train at Evreux.

A few minutes later the door was again dragged aside and another passenger came in. This time it was a hungry-looking, hatchet-faced man of about thirty, dressed in a shoddy grey suit that had seen much wear. In his hand he carried a cheap wicker basket fastened by a skewer, the sort of basket in which working men in France usually carry their food. Cub summed him up as a mechanic, an engineer of some sort. At any rate, he was cheerful.

'*Bonsoir, messieurs,*' he greeted loudly, putting his basket on the luggage rack. '*Mauvais temps, n'est ce pas?*'

'*Bonsoir,*' murmured Cub and Gimlet together. The other man, still buried behind his paper, did not answer.

The newcomer, naturally, took the remaining corner seat, which was opposite the man with the newspaper.

The train roared on. Gimlet sat still, his eyes half closed. The man with the paper continued to read. He seemed to be spending a long time over one page, thought Cub. So far he had not turned over. The latest arrival made himself comfortable with his legs along the seat and promptly went to sleep. He snored, gently. The train roared on.

Cub yawned, putting his hands in his pockets, for the night was cold, and although the heat regulator was 'on' the pipes gave out no heat. The next hour seemed like eternity. He tried hard to doze again, but sleep would not be courted. He was too alert; in fact, his nerves were humming. He knew not why, but a conviction came to him with increasing force that the scene in the compartment was not what it appeared to be; that it was, in fact, a scene in a play, in which everyone was taking a part. There were two or three things he would have liked to discuss with his chief, but private conversation was impossible, unless he whispered, and this was a course he preferred not to take. The man who was reading had still not turned over his page. He could, reasoned Cub, have read every word on it a dozen times. Once, snatching a glance, he saw that the man's eyes were not on his paper, but on him, although he looked away instantly their eyes met. Then there was the other man. He gave the impression of having boarded the train at Evreux. When he came in he had said '*Mauvais temps,*' which means bad weather. Normally a man would not make such a remark unless it was raining, or doing something violent; yet there was no sign of rain on the man's shoulders. His jacket and his hat were dry. Why, then, had he remarked on the weather? If it was raining at Evreux, and the black-coated man had boarded the train there, his hat would be wet, too. But it was not. Nor was his overcoat. It seemed to Cub that while both had sought to imply that they had got in at Evreux, they had, in fact, been on the train for some time. Gimlet had not moved. Like the mechanic, he appeared to be asleep.

At last, at long last, the train began to slow down. Cub moved the blind an inch and looked out. Dark storm-clouds were scudding across a sky about three-parts covered. Stars blinked mistily through the gaps. Below, the horizon was sharply broken by tall houses and chimney pots. Leaving the blind he tapped Gimlet on the knee.

'I think we're running into Paris,' he announced, speaking of course in French.

Gimlet drew a deep breath and sat up. '*Bon,*' he ejaculated, and started to move.

'Sit still,' said a harsh voice.

Cub's nerves twitched, stiffened. Turning his head he saw that the man in the black coat was no longer reading his paper. It had fallen across his knees. On it rested a hand, and in the hand was a heavy automatic. The muzzle covered Gimlet.

Cub's first thought was, 'So Paleface *did* recognize us after all.'

Gimlet spoke, still in French. 'If this is a hold-up you'll get little for your pains. I have no money.'

The man answered, his lips curling in a supercilious sneer. 'Bluff won't help you. Sit still until the train stops. When we go, we go together. If, before that time comes, either of you attempt to move, I shall shoot. Did you think you could so easily fool the Gestap—'

A muffled explosion cut the last word short. The black-coated man jerked convulsively. His pistol fell from his hand and clattered down. The body, quite slowly, subsided on the seat. The train bumped over a set of points and it rolled off on to the floor. From the jacket pocket of the man in the cheap suit a thin miasma of smoke was rising. With an alacrity that banished all pretence of sleep he stood up.

'I'm sorry I had to do this in your presence, *messieurs,*' he said tersely. 'But there was no other way.'

'Is this one of the men who were on the platform at Caen with *Generaloberst* Gunther?' asked Cub, suddenly understanding.

'He was. His name is Wilhelm Fluger of the Gestapo. My duty was to escort you to Paris. Had this German not molested you, you would not have known. There is no cause for alarm, but we must move quickly. The train has only a few hundred metres to go. Help me. Put off the light. Open the window.'

Cub jumped on a seat, and with his gun broke the single electric light globe. There was no switch. Gimlet went to the window. The blind went up with a rush. The window thudded down. Cold air poured in. The stranger caught the Gestapo man under the armpits, and Gimlet, seeing his intention, helped him. Together they lifted the body level with the window. For a second the shoulders rested on the frame.

'Now,' said the Frenchman.

The body slid through the window and disappeared. The man's hat and paper followed. The Frenchman pulled up the window, brushed his hands as if contact with the German had soiled them, straightened his jacket, put on his hat, took his basket from the rack and pushed open the door leading into the corridor. 'Adieu, messieurs,' he said calmly. Then he was gone.

'For heaven's sake!' gasped Cub. 'He was a cool customer. Who on earth was he?'

Gimlet shrugged. He himself looked a trifle shaken. 'A partisan, obviously. Probably a member of the Underground. We've heard a lot about what goes on in the occupied countries; now we've seen a sample.'

'But who put him on our trail?'

'Ask me something easier. We must have been followed, watched, when we left Numero's hide-out. Perhaps Numero himself set this fellow to watch us. Paleface must have been watched, too. I think it's pretty clear now that he recognized us when he looked in here, and tipped off the Gestapo man that we were on the train. Everybody watches everybody in France. What a life!'

'That fellow made no bones about plugging the Gestapo man.'

'Why should he? The Nazis aren't exactly lily-fingered. If French partisans employ the same methods, who is to blame them?'

'Not me.'

'Nor me, either. Look out – we're running in. Get ready for a quick move. Paleface is still aboard, don't forget. We must try to see him before he sees us, and keep clear.'

By this time the train was crawling into the terminus, the *Gare St. Lazare*. It stopped with a jolt. Gimlet looked into the corridor, left and right. 'Come on,' he said.

They joined the little crowd on the platform, moving towards the barrier.

CHAPTER FOUR

The Trap

Under grimy, shaded, overhead lights, the eastern terminus of the railway was almost as depressing as the station at Caen. At such an early hour, apart from the tardy passengers there were few people abroad. On the platform, inside the barrier, two storm-troopers stood watching the passengers file past. From time to time one of them would stop a traveller, apparently at random, and demand to see his travel permit. Cub and his leader escaped this ordeal. Their papers were in order, but – he knew there was always a 'but' when under the eyes of the notorious German secret service. The ticket collector examined their tickets carefully, but here again there was no difficulty, and Cub breathed a sigh of relief as they moved towards the massive portals beyond which lay the open air. From first to last, although he had kept sharp watch, he had seen no sign of Paleface. Gimlet gave it as his opinion – and it sounded feasible – that the man, unaware of the fate of his German associate, if indeed they were associated, had hung back to wait for him. At any rate, he did not appear; neither did the hatchet-faced mechanic of their brief but dramatic acquaintance; and Cub was content to leave it at that.

It was no longer raining, but the streets were still wet from a recent shower and ragged clouds gave promise of more to come.

'How do we get to the Opera?' asked Cub.

'We shall have to walk,' answered Gimlet. 'It's a fair step but I know the way.'

'That man Wilhelm Fluger. He will be missed.'

'Of course. They'll find his body on the line.'

'Then they'll start looking for us.'

'Probably.'

'The sooner we're out of Paris the better,' observed Cub.

'I agree – and the sooner I get back into my own clothes the better I shall be pleased,' asserted Gimlet. 'Let's get cracking.'

They set off through the dreary streets of what had once been the brightest capital of Europe, but now the crushing hand of war was everywhere apparent. What few people there were about moved through the hollow-sounding streets with weary tread or nervous haste.

It had turned six o'clock, with the eastern sky slowly turning grey, when Gimlet announced that the open space before them was the Place de l'Opera. The massive pile of the Opera itself loomed huge against the clouds. They walked on towards it. The city was just opening tired eyes for another day. An old man was dejectedly swilling the pavement in front of the Café de la Paix.

'When you look at this,' said Gimlet, as they walked on, 'say to yourself, but for a little band of winged warriors, this was London.'

'Ghastly thought,' muttered Cub, out of the corners of his eyes watching a Nazi patrol march past.

Gimlet stopped a man and asked the way to the Rue de Lorraine.

The man pointed. 'A la bas,' said he, curtly.

They turned into the street, a miserable little thoroughfare of dingy shops, many of them boarded up. Not a soul was in sight. Watching the numbers on the doors they proceeded to the one they sought, number 117. Cub noted that the door lay a little way back from the street, at the end of a short passage. Gimlet did not stop. He went on for another thirty yards before he pulled up. And he did not stop abruptly, but first slowed down, and finished in a convenient doorway.

'It seems all quiet,' he said softly. 'I've been thinking,' he went on. 'I've decided to tackle this job alone – at any rate, until I confirm that everything is okay. There is no need for us both to go. If the place is connected with the Underground movement you may be pretty sure that they won't let two strangers just walk into it. Again, although I don't think it's likely, there's just a chance that we may have been followed. You hang about outside and keep your eyes open. Should things come unstuck, go back to Caen and report to Numero Neuf. If I whistle, come right along.'

'Very good, sir.'

Without any attempt at concealment Gimlet walked back along the pavement to the cabinet-maker's establishment, and turning into the entrance alcove knocked lightly on the door. There was no answer, but almost at once the wan daylight at the street end of the passage was blocked out by a dark form. Another joined it, filling the entrance, and Gimlet saw with disconcerting clarity that his retreat had been cut off. If the passage was a trap, he was secure inside it. The two figures moved towards him, slowly, quietly, but with a sort of relentless deliberation, almost to touching distance. Then they stopped. A voice, coldly polite, inquired, 'Do you seek someone, *monsieur?*'

Gimlet answered: 'Naturally, or I should not have come to the door. Surely this is the house of Pierre Sabonier?'

'Is he a friend of yours?' asked the voice.

'No,' answered Gimlet, truthfully, for he could see no point in lying. 'But I have business with him. It happens that he is a friend of a friend of mine. But permit me, *monsieur* – and I am sure you will comprehend my curiosity – what is the purpose of these questions?'

'It is possible that we may be of assistance,' was the suave reply. 'Monsieur Sabonier is away from home. We also are friends of his, so if we can be of service, pray command us.'

Now Gimlet was in a quandary. He did not feel inclined to discuss his business with two absolute strangers whose faces he could not even see; but it was obvious that dissembling would get him nowhere. No matter whether these men were friends or foes a chance would have to be taken. It was imperative that he should make contact with the Underground, and if he abandoned this opening – even if he were allowed to do so – he would find himself at a loose end.

'I was hoping,' he said slowly, 'that Pierre Sabonier would be able to inform me of the whereabouts of a mutual friend.'

'Perhaps we can help. What is his name?'

'Monsieur Rouge.'

'Ah?' breathed the voice. 'In that case it is possible that we may help you.' Advancing to the door the man knocked on it thrice, a knock so peculiar that it was obviously a signal.

Gimlet heard, rather than saw, the door swing open. There was no light. Beyond the door was the darkness of the tomb. The figures moved towards it.

'Enter, *monsieur*,' said the voice. The words were spoken quietly, but in them lay a command that was not to be ignored.

'Certainly,' agreed Gimlet, observing that he was in no case to refuse.

Nothing more was said. All moved forward into the darkness. Behind them the door was closed. A key turned smoothly. A bolt slid home. The passage went on for some little way, then the voice said, '*Halte!*' The party halted. An electric switch clicked. The light flashed on, and this was the scene it revealed.

It was a room, equipped in the nature of an upholsterer's workshop, or warehouse, for scattered about – mostly packed against the walls to leave a clear space in the middle – was an assortment of furniture, either genuine antique or spurious. With this Gimlet was not concerned, for in view of Sabonier's trade such a picture was only to be expected. In the open space there was a heavy oak desk. Behind it was a chair. In the chair sat a man who might have been anything between fifty and sixty years of age, well dressed in a rather severe style. His face was that of a scholar, or at any rate of a man of considerable mental capacity. His most noticeable feature was a high dome of a forehead, due to partial baldness. He wore steel-rimmed spectacles, from behind which blue eyes of remarkable intensity regarded the man in front of him. At his elbow stood a slim youth of perhaps nineteen, with a dark, saturnine cast of countenance. There were two others in the room. They stood one on either side of Gimlet, and were evidently the men who had escorted him in.

The man in the chair was the first to speak. He spoke, as was to be expected, in French, the rather hard French of the North. 'I am sorry to put you to this inconvenience, to inflict upon you what must seem a melodramatic performance,' he said apologetically. 'But you are unknown to us, and we cannot afford to accept strangers at their face value. Now tell me, what is your business here?'

Holding the left lapel of his jacket Gimlet answered: 'I came here to see Monsieur Sabonier. If he is not available I will call some other time.' Had it been possible he would have retired, for he was by no means satisfied with the way things were going. Even if Sabonier was away, why, he wondered, did this man not proceed with the ritual prescribed by Numero?

'Sabonier is away,' went on the man in the chair.

'In that case I will wait,' decided Gimlet.

'You may have to wait for some time,' was the answer, spoken in a significant voice. 'You will be mortified to know that Sabonier committed an indiscretion which has resulted in his being apprehended by the police.'

This information only served to deepen Gimlet's quandary. It meant that either he would have to abandon his project or take the men who now confronted him into his confidence.

'I understand that through Sabonier you wished to make contact with Monsieur Rouge?' proceeded the man in the chair, in a prompting voice.

'That is so,' admitted Gimlet.

'Why are you so anxious to meet Monsieur Rouge?'

'I had some private business to discuss with him.'

'You know, of course, that Monsieur Rouge is not a healthy man with whom to associate … that he is suspected of subversive activities?'

'I have heard a rumour to that effect.'

'It was, perhaps, in this connection that you wished to see him?'

This, Gimlet perceived, was a leading question. He must now either deny or admit his mission. He made up his mind. 'Yes,' he answered firmly.

The man in the chair smiled. 'We begin to understand each other, I think.'

At this juncture another man entered the room from somewhere in the rear, and walking quickly to the man in the chair whispered in his ear. The man in the chair stood up. 'Excuse me a moment,' he said, speaking to Gimlet, and rising, followed the newcomer out of the room.

He was gone for some minutes. In the interval of waiting, without moving, Gimlet made a more thorough reconnaissance of that part of the room which could be seen without effort. And as his eyes wandered slowly over the odds and ends of furniture, littered with pewter, brass, and china bric-a-brac, they were arrested by a movement in one of the several mirrors of an ornate overmantel that stood askew in a broken wardrobe. Framed in the mirror was reflected a picture cast from an angle by yet another mirror which he could not see. For a moment he ceased to breathe, for the picture explained the situation perfectly – too perfectly. The reflection showed the interior of another room, a small one. At a table sat a man with a pencil poised over a writing pad, waiting. He wore the dark, sinister uniform of the Gestapo. Gimlet knew then that the interview was an interrogation, that the man's job was to write down everything that was said. He realized also that he had already said enough to convict himself.

His interrogator came back into the room and resumed his seat at the desk. 'So sorry,' he said casually. 'We were speaking, if I remember, of Monsieur Rouge? You wanted to see him? That might be arranged, although, of course, it would be necessary for you to give us an idea of your business, so that we might judge whether the interview you seek is justified. Monsieur Rouge is a busy man.'

'Before I tell you what I have to say to Monsieur Rouge, it would not be unreasonable, I think you will agree, if I ask you to tell me to whom I am speaking. There must be precautions on my side, as well as on yours.'

'Of course,' admitted the man in the chair readily. 'You are quite within your rights to make such a request. Our little play has gone far enough. Our masks may come off. We, here, are of the Underground – but you knew that. If you need proof I can perhaps provide it by informing you of your movements since you left the *Restaurant des Voyageurs*, at Caen, last night – or is that enough?'

'That is – enough,' said Gimlet slowly, striving to keep steady under the shock of this information.

'By the way, what happened to Catron – did he get through?' queried the man in the chair in an off-hand way.

'Yes,' lied Gimlet.

'Good. So the information he carried reached the British agent safely, eh?'

'Yes,' lied Gimlet again, determined if possible to mislead the enemy.

The man in the chair stood up, and came round to the front of the desk. 'You know what his information was, no doubt?'

'No,' replied Gimlet.

'Liar!' snapped the man, and struck Gimlet across the face with such force that he reeled. The men on either side caught him by the arms and

*The men on either side caught him by the arms and held
him while his pockets were emptied on the table.*

held him while his pockets were emptied on the table – his service revolver, among other things.

The leader of the enemy party regarded his prisoner with cold hostility. 'Now what have you to say?' he grated viciously.

'Nothing,' answered Gimlet.

'Who killed the passenger on the Paris train this morning?'

'Not me.'

'Lying swine!'

'You know your name,' sneered Gimlet.

The German drew a deep breath. 'Are you going to talk?'

'No.'

'You may change your mind about that.'

'Don't flatter yourself.'

'That's enough,' said the German harshly. 'Put him with the rest. We're catching a nice lot of rats in this trap,' he concluded, apparently for Gimlet's benefit.

Gimlet was led away. As he passed the door of the room in which the uniformed man was sitting he understood the situation even more clearly. For in the same room, smoking a cigarette while he perused a paper, was Paleface. He caught Gimlet's eyes in passing. He smiled – a sardonic, mocking smile.

'The game isn't over yet,' said Gimlet evenly, and passed on.

A door was unlocked and opened, disclosing a small room with bare, whitewashed walls. The only furniture consisted of forms, set round the room. On them, in various attitudes of despair, dejection and defiance, sat seven men, some dishevelled and unshaven.

Gimlet was thrust inside. The door slammed. Seven pairs of eyes regarded him with mixed emotions. All the expressions of human affliction were there – compassion, mortification, bitterness, heartache.

'Say nothing, *monsieur*,' breathed an elderly bearded man. 'The Nazis have a dictaphone. They listen to every word.'

Gimlet found a vacant seat on a form.

CHAPTER FIVE

Cub Sets the Pace

From the dark shelter of his doorway Cub watched his commanding officer enter the shop of Pierre Sabonier. Almost at once, to his alarm, he saw two figures appear from nowhere, as the saying goes, and follow him in. He tried to calm his fears by telling himself that these men were partisans, patriots, whose sinister movements were merely precautionary measures. And when nothing happened, and Gimlet did not reappear, it began to seem that this surmise was correct. Taking advantage of every doorway, Cub shifted his position, working nearer and crossing to the opposite side of the road to get an uninterrupted view of the establishment. Dawn was now breaking – grey, bleak, drear.

Five minutes later a man came walking briskly down the street, from the end at which they had entered it. At first Cub took little notice, supposing him to be a man on his way to work; but when, as the fellow drew near, he caught sight of his features, he crouched back with his brain whirling from shock. It was Paleface: he went straight to the door, knocked, and disappeared.

What to make of this Cub did not know. Could it be possible, he wondered, that this man, this supposed spy, was a member of the Underground after all? It began to look like that. If he were not, then there was something fishy about this cabinet-maker's workshop.

Another ten minutes passed, with Cub getting more and more uneasy, and then a second man appeared in the street, following in the footsteps of Paleface. He strolled rather than walked, hands in his pockets, as if on no definite errand. As he came into clear view Cub had another shock. It was their hatchet-faced accomplice of the train. Of his standing there was no doubt, thought Cub with a spasm of relief, for that very morning with his own eyes he had seen him kill a member of the Gestapo – if the black-coated man *was* a member of the Gestapo. The trouble was, reflected Cub, in this Underground war it wasn't safe to believe anybody or anything, not even the evidence of one's own eyes.

Hatchet-face walked on until he came level with 117. There for a moment he appeared to hesitate, to falter; then, to Cub's surprise, he went on, the speed of his steps increasing.

Keeping close against the wall on his own side of the road, Cub hurried after him. Apparently Hatchet-face heard the footsteps, for he snatched a glance over his shoulder, and seeing that he was being followed he broke into a run.

'Wait, *monsieur*,' called Cub, who also began to run.

The man halted instantly, as if he had recognized the voice. Turning, he stood back against a shop, waiting.

Breathing fast, Cub joined him. 'Why did you walk past 117 as you did?' he questioned tersely. 'I expected you to enter.'

The man caught him by the arm and drew him close against the wall. 'What are you doing here?' he asked sharply. Without waiting for an answer he went on, 'At this instant this is probably the most dangerous street in Paris. Where is your friend?'

'He went inside – number 117.'

The man's expression was like ice-water on Cub's heart. 'Then God help him,' he said simply. 'He is as good as dead.'

'What do you mean?'

'The Nazis are in there.'

Cub was shaken to the very soul. 'Are you sure?'

'But yes – *certainement*.'

'But you were going there yourself,' challenged Cub.

'True, but I took care not to go in when I saw ...'

'What did you see?'

'Little chalk marks on either side of the window. They are our secret warning. They must have been made recently, by friends, for the benefit of any patriot who thought of entering.'

'Did you see a pale-faced man on the train – he was on the platform at Caen, with *Generaloberst* Gunther—'

'And Wilhelm Fluger, of the Gestapo – the man I killed. Yes, of course I saw him. Fluger travelled on the train to keep him under surveillance.'

'He, too, went into 117,' said Cub, sick at heart, and in something like panic.

Hatchet-face shrugged. 'I did not know the Nazis were here. Why should I? As you are aware, I was in Caen last night. Two days ago all was well here, but the chalk marks can only mean that Sabonier has been arrested and the premises occupied by the Gestapo. The place is now a trap. They may have caught some patriots in it, but they will catch no more.'

'They've caught my chief, that's what concerns me,' said Cub bitterly. 'He walked straight into it. What can I do now, *monsieur* – I didn't catch your name?'

'You can call me Dominique.'

'Is there anything I can do? This is awful.'

'I can only tell you not to go near that shop, *mon camarade*. You would be as certain to find death waiting for you as if you jumped from the top of the Eiffel Tower. I was not told that you were coming here. My orders were to see you safely as far as Paris. Not that I could have done anything had I known, for I myself did not know about the Nazis being in until I saw the chalk marks. I had business with Sabonier.'

'Has the shop any other door?'

'I know of none.'

'Then I shall stay here to watch what happens,' decided Cub.

'I will wait with you – for a little while anyway,' stated Dominique. 'My headquarters will know about this already, so I need not hurry. By watching we may gather information about the prisoners the Nazis have taken. There is danger, of course. Others may be watching, both friends and foes – one cannot tell. We ourselves may be watched even now. Eyes are everywhere in my unhappy Paris.'

Half an hour passed. Nothing happened. A few pedestrians and a bread cart went through the street without stopping. An old woman swept her shop front. Another vehicle appeared, a small motor van with a longish black body. It was travelling slowly, and presently stopped outside number 117.

'What's that?' asked Cub.

'It is all over,' said Dominique heavily. 'That's the prison van. God knows how many Frenchmen have taken their last ride in it. It means that the prisoners are being taken away and the trap abandoned.'

'They will be shot, I suppose,' muttered Cub in a voice that he scarcely recognized as his own.

'*Sacré*! Instantly. The Boches do not believe in feeding those who are to die. I am desolated, but there is nothing we can do.'

'If that's how you feel about it you'd better go home,' declared Cub in a desperate voice. 'But I'm not going to stand here and watch my chief carted away without doing anything about it. None or all is our motto.'

'I implore you not to do anything insane. What can you do, alone?'

'I can at least kill a few Nazis,' answered Cub through his teeth. '*Au revoir, monsieur*.' He started off towards the van.

'Wait! *Tonnerre de Dieu*! This is madness, but I cannot see you go alone,' swore Dominique in a thin, hard voice.

'You'll lose your life if you come with me,' asserted Cub. 'I'm in no mood for finesse – the affair is too desperate.'

Dominique made a gesture of finality possible only to a Frenchman. '*Hélas*! We shall all lose our lives one day. What difference makes an hour or two, or a week or two? *Vive la France*!'

'Please yourself,' said Cub, still walking. 'But a little less of the heroics, my friend, or someone will hear you, and we shall be shot before we get to the place.'

As they drew nearer Cub appraised the situation. There had been with the van two men, ordinary German soldiers of the transport service. One had dismounted, had gone to the rear of the vehicle, and, having unlocked the door, went on into the shop. The driver, in greatcoat and field service cap, remained lolling at the wheel. He had left the engine running.

'What are you going to do now?' asked Dominique – a trifle sarcastically.

'Say what are *we* going to do. I will tell you. It is all very simple. Can you drive a van?'

'But of course.'

'You still have your pistol?'

'Certainly.'

'*Bon.* This is all we have to do,' said Cub. 'I will speak to the driver from this side. You will walk on, but hurrying round the back of the van, will come up quietly on the other side of the fellow. As he will be looking at me he will not see you. Hit him on the head with your pistol. When he falls, put on his greatcoat and cap and push the body under the van – clear of the wheels, so that you won't run over him when you start. Take your place at the wheel and leave the rest to me. When I say go, drive away. That's all.' Cub glanced at his companion's face. 'Try not to look so ill, *mon ami.* You look on the point of death.'

'I am,' answered Dominique simply. 'My brain tells me that this thing is not possible.'

'Mine tells me that it is – and there is no need for nervousness.'

Dominique drew himself up. '*Monsieur*! My *sangfroid* is unbelievable. Remember, if I die, I died for France.'

'I'll bear it in mind, but nevertheless, try not to die,' requested Cub. '*Voyons*! *A victoire*!'

They were now level with the van. Cub stopped, smiling at the German half sheepishly, half cheekily. 'Good morning, *Herr Hauptmann*,' he greeted confidently, for this was a game the Fleas had often played. 'Do I observe that you are collecting more material for the firing squad?'

The German threw him a surly, suspicious look, as if not sure how to take this sally. 'Yes,' he growled. 'And if you give me any of your sauce I'll put you in with them.'

'*Oh la, la!*' cried Cub, affecting horror. 'How about a cigarette to smoke your health?' he suggested roguishly.

'*Nein.*'

'Then the health of the Führer?'

'I'll give you a clip over the ear if you don't take yourself off.'

'So! I've been promised that before, but no one has been able to do it,' scoffed Cub, provokingly.

The German raised his hand for the blow. It never fell. The butt of Dominique's pistol came down on his head. The hand dropped limply, and the Nazi collapsed without a sound.

'*Bon ça!*' congratulated Cub tersely, and without waiting to watch Dominique's further activities, he walked to the rear of the van, where, hands in his pockets, he took up the attitude of an idle spectator; and it must be admitted that is precisely what he looked like.

He had not long to wait. Indeed, so soon was the shop door opened that, observing how finely cut for time had been the operation, his nerves tingled with mild shock.

A procession emerged from the cabinet-maker's house. First came a soldier, the driver's companion. He took up a position by the open door of the van, entry into which was facilitated by an iron footplate, and with a jerk of his thumb indicated that those who followed him were to get in. Behind him in single file came eight men with handcuffs on their wrists. Gimlet was the last of the line. He saw Cub instantly. For a split second their eyes met, but his expression did not change. Bringing up the rear, but not in the cavalcade, came two hard-faced civilians whose cropped hair and square-cut heads were sufficient to reveal their nationality. They came as far as the pavement, where they stopped to watch the prisoners file into the van. It was clear from the casual manner in which they did this that the event was no novelty, and nothing in the way of opposition was expected. As soon as the last prisoner had stepped into the van, helped unnecessarily by a vicious shove, the soldier slammed the door, and with his back to the lone spectator, who had been entirely ignored, reached for the lock to turn the key that was in it.

Cub snapped into movement like a steel spring released from tension. His hand came out of his pocket holding his automatic by the muzzle. Taking a quick step forward he slammed the German on the head in no half-hearted manner, and then, whirling round, blazed three shots at the two men in the doorway. In the face of this sudden attack they fell back into the passage. Whether they had been hit or not Cub did not know. He did not wait to see. Dashing along the side of the van to the front seat he leapt aboard shouting, '*Allez!*'

The van shot forward with such a jerk that he nearly fell out; but he managed to hang on and drag himself into the seat. In a detached sort of way he heard shots from behind, but as far as he could tell no bullet hit the van.

A procession emerged from the cabinet-maker's house.

'Steady, you maniac!' he shouted, for the vehicle was now travelling at a speed worse than dangerous.

Dominique was, in fact, driving like a lunatic, taking the most outrageous risks, tearing straight across narrow cross-roads without any regard for traffic, pedestrians or anything else. He was obviously beside himself with excitement. Cub, who knew the French temperament only too well – and it is never so wildly enthusiastic as when success is in sight – was prepared to make allowances; but not to this extent. 'Steady, fool!' he cried again, furiously. 'Everyone is looking at us. Do you want to tell the world what we are doing? Slow down!'

Dominique steadied the pace a little. His face was chalk white and his eyes ablaze. '*Sacré*!' he choked. 'The audacity. It was *superbe*! This will be the talk of Paris.'

'Then let us live to hear it,' snarled Cub, who could see nothing but disaster ahead. 'Don't talk. Watch what you're doing. Turn the van over and it will be the end of all of us.'

They missed a heavy farm cart, piled high with logs, by inches. Dominique's brakes screeched. The van skidded. Leaning out at a suicidal angle he yelled something at the driver of the cart.

Cub dragged him in.

'*Bon*,' said Dominique. 'I know that man. He is of the fraternity. He will block the road behind us with his cart.'

He slowed down to a more sensible pace. 'Where are we going?' he demanded suddenly.

'Why ask me?' rasped Cub. 'This is your city. The prisoners are handcuffed, so they can't step out into the street. Do you know anyone who can get the handcuffs off?'

'Yes, but I should be breaking orders.'

'What orders?'

'On no account to go near my district headquarters if I am pursued.'

'We don't know that we are pursued.'

'*Zut*! We shall be.'

'Dash that for a tale,' retorted Cub hotly. 'The circumstances justify anything. In five minutes the whole city will be buzzing. Where are these headquarters?'

'At the establishment of my brother, who is a builder of houses near the *Gare de Lyons*.'

'Is he of the Underground?'

'A section leader.'

'Then go there.'

'We will risk it,' decided Dominique, and swinging the van, which was running beside the river, across the first bridge, he tore on.

'How far away is the *Gare de Lyons*?' asked Cub.

'Less than ten minutes.'

Cub hoped sincerely that this estimate of time was correct, for almost everybody was looking hard at the conspicuous vehicle, the purpose of which was well known. Some people, more curious than the rest, stopped to watch it out of sight. There was this advantage, however; it was given priority in the traffic, sometimes by *gendarmes* on point duty, or the Vichy Militia which at important cross-roads supported them. Nevertheless, Cub realized that on this very account the course taken by the van would be traced.

'How are we going to get rid of the Black Maria?' he asked his companion.

'Yes, how?' returned Dominique vaguely.

'You tell me,' invited Cub. 'I'm not a Parisian.'

Dominique drove on, looking worried. 'It is a question,' he admitted.

'That's why I put it to you,' retorted Cub, with gentle sarcasm. 'If you can't handle it, I will.'

'There is another danger,' asserted Dominique moodily.

'What have you thought of now?'

'When we drive into the yard of my brother Felix it may be he will think we have come to make the arrest. *Je ne sais pas*. He is a furious fellow. He may shoot. Perhaps a bomb will be thrown. He has no love for the Nazis.'

'So I gather. All right. As you drive into the yard you'd better lose no time in getting rid of that hat and coat. Yell that we are friends, then jump down and release the prisoners. I'll get rid of this hearse.'

'How? It is not a thing to be put in the pocket – *hein*'

'I'll park it at a safe distance and then come back.'

'It might be possible,' agreed Dominique. 'But get ready. We have arrived.'

The van was now running through the unpretentious streets of a squalid quarter. There were only a few people about, and they, apparently, had guilty consciences, for usually the sight of the vehicle was enough to send them down the nearest side street. Dominique turned suddenly between open gates into a builder's yard and came to a skidding stop. A large board carried the notice:

Entreprise Felix Purcelle
Reparations et decorations.

Jumping down, Dominique tore off his overcoat, shouting. Some workmen, who had scuttled like rabbits at the van's appearance, stopped, looking back. Another man, swarthy, with bristling black moustaches, dashed out of the back door of the house, a revolver in his hand. There were a few seconds of confusion, understandable in the circumstances. Dominique continued to shout, beating his chest to emphasize his words.

'Release the prisoners!' called Cub, wriggling into the driving seat.

Dominique ran to the rear of the van and opened the door. '*Descend, messieurs,*' he invited urgently.

Gimlet was the first out. Cub, leaning from the seat, hailed him. 'You're in safe hands. I've got to get rid of this pantechnicon. I'll be back.'

The prisoners out, Dominique slammed the door. '*Avance!*' he shouted.

Cub revved the engine, spinning the wheel, and turning in a tight circle shot out through the gates into the narrow street. To his great relief not a soul was in sight, and he smiled grimly as he realized why. The arrival of the van had caused a prompt evacuation. He had no idea of where he was. Not that it mattered much, he thought, as he put his foot down on the accelerator and sped on, taking every turning that appeared, in order to leave a crooked trail.

It is a curious fact which has often been noticed, that almost all important railway stations are set in mediocre surroundings. At the best, small hotels and eating places hem them in. The *Gare de Lyons*, the great Paris terminus that serves the South of France, is no exception, as Cub noted when, shooting out of a miserable little street he saw the imposing building facing him across an open space of some dimensions. It was obviously a station, and recalling Dominique's remark, he assumed it, correctly, to be the *Gare de Lyons*. It would, he decided instantly, suit his purpose as well as anywhere. He was desperately anxious to get rid of the van, for every minute now increased the likelihood of its being stopped. Without slowing down he drove up a short slope to the front of the station, and stopped when further progress was barred by a line of stationary vehicles, most of them of the heavy transport type, some loading, others unloading. Taking off his jacket and carrying it under his arm – for he was afraid it might help identification – he jumped down on to the broad pavement and dived behind a stack of boxes, from where he made a swift survey of the vicinity. What few men there were about were busy on their jobs, and so far, he thought, had not noticed the arrival of the sombre vehicle. One person had, however. A boy. A thin, bright-eyed, ragged urchin of about fourteen, who had been engaged in sweeping the paving stones. He looked suspiciously from Cub to the van, and back again at Cub. This put a check on Cub's plan, which was to leave the locality with all speed. He knew that it could only be a matter of minutes before the van was discovered, when the boy would certainly be questioned. To confirm his fears, he could hear motor-cycles roaring up the station ramp.

He went straight to the boy, who was resting on his broom. 'Do you love France?' he questioned fiercely.

The boy's eyes opened wide. '*Mais oui.*'

'And you hate the Nazis?'

'*Mais oui.*'

'Then forget that you have ever seen me,' said Cub tersely. 'I am a messenger of the Underground and the Nazis are on my trail. Keep your head. Go on with your sweeping. I shall pretend to be working here.'

Whistling cheerfully, but with nerves braced and eyes alert, he created a task by stacking the boxes nearer to the wall. He knew the motor-cycles had stopped. He had heard their stands crash down on the off-side of the van. Footsteps approached. Voices spoke trenchantly in German.

'Here you, boy,' snapped a voice in bad French.

Cub turned. Three storm-trooper motor-cyclists, swastika-decorated, stood before him. One of them pointed a finger at the van. 'How long has that been here?'

Cub pretended to think for a moment. 'About five minutes, *Herr Leutnant.*'

'Are you sure?'

'Positive, *Herr Leutnant.* It nearly knocked me down it came in so fast.'

The urchin chipped in, shrilly. 'That's right. I saw it.'

'Who was driving?'

Cub answered. 'A stout man with a black beard, wearing a beret. He seemed much agitated, and swore at me for getting in his way.'

'That's right. A stout man with a black beard,' confirmed the urchin.

'Did he have a lad with him?'

Cub shook his head, looking at the urchin. 'I saw no lad – did you?'

The urchin shook his head vigorously. 'He had no lad with him – I would swear to that.'

'Which way did he go?'

Cub pointed towards what looked like a goods yard. 'He went that way, *Herr Leutnant,* walking like a man in a hurry to catch a train.'

'That's right,' chirped the urchin. 'That's the way he went. I saw him – the fat pig.'

This, apparently, was as much as the Germans wanted to know. One had already opened the van, to find it empty. The leader rapped out some orders about telephoning to headquarters and taking the police van back to the depot. Cub resumed his work, continuing with it until the Germans had departed, taking the van with them. Then he slapped his untidy colleague on the back.

'Thanks, my friend,' he said. 'Bravo! You were terrific.'

'Pah ! Don't speak of it. It was a pleasure,' announced the boy, grinning. 'I lie to them all the time, so that they go the wrong way and miss their trains. May I join the Underground?'

'Not today, but I'll remember you,' promised Cub. '*Au revoir.*'

'*Au revoir. Bon chance.*'

Cub made his way back to the builder's yard – not without difficulty, for he had taken more turnings than he could remember. However, a woman with a shopping basket directed him to the Entreprise Purcelle. Finding the heavy wooden gates shut he banged on them with his fist. A small door was opened cautiously. He went in. The door was shut behind him. The first man he saw was his chief, in blue overalls, sitting on a pile of planks talking to the hatchet-faced Dominique and his brother Felix. A mechanic, file in hand, was just walking away with the handcuffs.

Gimlet smiled. 'Grand work, Cub,' he commended. 'I shan't forget that. It was well thought out and brilliantly executed – real commando stuff.'

Cub flushed at this praise from one who seldom gave it. 'Thank you, sir.'

'Get rid of the van?'

'I took it to the station and handed it over to the Nazis, who are now looking for the driver – a fat man with a black beard, wearing a beret.'

'Good!' exclaimed Gimlet. 'We were waiting for you. I've told these gentlemen who we are. Monsieur Felix has been kind enough to offer us breakfast. Afterwards he is going to introduce us to the man we came to see.'

'Monsieur Rouge?'

Gimlet nodded. 'That's what they call him.'

CHAPTER SIX

Underground

Over a frugal breakfast of potato rolls and *ersatz* coffee, for which Felix apologized, Gimlet decided that his only course, if there was not to be an indefinite delay, was to take the Purcelle brothers fully into his confidence. He had already revealed his own and Cub's identity, so he now related how they had come to be associated with the Catron affair. When he had finished, Dominique departed on urgent business, leaving Felix to return the confidence.

He began by stating that he was a section leader of the Underground movement He had heard, he said, of the Grey Fleas of the North, but had hitherto taken the rumours of their exploits with a grain of salt. It now transpired that the escape of the prisoners from the Rue de Lorraine had been watched by Underground spies; the details had been reported to him, and he congratulated Cub warmly on the way he had handled so hazardous an affair. It was true, he confirmed, that Pierre Sabonier had been arrested on suspicion of being connected with the patriots. What neither Gimlet nor Cub knew – and this came as a pleasant surprise – was that Sabonier had been among the prisoners rescued. Felix admitted that he was worried about the arrest of the old cabinet-maker. Either a spy had penetrated their defences, or someone had been careless, he averred.

Gimlet reminded him of Paleface, whom he had mentioned in his report, pointing out that this man had been at Caen and also in the Rue de Lorraine.

'We shall have to find out who this fellow is,' declared Felix. 'From your description I do not recognize him. He must be a new man the Nazis have got hold of.'

'I think he's French,' put in Cub.

'So much the worse for him, if we get our hands on him,' said Felix in a hard voice. 'We do not murder our countrymen, you understand, even in such a case as this,' he added quickly. 'Even traitors have a fair trial. Broadly speaking such men come into one of two categories. There are the men – and you will find a sprinkling of them in any community – who would betray their own mothers for money. They neither deserve nor receive mercy. But there are others who are forced to work for the Nazis against their will. They are different. You may say, what power could force a man to thus play Judas to his country? The Nazis know. I put it to you, comrades, what would you do if you were told by the Gestapo that if you refused to obey orders, your parents, your brothers and sisters, your children, would all be shot, and your house burnt to the ground – *hein*? Remember, the Nazis carry out their threats. The plight of these unfortunates is terrible, and although we know what they are doing our hearts bleed for them. They are not to be judged by ordinary standards. We sometimes feel that there are people in England, which has escaped the horror, who forget this.'

Gimlet nodded. 'It is not so much that they forget, as because, never having faced such tribulations, they know nothing of them.'

Felix admitted the truth of this. 'In this war no man should judge his neighbour until he is sure that he knows all the facts,' he opined.

Another identity he revealed was that of the German who had been in charge of the trap that morning in the Rue de Lorraine. This man, he stated, was none other than Karl Bussemann, the hated head of the Gestapo in Paris. 'We shall deal with him when the time comes,' was the ominous threat.

'The question is, what should be our next action?' asked Gimlet.

'That will be for the executive committee to decide,' answered Felix. 'It is likely that you will be asked to attend and make your report in person. In fact, taking your willingness for granted, the arrangements are now being made by my brother Dominique.'

To this suggestion Gimlet readily agreed. Above all, he was anxious to know what information the unfortunate Catron had been carrying to Numero, at Caen, for transmission to the British authorities. It was obviously something of importance, he told Felix, so the sooner the information was across the Channel the better.

'It is a matter of the greatest urgency and importance,' admitted the builder. 'Being a section leader in the area most concerned I know what it is, but I regret that I cannot disclose it to you without the permission of the committee. They may do so. I do not know. It is not for me to say, *monsieur*. The lives of many brave men depend upon the tightness of our communications, you comprehend?'

'I understand that,' agreed Gimlet.

Soon after this Dominique returned. Addressing his brother he said, 'All is arranged. The committee was in session when I arrived, to discuss the betrayal of Pierre Sabonier. I am to instruct you to bring our allies before the committee instantly.' Looking at Cub he continued with a wry smile, 'Our little *affaire* in the Rue de Lorraine this morning has, as you would say, put the grease in the stove. Paris talks of nothing else. Men smile as they walk the streets, and when Paris smiles the Nazis rage. God knows how they know, but the street urchins are saying that the Fleas were responsible. At least, they call to each other that there are more fleas in Paris than ever before, and as they pass the German patrols they make pretence of scratching themselves. The Nazis glare, but can do nothing about it. Bussemann, they say, roars like a bull that smells blood. It would be a good thing, *mes amis*, not to fall into his hands at this moment. Every street, every road out of Paris, is watched.'

Felix rose. 'If the committee is waiting we must go. They are busy men.'

Cub wondered how, if the streets were being watched, they were to get to the place of the meeting. He was soon to learn.

Felix led the way to a shed in which was stored the sundry equipment of the building trade. While two workmen stood on guard at the door some planks were lifted aside, disclosing a manhole.

Gimlet threw a sidelong glance at Cub. 'This is where we go down the drain,' he murmured. 'I hope it isn't going to be a messy business.'

'It is an entrance to the old sewers of Paris,' explained Felix. 'You may have heard of them, perhaps? They are famous for their rats, and for the excellent mushrooms which before the war were grown in great quantities.

It happens that the temperature is perfect for their culture. Of course, it is many years since these old sewers were abandoned,' he added quickly. 'The Germans know of them, and have occupied a part for the storage of ammunition – which we shall blow up when the time is ripe. But there is a labyrinth of tunnels about which the Nazis know nothing. Only a few old Frenchmen can find their way about them and they act as guides. Alone, a stranger would soon become lost. It would not be a good place to die ... the rats, you understand? We French love the double meaning, and it is not for nothing that we call ourselves the Underground. Descend, *messieurs*.'

Dominique showed the way with a torch. An iron ladder made it possible to descend a vertical shaft to some twenty feet below ground level into the ancient sewer which, as a matter of detail, bore little resemblance to one. It was more like a bricked culvert, a narrow tunnel, just large enough for a man of normal stature to walk without stooping. The atmosphere was temperate, rather humid and oppressive, but not unduly so. The floor was dry.

An old man, blue-bloused after the French fashion, was waiting, lantern in hand. He touched a greasy beret with a respectful '*Bonjour, messieurs*,' waited until the manhole cover was replaced, then set off.

The walk turned out to be a long one – farther than Cub expected. He estimated that they must have travelled more than a mile. With secondary tunnels and drains branching off at all angles he was able to appreciate all that Felix had said about the place being a maze, although the old guide went on like one who is at home. More than once they passed long platforms, or troughs, which appeared to be filled with eggs. These were, Cub ascertained, the famous mushroom beds which before the war had supplied half the capitals of Europe with the popular delicacy.

'I suppose the Germans have the mushrooms now?' he observed.

'No,' answered Dominique. 'In the early days of the occupation they tried them, but the *champignons* did not agree with them.'

'Why not?'

'Because in some mysterious way a species of fungus got mixed up with the mushrooms. It happened to be a poisonous fungus,' he added naïvely. 'Of course, such a thing is possible at the best of times, while there are people who do not know the difference between a mushroom

An iron ladder made it possible to descend a vertical shaft ...

and a toadstool. That is what we told the Nazis, and all they could do was to leave the mushrooms for the French to poison themselves.'

'Did the French poison themselves?'

'What a question! Of course not. After that, by a curious chance, there were no more fungi.'

Cub laughed.

'The Boches invented the phrase "total war",' reminded Felix grimly. 'The Underground has accepted it, and being French, we have introduced into it some of that artistry for which we have always been famous. What is sauce for the goose is sauce for the gander, *mon ami*, and as all the world knows, French sauces are *par excellence*.'

At this point of the conversation the walk came to an end. The guide halted before a side turning where two sentries stood guard. Felix went on alone. In a few minutes he was back. 'Come,' he said, and the party moved forward towards an area of diffused light.

Cub hardly knew what to expect, but he was not prepared for the scene which presently met his gaze. He had rather taken it for granted that the Underground headquarters would be primitive in the extreme. It turned out to be very different. It might have been a military headquarters behind an army – as actually, of course, it was. There was radio, with operators at their posts. There was a telephone switchboard, with a chic brunette on duty. These things were noted in passing to an inner vault, where seven men sat round a table – one at the head and three on either side. There were extra chairs.

It was the man at the head of the table who held Cub's attention. His commanding yet dignified poise, the high intelligent forehead, the steady eyes and pointed grey beard, seemed familiar. He was not surprised when Gimlet stiffened to attention, saluted, and said, '*Bonjour, Monsieur le General*.'

The man at the head of the table rose and held out his hand. For an instant a faint smile softened the grave, care-worn face. 'So you recognized me, eh?'

Gimlet took the hand. 'No one who has ever seen General Roularde is likely to forget him.'

'Ah well, it is better to forget names and titles here,' was the quiet reply.

'My name is Monsieur Rouge. Please be seated. As you will easily believe, I am a busy man, and the affair in the Rue de Lorraine has caused me some extra work.' The General turned to Cub. 'So you are one of the Grey Fleas, eh? We have watched your exploits – oh yes, we heard about them – with interest. At one time we were tempted to affiliate the Fleas with the regular Underground, but in the end we decided against it for fear the added responsibility would curb your audacity. Congratulations, my son. My felicitations to the Fox when next you see him. But now to work. Time presses.'

Seated at the table Gimlet recounted his version of the Catron episode. 'What I am most concerned about is the information Catron was carrying to our agent in Caen,' he concluded. 'British Intelligence, not having received it, will be getting anxious.'

'Naturally. Is it your intention to return to England immediately, *capitaine*?'

'Yes.'

'Has this been planned?'

'Not exactly. I can get across the Channel if I can get to the coast. Before considering ways and means of doing that I decided to wait until my mission here was complete.'

'It is complete now?'

'Yes. To make contact with Monsieur Rouge was my objective.'

'Very well. You would, I imagine, be prepared to act as messenger?'

'Certainly.'

'Good.' The general glanced round the table. 'Is it agreed that we put Captain King in possession of the facts?'

Six hands were raised in acquiescence.

The general bowed, then looked at Gimlet and Cub in turn. 'You can both hear this,' he said. 'Should one fail to get through, the other may succeed. Here, then, is the information Catron was carrying.

'The situation which we are anxious to present to the British authorities embraces several issues,' the general began. 'You will have heard of the great Renault motor works here in Paris. They were bombed some time ago, but are now in partial production again, producing aero engines. To prevent a repetition of the air raids the Germans have resorted to a ruse forbidden by the rules of war – not that they have ever abided by any rules when it was to their advantage to ignore them. A British prisoner-of-war camp has been set up in the works. Nothing has been said of this in your newspapers, but the Nazis arranged that the British Government should hear of it. Your Bomber Command is now faced with the problem that if it attacks the works, the prisoners – who, incidentally, are mostly commandos – will be killed. So the works cannot be bombed, and it was left to the Underground to find a solution to the problem. We think we have found one. We plan to evacuate the prison camp, and simultaneously, with the co-operation of Bomber Command, destroy the works. Many escapes have been made by tunnelling out from the inside of a prison camp, but as far as I know, escape has not been made possible by a tunnel driven in from the *outside*. Our engineers have cut a tunnel. The head of it is now twenty feet below the yard which contains the dormitory, the hutment, in which the prisoners are housed. Any night we can break upward through the crust and get the prisoners away. But when this happens the bombers must strike immediately, otherwise the Nazis will rush in fresh prisoners and the raid will be foiled. The success of this scheme, even more than most military operations, will depend upon perfect timing – but I need not tell you that. Now we come to the difficulties. There are a hundred men in the prison camp. What are we to do with them when we get them out? True, we could take them to a place where they would be safe for a while, at any rate, but the problem is, how to feed them. In Paris today rationing is so strict that it is not easy for one man to keep body and soul together. To feed a hundred men even for two or three days would be impossible. We simply do not possess the food. To men of experience like ourselves it is easy to see what would happen if food was not forthcoming. One or two undisciplined fellows would go out to find food. They would be caught and the whole scheme would fall to the ground.'

'Apart from feeding them, where are you going to put all these men, anyway?' asked Gimlet.

'In the event of our plan being adopted we should hide them in an old abandoned cloth mill at Claire, on the edge of the Forest de Pareil – about twenty-five miles from Paris.'

'How do you purpose getting them there?'

A ghost of a smile played for a moment on the general's austere face. 'They will ride there on bicycles.'

Gimlet stared. 'A hundred British troops – riding out of Paris on *bicycles*? Pardon me, *monsieur*—'

'They will not be in uniform, of course. This is the idea. As you will know, road racing on bicycles has always been a popular sport in France. These races sometimes cover hundreds of miles – as the one from Paris to Nice. The Nazis, in an attempt to placate our people, have permitted such races, setting a limit of a hundred men in any one race. We are just within that limit. This is how it will go. The prisoners will be brought out of the camp through the tunnel into an old gymnasium from which the tunnel was started. There, each man will roll his uniform in a bag which we shall provide, and attire himself in racing clothes lent by the men who will lend the bicycles. At the blow of a whistle the race will start. The winning post, ostensibly, is opposite the cathedral at Rouen. It will take place at night – that is also a Nazi rule, so that it does not interfere with work.'

'It might be done, by gad!' muttered Gimlet enthusiastically.

'We have done more incredible things.'

'But what is going to happen when these men fail to arrive at Rouen? The Germans will know that they must have disappeared somewhere *en route*, and the game will soon be up.'

'A reasonable question, *mon capitaine*. We have not overlooked a contingency so obvious. The racers *will* arrive – but they will not be the ones who set off. You see, on the night of the operation, a hundred members of the Underground, all cyclists, will be hiding in the old mill. It is on the bicycles of these men that the prisoners will be racing. As each escaper arrives at the mill he will hand over his cycle, which will bear a number, to its owner, who will then continue the race. Thus, at the appointed time, the crowd that will collect in Rouen to see the finish of the race will not be disappointed. If all goes well, the Nazis, who are not overburdened with imagination, will not connect the mass escape with the race.'

'I must say that the idea of a hundred British troops riding out of Paris on bicycles under the noses of the Nazis fills me with joy,' stated Gimlet. 'But what next? Let us say that the prisoners are now hiding in the mill. What happens to them?'

'Precisely. Without food, which we cannot provide, in a day or two there would be trouble. We feel that in getting the men to the mill we shall have done our part. We must ask the British authorities to make arrangements for getting the prisoners to England.'

Gimlet thought for a moment or two. 'This mill must be a long way from the coast. Is there a field handy where aircraft could land?'

'Unfortunately, no. The country is wooded. It so happens that where there is a possible landing area we have no place suitable for hiding such a large body of men. There is a good landing place about twenty miles from the mill. Obstructions have been erected by the Germans, as elsewhere, to break up any British machine that tried to land, but it might be possible to remove these obstructions at a given moment. Our organization is now widespread and efficient.'

'If we used this landing field we should need transport to get the men from the mill to the spot. To march all that way would be to risk everything. Have you any form of transport?'

'No. The Germans have taken everything except a few farm carts – and they would be too slow.'

'Would it be possible to cut out the mill altogether – get the prisoners to ride direct to the landing field?'

'It might be possible, but it would complicate matters, particularly in respect of the time-table. In the first place, the landing field is nowhere near the Rouen road, to which the prisoners should keep. Again, some prisoners will cycle the distance much faster than others. It is a common mistake to attempt too much in one effort. Do not lose sight of the fact that the main military object of this affair is the destruction of the Renault works. Without appearing callous, I think you will agree with me that the ultimate escape of the prisoners to England, while greatly to be desired, is secondary. If Bomber Command raid the works, and provide transport planes for the prisoners, and guarantee perfect timing – well, let them try. But as you know, few operations work out exactly to plan. The unexpected always happens. Hold-ups are almost inevitable. Suppose the transport planes arrived and the prisoners were not there? Let us say that some unpredictable contingency arose to delay the escape. Again, the prisoners will not all arrive together; they will probably arrive in twos and threes over quite a period of time. What then? Obviously, the transport planes will not be able to sit in the field, waiting, and hope to escape detection. Radiolocation will spot the planes coming out, and note their whereabouts when they land. Within ten minutes German mobile units will be on the spot, and the scheme will end in disaster. It would be better to play safe – or as safe as is reasonably possible.'

Gimlet considered the problem for a minute.

'I think this matter had better be left to the Higher Command to settle,' he decided. 'The first thing is for me to let my people know about the scheme and hear what they have to say. With your permission I will start for home immediately.'

'If your Higher Command can think of a better plan, or devise modifications on the one I have just put forward, I hope they will not hesitate to say so. The great thing is not to incriminate – if it can be avoided – those of us who have to stop in France. Now about your return. You came to Paris from Caen, so presumably it is from somewhere near Caen that you will return to England?'

'Yes.'

'And you have made no arrangements for this journey?'

'None.'

'Will you leave it to us to prepare a programme? You would be well advised to do so. The Nazis must know that you are still in the city. Bussemann has seen you. Your description even at this moment is being broadcast. But do not let that worry you. We will arrange something. Getting our people in and out of the capital has to be done so often that it has almost become a routine job – a regular service. Such journeys are usually made after dark – it is safer. Let us make you comfortable for a few hours while my transport experts work out a route for you.'

'Is there a similar route by which I can return to you to report, after I have passed this information to my people?'

'Since you do not know exactly when that will be I think you had better use the *service reguleur*. It has succeeded admirably so far. Every night a special train carrying farm produce leaves Normandy for Paris. It picks up trucks along the route. You will wish to board it at Caen, where it arrives at eight-fifteen. All you have to do is to go to the porters' room under the east signal box at eight. There you will find a shunter. His name is Hilaire. Tell him that Monsieur Rouge wishes to see you in Paris and he will find a place for you in the truck that will be waiting for collection in a siding. On reaching Paris the train runs into a goods yard at the *Gare St. Lazare.* Friends will be there to meet you. From the station you will ride in a vegetable cart, or perhaps a milk float. Hilaire will have told the driver of the train that there is special freight on board, and the driver will pass the word to us. Do I make myself clear, *monsieur?*'

'Perfectly, sir,' answered Gimlet.

CHAPTER SEVEN

The 'K' Plan

The assertion of Monsieur Rouge, that getting patriots in and out of Paris had become a routine job, proved to be no idle boast. His experts, he had said, would work out a plan. This they did, and it operated with such precision that four-thirty the following morning found Cub and his chief on the outskirts of Caen. To Cub the experience was particularly interesting in that it revealed the wide ramifications of the Underground network. It was also an object-lesson to demonstrate the folly of trying to hold an entire nation in subjection.

The return journey to Caen began at dusk, when the travellers, rested and fed, were informed that all was ready for their departure. Having been wished 'Bon voyage' by Monsieur Rouge and the brothers Purcelle, they proceeded forthwith under the guidance of a man who was the very spirit of taciturnity. He rarely spoke. They never learned his name.

First there was a long walk through a 'drain' that ended where the effluent had originally discharged into the River Seine. Here they were provided with filthy overalls which they were told to wear over their clothes. Near at hand a barge had just finished discharging coal. They went on board. No one spoke to them or appeared to notice them.

'This business gets dirtier and dirtier,' remarked Gimlet in a voice heavy with disgust.

The barge cast off and chugged away downstream. On either side rose a fantastic silhouette of chimneys from the roofs of lightless Paris. Once, at a bridge, the barge was challenged, presumably by a Nazi sentry. The man at the wheel called out something. The barge did not stop. This, the first stage of the journey, was made with surprising ease.

It ended at Sèvres, home of famous china-ware. Gimlet recognized the outline of the great factory, which he had often passed in pre-war days. The barge crawled to a wharf and made fast. In front of the factory stood a line of vehicles. The guide furnished the information that this was a convoy of reconditioned lorries, driven by French drivers. Where they were going the guide did not say. He walked down the line to the last lorry, and, indicating that the others were to follow, climbed aboard. After a delay of about ten minutes the convoy started. A tiresome drive of about an hour followed; then the convoy ran through a large town. The driver of the rear lorry stopped to make – or pretended to make – an adjustment to his engine. The guide said quietly, '*Messieurs*, this is Mantes; we have arrived.' The party dismounted.

A short walk took them to a railway line, within sight of a station. The guide took cover beside a side-tracked goods train, and volunteered the information that this was the western railway.

'This is where I leave you,' he said. 'A goods train bound for Cherbourg will be along in a few minutes. At this place the train will slow down. It does so every night, in case there are passengers – you understand? You will travel with the guard. If you will tell him that you wish to descend at Caen he will arrange for the driver of the engine to slow down again just outside the town.'

Soon afterwards the goods train puffed into the station. After a wait of a few minutes it came on. The engine whistled, three short notes.

'All is well,' said the guide. 'That is the signal. *Adieu, messieurs.*'

'Goodbye, and thank you,' returned Gimlet.

The train came on, the engine hissing. As it rumbled on a figure could be seen leaning out of the guard's brake. Gimlet took a running jump and climbed aboard. Cub followed. The guard dragged him in. Then, to Cub's surprise – not to say consternation – a third figure rolled into the dimly lighted brake. It was a German soldier. Before Cub could recover from his shock the man had scrambled to his feet and made a swift sign to the guard.

The guard nodded, quite unperturbed. He slammed the door. Then, turning, he said calmly, 'Make yourselves comfortable, *messieurs.*' He looked at Gimlet. 'Where do you wish to descend?'

'Caen.'

The guard switched his glance to the German, who said 'Cherbourg.'

'*Bon*,' acknowledged the guard, and went on with his work.

Cub looked at Gimlet and back at the German. To his utter and complete amazement – although by this time he suspected the truth – the German deliberately winked. The idea of a German winking struck him as so incongruous that for a second or two he could only stare. Then, to cap all, the German said, in a casual voice, in perfect English, 'Do either of you fellows happen to have a cigarette on you? I've run out.'

Gimlet took out his case. There were six cigarettes in it. 'Take the lot,' he invited. 'I hope to be where there are plenty, before dawn.'

'Lucky devils. I may be here for weeks,' murmured the man in German uniform, taking three of the cigarettes. 'If you'll excuse me now I'll snatch forty winks. It's some time since I had any sleep.' He curled up in a corner, and lighting a cigarette inhaled the smoke with infinite relish.

Gimlet found a seat on a crate. He looked at Cub and smiled. 'Takes all sorts to make a war,' he remarked.

The train rolled on through the war-stricken night. After a while Cub, too, lay down and slept.

He was awakened by Gimlet shaking his arm. 'On your feet,' was the order. 'The guard tells me we're approaching Caen.'

Cub scrambled up. 'What's the time?'

'Half past four.'

The train slowed down. The guard opened the door. '*Bonjour, messieurs*,' he said evenly, as if all this was part of his everyday work. The 'German' was still fast asleep in his corner.

Wondering if he would ever see either of their fellow passengers again, Cub, with a jump, followed his leader to the permanent way. For a little while they lay side by side on the embankment, listening, watching the tail light of the train disappear.

'That was a knockout,' muttered Cub. 'I'm beginning to wonder if anybody in France is what he appears to be.'

'Quite a lot of people are not, evidently,' returned Gimlet. 'Well, let's move along to the forest and get in touch with Trapper. He'll be waiting.'

Cub followed his leader to the permanent way.

The journey to the Fleas' headquarters was accomplished in just under an hour, without incident, but the end provided a surprise. Not only was Trapper in the cellar under the ancient hunting-box, but Copper, and the man they knew as Numero Neuf.

Gimlet made no attempt to conceal his astonishment. 'What the devil's all this?' he asked wonderingly.

Numero answered. 'It's all very simple. As you know, I slipped home last night and reported what had happened to my headquarters. There was a quick conference, and it was decided that I should come back right away to keep in touch with you, for reasons which I will explain presently. We got here about two hours ago.'

'But I was going home myself,' declared Gimlet.

'I know, but there's a spot of bother about Catron's information not getting through. Headquarters thought it would save time if I came back and contacted you.'

'But how did you find your way here?'

'You sent this corporal of yours home, too, didn't you? He reported the position from your angle. Headquarters put two and two together, and as he was the only man who knew just where to find you they sent him back with me to act as guide.'

'Smart work. How did you get here?'

'Flew over – dropped by parachute.'

'But that's all very fine,' argued Gimlet. 'How the deuce am I going to get home? The corporal was going to pick me up in one of our boats.'

'That's what I told them, sir,' put in Copper. 'They said they would make other arrangements. The officer who I was to guide would give you your orders.'

Gimlet frowned. 'Give *me* orders?' He turned to Numero. 'I'm a soldier – or I thought I was one. I don't take orders from civilians, even if they are in the Intelligence Service.'

'I'm not a civilian,' said Numero quietly. He smiled. 'As a matter of fact, old boy, there's no need to keep it a secret any longer; I'm General Sir Saxon Craig, Assistant Director of M.I.5.'

Gimlet was frankly shocked. 'I'm very sorry, sir, but how was I to know?'

The general smiled again. 'You weren't. I pop to and fro from time to time to have a look at things with my own eyes. You'd better forget who I am, though. My contacts here only know me as Numero Neuf, so stick to that, if it's all the same to you.'

'It's all right with me,' agreed Gimlet. 'But I'm still at sea about this business.'

'Sit down and I'll tell you all about it,' invited Numero.

They made themselves comfortable.

'As I told you, we were more than a little worried about the non-arrival of this special information Catron was bringing us from Paris. You've been to Paris?'

'Yes.'

'And you made contact with the Underground as I suggested?'

'Not exactly. Sabonier was arrested just before we arrived – I'll tell you about that later on. Actually, it made no difference in the long run. We made contact with the Underground.'

'Did you see Monsieur Rouge himself?'

'Yes.'

'Did he give you the information?'

'Yes.'

'Splendid. Now, what's it all about?'

'Just a minute,' protested Gimlet. 'Let's get this straight, first. Am I to understand that *you* are taking this information home?'

'Yes.'

'Is there some particular reason for that?'

'Yes. You see – don't get upset – you may not be going home ... yet.'

'Ah,' breathed Gimlet. 'You'd better give me the low-down of the new idea.'

'It's quite simple, my dear fellow. We don't know what his Underground information is. You do. It struck headquarters that it might involve some job which you could handle; and as you are already on the spot it seemed pointless to bring you home. If you *can* handle the job you can go straight ahead.'

Gimlet frowned. 'That's pretty cool, sir. Am I a commando or an Intelligence agent?'

'I'm afraid that in this war, King, you have to be what the exigencies of the service demand,' said Numero earnestly. 'But suppose you tell me what this information is? If it turns out to be an obvious Intelligence job, and you'd rather not do it, so well and good. But if a military operation is called for I know of no one better qualified to handle it than you are. Now, what's the news?'

'You don't mind if I talk in front of my chaps – we work together, you know, and they sometimes have ideas?'

'Not in the least. They're under your command. You can tell them what you like.'

Sitting in the underground chamber, with Fleas on guard outside, Gimlet passed on the plan for the destruction of the Renault works and the disposal of the prisoners.

'So that's it,' breathed Numero, when he had finished. 'It's an ambitious scheme, by Jove, but it would be a fine job if we could pull it off. Of course, we knew about this revolting Nazi trick to prevent us from bombing the works.'

'Why did they choose the Renault works, in particular, to try it on?' asked Gimlet. 'There are other objectives.'

'True, but there is a special workshop in the grounds of the Renault factory where we have reason to believe that something of a very important nature is going on. We know which shed it is – we have air photographs on which it is marked. It may be that experimental work of some sort is going on inside, but we don't know, because only Germans are employed in it. One detail which Monsieur Rouge did not tell you is this. The prisoners, or most of them, are commandos taken in the Dieppe raid – the fellows who were subsequently shackled. They still may be, for all we know. A large proportion are Canadians, but there are some Kittens, your own fellows, among them. But let us get down to brass tacks. The job begins to look more and more like a military operation. What's your opinion of it?'

'In Paris the whole thing was sprung on me suddenly, so I hadn't much time to think about it; but I've turned it over in my mind since, and this is what I think. The Underground scheme is all right, but it doesn't go far enough. I can't help feeling that with a hundred good men this show should be turned from a defensive to an offensive one. We ought to be able to do quite a bit of damage before we withdraw. I've done too much running away, lately. If we must run, let's hit the Nazis a crack first, while we're on the spot. What do you say, you fellows?' Gimlet glanced at the three Kittens, who were standing by.

'Bash 'em all round the clock, sir, anywhere, any time, that's what I says,' answered Copper simply. 'Am I right, Trapper?'

'*Zut*! *I'll* say you're right,' answered Trapper.

'We've got some useful equipment hidden here in the Forest, sir, that we left the last time we were out,' reminded Cub.

'Give me a rough idea, King, of what's in your mind,' invited Numero.

'All right,' agreed Gimlet. 'In the first place it will be necessary for someone to enter the Renault works to release the prisoners. As the tunnel is ready, that should be easy. But I say, while we are inside, let's make a little smoke. With flares and grenades we could mark that special shed for the bombers with more accuracy than – with all due respect for them – our pathfinders. In short, while we're on the job, we might as well set the place alight. Having lit a signal for the bombers to do their stuff, all we have to do is to retire into the tunnel, which would be blown up behind us to prevent anyone from following.'

'How many men would you need for this party?'

'Myself and the three fellows I have with me should be enough. The scheme can then follow the French plan until the prisoners arrive at the old mill at Claire, where, in any case, we are supposed to take over. The snag that the Underground was up against was feeding the men while they were in the mill, and later, transporting them to a place where they could be picked up by our aircraft. The nearest field is some distance from the mill. Now, instead of all this messing about, I suggest that we use the German aerodrome at Rambours, which is a lot more convenient and has a safer landing surface.'

'But Rambours landing field is occupied by a German bomber group – some of the fellows who raid London.'

'Ho! So that's where they come from,' growled Copper. 'I've been waiting for a chance to call on some of these blokes who knocked our 'ouse about—'

'All right, corporal. Keep your imagination under control,' advised

Gimlet. He turned back to Numero. 'My idea is that we – that is, ourselves and the prisoners – seize this bomber station and burn it out. Then, before the enemy can reorganize, our machines come in and pick us up. I like the idea of using a German landing field. It would give the show a more stylish finish than lying in some stinking ditch, round some dirty meadow, getting our clothes all messed up – you know how it is?'

'But for such an attack you would need weapons – weapons for a hundred men.'

'There shouldn't be much difficulty about that. Machines could come over the mill and drop us the necessary small arms, grenades and what-nots. My fellows would have to change back out of their racing togs into their uniforms, of course. As I see it, it's just a matter of timing.'

'And at the finish there would be a hundred men to pick up – some of them casualties, no doubt.'

'Half a dozen Lankies,[*] or Wimpeys,[**] could do the job.'

'It would be a pretty piece of work if it came off,' agreed Numero. 'But what's Monsieur Rouge going to say about all this?'

'I think he'll agree. In fact, he told me that if we could think of a better plan than his he would be quite willing to adopt it. His only stipulation was, bearing in mind that his organization would have to stay in France, he didn't want it exposed to too much risk. I'll tell him that once our fellows are at the old mill he can retire from the scheme and leave us to our own devices.'

'All right. You work out the operation in detail – the time schedule, what you'll need, and so on. I'll take it home and present it to the Higher Authority for approval.'

'When are you going home?'

Numero looked at his watch. 'It will he light in an hour and a half. If you could work out your plan in half an hour I could get back tonight. I have a date with a pilot, at a field about three miles from here, just before dawn.'

'And are you coming back here again, to let me know if the plan has the approval of the departments concerned?'

* Lancaster bombers.
** Wellington bombers.

Numero considered the question before replying. 'Probably not. There's really no need. Knowing exactly what you have in mind it might be better if I stayed in the operations room and watched things from there. Some emergency might arise – you never know. Let's leave it like this. If a machine comes over and drops two flares, green changing to red, you'll know it's okay for you to go ahead. Should anything occur to cause me to alter my mind, and come over, the machine will drop a string of three flares, red only. In that case, should you wish to get in touch with me, you'll find me in my apartment in the Rue Basse, in Caen.'

'Good enough,' agreed Gimlet. 'I'll get to work on the plan right away.'

'When would you schedule this show to come off?'

'The bicycle race has been arranged provisionally for Sunday night. Monsieur Rouge said it could be postponed if necessary, but Sunday would be most desirable because it's the only night of the week that the works close down – which means that there will be no forced French labourers there then. Tomorrow will be Saturday. Sunday means a bit of a rush, but we ought to be able to manage it. It should give us time to get back to Paris and put the plan before the Underground Committee, anyway. As far as I, personally, am concerned, the sooner the better.'

'Fair enough,' concurred Numero.

'Just one other thing,' concluded Gimlet. 'There's an Air Force squadron attached to Combined Ops. Under the command of a chap named Bigglesworth. His outfit seems to know this game so well that they take it in their stride. They picked us up last time we were over, and I like the way they did it – no messing about. If you could arrange for them to handle the air side I'd feel there wouldn't be much chance of it going wrong.'

'You mean the chap they call Biggles?'

'He's the fellow. Tell him the story so that he can get his teeth into the whole set-up.'

'I'll see what I can do about it,' promised Numero. 'Get busy on the scheme. We'll call it the "K" plan.'

CHAPTER EIGHT

Saturday

The following day, Saturday, passed quietly. It was, Cub suspected, the lull before the storm. With a map in front of him Gimlet went over his plan again and again, estimating times and checking distances, looking for weak spots and trying to foresee every possible contingency that might arise. This was the 'K' plan, the plan that General Craig, or Numero Neuf, as he preferred to be called, had taken back to England for approval.

Gimlet knew from experience that in a scheme so intricate, involving a large number of personnel, should anyone fail in his duty, in no matter how small a degree, the whole plan would collapse and disaster would be shared by all. He was also well aware that be they never so carefully planned, operations seldom proceed precisely according to schedule; that a hitch here, a moment's delay there, could upset the entire timetable. The best that a commander could do was to try to anticipate such breakdowns and have an alternative plan ready.

Security was his main worry. The enemy was aware that something was in the wind, and would at that very moment be employing their tremendous resources to discover what it was: should they get one whiff, the faintest suspicion of the truth, even if the scheme were not fore-doomed to failure the hazards would be multiplied a hundredfold. Never had he been so anxious. This was not on his own account, nor that of the men who would be under his command. They all knew the risks they were taking and accepted them as an inseparable part of their job. His greatest concern was for those brave Frenchmen, the civilian members of the Underground movement. It would be upon them that the heavy hand of the Nazis would fall, should their complicity be suspected – and it probably would be, regardless of whether the scheme was a failure or a success. For the commandos it would be simply a matter of life or death in action. For the patriots it would not be so easy. Working all the while in the grim shadow of the execution yard, they would doubtless accept their fates with the high philosophy of true patriots the world over; but it would not end there, and they knew it. Their homes would be wiped out. Their families – wives, children, fathers, mothers, and even distant relations, most of them entirely innocent – would be questioned, tortured after the Nazi fashion, and at the end brutally murdered or thrown into a concentration camp, which was practically the same thing. Wherefore Gimlet, as never before, was desperately anxious that the operation should not, through any fault of his, come 'unstuck'; that no trail should be left which might lead back to the Underground. The onus of responsibility for this rested on his shoulders.

Not sharing the cares of leadership, Cub, Copper and Trapper suffered from no such pangs of apprehension. Their part was to obey orders. Although they did not discuss it, they knew well enough that their fate was in their leader's hands; and having complete confidence in him they were content to have it so. Wherefore, with a screen of Fleas thrown round the outskirts of the forest to watch for possible trouble, they sat under the ivy-clad wall of the ruin and talked of lighter matters, in the manner of old soldiers. While they talked, Trapper polished the little bow and arrows which were a part of his private equipment. After a while, to test the bow, he stuck the butt end of his cigarette on a tree about thirty paces distant for a target, and returning to the party impaled it at the first shot. The Fox, thinner than ever, moving with all the nervous awareness of danger of his namesake, joined them. He was just in time to witness Trapper's exercise in archery.

'*Enfin*, but I should like to know how you do that, *mon brave*,' he said admiringly.

'Pah! It is simple,' was the casual reply. 'All that is necessary is that you start practising when you are five years old. You practise every day for ten years. Then you begin to hit the things you shoot at. Then you practise every day for another five years, and hoopla! you cannot miss.'

Smiling ruefully the Fox found a seat with the others. '*Hélas*! I am several years too late in the starting,' he sighed.

255

'Where've you been to, Foxy me lad?' inquired Copper.

Fox shrugged. 'I go to the town, to take to the mother of the Grasshopper a tin of the bully given to me by *Monsieur le Capitaine*. Today she will eat well.'

'You've got a nerve,' returned Copper, grinning. 'Don't you bring no 'ounds this way, a fox-huntin'. Ha! That's a joke. Fox-huntin' – get it? You know what happens when they catch the fox? They cut his head and tail off, and then skin 'im – so they tell me. That's what old Gunther would do to you, me lad, if he got 'is 'ands on you.'

'Gunther will need a faster horse before he can catch me,' scoffed the Fox. 'Besides, he shouts so much with the rage that he sees nothing.'

'Ho! Is that so?' murmured Copper. 'Now who's trod on his toes?'

'The word is out that my cousin Edmond has gone to England to join the Fighting Navy. To do this he makes the general the big fool. *Oh la la*! The story goes round the town and everyone laughs. Even in Caen they still enjoy the joke. Ah! that Edmond – he is a droll one. Always they call him *le Tricher*.'

'What's that mean?' growled Copper.

Cub answered. 'The cheat.'

Copper frowned. 'I ain't got no time for cheats.'

'But it is good to cheat the Nazis, *mon ami*,' protested Fox.

'Tell us how Edmond pulls off his trick,' invited Trapper.

'*Alors*! This was the way,' asserted Fox. 'Edmond, he is by trade a man of the fish – no, the fisherman, *n'est ce pas*? He has an idea the most superb. *Tres, tres fantastique*. But first I must tell you that the *generaloberst* finds out that Madame Elise, she who in the old days keeps the Hotel Metropole, has buried in her garden her stock of fine old brandy, *le cognac – trés bon*. Over twenty dozens of bottles – *Oh la la*! The Nazis took the hotel from her, you comprehend? So that she has no business, no money. Gunther, he takes the brandy. Edmond, who thinks for a long time how he can get to England, now thinks how he can get the brandy. He has an idea. *Une chance*! He goes to the *generaloberst*, and says he knows a man, one who lives down the coast and before the war was a smuggler. This man has much money but no brandy. For the cognac he would pay a thousand francs the bottle. That is much money, even for fine cognac, and the *generaloberst* loves money. So they make the arrangement. Edmond takes a bottle and is to have a hundred francs for the business. He brings back the money, but Gunther gives him only ten francs, not a hundred. Then Edmond takes two bottles, and brings back to the general two thousand francs, saying that the customer will take all the brandy at the same price. Says the *generaloberst*, but you cannot carry twenty dozens of bottles so that no one shall see them in the transportation. Edmond answers, if you will give me a permit, *Herr Generaloberst*, I will take it in my boat. To this Gunther agrees, telling Edmond he is a smart fellow. So the permit is written and signed by the *generaloberst*. Edmond carries the brandy to the boat, in which all his friends who wish to go to England are already hiding. *Hélas!* He sails out and does not come back. He goes straight across *La Manche*.'

'What's *La Manche*?' demanded Copper.

'It's the French name for the English Channel,' explained Cub. 'It means The Sleeve. The Channel is supposed to bear some resemblance to a sleeve.'

'Ho! I get it. So Edmond had a card up his sleeve, as you might say. Ha! That's a good 'un. Laugh, everybody.'

Fox smiled. 'When Edmond lands in England he has brandy up both sleeves, *mon camarade*, which is even better, because the British Government gives him money for it and sends it to the hospitals. Now Edmond is in the Fighting Navy. What a man! What brains! What nerves! One day he will be president of France.'

'Swipe me with a blanket!' exclaimed Copper. 'But how did you get hold of this tale, if Edmond is in England?' he added suspiciously.

'Because, *mon ami* – and this is something Gunther does not know – in the middle of the night a friend of Edmond arrives at the house of Madame Elise and gives her twenty-four hundred francs from the British Government, which is payment for the brandy at a hundred francs the bottle – a fair price. He tells the story, and today all Caen talks of nothing else. So once more we twist old Gunther's nose. But he does not like this, and looks for an excuse to shoot hostages.'

'*Sacré!* Does he need an excuse?' asked Trapper.

'But yes. If there is no excuse it will be said that the shootings are because of the brandy, and the story might reach the ears of the Führer. Now he looks for Gimlet and some Kittens, who are known to be in Caen.'

'Strike a light! How does he know that?' demanded Copper.

The Fox shrugged. 'Ah! I do not know. Spies of the Gestapo tell him, perhaps.'

'What beats me is, why old Gumboil ain't rumbled this forest hide-out before now,' declared Copper.

'Many times they have been through it,' asserted Fox. 'When they look in one place we go to another.'

Cub joined in, smiling. 'Once or twice we have helped them to look, but their trouble is, they don't know what they're looking for. It would need an army to comb the place thoroughly. And suppose they did that? The Fleas would just move into the next forest. There are plenty of forests in France to choose from – and there are thousands of patriots hiding in them, too. What can the Boches do about it? Nothing. They need all the men they've got to guard the towns. After all, the Normans, who started out from Caen, you remember, tried pretty hard to find Robin Hood, who hid in Sherwood Forest, but they never did.'

'So now we're 'avin' a sort of return match, eh?' remarked Copper, grinning. 'Aw, let's forget the Jerries fer a bit. How about a slice of bully and a biscuit? I'm peckish. Blimey! Could I do with a basin o' fish and chips from old Ma Smith's joint down the Old Kent Road? Not 'alf I couldn't. Lovely grub. Might 'ave bin 'aving it, too, but for this perishin' war. Stop muckin' abart and get on with it, I say. Am I right, Trapper?'

'Are you right? *I'll* say you're right,' agreed Trapper warmly.

And so the day wore on until dusk dimmed the scene. And an hour after sunset, high up in a sky that was being scissored into sections by questing searchlights, came the signal for which they were all waiting – two flares, green changing to red.

'That's it,' said Gimlet cheerfully. 'Now we can go ahead. We move off in twenty minutes. We've got to be at the signal box at eight sharp.'

'How about togs, sir?' asked Copper.

'We wear uniforms,' answered Gimlet. 'This is a commando job now. Cub, you may have to do a spot of scouting, so you might keep your overalls on over your uniform for the time being. We shall need some equipment in addition to revolvers to crack open the Renault works – a couple of Sten guns, some grenades, and a signal flare or two should do us. We'll carry them in a sack. Everyone will take an emergency ration of biscuits for his own use.' Gimlet turned to the Fox. 'When we move off you might put a screen of Fleas out in front of us to pass back word if anyone is about. Our objective is the east signal box at Caen.'

'Oui, mon capitaine.'

'After we've gone you'd better come back here and lie low.'

'Oui, mon capitaine.'

A quarter of an hour later, the party, in single file with the Fox leading, started off through the leafy aisles of the silent forest. To anyone making such a march for the first time the experience must have been an eerie one, but to those now engaged the manoeuvre had become commonplace. There were occasional halts and brief delays, with signal calls and quiet conversations between the Fox and small figures that appeared out of the darkness, spoke fiercely, and disappeared whence they came. If ever there was any real danger the commandos saw nothing of it, and the railway line was reached without incident or alarm. The Fox had done his job well; he struck the track at a point about a hundred yards to the east of the signal box, which turned out to be the usual square, two-storied, box-like structure, with faint light showing through the glass sides of the upper part. Within the lighted area the spectral shape of the signalman could just be discerned as he went about his duties. A hundred yards or so beyond the signal box a few shaded lights revealed the position of the station. The time was five minutes to eight.

'Shall I have a prowl, sir, to make sure this shunter Hilaire is inside?' suggested Cub.

'Go ahead,' agreed Gimlet. 'A whistle will bring us along if it's all clear.'

Keeping close against the side of the low embankment, and from habit taking advantage of any cover that offered. Cub moved forward with cat-like tread towards the signal box, which, as he drew near, he observed, was of the standard type, the upper part, containing the signal levers, being reached by an outside staircase. Closer reconnaissance disclosed that the ground-floor cabin had its own door, and one window facing the track;

but as the window was blacked-out it was impossible to get a glimpse of the interior, or even a part of it. Advancing to the door Cub was about to try the handle when the sound of voices reached his ears. Listening, he made out that there were two men talking. One, he surmised, would be Hilaire. Who was the other? A platelayer or a porter, perhaps? It might be a friend; on the other hand, it might not. He decided to wait.

Five minutes dragged by, with a desultory conversation still being carried on inside. Cub knew that the others would be wondering what he was doing, but without taking a risk there was nothing he could do about it. If he went back to them to report, the second man might emerge the moment his back was turned, and still more time would be lost in ascertaining that he had departed. Another five minutes passed. It was now well after eight, and the train was due at eight-fifteen. Already the time would be short for the shunter to make the necessary arrangements. It seemed that the only alternative to going back to Gimlet to report, which would involve the loss of two or three more minutes, was to risk a peep into the cabin.

The crash of a signal lever, and the harsh scraping of a cable almost under his feet, brought his heart into his mouth, as the saying is. But it hastened his movements, for there was sound reason to suppose that the train just signalled was the one which they intended to board. After feeling to make sure that his uniform was not showing anywhere, he reached for the door knob.

Precisely at that moment the door was opened from the inside, with the result that he came into collision with a man who attempted to come out. With a grunt of surprise the man recoiled a pace into the room. Light struck his face. Cub recognized him instantly; and he knew from the expression in the man's eyes that he, too, had been recognized. It was Paleface.

Cub was probably the more surprised. He had almost forgotten the man, whom he supposed to be in Paris. The last time he had seen him was in the Rue de Lorraine, when he had entered Sabonier's shop. Anyway, all that mattered for the moment was that recognition had been mutual. Cub had no particular quarrel with the Nazi spy – at any rate, not just then, when there were other, more pressing matters to attend to; but he realized that if the man got away, within five minutes there would be a hue and cry.

Obviously, Paleface had to be stopped; and with this object Cub reached quickly for his gun, only to discover, to his chagrin, that it was under his overalls. Before he could do anything else Paleface had jumped forward, struck him a violent blow on the chest, and rushed out. Cub staggered, but grabbed the man in passing, and hung on. They both fell on the dirty gravel beside the track.

In the struggle that ensued Cub found himself fighting both an offensive and a defensive action. His antagonist, on account of age alone, was both heavier and stronger, and it was soon clear to Cub that he was likely to get the worst of the encounter; for which reason, had the circumstances been different, he would have been content to break away. But as things were, even though he was receiving punishment, he dare not loose his hold for fear the man should get clear and raise an alarm. So he had to hold on, and at the same time defend himself against injury – no easy matter, for his opponent struck out and kicked with desperate energy. The irony of the situation was, although Cub had help near at hand he dare not call for it because of the proximity of the station. From Hilaire – assuming that he was the other man in the ground-floor room – he could expect no help, for the simple and obvious reason that the shunter, never having seen him before, would not know whether he was a friend or an enemy. And yet, curiously enough, it was from this direction that assistance came; and it was forthcoming when Cub's flimsy overalls were torn away from his neck, exposing the uniform beneath. Hilaire stepped into the fray, and for this intervention Cub was thankful, for his plight was precarious. He had been holding Paleface by the throat in a frantic endeavour to prevent him from shouting; but the man had broken loose, and rolling over, was in a fair way to break Cub's back across the nearest rail of the steel track. It was at this critical juncture that Hilaire, muttering incoherently, took a hand by seizing Paleface by the hair and hauling him off, at the same time smothering his face with a lump of oily cotton waste. Panting, Cub staggered to his feet, and finding himself unable to whistle, croaked hoarsely for Copper. He then went to the assistance of the shunter, who by this time was finding that he had, as it is said, bitten off rather more than he could chew.

It happened, however, that the commandos, alarmed by the delay, were already moving towards the signal box when Cub called. They now arrived at the double, and the issue was soon settled. Recognizing Paleface in the light that streamed from the open door of the cabin, Gimlet grabbed him by the collar and dragged him off the shunter with a muttered 'Sock him, corporal.'

Copper swung a hook to the jaw that lifted the man off his feet before stretching him senseless on the ground against the wall of the signal box.

'I told that swipe, in Sabonier's shop, not to crow too soon,' muttered Gimlet.

'What do you want me to do with him, sir?' asked Copper calmly.

'Take care of him,' answered Gimlet curtly, and turning to Cub, demanded, 'Where the deuce did that stinker come from?'

'He came out of the cabin just as I was going in,' explained Cub. 'We knew each other. He had a crack at me and I tried to hold him. I daren't shout because of the station.'

Gimlet faced the shunter. 'Are you Hilaire?'

'*Oui, monsieur.*'

'We have urgent business with Monsieur Rouge. He told us that you could arrange the passage to Paris.'

'*Oui, monsieur.*'

Gimlet jerked his thumb towards the vague shadow in the upper part of the signal box. 'What about him?'

'He is a friend, *monsieur.*'

Gimlet pointed at Paleface. 'Do you know this man?'

'No, *monsieur.*'

'You have never seen him before?'

'No.'

'What was he doing here?'

'He came down the stairs from the signal box, just before this one arrived.' The shunter indicated Cub.

'What was he doing in the signal box?'

'He did not tell me.'

'What did he want?'

'At first he asked me questions about the trains. Then he told me he was of the Underground, and wanted to get to Paris.'

'And what did you say?'

'He did not give me the right signs, so I knew he was not of the Underground. I said I knew nothing of the Underground.'

'How do you know *we* are friends of the Underground?'

'Because I received a message to expect you, *monsieur*.'

'Good. Then that settles that. We've no time for talking – we're late now. Can you make the arrangements?'

'There are none to make, *monsieur*. The trucks are in the siding and the train's not yet in the station. Come this way.'

'What about him, sir?' put in Copper, jerking a thumb at the still unconscious spy.

'Obviously we can't leave him here to raise a stink. Confounded nuisance, but we'll have to take him with us. No matter. Monsieur Rouge would probably like a word with him. Lead on, Hilaire. Bring the sack along, Trapper.'

The shunter strode quickly down the line for a short distance towards the station and then turned into a siding where two goods vans were waiting. He opened the door of the nearest. '*Montez, messieurs*,' he invited. 'It is more comfortable to travel with the cabbages and watercress than with the milk churns which fill the other truck.' When the commandos had climbed aboard he added, 'I make a mark on the outside with chalk, so that those in Paris will know where to look for you. When the train arrives in the goods yard of the Gare St. Lazare, remain seated behind the crates. Friends will find you. Ah! here comes the train. *Adieu, messieurs, et bon voyage*. My service to Monsieur Rouge if you see him.' The shunter swung the heavy door into place.

Gimlet switched on a torch, keeping the light down. 'Tie the prisoner up in case he comes round at an inconvenient moment. I'm a bit worried at finding him here.'

'According to the Fox, Gunther knows we're back at Caen,' contributed Cub. 'Maybe Paleface was looking for us.'

'Well, now 'e's found us I 'ope 'e's 'appy,' remarked Copper, tying the man's hands behind his back. 'He'll be a bit more careful next time. What say you, Trapper – am I right?'

Trapper clicked his tongue. 'Sure, pal. *I'll* say you're right.'

A minute later the van jolted as the train shunted into the siding to pick it up. Buffers clanged. Coupling chains clanked. The train began to move.

'We'll stack these crates and sit behind them, in case some inquisitive blighter pokes his nose in,' decided Gimlet. He laughed quietly. 'Upon my life, I've gone to Paris a good many ways, but this is the first time I've travelled with the vegetables.'

'What time do you reckon we ought to arrive, sir?' inquired Copper.

'About four or five in the morning, I imagine.'

'Strike me purple!' muttered Copper in tones of deep disgust. 'Nine hours sitting on a basket of perishing cauliflowers. If my old Ma could see me now, she'd say—'

'It serves you right,' concluded Gimlet.

'That's it, sir. 'Ow did yer know?'

'Mothers all say that,' returned Gimlet evenly.

'I reckon they're about right, too.'

'Sure they're right,' put in Trapper moodily.

'Copper, you'll take the first watch,' ordered Gimlet. 'Keep an eye on the prisoner.'

'Aye aye, sir.'

'The rest had better try to get some sleep,' concluded Gimlet.

CHAPTER NINE

Warm Work at the Terminus

The journey to Paris was a tedious one. The train stopped often, and shunted to pick up more trucks of agricultural produce; and as its load increased its speed decreased. The prisoner recovered consciousness soon after the start. In the light of the torch which Gimlet turned on him he surveyed his captors with sullen, malevolent eyes. Once, Cub thought he caught a sardonic gleam in them, as though the man enjoyed some secret that was to his advantage. This produced in Cub an uneasy feeling, but he said nothing. Gimlet tried questioning the man, but neither threats nor the promise of fair treatment would induce him to open his lips. Later, this behaviour was to be explained, but at the time there was no clue to it. Gimlet came near to the truth when, speaking to Cub on one side, he remarked: 'I wish we weren't cluttered up with this fellow, but he's here, and short of murdering him, which isn't our way of doing things, there's nothing we can do about it. I've an uncomfortable feeling that he's got – or thinks he's got – a trick up his sleeve. He should be more scared than he is at the thought of being handed over to the Underground. They'll make him talk, I'll warrant. Hilaire said he came down into the cabin from the signal box. I wonder if the man there gave anything away, by accident? When people talk, they usually say more than they intend. There would be a telephone and a telegraph instrument in the signal box ... he may have spoken to Paris. But guessing won't get us anywhere. When we approach Paris we'll empty one of these cabbage crates and put him in it; that will keep him out of sight and at the same time prevent him from seeing anything. Remember to empty one of the crates, Cub – they're plenty large enough to hold a man.'

'I may as well do it now,' answered Cub.

As he moved to obey the order, he, too, made an observation which, in the light of subsequent events, showed sound reasoning.

'When we came from Paris to Caen, sir,' he said in a voice too low to reach the prisoner, 'we had a fellow-traveller – you remember the German soldier? I think the way he arrived, and got aboard, implies that the train is often used for getting people out of Paris. And didn't Monsieur Rouge say something about a regular service? This train back into Paris might be as commonly used. There may be more people aboard than we know about. That's nothing to do with us, but there's an old saying about the pitcher that goes too often to the well getting its handle knocked off.'

'Blimey! What's the matter with you?' growled Copper. 'Are you tryin' to give me a nervous breakdown? I remember a feller down the Old Kent Road—'

'Never mind about the Old Kent Road,' broke in Gimlet. 'If you start talking about nerves you're not likely to see it again.'

'True enough, sir,' agreed Copper heavily. 'All the same, if my old Ma could see me now she'd take a bottle of aspirins – s'welp me, she would.'

It had turned five o'clock when, in the darkness that precedes the dawn, the train crawled laboriously into the Paris terminus. As was to be expected, it did not run into the main passenger platforms. Gimlet, who was watching from the door, announced that they were going into the goods depot. Cub got a glimpse of a vast covered yard, dimly illuminated by the usual shaded lights. There were no platforms; the lines ran in between broad flagged pavements, with roads beside them, wide enough to permit the assembly of motor traffic for the collection of the rail-borne freight. The place wore a deserted, dejected appearance. There were no other trains.

Copper threw open the crate that had been emptied, and lifting the prisoner by the collar, ordered him to get in. Showing his revolver he made a promise, in a tone of voice not to be doubted, that 'one bleat would be all that was necessary to put him to sleep for a long time.' The man got into the crate, and Copper tied down the lid with the string that had been used previously for that purpose.

By the time this was done the train had almost run to a standstill; and

Copper lifted the prisoner by the collar.

it had gone far enough to reveal, through a blur of steam and smoke, a scene which gave Cub a sinking feeling in the stomach. True, the expected greengrocers' carts, and vans and barrows, were there to collect the farm produce. But they were not all. There were other things, and they needed no explanation.

The 'quay' into which the train had run was manned by a considerable reception committee. Uniforms predominated. There were Nazi uniforms, and uniforms of the quisling Feld Gendarmerie. There was also a sprinkling of civilians, some wearing swastika armlets. It was clear that the Nazis and their co-operatives had already been busy, and the precise situation, as Cub made it out, was this. The vans and carts, about a dozen of them, had arrived to meet the train. That some of the drivers were of the Underground, who had come more in order to pick up members of their organization, and refugees, than vegetables, was not to be doubted, although which they were, Cub, of course, had no means of telling. The Nazis had arrived, apparently a few minutes before the train, and had arrested certain suspected drivers or their helpers. At any rate some seven or eight men stood in line, some crestfallen, some protesting, some defiant, near their vehicles, which had been drawn up close together with their backs to the train in readiness to load up. Covering this line of men with rifles, under the direction of two swastika-decorated civilians, were several storm troopers. A third man, an officer of the Gestapo, was shouting at the prisoners in a bullying voice. Cub heard Gimlet catch his breath and mutter, 'By gad! It's Bussemann himself.' Around these central figures, at scattered points, as if to keep outsiders at a distance, were some uniformed members of the French Militia. Others, accompanied by civilians, had started to search the train, beginning at the engine. The engine driver and his fireman had already been dragged off the footplate. One man was on the roof.

'Strewth! They're goin' to ask us fer our tickets,' muttered Copper.

'Yes, it's a round-up,' said Gimlet in a hard voice.

'Zut! We chose the wrong train,' observed Trapper.

Confirmation of Gimlet's remark was soon forthcoming, in a short, intense drama. There was a shout; a scuffle. A man leapt from the train and streaked across the quay. Rifles cracked, making the lights flicker.

The running figure crumpled like a wet sack, skidded a little way across the greasy stones, and lay still. Men closed in on him. A murmur that was half a groan, half a gasp of compassion, broke from the line of men under arrest. Some moved. Voices snarled at them to stand still. Looking more closely at these men Cub's mouth went dry. He recognized Dominique, who had evidently come to meet them. Bussemann was questioning him in a loud voice. What answer Dominique made Cub could not hear, but stepping forward, Bussemann struck him a blow across the face with his gloved hand that sent him reeling.

Gimlet spoke. 'Things may not be as bad as they look,' he said quietly. 'We'll give them a run for their money, anyway. Listen carefully, everybody. Copper, when we break cover make for that light lorry at the end of the line. Don't let anyone stop you.'

'Aye aye, sir.'

'Having got to it your job will be to hold the Nazis off until everyone's aboard.'

'Aye aye, sir.'

'Knock off as many of the enemy as you can.'

'Yessir.'

'Start when you hear the bang of a bomb.'

'Yessir.'

'Trapper, you'll help me to cut a lane through this Nazi scum. Use a Sten gun, and hang on to the bag of equipment.'

'Sure, sir.'

'Cub, while we're dealing with the opposition you'll double to Dominique and tell him to get his friends to the end lorry. Having got them in, he'll take the wheel, ready to drive anywhere he likes. He knows Paris better than we do. That clear?'

'Yes, sir.'

'Good, then let's go.' As he finished speaking Gimlet took a grenade from the sack. Sticking his revolver in his belt, he leaned out of the door and flung the bomb along the side of the train towards the spot where the Frenchman had fallen, where his body was now being dragged away by several Nazis. The grenade struck the ground, bounced, and in a blinding flash of light, exploded.

Cub was prepared for a bang, but in the confined space of the yard the effect was shattering – literally shattering. Glass crashed, some falling from the roof. Several lights went out, darkening a scene already dim. The immediate result was confusion, and a rising medley of sounds. Into this Copper leapt out, shouting 'Gangway for a British officer!'

Hard on the reverberations of the explosion came the snarling of Trapper's Sten gun. Cub saw several Nazis fall, before his view was blotted out by Gimlet and Trapper jumping out together. Advancing, spasmodic flashes of yellow light lit the scene as their revolvers roared. Everything was noise, or so it seemed to Cub, as, automatic in hand, and feeling strangely unconscious of his limbs, he made a bee-line for Dominique, calling his name in a high-pitched voice. He tripped and fell over a fallen Nazi, and rising, was nearly deafened by an explosion almost in his ear. He did not see who had fired the shot, but he saw one of the civilian Gestapo taking deliberate aim at Gimlet. He fired from his knees; the man dropped his gun and staggered away, groping at the air. Springing up, Cub dashed on through a scene that was no longer real, but pure nightmare. Some of the detained Frenchmen were milling about as if uncertain what to do; others had thrown themselves flat to escape the bullets that were flying in all direc-tions. Some shots, apparently, were hitting the domed roof, for glass rained down. Cub caught Dominique by the arm. 'Keep your head!' he shouted. 'Make for the end lorry and get your crowd into it. You've got to drive!'

Dominique answered incoherently. He was, in fact, behaving like a man out of his mind, for which, admittedly, there was some excuse. In a frenzy of excitement he fired a volley of words at his companions, and spinning round, ran toward the lorry, with the rest streaming along behind him. Cub followed. Through a blur of smoke he saw that Copper had already reached the van. He was crouching near the tailboard, shooting with steady, methodical deliberation. Several bodies lay sprawled in grotesque positions along his line of fire. A Gestapo man was crawling towards a revolver that lay on the pavement in front of him. Cub took a running kick at the weapon. With a snarl of rage Dominique snatched it up and fired three shots at point-blank range into the Nazi.

'Go easy on the ammo, Frenchie!' growled Copper. 'Whatcher, Cub. How yer doin'? What a crimson beano!'

Cub thrust Dominique towards the driving seat of the lorry. 'Get in, but don't start till you get the word,' he ordered, and dashed back to the rear to see if the patriots were getting aboard. They were – one, limping, was being helped by the others.

Trapper appeared through the smoke, walking backwards, still firing the Sten gun in short bursts, spraying the train, and the other vehicles, evidently with the idea of forcing the enemy, who had taken cover, to keep under cover. In this he succeeded. The only Nazis Cub could see were casualties. Reaching the van, Trapper tossed his Sten gun in the back, and drawing his two revolvers began shooting at flashes that showed from time to time at different points.

'Where's Gimlet?' cried Cub, in a panic.

'Why ask me?' returned Trapper, between shots.

'Copper – Gimlet's down!' shouted Cub, and ran forward, looking at the figures on the ground. One seemed larger than the rest. It heaved, and rolled over. Cub caught sight of khaki tangled with dark blue, and running close, found Gimlet locked in a clinch with Bussemann. The German had just torn his right arm free. The hand clutched a revolver. Cub dare not shoot; the figures were too close. He seized the arm, forced it down on the stone pavement, and knelt on it, striking at the hand with the butt of his pistol. Gimlet twisted, and breaking free, struck at Bussemann's head as he rose. The German went limp. Cub sprang up, and in doing so caught a glimpse of his chief. He was in a fearful state. His uniform was filthy. His collar was twisted round the back of his neck. Hatless, his hair was plastered on his forehead with sweat. His face was black with the greasy grime of the quay.

'Disgusting business,' snarled Gimlet. 'How are things going?'

'Fine,' answered Cub. 'Everyone's at the truck. Dominique's waiting to start.'

'Okay. Let's go.'

They ran to the lorry, meeting Copper halfway. He turned back with them.

By this time the din had largely subsided, like a storm that blows itself out. There were still occasional shots, and the whistle or smack of a bullet; but as far as the fight was concerned, it was over – temporarily, at any rate.

Gimlet was well aware that the lull would not last long.

'Get aboard, everyone,' he ordered. 'I'm going in front with Dominique.'

Cub remembered something. 'What about Paleface – in the crate?'

'We can't stop for him,' rapped out Gimlet. He disappeared towards the front of the lorry.

Trapper had already climbed into the back. Sitting on the equipment sack, gun in hand, he kept close watch on the battlefield for further trouble. Copper swung Cub aboard and climbed in. 'Let 'er go!' he shouted.

The lorry shot forward. Through a scene now entirely deserted it raced through the station yard into the dark streets of the city. Where they were, or where they were going, Cub did not know. For one thing, he did not know Paris, and secondly, reaction from the fight left him slightly dazed. The lorry went on, through interminable streets, each one like the last – what little could be seen of it, for darkness still held the city in close embrace. The rescued Frenchmen seemed dazed too. None spoke. Only Copper appeared unperturbed, as if nothing unusual were happening. He nudged Cub playfully in the ribs with his elbow. 'How goes it, chum?'

'Frightful,' answered Cub frankly.

'Pah! You'll get used to it,' replied Copper. 'Blimey! You ought to have been in the Dieppe raid. Now that *was* a show. Am I right, Trapper?'

'*I'll* say you're right,' agreed Trapper, a smile twisting his scarred face.

'My knees have gone to jelly,' declared Cub.

'Jelly? What's that? I ain't seen none since the war started. Ha! What a joke.' Copper sighed. 'Strewth! Did I like jelly when I was a kid? My old Ma used to say—'

'Tell us some other time,' implored Trapper.

'Okay – okay,' returned Copper airily. 'Lumme, a bucket o' tea would go down well – not 'alf it wouldn't.'

He gurgled suddenly in his throat.

'What's funny?' asked Cub. 'Have I missed a joke?'

'I just remembered we left Paleface done up in the cabbage basket. S'welp me, what a present *he'll* be for someone buying a feed for the rabbits.'

'It was a bit tough on him,' commented Cub.

272

Copper chuckled. 'Tougher on the rabbits, chum. What say you, Trapper, old pal?'

'It's going to be tough on a lot of people in Paris, tomorrow, when the Nazis get busy looking for a bunch of commandos,' remarked Trapper.

'Aw! Forget it,' growled Copper. 'Hello – looks like we're arriving.'

The lorry had swung sharply into a drive, bounded by thick evergreen shrubs. It ran on a little way, then stopped, in darkness and in silence.

'I wonder where we are?' murmured Cub.

'What's the odds?' returned Copper. 'What I want's a basin of tea. What's the French for tea?'

'*Thé*,' Cub told him.

'That's lucky,' answered Copper. 'I ought ter be able ter remember that one. How about trying to scrounge a pot? A rough house always did give me dry tonsils.'

Gimlet appeared. 'Don't talk so much,' he ordered. 'We're there. Get yourselves tidied up. I've asked Dominique to arrange for baths.' He walked away.

Copper buried his face in his hands. 'Knock me over with a blanket,' he pleaded. 'Did yer 'ear that, mates? We blind our way into Paris, and all he can think to ask for is baths. What does he reckon we are – a bunch o' kids togged up fer a school treat? Baths on the brain, that's what he's got. Next thing he'll be tellin' us ter go out and get an 'air cut. Blimey, it's a bit 'ard.'

Gimlet reappeared. 'Were you saying something, corporal?'

'No, sir,' answered Copper. 'Just thinkin' aloud, as you might say.'

'Dangerous habit, corporal. You should cure yourself before someone hears you.'

'Yessir.'

'Come on – this way.'

CHAPTER TEN

Sunday

Copper did not get his basin of tea, for the simple reason that in enemy-occupied France tea had practically ceased to exist; but he had – they all had – some coffee which, as Copper remarked, while it was 'nothin' ter write 'ome about', was better than nothing. This they drank while resting in a large, well-appointed house, in front of which, it transpired, Dominique had pulled up. Where the house was situated, to whom it belonged, and what it looked like from the outside they did not know. A peculiar knock had brought a man to the door. With him Dominique had had a whispered conversation, as a result of which the commandos were invited in. Dominique disappeared, and presently Cub heard the van being driven away. What happened to the Frenchmen who were in it was a matter for conjecture. They did not come into the house, so it could only be assumed that they had dispersed to their homes, or had gone into hiding at some other place.

The commandos relaxed in a comfortable lounge for about twenty minutes, waited on by a woman who was attentive to their welfare but who said little; then Dominique returned, bringing with him his brother Felix. Felix was agitated. Dominique had told him of the affair at the Gare St. Lazare. All he could say about it was that it was *'fantastique,'* and this he said several times. He did not reproach Gimlet for what he had done, but it was clear from his manner that he regarded this sort of open warfare in the heart of Paris with no small trepidation. No doubt the fear of reprisals weighed heavily upon him. However, he greeted Gimlet warmly and with respect, and informed him that although Paris was being combed by the Nazis for the desperadoes who had created such havoc at the railway station, they were reasonably safe where they were. Monsieur Rouge had been informed of the circumstances, and as soon as the Executive Committee could be got together the commandos would be taken to Underground Headquarters. As Cub expected, this involved a journey through the sewer, a branch of which passed beneath the outbuildings of the house in which they had found refuge.

At nine o'clock they were all at Underground Headquarters, Gimlet in earnest conversation with Monsieur Rouge, a large-scale map of Paris and a plan of the Renault works on a table before them. Gimlet went over the modified plan in detail. Monsieur Rouge looked startled, and then dubious, when Gimlet came to the proposed attack on the Luftwaffe airfield, which had the double purpose of destroying the enemy bomber base and providing a landing ground for the British planes that were to take the commandos home; but when Gimlet pointed out that the Underground would have no hand in this, that it would, in fact, have already faded out of the picture, he made no demur, although he confessed that the audacity and magnitude of the operation left him somewhat breathless. Gimlet observed that in these very factors lay their best hope of success. The Nazis would hardly be expecting an enterprise so ambitious.

'The plan will operate tonight,' he went on. 'The race is due to start at eight-thirty, so I have fixed zero hour for eight. The bombers will arrive at eight-thirty-five. There is only one factor for which I have not been able to provide. It is this. We – that is, the three men here with me and myself – will be the last to leave the works. My intention is, unless we are prevented, to retire by the way we enter – through the tunnel, which you will then blow up to prevent the enemy from following should he attempt to do so. But the question is – and here I am hoping you will be able to make a suggestion – how are *we* to get from Paris to the old mill at Claire? The cyclists will have started. It is likely that they will be well ahead of us. At the worst, we shall have to cycle too; but no one knows what may happen in the works, and we may be in no state to cycle twenty-five miles. Also, we shall be in uniform, in order that the attack may be claimed as a legitimate military operation. That is as much for your benefit as ours. British commandos will carry the responsibility, so that the Germans will have no excuse for blaming or punishing the civil population of Paris. Of course, the Nazis will guess that the Underground had a hand in it, but if British commandos are seen, they will be regarded as the prime agents. Again, the Nazis do not like commandos, and if we were caught in plain clothes they would be glad of an excuse to tell the world that we were a gang of civilian cut-throats under arms, wearing uniforms only when it suited us. We are soldiers, and this attack will be made by soldiers. Do I make myself clear?'

'Perfectly, *mon capitaine*.'

'To return to the question of getting to Claire, it is important that I should be there when the cyclists arrive, to take control. Without motor transport I should arrive long after them – if I arrived at all. We have no transport in France, so in making my plan I had to rely on you to provide us with a vehicle large enough to hold five.'

'Five?'

'There will be four of us, but it will be necessary for us to have a guide, otherwise we may lose our way. Perhaps Dominique will oblige, assuming that he knows the road?'

In the absence of Dominique, Felix asserted that his brother would be willing to drive – if a car could be found.

'But surely you have a car of some sort?' queried Gimlet.

'It is not a matter of a car,' put in Monsieur Rouge. 'It is a matter of petrol.'

'What about the van we just arrived in?'

'Every German in Paris is looking for it. You would not get far in that.'

'A carpenter with some paint could alter the look of it by tonight.'

'That could be done, but there will not be more than a litre of petrol in the tank,' declared Monsieur Rouge. 'The Nazis hand out petrol only in sufficient quantity for a stipulated journey. The van might have enough petrol to take it to the outskirts of Paris, certainly not more.'

Gimlet thought for a moment. 'There should be plenty of petrol in the Renault works.'

Monsieur Rouge started. 'Surely you have enough to do without carrying petrol?'

'It could be done.'

'Perhaps.' Monsieur Rouge laid a finger on the map of the works. 'This is the petrol store, but it is in big tanks.'

'Is there no private garage?'

'Yes, at the house occupied by Herr Streiner, the German overseer of the works. He uses a big touring Renault car. Doubtless there is petrol in his garage.'

'Then we will see what can be done about it,' declared Gimlet.

'A point in your favour is that you will not have far to go,' observed Monsieur Rouge. 'The house and garage are near the experimental shed, which you intend to destroy.'

'You still don't know what's inside this shed?'

'No.'

'Very well, *monsieur*,' said Gimlet. 'We shall arrive, I hope, with petrol, so please have a vehicle waiting. There is one last thing that disturbs me,' he went on. 'As you have heard, the Nazi spy who we call Paleface, the man who tried to impersonate Catron at Caen, is in Paris. There is good reason to think that he was responsible for the searching of the train at the Gare St. Lazare this morning. At all events, he was in the signal box at Caen last night. We caught him, and brought him to Paris with us, but there was something in his manner, a sort of confidence, that makes me think he knew what was going to happen in Paris. We put him in a cabbage crate intending to deliver him to you, but in our hurried departure he was left behind.'

Monsieur Rouge looked concerned. A furrow appeared between his eyes as he glanced round the committee and back to Gimlet. 'What you tell us answers a riddle, *monsieur*. We have this man, but could not comprehend who he could be.'

'You've got him?' Gimlet looked amazed.

'After the affair at the station the vegetables were distributed as usual, although the retailers had to go to the station to get the produce,' explained Monsieur Rouge. 'One crate, when it was opened in a shop at Montmartre, was discovered to have a man in it. The man who found him, knowing for what purpose the train was sometimes used, asked him if he was of the Underground. He answered yes, whereupon, unknown to the stranger, the matter was reported to us. We gave instructions for the man to be brought here, and he should now be on the way. But in view of what you tell us he should be more closely guarded. What explanation he intends to give us when he gets here I cannot imagine, but he certainly seized a chance to get into the Underground and may have already seen and heard more than is good for any of us. We will attend to him. Meanwhile, as you are not likely to get much sleep tonight I suggest that you pass the day quietly in repose. Any difficulties as the result of this morning's affair will be reported to you. There is only one thing I fear.'

'What is it?'

'That the cycle race will be cancelled, if only as a form of retribution for the trouble at the station. The Nazis are mean in little things. If they can hurt us, they do.'

'Hm. That *would* be awkward,' admitted Gimlet. 'Nothing has happened so far, so they may let it go.'

'Let us hope so.'

Gimlet rose. 'That seems to be all for the time being, *monsieur*. We will leave the transport arrangements to you.'

'You may with confidence do so,' averred Monsieur Rouge.

Thereafter the day passed quietly enough. The commandos returned to the private house, where they had nothing to do except wait for zero hour. From time to time Dominique or Felix brought snatches of news about what was happening outside. As was to be expected, the affair at the Gare St. Lazare had created a sensation, and roused Nazi fury to boiling point. They were making ugly threats, and Cub wondered to what excesses their anger would lead them if, following the battle at the station, the Renault works project was successful. Bussemann was about with his head in bandages, Felix informed them. Rewards were out for the commandos, who were thought to be still in Paris. Anyone concealing them was promised instant death. Dominique may have hit a nail on the head when he said that what really upset the Nazis was not so much that there were British commandos loose in Paris, as the obvious inference that they were there for some special purpose, and the Nazis could not discover what that purpose was.

'They will, in due course,' murmured Gimlet drily.

The first disconcerting news came about six o'clock, when Monsieur

Rouge and Felix appeared together. One glance at their faces and Cub knew that something had gone wrong, but he would never have guessed what it was.

'The plan cannot go through,' said Monsieur Rouge abruptly.

Gimlet's eyebrows went up a little. 'Why not?'

'*Ecoutez*. I will tell you,' averred the Frenchman. 'I told you we had the man you call Paleface. He was brought to me for questioning. We, knowing what we did about him, and he, knowing the fate that we mete out to traitors, broke down, and in the hope of saving his life confessed everything. He is not true French, thank God, but half an Italian, from the Savoy. As you thought, in the first instance his task was to impersonate Catron, and work his way into the confidence of British agents and the French Underground. That does not matter now. What does matter is this. Permission to hold the cycle race tonight has not been withdrawn as we thought it might be, because the Nazis think, if they do not actually suspect, that it has some connection with Underground activities. They do not connect it directly with the arrival of British commandos at the Gare St. Lazare, but they are watching, and there is to be a check. At Villant, which is on the road to Rouen – between here and Claire, unfortunately – there will be a trap. Villant is about twenty miles from this spot. It is a small village. A short distance away there is a level crossing, with the usual small house in which lives the man who opens and shuts the gates. This house will he converted into a military post. The level-crossing gates will be shut. When the cyclists arrive there they will be stopped, examined and questioned. You see how impossible it is to go on. The scheme will be exposed immediately when it is discovered that the cyclists cannot even speak French.'

'Who is going to discover that?'

'The Germans at the post, of course.'

'And what do you think our fellows will be doing while the Germans are making this discovery – standing like a lot of sheep waiting for the butcher to drive them to the slaughter-house? My dear general, these men are commandos.'

'But they will not be armed.'

'Maybe not, but they've got hands, and you'd be surprised what they can do with them. But it may not come to that. *We* shall be armed, and we may be there first. How many Nazis will man this post?'

'We do not know – not many, probably, since the Nazis will hardly expect violence so near to Paris. If our information is correct it will be a small mobile unit from St. Armand, under the command of Hauptmann Hausmayer – a man of vile temper often chosen for such work.'

'The great thing in war is to give the enemy what he doesn't expect. On this occasion we shall do that, I trust, *Monsieur le General*. The scheme *must* go through.'

'Why not postpone it until things settle down?'

'Because the bombers will come, and I have no way of stopping them. Unless the prisoners are brought out of the works they are likely to be killed by our own bombs. That will not do. Whatever happens afterwards, the prisoners must be removed.'

Monsieur Rouge concurred, but he still looked worried.

'Let us go ahead and deal with trouble when we meet it,' suggested Gimlet.

'Very well, *capitaine*. Everything is in order. The engineers are standing by to break through the final section of the tunnel. The explosive charges are in place, ready to be fired when the prisoners have made their escape. We hope that the explosion will be thought to be a bomb dropped by the bombers, so that it will not be investigated. You understand that whatever else happens the tunnel must be destroyed rather than there should be a risk of it being discovered?'

'Of course. Let us meet at the head of the tunnel a few minutes before eight, with the engineers and mechanics at hand to strike off the shackles of any prisoners who may be so handicapped.'

'I shall be there,' answered Monsieur Rouge. He saluted and departed.

CHAPTER ELEVEN

Zero Hour

$\mathbf{A}$t a quarter to eight, with an engineer guide leading the way, accompanied by Monsieur Rouge, Felix and Dominique, Gimlet and his small party proceeded to the head of the tunnel. It bore no resemblance to the sewer system, being no more than a narrow passage driven through the bare earth, as if it might have been a giant rabbit burrow, although here and there, where faults in the subsoil made it necessary, the roof was shored up with timbers.

It was of some length – nearly a quarter of a mile, Cub estimated – and had its entrance in one of the several dressing rooms of a gymnasium. This building had been selected, Monsieur Rouge said, because, as well as being convenient, it was connected with the sewer. It was also the headquarters of a cycle racing club. A large assembly of cycles, therefore, would not invoke comment among the neighbours; or arouse the suspicions of the Nazis. The cycles were there, more than a hundred of them, with suitable racing kit, and sandbags, in which the prisoners were to carry their uniforms when they changed; and Cub marvelled at the new spirit that was rising in France, wherein men were willing to risk losing or lending their precious cycles, which could not be replaced, to strangers.

The commandos were equipped for their work. In addition to normal small arms and grenades, Copper and Trapper each carried a Sten gun and wire cutters. Thrust through his belt Copper also carried a short iron bar, bent and flattened at one end, which he called a 'jemmy.' It was, in fact, an improvised copy of the tool much favoured by burglars. Its purpose was to force the door of the prison hut should the key not be forthcoming. Balancing it in his hand Copper asserted that it would open anything.

The tunnel opened out at its head, forming a rough compartment some six feet high. In it a number of men, specialists in their trades, had assembled. All were quiet and serious, aware of the deadly peril in which the night's work would place them. There were two civil engineers, highly paid consultants in private life, who had been responsible for the construction of the tunnel. As yet they had no proof, but they were confident that the head of the tunnel was where they intended it should be – below the inside of the barbed-wire enclosure in which the prison hut was situated. There was also in attendance a blacksmith with a portable anvil, and a fitter with his tools, to remove the shackles from any prisoner who wore them.

Other conspirators remained in the gymnasium – one man, who spoke English fluently, to inform the prisoners when they arrived of what was happening, and two expert cyclists who were to lead the 'race.' They knew every inch of the road between the gymnasium and Rouen, having competed in many races. In the gymnasium yard stood the disguised van in which, if petrol could be obtained, Dominique would drive the commandos to the old cloth mill at Claire. Much depended on this petrol, for it was Gimlet's intention to get to the Nazi trap, the level crossing at Villant, and 'liquidate' it before the cyclists arrived.

Darkness had fallen. There was as yet no moon, but it was starlight, with little cloud and no threat of rain. This was important, for, as Gimlet remarked, weather conditions could play a vital part in the flying operations. Should the weather deteriorate, restricting visibility, the pilots might have difficulty in finding the mill, where they were to drop equipment, and in the landing operations on the enemy airfield at Rambours.

At a few minutes before eight, after looking at his watch, Gimlet turned to Monsieur Rouge and said: 'I think the sappers might make a start.'

Monsieur Rouge spoke to the engineers, who, requesting the others to stand aside, put together a clumsy but efficient wooden platform, large enough for three or four men to stand on together. Mounting this, they began driving upwards in a cavity where this work had been begun. Dirt and stones fell in a steady shower, and after a while the platform was raised higher. Very soon Cub could only see the legs of the men who were working. As they went higher they worked with more caution, sometimes pausing to listen. At last there was a significant silence. The men descended.

'*Voilà*! *messieurs*,' said one in a low voice. 'We are in the compound, correct to a metre.'

'Good work,' said Gimlet.

The engineer shrugged. 'When one has dug tunnels through mountains, a little hole like this is a simple matter. All is quiet.'

'How far are we from the prison hut?'

'Thirty paces, *monsieur*.'

Monsieur Rouge faced Gimlet and saluted. 'It is now for you to proceed, *capitaine*. We shall wait here. You understand that should you fail, or should the plan miscarry, you may not be able to return this way? The tunnel will be blown up, to prevent pursuit from reaching the gymnasium.'

Gimlet nodded. 'Quite right. At all costs the Underground must be protected.' He turned to his companions. 'You all know what we have to do. If I'm knocked out, ignore me; Copper will take over and carry on. Is that clear?'

'Aye aye, sir,' murmured Copper.

'Stand fast while I have a look round.'

In dead silence Gimlet mounted the platform. For perhaps a minute he remained motionless. Cub, standing below, could see a solitary star; it was like looking up from the bottom of a manhole. Then Gimlet descended and asked the engineers to enlarge the hole a trifle. This occupied only two minutes, for the surface crust broke away easily. The work done, Gimlet made a sign to the others to follow him and remounted the platform. He went no farther. Cub found himself with his head projecting above the ground in an extensive gravelled area, square in shape, which reminded him of a school playground. Its boundary, a thickly stranded barbed-wire fence, could just be discerned. At one point it was broken by a small box-like building, which Cub knew from the plan was the guard-house. He could not see the sentry, who presumably was standing at the far side of the hut, near which was the gate that gave access to the prison camp. There was a larger building near at hand, a long low structure about thirty yards distant. Not a light showed. All was silent.

'Get your bearings,' whispered Gimlet. 'The long building in front of us is the dormitory where our fellows are locked up. A sentry is patrolling it – he's round the back now. That small building over there is the guard-hut; we don't know how many men are in it, but there shouldn't be more than half a dozen at most. If it was only a matter of getting the prisoners away there would be no need for us to bother with them, but we've got to go out to the works, and we daren't leave enemy troops in our rear to cut off our retreat. Our first job is to get the prisoners out, and we shall have to do it without any noise. That line of buildings outside the wire, like a row of hangars, is the main works. The secret workshop is at the eastern end – somewhere about there.' Gimlet pointed. 'The manager's house is close by it. We shall be going there presently – or rather to the garage – for petrol. Well, it's time we were moving. Trapper, you go first and see what you can do about that sentry. He should come into sight in about thirty seconds, round the right-hand end of the dormitory.'

Trapper gave his Sten gun to Copper to hold, drew himself up to ground level, wormed his way out and lay flat. He reached back for the Sten, drew it beside him, and, still flat on the ground, merged into the darkness. The only sign of him was a slight hump that might have been an irregularity in the ground. Gimlet followed. Copper went next. Striving to steady his racing pulses, Cub drew himself up and lay flat. The show had begun. What had gone before was only the prelude. The events of the next half-hour, regardless of Gimlet's meticulous planning, were largely in the hands of the fickle gods who control the fortunes of war. Only one thing was certain. There could be no turning back.

The drama opened, as Cub expected it would, when the German sentry appeared at the end of the prisoners' hutment. His deportment was that of ninety-nine sentries out of a hundred when the firing line is far away, and, consequently, danger is not seriously considered. The man had his rifle at the slope, but he carried it carelessly, loosely, and walked in the manner of one who is bored by the dull routine of his job. Sometimes he stopped, and for want of any other entertainment gazed at the stars. Once he yawned loudly before walking on. In a way, while unpardonable, this attitude was understandable. The man's job was to keep the prisoners from getting out. It probably never occurred to him that there might be people outside anxious to get in. It is likely that his thoughts were far away – the thoughts of sentries often are. However that may be, about halfway along the hut he stopped, and leaning his rifle against the boards, stood gazing at some distant object.

Cub saw the hump that he knew was Trapper take shape. It became a kneeling figure. There was a vibrant *whang*; a thud; a gasp. Crouching low, Trapper ran forward, his knife swishing from its sheath. He did not need it. The sentry was dead, with an arrow through his heart, never knowing what had killed him. This Cub saw when, with Gimlet and Copper, he reached the hut.

Keeping close in the black shadow of the hutment they turned and stared at the guard-house, now about sixty yards distant, to confirm that their entry had not been observed. The silhouette of the sentry on duty at the gate could just be seen. He was walking to and fro across the gateway in a manner from which it was clear that he had no suspicion that anything was wrong.

'All right, Copper. See what you can do with that door,' ordered Gimlet.

Copper produced his jemmy. Inserting the thin end between the door and the jamb he put his weight on the iron. Greater and greater became the strain. The door creaked. The jemmy began to bend. Then, with a sharp, rending crack, the lock tore out and the door flew open.

Cub held his breath, for he felt sure that the sentry at the gate must have heard the noise. And apparently he did, for advancing a few steps he called, but without alarm: 'What are you doing, Fritz?'

Gimlet answered, 'Nothing. Sounded like one of the *Englanders* falling out of bed.' He laughed shortly.

The sentry laughed too, and walked back to his post.

'He'll be laughing the other side of his mug presently,' growled Copper.

While this brief conversation was going on there had been a certain amount of movement inside the dormitory. A voice, rich with trans-Atlantic brogue, drawled, 'What's the joke, Heinie?'

'Shut up and keep still,' snapped Gimlet, in English.

They went in. Gimlet closed the door. 'Listen, everybody,' he said tersely. 'We're commandos. Don't make a sound. Are you listening?'

A low chorus of voices answered 'Yes.' A single voice, thin with suppressed excitement, added, 'Cor lumme! It's Gimlet himself.'

'Are there any Kittens here?' queried Gimlet.

'Yes, sir,' came from several places.

'What about a light?'

'The switch is just inside the door, sir.'

'Can the light be seen from the outside?'

'No, sir – the hut's blacked out.'

Gimlet switched on the light, revealing a number of men in various stages of undress. 'Who's the senior N.C.O.?' he demanded.

A powerfully-built middle-aged man stepped forward. 'I am, sor. Sergeant-Major Macready,' came in a thick northern burr.

'Good. Listen, boys,' went on Gimlet, raising his voice a trifle. 'We've come to get you out of this. Slip into your battle rags and make it snappy. Our bombers are due in twenty minutes. Is anyone not able to walk?'

'We're all fit men, sor,' said the sergeant-major. 'Twenty-two men are wearing leg shackles.'

'The others will have to help them.'

'Yes, sor.'

'Go to it. We don't want any noise. No talking.'

There was a rush to get dressed.

Gimlet turned to Trapper. 'Stay here until the party is ready to move off, then get everyone to the tunnel. You will remain outside the entrance to cover our retreat in case we need support.'

'Very good, sir.'

Gimlet spoke to the sergeant-major. 'Keep your fellows together. As soon as they're ready to go, follow this man. You're going out through a tunnel. When you get to it you'll be told what to do by some members of the French Underground. Obey their orders. Presently you will be leaving Paris. Try to keep at the head of the party so that I shall know where to find you when I come along.'

'Yes, sor,' answered the Scot.

'Switch the light off, Trapper, while we go out, and shut the door behind us.'

The light was switched off.

Gimlet, with Copper and Cub, went out. Copper carried his Sten gun at the ready, but he did not need it. All was quiet.

'We'll tackle the guard-hut next,' said Gimlet. 'If we keep the hut between us and the sentry he won't see us. If he shows up on either side, drop flat. Come on – single file.'

Walking on their toes they made straight for the hut. There was no cover. Once, when the sentry appeared, they dropped, and lay still for about a minute. Then the sentry moved back behind the hut. They went on, and did not stop again until they were close against the wooden timbers of the hut, which was inside the wire. Advancing slowly and with infinite caution to the corner, it became possible to see that the barbed-wire obstacle that was used to fill the gateway stood slightly open, sufficient to permit the passage of one man at a time. The sentry, rifle at the slope, was twelve or fifteen yards distant, still walking away, slowly, to the limit of his beat. From within the hut came a low murmur of voices.

Cupping his hands round Copper's ear, Gimlet breathed: 'We've got to get this sentry before the boys start going across to the tunnel. Handle him, but no noise.'

Copper nodded, and moved forward to the corner of the hut.

The sentry had turned and was now coming back, still at the same pace. Each step occupied a second of time, and each second seemed to screw Cub's nerves a little tighter. The German, unaware of his peril, reached the hut. He turned about and 'ordered' his rifle. As the butt thudded on the ground Copper glided forward. Silent though he was, the sentry evidently heard something. Or he may have turned to enter the hut. Anyway, he turned; but by that time Copper was within striking distance. His fist flew out, and behind the punch was the skill, the force and timing, that can only be acquired, even by professional boxers, by long practice. His fist took the man on the jaw with a shattering crack that made Cub wince. He had heard the sound before. It always made him wince. It sounded frightful, he thought.

Copper reappeared dragging the unconscious sentry. He dropped the body, as if it might have been a sack of potatoes, at Gimlet's feet. 'Here you are, sir,' he remarked nonchalantly.

'How long will he be asleep, do you think?'

Copper's fist took the man on the jaw with a shattering crack.

'A fair time, sir, I should say,' replied Copper. 'I 'ad to 'it 'im 'ard, pore blighter.'

'Bring him along,' ordered Gimlet. 'Now for the fellows in the hut.'

'What are we going to do with them, sir – mop 'em up?' queried Copper.

'Not if it can be prevented. That would be a bit too much like murder,' decided Gimlet. 'I hope you'll be able to take care of them while Cub and I complete the operation. Then we'll lock them in and leave them to it.'

'They'll kick up a noise if we leave them, sir.'

'By the time we leave them there will probably be plenty of noise, anyway,' answered Gimlet evenly. 'Come on. Cub, as soon as we're inside, shut the door. We don't want any light showing.'

'Yes, sir.'

Revolver in hand, Gimlet led the way to the door. He reached for the knob. It turned. He opened the door an inch. The sound of voices swelled in volume, like a radio turned up. Then he pushed the door wide open, and with the same movement stepped inside. 'Keep still and don't make a sound,' he rapped out, in German.

There were five men in the guard-room – a sergeant, two others sitting at a small table playing cards, and two men lying in their bunks. The sergeant stood with his back to a small iron stove, arms folded, watching the card players. Weapons and equipment hung on a rack just inside the door.

When the commandos entered none of the Nazis moved. Their first reactions were natural enough. Their eyes opened wide. Their faces paled. The sergeant's jaw sagged. One of the card players half rose in his chair.

Gimlet's revolver covered him, and he sank back. Cub closed the door, and Copper deposited the unconscious sentry on the floor.

'One sound and you die,' said Gimlet with cold earnestness. 'Cub, is the key inside the lock?'

Cub looked. 'No, sir.'

Gimlet addressed the sergeant. 'Where's the key?'

The sergeant moved his lips. He seemed to be recovering from the first stunning shock. 'It isn't here.'

'You ask him, Copper,' invited Gimlet.

289

Copper stepped forward. His huge fist closed over the collar of the German's tunic and screwed it into a ball. He thrust his face forward, jaw belligerent. 'You 'eard 'im. Where is it, chum?' he questioned in a slow, deep voice.

Gimlet repeated the question in German.

The sergeant lost his nerve. 'The officer has it.'

Gimlet realized that this might be true. 'Where is the officer?'

'I don't know.'

'What time does he come round?'

The sergeant's eyes flashed to a cheap clock that hung on the wall. 'Any time, now,' he answered.

'Search him, Copper,' ordered Gimlet.

Copper's hands went through the sergeant's pockets. The key was not there.

'All right. We mustn't waste any more time,' asserted Gimlet. 'Copper, take care of this bunch. We'll collect you on the way back. Come on, Cub.'

Gimlet went out. Cub followed. Everything was still quiet. Looking across the barbed-wire enclosure it was possible to see the prisoners streaming towards the tunnel, where they disappeared like rabbits into a burrow. Trapper was standing by, watching.

'Things are going nicely,' remarked Gimlet. 'Let's see about finding some petrol.'

CHAPTER TWELVE

The Raid

Gimlet took a pace forward, to move off, but Cub caught him by the arm.

'Just a minute, sir,' he said tersely. 'Who's this coming – look, over to the right.'

Gimlet backed swiftly to the wall of the hut, staring in the direction indicated. Two figures had appeared, but beyond the fact that they marched in military style they were as yet too far away for details to be made out. They were coming directly towards the guard-hut, which, in the absence of other buildings, was obviously their objective.

It did not take Gimlet long to realize who they were. 'It's the orderly officer and the senior N.C.O. of the guard,' he announced. 'He's chosen a bad time to make his round. We'll wait here. Dear – dear … won't they be surprised to see us!'

Cub looked across the barbed-wire enclosure and saw prisoners streaming from the dormitory to the tunnel, at the entrance of which there was quite a group waiting to enter. It struck him that the approaching Germans could hardly fail to see what was going on, and he made a remark to that effect. Hardly had the words left his lips when, with a shout, the Germans broke into a run.

'This, I fancy, is where the balloon goes up,' said Gimlet quietly. 'Stand fast.'

At first it struck Cub as funny that the two Nazis should run straight towards them; yet it was natural enough, he perceived, that they should make for the hut, to turn out the guard.

'On second thoughts we had better warn Copper that there may be a

291

fracas,' decided Gimlet. 'Moreover, there may be some noise, and if we are inside it is less likely to be heard.'

'Those fellows will see the light when we go in,' Cub pointed out.

'They'll suppose we are sentries.' Gimlet laughed softly. 'One thing we can be sure of – they will not suppose we are what we are.'

They went inside, leaving the door closed, but not latched. The situation was precisely as they had last seen it. Copper, chewing a dead matchstalk, was covering the Germans, watching them with steady, pensive eyes.

'There are visitors on the way,' Gimlet told him. 'I think it's an orderly officer and an N.C.O. Leave them to me. You keep your eyes on these fellows.'

Copper spat out the matchstalk. 'Aye aye, sir.'

The German officer and his orderly sergeant – as the other turned out to be – did not walk into the guard-hut. They ran in, the officer in front, shouting something about *Englanders*.

Gimlet was standing just inside the door, a little to one side, gun ready. As soon as the Germans were over the threshold he kicked the door shut, and standing with his back to it, said crisply: 'Hands up – and keep them up. Cub, take their weapons.'

Cub obeyed. The Germans made no protest. They may have been too surprised. In fact, they looked dazed with shock, which in the circumstances was understandable. The spectacle of three uniformed British commandos, fully armed, must have been hard to believe.

Gimlet waved them back against the stove in line with the sergeant of the guard, and there they stood, still staring, as men might stare at an apparition. The officer's lips moved, but no sound came.

Gimlet held out a hand. 'The key of the hut,' he said curtly.

The German did not move.

'The key!' snapped Gimlet, with an edge on his voice.

The officer started violently, put his hand in his pocket and passed the key without a word. Gimlet tossed it to Copper. 'When the time comes for you to leave the hut, lock them in. Meanwhile, if they try any funny stuff, let them have it.'

'Aye aye, sir,' acknowledged Copper imperturbably. His expression did not change.

Gimlet beckoned to Cub and they went out. 'That's all right, but it's cost us five minutes,' he observed. 'We shall have to get on faster than this. The garage comes next. Bring that sack of equipment along.'

Comparatively speaking, it was no great distance to their objective, but in the circumstances it was far enough – the best part of two hundred yards. No time could be afforded for reconnaissance, apart from what could be seen as they approached. This was in a direct line, for there was no cover of any sort unless they made a considerable detour and came upon the house from the rear. The building was a black silhouette, unbroken by a light of any sort. All was quiet. The garage, a flat-roofed building detached from the house, was less than twenty yards away, and Cub was just congratulating himself that everything was going fine, that the sortie was going to be easy, when a sound broke the silence, one that put a different complexion on the situation and at the same time gave his nerves a jolt, so unexpected and so sharp was it. It was the unmistakable slam of a car door. He stopped abruptly, naturally, as did Gimlet. Staring ahead in the direction from which the sound had come he saw that the garage doors were wide open. The interior of the building was in pitch darkness, so that beyond that nothing could be seen. A second sound followed the first – the usual partner of it. The whirr of a starter. Nothing more was needed to indicate what was happening. Someone was in the garage. He had just got into the car with a journey in view. Who it was did not matter – it would certainly not be a friend.

Cub's common sense told him what would happen next. The headlights would be switched on. Gimlet evidently realized it too, for without a word they moved together, and they moved fast, making a dash to get clear of the garage doors. But they were too late. The lights flicked on, cutting a path through the darkness, so that for two seconds the commandos were revealed as clearly as though it had been daylight. They reached the dark area beyond the twin beams, but Cub knew that they must have been seen by the man in the car. What to do next he did not know, so he waited for his chief to give him a lead. This Gimlet did by running straight at the car – or, rather, into the garage, for all that could actually be seen were the headlights, which only served to make the darkness beyond them the more profound. From this darkness, above the purr of the engine, there now came a slight noise. It was brief – the mere click of a latch and a scuffle, as if someone had moved quickly. Silence followed. Gimlet reached the nearest door of the car and wrenched it open. Cub, following closely, saw that the vehicle was empty.

'He must still be in the garage,' breathed Gimlet. 'Watch your step.' Then, raising his voice, he said sharply in German, 'Come out or we shoot!'

There was no answer.

Crouching, Gimlet worked his way along the side of the car to get to the back of the garage. His torch sliced a wedge of light out of the blackness. The light moved slowly across the floor. It leapt to the rear wall, moved a little way, then stopped, stopped at an open door – an ordinary door. It was open. Further explanation was unnecessary. The man had gone.

'He must have bolted into the house,' said Gimlet.

'He saw us.'

'Of course he did. The game's up. We've got to move fast. We're behind schedule, anyway.'

As the words died on Gimlet's lips, as if to confirm them came the short ring of a telephone bell when the receiver is lifted. It came from the house, and was followed by a man's voice speaking in quick excited sentences.

'That's ripped it,' said Gimlet. 'We came here for petrol. Let's find some and get out.'

In the light of the torch Cub saw a pile of five or six cans. He made a dive for them, only to drop them one after the other with grunts of disgust as he realized from their weight that they were empty. There was a drum of oil, but that they did not need. Gimlet joined in the search. It was brief, and they soon knew the worst. There was no petrol. Gimlet turned back to the car, a big tourer, and looked in the back. 'Nothing doing,' he said, slamming the door. He ran his torch over the outside of the vehicle. It stopped at the running board. On it, clamped in a metal clip, was a fitted petrol can. The seal was intact. The clip was secured by a bolt, held by a nut. Having no tool, Gimlet tried to turn the nut with his fingers, but failed.

'There should be a spanner somewhere in the car,' said Cub.

'We haven't time to look for it,' answered Gimlet.

This was obviously true, for by now there was a considerable amount of noise, of one sort and another, outside, mostly in the direction of the house. Voices were shouting. Doors banged. Footsteps could be heard, running. A weapon cracked and a bullet came through the window of the garage, shattering the glass and ripping through the body of the car. Cub felt the wind of it on his cheek, so close to his head did it pass.

'Get in,' ordered Gimlet.

For a moment Cub did not understand.

'In the car,' said Gimlet shortly. 'It'll be quicker than walking and we may have a chance presently to get that petrol can off. Bring the equipment. We'll lob a cookie in that secret workshop and set a marker for the bombers whatever else happens.'

They scrambled into the car and slammed the doors. The engine was still purring. Cub could see a swastika pennant hanging limply from the radiator cap. Gimlet switched off the lights. The car moved forward, swiftly gathering speed. A bullet struck a metal part with a *whang*, but did no damage. Cub looked at his watch and saw that it was twenty-two minutes past eight. They were well behind schedule. However, he did not comment, for nothing he could say would help matters. He knew that the shooting must have started a general alarm, but nothing could be done about that, either.

Gimlet brought the car to a dry-skid stop flush against the wall, and under one of the windows of a long, low workshop that stood apart from the main assembly line. Painted on the wall in enormous letters, Cub noticed, in German and in French, the words 'Smoking forbidden.' No light showed, from which it seemed reasonable to suppose that work had been suspended in the building. He hoped so, at any rate, for Gimlet climbed on to the roof of the car, and without hesitation smashed the glass out of the window with the butt of his gun.

'Pass the bag,' he ordered.

Cub handed up the sack, and followed it. Gimlet's torch was probing the interior of the shed, but all that could be seen was a long test bench on which rested some laboratory equipment and a number of large glass jars.

'I should say they're experimenting with high-octane petrol,' remarked Gimlet, selecting some delayed-action grenades from his sack.

'There's a notice on the wall says no smoking,' said Cub.

Gimlet's torch was probing the interior of the shed.

'That doesn't apply to us,' returned Gimlet, with a suspicion of humour in his voice.

Cub was to remember this remark.

'Never mind me; keep a look-out, and stop anybody who tries to inter-fere,' continued Gimlet.

Turning, Cub faced a scene in which there were now several lights and a good deal of activity. Men were running about. Orders were being shouted, but in a way that suggested that although an alarm had been given, no one knew quite what the fuss was about. A hooter started hooting in short staccato blasts. Behind him Cub could hear Gimlet throwing things into the workshop. Then, to add a final touch, a siren wailed its hideous warning. In a few seconds all the Paris sirens were howling.

'The bombers are coming, sir,' he said, taking a quick shot at a man who came running along the side of the building towards the car.

'So I hear,' answered Gimlet evenly. 'There should be quite a noise here presently – yes, quite a noise. Pity we can't stay to watch. All right. That's all. Get back in the car. We'll get along.'

As Cub jumped down a machine gun started stuttering and a line of tracer bullets leapt from the front of the guard-hut towards the main gates of the works. Glancing, he saw that they were open. Headlights, of cars or motor-cycles, were pouring in.

'That sounds like Copper, warming up his gun,' remarked Gimlet, as he joined Cub in the car. He looked at his watch. 'By gad! It's turned half past. We're cutting it fine.'

'A bit too fine,' muttered Cub in a voice stiff with anxiety, for he could now hear the drone of the approaching bombers, a drone that grew relentlessly in volume, sinister, as inexorable as death itself. Punctuating the drone was the coughing and grunting of flak and the crackle of small arms. Lights flashed in the air as well as on the ground. Bullets were flying in all directions.

'Things are certainly beginning to hum,' said Gimlet, as he sent the car racing across the short distance separating them from the guard-hut.

Copper was squatting outside, firing short bursts at selected targets. From time to time he sent a burst into the secret workshop, from which crimson smoke was now billowing.

'Our lads upstairs should have no difficulty in seeing that, I think,' observed Gimlet as they got out of the car. To Copper he said, 'What about your prisoners?'

'I locked 'em in, sir, so I could come out and see what was cookin',' answered Copper.

'I see. Come here and see if you can unscrew this nut.' Gimlet pointed at the clip holding the petrol can.

Copper rose to his feet. As he did so there was a blinding flash, and an explosion of such violence that Cub was hurled backwards by the blast into the barbed-wire fence. For a few seconds he was too stunned to grasp what had happened, but in a vague sort of way he assumed that the bombers had arrived, and had started to unload. But as he unhooked himself from the wire he heard Copper say: 'Blimey! sir, what a beauty. What did you put in that one?'

'It wasn't what I put in it. It must have been something in the hut,' asserted Gimlet.

Looking across the open space Cub saw that the secret workshop was no longer there. A rain of burning debris was dropping on the place where it had been.

'Never mind about that – get this petrol can off,' said Gimlet to Copper. 'We've only two minutes left.'

Copper seized the nut between finger and thumb. Nothing happened. 'So you'd be awkward, would you?' he growled, and seized the nut for a fresh effort.

To Cub, this standing by doing nothing while Copper tried to unscrew the nut was the most nerve-racking part of the operation. All around them pandemonium reigned. The bombers were roaring almost overhead. Flak was lacerating the sky. Searchlights thrust waving fingers at the stars. Tracer shells cut curious curves across the dome of heaven. It was almost as light as day. Looking across the barbed-wire enclosure he could see Trapper standing alone at the entrance of the tunnel. Another figure appeared out of the ground. He recognized Dominique. Both of them started running towards the guard-hut.

'Here comes Trapper, sir,' he warned.

Gimlet looked round, and as he did so a sheet of flame leapt up behind the running figures, leaving a pillar of smoke hanging in the air. Again came the roar of an explosion.

'What the deuce was that?' muttered Gimlet.

Again Cub thought it must be a bomb from the first of the bombers.

Gimlet turned to Copper, still struggling with the petrol can. 'Pack up,' he said. 'We shall have to leave it. Come on.'

Trapper dashed up. 'The tunnel's gone,' he announced.

'Gone? What the devil are you talking about?' snapped Gimlet.

'Blown up, sir.'

Cub felt his stomach going down like a lift.

'*Monsieur*, it was the water,' cried Dominique. 'Monsieur Rouge sends me to tell you that you cannot pass.'

'Water?'

'There is an explosion,' gabbled Dominique. 'The earth shakes. It falls. A water main bursts. The tunnel is full of water. Monsieur Rouge cannot wait, or he is drowned. He says the tunnel must go. *Voilà*! The charge is fired.'

'That must have been the workshop going up, what bust the water main,' observed Copper dispassionately. 'Means we're shut out – or shut in, I dunno which.'

'Did the prisoners get clear?' Gimlet asked Dominique.

'But yes, *monsieur*.'

It took Cub a minute to realize the enormity of the disaster. Why did something always have to go wrong with military operations he thought bitterly. Something had certainly gone wrong this time. Yet no one could be blamed, for neither the explosion in the workshop, nor the result of it, could have been foreseen.

'What next, sir?' asked Copper.

The answer came from the sky, and it came with the shrill crescendo wail of falling bombs.

Trapper clicked his tongue. 'Here come the cookies,' he announced.

'Into the car, everybody,' ordered Gimlet. 'There's only one way out now, and that's through the main gate. That's the way we go. I'll drive. Dominique, sit next to me. I shall need a guide when we're out – Copper – Trapper, take the side windows and deal with any opposition. Look out! Duck!'

They all went flat, and an instant later, with a roar like thunder, the first stick of bombs straddled the works. The earth rocked. Blast swept the scene like a typhoon. The car nearly went over. There was a general scramble to get into it. The doors slammed, but such was the roar overhead that the sound was no more than the clicking of mousetraps. The car leapt forward into a hail of incendiaries. Fortunately, none touched it, and it raced on through a blinding glare, swerving wildly to miss the areas of fire. Two motor-cyclists shot out from behind a building and came tearing towards the car. Copper's Sten gun chattered and they crashed. There were others, but none attempted to interfere with the car. Indeed, although several Nazis were seen, they were more concerned with getting away from what was arriving overhead than anything else, for by this time, as Cub realized, the bombers' objective was no longer in doubt. Again the air was filled with the scream of bombs. When they burst, again the car, heavily loaded though it was, nearly went over. It ran on two wheels for some distance, and only Gimlet's experience as a racing driver prevented catastrophe. All around flames were leaping up.

'Blimey! Talk about falling backwards through 'ell,' muttered Copper. 'If my old Ma—'

'Don't tell us,' rasped Trapper.

'What's the matter with you?' snorted Copper.

'I'm scared stiff.'

Cub was glad to learn that someone else besides himself was scared stiff.

The car shot through the main gates at a speed which caused him to catch his breath. They stood wide open. No one attempted to stop it. In fact, not a soul was in sight. Cub was not surprised. From behind came a roar, a persistent roar, as if the earth itself was falling to pieces. Debris rained. Several pieces crashed on the roof of the car, without affecting it. Dominique's face was buried in his hands.

'Here, you, wake up and show me the way to the gymnasium,' said Gimlet.

'I was not asleep, *monsieur*,' said Dominique in a dull voice.

'Ho! I'll bet 'e wasn't,' put in Copper.

'Next turning to the right,' said Dominique.

Copper nudged Cub playfully in the ribs. 'I'll bet he'll think twice before he hooks up again with commandos,' he chuckled. 'My oath he will.'

'So shall I,' said Cub grimly.

CHAPTER THIRTEEN

Cub Springs the Trap

With Dominique saying, ' Left ... right ... left,' like a vocal puppet, the car sped on through abandoned streets. During the drive, which lasted only a few minutes, Cub did not see a single living soul. Not that this was any matter for wonder; with a cascade blitz in full swing on the threshold of the city the civil population at least would take cover. All anti-aircraft defences were in action, and flame flashed against a sky that glowed as though it might have been red hot, like a blacksmith's furnace, from the glare of the blazing motor works. The air quivered and rocked with the dreadful music of modern war. Smoke rolled and spread like the waves of a sluggish sea.

'Well, whatever else 'appens, we've knocked their blinkin' works fer six,' observed Copper, with deep satisfaction.

'We left those Germans locked in the guard-hut,' reminded Cub.

'What abart it?' demanded Copper aggressively. 'They locked our fellers in a barbed-wire cage – didn't they? Would they have cared if they'd been bombed? Not on your blinkin' life. Look what they did to our 'ouse, anyway. 'Bout time they rumbled that two can play at this game, I say – what say you, Trapper, old pal? Am I right?'

'Tch! *I'll* say you're right,' returned Trapper succinctly.

'*Halte!*' cried Dominique. '*Voilà!*' He pointed. '*La bas*. The gymnasium.'

Gimlet brought the car to a stop a few yards short of the building.

'Shall I have another go at gettin' that petrol can off, sir?' suggested Copper.

Gimlet thought for a moment. 'No. There's no point in it now. We shall do better with this car. With that flag on the bonnet we're not so likely to be stopped. Stand fast.' He ran down the path to the gymnasium.

He was away only two or three minutes. When he came back he said: 'The race started before the raid began, so the boys should be well on their way. This devil's din going on behind them should encourage them to make good time. The Underground are evacuating the gymnasium and setting fire to it, to cover up. The Nazis will think an incendiary got it. I said goodbye to Monsieur Rouge for all of us. He's satisfied that we've done a good job. I told him it was thanks to him. All right. Take over, Dominique. Head straight for Claire. Slow down as you pass the head of the column of cyclists – I want to speak to the sergeant-major. Your brother Felix says when you return to Paris go to his house by the Gare de Lyons.'

'They must have been surprised to see you, sir, thinking we were trapped in the works,' remarked Cub.

'They looked a trifle taken aback when I walked in,' admitted Gimlet. 'Go ahead, Dominique. Drive carefully.'

'*Oui, monsieur.*'

The car moved forward, smoothly.

Paris might have been a city of the dead. In the entire trip to the suburbs Cub saw fewer than a dozen persons, and these were civil defence men; taking cover in convenient doorways, they were evidently too taken up with the major event of the night – the raid – to stop a car carrying the Nazi pennant. The only traffic was fire engines, tearing towards the conflagration, and as they raced on through deserted boulevards Cub appreciated how right Gimlet had been when he predicted that the raid would prove a valuable ally. The bombers still droned overhead. Unmolested, the car ran on through the squalid north-western suburbs which, reluctantly it seemed, at length gave way to open countryside.

'You know the level crossing at Villant?' Gimlet asked Dominique.[*]

'*Oui, monsieur.* It is just beyond the village.'

'There should be a warning notice for motorists at a hundred metres.'

---

[*] In France it is customary for road danger signals to show the distance to the object – school, dangerous turning, level crossing, or whatever it may be.

'*Oui, monsieur.*'

'Stop when you come to it.'

'*Oui, monsieur.*'

Soon after this they caught up with the tail end of the 'race.' As the car overtook the cyclists Copper leaned out and offered words of encouragement and advice. Occasionally he recognized a Kitten, and exchanged enthusiastic greetings with him, at the same time keeping Trapper informed as to the identity of the rider. Once – for the first time in the operation – he got really excited. 'Blimey! There's Shorty Hughes – or else his ghost!' he cried. 'Watcher, Shorty!' he hailed. 'What are yer doin' on that grid? They told me you was dead as spam, in the casino at Dieppe.'

'Indeed to goodness I am,' returned Shorty. 'I'm just looking round to see how you get on without me, look you. How about getting out and letting me have a ride, you big flatfoot?'

The progress of the car put a stop to this interesting but unprofitable conversation. The cyclists were strung out for a distance of half a mile, and when the head of the column was reached Dominique slowed down to the same speed so that Gimlet could speak to Sergeant-Major Macready, and the French guide who rode beside him. He told them of the trap ahead, and warned them to stop at the level-crossing sign, unless they got a signal that it was safe to proceed. The car went on again for about ten minutes, when Dominique, slowing down and calling attention to a red light in the road ahead, said: '*Voilà, monsieur*! The crossing. The gates are shut.'

'Pull into the side of the road and stop,' ordered Gimlet.

''Ere we go again,' sighed Copper.

The car stopped. Overhead the bombers were droning home.

Gimlet turned to those behind. 'We'd better have a look at this crossing before we go any farther. Our boys are only a mile or two behind, so we can't afford much time. Monsieur Rouge said that according to Paleface the post was manned by a small mobile unit from St. Armand, under a fellow named Hausmayer – but a lot depends on what he calls small. Cub, you've had a lot of practice at this sort of thing; would you like to run along and cast an eye over the set-up?'

'Certainly, sir.'

'Don't take any chances and be as quick as you can.'

'Yes, sir.'

Cub got out of the car, closed the door quietly, and making for the hedge which lined the road, moved quickly but quietly towards a cottage that stood beside the crossing, and in normal times was occupied by the gate-keeper. Any slight noise that he made was smothered by the drone of the bombers. It occurred to him that this factor should help him in another way; it seemed likely that the entire post would have assembled to watch the sky for possible combats with night fighters, and if the Germans were watching the sky they would not be paying much attention to the road. In these assumptions he was right, but he was not prepared for the sight that met his gaze when, getting through the hedge and skirting the tiny garden of the cottage, he dropped flat and wormed his way forward until he could see the railway line. The first thing he saw was a double line of motor-cycles, on their stands, parked beside the track. Running his eyes over them he counted forty-eight, which meant that there must be that number of enemy troops there. This shook him more than a little, for he knew that Gimlet did not expect anything like that number. Rising a little, he could see the troops assembled in a little crowd, without any sort of order, on the line in front of the cottage. As he expected, their faces were turned upwards. From them came a buzz of conversation. This was really all he needed to know, but he paused for a moment to make a survey of the cottage before retiring. He ran the last forty yards to the car.

'Well?' greeted Gimlet.

There are at least forty-eight men of a motor-cycle unit,' informed Cub.

Gimlet started. '*How* many?'

'I counted forty-eight motor-cycles parked beside the track. The men are standing in a bunch near the gate.'

'Good Lord!' Gimlet's tone of voice expressed his surprise and concern. 'We can't handle that lot – and get away with it.'

'I don't see why not, sir,' growled Copper.

'I do,' put in Cub. 'The moment we started anything someone would go to the phone and report what was going on. That would bring reinforcements.'

'So the cottage is on the phone?' queried Gimlet.

'Yes, sir. I saw the wire.'

'That makes it worse,' rejoined Gimlet. 'Either Paleface was misinformed or else he lied. This is a bigger show than an ordinary police trap. Of course, Bussemann may have increased the scope of the thing after the affair at the Gare St. Lazare.'

'May I make a suggestion, sir?' requested Cub.

'I'd be glad of one.'

'Why not give the post a miss altogether? I mean, there's no reason why the cyclists should use the level crossing. Their racing bikes weigh practically nothing. Our chaps could dismount here, pick up their bikes, walk across the fields for, say, a quarter of a mile, cross the railway line, and then strike diagonally to hit the road well beyond the crossing.'

'Blimey! It's simple,' muttered Copper.

Gimlet shook his head. 'No. Sorry, Cub, but that won't do. This race must end at Rouen. What do you suppose would happen when the French cyclists arrived at the winning post without having gone through this gate? The Nazis aren't fools. They would know that the trap had been deliberately avoided, and they wouldn't be long discovering that. They would probably discover it even before the cyclists got to Rouen. The Frenchmen who are taking over the bikes would be questioned. What possible reason could they give for leaving the road? None. The Nazis would guess what had happened and shoot the lot of them. No, we can't let the Underground down like that.'

'I see that now, sir,' agreed Cub.

'My original idea was for us to storm the post, so that the show would be attributed to British commandos – nothing to do with the race. But I did not expect to have to deal with more than half a dozen men.'

'Why not wait for the boys to arrive, and then attack the post in force?' suggested Trapper.

'That won't do either,' declared Gimlet. 'At all cost the cyclists must be kept out of this. That phone is the snag. One word to Paris that the post was being attacked, and the cyclists were going through, and the game will be up. Nazi troops would converge on the area and everyone would be wiped out, long before we could get to the mill, let alone the aerodrome. I see nothing else for it but a legitimate commando attack on the post, although four against forty-eight is a pretty tall order, even taking into account the advantage of surprise.'

'Just a minute, sir, before we take on anything as desperate as that,' demurred Cub. 'Let's try a ruse first, *à la* Fleas.'

'Ruse?'

'Yes, sir. You see, when I was with the Fleas we had to rely all the time on cunning. We had no weapons to fight battles, although as a matter of fact, from what I've seen of the Germans, it's easier to trick them than fight them. Their discipline is marvellous, so marvellous that it never occurs to them to question an order from a senior officer – you know that, sir. The Fleas always tried to take advantage of that, and we usually got away with it. If my ruse fails we can always fall back on fighting.'

'What's the ruse?'

'Simply this. You go back to the public call box outside the village post office and ring up Hauptmann von Hausmayer, who's in charge at the level crossing, and say that you are Bussemann, speaking from Paris. Or if you can't imitate Bussemann's voice say you are Major somebody or other, any senior rank, speaking for Bussemann. Say that owing to the raid the race was cancelled. That shouldn't be hard to believe. They must have heard the din from here, and I'll bet anything Hausmayer will believe it. You simply tell him to pack up, return to barracks, and stand by for orders. The Nazis will depart, leaving everything quiet for the boys to go through. It may be hours before they discover the trick.'

'Strewth! For a nipper you certainly get bright ideas,' asserted Copper, in a voice of astonishment.

'I see a snag,' said Gimlet. 'Suppose they do pack up – and come this way. They'll run straight into the race.'

'Monsieur Rouge said the troops were from St. Armand. That's the other way.'

'*Oui. C'est ça,*' confirmed Dominique.

'It sounds too good to be true, but I'll try it,' declared Gimlet.

'All you stand to lose is a few minutes of time,' averred Cub.

306

'If this comes off I'll see you get a stripe on your sleeve,' promised Gimlet.

'And if it don't I'll see you get one across the backside of your pants,' said Copper, grinning.

'Back the car, Dominique,' ordered Gimlet.

The car backed slowly down the road until it was opposite the call box. Gimlet got out. 'Stop the cyclists if they get here before I'm back,' he commanded, and he went on to the phone.

A minute passed ... two minutes. The head of the column of cyclists appeared. Copper jumped out and held up his arms. ''Arf a mo, sergeant-major,' he said. 'Gimlet's orders are that you stand fast while we clear up a spot of trouble. Tell the boys to dismount where they are, to stop 'em piling up in a mob. No talking.'

Gimlet reappeared. He was smiling. 'Swallowed it, hook, line and sinker,' he said, tersely. 'Hark!'

From the darkness ahead came the throb and clatter of motor-cycles being started up.

'If they do come this way we're goin' ter 'ave a picnic,' asserted Copper, holding his gun forward to cover the road.

The throb of motor-cycles grew into a roar, drowning even the drone of the bombers. It rose to a high note, then started to fall. It became a hum. The hum faded. Silence fell.

'Gorne, by thunder!' said Copper in tones of stark incredulity. 'If I wasn't 'ere ter see this with me own eyes I'd never 'ave believed it, s'welp me. Strike me scarlet! If they'd make Cub a general there wouldn't be no need to fight no more crimson battles.'

'Don't chatter so much,' admonished Gimlet. 'Let's push along and see what's happened. The red light has gone, so they must have opened the gate before they left. Sergeant-major, bring the column along slowly. The all-clear signal will be a hoot on the klaxon. We've lost some time, so try to make it up.'

'Yes, sor,' answered the sergeant-major.

The others got back into the car. Dominique drove on, somewhat nervously. Nothing happened. The car bumped slowly over the rails. Still nothing happened. Not a soul was in sight. The car crawled on a little way and Gimlet gave the order to stop.

'We'd better have a look round,' he decided. 'We're not in any hurry – we shall easily overtake the cyclists. Sound the klaxon, Dominique.'

Dominique obliged. Leaving him in the car, the others walked back to the level crossing, across which the race was now proceeding at a good speed.

'What a picture,' murmured Copper as they stood and watched the cyclists go past. 'If I told my old Ma about this she wouldn't believe it.'

'Neither would anyone else,' returned Gimlet drily. 'Let's have a look round.'

A quick inspection of the scene revealed nothing of interest. Inside the deserted cottage the telephone bell was jangling in the persistent manner of such instruments. Gimlet opened the door and picked up the receiver.

'*Jahwohl, Herr Kommandant*,' he said in a gruff voice, and hung up.

'What was that about, if I may ask?' inquired Copper.

'Somebody wanted to know if everything was all right. I told him yes.'

Copper grinned. 'Well, that wasn't no lie.'

'Let's get along.'

They went out. As Trapper closed the door behind them Gimlet stiffened. 'What's this coming?' he muttered. 'Sounds like somebody in a hurry.'

Down the road, from the direction of Paris, came the hum of a powerful car.

'It may be nothing to do with us,' observed Gimlet. 'Stand back close against the wall. We shall soon know.'

They knew within a minute. A car pulled up with a grinding of brakes and two men jumped out. Both wore uniforms. One was hatless – his head was in bandages. Cub recognized Bussemann. Running up the track, to stop within a dozen paces of the commandos, the German shouted furiously, almost hysterically, for Hausmayer. It was clear from his manner that the absence of personnel was beyond his understanding. In fact he said so in a high-pitched voice to his companion, an army major. At the same time it was evident that he did not expect trouble, much less danger.

Gimlet whispered to Copper. 'You get the driver of the car. It mustn't get away.'

Bussemann yelled again for Hauptmann Hausmayer.

Gimlet took a pace forward. ' He isn't here,' he said evenly.

The two Nazis spun round as if they had been shot. Cub distinctly heard them catch their breath when they saw the slim figure standing there. Gimlet's gun was in his hand.

'Hausmayer's gone back to barracks,' he said casually. 'I told him to go.'

'He – I – you – what…?' Bussemann groped for words with conspicuous lack of success.

'You remember me, of course?' continued Gimlet imperturbably. 'You hit me across the face – remember? Well, it's my turn to do the slapping. We're just moving off, and you're coming with us. I know several Frenchmen who will be delighted to have a word with you, now you haven't a company of bayonets to back you up – you thug.'

Bussemann's companion was responsible for what followed. It may be that he thought that with luck he might reach the car. Maybe he thought that in the tricky light the commandos would miss him if they shot at him. What he thought will never be known. He jumped sideways, and ran. Gimlet's gun blazed and he crashed across the rails. Bussemann snatched at the opportunity to grab his automatic, and it might have gone badly with Gimlet had not Trapper fired. He used the Sten gun, which all this time he had been holding in his hands. He fired a burst of five shots. Bussemann spun round, stood upright for a moment, gasping, then dropped like a coat falling from a peg. He did not move again.

'Thanks, Trapper,' said Gimlet quietly. 'Maybe it's better this way. I hope Copper hasn't killed the driver of that car – I expect there was one. I want it to be known that this was a Commando job – not the Underground.' As he spoke he walked quickly towards the road.

The car was there. A man was lying along the running board and Copper was sitting on him. 'What do you want me to do with this pipsqueak, sir?' he inquired.

'What is it, exactly?'

Copper examined his prisoner, who offered no resistance. 'It's a soldier, sir,' he announced. 'Just a common gorblimey private.'

'Put something in his mouth, tie him up, dump him in the cottage and lock him in,' ordered Gimlet. 'Somebody will find him sooner or later. By that time we shall be well on our way.'

'Aye aye, sir.' Copper set about his task, while Gimlet punctured the two rear tyres of the car by the simple expedient of sticking his dagger into them. This done, he took a piece of chalk from his pocket and made his mark, a rough drawing in the shape of a gimlet, on both sides of the car. 'That should leave the Nazis in no doubt as to who did the job,' he remarked.

Copper walked over to the cottage with the prisoner slung over his shoulder like a sack of flour. He tossed his burden inside, shut the door and locked it. Whistling under his breath he returned.

'All right, let's get along,' ordered Gimlet, and led the way back to Dominique, whom they found, what with the delay and the shooting, in a state bordering on panic.

'What was that shooting?' he asked anxiously.

Copper answered. 'That was Bussemann.'

Dominique stared. 'What of him?'

'Aw, nothin' much. 'E just rolled up in time for a busman's holiday, that's all.'

'He's gone where he has sent a lot of other people,' put in Gimlet.

Dominique shook his head. 'I don't get it.'

Trapper clicked his tongue. 'Bussemann did.'

'What-ho, that's a good 'un,' chuckled Copper. 'I must remember that—'

'Stop chattering and get on with the job,' ordered Gimlet curtly.

'Aye aye, sir.'

'Drive on to the mill, Dominique.'

'*Oui, monsieur – tout de suite.*'

The car cruised up the road.

CHAPTER FOURTEEN

The Muster at the Mill

The old cloth mill turned out to be a much larger building than Cub expected. Situated on the north bank of the Seine, it was in fact a place of considerable size, and in its heyday must have been a factory of importance. But that, judging by appearances, was a long time ago – unless, being built of wood, it had easily become dilapidated. It was now little better than a ramshackle ruin – not that this mattered in the slightest degree as far as the scheme was affected. It lay about a quarter of a mile from the main road, and could be reached only by a single drive, much overgrown in places, for the adjacent country was thickly, although not entirely, wooded. Looking at the towering silhouette as it came into sight, balanced precariously, as it seemed, on the bank of the wide, turgid river, the thought occurred to Cub that no building could have been more appropriate to their design, either in practical utility or appearance; as a base for plots and a rendezvous for plotters it was the perfect setting.

Bearing in mind the swastika decorations of the car, Gimlet requested Dominique to stop some distance short of the mill, to avoid starting anything like a false alarm among the patriots who would certainly be on the watch.

'We shan't need the car again, I hope,' he told Dominique as he walked on. 'I shall have to leave you to dispose of it.'

'But certainly, *monsieur*,' answered the driver readily.

'Will you destroy it?'

'No, *monsieur*. Our method is to take marked cars to pieces, and distribute the component parts in many places until such time as they may again be required.'

'Good idea,' opined Gimlet.

At this juncture they were challenged by an invisible sentry. Having given the password they were escorted, by two men who then appeared, to the mill, where, in the light of a few candles stuck on convenient shelves, a remarkable sight was revealed – a hundred men of all ages in skimpy racing clothes, sitting about on dilapidated looms and derelict machinery. Each man carried his identification number on a white card. It was the first time that Cub had seen the Underground in force, and he found the spectacle inspiring. Enthusiasm and high spirits were apparent everywhere. There was no sign of nervousness or fear.

An elderly man in ordinary clothes came forward and announced that he was in charge of the party while it was at the mill, whereupon Gimlet informed him that the cyclists were approaching, information that was received by the assembly with obvious satisfaction. Gimlet went on to say that while they were waiting he would like to make a few remarks to the partisans, a suggestion that was welcomed by a quiet buzz of applause. Standing on a broken loom of obsolete pattern he addressed the meeting:

'Men of France and comrades in arms,' he began. 'This has been a great day for us and a bad day for the Nazis, for we have struck the enemy a blow where it will hurt for a long time. Presently we must part, but that does not mean that we shall not meet again. Soon, in a few weeks, a few months, perhaps, by our efforts and yours, the vandals from across the Rhine who now defile your soil will be flung back whence they came, except those, like the scoundrel Bussemann – now dead on the railway line at Villant – who leave their bones in the land they came to despoil.' (This tit-bit of news was greeted with another burst of applause.) 'I hope one day we shall meet again in a Paris that is free, when we will celebrate this occasion in a manner worthy of it. You all know why we are here,' continued Gimlet. 'If our project is to succeed every man must play his part, cost what it may, even life itself – and that, after all, *messieurs*, is but a small price to pay for such a reward as we hope to secure. In a few minutes the British prisoners from Paris will be here. Take your cycles and complete the race, a race which, you may be sure, will in due course find an honoured place in the history of France. No doubt when you reach Rouen you will be questioned about an incident that has occurred at the railway crossing

312

at Villant. All you have to say is that when you rode through no one was there. If there was trouble you saw nothing of it – which will be true. Stick to that story and the Nazis will have nothing against you. That is all, except that on behalf of your British comrades who are sharing with you the perils of this night, I thank you for your courage, your loyalty, and your co-operation. When my men arrive, take your cycles and go about your business quietly, and without loss of time. Goodbye, and good luck.'

Gimlet stepped down to a quiet but fervent murmur of approbation. After a glance at his watch, to the leader of the French party he said questioningly: 'You will not be going on with the cyclists?'

'*Non, monsieur*. It happens that I have a cottage near by, so I was asked to superintend events here.'

'Then you must know the district very well?'

'*Mais oui, monsieur*. Every centimetre of it.'

'I'm expecting some supplies to be dropped by air. An open space, not too large, surrounded by trees so that a ground signal could not be seen except from above, would be the most suitable. Do you know of such a place, near at hand?'

'I know the perfect place,' answered the man without hesitation. 'It is only a few minutes' walk.'

'Would you show it to one of my men, so that when the time comes for our machines to arrive – which will be in about fifteen minutes – we shall know where it is?'

'Certainly, *monsieur*. Instantly.'

'Go with him, Cub,' commanded Gimlet. 'Mark the place well. You'll have to find your way back to it when the planes are due.'

Cub accompanied the guide to the spot, a woodland glade perhaps two acres in extent, noting carefully the direction and distance. They were away only for a few minutes, but returned to find a scene of great activity, and, at first glance, confusion. The cyclists had begun to arrive. Activity there was, but not confusion. Gimlet called the number of each cycle as it entered, and the Frenchman bearing the same number came forward to claim it. He would wait for the commando to remove his uniform bag, then ride away. Thus, as one came, one departed, so that the number of men in the mill remained the same.

'Get our fellows into their uniforms as quickly as you can, sergeant-major,' Gimlet told the senior N.C.O. 'I shall want some of them to go out and bring in the equipment that is being delivered by air. The planes are due in ten minutes.'

As soon as the first dozen men were properly dressed, Cub, with his torch ready for use, led them to the fringe of the glade. 'Tell your chaps to mark the stuff as it comes down,' he told the sergeant-major, who was with him. 'We'd better keep close against a tree or we may get a case of rifles on our heads. The equipment will come down on parachutes, of course, but even so it will land with a tidy bump.'

They had not long to wait. As soon as Cub heard the machines coming he ran into the open, winked the prearranged signal – the letter K, in Morse – several times on his torch, stuck the torch into the ground with the light pointing upwards, and bolted back to his tree. The first machine roared over. It was not seen, but as the roar receded there was a double bump, as if two heavy objects had struck the ground. Some commandos ran out and came back staggering under heavy loads. By that time the second machine was nearly overhead. More bumps. More loads were brought in. This was repeated six times. Only one load missed the glade; it crashed down into a tree, but its weight carried it through the branches and it was quickly found. More commandos arrived and the equipment was carried to the mill, by which time the noise of aircraft was a distant drone.

'The machines were dead on time, sir,' Cub reported to Gimlet. 'Here's the equipment.'

'Just like blinkin' clockwork,' remarked Copper.

'That's the way things *should* go, when you have the right men on the job,' asserted Gimlet.

'Two packages seem lighter than the rest,' remarked Cub. 'They're sacks. I don't know what's in them.'

'Unpack them and find out.'

'Yes, sir.'

There was a gasp of astonishment and delight that ended in laughter when the first sack was unpacked. It brought Gimlet over in a hurry.

'What have you got there?' he asked sharply.

'Hams, sir,' reported Cub weakly. 'Four hams and about twenty pounds of cheese. From the feel of the other sack I should say it contains loaves of bread.'

'That wasn't in my schedule,' declared Gimlet, 'but it's nice to have it all the same. I'll wager that was Bigglesworth upstairs – this was his idea.'

'Not a bad idea either,' murmured Copper. 'What say you, Trapper? Am I right?'

'Sure – every time,' confirmed Trapper.

'Has everyone arrived, sergeant-major?' asked Gimlet.

'Yes, sor.'

'How many men?'

'One hundred, sor.'

'Anyone not changed yet?'

'No, sor. We're pretty well ready to move off.'

'Good. Make up this food into one hundred and four rations, and be quick about it. It can be eaten right away – but don't get the idea that this is a picnic. We've a long way to go yet. Anyone who isn't ready to march in ten minutes will be left behind.'

'Very good, sor.'

Gimlet sat down, lit a cigarette, and with a faint smile on his face watched knives making short work of the hams, the cheese, and the bread.

'Marvellous what a bite o' grub'll do, ain't it, chum?' remarked Copper to Cub, between bites of an enormous sandwich. 'Nothin' like a scrap to give you an appetite.'

'So I notice,' assented Cub, eating ravenously.

Ten minutes later Gimlet rose. 'All right. Finish up. Hand out the equipment, sergeant-major, and get the party on parade.'

'Yes, sor.'

The meal came to a hasty conclusion. Rifles, automatics, Sten guns and grenades appeared, and were passed from hand to hand. This done, the sergeant-major mustered the parade in a double line. He called the troop to attention, made his inspection, and reported to Gimlet, 'All present and correct, sor.'

Gimlet stood the parade 'at ease', and addressed it quietly.

'This is the position,' he announced. 'We've got a four-mile march ahead of us. The objective is the German-occupied aerodrome at Rambours, which is one of the bases from which enemy bombers operate against Britain. Our job is to capture the airfield and liquidate it – or at any rate hold it long enough for our planes to pick us up. Obviously, if we don't capture the airfield our planes will not be able to land, and if they don't land we shan't be going home. I needn't tell you what is likely to happen if we find ourselves stuck in France, so when we go into action it will be up to every man to hit hard and keep on hitting until the enemy has had enough. When you get the signal to break off, disengage and retire on a rallying point which will be selected when we arrive. Lose no time, because the same signal will bring the planes down. Keep off the landing area. There may be casualties. I don't want anyone left behind. Those who aren't hurt will bring in those who are. As I shall have to maintain control of the operation and act as liaison with the aircraft I shall not be able to lead the attack in person – but I shall be watching. When we leave here we shall travel cross-country to avoid being seen. The march will be made in silence – and when I say silence I mean silence. If I hear any talking in the ranks the men responsible will go home under arrest. No smoking. Corporal Collson, Private Troublay and Cadet Peters will remain with me for special duties. That's all. Any questions?'

'What about prisoners, sir?' asked a lanky, loose-limbed commando.

'There shouldn't be any,' answered Gimlet. 'If there are – well, some of you will have to give them your places in the aircraft.'

'Then there won't be any,' growled the commando, to a titter of mirth.

Gimlet took out his pocket compass, nodded to the sergeant-major, and strode to the door, followed by Copper, Trapper and Cub.

The sergeant-major called the parade to attention. 'Ye all heard what the C.O. said about talking,' he rasped. His eyes wandered threateningly down the line. 'I don't want to have to remind anyone. Left turn. Forrard.'

In silence the commandos filed out into the night.

CHAPTER FIFTEEN

Grand Finale

To Cub, the march across the silent countryside had the illusory, unsub-
stantial quality of a dream remembered long afterwards. For this, no
doubt, the lack of sound was largely responsible. Gimlet strode on ahead.
Behind, in double file, like phantoms of the night, came the commandos,
silent, grim, accoutred as if they might have been invaders from another
planet. The moon, a slender crescent, swept up from a distant cloudbank,
and hanging like a fiery sickle in the sky cast a pallid light upon a landscape
typical of northern France – vast hedgeless fields, wide sheets of reed-
fringed stagnant water, and twin lines of poplars that accompanied roads
as straight as railway tracks. Once, the horizon was broken by a stand of
elms, the branches blotched in uncouth patterns by clumps of mistletoe.
Although Cub was familiar with such scenery, after a time a feeling came
over him that this was not really happening; that it was all a story, a fairy-
tale, in which he was one of the characters, forced by an evil power against
his will to play a part, and that was to march, and march, and keep on
marching to eternity. Time no longer meant anything. There were moments
when he wished something would happen – moments indeed when he felt
that if something did not happen to break the hideous spell of silence he
would scream. But no. The only sound was the monotonous tramp-tramp,
tramp-tramp of martial feet on new-ploughed earth or the swish-swish,
swish-swish of the same feet brushing through grass or stubble.

Yet the march lasted only an hour and ten minutes. Then, from beyond
a horizon formed by a long fold in the ground not far ahead, there came
a sound which with one stroke banished all sensation of unreality. It was
the snarling of an aero engine being started up. Another joined it. A glow

317

of light appeared in the sky, to cast the little hill ahead in high relief. Gimlet raised his hand. The column halted. There was a rustle, a sigh of a hundred indrawn breaths. Gimlet turned and spoke in a low voice to Cub. 'Go ahead and see what you can make out. Don't show yourself against the skyline. We shall follow on, slowly.'

'Yes, sir.'

Cub went forward at the double, but when he neared the rising ground he dropped flat and dragged himself with his elbows to the top. He was not unprepared for the scene that greeted his eyes – except in one respect. He knew, of course, that there would be an airfield. And an airfield was there, with a line of hump-backed hangars, hutments in regular order, and a wind-stocking pole standing stark against the sky. There were aircraft, most of them parked round the perimeter of the landing area. That, too, was to be expected. What did surprise him was the amount of light, which enabled him to see these things. It was mostly concentrated on the concrete apron in front of the hangars, where three twin-engined bombers were being started up. Another was being fuelled from a mobile tank. Three men in flying kit were cutting across a runway towards another bomber, followed by a tractor trailing a load of bombs. A vehicle of some sort was cruising towards the airfield along the hedgeless accommodation road which served the camp. The main road, Cub knew from the map he had studied, was nearly a mile away. The nearest bomber, a Messerschmitt 410, was not more than fifty yards from where he lay. He could see no one near it. There was another machine about the same distance beyond it. There was no sign of the crew.

From all this Cub soon came to two conclusions. The first was that preparations for a raid were in progress – had just begun. The second was that no British aircraft was near, or the lights would be dowsed. In short, the squadron was casually getting ready for a sortie with no fear of inter-ruption. That, for the present, was as much as he needed to know, so after backing away from the skyline he returned to the troops, who had moved nearer and had dropped to the prone position. He found Gimlet and made his report.

'Sounds like money for jam, sir,' remarked Copper, who listened.

'I think it's safe for you to advance to the ridge, sir; from there you could see things for yourself,' suggested Cub.

Gimlet stood up. 'Sergeant-major, tell all N.C.O.s to join me here,' he ordered. With the aero engines ticking over there was no possibility of being heard.

Word was passed back down the line and the N.C.O.s came forward. They advanced with Gimlet to the brow of the rise, where they lay flat, looking at the scene before them. Cub went with them.

Gimlet considered the airfield for a good three minutes before he spoke. 'I fancy we've got them cold,' he said softly, looking at his watch. 'Our machines are due in eighteen minutes,' he went on. 'That means they'll be crossing the coast in about eight minutes. As they will be on a course for this district the airfield will be warned, and we may expect the lights to go out. The bombers may try to get away before our fellows arrive or they may decide to pack up and lie low until they have gone. If we strike first they won't be able to do either; but if we're going to do that we shall have to move fast, to get into position. This is how we'll handle it, but the action will not start until I fire a green light from this point. Sergeant-major, I shall hand over the main assault to you. Take fifty men, and without being seen get within striking distance of those hangars. Cut any telephone wires you see to prevent the enemy from calling for help. When the action begins, deal as you think best with any opposition and do as much damage as you can. Set fire to anything and everything, particularly the oil and petrol stores if you can locate them. I shall detail Sergeant Brown to follow you up with ten men and give support should you need it. They can pick up your casualties, if any. Keep off the landing area or you may be knocked down by our planes coming in. Rally here when I fire a red light. Watch for it. That clear?'

'Yes, sir.'

'All right – move off.'

The sergeant-major backed away and disappeared into the darkness.

Gimlet continued. 'Sergeant Brown, take ten men and support the sergeant-major. Keep your fellows together and hold them back unless you see that the sergeant-major's force is in trouble. If that happens, attack from a flank. Keep off the landing area and rally on the red light. Move off.'

The sergeant retired.

'Corporal Collson, as your home was blitzed, I've reserved a job for you that you should enjoy,' continued Gimlet. 'Take thirty men, and working your way round the boundary of the airfield, leave one or two with every aircraft, according to the strength of any opposition you may encounter. Actually, I don't think there is anyone near the machines parked on the perimeter. When the action signal is fired – not before – the job of your detachment is to destroy the machines. Set fire to them – smash them – riddle them with bullets. Don't try to do too much yourself; stand where you can keep things under control, and hold a few men back to cut down the enemy if he tries to interfere. Rally on the red light. Don't get in the way of landing aircraft. Bring your casualties back with you. Go ahead.'

Copper spat on his hands. 'This is hoopla for chocolates,' he whispered hoarsely to Cub in passing.

One N.C.O. remained – a lance-corporal wearing the kitten cypher on his arm. Gimlet tossed him a greeting. 'Hello, Corporal Miles. Nice to see you again. How are you?'

'Fine, sir, thanks.'

'Sorry I lost you at Dieppe.'

'My own fault, sir. I got too far and couldn't get back.'

'Don't make the same mistake tonight. I'm holding ten men in reserve. Go back to them, stand fast, and tell them they may get their chance presently.'

'Yes, sir.'

Again Gimlet looked at his watch. 'Four minutes to go. It will be interesting to see how the enemy deals with a show like this. We ought to be able to do him a lot of mischief – quite a lot of mischief.'

'Yes, sir,' agreed Cub – a trifle dubiously.

'What beats me is, why Jerry doesn't keep a better guard,' murmured Trapper.

'If the Nazis put a cordon of sentries round every airfield he's holding he wouldn't have any men left to do the fighting,' returned Gimlet.

'Looks like in the next war everyone not flying will be guarding airdromes,' observed Trapper moodily.

'Never mind the next war, let's get on with this one,' said Gimlet curtly. Taking his signalling pistol from his pocket he stood up. With his eyes on the watch on his left wrist he raised his right arm. There was a flash and a report. A brilliant green star appeared in the sky, smoking as it described a graceful parabola before starting to fall.

Cub held his breath, staring all eyes, as the saying goes, wondering what would happen next.

Actually, in the event, things did not happen as fast as he expected. At first, the Germans on the concrete merely stopped what they were doing and gazed up at the light, probably wondering what it signified. Some may have guessed, for soon there were shouts, followed by a general move towards the hangars. An officer ran out on the concrete. He shouted an order. A whistle blew. Then, above all other noises came the satanic chatter of a Sten gun. Another joined it, and another. Small arms crackled. Tracer swept the tarmac. A cloud of bullets struck the mobile petrol tank like a flail. A trickle of blue flame appeared. It became a stream. With a terrific *whoosh* the tank blew up in a blaze of ghastly blue light, throwing blazing petrol on all sides. The bomber near which it was standing was drenched. Yellow flames appeared in the blue. Fires appeared in other places, in hangars, in workshops, to bathe the scene in a lurid light that grew ever brighter. Commandos appeared, running along the concrete, shooting as they ran. They seemed to be meeting with little opposition; ground crews and air crews who had been working on the machines scattered like wisps of snipe – those who had not fallen. Cub, watching, could almost feel sorry for them. The surprise was complete. It must have been shattering. Probably few, if any, of the men on the airfield carried weapons. Later, armed and organized, they might put up a stiffer resistance, but caught as they were, utterly unprepared, there was little they could do except run for cover. The result was confusion approaching panic. Cub could imagine the same thing happening on any airfield, in any country, suddenly attacked by a strong body of trained men in the dead of night. Even paratroops, he reflected, could not reach an objective without their aircraft being spotted by radio-location operators, and a hot reception prepared. But for an airfield, far from the sea, far from any fighting front, without the slightest warning to suddenly be stormed by commandos, must be outside even Nazi calculations. They would wonder where on earth – or heaven – the commandos had come from.

The light grew brighter as more buildings were fired. The crash of grenades punctuated the now incessant rattle of small arms. More fires appeared on the perimeter of the airfield as the aircraft parked there were attacked by Copper and his detachment. Here, there had been little shooting, and Cub imagined that Copper had had an easy task – as later was confirmed. The airfield was soon ringed by flames. The buildings were an inferno. Cub, although he knew that success had crowned their efforts, was appalled by the fearful spectacle presented. Gimlet was watching, apparently unconcerned. The reserve troops had moved up to see what was going on. Some were muttering.

Gimlet turned and spoke to them. 'Sorry, you fellows. I know it's hard to watch the fun without taking a hand, but that's how it is. Keep your eyes open for casualties coming back; you can help them.' He looked at his watch. 'Our planes should be over in three minutes – and they won't need pathfinders to guide them, by gad! This bonfire must be visible from the coast. Keep your heads down, or some of you will be stopping these stray bullets.'

The bullets to which he referred were those bursting from the exploding ammunition in the gun turrets of the blazing aircraft.

'What are those lights, sir?' Cub pointed beyond the hangars, where a string of lights were moving.

'Headlights,' answered Gimlet. 'Either enemy reinforcements or fire-fighting appliances – perhaps both. Every enemy unit within fifty miles must see this glare.

Odd commandos were now beginning to trickle back, some limping, or walking with difficulty; others were being helped, and Cub realized that they had not had things entirely their own way. Soon there was a line of figures on the ground at the rallying point, some laughing, some groaning, some swearing, as the reserve troops applied first aid. Gimlet went to them. 'All right, boys. With luck we'll have you in hospital in half—'

The rest of the sentence was lost in a violent explosion as one of the bombers on the tarmac, one that had taken fire, blew up – or rather, the bombs that it had taken aboard went off. Fortunately, they were only canisters containing incendiaries, or the result might have been serious for commandos in the vicinity. As it was, the incendiaries – perhaps allocated for London – were scattered far and wide, to illuminate the landscape in an unearthly flickering glare.

'Blimey! Talk about Brock's blooming benefit! The old Crystal Palace never put on a better show, not even when it went up itself,' called a voice, and looking round Cub saw Copper walking back, followed by his detachment. One man was being helped by two others.

A sound overhead took Cub's eyes upward. It was the drone of aircraft, flying low. Light from the ground was reflected on the underside of the machine as it turned.

'Dead on time,' said Gimlet. He raised his right arm and a red flare soared upwards. He beckoned to Copper. 'Take your men and cover the sergeant-major's withdrawal,' he ordered. 'Keep off the grass.'

'Aye aye, sir.' Shouting to the others to follow, Copper went off at the double to meet the troops who, having seen the red light, were now retiring, most of them walking backwards, some still shooting, some holding an arm across the face to protect it from the heat of the conflagration.

Cub noted that the lights on the road were getting dangerously close, and he was about to remind Gimlet of them when they scattered. The nearer noises made it impossible to hear anything, but he saw tracer cutting through the sky above the road. He had no time to work out what this might mean, for events close at hand compelled his attention. The first aircraft, a Wellington, was just landing. Commandos were rallying in a steady stream – Copper and his men with them. Only a few, he was relieved to note, were being carried. The Wellington, having landed, swung round and taxied quickly towards Gimlet, who was waving a torch. Leaving the engines running the pilot jumped down, paused to light a cigarette, and walked on.

'Is that Captain King?' inquired a voice.

'King here,' answered Gimlet. 'That's Bigglesworth, isn't it?'

'Right first time,' answered the pilot cheerfully. 'Everything under control?'

'Yes, going nicely,' returned Gimlet.

'Fine. We had no difficulty in finding you. You gave us quite a mark to fly on.'

'Burns nicely, doesn't it?'

'Very nicely,' agreed Biggles. 'My fellows will follow me in. I've brought six machines. They'll take twenty men each at a crush. Oh, by the way, there is what I take to be an enemy relief party coming up the road, but I don't think we need worry about it. I detailed some of my boys, flying Mosquitoes, to take care of the surrounding country, in case outsiders tried to crash into the party. All the same, it would be a good idea, don't you think, if we started to get the wounded away? There's the machine, wearing a red cross, just coming in. There's a doctor on board with bandages and things.'

'You think of everything.'

'Not everything – but we try.'

'Are you anxious to push off right away – I mean you, personally?' asked Gimlet.

'Good lord, no. I shall stay and see the show through. Take you home if you like.'

'Thanks. I'll accept that offer. By the way, is Bertie Lissie with you?'

'Yes, but he's in a hurry to get back – got a foxhound bitch due to whelp tonight, and won't trust the vet to handle it.'

'Quite right. If the bitch knows him she'll probably do better than with a stranger. Tell him I hope he gets some nice pups.'

'You'll probably see him yourself when we get back.'

'I might give him a hand.'

'He'd be glad, I'm sure.'

'We shall need the pups. Be pretty sickening, by gad, if after all this sweat there was no huntin'.'

Copper nudged Cub. 'Blinkin' marvellous, ain't it? Foxhound pups. That's all they think about. How's yer horses? What's the fishin' like? Strike me puce! One day they'll wake up with a jerk and discover there's a war on.'

'Don't let them kid you, Copper,' returned Cub. '*They* know there's a war on. Lord Lissie's pack of hounds means as much to them as the Old Kent Road does to you. It's just a matter of taste.'

'Maybe – maybe, but I'd sooner go to the dogs at Clapham stadium and do my fishin' with a pile o' chips,' growled Copper.

Biggles was still talking to Gimlet. 'I'd better get along to keep an eye on things. See you presently.' He strolled away.

Gimlet turned to Copper. 'Don't stand there dreaming, corporal. There's plenty to do.'

'Aye aye, sir.'

Eighteen wounded men, the total number of casualties, were lifted into the ambulance machine, which at once took off and disappeared into the night. One by one the other aircraft taxied over, took its complement from the commandos who had mustered in single file under the critical eyes of the sergeant-major, and took off. Presently only one Wellington remained. Sixteen men stood by, including Gimlet, Copper, Trapper and Cub. Occasionally a shot whistled from the direction of the hangars, but of organized resistance there was none. Bursts of machine-gun and cannon fire came from the distance as Mosquitoes harried vehicles that attempted to approach.

Biggles joined the party and spoke to Gimlet. 'Ready to move off?' he inquired.

'Yes. I don't think there's any more we can do here,' answered Gimlet.

'Then let's get along.'

The party filed into the Wellington. Cub found a seat on the floor with Copper and Trapper. It vibrated as the engines roared and bumped a little as the machine took off; then it settled down in steady flight, climbing for altitude.

A hatless, ginger-haired flying officer appeared from the forward part of the aircraft. 'Everyone all right?' he inquired brightly. Then, as his eyes fell on the three comrades, he went on, smiling, raising his eyebrows. 'What – you again? You'd better take season tickets.'

'We will when you put on a restaurant car, sir.' returned Copper promptly.

'It's hardly worth it on these short runs,' bantered the officer. 'Besides, it's better to eat on the ground – you're not so likely to spill the soup. Dinners will be waiting when we get down. We ought to be home in twenty minutes.'

Copper looked pained. 'Is there any doubt about it, sir?'

The officer nodded. 'Rather. The Nazis don't really approve of our going to and fro like this. Sometimes they try to stop us. But don't worry – you've got the best pilot in the service at the stick.' The officer smiled again and went back.

'Cheerful coves, ain't they?' remarked Copper.

If the Nazis did try to stop the aircraft those in the cabin had little indication of it. The machine turned sharply once or twice, and for a little while, for about a minute, flak barked its throaty cough. That was all. Soon afterwards the bellow of the engines sank to a contented purr; the floor of the aircraft tilted down; the wheels rumbled as they ran over the ground; movement stopped.

''Ome,' said Copper dispassionately. 'Anyone got a pencil?'

'What on earth do you want a pencil for?' demanded Cub.

'To drop a line ter my old Ma before she rolls up at the War Office to ask 'em what they've done with 'er little boy. Never forget to write ter yer Ma. Am I right, Trapper, old chum?'

'You're always right,' asserted Trapper.

Gimlet's head appeared in the doorway. 'Dinners are waiting, so get yourselves cleaned up and washed.'

'This everlastin' washin',' muttered Copper. 'A spot of clean dirt never stopped my teeth workin'.'

Gimlet reappeared. 'Did you say something, corporal?'

'No, sir.'

'Just thinking aloud again, eh?'

'Yessir.'

Gimlet smiled and turned to Cub. 'I've been asked to pass you an item of news that should please you.'

Cub's eyes opened wide. 'Me, sir?'

'Your father came home from Spain by air two days ago. He's here, in the officers' mess, waiting for you. I promised you a stripe, but it seems you won't need it – he's talking of your going to an officers' training unit. Make haste.' Gimlet departed.

Copper glared at Cub. 'Ho! So stripes ain't good enough for yer? Goin' in fer pips, eh? Maybe you think me and Trapper are goin' ter salute you? Pah! Don't make me laugh.'

Controlling his expression, Cub nodded seriously. 'Do you know the first order you'll get from me?'

'What?'

'Get your hair cut,' snapped Cub, imitating Gimlet's manner. Laughing aloud and dodging Copper's fist he jumped down and ran towards the officers' mess.

GIMLET COMES HOME

Trapper threw himself on the ground.

CHAPTER ONE

A Mystery Needs Explaining

Nigel Norman Peters, better known in his disbanded Commando unit as 'Cub', halted in front of the Ritz Hotel in Piccadilly, and inclined his head towards the massive portal. 'This is it,' he announced.

His two companions, ex-Corporal 'Copper' Colson, of Bow, London, late of the Metropolitan Police Force, and taciturn ex-Trooper 'Trapper' Troublay, of Canada, both one-time members of the Commando troop known as King's 'Kittens', looked at the door, at the attendant commissionaire, and back at Cub.

Copper spoke, and he spoke with feeling: 'Not fer me, mate. That ain't my joint.'

Cub smiled. 'What's the matter – scared?' he bantered.

'Scared stiff,' admitted Copper, eyeing the commissionaire with hostile suspicion.

Trapper shrugged, as only a French-Canadian can. 'For me, I'd rather go through Dieppe again than winkle my way through this place.'

'All right,' agreed Cub lightly. 'I'll go in and find Gimlet, and tell him that for the first time you're windy of following him.'

'It ain't that I'm so windy – but look at us,' complained Copper.

Cub raised his eyebrows. 'What's wrong with us?' he demanded, a justifiable question, for all were neatly dressed in dark lounge suits, their demobilisation outfits. Admittedly, Copper's right jacket-pocket bulged in a rather slovenly manner, due to the presence of a Service automatic which he had retained, either as a souvenir or because, as he once remarked, after five years of having it on him he felt undressed without it. The Indian hunting-knife which Trapper carried on his belt was only revealed when he put a hand in his trousers pocket for some small change. For sentimental reasons Cub still clung to his little Mauser thirty-eight, but its presence in his hip-pocket would not have been suspected. On the whole, as he pointed out, there was nothing wrong with them.

Copper braced his muscles like a man confronted by mortal danger. 'Right you are, Cub,' he said shortly. 'I'll try it. You lead the way. But if anyone tries any half-larks with me—'

'They won't, don't worry,' Cub told him, laughing. He went in, the others following, and deposited their hats in the cloakroom.

Copper let out a stifled shout as his eyes met those of the cloakroom attendant. 'Blimey! Look who's 'ere!' he cried. 'If it ain't Shorty Hughes.' He gave the attendant a friendly push that sent him reeling. 'Whatho, Shorty, me old Hun-hunter. How goes it?'

Private Hughes, late of the Royal Welsh Fusiliers, looked up and down the corridor with a nervousness he had never shown in Normandy. 'Shut your face, you big lout,' he snarled. 'What is it you want to do – get me the sack, look you?'

'Who'll give you the sack?' enquired Copper belligerently.

'The manager.'

'Where is 'e? Who does 'e think 'e is? Let's knock 'is block off.' Copper looked round, presumably for the manager.

'Behave yourself,' requested Cub curtly. 'This isn't a raid.' To Shorty he explained that they were there by appointment to dine with their old C.O., Captain Lorrington King, D.S.O., more often known to his Commandos as 'Gimlet.'

'Then push along to the grill-room and leave me alone,' muttered Shorty. 'I've only had this job a week, and if I lose it my missus 'll tear the hide off me.'

'Serves yer right fer getting hitched,' said Copper coldly. 'We ain't got jobs at all, yet. Still, we've got a bit of dough left, so why worry. So long, Shorty. If you dish out your tickets like you used ter dish out machine-gun bullets, you'll do.'

Cub walked down to the grill-room, where the party was intercepted by the head waiter.

'We are guests of Captain King,' explained Cub.

The waiter glanced at a card which he held in his hand. 'That's right, sir. A table for four. This way, gentlemen, please.'

Copper nudged Cub. 'What do yer know about that?' he whispered hoarsely. 'He mistook us fer gentlemen.'

The waiter pulled out three chairs with the dexterity of long practice. 'Captain King hasn't arrived yet. Can I get you anything while you're waiting?'

'Yes, you can bring me a pint,' answered Copper promptly.

The waiter looked pained. He winced. 'A pint of what, sir?' he enquired frostily.

'Anything you like, old cock,' answered Copper cheerfully. 'I ain't particular.'

'Very good, sir.' The waiter drew a deep breath and departed.

'Not a bad sort of cove,' observed Copper as he sat down. 'Did yer notice 'im call me sir? Maybe he was in the Guards. They still call N.C.O.'s sir at the depot, I hear.' He looked around. 'I remember once heaving a sticky-bomb into a gin palace like this at a place called Le Touquet. Didn't 'alf make a mess and no blinkin' error. Cleared the Jerries out, though.'

The waiter returned with a tankard which he put on the table, and after a sidelong glance at Copper withdrew.

Copper drank deeply. 'Wonder 'ow long Gimlet's going ter be?' he remarked. 'I'm ready for me rations. It ain't like Gimlet not ter be on parade at the time shown in orders. He said seven sharp. It's five past. That ain't like 'im. There's somethin' queer about it.'

'Give him a chance; he's held up in a traffic jam, perhaps,' suggested Cub. 'He'll be along.'

Minutes passed. The grill-room was beginning to fill. Copper fidgeted. 'Quarter past,' he muttered, glancing at his watch. 'There's something funny about this. I don't like it. Gimlet once had me on the mat for being thirty seconds late on parade – and we hadn't had no sleep fer two nights. I hope this place ain't made 'im soft.'

'Tch! Nothing would make Gimlet soft,' put in Trapper quietly.

More time passed. The room was full now and the waiters busy. There was an appetising smell of food.

'Here, I'm getting peckish,' growled Copper. 'How about slipping out ter some little joint fer a plate of fish and chips while we're waitin'?'

'Gimlet must have had an accident,' decided Trapper.

A quarter of an hour later Copper said: 'Ten to eight. I don't like it.'

All Cub could say was: 'We'll give him till eight, anyway.'

At eight o'clock the waiter approached the table.

Said Cub, in a low voice, seeing him coming: 'He's going to say that Gimlet has rung up to say why he couldn't come. I was wondering why he didn't ring up.'

Cub's guess was wrong. The waiter came to seek information, not to give it. 'Have you heard anything of Captain King?' he enquired.

Cub answered. 'Not a word.'

The waiter went on. 'The chef is getting worried. The captain came here in person and ordered special dishes. They will be ruined.'

'I don't like it,' muttered Copper.

'Don't keep saying that,' reproved Cub irritably. 'I'll admit it's queer, but there is probably a simple explanation. Gimlet wouldn't leave us sitting here if he could get in touch with us. Yet he must be in London, and in London one is seldom far from a telephone. It certainly is odd.'

In the end the party waited until nine o'clock. Then Copper got up. 'Gimlet ain't comin',' he asserted. 'If 'e was comin', he'd be 'ere. Am I right, Trapper?'

'Sure you're right,' agreed Trapper without hesitation. 'Let's go.'

They went out, found a small café, and had a cheap but satisfying meal. The conversation still ran on Gimlet's unaccountable failure to turn up at a reunion party which he had suggested and arranged.

'Could we have made a mistake in the date?' suggested Copper.

Cub shook his head. 'No. He said "Wednesday, seven sharp", and the waiter at the hotel knew about it. We couldn't both be mistaken. This is the day right enough, and when Gimlet fixed it he intended to be here, there's no doubt of that. Something must have stopped him. What was it, I wonder?'

'Nothing,' muttered Copper. 'I never knew anything stop Gimlet when he wanted to get some place.'

'All the same, something *has* stopped him,' said Cub. 'We'll go back to the Ritz a bit later on to see if they've heard anything. Ten to one there'll be a message.'

But when, just before eleven, the party returned to the hotel, it was only to be informed that no message had been received from Captain King. The manager was somewhat concerned because – as he now divulged – Captain King had booked a room at the hotel for the night. He had not claimed the room. It was very strange, the manager thought, because Captain King was an old client who did not do that sort of thing.

'Strange!' exclaimed Copper. 'I should say it's more than that. It's phoney, that's what it is. I don't like it.'

'Had Gimlet been involved in an accident, providing he wasn't unconscious he would ask the police to let us know, or let the manager here know, what had happened,' opined Cub pensively. 'Of course he may have gone back to his home in Devonshire for something. But there's nothing we can do about it.'

'Ho! ain't there?' muttered Copper. 'If something's happened to 'im in Devonshire, what's wrong with slipping down to report fer duty, as we might say? I reckon he'd be glad ter see us, fer old times' sake.'

'Yes, we could do that,' agreed Cub. 'We could go down on the first train in the morning. It would be a trip, anyway.'

'*Bon*,' declared Trapper. 'We can sleep at the Y.M.C.A. tonight and take our small kit with us in our haversacks when we leave. How about rations? We'll take some along, I reckon; then we shall be all right whatever happens.'

'We shan't need rations,' averred Cub. 'There are still plenty of eating places in the country.'

'Yes, and by Jumbo, don't they know 'ow ter charge,' sneered Copper. 'You please yerself, but I ain't bein' stung by no lily-fingered soup-wallah. I've managed fer meself all right fer the past five years, and I reckon I can go on doin' it. If you've got yer grub on yer back, you always know where you are. Am I right, Trapper, old chum?'

'Sure, pal, you were never more right,' drawled Trapper. 'We don't have restaurants in the backwoods where I come from. We learn to do without 'em. When I travel, my kit goes with me, and that includes rations – and I can still travel light.'

'Okay,' agreed Cub. 'Maybe you're right. It's nice to be independent, anyway.'

'Nothing nicer,' murmured Trapper.

And so it came about that when the first west-bound train left Paddington the following morning three seats were occupied by passengers who, now that the time had come, were a little nervous at their temerity. But, having started, they went on, and by noon were in the village of Lorrington. At twelve-thirty they were ringing the front-door bell of an imposing Elizabethan manor which they had been informed was Lorrington Hall.

The door was opened by a man in black clothes whom Cub presumed to be the butler. There was nothing of the jovial countryman about him. On the contrary, he was a small, hard-faced little man with a sallow complexion and dark active eyes that surveyed the callers with suspicion if not actual hostility. His manner was in accord with his appearance.

'Yes, what is it?' he asked sharply.

Cub answered. He did not say much, for one thing because he did not like the man and half expected a rebuff. He merely explained that they were old comrades of Captain King. They had called to see him.

The butler's manner remained uncompromising. He told them, shortly, that Captain King was not at home.

'Do you know where he is?' asked Cub.

'Captain King does not tell me his business,' answered the butler stiffly.

'When are you expecting him back?'

The door started to close. 'He may be away for some time – that's all I can tell you. Good day.'

'Thanks,' said Cub, and turned away.

'That poodle-faker wants his face pushing in,' rasped Copper, staring at the closed door. 'Looks as if we've come all this way fer nothin'.'

'This gets odder and odder,' said Cub as they started back up the drive. 'What can Gimlet be doing?'

'There's somethin' fishy about it,' declared Copper. 'I don't like it.'

'I can't believe that Gimlet would let us down,' put in Trapper moodily.

'Nor he wouldn't,' growled Copper.

Near the gate a youngish man, in well-worn khaki battle-dress with Service insignia removed, was trimming the edge of the drive.

Copper accosted him with the easy confidence of one soldier addressing another. 'Say, chum, when did you last see your boss?' he asked. 'We served under 'im in the recent fuss, and we thought we'd like ter see 'im.'

The soldier stopped work, leaning on his hoe. 'I saw him three days ago. I drove him to the station when he went off to Scotland.'

Cub started, a puzzled frown lining his forehead. 'Off to *where?*'

'Scotland.'

'Blimey!' ejaculated Copper. 'What did 'e want ter go there for? We 'ad a date with 'im in London.'

'He said something about seeing some old comrades in London,' admitted the soldier. 'He said he thought he had time to slip up to Scotland first and look over the property.'

'Property? What property?'

'It seems his uncle died while he was away at the war, and left him a big property up in the Highlands – grouse moor, deer forest, lodge, and all the rest of it. There was a bit in the paper about it. I cut it out. I think I've still got it.' The soldier took a much-worn wallet from his pocket, selected a slip of paper from sundry photographs and letters, and handed it over.

Cub took it and read it with interest. From time to time for the benefit of the others he made a comment. 'House called Strathcarglas Lodge ... near a place called Auchrory ... nearest station Tomnarrow. Phew! An estate of nearly a hundred thousand acres.'

'Make a good Commando battle-training ground,' suggested Copper. 'Maybe that's his idea.'

'You can keep the paper if you like,' offered the soldier. 'I've done with it.'

'Thanks.' Cub did not really want the clipping, but to be friendly he folded it and put it in his pocket.

Copper jerked a thumb towards the house. 'That nasty-looking head-cook-and-bottle-washer who runs your show wants 'is mug pushin' in,' he remarked. 'Why didn't he tell us the boss 'ad gone ter Scotland? Did 'e know about it?'

'I suppose so. Maybe he thought you were just touting for jobs and it was no business of yours.'

Copper's shrewd Cockney eyes narrowed. 'Not our business, eh? That's where 'e's wrong. And suppose we was toutin' fer jobs – who's got a better right?'

'No one,' admitted the soldier warmly, eyeing Copper's massive figure. 'Haynes – that's the butler – is a queer type. I don't like him and he doesn't like me; but I can't afford to fall out with my job.'

'Did your boss say anything else when he went off?' asked Cub.

'He said I was to have the car at the station to meet him off the noon train today.'

'Come to think of it, I saw you at the station,' observed Copper. 'I didn't recognise you just now in yer workin' kit.'

'That's right. I was at the station.'

'That was the train we were on,' declared Cub. 'Gimlet wasn't on it.'

'You're telling me he wasn't!' muttered the soldier. 'I've mucked up the car for nothing.'

Copper turned towards the gate. 'Well, so long, chum. We'll be on our way.'

'My name's George Vass,' called the soldier. 'If I can be of any help, let me know. So long.'

'S'long.'

Copper walked on, his forehead creased by the effort of deep thinking. 'I don't like it,' he muttered. 'Gimlet can't 'ave changed so much that 'ed say one thing and do another. No bloomin' fear. It's fishy, mates ... fishy, that's what it is. Well, let's get back ter London town.'

'And when we get to London, what then?' asked Trapper.

'We could call at the Ritz to see if he's been there – that's about all we can do,' suggested Cub.

'All right. Let's do that,' agreed Copper. 'But I don't like it.'

'So you said before,' murmured Cub.

The party returned to London, and that evening made enquiries at the Ritz. Nothing had been seen or heard of Captain King. The reserved room had not been claimed. The manager was rather annoyed about it.

'Strike a light!' muttered Copper. 'That beats anythin' I ever 'eard of.

Why, we might 'ave lain sittin' in that place waitin' till now, swelp me. That ain't like Gimlet. Something's 'appened to 'im, I'll take my oath on it.'

'I think you're right,' said Cub. 'There is something queer about it. Even if Gimlet went to Scotland he could have sent us a wire. He must still be there. Why doesn't he get in touch with us?'

'There's only one answer ter that,' asserted Copper. ''E can't, and you can bet yer sweet life on that. And I'll tell yer somethin' else. I'm goin' up there ter find out why. What's the name of this place 'e went to, Cub?'

Cub referred to the clipping. 'Strathcarglas Lodge. The nearest station is Tomnarrow-on-Spey.'

Copper looked at the others. 'Well, what about it? I ain't never bin ter Scotland, but I knew some of the boys in the Fifty-first Highland Division, and I reckon it's time I saw where they came from.'

'Tch! What are we waiting for?' asked Trapper. 'Let's shove along. There's too many people in London to suit me, anyway.'

'When I was a kid I used ter sell papers outside Euston Station,' said Copper. 'There was a fast train north at seven-twenty. We can just do it, and have time ter pick up some grub at the coffee-stall outside. Come on.' He made a run for a passing bus.

And that is how it came about that shortly before eleven the following morning found three strangers, with haversacks slung, and raincoats over their shoulders, standing on the little lonely platform of Tomnarrow station, watching the train puff out of sight on its unhurried run to Aberdeen. The travellers, with their war gratuities sadly depleted, looked about them for a town or village. There was none. The tiny station stood alone, in the centre, it seemed, of unlimited solitude, a silent world of rounded purple hills that towards the east rose ever higher to merge at last into a group of rugged peaks. A questing buzzard floated past on lazy wings. After the noise and bustle of the south, Cub found the complete absence of sound almost uncanny. Only one other human being was in sight. A man, the station-master or porter, was walking towards his little grey stone house.

'Blimey! Where 'ave we got to?' enquired Copper plaintively.

Cub inclined his head towards the solitary man, who had now started to stack peat against a shed. 'Let's ask him,' he suggested.

CHAPTER TWO

First Reconnaissance

They soon came up with the man, a lean, weather-bronzed Highlander. He turned when he heard them coming, slowly, as if time was a thing of no account.

'Can you direct us to a lodge called Strathcarglas?' requested Cub.

The Highlander, evidently a man who used words carefully, considered the question and the questioners. He pointed to a narrow heath-fringed road that wound an undulating treeless course across the moor to disappear into distant hills.

'How far is it?' asked Cub.

Again the man gave the question some thought before answering in the true soft Highland brogue. 'Seventeen miles.'

Copper drew a deep breath. 'Seventeen ... stiffen the crows!' he exclaimed. 'I swore when the war was over that I wouldn't do any more walking.'

Further enquiries produced further facts. The village of Auchrory lay at a distance of twelve miles. It was not actually a village but a district, a few crofts scattered along a glen – Glencarglas, the valley of the River Carglas. There was no transport available between the station and the glen; there never had been, and – added the man – it was to be hoped that there never would be. Motor-cars ran over the sheep and disturbed the grouse. The shooting lodge, Strathcarglas, was five miles beyond the village.

'The new owner of the lodge was here the other day,' prompted Cub, seeking information.

'Aye. Frae London.'

'Did you see him?'

'Aye. I mind him fine.'

'How did he get to Auchrory?'

'He walked.'

'When did he come back?'

'He hasna come back.'

'He might have come back without you seeing him,' suggested Cub.

'Och! If he'd come back this way, I'd have seen him,' said the Scot. 'Unless he went across yon hills to Deeside,' he added.

'Is that the nearest place in the other direction?'

'Aye.'

'How far is it?'

'Forty miles.'

Cub was slightly incredulous. 'Do you mean – if we started across the hills there is nothing for forty miles?'

'A croft or two maybe, or a stalker's hut for the red deer on yon high tops.'

'Did the gentleman who came here say anything to you before he started walking?'

'He asked the road.'

'What did he do about his luggage?'

'Och, he carried it. 'Twas only a bag.'

Cub looked at the others. 'That settles it. Gimlet went this way, and he hasn't come back. It's pretty certain he'd come back the way he went.' To the man he said, 'Is there a tavern or an inn at Auchrory?'

'Aye, there is that. The Glencarglas Arms. A mon named McTaggart keeps it now since old Coutts died sudden twa years back.'

'I see. Thanks very much.' Cub turned back to the others. 'We'd better start walking.'

'Aye,' said the Scot, 'ye'd better away. 'Tis a fine dee, but the weather on yon hills is not to be trusted at this time of the year. She changes quick.'

'What are those mountains?' enquired Cub, pointing to the east. He used the word 'mountains' naturally, for that is what in fact they were, although he noticed that the Scot referred to them as hills.

'The Cairngorms.'

'And that's the direction of Auchrory?'

'Aye.'

Cub glanced at the blue sky overhead and smiled. 'A little rain wouldn't hurt us,' he remarked.

'When it rains doon here 'tis snow on the hill, or maybe hail, which is worse. The hail cuts the face off ye,' explained the Highlander. 'If ye're caught on the hill by the weather, ye dinna last long. If the clouds come down, make for the glen, or find a ledge and stay there; for there are places where if ye fall ye can fall an awfu' long way. Watch the deer. If ye see them coming doon the hill ye'll know a change is on the way.'

'Thanks,' said Cub. He paid little attention to this advice at the time, but he was reminded of it later.

'Come on,' said Copper impatiently, 'let's be moving.'

As they started down the road, for the first time Cub found time to appreciate the scenery. As he remarked to the others, he had no idea that such wild solitude was to be found in the British Isles.

'What's the odds?' growled Copper.

'The trouble with you is you've no imagination,' retorted Cub.

'There are bigger places in Canada,' observed Trapper casually.

'That may be, but this isn't Canada,' answered Cub, surveying the panorama ahead with interest and not without concern, for the road, which could be seen for miles except where it dived between the hills, seemed to have no end.

For its greater part the road wound a serpentine course between heather-clad hills, but there were places where, its way barred, it was forced to climb high to surmount them. At more or less regular intervals tall posts accompanied the road on its winding way, and these puzzled Cub until Trapper announced their purpose.

'We have them on open roads in Canada,' said he. 'They mark the road when she is under snow.'

As the time of the year was late September, the heather was beginning to fade, but predominant colour was still purple. Only the distant Cairngorms, towards which they were marching, were blue, navy blue, hard and clear-cut against the sky. The nearer, lower hills, bathed in autumn sunshine, seemed friendly enough, being for the most part smooth, rounded contours, curiously blotched, like war-time camouflage, with dark patches where the heather had been burnt, to provide – as Cub learned later – grazing for sheep and resting-places for young grouse. Sometimes as they walked on, a cock grouse, master of a covey, would leap into the air, and remain poised for a moment on hovering wings, to survey the intruders before sinking back out of sight into the heather. The curious, strident crowing of these birds seemed to go with the landscape, thought Cub, as they trudged along. Very soon the sound, by constant repetition, became part of it. It was, in fact, the only sound. There were, he noticed, places on the sides of the hills where the eternal heather was streaked with vivid yellow or green. He had no idea what caused this, but here again he was soon to learn. Once, at a tremendous height, a bird, that from its size could only have been an eagle, passed over on rigid pinions. For a little while the grouse fell silent.

Copper mopped his face with a large handkerchief, for the sun blazed down on the open road with surprising force. 'We must be nuts,' he muttered petulantly. 'As if we ain't done enough marchin' ter larst a life-time. If my old Ma could see me she'd think I was outer me mind – my oath she would.'

'Then let's go back,' bantered Cub.

'What!' Copper glared. 'Me go back! What we start we finish. Am I right, Trapper, old pal?'

'Sure you're right,' agreed Trapper without enthusiasm.

The party strode on.

'I'm trying to work this problem out,' said Cub presently. 'Gimlet travelled to Scotland on Monday. His intention must have been to spend Tuesday here and catch the night train back, arriving in London in plenty of time for our party. He intended staying the night at the Ritz and catching the early morning train back to Devon. We know that because he arranged for George Vass, his chauffeur, to meet him. Something went wrong with the timetable. What was it? All I can think of is, he didn't know it was seventeen miles from Tomnarrow station to the Lodge. If he did, then he must have reckoned on getting transport, otherwise he would have realised that it was impossible for him to get from the station to the Lodge, look round, and get back to the station the same night. That's all right so far as it goes, but he would have discovered all this at Tomnarrow station, before

343

he started for the Lodge; in which case he would have sent us a wire calling the party off. I'm convinced that either he would have postponed his trip to the Lodge and gone back to London on the next train, or he would have let us know. In any case, even if he had done none of these things, why is he still here? Why didn't he catch the London train yesterday – or today? Today's Friday, and he's still missing. He's been missing since Tuesday, when he left the station, until now – Friday afternoon. Of course, there may be nothing to it. We may find him at the tavern, the Glencarglas Arms. He may be at the Lodge, but as we don't know whether it is furnished or not or if there is any staff there, it's no use guessing about that. I still think it's queer. It isn't like Gimlet to stay on up here without a word to let us know what has happened. Well, he'll be surprised to see us. We shall find him, of course. There can't be so many strangers in these parts that the locals don't notice them. In fact, I should say a stranger here is an event.'

It had turned three o'clock when the travellers reached what they took to be Auchrory; at least, for some time they had been passing an occasional grey-stone croft, usually some distance from the road, although fields of arable land were few and far between. Sheep, wandering on the hillside, or shaggy long-horned Highland cattle deep in a glen, were the only stock. Cub noticed an isolated cottage that had been turned into a little general shop. A red posting-box had been let into the front wall.

Eventually, ahead, at a bend in the road where the glen with outcrops of naked rock rose almost sheer, they observed what they assumed to be their objective, the Glencarglas Arms, a long, low building of some size, with a thick-slated roof, standing with its feet almost in the heather. Out-buildings formed a rough square behind the main premises. There was no garden, not even an apology for one. The only growth that appeared to flourish was dank moss. So much could be seen at first glance.

'That must be the pub,' said Copper.

Cub agreed.

As they drew nearer, two other features were revealed. For some time Cub had been conscious of a sound which, as they walked on, increased in volume. It was not unlike the noise made by a distant train. Now he saw the cause. It was a river, a turbulent stream that came pelting between the hills to skirt the tavern and go plunging on under an ancient single-span stone bridge to an unknown destination. This river had nothing in common with leisurely, reed-fringed southern streams. Its way was hard, for it was governed by rocky banks which controlled its width from ten to thirty yards. Fallen rocks impeded its progress. The water was clear but dark peaty-brown in colour. In the widest places it was shallow, but where it was hemmed in by rock it formed deep, sinister pools.

There is always a fascination about a river, and Cub stopped to look at it. He himself had had few opportunities for fishing, but his father was a keen fisherman, and from his conversations he had learned a good deal about the art.

'This must be the Carglas,' he remarked. 'There will be trout in that river – probably salmon, too. Pity we didn't bring a rod. The river, I suppose, accounts for the inn.'

'What do you mean by that?' demanded Copper.

'The Glencarglas Arms is obviously a fishing hotel. There's no other reason for a pub to be here. You'll find these fishing hotels all over Scotland. I know, because my father used to come up here a lot. He was going to bring me, but the war put an end to that.'

The second feature to present itself was a road, a side turning; or, not to create a wrong impression, a track. Joining the road at right angles it twisted across the moor for a short distance before losing itself in the hills. At the junction of the two roads a notice-board had been erected. It bore two words: Dangerous Road. Cub looked at the notice, then at the track. He walked a pace nearer and looked again.

'Why stick that notice up?' questioned Trapper. 'Who'd want to go up there, anyway?'

'You never know,' answered Cub. 'In normal times cars use these side roads, cars belonging to shooters who want to get to the grouse moors, or fishermen who want to get higher up the river.'

A small boy came along the main road, driving a black cow. Cub accosted him, pointing up the track. 'Where does that road lead?' he asked.

'To the Lodge,' was the answer.

'What lodge?'

'Strathcarglas.'

'Then that's the way to Gimlet's property,' said Copper.

345

'Must be,' returned Cub.

'What about it? Shall we tackle it now?'

Cub glanced at the sky and saw that it was clouding over. 'We haven't a lot of time if we don't want to get caught out for the night,' he answered. 'We'd better go to the pub, first, to see if they can put us up. While we're having something to eat, we can decide whether we go straight on or wait until tomorrow. The chances are that we shall find Gimlet staying at the pub. If the Lodge hasn't been used for some time, it's unlikely that there will be any staff there, and if there's no staff Gimlet won't be likely to stay there. It's almost certain that he'd stay at the inn. Let's go and ask.'

They walked on to the tavern. As they drew nearer Cub paused again, this time to watch a man who was fly-fishing a pool just above the hotel.

'Looks like you were right, Cub,' observed Copper. 'This must be a fishing pub.'

'That's funny,' murmured Cub, half to himself.

''Strewth! What's wrong now?' grunted Copper. 'According to you there's always somethin' funny about somethin'.'

'There's something queer about this place, anyway, said Cub quietly.

'What are you gettin' at?' demanded Copper.

'To start with, look at that fellow fishing,' invited Cub. 'Most people who fish in Scotland, whether they are locals or visitors from the south, are real fishers. That fellow doesn't know what he's doing. I'll swear he's never fished before. That's a salmon rod he's using. He's fishing a fly straight upstream, and that's something you just don't do. Not that he can cast a fly, anyway.'

'Perhaps he don't know any better?' suggested Copper.

'The man who keeps the pub should know. Why doesn't he tell him? Another thing that's queer is that lane we've just passed.'

'What about it?'

'The notice about the road being dangerous is new. It has only just been put up. Who would put it there, and why?'

'You tell me,' suggested Copper.

'Obviously, it would only be put there to stop people using it.'

'Who would want to use it?'

Cub shrugged. 'I don't know. But someone *has* used it, and recently.'

Copper raised his eyebrows. 'How do you know that?'

'I noticed motor-car tyre tracks in the mud – not one mark, but several.'

'That bloke at the station said there wasn't no transport on this road,' remarked Copper.

'And since we haven't met or been overtaken by a single vehicle, it seems that he is right,' replied Cub. 'That there are tyre marks on the track leading to the Lodge seems all the more queer. I may be crazy, but there are things about this entire set-up that don't hang together. Remember, it was somewhere about here that Gimlet disappeared. If he isn't at this pub or if he doesn't soon turn up, I shall be more than ever convinced that this place isn't what it seems. Let's go to the pub and make some enquiries. Leave the talking to me. I have a feeling that we ought to be careful.'

Entering the hotel, they found themselves in a small hall. A door, standing wide open, gave access to a bar. There were no customers in it, but a middle-aged man in his shirt-sleeves sat behind the bar, reading a newspaper. He glanced up when the newcomers entered and rose to his feet. There was nothing remarkable about the man. In fact, his general appearance was what might have been expected.

Cub came straight to the point. 'Can we stay the night here?'

The answer was even more to the point. 'No,' was the curt reply.

Cub looked surprised. 'Why not?'

'Full up.'

'Oh!' said Cub. 'In that case, can we have something to eat and drink?'

The man thought for a moment. 'I could let you have a bit of bread and cheese,' he answered slowly. 'And I've got some beer.'

'All right. Bread and cheese will do,' returned Cub. 'I'd rather have a pot of tea than beer.' He sat down.

The man nodded and disappeared into the back regions.

Cub looked at the others. 'He's lying,' he whispered. 'He isn't full up. There must be eight bedrooms at least. If this place was full, the hall would be littered with rods, gaffs, fishing-bags, mackintoshes, and all sorts of clobber. I've seen fishing pubs. There wasn't a single hat or coat on the hall-stand. I'll tell you something else. That fellow's name may be McTaggart, but he's no Scot.'

The hotel keeper came back with three plates of bread and cheese, to which presently he added cups and saucers and a pot of tea. Having put these on a small table, he retired behind the bar.

'Where are you making for?' he asked in a casual voice.

'Nowhere in particular,' answered Cub. 'We were hoping to find a man here whom we thought might give us a job.'

There was a short, curious silence.

'Oh!' said the man slowly. 'What was his name?'

Cub looked up. 'Captain King,' he said distinctly.

The man, who was wiping down the bar with a rag, stopped short. His head came round so that his eyes met Cub's. 'King,' he said slowly, as if weighing the word.

'That's right – King,' repeated Cub. 'Has he, by any chance, been here?'

The man shook his head. 'No. No, he hasn't been here.'

At this junction the man who had been fishing came in. He found a seat at the end of the bar and ordered a glass of whisky. With the glass in his hand, he contemplated the travellers thoughtfully.

Cub returned the inspection. The man, a big florid fellow with a heavy fair moustache, wore tweeds; to be precise, the garments commonly called plus-fours. He was, in fact, dressed for the country, but it seemed to Cub that he did not wear his clothes like a countryman. It was hard to say exactly what caused this impression. Perhaps the man was too immaculate to be a genuine fisherman. His plus-fours were cut in an exaggerated fashion. His tie was too loud. With one thing and another, Cub formed the opinion that this man was pretending to be something that he was not.

The man spoke first. 'You boys going far?' he asked carelessly.

'It all depends,' answered Cub cautiously.

'Depends on what?'

'How we get on.'

'So you're on the loose, eh?'

'More or less.'

'Ah-ha.' The man sipped his whisky. 'Not running away from – anything ... are you?' he suggested slyly.

'Why – are you?' returned Cub curtly.

The man's expression changed. He frowned. 'I just wondered what you were doing here, that's all.'

'We're minding our own business,' replied Cub softly.

'Quite right. No offence meant.'

Cub went on with his bread and cheese. Presently the man got up and went out. The barman leaned on his bar, apparently reading his newspaper, but, Cub thought, actually paying more attention to them than the occasion warranted.

Cub broke the silence. 'There's a lane turns off to the right, just above the hotel. Where does it lead to?'

'Nowhere,' was the half-humorous reply.

'It must have led to somewhere sometime?' suggested Cub. 'Else why put a notice up saying the road is dangerous?'

'The road is dangerous,' answered the man. 'There are places where it has almost disappeared. I've never been up it myself, but they say it leads to an old disused tin-mine. Hasn't been worked for years, of course.'

'Why of course?'

'Because the metal petered out, I suppose.'

Another short silence. The travellers finished their meal.

'Sure you can't fix us up for the night – we aren't particular where we sleep?' said Cub.

The man shook his head. 'Sorry. Haven't a corner anywhere.'

'In that case we'd better push along,' murmured Cub, taking out some money to pay for the meal. A coin fell on the floor and he stooped to pick it up.

The others rose, and with a nod they all left the hotel.

Close outside the front door the fisherman had left his rod – at any rate, a rod stood there, fourteen feet of cane, leaning against the wall. As Cub drew level, he stopped to look at it. He reached out, took the gut cast in his hand and allowed it to run on to the fly, which he examined with interest.

'What's the idea?' enquired Copper sarcastically. 'Thinking of tryin' your luck?'

'No,' answered Cub, speaking softly. 'That cast confirms my opinion that the man using it is no fisher. No fisher ever tied knots like those. If he hooked a fish they'd slip, so whether he knows it or not he's wasting his time. And the fly isn't the sort of lure I'd use on a day like this.' Cub parted his lips as if to continue his criticism, but changed his mind, and after a quick glance at the door walked on. Nor did he speak again until they came to a bend in the road, where a shoulder of rock hid the hotel from view. Then he turned to the others. His manner was crisp.

'Copper was right at the beginning,' he said tersely. 'This place is phoney. Those men are lying – both of them. Gimlet's been to that pub. After walking twelve miles from the station he was bound to call there, if only for a drink. That man calling himself McTaggart is no Scot, and the fellow pretending to be a fisherman is a fake. It sticks out a mile. We needn't argue about it. Gimlet has been to that pub. I *know* he's been there. If he did nothing else, he sat in that bar and smoked a cigarette.'

'How do you know that?' demanded Copper.

Cub held out his right hand, open, palm upwards. 'I picked this up from a join in the linoleum,' he said quietly. 'A matchstalk,' murmured Copper.

'A match torn from a *book* of matches,' corrected Cub. 'Read the name on it.'

Copper looked at some tiny printed words on the side of the minute slip of pasteboard; and as he read them he drew in his breath sharply.

'Ritz Hotel, London,' he breathed. He turned slowly to stare at Trapper. 'Cub's right,' he muttered. 'Swelp me!'

CHAPTER THREE

The Reconnaissance Yields Results

'I think we take a hand in this,' said Trapper, softly but meaningly, when the full significance of the discovery had been realised.

'That lying swine in the bar,' growled Copper. 'For two pins I'd go back, cut his feet off at the ankles, sharpen the stumps and hammer him into his own backyard.'

'We shan't get anywhere by resorting to violence – at any rate, not at this stage,' said Cub. 'Let's use our heads. This is how I see it. Gimlet came here. He went to the pub, as he was bound to, if only for a drink and to ask the way. He might never have got beyond it, or he might have gone straight on to the Lodge. He hasn't gone back to the station. Incidentally, talking of the Lodge, you'll notice that the barman didn't say anything about it when I asked him where that tract led to. He said it went to an old mine – which may, of course, be true. But why didn't he mention the Lodge, which is a more important building than an abandoned mine? He must have had a reason for not mentioning it. That boy I spoke to said the Lodge was up there; he's a local kid and I bet he was telling the truth. It all smells fishy to me. I feel it in my bones that these people are in some way mixed up with Gimlet and the Lodge. How, I can't imagine. But there it is. It was obvious that he didn't want us hanging around here. What are they up to? They can't be highway robbers – that sort of thing is past and done with, even in remote Scotland, where I believe it was once a profitable line of business.'

Copper struck his thigh a violent blow. He became suddenly excited. 'Holy winkles!' he cried. 'I've got it.'

The others looked at him in astonishment.

'Now what have you got?' enquired Cub.

'That barman,' said Copper fiercely. 'When I first went in and clapped eyes on him, I said to myself, I've seen that chivvy before. In the Force we're trained to remember faces, you know. It's over five years since I was a London bobby, but I ain't forgot. All the time I was inside I kept wondering where I'd seen 'im before, but I couldn't remember. Now I've got 'im.' Copper leaned forward and went on in a hoarse whisper. 'Do you remember just before the war there was a scare about two criminals who got away from Dartmoor? Both were in for a long stretch. Forsyth and Burke were their names. It all comes back to me now. When they were on the run Forsyth shot a policeman. With half the country lookin' for 'em, they managed to get to Scotland and find a hide-out somewhere in these parts – in an old ruined croft right off the map. But as it happened, two keepers see smoke comin' out of the chimney and went to find out what was goin' on. Forsyth and Burke must 'ave seen 'em comin'. They opened up on 'em. One of the keepers was hit. He died later. The other went ter fetch 'elp, but by the time he'd got it, the crooks were away again. They took ter the hills – there was nowhere else. But the game was up. Forsyth was run down and shot dead by a policeman – near Aberdeen, I think it was. But Burke got away, and as far as I know 'e was never rounded up. The war came along and the story sort of faded out, but during my last few months in the Force I see Burke's photo every day, on the divisional notice-board, amongst the wanteds. That man inside the pub is an older-lookin' fellow than Burke – but then 'e would be, after six years. He's grown a moustache, too, but I'll take my davy that's 'im. I'll let the Yard know about this.'

'Just a minute,' put in Cub, who had listened to this recital with wonder on his face. 'Not so fast. This handing over of a wanted man, if it is Burke, may be all right; but we came here to find Gimlet. Calling in the police at this stage will throw the wrench into the gears. There will be a general rumpus and Gimlet may disappear for good.'

'True enough,' agreed Copper with some reluctance.

'We can afford to bide our time,' Cub pointed out. 'Burke, who must have changed his name to McTaggart, doesn't suspect that we've spotted him. He'll hang on here. I think it will pay us better to play fox for a bit before calling in the police.'

Trapper nodded. '*Zut!* I think so. What shall we do, then?'

'Personally, for a start, I'm in favour of exploring that road that leads to the Lodge,' advised Cub. 'We might have a look at the Lodge itself, in the hope of locating Gimlet or picking up the trail. The weather is still fair. We've got rations, and we can sleep rough if necessary. We've done it before often enough.'

'Burke's an old lag,' muttered Copper. 'Once a crook always a crook. If he's 'ere, then there's a racket of some sort goin' on – you can bet yer life on that.'

'Gimlet must have blundered into it,' opined Cub. 'Let's try the Lodge. It won't do to be seen going up that lane, but if we cut round the back of the hill behind us and then swing to the right, we ought to strike the track well up the glen, out of sight of the pub.'

'Okay,' agreed Copper. 'Let's march. I'm aching fer action now I know what's what, but we ain't got too much time if we're goin' ter give the Lodge the once-over before it gets dark.'

Without further parley they set off, following the course of a burn that babbled round the foot of a hill, which they kept between them and the tavern. This brought them to a growth of stunted birches, and using these for cover they swung round behind the hotel and struck the track some distance above it. In order to reach the track, however, they had to wade the river, which, it was now revealed, followed the same course as the rough, stony road. Or it might be more correct to say that the track ran through the same deep glen as the river. There was no difficulty in fording the river at some broad shallows. Presently it was possible to see that the water, in its headlong rush from the hills, had cut a deep gorge into the earth. There were places where the sides of this gorge were sheer cliff, glistening with dripping peat-water that drained out of the hill above; there were also places where the banks, less sheer, were clad in dense stands of spruce, larch, and fir, with the result that the scene presented was wild in the extreme. And as the party proceeded, the picture, instead of softening, became ever more harsh and forbidding. The cliffs towered for three hundred feet or more, so that the river at the bottom appeared to be no more than a brook; the noise of its turbulent progress was always audible.

'Strike a light!' exclaimed Copper once, keeping well away from the lip of the chasm at a point where a landslide had carried half the track away with it. 'No wonder they said the road was dangerous. I'd be sorry to bring a jeep along here on a dark night – my oath, I would.'

'All the same,' Cub pointed out quietly, 'cars do come up here. You can see the tyre marks. Look here.' He pointed at some soft ground caused by water oozing out of the heather across the track. Such places were common. No effort was required to see the wheel tracks, for the imprint of the tread of the tyres was plain enough. 'The people who use this road must know it pretty well,' went on Cub. 'There are places where there are not more than six inches to spare between the bank and the edge of the cliff. Even knowing the road one would have to drive slowly and carefully.'

'You're telling me,' muttered Trapper. '*Ma foi!* This reminds me more and more of the foothills of the Rockies.' He frowned suddenly, his eyes still on the ground. 'But nobody said anything about a farm up here,' he murmured.

'Farm? What about a farm?' enquired Copper.

Trapper stooped and picked up three or four grains of corn, which on closer examination turned out to be barley. It was quite clean and fresh, because – as Trapper pointed out – it had not been pressed into the mud. It lay on top and had obviously been dropped quite recently. 'Barley to me means a farm,' he asserted. 'Threshed barley would hardly be coming *up* this track. It must have been on its way to the main road – which means, I think, that there must be a farm up here, some place. Not only a farm but land good enough to grow corn.'

'You ought ter be a blinkin' detective,' averred Copper. 'Suppose there is a farm. What about it?'

Trapper shrugged. 'Nothing. I do not know Scotland, but there seems something wrong about this. The moor does not look to me like arable land. And if there is a farm, why were we not told of it? Why didn't the boy mention it?' He studied the road again and the surrounding country. 'This does not look to me like a farm track. What sort of farmer would let his road get in such a state?'

'When we see him, you can ask him,' suggested Copper with mild sarcasm.

They went on, scanning the track ahead for the first glimpse of the

Lodge. For a time, as the light slowly began to fade, they saw nothing – nothing, that is, except the wild creatures that had found safe sanctuary in the remote glen. Foxes, stoats, mountain hares, and rabbits were common. Once, rounding a bend, a golden eagle that had been standing on the edge of the precipice launched itself into space on majestic wings; on another occasion a roe-deer bounded away into the cover of a wood. Trapper watched it go with reflective eyes, and a little later, with his jack-knife in his hand, disappeared into a copse, to return with a stout ash wand some two and a half feet long. This, as he walked, he proceeded to trim. From time to time he made other sorties, and returned with smaller sticks, always straight ones.

The others knew what he was doing, for in the past they had had ample opportunity of observing his masterly skill with the primitive weapon known as a bow and arrow.

'What's the idea?' enquired Copper, after a wink at Cub.

'I could live in this country without money,' said Trapper simply. 'I have lived for weeks in territory where there is less game. Our rations will not last long – unless we add to them a little fresh meat, or perhaps fish.'

'That would be poaching,' warned Cub.

'This is Gimlet's property,' returned Trapper. 'If he is not available for us to ask his permission to hunt, we shall have to hunt without his permission. But he will not mind. He would not have old comrades starve to death. Besides, what is a rabbit, more or less?' He went on trimming his stick. 'I wish I had brought my bow. But how should I know I might need it? Still, I always have arrow-heads and feathers in my kit. Tch! You will see.'

A few minutes later he stopped, picked up another grain of barley, and after a glance at it tossed it aside. 'Someone has been this way lately,' he announced. 'Barley does not travel by itself.'

'Why lately?' asked Cub.

'Because corn would not lie for long on this track without a bird finding it,' answered Trapper.

'So what?' queried Cub. 'Barley is a common enough crop in Scotland.'

'Still, I don't see any farm,' murmured Trapper, walking on.

Twilight was softening the harshness of the scene when, turning a corner, Copper uttered an exclamation and pointed up one of the mysterious little side glens which had at frequent intervals invited attention and speculation as to where they ended. Standing in this particular glen, which, treeless, was as bleak as anything that could be imagined, bounded by dark hills that bore many scars, was a fairly extensive stone building, grey, dilapidated, as cheerless and forlorn as an abandoned prison. There were no windows. An arched entrance, gaping like a mouth that would not shut, gave access to it. The merest outline of an overgrown track, leading to this entrance, could just be discerned.

'Swelp me!' muttered Copper. 'That ain't a house. What can it be, stuck away up there?'

'It certainly isn't a farm. I'd say it's the tin-mine Burke spoke about,' guessed Cub.

'Then he wasn't lying about that.'

'Apparently not. The place, whatever it is, is deserted.'

Copper surveyed the building, which stood at a distance of perhaps a quarter of a mile. 'My gosh!' he breathed. 'I never saw a drearier-lookin' place than that. What a spot fer a murder. Fair gives yer the shivers ter look at it, don't it?'

'It certainly does,' agreed Cub, who was examining the ground closely. 'The wheel tracks don't go up to the mine – they go straight on. Wait! Yes, they do, by Jove! That's queer. What do you make of that? Most of the tracks go straight on, which means, I imagine, that the Lodge is still somewhere ahead; but there are two sets of tracks leading to the mine – or maybe it's one up and one down. Anyway, somebody has been up here, and lately, too. You can see where the wheels have cut into the moss.'

Copper still stood staring at the building. 'This beats cockfighting,' he remarked. 'I wonder...?'

'You wonder what?' queried Cub.

'What fools we should look if we was makin' a mystery outer nuthin' – if Gimlet suddenly came strollin' round the corner and said, Come on, boys, you're just in time fer supper.' He turned a knowing eye on Cub. 'It's easy ter let yer imagination run away with yer. I've 'ad this sort of thing before, when I was in the Force. There's always somethin' creepy about an empty house.'

A golden eagle flew majestically over their heads.

'So far as this one is concerned, we can settle any argument in ten minutes,' replied Cub. 'Let's have a look at the place. What have we to be afraid of, anyway? If there's nothing here, well, we'll just carry on to the Lodge.'

'Okay,' agreed Copper.

The party turned off the track and headed direct for the building.

'Don't you think we ought to be a bit more careful how we approach?' suggested Cub.

'No,' answered Copper shortly. 'We ain't in France now. I've done with soldiering.' He tapped his pocket. 'If anyone wants ter start an argument with us, why, 'e can 'ave it – my oath, he can, after us paddin' the hoof all this way. Am I right, Trapper?'

'Sure you're right, pal,' agreed Trapper.

They went on, their feet making no noise in the lush moss. The only sounds were the murmur of an unseen burn and the resentful cackling of grouse deep in the heather. The building did not improve on closer acquaintance; it remained as silent, as cold, as cheerless, as dead as the boulders that lay around it.

Copper made straight for the entrance. At a distance of ten yards he stopped to make another scrutiny of the pile. 'What a' 'ole,' he muttered. 'Blimey! What a' 'ole.' He strode on through the entrance, which now took the form of a short tunnel giving access to a central courtyard of some size. The others followed closely, their footsteps echoing with a hollow sound as they passed through the tunnel into the yard, which was bounded on three sides by long low buildings now in the last stages of dilapidation. The walls, built of local stone, were more or less intact, but the roofs had collapsed, or had been blown down, exposing the broken wooden skeletons of the roof-trees. A doorway, with its door hanging drunkenly on one hinge, invited exploration. Copper went through and into the building. It was empty. There were signs of oil stains on the earth floor as if the place had once housed machinery, but if so the machines had been taken away. The scars on the hillside beyond were now obvious excavations, presumably where ore had been mined. Some took the form of short caves driven into the hillside.

The centre of the courtyard was occupied by a conspicuous feature – a rough wooden structure with a roof, now awry, that had once covered a windlass of some size, so that the whole thing had the appearance of a large well. A rusty steel cable, broken off short, hung from the wheel over a vertical shaft, and this, Cub surmised, was the original mine. He walked up to it and looked down. This at first was no more than idle curiosity, for he was satisfied that the place was, in fact, an abandoned mine of some sort. But then, as he stood there, he saw something else, something that raised his casual curiosity to a spirit of definite enquiry. The earth round the edge of the shaft was soft. In it, clearly imprinted, was the mark of a heavy nailed boot. The astonishment of Robinson Crusoe on first observing the footprint on the beach of his desert island was no greater than that of Cub when his eyes fell on this significant sign of human activity. The boot print was on the very edge of the mine and pointing towards it. It could only mean one thing.

Advancing a pace and taking his pocket torch in his hand, Cub turned the beam down the shaft, in order, if possible, to ascertain the depth of it – a natural enough thing to do. The shaft turned out to be more shallow, much more shallow, than he expected. He judged it to be about twenty feet deep. His curiosity satisfied, he was about to turn away when an object at the bottom caught his eye. He looked again. He stared, stared hard, while a sensation like pins-and-needles crept down his spine.

'Copper,' he called in a queer strangled voice, 'come here.'

Copper came, increasing his pace when he saw the expression on Cub's face. 'What is it?' he asked quickly.

Cub passed the torch with a hand that was no longer steady. 'Look down that shaft,' he requested. 'I thought I could see – something. Can you – or am I imagining things?'

Copper looked down the shaft. He stiffened. Then, lying flat and extending his arm to full length, he looked again. Suddenly he scrambled to his feet. His face had lost its colour. 'You ain't seein' things, mate,' he said tersely. 'There's a corpse down there. Some poor blighter must 'ave fallen in ... or else ...'

For several seconds they stared at each other in mute horror.

'What are we going to do about it?' asked Cub through dry lips.

'We've got ter get 'im up,' declared Copper. 'We can't leave 'im there. This looks like bein' a police job, after all – my oath, and not 'alf.'

'How are we going to get him up?'

'There's only one way,' asserted Copper. 'One of us will 'ave ter go down. I'll go.' He ripped off his coat.

'It's a long drop,' warned Cub.

'Gimme your belt,' ordered Copper. 'And yours, Trapper. Now the slings off the 'aversacks – that ought ter just about do it.'

With hands deft from long Commando training Copper buckled the three belts together, and to the end buckle linked the haversack slings, so that he soon had a rope about eighteen feet long. One end he took in his big hands with a firm grip. 'Let me down slowly,' he commanded. 'I don't want ter land on top of the poor cove. When I sing out okay, haul away. Stand fast.' With the rope in his hands and the others hanging on, Copper disappeared over the edge of the shaft. Slowly the improvised rope ran out. There was a short delay. Then a voice came up from the depths. 'Okay – haul away!'

Trapper and Cub, with their feet braced against a rough brick coping, not without effort, hauled up a heavy weight.

'Easy does it,' said Trapper, through his teeth, as a limp body came into view. 'Hold tight!' Releasing his grip on the rope, he reached out and caught the body by the jacket in the small of the back.

The entire body came into view, to flop like a sack on the dank earth. It rolled a little and lay face downward. Without speaking, Trapper turned the body over so that the face was exposed. His breath hissed through his teeth.

'My God!' cried Cub in a choking voice. 'It's Gimlet!'

'Let's get Copper up,' said Trapper through tight lips.

CHAPTER FOUR

Activity in the Glen

A moment of wild, almost frenzied energy, and Copper, pale-faced, grimed with mud, came scrambling over the edge of the shaft. He went straight to Gimlet, muttering, 'How is he?'

'Isn't he dead?' cried Cub, who had taken this for granted.

'He wasn't a minute ago,' answered Copper. 'His heart was beating – I felt it. I don't fancy he's been down that hole for very long. He's in a mess, though.'

This last remark needed no qualification. Gimlet's face was ashen. There was a bruise on the side of his face and a line of congealed blood from his forehead to his chin. His hair was matted with blood, or mud, or both. His clothes, a grey lounge suit, were caked with mire. A quick examination disclosed no other wounds; nor, as far as could be ascertained, were any bones broken. Cub soaked his handkerchief in a nearby pool and bathed the pallid face.

'What are we going to do with him?' he asked hoarsely.

'Yeah, what?' queried Trapper.

'We ought ter get 'im to a hospital, or a doctor, right away,' declared Copper.

'We've got to be careful,' put in Cub quickly. 'Don't let's kid ourselves. Gimlet didn't *fall* into that hole. Left alone, he'd never have come this way. He was brought here and thrown in. And if he was thrown in, those people at the pub had a hand in it. Who else could it have been? The pub is the only house for miles, yet obviously we can't go there. We can't even get on the road without them seeing us. We shall have to think of something, but that's no use. We must get him somewhere safe until he recovers consciousness and is able to tell us what all this is about.'

361

'How about one of the crofts we passed on the road?' suggested Copper.

'The nearest one must be close on four miles from here; that's too far. Besides, news travels like radio in these rural districts. The people at the hotel would soon get to hear of a wounded man being carried off the moor.'

'Then where can we take him?' Copper looked helplessly round the darkening landscape as if seeking inspiration from it.

'He'll have to stay here – I mean, in there,' growled Trapper, nodding towards the main building.

'I think that's the only answer,' agreed Cub. 'We can't carry him fifteen miles to the station, that's certain. This seems to be the only place, but it's dangerous.'

'Dangerous? How?' demanded Copper.

'In the first place, we shall have to light a fire if we don't want Gimlet to die from exposure, and a fire would be seen by anyone on the track – and we've got a good idea of who's using the track,' asserted Cub. 'In any case, the skunk who hit Gimlet on the head may come back to see if he's still alive.'

'Ho! That suits me fine,' grated Copper. ''E'll find something 'e don't expect if 'e comes back 'ere, my oath 'e will.'

'Let's take him in and see what we can do for him,' said Trapper. 'I'll go farther up the glen to see if I can find a better place. *Alors*, it may be there is a cave, or a ruined croft, or something.'

They carried Gimlet, who still showed no signs of recovering consciousness, into the building, and, making a bed of raincoats and jackets on the hard earth floor, got him as comfortable as the circumstances permitted. Cub tried chafing his hands, but without effect. Trapper went off. Copper went over Gimlet again and discovered a small mat of bloodstained hair on the back of his head: Cub resoaked his handkerchief and cleansed the wound.

'It's clear enough what happened,' said Copper viciously. 'Some skunk lambasted 'im on the back of the skull and knocked 'im out. Gimlet couldn't 'ave bin expecting it or the bloke who did it wouldn't 'ave got away with it so easy. Then 'e was dropped down the shaft. Lucky no bones are broke. If that crack on the nut 'as fractured 'is skull, this is goin' ter be a long job; but it may only be concussion.'

Trapper dragged the body out of the pit.

'A question is, how long has he been down that hole?' queried Cub.

'Not very long, I'd say, otherwise 'e would be stiff by now,' answered Copper pensively. 'Look at it this way. 'E travelled ter Scotland, as we know, on Monday, arriving Tuesday. Let's say 'e got ter the pub durin' the afternoon, the same as we did. Today's Friday. Call it three days 'e's been 'ere. I reckon 'e couldn't 'ave been lyin' down that hole longer than yesterday. What could 'e 'ave been up to on Wednesday? No wonder 'e didn't turn up fer the party.'

'We aren't likely to know any more until he wakes up and tells us,' rejoined Cub moodily. 'We'd better risk lighting a fire to keep him warm.'

Copper felt in Gimlet's breast pocket, half took out a wallet and allowed it to slide back. 'Robbery wasn't the motive, anyway,' he observed.

At this juncture Trapper hurried in with good news. He had, he said, found a hut higher up the glen. It was round the corner, out of sight of the mine and the road. It was just a plain stone building, but there was, among other things, a stove. The door had been locked, but he had forced it open.

'That will be a deerstalker's hut, I expect,' remarked Cub. 'They put them about the moors in case the hunters get benighted or caught in bad weather. Let's get him along.'

With the raincoats arranged as a sling, Gimlet, still unconscious, was transported to the new quarters, with which Copper and Cub expressed themselves well satisfied. They had good reason to be satisfied, for nothing they could have hoped for would have better suited their purpose. There was a stove, a table, and two forms for seating. Even more important, there was a charred, battered kettle, an old iron saucepan, a frying-pan, a teapot, and two cups. Two small tins were found to contain a small quantity of tea and sugar. There was a bottle of salt and a supply of dry sticks for firewood.

'Blinkin' marvellous,' declared Copper. 'Someone must 'ave known we was comin'. I'll soon 'ave a fire goin'. Fill the kettle, Cub; we'll see what some 'ot water will do. What are you up to, Trapper?'

Trapper was finishing an arrow with feathers and a barb which he had taken from his haversack. 'I think perhaps a little fresh meat, for soup, would be *bon*,' he answered.

'Okay,' agreed Copper. 'Let's see what we've got in the grub line ourselves.'

Now, when they had packed their haversack each had provided himself with the type of 'iron' rations most suited to his taste. Inroads had been made into these during the long train journey to Scotland, but, nevertheless, the bags yielded a fair assortment of foods – an assortment which would have been a guide to the nationality of the selector. Copper produced some bread (very stale) and cheese. From a greasy newspaper he turned out some chipped potatoes, the fish counterpart of which he had already consumed. He also had an onion. Trapper's contribution was a sausage, a tin of meat-paste, some biscuits, a tin of sweetened condensed milk, and coffee essence. Cub, rather shamefaced, could only provide a rather battered lump of cake and three bars of plain chocolate. The accumulated result was, as Copper remarked, nothing to shout about, but it was better than nothing. Trapper departed to augment the larder, and the others turned their attention to Gimlet, who was now moaning feebly.

'That's a good sign,' stated Copper. 'I reckon 'e won't be long now comin' round.'

Actually it was two hours before Copper's sanguine prophecy was fulfilled. Trapper had long ago returned, carrying what Cub took to be a small leg of mutton, but which turned out to be a tiny haunch of venison. The carcass of the roe-deer that had provided this was hanging outside, Trapper informed them.

Cub perceived that in the circumstances in which they found themselves, Trapper's long experience as a hunter was likely to be put to good practical use. 'At last you're living up to your name,' he remarked, smiling.

'We do not starve, I think,' returned Trapper complacently. 'What Gimlet will need when he comes round is soup, hot soup.' He went out with the saucepan for water from a nearby burn.

Later, Gimlet, who for some time had been stirring uneasily, opened his eyes. At first there was no recognition in them, although this may have been due to the absence of light, for the only illumination was the glow of the fire through the open flap at the bottom of the stove. Without using Cub's torch, the battery of which would soon have been exhausted had it been kept on all the time, there was no way of improving this.

Copper knelt beside Gimlet. 'How are yer feelin', sir?' he asked gently.

Gimlet started. He tried to sit up, but sank back. In his eyes dawned the light of full consciousness. 'Am I dreaming, or is it Copper?' he said in a weak voice.

'We're all 'ere, sir. You're okay now,' answered Copper.

Gimlet's eyes went round the party. 'Hello, Cub. Hello. Trapper.' Then, after a pause, 'Where are we?'

Cub answered. 'In Scotland, sir. Somewhere near Strathcarglas Lodge.'

'How in the name of all that's miraculous did you get here?'

'Oh, we just followed you up, sir,' announced Copper breezily. 'When you didn't turn up fer the party, we knew somethin' was wrong. Old soldiers ain't absent from parade without good reason.'

'I'm sorry about the party,' said Gimlet, trying to raise himself.

Copper propped him up, using the haversacks as a back-rest. 'What happened to you, sir?'

Gimlet wrinkled his forehead in an effort to think. 'I'm trying to remember. Where did you find me?'

'At the bottom of an old mine.'

'Good God!' Gimlet looked startled and amazed. 'And where are we now? Whose house is this?'

''Tain't a house, sir. It's a hut near the mine. Take it easy, sir. Presently you can tell us all about it.' To Trapper he said. 'Get some soup in a cup.' Then, turning back to Gimlet, 'How do you feel, sir?'

'Not too bad,' returned Gimlet, putting a hand to his forehead. 'My head's opening and shutting.'

'I don't wonder at that,' replied Copper. 'Someone pasted you on the back of the skull.'

'So that was it,' murmured Gimlet.

Trapper dropped on one knee and handed a cup of soup to Gimlet, who sipped it. There was a short silence until he had finished. 'That's better,' he declared. 'Give me a cigarette, someone. You'll find a case in my jacket pocket.'

The cigarette was soon got going. Gimlet took a few draws.

'What's this all about, sir?' asked Copper.

Gimlet exhaled smoke. 'I haven't the remotest idea,' he surprised everyone by saying.

'You mean – you don't know?' returned Copper incredulously.

'I have no more idea than you have,' said Gimlet weakly. 'I'll tell you all I know – it won't take long. I came to Scotland on Monday to look over some property that was left to me while I was away at the war. It was my intention to return for the party. I thought I had plenty of time. I got here on Tuesday, and walked along the road to the hotel.'

'The Strathcarglas Arms,' murmured Cub.

'That's right. I went in for a drink, to ask the way and to see if they could put me up for the night.'

'Who was there?' asked Copper.

'There were two men – one man behind the bar, and another fellow, a fisherman, I think.'

Copper nodded. 'Go on, sir.'

'I don't believe in telling everyone my business, so I didn't say much,' resumed Gimlet. 'Without mentioning my name, I said I was interested in a grouse moor and thought of looking over the Glencarglas property; whereupon the barman said he would be glad to run me up to the Lodge in his car – an offer which, naturally, I was glad to accept. The chap went on to say that, as it was getting late and the road was in a dangerous state, it would be better if we went in the morning. He said that, after seeing the Lodge, he would run me back to Tomnarrow station in time to catch the London train. This sounded a very reasonable suggestion and I agreed. I stayed the night at the hotel. That's really all there was to it. In the morning we set off. The fisherman chap said he would come with us for the ride. He had never seen the Lodge, he said, or the country behind the hotel.'

'The lying hound,' muttered Copper.

'So he came,' continued Gimlet. 'I sat in front with McTaggart; the fisherman chap – I think he said his name was Smith – sat behind. We seemed to go for some distance. I remember admiring the landscape ... and ...' Gimlet puckered his forehead. 'I can't remember anything after that.'

'Ah,' breathed Copper. 'That's because the fellow in the back seat bashed you on the head.'

Gimlet thought for a moment. 'I suppose that was it. I remember going up the road well enough, but from then on my mind is a complete blank.'

'I can tell you what happened after that,' said Copper. 'They took you up to the mine and chucked you down the black hole of Calcutta.'

'But why?'

'That's what we've got to find out and, if I know anything about it, we shan't be long,' asserted Copper. He went on to give an account of their own adventures, concluding with his suspicions of the man Burke, alias McTaggart.

'If you are right about this, it puts the affair on a different, not to say serious, footing,' remarked Gimlet.

There was silence for a little while. The firelight cast a crimson glow across the floor, and the homely smell of burning wood filled the hut. Gimlet drank another cup of soup and declared that it had put new strength into him. He smiled when he was told what formed the base of it – the venison that Trapper had procured. After a while he sat up. He admitted that he felt a bit shaky, but nothing worse than that. 'What's the time?' he enquired.

Cub looked at his watch. 'Ten o'clock.'

'I suppose we'd better stay the night here,' decided Gimlet.

'That's the idea, sir – there's nowhere else,' said Copper. 'Are you fellows in a hurry to get back to London?' questioned Gimlet.

'No, sir. Our time's yours as long as you want it,' replied Copper.

'In that case, we'd better work out some kind of plan – I mean, how we are going to start sorting this business out,' suggested Gimlet.

'I think it would be better if we left that until the morning, sir,' advised Cub. 'No doubt you will be feeling more yourself then.'

'Perhaps you're right,' agreed Gimlet. 'There isn't much we can do tonight, anyway.'

'I'll bring in some heather and make some beds,' offered the practical Trapper.

It did not take long to make the hut snug for the night. The fire was allowed to die, and everyone settled down for the night.

Whether Cub actually went to sleep or not he could not afterwards remember; nor had he any idea of how long the hut had been silent; but he was suddenly aware that Copper, who lay next to him, was listening. He had raised himself slightly and his breathing was suspended.

Trapper must have heard something, too, for after a few seconds he whispered, 'It's a car.'

By this time Cub could hear it – the purr of a car running in low gear. The sound was some distance away, but there was no mistaking it.

Gimlet did not speak. His easy and regular breathing suggested that he was asleep.

'Let's see what goes on,' said Copper softly, getting up.

Cub rose, too. They went outside, closing the door quietly behind them. It was at once possible to locate the sound of the engine. The vehicle was on the road leading to the Lodge, not far from the point where they had left it to reach the mine.

Without a word Trapper set off at a dog-trot, the others following. The night was clear, with bright starlight, although the moon had not yet risen, so it did not take them long to reach the mine. They reached it just in time to see what appeared to be a large touring car pass across the bottom of the glen. It was travelling towards the main road – that is, the road on which the hotel was situated, so it had obviously come from higher up the glen, from a district which the comrades had not yet explored. The car carried no lights. In spite of the state of the road, it was travelling fairly fast. It went on. The sound of its engine faded and eventually merged into the silence.

'No use chasing it,' said Copper.

'That fellow must know the road well to travel on it at night without lights,' remarked Trapper.

'Why no lights, anyway?' put in Cub. 'There's no law against headlamps, and they would certainly make driving easier. That in itself is fishy.'

'You've said it,' asserted Trapper. 'That driver doesn't want to be seen, and in country like this, where there are no lights, headlamps would look like lighthouses. They would soon be spotted by somebody, and, having nothing else to talk about, the locals would soon start wondering about them.'

'That car must have been up to the Lodge,' conjectured Cub.

'Looks like it,' agreed Copper. 'It was a big car, too.' He turned back

369

up the glen. 'This gives us something else to think about,' he remarked pensively.

Gimlet was awake when they got back to the hut. 'Where have you fellows been?' he demanded.

Cub told him about the car.

'Looks as if somebody is using my Lodge without permission,' said Gimlet thoughtfully.

'Is there anybody there, as far as you know?' questioned Copper.

'Not a soul,' replied Gimlet. 'The place is fully furnished, but it has been shut up since the first year of the war. There was a caretaker, of course, but he died some time ago and, owing to the war, he couldn't be replaced. There's no one there now.'

'That, I should say, is where you're wrong,' observed Copper. 'What say you, Trapper? Am I right?'

'Tch! Every time,' responded Trapper.

'Well, there's nothing we can do about it tonight, so let's get in all the sleep we can,' advised Gimlet.

The party settled down. Silence fell, this time a silence that was to remain unbroken until dawn.

CHAPTER FIVE

Cub Goes Alone

Trapper was the first to wake. No one saw or heard him get up and creep quietly out of the hut. He announced his return, however.

'Come on, you guys, show a leg,' he requested. '*Enfin*! Daylight's running to waste.'

Cub, opening his eyes, saw him standing in the open doorway, bow in one hand and a string of four gleaming speckled trout in the other.

'Here's breakfast,' said Trapper, tossing his catch on the table.

Cub pulled on his shoes, got up, and, going to the door, inhaled the crisp morning air with satisfaction. Day was dawning and the sky was pink with the glow of it. A slight frost had spread a gossamer film over the heather. The atmosphere sparkled. The babble of a nearby burn took on a joyous note. Birds were astir. A mountain hare, probably disturbed by Trapper, lolloped to a distant ridge, where it turned to watch the invaders, its long ears twitching like semaphores.

Gimlet was still sleeping comfortably. His breathing was easy and regular.

'We shall need some more wood for the fire, Cub,' announced Copper. 'There's plenty down at the old mine – those rotten roof battens will do a treat.'

'I'll fetch some as soon as I've had a wash,' promised Cub. Taking soap and towel from his haversack, he walked over to the burn, where Trapper was already shaving in the crystal water, and made a quick toilet. This done, he set off down the glen on his errand.

Perhaps it was the clean fresh air that exercised his mind and put a spring into his stride; it may have been that his brain, refreshed by sleep, was working more smoothly than on the previous evening. Anyway, as he walked he found himself considering the mystery of Gimlet's misadventure from a new aspect. In describing what had happened, Gimlet had implied, if he had not actually stated, that he did not mention his name at the hotel. He had not divulged that he was the new owner of Strathcarglas. He had merely asked the way to the Lodge. Yet, judging from what had happened afterwards, it seemed probable that Burke and his fishing friend knew who he was. At least, it did not seem feasible that they would murder a casual wayfarer. The more Cub pondered over this, the more he became convinced that the people at the hotel knew Gimlet for whom he was. Indeed, it was practically proved by the fact that when, on the occasion of their visit, he had mentioned Captain King, the publican had stated definitely that he had not seen him. Had he not known Captain King, the natural question he would have asked was, Who is Captain King? Yes, decided Cub, the people at the hotel had known who Gimlet was when he arrived. Apparently they were not surprised to see him. It looked as if they had been prepared for his arrival. But how did they know he was coming? Who could have told them? Was there, somewhere, a spy ... a confederate who...? Cub remembered the butler at Lorrington Hall. The fellow had lied to them when he had said that he did not know where his master was. Why should he lie? He must have had a reason. Was it because...?

Cub was jerked from his reverie by a shock so rude that these vague suspicions were erased from his mind in an instant of time. Curiously, perhaps, as he had rounded the bend that brought the old mine into view, no thought of danger was in his mind. He supposed – without justification, as he afterwards realised – that he was alone in the glen. His surprise, therefore, was in the nature of a shock when, rounding the bend, he saw a man beyond the mine running towards the road. Cub assumed, naturally, that the man had seen him, and was running away in order to escape observation; and his first reaction was to give chase, even if only to get a better sight of the man, who, he felt sure, he had never seen before. He was dressed in a dark lounge suit of town cut, so it was certainly neither of the men he had seen at the hotel. Of that he was sure. Hurrying on towards the mine he could see, through the archway in the main building, a car standing on the road. Realising that he had no chance of overtaking the man, Cub stopped. It also occurred to him that he might be ill advised to show himself. And it was as well that he did stop. For hardly had he come to a standstill when a violent explosion somewhere near at hand hurled him into the heather. Slightly stunned, wondering what could have happened, he raised himself on an elbow just in time to see the car disappear beyond the hill on the right-hand side of the glen – that is, in what he supposed to be the direction of the Lodge.

Cub's first impression was that he had stepped on a land mine, or a booby trap, set by the man who had run away. This opinion did not last long, however; for, looking round, he saw something that more or less explained what had happened. A cloud of smoke was drifting up from the mine shaft – or where the shaft had been, for the hole was no longer there. The sides had caved in and the superstructure had been blown down.

It did not take Cub long to grasp the fairly obvious truth of the affair. The man had thrown a bomb or had fired an explosive charge in the mine, to destroy forever all trace of what lay – or what he supposed lay – at the bottom of it. Gimlet's body. Had Gimlet not been found murder would have been committed and all trace of the crime wiped out. Gimlet's bones would have lain deep in the earth, beyond possibility of discovery, till the end of time. Cub went cold as this gruesome yet undeniable fact penetrated his racing brain. Shaken, he was picking himself up when Copper and Trapper came pelting round the corner.

'What was that – who did it?' demanded Copper fiercely, looking round, gun in hand.

Cub pointed to the remains of the mine. 'Take a look at that,' he invited. 'A fellow bombed it – to bury Gimlet, I imagine. At least, I can't think of any other reason.'

'Did you see him?'

'Yes. He had a car on the road. I was just in time to see him running towards it.'

'Did he see you?'

Cub hesitated. 'I don't think so. At first I thought he was running because he had seen me, but his back was towards me when I came round the corner, and I don't remember him looking round. Thinking it over, it seems more likely that he was running away from the explosion which he knew was coming.'

'Who was he?'

Cub shook his head. 'I don't know. I've never seen him before.'

'It wasn't one of the fellows at the pub?'

'No – I'm sure of that.'

'Then there are three of them in it, at least,' declared Copper. He took another look round. 'Well, it's no use hanging about here. Let's get back. We might as well take some firewood.'

Loaded with fuel, they returned to the hut.

Gimlet was anxiously awaiting their return. Cub described what had happened.

'Good thing you fellows came along when you did, or you'd have been a long time finding me,' remarked Gimlet drily. 'I'm much obliged to you.'

'Don't mention it, sir,' replied Copper, grinning.

Cub stepped into the conversation. To Gimlet he said, 'May I have a word with you, sir?'

'Go ahead,' invited Gimlet. 'What is it?'

'It's about your butler at Lorrington Hall.'

Gimlet's eyebrows went up. 'What on earth has he to do with this?'

'I don't know, but I have an idea he might be in it,' answered Cub. 'Did he know you were going to Scotland?'

'Of course. He has to know my movements in order to run the house.'

'He told us he didn't know where you were,' stated Cub. 'But we'll let that pass. Did I understand you properly when last night you said you did not tell the hotel people who you were? You said, if I remember rightly, that you didn't believe in telling people your business?'

'That's right.'

'You didn't mention your name?'

'I did not.'

'But they knew who you were.'

'Did they? What makes you think that?'

'In the first place, you are not going to tell me that people sit beside a public highway and murder passing strangers. Secondly, when I asked if they had seen you, they said no. If Burke hadn't known who you were he would not have said that. He would have said, Who is Captain King? or something of that sort. I'm convinced that not only did they know who you were, but they knew you were coming. Everything points to it. The reason they decided to murder you was because they knew you were the new owner of Strathcarglas. Very well. If they knew you were coming, how did they know? Obviously, someone must have tipped them off. It must have been someone at Lorrington Hall. We know that Haynes, your butler, is a liar, so suspicion is bound to fall on him.'

'There was no reason why he should tell you, a stranger, where I was,' Gimlet pointed out.

'Perhaps not, but he needn't have lied about it,' persisted Cub. 'He said he didn't know where you were. That was a lie. If he didn't like the look of us, he could have told us to mind our own business. How long has he been in your service?'

'Not very long – about two months.'

'How did you come to take him on?'

'My old butler died while I was away at the war. I was thinking of advertising for a new one when, by a curious coincidence, this fellow Haynes turned up, seeking employment.'

'I have a feeling that that was not such a coincidence as you supposed,' averred Cub.

'Anyway, his references were excellent, so I took him on,' concluded Gimlet.

'His references were bound to be in order,' declared Cub. 'Anyone can forge references.'

'Well, all I can say is, he has been satisfactory in every way.'

'Naturally, he would be,' said Cub cynically. 'You can think what you like, sir, but I shall keep this chap in mind. Apparently you made up your mind suddenly to go to Scotland?'

'Yes, on the spur of the moment.'

'Then there would not have been time for anyone at Lorrington Hall to write a letter here, saying you were on your way? It must be a two or three days' post.'

'Probably, but there are such things as telephones, don't forget.'

'Not here,' argued Cub. 'The pub isn't on the 'phone. I noticed that.

There were telegraph wires along the road, but only as far as the cottage with the red posting-box outside. I noted the post-box in passing, thinking the cottage must be the local post-office, in case I wanted to send a letter home. It's about half a mile up the road from the pub.'

Gimlet shrugged. 'Very well. Anyone wanting to get an urgent message through could have sent a telegram.'

'In which case a record of it would be kept,' declared Cub. 'It would be interesting to know if such a telegram was sent.'

'I doubt if the postmaster, or whoever lives at the cottage, would tell you.'

'He might. There would be no harm in trying,' asserted Cub. 'Country people are usually ready to gossip, and up here they can't handle so many telegrams that they forget about them. I'll tell you what, sir; we're in no great hurry, and you'll need a bit of time to recover your strength. After breakfast, how about me going along to the post-office and having a word with the man there? By cutting across the moor I could get to it from the back, so the people at the hotel wouldn't see me – not that it would matter a great deal if they did. After all, they don't know anything about me or why I came here. I could be back in a couple of hours or so.'

'I'll come with you,' said Copper and Trapper together.

'No need for that,' disputed Cub. 'If we're seen walking about in a mob, Burke might get suspicious – and so might the man at the post-office. One person could get into his confidence where two or three might cause him to shut up like an oyster. I had some experience of that sort of thing when I was in the Fleas.[1] I'd rather go alone. Anyway, it's better for Copper and Trapper to stay here with you in case of trouble.'

'All right,' agreed Gimlet thoughtfully. 'There may be something in what you say. I don't see that any harm can come of making enquiries. Don't be too long away.'

'I ought to be back in a couple of hours,' said Cub. He turned to Copper. 'By the way, what was that man Burke in prison for?'

Copper screwed up one eye. 'Now, what makes you ask that?'

1 See *King of the Commandos*.

'Because,' answered Cub, 'I once read in a book that most criminals specialise in one particular racket, and stick to it.'

'That's true enough,' admitted Copper. 'But I'm afraid that ain't goin' ter help you in this case. Burke's racket was all washed up soon after he was arrested.'

'What was it, exactly?'

Copper scratched his head. 'I don't remember the details, but to the best of my recollection Burke was mixed up with a big American rum-running gang, when they had prohibition in the United States. He was a sort of special agent for the gang over this side, sending the stuff out to them or something of the sort. The New York police asked us to pick him up. When America repealed the prohibition law, the rum-running racket ended and the big booze bosses faded out.'

'I see.' Cub sat at the table and made short work of one of Trapper's trout, with a cup of tea.

'That's all the tea we've got,' remarked Trapper.

'Another reason why I should slip down to the post-office,' returned Cub. 'It's a little general store as well. I'll take my haversack and pick up some tea and sugar, and tinned milk, and anything else they have in the grub line.'

'Don't forget coffee,' murmured Trapper.

'Bring me a couple of packets of fags,' requested Copper, laying half a crown on the table.

'Okay.' The meal finished, Cub rose and slung his haversack over his shoulder. 'Shan't be long,' were his parting words as he strode off down the glen.

CHAPTER SIX

The Post-Office has Visitors

The weather remained fair, and Cub, travelling cross-country to avoid the hotel, had no great difficulty in reaching his objective. But it took him longer than he expected, for the natural obstacles in his way were not so easily overcome as he had supposed; not that he had given any serious thought to them. But it was his first experience of travelling in the Highlands off the beaten track, and he soon discovered that this was something not lightly to be undertaken. As it happened, and as he was to perceive later, this short experience was to stand him in good stead.

First there was the heather. It was higher, much higher, than he had supposed. And thicker. The tough woody stems dragged at his legs so that at each step he was forced to pick up each foot almost vertically. The ground from which the heather sprang was not, as he had imagined, soft earth. There were invisible boulders and outcrops of rock, usually set at oblique angles, expressly, it would seem, to impede progress. Burns gurgled and chuckled deep in the heather, in which they had cut beds in the manner of slit trenches. These trenches could not be seen because the heather met over them, and therein lay the danger of a false step, which could throw a traveller on his face and possibly break a leg. Last, but by no means least, there were the bogs. From the road the slopes of the hills appeared dry enough, but this again was a trap for the unwary. Fortunately the bogs were advertised by areas of sphagnum and stagshorn moss, forming the bright green and yellow streaks that Cub had already observed. These gave no indication of the soft mud that lay beneath them; but after once or twice floundering above his knees in mire, Cub soon learned to avoid such places. In due course he saw the road below him and the little shop that was his objective. Descending the bank, he made his way to the door.

The cottage, as he had surmised, was the sub-post-office of Auchrory. It was tended, he found, not by a man, but by a little grey-haired old woman who, looking at him over her glasses, greeted him cheerfully enough.

Now, on the way Cub had thought out his line of approach, and this he now proceeded to follow. He started by making his purchases, and while he was being served with these he had no difficulty in opening a conversation. As he packed his haversack, selecting things which he thought might be useful, not forgetting Copper's cigarettes, he spoke of the weather, the beauty of the glen, and passed on to discuss the fish in the river. 'I saw a gentleman fishing a pool lower down,' he remarked. 'Does he have any luck?' He gave a brief description of the man in plus-fours.

'That will be Mr Smith,' said the postmistress. 'No. I don't think he catches many fish.'

'He stays at the hotel,' prompted Cub.

'Aye. He does that.'

'Has he been here long?'

The woman's reply surprised Cub. 'Aye. He's been with us now for ... it must be getting on for eighteen months.'

'Then he must have been here when fishing was out of season?' murmured Cub.

'Aye. But he's not only a fisher, ye ken. He's in a line of business here. Everyone knows Mr Smith.'

'In business – here?' Cub was incredulous.

'Aye. He buys all the barley from the braes. Pays good prices, too. We should be sorry to lose Mr Smith.'

The word barley struck a sharp note in Cub's memory. He remembered the grains of barley on the track leading to the Lodge. 'And what does he do with all this barley he buys?' he questioned, hardly expecting an answer.

'Och. He makes it into dog biscuits,' returned the old woman.

'So he's ... a dog-biscuit ... manufacturer?' muttered Cub, conscious of a feeling of frustration. This was certainly not what he expected. No trade could have sounded more prosaic.

'Aye. A lorry comes once a week for the barley, regular as clockwork,' went on the postmistress. 'Mr Smith, he lives at the hotel to be handy for it.'

'I see,' said Cub slowly.

'And what would you be doing in these parts, young mon?' asked the postmistress, who seemed to have nothing else to do but talk.

'I was expecting to meet a friend here,' answered Cub. 'He was to have sent me a telegram if he couldn't come. Have there been any telegrams in lately?'

'Telegrams? Bless you, no,' was the reply. 'We don't get many of them things here. One came on Monday for Mr Smith and I haven't had one since.'

Cub's nerves tingled. 'So Mr Smith had a telegram – about the barley, I suppose?'

'Och, no. 'Twas to say royalty was on the way, although what royalty would be coming to Glencarglas I dinna ken.'

Cub blinked, frowning. Royalty ... again he was conscious of a sense of disappointment.

The old woman chuckled. 'I'm minded it's the king hisself coming to see us,' she joked.

Cub heard only one word. The word was 'king.' Again his nerves tingled. Royalty ... King ... So he had been right, after all. Royalty was obviously a code word for king – Gimlet King. 'Now, who would send a telegram like that?' he asked carelessly. 'Some silly southerner, I suppose?'

'Aye, the telegram came from the south,' confirmed the old woman. 'I ken the place well. 'Twas handed in at Lorrington, wherever that may be. You'd know it, perhaps?'

Cub did not answer at once. He was thinking hard. He now had the information he wanted, and there seemed no reason to linger. He half turned, and then decided to try one last shot.

'Yes, I know this place Lorrington,' he asserted. 'In fact,' he added, truthfully enough, 'I have a friend there. But he wouldn't send such a daft wire. Who could it have been, I wonder?'

'I can verra soon tell ye,' declared the willing postmistress, opening a folio and turning over some papers. 'Ah. 'Tis here the noo,' she went on, picking up a flimsy. ''Twas sent by a Mr Singer.'

'Singer?'

'Aye, Singer. 'Tis the last word on the telegram. You'd know him, maybe?'

Cub shook his head. 'No, I've never heard of him.'

The postmistress suddenly looked past Cub's shoulder and smiled. 'Och! Here's Mr Smith,' she exclaimed. 'Na doot he'll tell ye all about it.'

Cub started and, swinging round, found himself face to face with the last man he wanted to encounter at that moment. It was, as the old woman had said, Mr Smith, of the Glencarglas Arms, still in his vulgar plus-fours. Cub could have kicked himself for his carelessness in being so caught off his guard.

Smith paid no attention to Cub beyond a swift suspicious glance. His eyes moved on to the postmistress. 'What is it I can tell you about?' he asked sharply.

'Och. The young mon here—' began the old woman.

Cub broke in. The old woman's prattle, while it had suited him until now, was, he thought, likely to become embarrassing. 'I must be getting along,' he announced. 'Good day.'

'Guid dee to ye,' called the old woman cheerfully.

Cub departed. He strove to keep his actions natural, but aware that Smith's eyes were on him he was for once self-conscious. However, the man made no attempt to detain him, so he went on to the road, where now stood an old, rather dirty car, a Buick – presumably Smith's. Turning to the right he strode away in the direction of the inn, and the lane that led to the Lodge. Once out of sight of the post-office, a matter of a few yards, he increased his pace. He chose the road because now that he had been seen by Smith there was no point in taking to the moor, and he was anxious to get back to report the result of his enquiries to the others. Apart from which he had no desire at that moment to find himself involved in an argument with the alleged barley dealer.

He had not gone far when he heard the car, or a car, cruising down the road behind him. He assumed, correctly as it turned out, that it was Smith, who had not stayed so long at the post-office as he hoped he would. Cub thought swiftly. Two courses were open to him. The first was to turn off the road on to the moor, where the car would not be able to follow. But he realised that Smith must have already seen him, and he recoiled from the idea that the man might think he was afraid of him; that he was running away from him. The second course was to stay on the road, to ignore the man, or, if he was accosted, to bluff the business through. If a conversation ensued Cub thought he might learn something. So this was the course he chose.

The car stopped beside him abruptly as the brakes were applied, and a glance over his shoulder revealed Smith sitting at the wheel. But the barley buyer did not remain long in that position. The car door was thrown open and he stepped out – stepped out with a business-like alacrity. His eyes were on Cub's face, and Cub did not like the expression in them at all. He perceived that something more than argument was probable. He glanced down the road. Not a soul was in sight.

Smith opened the conversation. 'Going far?' he questioned in a hard voice.

'No, not far,' answered Cub, adopting a nonchalant attitude.

'No matter. Get in and I'll give you a lift.' The tone of Smith's voice when he said this made it clear that it was an order, not an invitation.

'I'd rather walk,' replied Cub. 'Thanks, all the same.'

'I said *get in*.' This time there was a real edge on Smith's voice.

Cub raised his eyebrows. 'Are you telling me what I can do?'

'I am,' was the harsh reply. 'You're going for a ride. Quit yapping.' Smith now backed up his argument by producing a Colt automatic – a big, heavy weapon.

Cub smiled faintly. 'What are you going to do with that blunderbuss?' he bantered. 'And where do you think you are – Chicago?'

Smith's face set in even harder lines. 'This isn't an ornament,' he grated.

'I can see that,' conceded Cub. 'But tell me,' he went on, 'why are you so anxious to take me for a ride?' This really was to gain time, for he saw that his position was really serious, and he was thinking fast.

'I want to talk to you, my cock, that's why,' answered Smith crisply. As he said this, into his eyes, which up to now had been frankly hostile, crept a look of curiosity. 'I thought you said you came here to mind your own business?' he challenged.

'That's right,' acknowledged Cub.

'You didn't act that way in the post-office,' rasped Smith. 'You seemed more interested in *my* business.'

Cub expected this. No doubt the old woman in the post-office had given the man the gist of their conversation. 'No,' he parried, 'I'm not interested in barley. I thought your line was something more remunerative,' he added slyly.

A puzzled frown that might have been genuine – at least Cub thought so – lined Smith's forehead. His manner became almost confidential. 'Y'know, I can't get you weighed up,' he confessed. 'You're too young to be a—'

'Cop?' suggested Cub naïvely.

The word darkened Smith's brow again. 'Okay, cop if you like,' he rapped out. 'But why am I standing here arguing with you? Come on, get in; we'll soon get to the bottom of your little game.'

Now Cub had already resolved that whatever happened he was not going to get into the car. Remembering what had happened to Gimlet, it was too much like taking a running jump into the lion's den. Where Smith would take him or what he would do, he did not know; but he could guess. So he determined to stay out. While they had been standing there, the sky in some mysterious way had become overcast. The tops of the hill were lost in a grey mist that came rolling down into the valleys, reducing visibility to about a hundred yards. Cub perceived that if he could get outside that distance he would be safe, for Smith would not be able to see him, and even if he gave chase it should not be difficult to elude him. The difficulty was the automatic which Smith still held in his hand.

'Come on, get moving,' ordered Smith impatiently.

'Okay – okay,' agreed Cub, taking a step nearer to the car. 'There's no hurry, is there? Put that gun away; it scares me. Besides, someone might come along the road.'

Smith smiled cynically and put the gun in his pocket.

'I'll tell you something else,' went on Cub evenly. 'That cannon of yours is too big, too clumsy, for real fast work. It isn't the size of the bullet that counts; it's where you hit your man. You ought to try something smaller – like this.' Cub's hand slipped easily into his pocket and came up holding his thirty-eight. The muzzle covered Smith. 'See what I mean?' he concluded blandly.

Smith's face was a study. 'Why – why – you little rat,' he choked.

'Now – now, no hard names,' chided Cub. 'I didn't call you names, did I? By the way, don't forget what I said about hitting your man in the right place. If you have any doubts as to whether I can do that I'll be pleased to give you a demonstration. Keep your hands away from your pockets and turn round.'

Smith glared.

Cub's manner changed. 'You heard me,' he snapped, jerking up the muzzle of his pistol.

Smith turned.

'Don't be in too great a hurry to see where I'm going or you'll get that demonstration I spoke about,' warned Cub. 'Just stand still and you'll be all right.' He started backing away from the road, up the hillside into the mist.

He had covered some seventy or eighty yards before Smith turned. By that time the man and his car were mere vague shapes in the mist. The heavy Colt roared, and a bullet zipped into the heather not far from where Cub was still climbing. But Cub only laughed and ran on. In a few seconds he was out of sight of the road. All he could see was the thin grey mist that enveloped him. Well satisfied with the way he had handled a difficult situation, he struck off on a course for the hut.

After a few minutes, hearing no sound of pursuit, he dismissed Smith from his mind. Smith, having a car on the road, would not be likely to follow him, he thought. It was more probable that he would go as quickly as possible to his friend Burke and tell him what had happened. Cub was quite sure now that some shady business was afoot. When the postmistress had first made mention of the barley buying he had wondered for a minute if the man was honestly engaged in business; but Smith's subsequent actions banished such a notion. Barley buying did not call for the employment of a heavy automatic, pondered Cub, as he strode on, dodging the obstacles he had learned to avoid.

Just when the thought first occurred to him that he was off his course, he could not afterwards recall. The mist persisted; indeed, it thickened, and the temperature dropped several degrees, so that the air was both damp and chilly. All he could see was heather, and as this all looked alike there was nothing to guide him. It was an uneasy feeling inside him rather than the sight of any definite object that made him steady his pace and look around for a landmark. He could see nothing that he could recognise; and when, soon afterwards, he found himself confronted by a towering crag, beyond which the ground fell away into a deep gulley, he knew that he was wrong. He had never seen this particular spot before. Changing direction to avoid these obstacles, he plunged on for the best part of an hour. Then he stopped again. He considered each direction in turn, and as he concluded his inspection he was conscious of a sinking feeling in the stomach. One way was as good as another. What was even worse, all sense of direction had departed. And direction, he became painfully aware, might be north. Or south. There was no indication. Absolutely none. It was a nasty moment – one that many a traveller in the Highlands has experienced. It seemed useless to go on, because for all he knew he was travelling in the direction opposite to the one he wished to take. Yet it was futile to stand still.

He remembered the advice of the man at that station. He could not find a ledge under which to take shelter, so he squatted down on the damp heather, hoping that the mist would lift. Chafting at the delay, he sat there for nearly two hours, and by the end of that time his irritation had turned to vague alarm. Suppose the mist did not lift? It might, as he was well aware, persist for days. It had turned bitterly cold. His limbs were becoming numb. He stood up and stamped to restore his circulation, angry now at his foolish predicament.

It began to rain. Not big drops, but a clammy soaking drizzle, so that he was soon wet as well as cold. The drops grew larger and turned to sleet, tiny particles of ice that hissed as they pattered on the heather. When the sleet turned to snow he could hardly believe it. It seemed ridiculous at that time of the year. The snow did not lie – at any rate, on the heather. In some strange way the heather seemed to absorb it. He remembered that he was not in England, but in the Highlands of Scotland, at an altitude of something over two thousand feet. It made, as he perceived with dismay, a lot of difference.

Bullets zipped into the heather not far from Cub.

Finding the cold intolerable he began to walk, feeling that if his senses would not help him luck might. Anyway, he decided, anything was better than sitting still and slowly freezing to death. Bending his face to the weather he floundered on through a grey-white world. Earth and air were the same colourless hue.

Pausing to get his breath, for the going was heavy, he started back in affright when vague shapes loomed suddenly in front of him. He laughed foolishly when he recognised the shapes for a stag leading a herd of hinds. Again he remembered the advice of the man at the station. The stags were coming down from the high tops. The information, he thought bitterly, had come too late to benefit him.

Somewhere on the hillside a grouse cackled harshly.

Silence fell. The persistent unchanging hiss of the snow could hardly be called a sound.

CHAPTER SEVEN

Copper Makes a Call

At the hut, Copper waited with some impatience for Cub to return. Not that there was any particular reason for impatience. A vague suggestion had been made that they might walk as far as the Lodge, but it was not pursued. Gimlet, now on his feet, was fast recovering from his misadventure, but there was obviously no point in taxing his strength without a good reason. Trapper killed a rabbit, skinned it, and made a stew in the saucepan for lunch. And so the morning wore on, with the weather slowly deteriorating. Copper eyed it with misgivings.

'What 'e'll do is mess about and get himself wet through,' he remarked, obviously referring to Cub. 'What's 'e up to?'

When the mist rolled down the hills, enshrouding the landscape in its clammy folds, he expressed his views more strongly. 'He said 'e'd be a couple of hours,' he muttered. ''E's been more than four.'

Trapper looked up from the arrow he was refeathering. '*Tiens*! If he's got any sense he'll stay where he is,' he drawled. 'If he tries short-cuts across the moor in this fog he may wish he stay at home – *hein*.' He joined Copper at the door.

A minute or two later as they stood there, gazing down the glen hoping and expecting to see Cub emerge from the mist, there came the sound of a distant shot.

Trapper looked sharply at Copper. Copper looked at Trapper, a question in his eyes. 'What was that?' he demanded.

'Someone shoots,' answered Trapper.

'I worked that out fer meself,' replied Copper. 'Who was it? – that's what I want ter know.'

'A poacher, maybe.'

'Poacher my foot,' growled Copper. 'Poachers use shotguns. That wasn't a shotgun. That was a rifle or a heavy pistol. Don't tell me it wasn't – I've heard enough in my time. I don't like it.'

Gimlet joined them at the door. 'What don't you like?' he enquired.

'Someone has just fired a shot, sir.'

'I heard it.'

'I made it out ter be a pistol shot,' said Copper. 'You can't mistake that short, flat bang.'

'What of it?'

'Cub may be in trouble. The report came from his direction.'

'*Tch*! He can take care of himself,' put in Trapper.

'I'm not so sure of that,' returned Copper. 'Why was there only one shot? It wasn't Cub's gun. That makes a crack like a whip. If somebody took a shot at Cub, why didn't he shoot back, eh?'

Nobody answered the question. Copper stared in the direction from which the report had come, the expression on his face suggesting that he was wrestling with a difficult problem. Suddenly he reached a decision. 'I'm going ter see if 'e's all right,' he declared. 'I don't like it. I might as well go as stand here doin' nothing.'

'You stand a poor chance of finding him in this fog,' said Trapper.

'If 'e's all right, I reckon I shall meet 'im comin' up the road,' asserted Copper. ''E won't be such a mug as ter leave the road in this muck. I'll go as far as the post-office.'

'Mind the people at the hotel don't see you,' warned Gimlet.

'Not in this fog they won't,' stated Copper. 'And if they do – what of it?' he demanded aggressively. 'Whose property is it, anyway? If anyone wants any back-chat with me, 'e can 'ave it. I never said no yet to anyone who fancied his chance. S'long.' He set off.

The sleet which started soon afterwards damped his ardour somewhat, but he kept going, and, without seeing any sign of Cub, in a trifle under an hour he reached the post-office. He went straight to the door and walked in. The postmistress, from behind the counter, greeted him with a smile.

Copper did not beat about the bush. 'Did you 'ave a young feller 'ere this morning, ma'am?' he enquired.

'Aye. There was a young mon here a while back.' The old woman gave a pretty accurate description of Cub.

'That's 'im,' confirmed Copper.

'Then you must be the gentleman he was expecting to meet here?' conjected the postmistress.

'I dunno about that,' answered Copper bluntly. 'What I want ter know is, what 'appened to 'im?'

'Och, he went away down the glen.'

''Ow long ago?'

'Some time now.'

'Was 'e 'ere long?'

'Aye, he was that. Half an hour maybe. We were talking about Mr Smith of the Glencarglas Arms. He went off when Mr Smith came in.'

Copper had half turned to the door. He came back. 'What was that you said?'

'I said the young mon went off when Mr Smith came in.'

'I see.' Copper spoke slowly. 'And what about Mr Smith – where did 'e go?'

'Away doon the glen.'

'How long was that after my chum 'ad gone?'

'Two or three minutes.'

'Was that before or after that shot was fired? You must 'ave heard it?'

'Yes, I heard it – it made me jump,' admitted the postmistress. 'It would be about five minutes after they left here.'

'Ah,' breathed Copper. 'Did Mr Smith come back?'

'No. He was in his car.'

'Oh, 'e was, was 'e?' Copper nodded thoughtfully. 'Thanks, ma'am, I'll be gettin' along.'

Leaving the post-office he strode down the road towards the hotel. He had no fixed plan. He was by no means sure what he was going to do, but the information he had acquired convinced him more than ever that Cub was in trouble; that the shot had some connection with him. Fine snow was now falling, but he ignored it. He walked with his eyes on the road, thinking he might see car tracks or oil stains if the car had stopped.

He found both. And he found something else, something that, as he stooped to pick it up, made him catch his breath. It was an expended brass cartridge, calibre forty-five. His face set in harder lines as he looked at it, for his worst fears were now confirmed. After listening for a few moments, for it was impossible to see more than a few yards, he quartered the area carefully, afraid of what he might find. He fully expected to come upon bloodstains, and he was relieved when this sinister expectation was not realised. He returned to the place where he had found the cartridge, and there he stood for a full minute. 'He walked into trouble all right,' he told himself.

Now Copper, as we know, was a simple man. Anything in the nature of finesse, of intricate planning, filled him with contempt. For Copper, the shortest and quickest way to his objective was the only way. If Cub had run into trouble, he reasoned, it would be with Mr Smith or someone at the hotel. Obviously, the hotel was the place to look for Cub. He set off.

Had it not been for an old, dirty, Buick car, that stood in the yard, the hotel, when he reached it, would have appeared entirely deserted. Not a soul was in sight. The door, he discovered, was locked. Undeterred, he banged on it with his fist. No one came, so he used the toe of his boot. The door was opened by Burke. 'We're closed—' he began, and would have shut the door in Copper's face had he been quick enough.

Copper's heavy boot prevented this. 'Not so fast,' he growled. 'What's wrong with you? You act like you was scared of somethin'. I've come 'ere ter ask you a question or two, mate, and I ain't going till I've asked them – see?'

Burke hesitated for a moment. Then he stepped back, opening the door wide. 'Come in,' he invited smoothly.

Copper went in. They went through to the bar, against which Smith was standing, a glass in his hand. Leaving the door open, Burke retired to his usual place behind the bar. Smith remained where he was.

Copper accosted him bluntly. 'You're Smith, ain't you?'

'That's my name,' was the answer.

'I'm lookin' fer that kid who you saw at the post-office this mornin',' said Copper shortly.

'What kid?'

'Don't give me that,' flashed back Copper. 'You know the kid I mean.'

'Why ask me?'

'Because you was the last ter see 'im.'

'Yes, I did see him,' admitted Smith. 'So what? He isn't here.'

Copper took a pace nearer. He was getting angry. 'What did yer do with 'im?'

'Why should I do anything with him?'

'Maybe you know that as well as I do.' Copper got down to brass tacks. 'You carry a gun, don't you? – come on, no lies; I can see your pocket bulging. Don't try ter pull it on me though. I was a Commando for five years and I ain't forgot what I learnt. Now then, you shot at that boy, didn't you?'

'No.'

'You're a liar. What *did* you shoot at?'

Smith faltered. 'Who says I shot at anything?'

'I do.' Copper tossed the empty cartridge on the counter. 'What 'ave yer got ter say about that, eh? Don't tell me you go out shootin' at cock-robins.'

'The last I saw of the boy he was running up the hill,' muttered Smith sulkily.

This was, as we know, the truth, but Copper may be pardoned for refusing to believe it. 'I ain't leavin' this house till you tell me where 'e is,' he said grimly. 'And I ain't goin' ter wait long. I'm in a hurry – see? You give me any more lies and you'll be sorry – my oath, you will. Now, what abart it?'

What Smith's reply to this would have been is a matter for conjecture. He never made it, for at this juncture a light lorry pulled up outside the hotel. The driver got down, stretched himself as if he had travelled a long way, and came into the bar. He paused on the threshold when his eyes took in the scene before him.

'What goes on?' he asked suspiciously.

Copper answered with easy familiarity. 'It's all right, mate. Nothing to do with you. You keep out of this and you'll be all right. I'm just havin' a bit of an argument with these two birds.' This said, he turned his back on the newcomer and paid no further attention to him. Consequently he did not see the swift meaning glance that passed between the driver and Burke. Nor did he see Burke nod significantly.

Copper had reopened his interrogation of Smith. 'Come on, out with it,' he ordered, and then paused, waiting for the answer.

Smith laughed.

'What's the joke?' demanded Copper.

'You'll find out,' sneered Smith. His eyes were looking past Copper's shoulder.

Suddenly Copper understood. He whirled round. But he was too late. He caught a fleeting glimpse of a heavy spanner upraised. Before he could make a move to defend himself, it crashed down on his head. The world seemed to explode in a flash of crimson flame which, spinning and contracting, became darker and darker until it ended in black night.

He slumped heavily to the floor and lay still.

CHAPTER EIGHT

Cub Goes Too Far

L ost on the hill, Cub walked on. Blundered would perhaps be a better word, for now that he was getting tired the strain of dragging his legs through the deep, shrubby heather became more acute. Moreover, the ground was seldom level; always it appeared to slope one way or another. If he went up, the cold became more intense; if he went down the hill, invariably he found himself faced by a torrent too broad or too deep to ford without wading in icy water. So in the end he scrambled transversally across the face of interminable hills, one foot lower than the other, a laborious business, but one which, at least, kept him reasonably warm. All the time he hoped that either the weather would clear or he would come upon some landmark which would give him his position. He lost all count of time. It seemed to him, in his impatience and distress, that he had been walking for days rather than hours. Occasionally he paused to rest, and when he did this his breath hung in the air like smoke.

When at length the light began to fade he became seriously alarmed. The temperature dropped still lower. This, in the end, may have been his salvation, for the snow, after persisting for a while as tiny frozen particles, stopped. As darkness fell, the air cleared. Miraculously, it seemed, stars appeared overhead. The moon had not yet risen, but as the frost conquered the humidity visibility improved. The scene around him lay open to his anxious eyes.

The panorama was much as he expected. It was not one to excite enthusiasm. He was alone in the centre of a silent world, his horizon on all sides bounded by dark, rounded hills. The question now arose, which direction should he take, for one way was as good an another. True, the stars gave him the points of the compass, but as he did not know the general direction he had taken since leaving the road, this was of scant assistance. Not a light showed anywhere. Ragged clouds still drifted low across the sky, giving promise of more snow to come.

In the end he did what in the circumstances was probably the wisest thing, he climbed to the summit of the nearest hill to get a wider field of view. In this he was successful. From his eminence he could just discern the general line of a deep valley running from north to south which he knew could only be Glencarglas. To support this opinion there were places where starlight glistened faintly on the turbulent waters of the River Carglas. There could not, thought Cub, be two rivers of such size in the district. Anyway, he decided, this was a risk that would have to be taken. He could not see the hotel. It was too dark for that, or, as the hotel lay deep in the valley, his view might have been interrupted by an intervening hill. He did not know. But the course of the glen gave him his approximate position, and he decided to work on that. There was no point, he reasoned, in going back to the post-office in the upper part of the glen, for this was now miles out of his way. It would be easier and quicker, he thought, to take a line that was bound, sooner or later, to cut across the lane leading to the Lodge. Once he found the lane, it would be a simple matter to locate the hut. He wondered what the others would be thinking about his long absence. Naturally, they would be anxious. The sooner he was back with them the better. Anyway, he needed food, and he needed it badly.

Confidently now he set off, strength restored by the knowledge that his ordeal was nearly over.

In this, as it turned out, he was mistaken. It was, he found, one thing to plan a direction, but quite another matter to follow it in a direct line. Burns, which always seemed to flow through a deep gulley, and steep faces of rock, and valleys between the hills, all necessitating detours, impeded his progress and threw him constantly off his course. Occasional flurries of frozen snow urged him on, however, and in due course he reached his objective – the track leading to the Lodge. He switched on his torch and looked at his watch. The time, he observed with some dismay, was eleven o'clock.

Having reached the track, he surveyed it with fresh misgivings. It was hard to say for certain because the landscape was so much alike, but he had a feeling that he had not seen this particular stretch before. A little way to the right the track took a sharp bend, and with the object of seeing what lay beyond he walked along to it. One glance was enough, for there before his eyes was something he had certainly not seen before. At no great distance loomed the bulk of a house of some size, almost a mansion; and it did not take him long to realise that this could only be Strathcarglas Lodge. He perceived that he must have struck the track some distance above the turning that led to the mine and the hut.

He observed that whoever had built the Lodge had had an eye for effect. No aspect could have been more inspiring. The approaching track, which at one time must have been a well-made drive, swung round the sharp corner so that the first view of the house was presented, suddenly, in its entirety. On the right-hand side of the drive, the bank, which rose almost sheer, was clad in a dense coppice of sombre firs. On the left the ground fell sharply into a fearful gorge, with the torrent of the Carglas thundering round and over a chaos of fallen rock in the depths.

His first inclination, a natural one, was to turn back and carry on with his original project, which was to get back to the hut where he had no doubt the others were impatiently awaiting his return. Then he remembered that none of them, not even Gimlet, had seen the Lodge. It struck him that as he was now so close he might as well cast an eye over the place, if only from the outside. It would not take ten minutes, and as he had been away for a matter of hours, a few minutes more were neither here nor there. Even then he hesitated. He was tired and hungry. Was it worth while? He decided that it was. It should be possible to learn without much trouble whether or not the place was occupied. If it was occupied there would be lights. That would be useful information to take back to Gimlet.

Having made his decision, which, although he had no reason to suspect it, was to have far-reaching results, he advanced cautiously on the Lodge, a massive stone pile with a turret at either end. A thin powdery covering of snow lay on the road, so he left it for the grass verge, where there was also a little snow but not enough to make footmarks conspicuous. His eyes were on the building. Not a light showed anywhere and, as far as he could see, no smoke came from the chimneys. Silence reigned.

His approach became even more cautious as he neared the building. Occasional groups of fir trees offered cover, and of these he took full advantage. From a distance of twenty or thirty yards, first he surveyed the house from the front. There was not a sign of life anywhere. Rather nervously he walked forward and tried the front door. As he expected, it was locked. His listened at the windows, but no sound of voices or of movement came from within. The whole place had a hopeless, abandoned look. Following the weed-conquered drive he made his way round to the back premises, but here he was confronted by a more difficult proposition, for the outbuildings were numerous and extensive, as was only to be expected at a building of such importance. They formed a quadrangle round an open courtyard. What they comprised he could only guess. They appeared to be stables, harness-rooms, kennels, wood sheds, and the like. No sound of life came from any one of them. He noted that some of the windows were curtained while others were not. Many were broken. It was a dismal picture, more depressing than the open moor. Such neglect conveyed an atmosphere of things past, of things dead and forgotten; the heather was at least alive, something of the present.

He turned his attention to the house. From this aspect it was, of course, less pretentious than the front, otherwise it was much the same. Not a light anywhere. Not a movement. Not a sound. Satisfied with his inspection, he turned away, but as an afterthought he walked across and tried the back door. His nerves tingled when it opened easily. He closed it again, quietly, and for a minute stood listening there, aware that his heart had increased its tempo. The door was unlocked. That, surely, was a sign of occupation? Or was it? It didn't necessarily follow, he decided. Very quietly he opened the door again and, taking a step forward, listened. Nothing happened. A deathly silence, the chill silence of a tomb, worried his eardrums.

Again he hesitated. Perhaps, after all, there was nothing to fear. Taking out his torch he switched on the beam and saw in front of him a short stone-flagged passage, with, as far as he could make out, a turning on either side at the far end. Closing the door behind him he walked on tip-toe to the end of the passage. To left and right now ran what was obviously a main corridor. He turned to the right. A door stood ajar. Encouraged by the utter absence of sound, he looked inside. It was obviously the dining-room. A massive table occupied the centre of the room, with chairs round it, all deep in dust. Heads of stags long dead stared down with glassy eyes from the walls. A picture had fallen and lay in a litter of fallen glass. From the mantelpiece a stuffed wild-cat, its back arched, teeth bared in a long last fixed snarl, glared at the intruder in dumb fury.

He returned to the corridor. Still no sound came. He would almost have welcomed one, so grim and unnerving was the silence. Just in front of him a flight of broad oak stairs gave access to the next floor. There seemed little point in going up. Had anyone been upstairs, he thought, he must have heard some movement.

Turning back along the corridor he found himself in the kitchen, an enormous chamber with a great iron range that would have cooked for a troop of Commandos. An enormous dresser, devoid of ornament, entirely occupied the end nearest to him. There was a long table of plain, scrubbed deal, and it was this that held his attention, for here at last were signs of life – an empty whisky bottle, some beer bottles, and half a dozen tumblers. A candle had been struck in an empty bottle. Cigarettes had been stubbed on the table. Ends lay about the floor, as they might lie in the bar parlour of a public-house. Visitors there had certainly been, thought Cub. Who were they? How long ago?

The next thing he noticed – and he made the discovery with fresh trepidation – was that the room was blacked-out. Not only blacked-out, but blacked-out with a good deal of care. Heavy curtains that obviously did not belong to the kitchen, but had been brought from another part of the house, had been nailed up to completely cover the windows. It was evident, as he now realised, that had lights been on in the kitchen he would not have known it when he was outside. What, he mused, was the object of such an elaborate arrangement? The answer was not hard to find. To prevent any ray of light from being seen outside. What light? No form of illumination was there, except a candle.

Cub decided that he had learned enough to go on with. He would come again, with the others; and in daylight they would be able to make a more detailed inspection. The outstanding fact was, there was no one in the building. This did not fit with the theory he had formed, but there was no getting away from it. He would get back to the hut. He turned to go.

At that precise moment, that which he had at first expected, but which he had now dismissed from his mind, happened. There came a sound – a series of sounds; strange sounds. They came from outside, and he stiffened to attention, listening, trying to sort out the medley of noises that now came clearly to his ears. They reminded him of something he had heard more than once in France during the war – the arrival of a train of horses or mules. He knew, of course, that such an idea was too fantastic to be entertained; yet it was of such an event that the sounds reminded him. Switching off his torch he went to a window that overlooked the courtyard and, carefully lifting the curtain aside about an inch, peeped out.

It was, of course, dark outside, and at first he could only discern a number of dark figures; but as his eyes became accustomed to the darkness these took shape, and he saw with no small astonishment that his guess had not been far wrong, after all. There, standing head to tail in the courtyard, obviously having just arrived, were three ponies, heavily laden with loads which, apart from the fact that they were bulky and heavy, were too indistinct to convey any idea of their contents. With the ponies were four men. The arrival of men in such strength was something on which he had not reckoned, and he viewed them with apprehension. Who they were, where they had come from, and what they were doing, he had no means of knowing. For the moment he was content to watch, wishing that Copper or Gimlet was at his side to lend him support.

There was nothing remarkable about the proceedings that followed. A man opened the door of one of the outbuildings – presumably a stable. The ponies were led in. The door was closed. There was a short pause. Then the stable door was opened and the ponies were brought out, now without their loads. Two men took charge of them. After a brief conversation in low tones, they walked away and were soon lost to sight in the surrounding gloom. The two men who remained, to Cub's consternation, walked over to the house – worse, to the back door. It was opened and shut. Boots scraped on the stone floor of the passage.

For an instant Cub stood still, nerves quivering, muscles tense. He hoped, hoped desperately, that the men would go to some distant part of the house, leaving him at liberty to retire by the way he had entered. He was not kept long in suspense. His hopes were dashed. The men, talking in low tones, came towards the kitchen. A sea of light announced their approach.

Cub had already left the window. He stood behind the door. In this position, he realised, discovery was inevitable. Where else could he hide? He could see only one place, and it was, on the whole, a good place. The top of the dresser was long enough and wide enough to hold half a dozen men. In a flash, using the shelves as steps, he was on his way up. Reaching the top he lay flat, vainly striving to stop the pounding of his heart, for although he had done his best to be quiet there had been a certain amount of noise. One of the shelves had creaked under his weight. The men were then only just outside the door.

'What was that?' said one.

'Rats, I expect,' was the reply, made in a voice with a pronounced American drawl. 'The place is lousy with them.'

So far all Cub had seen was the play of light on the ceiling; now, moving his head a trifle, he saw that this was cast by an electric lamp of the hurricane type and of considerable power. A moment later he saw the men. Both wore overcoats with the collars turned up, and soft hats pulled well down, so it was not possible to see much of them. One, who had his back to him, was a tall, burly fellow, whose movements were slow and ponderous. The other, facing him, was as different as could be imagined. He was a dapper, sleek little man, immaculately dressed, whose actions when he moved were as quick as those of a weasel. His face was pale, sallow, with a pronounced shaving mark. He wore a tiny black moustache, cut straight, on his upper lip. The eyes were dark, long and narrow, heavily lidded, under black brows. A Latin type, thought Cub; probably an American with Italian ancestry. He reminded Cub vaguely of an American dance-band conductor – the last type he expected to see on a Scottish moor.

The big man carried the lamp. Said he, as he stood it on the table: 'Billy ought to be here with the car. I hope he ain't going to keep us waiting. This is a hell of a hole. Gives me the jitters.'

The other took a silver flask from his pocket and poured a generous measure of the contents into two of the glasses, one of which he passed to his companion. 'He won't be late,' he said in a quiet voice but one which carried authority. Intuitively Cub judged him to be the leader. 'No, he won't be late,' he went on in his pronounced American twang. 'He knows I want to see him about these three strangers who are hanging about. There's something queer about it. We've no sooner got rid of one than three more turn up. Well, if they get in our way, they'll go the same way as the other.'

The big fellow laughed unpleasantly. 'That was a good idea of yours, Slim. It'll be a long time before anyone finds *him*.'

'It saved digging a hole,' returned the man named Slim, with an oily smile.

This half confirmed what Cub already suspected; this was the man who had bombed the mine.

He was feeling better. His breathing was easier. Not once had the men glanced in his direction. It was evident that they suspected nothing. From their conversation it was clear that they expected someone, a man named Bill. Cub hoped that he would come, after which they might all depart, for he was far from comfortable. He had not long to wait.

'Billy will be busy bringing up the rest of the barley,' said the big man.

Slim inclined his head at a listening angle. 'This sounds like him now,' he remarked.

Cub heard the purr of a car outside. A door slammed. Voices spoke in the courtyard, revealing that at least two more men were arriving. He heard the back door open and shut. Footsteps approached with a curious shuffling noise, as if one was reluctant. Slim opened the door from inside.

Three men entered. One was the barman, Burke. Another was the man called Smith. Both carried guns. As Cub's eyes fell on the third man he had to clench his teeth to choke back a cry. It was Copper; Copper, pale, his face streaked with dirt and a livid bruise on one cheek.

CHAPTER NINE

Hot Work in the Kitchen

To say that Cub was shaken by this utterly unexpected development would be understatement. He was shocked. To use a well-worn expression, he could hardly believe his eyes. Indeed, for a few seconds he was so completely flabbergasted that his brain seemed temporarily paralysed. It may have been the smooth monotone of Slim's voice that restored his power to reason.

Said Slim, 'Well – say! What have we got here?'

'He's one of the three I told you about,' answered Smith.

'Who is he?'

'He won't say. I thought you might be able to persuade him to talk.'

'Why, sure. That shouldn't be hard,' drawled Slim.

'I had a shot at the young 'un this morning, but he got clear,' went on Smith. 'He carries a thirty-eight and seems pretty smart with it.'

'H'm. So they're heeled, eh? What about this one?'

Smith laid Copper's forty-five on the table. 'I found this on him.'

'Does he know how to use it?'

Smith grinned. 'He didn't get a chance.'

'Tell me about him,' invited Slim.

'The young 'un spent some time this morning in the post-office, making enquiries about us,' explained Smith. 'That fool woman told him plenty. She talks too much. I arrived in time to hear the tail end of the conversation. When he left I followed him down the road to have a word of two with him, but before I could open my mouth he pulls a gun on me – pulled it like he knew how to use it, too. How was I to know he carried a rod?'

Cub smiled faintly at this distorted description of the affair on the road.

'I couldn't do anything,' went on Smith. 'He pulls out across the heather; I went after him, but I lost him in the blasted fog. So I went back to the pub. Presently this fellow comes along and starts shooting off his mouth, asking where the kid was. Things looked awkward for a bit, but luckily Larry happened to turn up with the lorry. Seeing what's going on, he crowns bigmouth here with a spanner and puts him down for the count.'

'How much did the young 'un learn at the post-office?' asked Slim.

'As much as the old woman knows, I reckon. That isn't much, but it's enough. She told him about the barley, and about the wire I had from Singer; that's what they were talking about when I went in. He didn't hear me come in – I took care of that. He shuts up, of course, as soon as he knows I'm there. I couldn't give it to him in front of the old woman, so I let him get a little way down the road, then I went after him. He got away. It was the blasted fog that did me.'

'Which way did he go?'

'Up the hill and across the moor, as far as I could make out. I reckon he must be somewhere on the moor now.'

Slim nodded. 'Okay. We'll find him, then we'll deal with him. There's another somewhere. Keep your eyes skinned for him. You'd better go on with your fishing so that you can keep an eye on the road. There may be more of them, for all we know. Did this fellow let anything drop when he was yapping?'

Smith thought for a moment. 'He said something about being a Commando for five years.'

Slim started. 'Why didn't you say so before?'

'Why, what's the angle?'

A sneer curled Slim's lips. 'It's a good thing I'm here to do the thinking for you. King was in the Commandos, wasn't he?'

'That's right.'

'Well, there's your hook-up.'

'You mean – King brought a bunch of Commandos up here with him?' Smith looked startled.

Slim nodded thoughtfully. 'It could be. We'd better find out. I guess this fellow will tell us.' He glanced at Copper.

'You guess again, slimy,' growled Copper.

'Do you think you can make him talk?' questioned Smith to Slim.

'I've been known to make dumb men talk,' boasted Slim. 'Okay. Leave this to me. You two had better load up with the vinegar and get along.'

'Can't I stay and watch the fun?' complained Burke.

'There's no sense in wasting time. Larry will want to be getting back. I'll put you wise when I know what I'm going to find out. You and Billy get back and watch things at your end.'

'If you say so,' agreed Burke. He went off, Smith following. There was a certain amount of noise in the courtyard. Car doors slammed and a vehicle was driven away. Only Slim, his big companion, and Copper remained.

Speaking to his assistant, Slim said, 'Okay, Tiny; let's get busy.' As he spoke he produced an automatic from his armpit and with it motioned Copper towards a chair. 'Sit down,' he invited in a smooth, oily voice. 'No need to get tired standing up.'

Cub, who had all along wondered why Copper had remained so passive, now saw the reason. His wrists were tied together behind his back.

Copper drew a deep breath and sat down. 'It's all the same to me,' he said evenly.

Slim smiled. It was not a friendly, not a pretty smile. His top lip curled, showing white teeth. His eyes, under their heavy lids, were as cold as those of a snake. With studied deliberation he laid his pistol on the table and from somewhere in the region of his hip produced a narrow-bladed stiletto. He whetted it slowly, almost lovingly, on the palm of his left hand, and then held it up in front of Copper's face. 'See this?' he enquired.

'I ain't blind,' answered Copper shortly.

'You soon will be – unless you answer my questions,' returned Slim softly. 'And that's only the beginning. And I ain't kiddin'. Now, let's make a start. Where do you come from and what's your racket?'

Copper sneered. 'So you think you can make me squeal? You've got the wrong man, fish-face. I've used better men than you for sandbags.'

Slim's nostrils quivered. 'So that's how you feel, is it?' he almost whispered. He took a pace nearer.

With what emotion, not to say consternation, Cub watched the impending drama can be better imagined than described. He came near to panic. Of one thing he was certain. Slim, as he had asserted, was not kidding. A man with such eyes was capable of any devilment, he thought. The very way he handled the knife was sinister. It was evident that unless something was done and done quickly, Copper would be mutilated. That at any cost must be prevented. Copper would not talk. Cub was certain of that, too. Nothing would make him open his lips. By nature he was as stubborn as only a Cockney can be, and neither threats nor punishment would move him. It was clear that only direct action could prevent a tragedy. Cub had no hope of achieving anything by mere words. This, he felt sure, would only expose his position to no purpose. This left only action, and the only action likely to succeed was the use of weapons. There seemed no point in shooting the big man, leaving Slim on his feet, for of the two Slim was the most dangerous, the most to be feared. That he thought nothing of murder was evident from his treatment of Gimlet. Yet Cub dare not shoot Slim for fear of hitting Copper who was directly behind him. There was, he decided, only one way to handle the situation. It would at least put a stop to the present proceedings, although what would happen afterwards was a matter for speculation.

Very gently, hardly moving his body, he slid his right hand into his pocket and drew out his thirty-eight. Extending his arm he took careful aim at the electric lamp, which still stood on the table not far from Copper, where the big man – Tiny, Slim had called him – had put it. Out of the corner of his eye Cub saw the stiletto move. His finger tightened on the trigger. The weapon blazed. Mingled with the report came the crash of splintering glass. The room was plunged into darkness. In a moment of inspiration Cub yelled, 'Come on, get 'em, boys!' This was to create an impression that he was not alone, and the ruse, judging by what followed, may have succeeded.

From the darkness came a shout of alarm. Slim cried, tersely, 'Beat it!' Footsteps clattered in swift movement. There was a crash and a curse as someone collided with the table. A gun roared and Cub flinched as a stream of sparks leapt towards him. The bullet smashed into the dresser. Cub snatched a quick shot at the flash and took a flying leap to the floor. He landed heavily and fell. Someone fell over him and he twisted as he rose. Again a gun streamed flame, this time from somewhere near the door, and a bullet ricocheted, whining shrilly, from floor to ceiling. Again Cub fired at the flash, and keeping low scrambled in the direction of Copper, whose voice, adding to the uproar, was yelling: 'Let 'em have it, kid, let 'em have it!' A bullet crashed through the bottles on the table. Glass flew. Pieces tinkled on the floor. Then, as suddenly as it had started, the commotion subsided.

Cub paused, tense, braced for quick movement, as the unnatural silence fell – a silence more dramatic than the din had been. Somewhere liquid was splashing gently on to the floor. Apart from that the only sound he could hear was someone breathing. Who it was he did not know. He himself held his breath, pistol at the ready, finger crooked. Nothing happened, so feeling his way he crawled to Copper, and taking out his knife cut free his wrists. He heard Copper get up. The chair went over. It seemed to make an extraordinary clatter. Again Cub crouched, waiting. What Copper was doing he did not know. From somewhere in the direction of the door, or from the passage, came a rustle of stealthy footsteps.

'Watch out, Copper,' said Cub in a tense whisper. 'We'll show the dirty rats,' returned Copper, in a voice vibrant with anger.

'They're in the passage,' warned Cub.

'That suits me,' muttered Copper. 'Come on.'

Cub heard him move forward. Groping his way he followed, but the darkness pressed on him. Such conditions were impossible, hopeless, he thought. Presently they would be shooting each other. He felt in his pocket for his torch. 'Copper, where are you?' he called.

CHAPTER TEN

Gimlet Takes a Hand

It is not to be supposed that while these events were occurring Gimlet and Trapper were at the hut doing nothing or merely stoking up the fire. They had, it is true, remained at the hut long after Cub had departed; and after Copper had gone to look for him it was some while before his prolonged absence was considered worthy of remark. As the afternoon wore on, however, and twilight began to dim the scene, Trapper looked up the glen with increasing frequency. At last he went to Gimlet, who was sitting by the fire, and said, 'Copper should have been back some time ago – if he was able to get back. This staying away is bad. It is not like him. Something is wrong or he would be back.'

'I've been thinking the same thing for some time,' returned Gimlet. 'I should have done something about it before this had I been able to think of anything to do. There didn't seem any point in wandering about in the fog with no particular objective. I'd rather not go near the pub just yet. I'm sorry I let Cub go off alone, in the first place. What's the weather doing now?'

Trapper smiled wanly. 'It has done everything – fog, rain, sleet. There has been a little snow, but it has stopped and the sky is clearing.' He went to the saucepan on the stove and stirred the contents. 'They will be hungry, those two. My beautiful soup, she is ruined. Soup will not keep hot for ever.'

Gimlet thought for a little while. 'We'd better have a look round,' he decided. 'I'll write a note and leave it here in case either of them comes back, then they'll know what we're doing. While I'm doing that, you might make a sortie as far as the road to see if you can see any sign of them.'

407

'Okay, sir,' agreed Trapper.

'Don't go too near the pub and don't be too long away.'

'If I'm not back in an hour, sir, you'd better start looking for me too,' replied Trapper. He went out and set off down the glen.

He had an open mind about the probable result of his investigation. He would not have been surprised to meet Copper or Cub, yet, paradoxically, he was not very hopeful of finding them. They were in a big country and they might be anywhere in it. Had it not been for the revolver shot earlier in the day, he would have concluded that Cub had got lost in the fog, and Copper, looking for him, had made the same blunder. He knew only too well from his experience in the backwoods of Canada how easy it was to become lost in country without conspicuous landmarks. But he did not like that pistol shot.

He reached the mine. Finding nothing there, he went on to the road. He looked up and down. A little snow lay about. He examined that nearest to him, but it was unbroken by a mark of any sort except in one place where a rabbit had crossed a smooth patch. He walked a little way towards the tavern, but finding nothing he turned and walked back the other way, passing the glen that led to the mine, and so on into country new to him. He did not go very far, for it was now dark, and while the stars and the snow between them made it possible to see a little way, he could not see enough to make further exploration worth while. Moreover, it was time, he decided, that he returned to the hut. Before turning he subjected the track ahead to a final close scrutiny. A mark in the thin film of snow some distance away attracted his attention. Taking care to leave no trail himself, by keeping to the heather, he walked up to the mark and saw at a glance that it was a human footprint. There were, he now observed, several footprints, some more clearly defined than others. He bent over the clearest one he could find, and striking a match, which he shielded with his hands, examined it minutely. Drawing a deep breath, he straightened his back and stared up the tracks; then, as if he had reached a decision, he swung round and made the fastest time he could to the hut.

Gimlet was there, waiting. 'Any sign of them?' he asked.

'Plenty,' answered Trapper. 'Cub has been back this way.'

'How do you know?'

'I found his tracks in the snow. They come down the hill and strike the track some distance above the turning to the mine. He was lost, I think. Instead of the tracks coming this way, as they should have done, they go the other way. They go – but they do not come back.'

'Then he must still be up there somewhere.'

'Nothing is more certain.'

'You're sure they're his tracks?'

'It is impossible to be mistaken. Always the heel of his right shoe is worn, where he twists a little on it as he walks.'

'Were there any other tracks?'

'I did not see any. He was alone. He did not hurry, either. The tracks show that he waited a little while, as if in doubt.'

Gimlet pondered. 'I think it's all very strange,' he murmured. 'We can only conclude that something must have happened or he would have come straight back. The thing becomes more and more perplexing. You didn't see any sign of Copper?'

'Not a thing.'

Gimlet rose. 'We have at least something definite to go on now,' he said. 'We'd better try to follow up Cub's tracks. I've written the note. I'll leave it here on the table. Let's go.'

They left the hut, but they had not gone a dozen yards when Trapper caught Gimlet by the arm. '*Tch*! Here comes the car again,' he whispered.

Standing still, they could hear the car distinctly. It was possible to tell the direction it was travelling from the sound. It was going up the track from the main road towards the Lodge. They hurried forward, hoping to catch sight of it, but by the time they had reached the old mine it had gone past. The purr of the engine faded.

Trapper said nothing. He strode on to the track, where the marks of the tyres were plain to see. Still without speaking he walked on to the footprints which, he had asserted, could only have been made by Cub. The moon had not yet risen, but even in the wan starlight the dark tracks in the white snow could be followed without difficulty. 'See,' he said. 'He came down the hill from the right. What he was doing on that hill I do not know, for it is not the direction of the post-office. But he may have been lost. He reaches the tracks, he hesitates a little while, and then goes on.'

'All right. Follow his trail as far is it goes,' ordered Gimlet.

They had not travelled very far when a sharp sound, no great distance ahead, brought them to a halt.

'That was a car door being slammed,' stated Gimlet.

'Yes. Now the engine has started. The car may be coming back. Yes – she comes,' snapped Trapper. 'Quick!' They just had time to throw themselves in the deep heather at the side of the track when the car appeared round the bend about a hundred yards ahead of them. They lay still as it came on, travelling fairly fast. Carrying no lights, it passed them quickly and disappeared from sight down the track.

Gimlet got up. 'Could you see who was in it? I couldn't.'

'No,' answered Trapper. 'I looked hard, but I couldn't see a thing.'

'Pity,' murmured Gimlet. 'No matter. Let's push on. That car started from somewhere not very far in front of us. I don't think we have much farther to go.'

With some difficulty Trapper picked up Cub's tracks again, on the verge, and, following them, soon came to the bend. He stopped and clicked his tongue, pointing. Words were unnecessary.

'The Lodge, by Jove!' muttered Gimlet. 'So that's the answer. It will be interesting to see just what is going on here.'

Trapper advanced, still following the tracks. He looked at the spot where Cub had made his first survey in front of the Lodge. This yielded nothing, so he went on round to the rear. But he stopped abruptly, with a low whistle of surprise, when he reached the courtyard.

'What is it?' asked Gimlet, catching up with him.

Trapper waved an eloquent hand at a medley of tracks that had almost trampled out of existence the thin mantle of snow. 'Sacré! Someone has been busy here,' he ejaculated. 'If—'

He got no farther. Whatever he was going to say was cut off short by the crack of a firearm inside the house. It was followed by a shrill muffled cry. Came another shot, a heavier report this time, and another, and another, and another. A moment later a door was flung open and two men dashed out. In a flash, before either Gimlet or Trapper could recover from their astonishment at this unexpected development, they had vanished into an opening between the outbuildings and the house. Their footsteps could be heard running on.

Trapper would have followed, but Gimlet held him back. 'Steady,' he cautioned. 'One of those fellows was carrying a gun – I saw it in his hand. I fancy that first shot was Cub's thirty-eight. We'd better see what's happened inside before we start chasing about the moor in the dark.'

The back door had been left wide open. Gimlet went in, Trapper close behind. They felt their way down a short corridor. Vague sounds came from the left, so they turned in that direction. Then, in the darkness ahead someone spoke. Unmistakably it was Cub's voice. 'Copper, where are you?' it called.

Gimlet relaxed. 'Okay, Cub. Go easy with your gun. It's me – Gimlet,' he said quickly.

There was a gasp in the darkness. A torch flashed and the scene was revealed. The most conspicuous object in it was Copper, a chair raised above his head as if to strike. Seeing Gimlet, he lowered it, slowly, like a man who doubts his eyes.

'Sufferin' whelks!' he muttered. 'Another second and I should have brained you, sir.'

'How the deuce did you get here?' demanded Gimlet crisply. 'What's going on, anyway? Can't we have a proper light?'

Trapper struck a match, and, seeing the candle on the table, lit it.

Gimlet looked at Copper and Cub in turn. He looked at the smashed lamp, splintered wood, and broken glass. 'Are you both all right?' he asked. 'You seem to have been having some fun here.'

'Right as rain, sir,' answered Copper cheerfully.

'Then perhaps you wouldn't mind telling me what all the fuss was about?'

Copper looked at Cub. 'You tell him,' he pleaded.

'It's a bit hard to know where to begin,' said Cub. 'I don't know anything about Copper. I only know what happened to me. But there are two men in the house.'

'They've gone,' interrupted Gimlet. 'They went in such a hurry that I doubt if they'll come back. Were they doing the shooting?'

'I started it,' admitted Cub. 'A little while ago there were some other men in the yard, with a string of ponies.'

Trapper butted in. 'With what?'

411

'Another second and I should have brained you, sir.'

'Ponies.'

'You do not see very well in the dark,' said Trapper. 'They were stags; come down from the hill for shelter, no doubt.'

'Are you telling me that I don't know the difference between a horse and a stag?' demanded Cub indignantly.

Trapper shrugged. 'There have been stags in the yard.'

'They were horses when I saw them,' snorted Cub.

'Don't argue,' broke in Gimlet curtly. 'We'll settle that later. Trapper, wedge a chair under that door handle so that no one can open it. Let's get down to brass tacks. What happened to you, Cub? Why did you come here?'

'It's rather a long story,' answered Cub. 'Those fellows might come back, and there's quite a gang of them. Wouldn't it be better to go back to the hut before we start comparing notes?'

'Leave my house?' retorted Gimlet with some warmth. 'Certainly not. What the deuce next? This happens to be my property, as that bunch of thugs who have been using it without my permission will presently find out. We'll stay here; but that doesn't mean we need live in this disgusting mess.' Gimlet eyed the dirty glasses and broken bottles with disapproval. 'In the morning we'll get the place tidied up. There should be mattresses and blankets upstairs, so there's no reason why we shouldn't be quite cosy. More important still, there's a bathroom. I need a bath. You look as though you could do with one, too, Copper. And see about getting your hair cut.'

'Yessir.'

'We can collect our kit from the hut in the morning.'

'Yessir.'

'I got quite a few things from the shop,' interpolated Cub. 'Tea, sugar, flour, some candles and so on. They're in my haversack. I left it on top of the dresser.'

'Good.'

'Did you get my fags?' enquired Copper.

'I did,' answered Cub. 'And, knowing your low taste, I also got you a jar of pickled onions.'

'What-ho! Onions, eh? There ain't no nicer fruit.' Copper climbed on the dresser and, lifting down the haversack, emptied the miscellaneous contents on the table. 'Strewth! We'll be able ter live like blinkin' dukes,' he observed.

Gimlet frowned. 'All I ask is that you don't eat onions for breakfast,' he said coldly. 'Go ahead, Cub. Tell us what happened to you.'

Without omitting anything of importance, Cub gave an account of his adventures from the time he left the hut up to Gimlet's arrival at the Lodge.

When he had finished, Gimlet turned to Copper. 'What about you?'

Copper told his story.

'Well, well,' murmured Gimlet at the end. 'This begins to get exciting. It looks as if we may have bigger game than grouse to shoot at. There are still a lot of pieces missing, but our jigsaw puzzle is beginning to take shape. As far as Trapper and I are concerned, there was nothing remarkable about our turning up here. Trapper went out to look for you and found your footprints in the snow. Naturally, we followed on. It's all turned out for the best. There wasn't room to swing a cat in the hut; this will make a much better headquarters. It's no use starting anything tonight, but in the morning we'll get down to things. Tracks in the snow should show us the way those fellows went. Meanwhile, we'd better get some sleep. Copper, make a raid upstairs for blankets. Cub, you should find a broom in the scullery; get this pigsty mucked out; we can't sleep on broken glass. Trapper, get a bucket of water.'

As they went about their tasks Copper whispered to Cub, 'The skipper's more like his old self. We look like havin' a busy day tomorrow.'

Trapper was the last to return. 'We were both right about the stags and horses,' he told Cub with a smile.

'Don't talk nonsense – how could you both be right?' enquired Gimlet, who had overheard.

'*Zut*! The hoof marks were those of stags,' answered Trapper. 'But a heap of horse droppings gave the game away. It's an old Indian trick – to have ponies shod with shoes the shape of stag's hooves. People looking for ponies don't follow a trail made by a stag. *Enfin*! One of these guys, at least, has brains, I think. Stags are common here. No one would think much of any marks they made; but horses – that would be different.'

This announcement was greeted by a short silence. It was broken by

Gimlet. 'You're right about someone having brains,' he said seriously. 'We shall have to watch how we go. Did you lock the back door behind you?'

Trapper put the key on the table.

'I ain't sorry Slim forgot to take my gun with him; I've got an idea I shall need it,' said Copper grimly, as he picked up the pistol, which had been left on the table, and put it in his pocket.

Gimlet nodded. 'It wouldn't surprise me if you're right,' he said quietly. 'But that's enough for tonight. Let's turn in.'

CHAPTER ELEVEN

Gimlet Sums Up

In spite of the lateness of the hour at which they had retired, Gimlet was early astir the following morning, getting the place 'organised', as he said. With blankets folded and mattresses stacked under the long table, everyone was soon busy on a task. Cub tidied up. Copper prepared breakfast. Trapper went off to the hut to fetch the things that had been left there. He brought back a brace of grouse for the pot and some disturbing news. The wind had swung round to the west, causing a sharp thaw, with a result that the snow had gone and all tracks with it. Not a footprint remained.

'That means we shan't be able to trail the guys who were here last night,' he observed, pulling up a chair and reaching for the coffee.

'Pity about that,' murmured Gimlet. 'Before we start wandering haphazard about the moor, we'd better talk things over and try to arrive at some sort of plan. We've quite a lot of information now, but it needs sorting out. I've been thinking it over.' He poured another cup of coffee and lit a cigarette. 'The main factor is, we are up against a big thing; let us have no delusions about that. No ordinary racket would bring American gangsters here. Moreover, if that fellow Smith has been here for eighteen months, as the post-woman says, the business, whatever it is, has been going on for some time, and must now be well established. And remember, it's a racket big enough to make murder worth while. Secondly, it must be highly profitable to support the big gang which we know now is at work.'

'I reckon that there are eight of 'em in it that we know of,' put in Copper.

Gimlet resumed. 'There's Slim, whom we have good reason to suppose is the boss. There's the fellow who was with him last night – Tiny. There's

Burke and Smith at the hotel; there's the man Singer who sent the wire from Lorrington; there's Larry, the truck driver; and finally, there are the two unnamed men whom Cub saw go off last night with the ponies. As Copper says, that tots up to eight, and there may be more. I think it's highly probable that there *are* more. Now, let us try to figure out how the organisation works. It seems pretty clear. Singer, who may, as Cub suspects, be Haynes my butler, looks after things at Lorrington, in case trouble of any sort promises to start there. His chief job may have been to watch me and keep the gang informed of my movements. While I was away at the war, it was unlikely that I should trouble them, but once it was over the gang must have known that it was only a question of time before I came here. So they planted Haynes, alias Singer. He did his job all right, too. As soon as he knew I was bound for Scotland, he sent off a wire, with what results we know. It would have been risky to bump me off at Lorrington, where I'm well known and where there are always people about. Here it would be a fairly simple matter, and, in fact, if you fellows hadn't turned up they would have got away with it. Larry drives the truck, so we may assume that he is the contact man between here and the south. Smith and Burke handle the hotel. That arrangement serves a double purpose. The gang had to control the hotel, otherwise there might have been all sorts of people staying there for the fishing, and someone, spotted the traffic between the hotel and the Lodge, might have wondered what was going on. From the hotel Burke and Smith can watch the road; at the same time they are in an ideal position to operate up and down the glen, using an old Buick car for the purpose. The rest of the gang is some-where up here. Just where, we don't know. Nor do we know what they are doing. That's what we've got to find out. Where the Lodge comes in isn't clear, although the indications are that it is a sort of halfway house between the pub and Slim's end of the glen. The road goes no farther than this, remember, so the car couldn't get past this point. Beyond here they use ponies, shod with fake shoes. As Trapper has pointed out, deer tracks are too common in these parts to call for comment, but too many pony tracks might excite the curiosity of a passing keeper or shepherd. Thinking over what Cub saw going on in the yard, it would seem that some product is being manufactured away up the glen, something heavy enough to need horse transport to carry it over country where mechanical transport could not operate. The question is, what are they producing? The only clue we have is that it may have some connection with barley, although that is by no means certain. The local people think it is dog biscuits, which would account for the comings and goings of the lorry; but I don't think we need pay any attention to that. That, obviously, is a cover-up. The barley business may be merely a blind.'

'Slim referred to the stuff as vinegar,' put in Cub.

Gimlet smiled cynically. 'My answer to that is, as Slim would probably say, hooey.'

'Just a minute,' interposed Copper. 'They make malt out of barley, and they make vinegar out of malt. I've seen the words "pure malt vinegar" on the bottles in old Ma Smith's fish-shop thousands of times.'

Gimlet shook his head. 'These people are not likely to bother about a commodity that can be bought for a shilling a bottle,' he observed drily. 'It's more likely Slim has set up a press for making counterfeit silver coins. In bulk, they would weigh heavily.'

'About this fellow Slim,' said Copper. 'One of the big noises in America during the gangster days was a chap named Slim Delano. I never saw his picture, but I'm wondering if this Slim could be the same chap.'

'Might be.'

'He was wanted for a nice crop of killings; but I don't think they ever got him,' went on Copper.

'That fellow last night had the face of a killer, if ever I saw one,' murmured Cub. 'Delano sounds Italian, and Slim – our Slim – certainly looked like an Italian.'

Gimlet nodded. 'It's worth bearing in mind.' He looked at Copper. 'What about this chap Singer? That obviously is a nickname, too. Queer how crooks adore nicknames. Does Singer suggest anything to you?'

Copper thought for a moment. He shook his head. 'I can't say as it does.' He grinned. 'Unless it's anything to do with Sing-Sing, the big jail in America.'

Gimlet smiled. 'There might be something in that.'

Cub stepped in again. 'But surely, sir, with all these crooks about our proper course would be to go to the police.'

'And tell them what?'

Cub faltered. 'Well – that the country is crawling with crooks.'

'And what charge could we or the police bring against them? In order to arrest a man you have to bring a definite charge. What can we accuse these people of? Buying barley? Making vinegar? No, that won't do. The police wouldn't issue a warrant without more information than we can provide. If they did and if at the finish they could prove nothing, the crooks might turn round and bring an action for wrongful arrest.'

'The skipper's right,' muttered Copper. 'I've been in the Force and I know. We've got to know more about this racket than we do at present before we can call in the police. Of course, the police might send a man along to have a look round, but all that would do would be to warn the crooks that the police were on the job. They'd either lie low for a bit or fade out.'

'It might clear them off my property, but after the crack they gave me on the skull I don't feel inclined to let them off so easily,' said Gimlet.

'But if this fellow McTaggart is really Burke, then he's a wanted man already,' argued Cub.

'True enough,' agreed Gimlet. 'Then what? The police arrest Burke – and the rest slide away. That won't do. We've got to get the lot while we're at it.'

'Dash it all, we could have them arrested for assault,' persisted Cub.

'Could we prove that?' asked Gimlet. 'I doubt it. A clever defending lawyer would ask the jury what possible motive had his clients for interfering with us. We should have no answer to that. In Copper's case, the three men who were present would swear blind that he was lying or that he was drunk. It would be three against one, and I doubt if any magistrate would convict on such questionable evidence. There was no question of robbery involved. They were too clever to touch my wallet. And look at this place. Apparently they haven't touched a thing. Why? Obviously, because someone might come here, and if anything was missing the police would be informed. The crooks wouldn't want that to happen. They'd be fools to spoil a first-class racket for the sake of a silly burglary – and they know it. They have used the house, we know, but we couldn't prove it, and if we did it would amount to nothing. So, taking one thing with another,

I think we can do without the police – at any rate, for the time being. We managed without the police in the old days in France, and I still prefer to think that we can look after our own affairs.'

Cub tried again. 'If this gang is operating up the glen, then they must have a house, or a farm, or some sort of building to work in. They wouldn't be likely to live in the open – not this weather.'

'They might be in a cave,' suggested Copper.

'Slim didn't look to me as if he had just stepped out of a cave,' asserted Cub sarcastically. Speaking to Gimlet, he went on. 'Do you know of any building higher up the glen, away in the hills perhaps?'

'I've never heard tell of anything of the sort,' answered Gimlet. 'But that, of course, isn't to say there is nothing. Remember, I've only just taken over the property. I've never been here before. I knew I had relatives here, that's all, but I wasn't particularly interested. I never expected to inherit the property. It only came to me because the two heirs next in line were killed in the war.'

'What about a map?' suggested Trapper, always practical. 'There should be a map of the estate – huh? That might tell us something.'

'It's an idea,' agreed Gimlet. 'There might be a map in the library. It's more likely, though, that any maps of the estate will be with the deeds, in the lawyers' office, and that's in London.'

'Then if it's no use sitting here, let's get after 'em,' suggested Copper bluntly.

Gimlet lit another cigarette and flicked the match into the fireplace. 'No hurry,' he replied casually. 'It's always a good thing to consider the enemy's point of view. After last night's affair, they must be wondering at the sudden invasion of their hide-out, just as much as we are wondering what they are doing. Don't forget they imagine I am under twenty feet of rock and rubble. What a shock they'll get when they see me. They have evidently been in the habit of using this room as a meeting-place. What will they do now someone is in residence?'

'How will they know we're here?' asked Copper.

'Unless I've missed my guess, Slim would send a man out this morning as soon as it was light enough to see, to find out if anyone was here. The fellow would see smoke coming out of the chimney and go back to report it. Slim's problem would then be to find out who is here – how many there are of us. He only knows of two – Copper and the person who shot at the lamp from the top of the dresser. Cub says he shouted something about "get 'em, boys"—'

'I did that, hoping they'd think the place was surrounded by police,' explained Cub.

'From the way they bolted I imagine they thought something of the sort, too,' said Gimlet, smiling.

'It was to stop you living here that they tried to bump you off,' Copper told Gimlet.

'I don't think there's much doubt about that,' conceded Gimlet. 'Now they'll be wondering how many more people they've got to bump off. That's why I think it might be a good plan – to use Mr Churchill's expression – to let them stew in their own juice for a while. We're in no desperate hurry. That won't suit them, though. They'll want to get on with their racket, whatever it is, but they won't dare to make a move while they realise that an unknown number of people are at the Lodge, sitting astride their lines of communication, so to speak.'

'Burke and Smith, down at the pub, won't know anything about that,' Cub pointed out.

'Not unless Slim has let them know and ordered them to keep clear. If he hasn't, Burke and Smith may roll up here; in which case we shall be only too happy to receive them.' Gimlet got up. 'For a start, it might be a good idea if we explored the house. Even if we learn nothing, we shall at least know our way about. Come on.'

An hour was spent exploring the Lodge from cellar to attic, and the outbuildings. The result was disappointing. It yielded absolutely nothing – that is, nothing in the way of a clue to the racket. It was a depressing reconnaissance. No spectacle could have been more melancholy than the dismal state into which the house had fallen. Except for one or two places where the rain had entered – probably due, as Gimlet pointed out, to the guttering being choked with dead leaves – there was nothing much wrong with the main structure. But dust lay thick on the furniture; there were places where plaster had fallen from the ceiling and soot from the chimneys, so that the general impression of neglect made everything look worse than it really was. There were, however, two items of passing interest. The first was the gun-room, which created a burst of enthusiasm, for there was an armoury of weapons in glass cases round the walls; shotguns of various bores and rifles with calibres ranging from light twenty-twos to forty-fives. Gimlet said the heavier weapons were for deer-stalking. There was ammunition, too, in the cupboards.

'I wonder Slim and his mob didn't help themselves to some of these,' remarked Copper, taking down a Mannlicher thirty-thirty automatic lever-action deer rifle, and looking through the barrel with professional aptitude.

'That Slim hasn't touched them all goes to show what a shrewd fellow he is,' returned Gimlet. 'Remember what I said in the kitchen? The lawyers are bound to have an inventory of the contents of the Lodge. Slim isn't such a fool as to risk a charge of housebreaking while he's on a much better proposition. What would they do with weapons of this sort, anyway? Slim carries all he's likely to need, under his armpit or in his pocket. Still, it's nice to know that if it comes to open war, we shan't be short of equipment. Help yourselves to anything you fancy.'

Copper took a twelve-bore sporting gun. 'Give me a double-barrelled scatter-gun and buckshot for close work,' he declared. Trapper said he would take the Mannlicher. Cub selected a heavily built Remington twenty-two repeater with a bolt action and telescopic sight. Gimlet said he wouldn't bother just then. If it came to shooting, he would see about it.

The second item of interest was a bed which, from the crumpled heap of blankets that lay on it, had been used. Several match-sticks and cigarette ends on the floor lent colour to this view. From the dust and a small quantity of plaster that lay on top of the blankets, this was evidently some time ago.

Cub put forward a theory. 'What happened here, I should say, was this,' he observed. 'When Burke was on the run in Scotland he came across this place and decided that it was a lot more comfortable than sleeping rough on the open moor. He stayed here for a while and used this bed. Walking about the hills looking for food, he tumbled across something that gave him his big idea. It was too big to start single-handed, so he got in touch with his pals across the Atlantic, and they, being out of a racket on account

of prohibition coming to an end, came over here and joined him. They got
the thing going, and they've had it all their own way ever since. When the
war ended they knew you'd be coming here, so they planted Singer to tip
them off when you headed north. All went off as arranged, but what they
didn't reckon on was the three of us following you up. As you say, that's
got them guessing.'

'I don't think you're far wrong,' agreed Gimlet. 'It must have been something like that.'

They turned their attention to the library.

''Strewth!' exclaimed Copper, looking round the shelves with their vast
array of books. 'We shan't get short of reading if things get dull – my oath
we shan't.'

'I don't think we shall have much time for reading,' returned Gimlet
quietly. 'There's just a chance that we may find a map here, but it's a bit
hard to know where to start looking.'

'Don't you think it's time, sir, we started lookin' fer Slim and 'is pals?'
muttered Copper impatiently.

Gimlet dropped into an easy chair. 'I've no intention of looking for him
– not yet, at any rate.'

'Not – look for him?' Copper seemed astonished.

'I'd rather he came here, to us.'

'You think – he'll come – *here*?' Copper was frankly incredulous. 'Slim
didn't strike me as being crazy.'

'Put it this way,' went on Gimlet. 'In the first place, I don't think you
quite realise what you're talking about when you speak of looking for
anyone in a region like this. My estate alone is nearly as big as a normal
English county. And it isn't flat, open country. None of it is level. It's either
mountain or valley, and, as Cub had already discovered, the going isn't
easy. An army could search these hills for a week without finding a man
who happened to get lost. That's why, in days gone by, a clan could make a
cattle raid and disappear as completely as if the earth had swallowed them
up – that's really what it amounted to. What hope have we, then, of finding
Slim, who has no doubt taken care to camouflage his hide-out? Another
point is, he might occupy this house during our absence, in which case it
would be a sticky job to get back into it. If we had something to go on it

would be different, but we have absolutely no idea where to start. There's another point. Suppose by some miraculous chance, we did run into Slim and his associates; what then? What could we do?'

'Do? Why, knock their blocks off; what else?' replied Copper promptly.

Gimlet frowned. 'Don't be ridiculous, Copper. The war's over. If we start making a private battlefield of the Highlands, it will be us the police will be looking for. According to the law, we should only be justified in employing force if we were attacked. In other words, in this country you can't start shooting people unless they try to kill you.'

'I get it,' replied Copper bitterly. 'We stand up and let them have first crack at us. If they miss, we have a go at them. Blimey, sir, what sort o' war do yer call that? There wasn't nothin' like that in *my* trainin'. Shoot first and say you're sorry afterwards has always been our motto – what say you, Trapper, old pal? Am I right?'

'*Tch*! Every time,' responded Trapper faithfully.

'Well, I'm afraid I must rule that out at Strathcarglas,' insisted Gimlet.

Copper shook his head sadly. ''Strewth! I call that a bit 'ard. For five blinkin' years we've risked our precious 'ids killin' the King's enemies; now we're not allowed ter knock off one or two of our own. It ain't fair – no, my oath, it ain't.'

'Still, that's how it is; that's the law,' said Gimlet. 'Don't worry though, I think you'll get your chance before this business is over.'

'If we can't go gunnin' fer Slim, how are we goin' ter get a chance?' demanded Copper.

'I've already told you,' answered Gimlet evenly. 'We'll stay here and let Slim come to us. He won't run away, don't worry. He's not going to abandon a valuable racket on our account. At the moment, like us, the enemy will be talking it over. While we stick our toes in here, they won't dare to carry on with the racket. They'll soon get tired of that. What, then, will they do? They'll come here and try to shift us.'

'What they'll do is try to bump us off, in case we go to the police and kick up a stink,' asserted Copper.

'I think that's more than likely,' admitted Gimlet. 'I hope they'll find we are not so easy to bump off as all that.'

'When do you think they'll come here?' asked Cub.

'They might come any time. After all, we haven't attempted to conceal our presence here. Confound them; I'm not going to hide in my own house. I don't think it's likely that they'll come in daylight, for fear we spotted them coming. They're more likely to come after dark. Presently we'll arrange things to ensure that they get an appropriate reception. Incidentally, by the look of the sky we're going to have some more snow. I'll have another look to see if I can find a map. Trapper, I think it would be a good plan if you took your bow and stocked the larder, just in case we found ourselves besieged. Copper, go up to one of the turrets and cast an eye over the landscape. We should look silly if we allowed ourselves to be taken by surprise. Cub can stay here with me. After that, we'll go back to the kitchen; it's warmer there. Later on we'll arrange things so that if we should have visitors, we'll be able to keep the party in order.'

For more than an hour Cub helped Gimlet to search the library for a large-scale map of the district. The quest, to Gimlet's disappointment, proved unsuccessful, so they gave it up and returned to the kitchen, where they found Trapper skinning a rabbit. A hare, hanging on a peg with the grouse he had killed earlier in the day, showed that he had not wasted his time.

Presently Copper came in and reported that although the turret commanded a fine view of the moor, and he had watched patiently for a long time, he had seen no sign of life anywhere.

'All right,' said Gimlet. 'As soon as Cub has finished his lunch he'll relieve you. After that, we'll take regular watches till sundown. Then we'll fix things ready for the night. I don't think Slim will disappoint us. From what we know of him, he doesn't seem to be the sort of man to tolerate opposition for very long.'

CHAPTER TWELVE

Slim Makes a Proposition

Within the kitchen of Strathcarglas Lodge silence reigned. Gimlet sat in a chair near the range in which a small fire smouldered, reading a book which he had brought from the library in the light of a candle that stood on a corner of the table near his elbow. Cub, also reading, shared the candle. Trapper, in his shirt-sleeves, with infinite care and patience whittled a new arrow. To a casual visitor it would have been a homely scene in a peaceful setting.

Gimlet looked at his watch. 'Ten o'clock,' he announced in a low voice. 'Your turn, Trapper.'

Trapper rose, put away his knife, donned his jacket and walked over to the door. All this he did very quietly. In his final exit from the room he made no more noise than a shadow, this being largely due to the fact that he wore his socks over his shoes.

A minute later, moving with the same uncanny silence, Copper entered. 'All quiet, sir,' he reported in a low voice. 'Sky overcast. Black as pitch, but the moon's just comin' up. Feels like snow.' He sat down and lit a cigarette. 'If my old Ma could see me she'd wonder what the blue blazes I was playin' at,' he observed reflectively.

No one answered.

Ten minutes passed with hardly a sound. Then Trapper came back. He still moved quietly, but now, as he closed the door behind him there was a quality of urgency in his manner. '*Ma foi*! You are right, sir,' he breathed. 'They come, I think. I hear a movement on the moor. A grouse has just gone over, flying low. I hear her wings.'

426

Gimlet stirred. 'That's it. That bird wouldn't have moved at this time of night if it hadn't been disturbed. Did you close the back door?'

'I closed it but I did not lock it, as you ordered.'

'You've no idea how many there are of them?'

'No.'

'Never mind; you should be able to find out; let us know by the signal we arranged. Mark the direction they take when they leave. That's the main object of this performance. But don't let them see you.'

'We look like havin' a lively time if the whole mob turns up,' muttered Copper.

'We'll risk that,' averred Gimlet. 'All right, everybody. Action stations.' Gimlet himself did not move. 'Remember, do nothing unless you get a cue from me, or unless it becomes obvious that the situation is out of hand,' he cautioned. 'Otherwise, not a sound.'

Trapper went out by the door through which he had entered. Cub went over to the big dresser, the lower part of which was a cupboard of some size. Earlier in the day it had been half filled with old-fashioned cooking utensils – saucepans, stewpans, and the like, but these had been removed to the scullery, where, arranged inside a door that gave access to some outer domestic offices, they ensured that no one could enter without making a good deal of noise. Cub crawled into the cupboard, pulling the double doors behind him until they were within an inch of being closed. Copper moved to a pantry and did much the same thing, that is, he pulled the door to without latching it, leaving a narrow crack through which, from the inside, he could see into the kitchen.

These were the dispositions which, earlier in the evening, had been arranged and rehearsed with a good deal of care. The weapons selected in the gun-room, loaded, were already in their respective places. Only Gimlet was, or appeared to be, unarmed. He did not move from his position in front of the fire except to turn the chair a trifle more towards the door which gave access to the corridor leading to the back door. The candle still burned, casting distorted shadows on the walls. Silence settled again on the scene. So still and quiet was it that a cinder, falling from the fire, made an astonishing amount of noise.

Five minutes passed and still the silence persisted; but at last it was broken. The door handle moved, making a noise so slight that in the ordinary way it would not have been noticed. Gimlet smiled faintly as, glancing at the source of the noise, he saw the handle slowly turning.

'Come in, Mr Delano,' he called in a clear voice.

The door handle stopped abruptly. There was a short pause. Then it was turned sharply and, with a bang, the door was flung wide open.

Gimlet did not move a muscle. Out of the corners of his eyes he could just see someone in a half-crouching position, one hand thrust forward, in the dark corridor.

There was another minute of palpitating silence. Nothing moved. Then, with an almost imperceptible gliding movement, an automatic held in front of him like the head of a snake about to strike, Slim advanced into the room. His eyes were on Gimlet. They never left him. They rested on his face as if it exercised upon him some fatal fascination. His own face, sallow at the best of times, was ashen. Cub, from where he squatted, could see the muscles of his jaws working. Still Slim stared, and stared, and stared again at the man sitting motionless in the chair.

Gimlet spoke again. 'Aren't you getting rather a big boy to be playing at soldiers, Mr Delano?' he murmured in a voice tinged with sarcasm. 'Or are you pretending to be the big bad wolf trying to frighten somebody? Come – come; put that nasty-looking weapon away. What are you going to do with it? You can't kill the same man twice.'

Slim drew a deep breath. He made a beckoning movement to someone behind him. Tiny appeared in the radius of light, his lips parted, eyes wide, sweat running down his face.

'Let's get outa here, boss,' he pleaded in a tremulous voice.

'What's the hurry?' enquired Gimlet.

Slim found his voice at last. 'What are you doing here?'

'Waiting for you.'

'Waiting – for us? Pah! Don't give me that.' Slim's voice was heavy with sarcasm.

'What I am going to give you eventually, Mr Delano, will probably surprise you,' replied Gimlet easily.

'Where did you get hold of that name?' demanded Slim viciously.

'The dead know everything,' bantered Gimlet.

'You ain't dead,' said Slim, showing his white teeth.

'Maybe it's his brother,' suggested Tiny. 'Watch he don't pull a gun.'

'Had I wanted to pull a gun on you, Tiny, you wouldn't have got as far as this,' said Gimlet. 'I could have dropped you cold as you came in the back door. Why do you think I left it unlocked? My sentries warned me you were coming.'

'Sentries?' questioned Slim.

Gimlet smiled faintly. 'The grouse. Every one is a sentry, and there are hundreds.'

Slim suddenly got angry, or perhaps he tried to cover his discomfiture by a show of anger. 'Quit fooling,' he snarled. 'How did you get here?'

'I just pushed aside twenty tons or so of rubble and walked along,' answered Gimlet nonchalantly.

'And you reckon you can get away with that?'

'Suppose you tell me what *you're* reckoning on?' suggested Gimlet. 'After all, this is my property. You are the intruder, not me. You're house-breaking at this very moment. What are you going to say if I call in the police?'

'You ain't calling the cops,' asserted Slim.

Gimlet raised his eyebrows. 'How do you know what I'm going to do?'

Slim hesitated again. 'Because I made a mess of putting you out of the way once doesn't mean I shan't do better next time.'

'You'd be silly to try anything like that again, Mr Delano,' replied Gimlet. 'You're not in America now, you know. Our police take a very poor view of murder, and unfortunately for men of your type they cannot be squared. Suppose you stop making threats you can't carry out and tell me what's on your mind.'

'You are,' snapped Slim. 'You're in my way.'

'You've already made that abundantly clear,' answered Gimlet smoothly. 'But there are two angles to that. You may be in my way. I object to anyone, much less a bunch of crooks, using my property as if it were their own.'

Slim stared. 'Crooks? What sort of talk's that?' he demanded.

'You should know,' replied Gimlet. 'Now tell me, Mr Delano, what are you doing on my property that you are so anxious to stay on it?'

Slim frowned. 'Are you kidding?'

'No,' returned Gimlet. 'I was never more serious.'

'Suppose we say that's my business?' suggested Slim. 'This place suits me. I like it, and when I like a thing I'm always willing to pay for it. That's fair enough, ain't it?'

'The reception I received when I first arrived didn't give me that impression.'

'Bah! That was Billy Smith. He acts kinda impetuous. I'm different. Suppose you and me get down to cases and get things fixed up as between gentlemen?'

The ghost of a smile crossed Gimlet's face. 'Go ahead.'

'I've done pretty well in this country since I came over here, I'll own to that,' went on Slim.

'How did you get into this country, with a war on?' asked Gimlet curiously. 'You've been here for some time, I understand.'

'Why, that?' Slim laughed shortly. 'Nothing to it. I joined the army to fight the Nazis.'

'I see. And when you got over here you deserted?'

'Put it that way if you like.'

'Go on.'

'What I was going to say was, suppose you let me hire this dump and you go some place else and forget about it? I ain't mean. I'm thinking of real money. How about ten thousand bucks for a year's hire and no more questions asked? How's that?'

Gimlet shook his head. 'Nothing doing, Mr Delano. I'm not for sale – neither is Strathcarglas.'

'Make it twenty thousand.'

'Not for twenty million.'

'What's wrong with my money?'

'Since you ask me, Mr Delano, I don't think I should like the smell of it. Let me be frank. I don't like you and I don't like your friends. In fact, I dislike you so much that by the time I've finished with you I hope you will be swinging on a well-built British gallows, or burning in one of your own electric chairs.'

Slim drew a deep breath. 'So that's how you feel?'

'That, Mr Delano, is exactly how I feel. I hope I have made myself clear?'

'You've decided to stay here – huh?'

'Precisely.'

'And you reckon I'll let you?'

'You barely come into my calculations.'

Slim took a swift glance round the room. 'I guess I've got you where I want you right now,' he drawled.

'You're not very good at guessing, Mr Delano,' said Gimlet gently. 'It would be more in accord with facts to say that the reverse is the case.'

'Is that so?' Slim spoke slowly. His eyes were never still. For the first time it seemed to occur to him that he might be in a trap.

'My advice to you, Mr Delano, is that you depart as quietly as you came. Of course, if you'd rather have it the other way, go right ahead.'

'Yeah?' Slim's lips closed in a thin line. He half raised his pistol. 'What's to stop me letting you have it?'

'Several things.'

'Where are they?'

'Oh no, Mr Delano, I'm not showing you my hand,' replied Gimlet. 'Perhaps I'll show you one card.' Gimlet inclined his head towards the scullery door. 'Copper,' he said quietly.

The muzzle of Copper's twelve-bore appeared, covering Slim. The scullery door opened slowly, revealing Copper on the threshold. His face was a mask.

'You want me, sir?' he asked, without taking his eyes off Slim.

'I may. Stand fast.' Gimlet looked at Slim. 'Is that enough or would you like to see some more?'

Slim swallowed hard. 'Okay,' he said in a voice that had acid in it. 'I get it. But don't get the idea I've finished with you.'

'I hope you will not be so ill advised as to suppose that I've finished with you, either, Mr Delano,' answered Gimlet quietly. 'I'm glad we've had this chat. We understand each other now, I think.'

'I ought to have made sure of you first time,' grated Slim through his teeth.

'Quite right. You should. A lot of men, better men than you, Mr Delano – many of them, alas, no longer with us – have thought the same thing.'

'I'll get you yet, you smug Britisher.' Slim's face had turned pale again, this time with anger.

'Don't get abusive, Mr Delano. Abuse is cheap. And suppose we leave nationalities out of it. You're just as much an enemy of your own country as mine. You see, I know quite a lot about you.'

Slim drew himself up and put his pistol in its holster. 'Okay,' he muttered. 'You win this time – but I ain't finished.'

'Neither have I, Mr Delano,' answered Gimlet smoothly.

Slim turned to the door. 'Come on, Tiny, let's get outa this.'

'My tall friend will see you off the premises,' said Gimlet, inclining his head towards Copper. 'He's a short-tempered fellow; when he gets upset he suffers from a twitching finger, so be careful not to annoy him.'

Slim, followed by Tiny, walked to the door. 'You ain't seen the last of me,' he promised viciously.

'And you haven't seen the last of me, Mr Delano,' answered Gimlet.

Slim and Tiny went out. Copper followed close behind, the muzzle of his gun never far from Slim's back.

Gimlet settled back in his chair and lit another cigarette.

Nevertheless, in spite of his careless attitude it was evident to Cub that he was listening intently. He listened for some time before he said: 'All right, Cub. You can come out now.'

As Cub emerged from his hiding-place, Copper came in, grinning. 'They've gone, sir – gone as quiet as lambs.'

'I wouldn't call them lambs,' answered Gimlet. 'Call them a couple of snakes that have had their tails trodden on. They're just about as venomous. Any sign of Burke or Smith?'

'No, sir. The yard's clear.'

'Then we may take it that Slim ordered them to keep out of the way. Or maybe it wasn't the night for them to come here to collect their famous vinegar.'

'The weather don't look too good,' said Copper. 'It's tryin' to do somethin', but I ain't sure what.'

Nearly an hour elapsed before Trapper reappeared. From the state of his feet and legs he had obviously been on the moor.

'How did you get on?' asked Gimlet. 'Which way did they go?'

'They went straight up the glen,' answered Trapper, sitting down. 'I followed them a fair way, but *alors*, it started sleeting and I lost them in the murk. I dare not get too close because I was following them more with my ears than with my eyes, and there were places where the river made so much noise that it drowned all other sounds. But I know just where I lost them and I know the general direction they were heading.'

'Good,' murmured Gimlet.

'It seemed a pity ter have ter let 'em get away,' said Copper sadly, shaking his head.

Gimlet smiled. 'That's probably what they're thinking about us.'

'What will Slim do next, do you reckon?'

'He'll come back,' returned Gimlet without hesitation.

Cub looked up. 'Do you really think so?'

'Without a doubt. He knows well enough that we're not likely to run away, and obviously he can't leave us here. He's got to move us in order to carry on, and he won't hesitate to employ the dirtiest gangster methods to do it.'

'And what'll we do?' questioned Copper.

'We shall stay here.'

'Suppose he sets the house on fire?'

'And bring a crowd here to watch a spectacle which would be seen for miles? Not likely. He wants to discourage visitors, not encourage them. Besides, he wants to use the house himself.'

'What will he be most likely to do, then?'

'There are several things he could do,' asserted Gimlet. 'We know he has explosives, because he bombed the mine. American cracksmen have a strong affection for nitro-glycerine, for safe busting and similar playful diversions, so one thing he could do would be to come back here, and toss a bomb through the kitchen window. That would be the quick and efficient way, because it would remove us all at one stroke – that is, if we were here. It won't work, for the simple reason that we shall shift our quarters to another part of the house. A slower way would be to snipe us one by one.'

'Ah! What do we do if he starts that?'

'We snipe back.'

433

'But I thought you ses we wasn't ter make the place a battlefield?'

'If he shoots at us we shall be in order in shooting back. That, in the eyes of the law, would be justifiable homicide. You were talking of attacking them. I'm talking primarily of defending ourselves. As things stand, if we attacked we would probably be left with casualties which we should find hard to explain to the authorities. If Slim attacks, his casualties will be his own affair. I don't know what he'd do with them, and, frankly, I don't care.'

'Sufferin' winkles!' growled Copper. 'This is a new line of soldiering fer us – waitin' ter be attacked; my oath it is.'

'Don't get upset about it, I didn't mean that literally; I was referring particularly to the use of lethal weapons. It isn't for us to start using them. We may manage without. But if Slim starts any really rough stuff, we'll hand him back everything we've got.'

Trapper grunted. '*Bon, ça.*'

'I should thunderin' well think so,' muttered Copper irritably. 'Does this mean we stay here all the time?'

Copper drew a deep breath. 'Thank gawd fer that. I thought from the way you spoke we wasn't goin' ter do no strikin'. What do we strike at first?'

'We can't really do any serious striking until we know what their racket is,' answered Gimlet. 'That is now the dominant factor. If we could find out what they are doing, we might have reasonable grounds for assault. One way to get that information would be to ambush the ponies and examine their packs, or intercept the car between here and the hotel, or stop Larry on the road to see what he has in his truck. I doubt if we have any right to stop the lorry on the road; if it came to a court case that could be made to look like highway robbery. But the lorry will have gone by now. Slim said last night that Larry was in a hurry to get back. It's a pity he didn't say where he was going.'

'London, probably,' put in Cub.

'I doubt it,' said Gimlet pensively. 'London is six hundred miles away. If Larry has gone to London, it will be at least four days before he's back. Even then, to do the trip in that time would require two drivers; I understand Larry was alone, so it doesn't look like London. It's more likely that he operates to Aberdeen or Perth, or some big town, and puts his cargo on rail for its final destination. In that case, he should soon be back. Which way was the lorry facing, Copper, when it stopped – towards Tomnarrow or Deeside?'

'Tomnarrow.'

'Then, it looks as if Larry had come in from Aberdeen. If he's putting the stuff on rail there, we ought to be able to trace it – but we'll talk about that later. Another thing we might do is tackle the car between the hotel and here, next time it comes. That would be on my property. But it's unlikely that the car comes up here every night, and we don't know the nights on which it does come. We can watch for it, but I doubt if Slim will allow it to come up while we're here.'

'How about attacking the pub?' suggested Copper.

'I doubt if we should find anything there.'

'We could grab a couple of prisoners.'

'At the moment prisoners are the last things we want to be bothered with, unless we can scoop the whole bunch at one go.'

'How about grabbing Singer and making him squeal?'

'He might not squeal. Anyway, we've no time to go to Devonshire. Here we are, on the main field of operations, and I don't feel inclined to leave it. If we left, it might look as though we were running away.'

'Blimey! We don't want 'em ter think that,' declared Copper emphatically.

Gimlet looked at his watch. 'It's getting late. I'll think things over and have a plan ready by the morning. Let's get this kit shifted to one of the turrets. It's a nuisance, but I'm afraid we shall have to mount a guard to see that the enemy doesn't break in on us. Let's be moving. This kitchen is no longer healthy. Cub, you go first with your torch and light the way.'

CHAPTER THIRTEEN

Slim Comes Back

Cub was awakened by an explosion of such violence that he was literally hurled from sleep to wakefulness. Such was the concussion, and so alarming the vibration, that his first thought was that there had been an earthquake and that the house was falling down on him. Then, remembering where he was, the thought flashed through his mind – Gimlet was right; thank goodness, we weren't in the kitchen. By that time, of course, he had realised that a bomb had exploded in some part of the house, and, recalling Gimlet's words overnight, he guessed it was the kitchen. He scrambled up. The others were already on their feet. There was no light in the turret, but he could just see their figures outlined against the windows, although it was still dark outside. Copper was absent. Cub remembered that he had offered to do the dawn guard.

'Take it easy,' came Gimlet's voice. Without opening a window, he was trying to see down into the grounds.

'Where was it, do you think?' asked Cub.

'In the kitchen, I fancy. Trapper, go and see if Copper's all right. I warned him to keep clear of the back premises.'

'Here, take my torch,' offered Cub.

Trapper hurried off. Cub joined Gimlet at the window. He saw that the sky had almost cleared; a few stars sparkled frostily; a crescent moon was dying behind the Cairngorms, throwing their serrated peaks into sharp relief. Between the Lodge and the mountains the landscape rolled away like a vast crumpled blanket.

Cub tried to see the hands of his watch, but could not. He dare not strike a light for fear it would be seen from outside and draw a pistol shot. 'I was trying to make out the time,' he told Gimlet.

'It can't be far short of dawn,' answered Gimlet. 'It's hard to see anything, but keep your eyes open. Tell me if you see a movement. Don't make a noise and don't show yourself.'

Cub stared down into the overgrown grounds surrounding the Lodge. He could see nothing beyond the vague shapes of shrubs and trees; for the rest, the scene was as lifeless as the surface of the moon.

'I should say they're gone,' he said in a low voice.

'I shouldn't,' answered Gimlet. 'It's more likely that they'll wait to see how much damage they've done. They'll have to find that out sooner or later. They're too smart to show themselves too soon, in case their squib failed in what it was intended to do. I hope Copper's all right.'

Trapper came back. '*Zut*! The kitchen's had it,' he reported. 'She is one beautiful mess.'

'Never mind that. What about Copper?' asked Gimlet. 'He was in the hall. He says the blast knocked him over backwards, but he's all right.'

'What's he doing now?'

'Waiting in the corridor by the kitchen, hoping, I think, to see someone to shoot at. *Mot de Cambronne*! He is angry. He swears like a lumberjack who drops an axe on his toe.'

'We might as well go down and see what's going on before he gets into mischief,' decided Gimlet. 'Go quietly. I don't want the enemy to hear us moving about. If they hear us, they'll keep clear. I'd rather they thought they'd wiped us out.'

They went quietly down the stairs and found Copper kneeling in the corridor, gun ready for action, watching the kitchen – or what remained of it. The room was a wreck, a litter of plaster, splinters of wood and broken glass. The heavy table had been overturned, and the ceiling sagged towards a corner, where a section of the wall had been blown clean out. Framed by jagged walls, in the outer darkness was an area of overgrown lawn, a shrubbery, and beyond this a copse of Scotch firs.

'See anything?' Gimlet asked Copper in a whisper.

'If I could I should be pumping lead,' answered Copper viciously. 'That bang blame near blew my eyeballs out of the back of my head. How about goin' out fer 'em and doin' a little moppin' up?'

'That's just what they'd like us to do,' replied Gimlet. 'One step outside that wall and you'd run into a piece of metal coming the other way. We'll leave them to do the investigating. Be patient and you may get a shot. It will be getting light presently. What size shot have you got in that scatter-gun?'

'Buckshot, sir.'

'All right. If you shoot, aim low. We don't want any stiffs left on our hands.'

There was a short interval. Nothing happened.

'I think we might hasten the proceedings if you did a little quiet moaning, Copper,' suggested Gimlet.

Copper looked up. 'What's the idea o' that, sir?'

'It should make them impatient to count the casualties. They may suppose that we were together, and if they got one they probably got up all. Go ahead. Trapper, you watch the rear; we don't want them slinking in on us another way.'

Copper's idea of a moan was so horrible that Cub recoiled in momentary alarm.

'Go easy, don't overdo it,' muttered Gimlet. 'I said moan, not howl. They'll think they've killed the cat.'

'Sorry, sir.' Again Copper rendered his version of a human being in agony.

Gimlet stopped him. 'That's enough,' he said shortly. 'I can't stand it.'

'I was doin' my best, sir,' whispered Copper in an injured voice.

'Then all I can say is, thank heaven you didn't do your worst,' adjured Gimlet curtly. 'Quiet now.'

Cub was watching the trees. He thought he saw a shadow flit from the trees to the shrubbery. 'I think they're moving,' he breathed.

A minute later a figure took shape in front of the shrubbery, a distance of about fifty yards. This time there was no doubt about it. Presently it was joined by another. The two held a whispered conversation and then made a cautious approach. A torch flashed, cutting a wedge of light between the men and the hole in the kitchen wall. Evidently they did not believe in taking chances, for they stopped again, the torch exploring the premises.

Gimlet spoke softly. 'All right, Copper; let 'em have it. Keep low. You ought to wing a brace with a left and right.'

The twelve-bore roared a double report. On the tail of the explosion came a yell of pain, or fear, or both. The flash of the gun momentarily blinded Cub; when he could see again the men had gone. A noise of groaning, cursing, and crashing came from the shrubbery.

'You seem to have stung one of them, anyway,' remarked Gimlet lightly. 'You might try browning the bushes to expedite their departure.'

'Shall I follow up, sir?'

'Certainly not. Keep under cover. We don't know how many men there are in those trees.'

As if to confirm Gimlet's warning, a spurt of flame jabbed the darkness from the base of the trees. A bullet smacked against the kitchen wall.

'See what I mean?' murmured Gimlet. 'We must discourage that sharp-shooter. Try a couple of shots at the next flash.'

A moment later a firearm flashed in the trees, three quick shots. They did no damage.

Bang – bang blazed Copper's gun. The pellets pattered against the boles of the firs like wind-driven hail.

There were no more shots.

'That seems to be all – for the time being, anyway,' observed Gimlet. 'Now they know we're still on our feet they'll make what the High Command used to call a strategical withdrawal. The stars are paling. They won't dare to stay in range after daylight. I think we might see about a bite of breakfast. You can attend to that, Trapper. Cub, you mount guard in the turret. Copper, take care of the east end of the house; the library window will be your best place. I'll bring your breakfasts to you when I've had my bath. Keep your eyes open. Slim is probably feeling pretty sore. Presently he'll get really nasty.'

Cub went up to the turret, and from its narrow windows watched the dawn break, cold and drear, over the lonely moor. He had one fleeting glimpse of the enemy. Two men, helping a third, showed for a moment on the brow of some rising ground a good mile up the glen. He had time to observe that they were walking away from the Lodge, before a fold in the ground hid them from view. He did nothing about it. The distance was far beyond the range of his little twenty-two, even if he had felt like shooting. But he told Gimlet about it when presently he arrived with a jug of tea, some home-made buns and a leg of cold rabbit. 'I rather think one of the men was Slim,' he concluded.

'He probably came to watch the proceedings,' answered Gimlet. 'We shall see more of him, but not just yet, I fancy. I'll relieve you presently to give you a chance to stretch your legs.'

Still watching the moor, Cub ate his breakfast; and as he watched he found time to think. He considered the affair from every angle, and, pondering, a new thought occurred to him. Burke had used the house as a refuge when he was being hunted by the police. Of that he felt reasonably certain. During this period Burke had had a brainwave, or had discovered something that had led to the organisation of the racket. Gimlet had agreed with this theory. But up to now Cub had rather assumed that the discovery had been made on the moor. Now, thinking it over, it seemed just as probable, if not more likely, that he had made his discovery in the Lodge. What that discovery was Cub still hadn't the remotest idea, but he perceived that it was the key to the whole situation. The moor, seldom visited by a human being, was an ideal place from which to run a racket. Or was it? He was not so sure of that. Most rackets were run in big cities. Slim was a typical city rat. Surely, thought Cub, he must hate this unnatural solitude, this banishment from the bright lights and gay life to which he was accustomed. It would have to be a powerful incentive indeed to cause such a man to live in a remote Scottish glen. There could only be one incentive, the only impulse men of that type acknowledged. Money. Slim was making money, big money, or he would not stay there. And he was making money in a manner that would not be possible in a city.

Following this line of thought, Cub decided that the glen was not only associated with the scheme for making easy money, but that it formed an integral part of it. That it was, perhaps, the very foundation of it. Here, in the unbroken solitude of a deep ravine or amongst the frowning crags of the high tops, Slim could do something that could not be done in a city; something, in fact, that could not be done anywhere else. Yet, reasoned Cub, the remoteness of the glen could not in itself be a sufficient reason. There were other places just as lonely. Why was he so desperately anxious to defend this particular locality? It looked as if the scheme upon which he was engaged could only be operated at Glencarglas; which in turn implied that there was something on Gimlet's estate that did not occur anywhere else. What could it possibly be? That question was not so easy to answer. The only things that occurred in abundance were things not likely to interest Slim – water, rock, heather, and the peat in which it flourished. Water in quantity was available anywhere. Rock was common enough. Heather grew all over Scotland. Peat could hardly be called rare; it was used as fuel in many places. It might be used to stoke a furnace. A furnace for what? There was, or had been, tin in the glen. Tin was quite valuable, but hardly of sufficient value to interest Slim. Was there gold, or some other precious metal, on the estate? It was possible but highly improbable. Thus pondered Cub, but in this direction he could get no farther.

He tried another line of thought. If Burke had made his big discovery either in the house or on the moor, there seemed to be no reason why they should not, by exploring, make the same discovery or hit on a clue to it. To go over the entire moor, as Gimlet had pointed out, was hardly a practicable proposition. It would take too long. Besides, the moor was now dangerous ground. But they had possession of the house, and it was open to investigation. There was, for instance, the room that Burke had used – or the room they presumed he had used. They had been in it once, and then only for a short time, during which they had given it no more than a cursory glance. Even if Burke had made his original discovery on the moor, Cub thought, it seemed feasible that he would return to the house to think it over. If he had, then there was just a chance that he had left some indication of it behind. A clue, however insignificant, might put them on the track.

So soliloquised Cub as he sat in the turret, his eyes working methodically over the eternal heather. Only once was his attention stimulated, and that was when a covey of grouse got up from behind a ridge in the middle distance, to skim on robust wings to another hill. He focused his eyes on the spot, and smiled when an old dog fox showed itself for an instant on the skyline, muzzle pointing in the direction of the birds he had failed to surprise.

Gimlet came in. Cub told him he had nothing fresh to report. Gimlet sat down, saying that he would take over for an hour, but Cub was not to leave the house.

Cub had no reason to leave the house. 'I shall be within call,' he promised, and, leaving the turret, he made his way to the room Burke had supposedly used. As his eyes swept over it again, his first sensation was one of disappointment. There was very little furniture in the room, and it seemed to him that the chances of finding anything was small indeed. However, he set about his task, searching the room systematically inch by inch, exploring the fireplace, running his fingers round the picture-rail and standing on a chair to examine the top of the wardrobe. This producing no result, he picked up the match-sticks and cigarette ends. They told him nothing. Two of the cigarette ends bore the name of the makers, but the brand was so common that they conveyed nothing. He left the bed until last; one by one he removed the blankets, shaking each one out for anything it might contain within its folds. Nothing fell out. At last only the mattress was left. It was a very ordinary affair. He felt it, pummelled it. He prodded it with the point of his knife for any hard object. Finally, to examine the underside he turned it over. As he did this his heart gave a bound. Here at last was something. Again he was swept by disappointment. It was only a book; a book in a cheap-looking old-fashioned binding. Its style suggested the Victorian period. He picked it up, and the title at once killed any hope that may have lingered. It was: *A Short History of the Western Highlands*, by the Reverend James McPherson-Smith. The date was 1852. It was fairly evident that it had been brought from the library, thought Cub. Burke must have brought it up to read, to while away the time when he was in hiding. There was always a chance, of course, that it had been put there before his time by whoever had occupied the room. Still, it was the sort of book Burke might read, considering his position. But why should he conceal it under the mattress? Why not leave it on the bedside table or the chest of drawers? Why hide it? – for there could have been only one object in putting it under the mattress.

Cub examined the book with renewed interest. A table of illustrations referred to a map at the end. Cub remembered that they needed a map and turned to the place indicated. The map was not there. That there had been one was apparent from the rough edge where it had been torn out. Turning to the contents page, his eyes ran down the chapter headings. Most of the districts named were unknown to him. But not all. One caused him to stop abruptly. He had good reason to know the place. The chapter was headed, 'The Story of Glencarglas'.

Cub, conscious that his heart was beating faster, feeling that at last he was on the trail of something, went over to the window and, finding a seat on a flimsy bedroom chair, began to read.

He was still reading when the door was pushed open with some force and Copper came in. He regarded Cub with irritable disaffection. 'What's the idea?' he demanded. 'Didn't you hear us calling you?'

Cub started. 'Sorry. No, I didn't hear a thing.'

'Well, come on. Gimlet's waiting.'

Putting the book in his pocket, Cub followed Copper to the turret, where he found Gimlet and Trapper.

'Where the deuce have you been?' demanded Gimlet crisply. 'I've been trying to get everybody together to outline my plan of campaign.'

'Sorry, sir. I didn't hear you.'

'What were you doing?'

'I was reading,' said Cub contritely.

'All right. Sit down and listen. This is my idea.'

'Before you go into that,' said Cub meekly, 'I have some information which I think you should know.'

Gimlet threw a glance at Cub and, noting the expression of his face, frowned. 'What's happened?'

'Plenty,' replied Cub a trifle breathlessly. 'I think I've got Slim and his gang weighed up.'

'Meaning what?' asked Copper.

'I know what they're doing.'

Gimlet stared. 'You *what*?'

'I've rumbled their racket.'

'And just how did you do, that?' asked Copper, with more than a suspicion of incredulity in his tone.

'Mostly by what is commonly known as putting two and two together and making them add up to four,' answered Cub. 'There was, I own, a little luck attached to it,' he added modestly.

'Out with it,' requested Gimlet.

A curious, half-embarrassed smile spread over Cub's face. 'Just a minute, sir. First of all, did you have an ancestor by the name of Cunningham-King?'

'Not exactly an ancestor,' replied Gimlet. 'The Cunningham-Kings were a different branch of the family. They were the people who originally owned this property. In fact, the uncle who left it to me was a Cunningham-King.'

'His grandfather would have the same name?'

'Of course.'

'And his son built this place?'

'So I believe.'

'He must have had a lot of money to build a place this size?'

'He had. The Cunningham-Kings were never short of cash.'

Cub's smile broadened. 'I'll bet they weren't. Do you know how they made it?'

'I've never been sufficiently interested to enquire.'

'If you had, you might have guessed what was going on. Would you like to know?'

'Now that the property has come to me, yes. What on earth are you driving at?'

'I'll tell you,' replied Cub, taking the book from his pocket. 'I found this under the mattress in the room we thought Burke had occupied. I can't truthfully say that I was looking for it, but I was looking for something. This is what I found. It's a history of the Western Highlands, written in 1852. Keep the date in mind. In the book there is a chapter on Glencarglas. I'll give you one paragraph. It should be enough.' Cub started to read. '"Although the private distillation of whisky in the Highlands had been terminated by Act of Parliament, the practice was continued until recent times in many a lonely glen, and of these Glencarglas was one of the most celebrated. The efforts of the Preventive Service to stop it were for many years in vain. Collisions between officers of the Crown and the convoys taking the illicit spirit to market were common. Blood was shed on more than one occasion. Night after night, guided by spies and guarded by scouts, ponies laden with the illegal produce of barley made their way by devious routes through the Eastern Highlands to the big cities of the south. Wits were matched against wits. One trick that long escaped detection was the shoeing of the transport ponies with shoes made to resemble the hooves of deer. This, it is said, was first practised by Mr Cunningham-King of Glencarglas, whose distillery was hidden deep in the fastnesses of the glen, in the shadow of the Cairngorms. Only when Mr Cunningham-King joined the ranks of those who, realising that in the end they were bound to lose the fight, applied to the government for an official licence, was the whereabouts of the distillery revealed. For many years this had been known only to the small handful of trusted servants who worked it. We are glad to be able to record that thereafter Mr Cunningham-King conducted his business in a proper manner, so that the sinister reputation of Glencarglas was soon forgotten. This gentleman lived to amass an honest fortune for the well-being of his family and the prosperity of the glen. The distillery is no longer in use. The eldest son, Mr Neil Cunningham-King, has recently pulled down the farmhouse that was the family home, and on the site erected a fine hunting-lodge which he has named Strathcarglas".'

Cub stopped reading and looked up. 'I don't think I need go any further,' he said quietly. 'Burke learned of the old distillery. He found it. He turned the clock back a hundred years, and with his pals started turning out illicit spirit. He's still doing it.'

There was silence for a full minute. It was broken by Copper.

'Whisky,' he breathed. 'Well, strike me purple! Scotland – barley – malt – it was stickin' out a mile. We were all round it and we couldn't see it, 'swelp me. Whisky costs next ter nothin' ter make, I'm told, but it fetches a fiver the bottle, black market, in London.'

'The duty alone is about eight pounds a gallon,' put in Gimlet. 'Not that Slim would bother about a detail like paying excise duty. Nice work, Cub.'

'Having been in the booze racket, the idea would naturally occur to Burke,' went on Cub. 'He knew it would appeal to Slim. They must have been having the time of their lives. No wonder they didn't want visitors at Strathcarglas.'

'But if the distillery was so hard to find, how did Burke find it – huh?' grunted Trapper shrewdly.

'There was a map in the book on which I imagine the exact location was marked.'

'Ah!' breathed Gimlet. 'Where's the map?'

Cub shook his head. 'That, I'm afraid, is a question I can't answer. Burke must have torn it out. At any rate, it's gone.'

CHAPTER FOURTEEN

Commando Work

C ub's final announcement was followed by another short silence. Trapper clicked his tongue. 'Now we know the racket, perhaps we should tell the police – huh?' he suggested tentatively.

Copper shook his head. 'They'd laugh at you. Before they'd believe a tale like ours, we should have to show 'em the distillery and a barrel of booze; and we couldn't show 'em either. So what? Suppose we tell the police that it's up to them to find the distillery. From what the Skipper says they'd have no more hope of doin' that than we have. According ter the book, the reason why the distillery lasted for so long in the old days was because it couldn't be found.'

'I'm afraid Copper's right,' said Gimlet thoughtfully. 'Our tale would take a bit of swallowing. When we call in the police we've got to be able to prove our story, and the only way we could do that would be by showing them where the racket is being carried on. At the best, the police would start wandering about the moor, and the sight of the blue uniform would be enough to send Slim and his gang into hiding. No, we've got to find the distillery, and unless we're prepared to spend weeks hunting for it there's only one way of doing that. We've got to get that map. If Burke took it, then the chances are he still has it.'

'Burke ain't far away,' suggested Copper pointedly.

'That's what I was thinking,' murmured Gimlet. 'All the same, it wouldn't be much use calling at the hotel and asking him to let us see it.'

'I wasn't reckonin' on doin' anything like that,' muttered Copper.

'No, I don't suppose you were,' returned Gimlet, smiling.

'I'd grab 'im and make 'im squeal.'

447

'Exactly. In view of what we know, I think we're justified in taking a fairly strong line; and, having started, we've got to go on or our birds might take fright. The thing looks like ending at the distillery. I'm wondering how many men Slim has there. Frankly, I've no idea how many hands it takes to run a private still.'

'Not many, according to the book,' put in Cub. 'The book says that in the old days it was run by a handful of men.'

'That's true,' agreed Gimlet. 'No matter. If it came to a show-down, we should have to take our chance on that. But first, a visit to the hotel seems indicated. I wouldn't attempt it in daylight, because they'd probably see us coming. Tonight, just before the official closing hour, would be our best-time. That is, just before ten. There is this about it. We do at last know what we're looking for. I doubt if Slim will try anything more today, but we'd better keep watch. Tonight we'll see what the hotel can be made to produce.'

This belief, that Slim would not attack again that day, turned out to be correct. Strict watch was kept, but nothing was seen. Trapper made a short sortie for food without encountering any opposition. The weather remained fair. At last the day died with the sun and the long-drawn twilight came to an end. Gimlet waited until nine o'clock, and then announced that zero hour had arrived. He admitted that he had no definite plan. 'We'll wait to see how the land lies before we settle on a line of action,' he asserted.

Leaving the house was a tense moment. Taking their weapons with them they used the front door, the key of which was on the inside. They did not all go together. Copper went first and, having reached cover without alarm, the others followed one at a time. All remained quiet, so in single file, at intervals of a few yards, they set off down the track towards the hotel.

It was a strange march. The gentle sighing of the breeze in the gloomy pines on the one hand and the sullen swirl of the river on the other. These were the only sounds. Never, thought Cub, had he seen anything quite so grim, so relentlessly impersonal, as if conscious of their age, as the hills that loomed darkly on their flanks. They made a man feel very conscious of his puny existence, he decided.

Gimlet called a halt about a hundred yards short of the inn. 'It's ten to ten,' he announced. 'For a start, we'll go to the yard and see what there is there. I expect we shall see the Buick. The lorry might have come back. If it is there, we shall know Larry isn't far away. Then we'll look at the house. By law the bar is supposed to remain open until ten, in which case we shall find Burke, and probably Smith, in it. On the other hand, it's quite likely that they have locked up. They don't want outside business. Keep on your toes. They may be watching.'

Still in single file, but closer now, they walked on towards the building, the silhouette of which they could see in front of them.

'Like old times, ain't it?' breathed Copper in Cub's ear.

Proceeding with increasing caution, they reached their first objective, the hotel yard, without interruption. The Buick was there. The doors were not locked, and a quick scrutiny in the light of Cub's torch revealed nothing of interest. The doors of the outbuildings were locked. Peering through a window, again using his torch, Cub saw many sacks of what was obviously corn, piled high. 'I imagine that's barley,' he whispered. 'They must be distilling in a pretty big way or they wouldn't have laid in such a stock.'

They turned their attention to the house, starting at the front. The window of the bar was blacked-out, but narrow strips of light framing the blind showed that there was a light inside. From the room came a murmur of desultory conversation. It was possible to distinguish two voices, but what they said could not be heard. Gimlet went on to the front door and tried it. 'Locked,' he whispered. 'Go round to the rear, Copper, and try the back door. Take a look at the windows in passing.'

Copper was away about three minutes. He came back with the information that the back door was also locked, and all the windows, so far as he could see, were shut.

'Then it looks as though we might as well use the front door,' decided Gimlet. 'What we must do, at all costs, is prevent a stampede. Neither Smith nor Burke must get away down the glen to warn Slim that we're on the move. Do you think you can open this door, Copper, without making a noise?'

'If it ain't bolted, I can do it,' answered Copper. 'Show us a light, Cub.' As he spoke Copper took out his jack-knife and, opening the marline-spike, bent the point at right angles against the wall. This done to his satisfaction he inserted it in the keyhole, Cub helping him by holding the torch close. There was a short interval during which the spike could be heard probing the lock.

'Can you manage it?' asked Gimlet anxiously.

'Easy as winkin',' answered Copper confidently. 'It's one of the old-fashioned sort.' As he finished speaking there was a faint *snick* in the lock. 'That's her,' he announced, bending straight the spike of his knife and replacing it in his pocket.

Gimlet tried the door. It opened easily. Instantly through the narrow opening came the sound of voices, amplified.

Beckoning, Gimlet withdrew for a few yards. 'It's no use messing about,' he said in a low voice. 'We've got to take what we want, if it's here, by force; but I don't want any shooting unless one of these fellows pulls a gun and looks like using it. If it comes to a rough house, use your fists.'

Copper held up a fist that looked like a leg of mutton. He kissed it affectionately. 'All ready and waitin', sir,' he announced. 'Last time I was 'ere they slammed *me*, and I ain't forgot it. No one slams me and gets away with it – my oath, they don't. Am I right, Trapper?'

'Every time,' breathed Trapper.

'Burke may have the map on him,' went on Gimlet. 'In that case it should be easy, but if it's hidden somewhere in the house it may take us longer to find it. Now, this is the line-up. Trapper, go round to the back door and see that no one leaves. Cub, as soon as we're inside, close the door behind us and stand guard over it. Don't let anyone in or out.'

'Right you are, sir.'

Trapper went off to the back and Gimlet returned to the front door.

'You take my gun, sir,' urged Copper.

'No – no. I shall be all right,' murmured Gimlet.

They moved forward. Cub brought up the rear. With nerves tingling he watched the others quietly enter the hall and stand still. It was unlighted. Following, he closed the door gently and stood with his back to it. Three paces distant the bar door stood open. Light from the room fell athwart the hall. From the bar, too, came voices. Burke and Smith were talking.

'Well, I don't like it,' Burke was saying. 'The cops may have nothing on you, but they've plenty on me. If you want my opinion, Slim's losing his nerve. He says he's done for King – and what happens? King's still walking about. Then look at this bomb business this morning. What good did it do? Slim and Tiny should have finished the job when they had 'em all together in the kitchen. Why didn't they?'

Smith answered: 'I spoke to Tiny about it. He says this fellow King is no ordinary guy. There's something about him that makes you think twice before you try anything. He says you can't tell whether he's pulling a bluff or not. He's as cool as they come.'

'Well, what's Slim doing about it? I don't feel happy while they're in that house.'

'Slim knows all about that. He promised to fix 'em.'

'I wish he'd get on with it.'

'Aw, stop squawking. Give him time. Your nerves ain't what they used to be, either. I own that Singer was right about this chap King.'

'Suppose he turns up here? You never know. What are we going to do, just the two of us?'

'Do? Give me the chance.' Smith laughed. 'I'd soon show you what I'd do.'

Gimlet had taken a pace or two forward. He pushed the door with his toe so that it swung slowly open, revealing the two men sitting on stools on the customer's side of the bar. Another pace took him to the threshold. The movement must have caught the eyes of both men, for their heads turned sharply.

Gimlet spoke quietly. 'You're in luck, Mr Smith. This is your chance.'

Smith did not move. His eyes went round. His mouth opened. His jaw sagged. Burke, too, appeared to be frozen in his chair.

'If you're wise you'll do nothing, either of you,' said Gimlet, walking in into the room.

Neither of the men did anything. Their eyes switched to Copper, who, gun under arm, walked in on Gimlet's heels. All this Cub could see plainly from his position in the hall.

Gimlet went on in the tones of a kindly master addressing his pupils. 'I want you both to put your hands on your heads and then stand over here with your backs to the wall.'

Neither moved.

'I'm an impatient man,' warned Gimlet, with steel creeping into his voice.

Burke put his hands on his head. 'Go easy, gov'nor,' he said nervously. 'I haven't done any harm.'

Gimlet inclined his head towards Copper. 'See if you can induce Mr Smith to be more obliging,' he requested.

Copper stepped forward. 'You 'eard 'im,' he growled. 'Get your 'ands up and smart's the word.'

At last Smith moved. With a lightning sweep of his left hand he flung the muzzle of Copper's gun aside. His right hand shot down to his pocket.

Copper's right hand also moved. It swung up with the vicious force of a kicking mule and made contact with Smith's chin with a noise like a golf-club striking a ball. The blow lifted Smith clean off his stool. He and the stool struck the ground with a crash.

Copper turned a grim face to Burke. 'I 'ope you've got more sense than ter try a balmy trick like that,' he said casually. 'Behave yerself and do as you're told, and we shan't 'urt a 'air of yer 'ead.'

Burke, with his hands raised, walked stiffly to the wall and turned to face the room.

'That's better,' said Gimlet approvingly. 'Copper, to save any further misunderstanding, you might collect any hardwear these gentlemen may be carrying.'

Copper stood his gun in a corner. Then, stooping, he removed Smith's heavy automatic and put it in his own pocket. From Burke he took a revolver and handed it to Gimlet. 'Souvenir for you, sir,' he said.

Addressing Burke, Gimlet went on. 'Now, Mr Burke – I think that's your name, isn't it? – I want you to empty your pockets. Make a clean job of it because my corporal here will check up and, as you may have noticed, he takes a poor view of disobedience.'

Burke obeyed without a word.

'Don't forget the breast pocket,' reminded Gimlet.

Burke handed Copper a wad of papers.

'Just glance through those, Copper, and see if there's anything of interest,' ordered Gimlet.

Copper went through the papers one by one. He put them on the bar. ''Tain't 'ere, sir,' he announced.

'It may be in his room,' suggested Gimlet.

'What are you looking for?' asked Burke sulkily.

Gimlet answered: 'I'm looking for a scrap of paper that happens to be my property. It's a little map. You stole it from my lodge, remember?'

Burke did not answer, but from the expression on his face, Cub, who was watching, knew that Gimlet's arrow had gone home. Apparently Gimlet realised it, too. 'Cub,' he said, 'you seem to be good at finding things. Slip up and try the bedrooms. We'll take care of things here.'

Cub moved towards the stairs which, as is commonly the case, went up from the hall. But with his foot on the bottom step he halted, head turned towards the front door from the region of which had come an unmistakable sound. A motor vehicle of some sort had pulled up either in the road or in the yard. Cub realised, for it was evident, that if a vehicle had stopped someone was coming to the hotel. Gimlet realised it, too, and spoke sharply.

'Copper, get rid of that,' he said, pointing to the inert form of Smith, who still lay where he had fallen.

Copper reached down, took the man by the front of the jacket and with one heave swung him up and dropped him over to the other side of the bar, where, of course, he could no longer be seen.

'You can put your hands down, but be careful what you do with them,' Gimlet told Burke curtly.

'Shall I lock the door?' asked Cub urgently.

Before Gimlet could answer the front door was opened, and from the confident way it was handled it was at once evident that the newcomer was no stranger. Slamming the door behind him he strode straight towards the bar; but on the way, as was inevitable, he caught sight of Cub. He hesitated in his stride. 'Who are you? I've never seen you before,' he said, and went on quickly towards the bar as if to take up the question with the proprietor.

As he entered the bar a voice, Copper's voice, exclaimed, 'Well, if it ain't our old pal Larry! You've seen *me* before though, ain't you?'

Larry took one glance at Copper's face and moved swiftly; but not swiftly enough. His right hand flashed towards his pocket, but Copper's arm shot out and his huge hand closed over the arm. 'Easy, mate, easy,' he said in a low drawl.

Larry struggled, but to no purpose. Copper's arms closed round him, holding him in the embrace of a bear, pinning his arms to his sides. Cub, watching, could see Copper's arms slowly tightening. And as they tightened Copper spoke softly, almost soothingly. "It me on the back of the 'ead when I wasn't lookin', didn't yer? 'It me 'ard. I don't like people doin' that ter me. It ain't friendly. 'Ave another good look at me so as you won't ever forget me, because you're goin' ter remember me, chum, yes, fer a long, long time.'

Larry's face was contorted with pain and fear. His lips were curled back, showing decayed teeth; his eyes bulged; the veins in his forehead stood out under the frightful strain that was being exerted on his body. A long-drawn gasp was forced from his lips as if his lungs were being crushed.

The end came suddenly. 'Let this learn yer never ter 'it a man on the 'ead when he ain't lookin',' crooned Copper. With a swift movement he released his grip and took a pace back, leaving Larry standing just as he had been held, with his arms against his sides. His left fist slammed into Larry's solar plexus, causing the wretched man to fold like a jack-knife. A split second later his right fist swung up in a vicious hook to smash into the middle of Larry's face. Like a discarded scarecrow the unconscious man went backwards through the furniture and slithered along the floor until he was brought to a stop by the wall.

Copper brushed his palms together. 'That should learn 'im,' he observed with quiet satisfaction.

'By James! I hope you haven't killed him,' said Gimlet anxiously.

'Killed 'im? Bah! It takes more than that ter kill a rat,' sneered Copper.

Then the atmosphere stiffened to a deathly silence as a voice said, 'What's going on here?'

Cub started violently and, looking in the direction from which the voice had come, saw that the front door was wide open. In the hall stood the very last man he expected to see. It was a policeman.

The officer took a step nearer the bar. He looked at Cub; from Cub to Gimlet; from Gimlet to Copper, and from Copper to the body on the floor. He surveyed the broken furniture. Finally his eyes came to rest on Burke in a manner which suggested that he knew who was the proprietor. 'What's going on here?' he repeated.

'Nothing,' answered Copper. He made a gesture. 'We had a little argument, that's all.'

The constable looked surprised – as well he might. His eyes went back to Larry. 'What's he doing there?'

'Having a rest,' answered Copper. 'He's tired.'

Gimlet joined in. 'Between ourselves, officer, the man's drunk. He ought to be locked up for driving in that condition.'

'What are you doing here?' demanded the policeman. 'It's after closing time.'

'We're residents,' parried Gimlet.

Burke found his voice. 'That's a lie,' he said loudly. 'They're not staying here. I've told them a dozen times to go, but they won't.'

The officer nodded like a man who at last has a perplexing situation appraised. 'Oh! So that's it,' he observed. Like most policemen he was inclined to be tolerant. 'Come along now, gentlemen, please,' he requested. 'Don't let's have any more trouble.'

'I'll take care of him,' said Burke, nodding towards Larry, who was now showing signs of coming to his senses.

Cub perceived that Gimlet was, as it is said, in a cleft stick. It was quite certain that if they left the house they would not be able to get back into it; Burke would see to that; yet to refuse to obey the law was to lay themselves open to arrest.

Gimlet spoke again. 'I'm afraid this was really my fault, officer,' he said apologetically. 'We've all walked from Tomnarrow station and we can't get any farther tonight. Perhaps I didn't make it clear that we want to take rooms.' Gimlet turned to Burke. 'Did I, Mr – er—?'

'McTaggart's the name,' said Burke, with a nervous start.

Gimlet turned back to the policeman. 'You know, I can't help feeling that I've seen Mr McTaggart before,' he said blandly. 'I wonder where it could have been?'

'What's the odds?' put in Burke quickly. To the constable he went on. 'It's all right. If these gentlemen are so anxious to stay, I'll fix them up.'

The policeman looked from one to the other. 'Are you sure you can manage them?' he questioned dubiously. It was apparent that he was by no means satisfied with the explanation given.

Gimlet clinched the matter by taking a visiting-card from his wallet. 'Here's my card, officer. I'm the new owner of Strathcarglas. I hope you'll look in and see me some day when you're passing.'

The policeman's manner became respectful, but there was still a shade of suspicion in his voice when he answered. 'Why didn't you say that before, sir? I'll let the Inspector know you've arrived.' He turned to the door. 'Good night, sir,' he said over his shoulder.

'Good night, officer,' returned Gimlet.

The policeman went out. Cub saw him to the door and came back to the bar. 'He's gone towards Deeside on a bicycle,' he reported.

'This is a more popular establishment than I had supposed,' murmured Gimlet drily. He moved close to Cub and went on in an undertone. 'Slip out and see where Larry left his truck. You might have a look at what he has on board at the same time.'

Cub was soon back. 'The lorry's in the yard,' he reported. 'There are six casks in it – empty. They reek of whisky.'

'Any labels on them?'

'No – no mark of any sort.'

'I see. Close the door in case we have more visitors and we'll see about the map.'

At this stage Smith appeared behind the bar, walking stiffly from the back premises, an expression of chagrin on his face. The reason for this was soon apparent. Close behind him, the muzzle of his gun in the small of his back, was Trapper.

'Where did you find him?' asked Gimlet.

'Tried to slink out of the back door, sir,' explained Trapper.

'Good thing you were there,' observed Gimlet. 'You can stay here now with Copper to take care of this bunch. We've wasted a lot of time and we still haven't got what we came for. We shall have to get busy.'

CHAPTER FIFTEEN

Gimlet Takes the Trail

In the end Cub found the map, but it is doubtful if he would have done so had not Copper intervened.

For half an hour after the constable had gone Cub searched with hopes that waned as each successive room proved barren of results. He ransacked Burke's sitting-room, his bedroom, and even the kitchen – all in a wretched state of untidiness and not to be associated with a decently run hotel. Gimlet, growing impatient, joined him, and together they devoted another half-hour to the search, covering much of the same ground again. One thing of interest did come to light. In a writing-desk in Burke's sitting-room they found a large packet of printed labels. The address was the same in each case: Bechenstein & Co., Pure Malt Vinegar Works, Slavonia Street, Soho, London.

'Vinegar – fiddlesticks,' said Gimlet. 'I'd say these are the labels that Larry tacks on his casks when he takes them from here. This precious vinegar establishment must be the headquarters of the distributors in London. I'm glad we've got it. They'll be in the bag, I hope, with Slim and his friends, at the finish.'

Cub was prepared to abandon his quest when, soon afterwards, Copper put his head round the door. 'Any luck?' he enquired laconically.

'No,' retorted Cub.

'Strike me purple,' muttered Copper. 'We shall be here all night at this rate. Look's as if I shall have ter do somethin' about it. Hold 'ard – shan't be long.' He withdrew.

The significance of this remark did not dawn on Cub until afterwards.

Within five minutes Copper was back. 'The map's in the lining of the old jacket hangin' behind Burke's bedroom door,' he astonished Cub by saying.

Gimlet turned suspicious eyes on Copper. 'How did you learn that?'

'Burke told me,' answered Copper, gazing at the ceiling.

'Ah!' Gimlet nodded slowly. 'I thought so. Did you ...'

'Did I what, sir?' Copper affected a look of injured dignity. 'I just asked 'im and he couldn't tell me fast enough.'

'I see,' said Gimlet grimly. 'What did you do to Burke to induce him to part with that valuable information so readily?'

'Do to 'im sir?'

'You heard me. Did you hurt him?'

'Hurt 'im, sir?' Copper looked shocked. 'Why, I wouldn't 'urt a fly – you know that, sir.'

Gimlet's eyes glinted. 'Tell the truth.'

Copper smiled sheepishly. 'Between ourselves, sir, I own that I did 'ave ter persuade 'im – although mind you, I asked 'im kind enough at first.'

'What did you do?'

'It was a little trick Trapper showed me once. 'E ses an Indian showed it to 'im. Never fails, 'e ses. Maybe he's right, too. Leastways, it didn't fail with Burke.'

'I've told you before that I won't tolerate such methods,' said Gimlet sternly.

'What about Slim's methods, sir?' said Copper in a hurt voice. 'What about the way he asked *me* questions? Blinkin' bodkin in 'is 'and, 'e had. Was goin' ter prod out my blinkin' eyeballs, 'e was. I didn't need no knife. Besides, time's gettin' on, sir. We don't want ter be messin' around 'ere all the bloomin' night, do we?'

'No, we do not,' agreed Gimlet. 'We've been here too long as it is. I'm by no means certain that the police officer was entirely taken in by our story. He was no fool. It wouldn't surprise me if he came back. There's always a chance that Slim may turn up here, too. Cub, slip upstairs and see if that map is where Burke says it is.'

In a few minutes Cub was back, the map in his hand. 'Yes, here it is,' he said. 'Burke wasn't lying.'

'I didn't think he was,' put in Copper. 'I told him if he wasted my time, I might turn nasty.'

Gimlet glanced at the map and put it in his pocket. 'This is what we want,' he asserted. 'Let's be moving.'

'What about the prisoners?' asked Copper.

'They're coming with us,' decided Gimlet. 'We're not going to leave them here so that they can take a short-cut to Slim the moment our backs are turned. They know too much. If Slim got wind of what was happening, he'd either lie in wait for us and pot us from cover, or he'd be off faster than a hunted stag. A few hours in one of the Lodge cellars won't do the prisoners any harm; in fact, it will give them time to cool down and think things over.'

'It's a fair step back to the Lodge,' remarked Copper.

'I've no intention of walking if that's what is worrying you – not with a Buick standing in the yard doing nothing,' said Gimlet.

'That's more my idea of travellin',' approved Copper. 'Then let's get along.'

That concluded the business at the hotel. The three prisoners, two of them looking decidedly the worse for wear about the face, were escorted out by Copper, who, having opened the breech of the twelve-bore to prove that it was loaded, told them in terms they could not possibly misunderstand what would most certainly happen to them if they tried what he called 'half larks.' These threats did not fall on deaf ears. It was obvious to Cub that the men were really scared of Copper – as indeed they had good reason to be. Even Cub was by no means sure that Copper was bluffing. Apparently the prisoners by mutual consent, decided not to run the risk of finding out.

Gimlet locked the hotel door, put the key in his pocket and led the way to the car, where he ordered the prisoners into the back seat. Copper and Trapper sat facing them. Cub sat next to Gimlet, who drove, and was soon on the way to the Lodge.

The journey was uneventful, but as the car slowed to a stop in the courtyard there was a curious incident. Gimlet had swung open the door preparatory to getting out when a man – it was too dark to see his face – stepped from the shadow of a wall and said, 'What's the idea of coming up here? The boss said you was to stay put till he gave the word to move.' It was evident that the man was one of Slim's watchers, who thought he was talking to Burke or Smith.

Gimlet got out. 'Is that so?' he said evenly. 'Well, from now on I'm the boss, and you'll take orders from me. Stand still – unless you want some cold night air letting into you.'

The man did not move. He may have been too dazed with astonishment, or perhaps the sight of Copper's twelve-bore, as he got out, had something to do with it. Trapper relieved him of an automatic. The man did not resist. Apparently he did not feel inclined to take on four armed men, men who spoke in a disconcertingly businesslike way. This was understandable. It takes a good deal of nerve to accept odds of four to one. So another prisoner was added to the party which, in the light of Cub's torch, was marched to a wine cellar, where Gimlet spoke quietly but in a voice that discouraged argument.

'I want you men to understand clearly that we are no amateur performers,' he said. 'Even though you were dodging the war in a Scottish glen, you must have heard of Commandos. Well, we're Commandos; and Commandos don't talk for the pleasure of hearing their voices; nor do they carry weapons for ornament. They know how to use them, and on the slightest provocation they do use them. Make no mistake about that. Disobey my orders and I won't be responsible for the consequences. To remove temptation, I'm going to have you tied up. My men are experts in tying knots, so the ropes won't hurt you unless you try to get them off, in which case someone is liable to get strangled.' Gimlet turned to Copper. 'I'll leave that to you,' he ended. 'Some bell-cords from upstairs should suit your purpose. Trapper will give you a hand. Lock the cellar door when you leave. You'll find us in the library. Come on, Cub.'

In the library, by the light of a candle, they examined the map. And there, soon afterwards, Copper and Trapper joined them.

'Did you get the prisoners settled comfortably?' asked Gimlet without looking up.

'Aye, aye, sir. I don't think they'll go far,' answered Copper.

'All right. Now pay attention,' Gimlet marked a spot on the map with the point of a pencil. 'Here's the Lodge.' He moved the pencil. 'Here's our objective – the old distillery. The distance is about five miles. It's away up the glen. There's no road, not even a track. The moon should be up, but across difficult country, with probable obstacles, to get there will probably take not far short of two hours.' He looked at his watch. 'It's two o'clock now. We should be on the spot by four or soon afterwards. I think we've time for a cup of tea and a biscuit before we move off.'

'And what's the plan when we get there, sir?' asked Copper.

'We'll have a look at the place and go straight on in. It's no use messing about. We'll avoid shooting, if it is possible. We shall be dealing with desperate characters, some of them hard-boiled gunmen, no doubt, so we may have to shoot it out. I'd prefer to take prisoners and hand the whole thing over to the police; but if they want to fight, that's the way it will have to be. Any questions?'

There were no questions, so the party adjourned to the kitchen, where Trapper soon had a kettle on a brisk fire. Cub mounted guard.

Half an hour later, in single file with Copper leading, they set off up the glen. A few flakes of snow were falling in a leisurely fashion, but nothing, as Gimlet remarked, to worry about.

Cub had made many night marches, but none like this, and none so hard. Usually they had been made across the cultivated fields of France, over country that he knew. The risks may have been greater, but the actual going had not been heavy. Here the going was exhausting. For this the heather was partly responsible, but steep gradients, up and down, did nothing to improve matters. Soft marshy ground was not uncommon. Outcrops of rock had to be surmounted or by-passed. Burns, with beds of slippery boulders, had to be crossed. Cub found it hard to believe that all this was happening in Britain. One thing he did find easy to believe was the reason why, in the old days, the preventive officers had been unable to locate the distillery.

After an hour of unbroken progress, Gimlet called a halt. The others were panting, but he appeared to suffer no distress. 'Tough going, eh? But we'd better push on in case the snow starts in earnest,' was the only remark he made.

The party, after a short breather, pushed on.

Another hour passed. Cub had lost count of time; the feeling was coming over him that he had been marching all night; but the fact that

Gimlet was now advancing with more caution told him that they must be nearing the objective. He was not sorry.

At length Gimlet halted. 'We can't be far away,' he said softly. 'I rather thought we should be able to see the place from here, although we can hardly expect them to be showing lights. Let's move up to the top of the hill – we should get a wider view.' He indicated some steeply rising ground on their right, and in this direction they turned. Near the top Gimlet halted again and surveyed the landscape as far as it could be seen. 'Queer,' he said in a puzzled voice. 'If the map is right, it should be here or hereabouts.'

'Perhaps the map isn't right,' suggested Cub.

'If it ain't, we're sunk,' observed Copper gloomily.

'Just a minute,' said Cub tersely. 'I can smell something. There's a smell of burning. I thought I caught a whiff of it just now, but I got it then distinctly.'

'*Tch*! Cub's right,' asserted Trapper. 'It's peat. We must be close.'

'What's that dark patch over to the left?' asked Gimlet.

Copper walked towards it, but after taking a few steps he drew back with a half-strangled cry of alarm. He came back quickly. 'My gawd! I very nearly went over!' he exclaimed in a startled voice. 'There's a socking great hole in the ground. There's smoke comin' out of it.'

Gimlet made a slow advance towards the spot, the others keeping him company. He paused near what Copper had correctly described as a socking great hole in the ground. From it a thin miasma of smoke was issuing. 'This must be it,' he whispered. 'This is the smoke from their boiler fire. I don't see that it can be anything else. It comes up through a flaw in the rock. But how the deuce do we get into the place?'

The answer to this question was not so hard to find as they expected. Further cautious exploration revealed a gorge, a fearful gash in the side of the hill on which they stood. From the darkness of the depths, for they could not see the bottom, came the burble of running water.

'Either the distillery, or the entrance to it, must be in that ravine,' declared Gimlet. 'The next question is, how do we get into it? Time's getting on. If we're caught up here in daylight, we shall lose our chance. Copper – Trapper, go along to the right and see if you can find a way down. There should be a path somewhere. Take care you don't go over.

They marched cautiously through the glen.

Don't go too far. Rally at this point. I'll go with Cub to the left.' Beckoning to Cub, Gimlet started exploring the lip of the chasm on their left hand.

They went some little way, slowly, for the nature of the ground discouraged hasty movement; but of a track or path leading down there was no indication. In some places the drop was sheer cliff; elsewhere the slope was too steep to be tackled in the dark without careful preparation.

'Of course, the only entrance may be at one end or other of the gorge,' remarked Gimlet. 'The snag is, we've no idea how far away that may be. It's snowing faster than it was, too. Confounded nuisance. We'd better start working back!'

'Just a minute, sir,' whispered Cub. 'What's that a bit farther on? Looks as if the ground slopes a bit more easily.' He walked on to the spot and saw that his supposition was correct. A wide slide of loose shale fell away into the gloom of the ravine. There were places where a descent might be attempted, but still nothing resembled a path. He went a little farther and, peering down, made out what he took to be the faintest outline of a trail running transversely across the slide. 'Does that look like a path to you?' he asked Gimlet who had followed him.

'It's hard to say,' was the reply.

'At a pinch that could be a way down,' declared Cub. 'It seems to slope up towards the right. I wondered if we could have passed the beginning of the path without noticing it?'

'If so, we should probably pass it again on the way back,' murmured Gimlet.

'We could easily get over that,' asserted Cub. 'I'm pretty sure I could get down to that path – or whatever it is. If I could get on it, by taking the upward slope it should bring me to the top. By keeping level you could watch me, and so we should discover where the path starts. Then we could collect Copper and Trapper and all go down together.'

'Have a go at it if you like,' invited Gimlet, 'but for goodness' sake watch your step. Shale is tricky stuff.'

'We shall have to try something pretty soon, anyway,' declared Cub. 'With luck I might strike the quickest way to the bottom.'

In the event he did, but not in the manner he expected.

As soon as he started down the slope, a slope of perhaps forty-five degrees, he realised that the shale was more treacherous than he had supposed. Several small pieces, disturbed by his feet, went clattering to the bottom. The only comfort he derived from this was the knowledge that the bottom was not so far down as he had thought. More slithers of shale sliding away caused him to pause and reflect on the risk he was taking. Common sense adjured him to turn back; and indeed he would have gone back, but glancing up he formed the opinion that it might be harder to get to the top than to go on down to the path. The fact that he could see now that there was a definite path just below him was the deciding factor. He went on. Instantly, more shale began to slide. More and more pieces clattered down. He found that he could not stop, much less get back. He could hear Gimlet calling to him from above in a voice brittle with alarm, but he was no longer in a case to heed warnings. The whole slope in his vicinity was on the move. He dropped his rifle and clutched at an isolated tuft of heather, but its roots were in the same unstable foundation as himself, and the shrub came away in his hands. In sheer desperation he threw himself backwards, flat on his back, but this did not stop the movement. At a speed still slow, but increasing, the landslide went on inexorably. There was a brief respite when his feet struck the path. He clung to it with the tenacity of despair; but a piece of shale striking him in the face caused him to release his hold. His speed increased. With a crash and clatter, and avalanche of loose shale, bearing Cub with it, rolled on down the slope into the ravine.

CHAPTER SIXTEEN

Cub Takes a Chance

That Cub was not seriously hurt in his fall was due to two reasons. The first was that the slide, as is commonly the case, fanned out at the bottom to a shallow heap of detritus, which first slowed down and then finally stopped his progress; and the second, that the slide ended in a peat hag. He did not know this. He knew nothing of peat hags, although he was vaguely aware that there must be places where peat was cut. At first, as he sat up, slightly dazed, he was only aware that he appeared to be sitting on a monstrous sponge.

It took him a minute to collect his senses, a minute during which he automatically tested his limbs to make sure that none was broken. Finding none, to his great relief and no small surprise, he looked about, and saw that he was, as he expected, at the bottom of the ravine, which was wider than he had supposed. He observed with mingled feelings of alarm and thankfulness that had he gone a little farther he would have finished in a burn. It looked cold and grim.

That he had made a good deal of noise in his descent he was painfully aware; so much noise, indeed, that anyone within a fair distance must have heard him. What Gimlet was thinking he could only surmise. He hoped that he would not attempt to follow him down the treacherous bank. Not that he was happy at being alone. Somewhere, at no great distance, was the distillery. There was just a chance that the clatter of the falling shale had been drowned by the babble of the burn, but he dare not count on this. Unless the men in the distillery were making a lot of noise themselves – and there was no reason to suppose that they were – they must have heard his precipitate arrival.

In this assumption he was correct, as he was presently informed. With the intention of looking for his rifle, he stood up and started walking along the peat towards the bottom of the slide; but before he had taken half a dozen paces he put his foot into a hole and found himself up to the knees in icy water. He did not mind the water, but he nearly broke his leg. As it was, he stumbled forward, and as he picked himself up he saw that the hag was pitted with such holes. He had already decided that a Scottish moor was not a thing to be trifled with, and this convinced him more than ever that he was right. Uncomfortable and feeling rather sorry for himself, he was about to resume his search when he heard voices approaching. The dampness of the peat was no longer a matter for concern. He dropped flat and waited, hoping to escape detection. He had no intention of taking on the crew of the distillery single handed.

'I guess it was somewhere about here,' said a voice which he recognised at once as Slim's.

'Another goldarned landslide,' answered another voice. 'The stuff's always falling. One of these days someone's going to get crowned with a hundred tons of rock.'

Cub could just make out two men standing a dozen paces away, surveying the slide. They continued their conversation.

'It must have been a fair lot came down just now,' said Slim. 'Wonder what caused it?'

'Might have been anything. I've seen a rabbit knock lumps down.'

'I'm thinking about that bunch at the Lodge,' said Slim, with concern in his voice. 'Well, they won't be there much longer. Tiny's going to clean 'em up. He knows how. Let's get back.'

The men walked off up the ravine in the direction from which they had come. Cub watched them, sitting up to see better. Little moonlight penetrated into the bottom of the gorge, however, and he soon lost sight of them. But, still watching, he saw something that aroused his curiosity. It was a beam of light that came and went as if a door had been opened and shut. This put him in something of a quandary. He would have asked nothing more than to get back to the others; and this was the course dictated by prudence. But the problem was, how to get to them? He did not relish the idea of trying to climb back up the slide, and he knew of no other way of getting to the top. He realised that there must be a proper path down, but it might take him the rest of the night to find it. The others would, he reflected, be certain to come down to him sooner or later. Gimlet had witnessed his misadventure and, before doing anything else, would come to his aid. Perhaps, after all, his best plan was to wait. This he decided to do.

Presently, as he sat there, it struck him that instead of doing nothing he might as well try to locate the spot, the source of light, where Slim and his companion had vanished. This would be useful information, the first thing that Gimlet would want to know. Rising, he began to walk cautiously towards the spot. As near as he could judge, it was between fifty and sixty yards away.

For a time all went well. There was no movement anywhere. Thinking that the burn would cover any noise that he might make, he advanced with more confidence. Not that he in any way relaxed his caution. Nearing the spot he halted, peering into the gloom ahead. The gorge still ran on, but just in front of him there appeared to be something on the right. It was hard to make out what it was. At first he thought it must be a mass of rock jutting out from the cliff, which at this point rose almost vertically; but it had a certain regularity, a squareness, that discounted this. Advancing a pace or two nearer, he perceived that the mass was rock, but it was a building of some sort, constructed, as far as he could see, of the same rock as the cliff, against which it leaned. It struck him that from the point of view of camouflage, this must be a perfect example. Old Cunningham-King, when he built this retreat, knew what he was doing, thought Cub. No wonder it baffled the Excise officers. He went still nearer, and at last a tiny chink of light revealed what he supposed to be the place where the two men had disappeared. Further investigation showed that it was, in fact, a doorway, or rather, a wide arched entrance, overhung with a large tarpaulin, provided for black-out purposes – at least Cub could think of no other reason for it. Somewhere not far away a small engine was humming; precisely where, and for what purpose, was not apparent.

The temptation to return now to the others reasserted itself; but the temptation to see what lay beyond the chink of light, where the tarpaulin curtain fitted badly, was irresistible. It would not, he told himself, occupy more than a few seconds of time. It was a risk, but a risk worth while. A swift glance up and down the ravine gave no hint of danger. Everything looked quiet, deserted, harmless. Moving quickly now, he went forward and put his eye to the narrow strip of light.

The result was disappointing. He found himself looking into a fairly extensive chamber with an arched roof and bare whitewashed walls. Devoid of furniture, it appeared to be something in the nature of a vestibule, the sort of place where at a railway-station goods are loaded. But here the only goods were a number of barrels on end against the wall on the left. Cobwebs hung in festoons from the roof, giving the place a long-neglected appearance. The only other objects of interest, very mild interest, were a number of doors, four in all. One was open. It revealed a passage, like a tunnel, leading farther into the building. The three other doors, small wooden doors, were shut. They were painted dark red, and each bore a notice in white letters – curious, old-fashioned letters. On one: Duty Free Warehouse. On another: A Malt House. On the other: A Racking Store. Just what these notices signified, apart from the fact that they were obviously to do with the process of distillation, Cub did not know. Nor did he particularly care. This, without doubt, was Slim's workshop. That was all that really mattered. One thing that did surprise Cub was the lighting. An unshaded electric bulb hung from the ceiling. Evidently the distillery produced its own electricity, he thought. A plant would not be difficult to install. It would be useful for more purposes than one. He could still hear an engine running, and decided that it must be a small turbine, or dynamo, operated perhaps by the burn.

This was as much as Cub wanted to know – at any rate, for the time being. Well satisfied with his inspection, he decided to return to the slope to see if Gimlet had arrived. It was there Gimlet would look for him. Deep in thought, he turned away, and at his first step collided with someone who had just arrived. Surprise seemed to be mutual. Then the man made a grab at Cub, at the same time letting out a yell. Cub sprang back to avoid the hand, for he recognised the voice and figure. It was Tiny. Thereafter things moved faster than they can be narrated.

In jumping backwards Cub fell against the tarpaulin, which must have been carelessly fastened. Anyway, his weight was sufficient to bring it down. It fell across him, and on Tiny, burying them under its slack coils. After a moment of confusion Cub was clear first, but Tiny was only a split second after him, and he, seeing that Cub was bent on escape, flung out his arms to prevent it. Cub realised only too well that if once those big arms closed round him he would be finished. He backed into the distillery, the only way he could go, looking desperately for another means of escape. Tiny evidently realised what was in his mind, for his hand went to his pocket and came up holding a gun. Cub, side-stepping, whipped out his thirty-eight. Two shots sounded as one. Tiny's bullet snatched at Cub's sleeve in passing. Tiny dropped his pistol and staggered back, cursing luridly. But he still occupied the entrance.

At this junction Slim appeared, running, at the entrance to the inner passage. There were others behind him – more, Cub realised, than he could cope with. He could not remain where he was, and with his line of retreat to the ravine cut off he made a bee-line for the nearest available door, which happened to be one marked A Racking Store. He had no idea what a racking store was, but at that moment any room was better than the one he was in. As he slammed the door behind him a bullet bit into it – sufficient proof that Slim meant business. Before him was a plain corridor that long ago had been whitewashed. Its whiteness had succumbed to dust and dirt. Along this he sped, expecting that Slim would follow, expecting every instant to feel a bullet boring into his back. He heard the door behind opening. Confronting him at different angles were two more doors, one labelled A Mash House and the other A Draft House. For no particular reason he dived into the mash house. Again a bullet followed him, but he would not risk exposing himself by shooting back. He found himself in a square room with most of the centre occupied by a strange-looking metal contraption. At the far side a stepladder mounted upwards. He went up the ladder, thinking that the top would be as good a place as any to hold his ground. Around him all he could see was a shadowy expanse of wooden floor with another flight of steps leading still higher. In the distance he could hear heavy footsteps pounding and men calling to each other. It seemed that for the moment the enemy had lost him but were hunting for him. Eventually, of course, they would find him, unless he could get out of this maze, which did not seem likely. He considered the situation. Not that it needed much consideration. He was in the distillery. So much was certain. He had been anxious to find it; now he was even more anxious to get out of it. The chances seemed slender. He had no idea of his position in relation to the entrance. He only knew that it lay somewhere below him. A distillery, it was clear, resembled nothing so much as a rabbit warren. It was all doors and corridors. He doubted if he would be able to get out even if there had been no opposition. He could still hear people moving about, so he decided that his best plan was to remain where he was until something happened. He put his torch, which he no longer needed, in his pocket.

He had not long to wait. Somewhere above him a door creaked. Footsteps, stealthy footsteps that a man makes when he tries to move quietly, followed. He perceived that he had enemies above him as well as below. Looking up to the head of the steps that rose from the floor on which he rested, he saw a man looking down. The man shouted, 'Here he is!' and Cub knew that he had been seen. The words were followed by the roar of a gun and a bullet came close enough to Cub to sting him to retaliation. He took quick aim and fired. Blended with the shot was the sickening *phut* of a bullet ripping through flesh. He did not wait to see the result, but keeping close to the wall darted across the floor. His eyes being upturned to the danger area, he did not see a square opening in the floor in front of him. The first he knew of it was when he stepped into space. The next instant he was sliding down a chute that sagged under his weight, with his eyes and nose full of dust. It was a terrifying sensation while it lasted; fortunately it did not last long; he shot out on to a heap of something soft. The warm sickly smell of malt filled his nostrils.

He felt quickly for his torch, for he was now in darkness, and switching it on he observed that he was in a cask of such enormous dimensions that for a moment he was dismayed. The sides rose far above him. Fortunately, at one place, apparently where the malt had been tipped in, the stuff was piled high. Staggering, sliding, his feet sinking deep into the malt that subsided under his weight, he scrambled to the top of the heap, from where, to his relief, he found he could clamber over the side. He found himself on a wooden floor, in a place that had the appearance of a barn. There were doors round the walls. As before, they bore names that meant

471

nothing to him. Opening the nearest, which happened to be labelled A Still Room, he gazed into an apartment larger than anything he had yet seen. He could see clearly, for the place was lighted by several grimy electric bulbs. What he saw was not so much a room as a large area, the ceiling far above and the floor far below, the whole criss-crossed with innumerable pipes, single pipes and pipes that writhed in bunches, like snakes. The place was a bewildering maze of pipes, but the most conspicuous object was a huge copper dome, shaped like a retort.

Cub was in no mood to speculate on the purpose of these things. More important were flights of steps, some going up, others going down. A flight near at hand ended near what seemed to be two great black beehives. Still concerned only with getting out of the place, he went down the steps, which ended on a stone floor. The nearest black bee-hive radiated heat, and he realised that it was a furnace. Not far away was a vaulted entrance. Stepping over coils of pipes he walked towards it.

It must not be supposed that while all this happened the distillery was quiet. There were shouts. Men called to each other. Feet clattered up and down steps. These sounds suddenly rose to a pandemonium, during which occurred a volley of shots. Among the shots was the heavy boom of a twelve-bore. Then a voice bellowed, 'Cub, where are you?' and Cub smiled weakly from relief. Copper had arrived.

Advancing to the vaulted entrance, he shouted: 'Hi! Copper!' At the same time he stood ready to take cover, for it seemed not unlikely that Copper, following his avowed principle, would shoot at the first figure he saw and ask questions afterwards. Walking on down a broad white-washed corridor he came upon the body of a man, a man he had certainly never seen before. He was a negro. He lay huddled against the wall, a razor near his hand. Walking on he caught a fleeting glimpse of Slim, who darted from one door to another across the passage. More shots were fired, the reports seeming to come from different directions. Suddenly, out of a side door, burst Gimlet.

Seeing Cub, he hurried to meet him. 'What the deuce do you think you're playing at?' he demanded crisply. 'Why didn't you wait for us?'

'I wasn't given the chance,' answered Cub.

'Have you seen Copper?'

'No, but I've heard him.'

'So have I. He'll make a shambles of the place with that scatter-gun of his if I don't stop him. My orders were that we should stay together, but when the shooting started we got split up; this place has more holes and corners in it than the Maginot Line. Where were you going?'

'I was trying to find my way out of this labyrinth. Do you know the way out?'

'I think so. We'd better head that way. If we don't get together, we're likely to be shooting each other.' Gimlet turned about and walked down the passage.

They came upon another man, dead or unconscious, sprawled across the floor.

'I fancy Copper's been this way,' observed Gimlet grimly.

After passing through numerous doors they found themselves, to Cub's relief, in the vestibule from which he had started his tour of the distillery. Tiny was there, propped up against the wall, supporting himself with his hands. Blood had run from his fingers to make a little pool on the floor. His face was grey. His eyes were open but lustreless.

Gimlet looked at Cub sternly and indicated the man with a jerk of his thumb. 'Did you do that?'

'I may have done,' admitted Cub. 'I had a crack at him, but he shot at me first.'

Gimlet turned to Tiny. 'Hi, you, where's Slim?'

'Gone,' was the reply in a dull voice.

'So he's pulled out, eh?'

'Yeah. Left us ter take the rap, the cheap double-crosser.'

'Anybody with him?'

'No.'

Gimlet went to the entrance and looked out. The grey light of dawn was creeping into the ravine. More snow had fallen. I think Tiny's telling the truth,' he told Cub when he came back. 'I can only see one set of foot-prints.' He went to the inner passage and shouted, Copper!'

A minute later Trapper appeared. 'Did you call, sir?' he enquired.

'Where's Copper?'

'*Enfin*! The last I see him he is chasing a man up and down ladders.'

'The fool. He'll lose his life in this warren.'

Cub opened another door and listened. In the distance he could hear Copper still shouting, 'Cub!'

'Here we are!' yelled Cub. 'This way.'

An answering yell told him that he had been heard. Soon afterwards Copper appeared, grey with dust and cobwebs. 'Blimey! What a rounda-bouts,' he muttered. 'Passages everywhere and none of 'em leading anywhere.'

'Never mind that,' interposed Gimlet curtly. 'Slim's got away. He'll make for the Lodge and then for the hotel. I'm going after him. You stay here with Trapper. Collect the casualties and do what you can for them, but don't trouble about anyone else who may be inside. They can't get out while you're here.'

'Aye, aye, sir.'

'We'll get in touch with you as soon as we can,' promised Gimlet.

'Aye, aye, sir.'

'Come on, Cub.' Gimlet strode out into the cold grey dawn. 'I imagine Slim knows the best way,' he said tersely. 'We'll follow his tracks. He can't have got more than ten minutes' start.'

CHAPTER SEVENTEEN

The Round-up

'How did you get down here?' asked Cub, as they followed Slim's tracks down the ravine.

'Nearly broke my neck sliding down that confounded toboggan run,' answered Gimlet. 'I couldn't find any other way down. Copper and Trapper must have heard me and followed me – I haven't had a chance to ask them.' Gimlet pointed, his finger indicating a line of tracks that mounted upwards. 'Apparently that's the path. We might have been hours finding it. No sooner were we down than we heard shots. Guessing that you had started something, we hurried along to see what was happening.'

It seemed to Cub that the return journey was not as bad as the outward trip. For one thing, it was slowly getting light, and for another, Slim took an easier route. It was some time before they saw him, but eventually they caught a glimpse of him as he topped a ridge about half a mile ahead. He paused to look back, and they knew from the way he turned and went on that he had seen them.

'He won't stay long at the Lodge,' prophesied Gimlet. 'He'll make for the hotel, supposing Burke and Smith to he there.'

'If he gets to the Lodge first, he'll beat us,' asserted Cub. 'He'll spot the Buick in the yard and use it.'

'In that case, we've got to beat him to the Lodge,' declared Gimlet, setting such a pace that Cub found it hard to keep up. In fact, he could not keep up, but gradually dropped behind. In half an hour he was nearly thirty yards in the rear, but he put on a spurt down a slope and made up some ground. He saw Slim running across the open moor, still with a lead

475

of several hundred yards. Seeing his pursuers, Slim turned and fired two shots. They went wide, kicking up the snow some distance away.

'Silly fool, shooting at that range. Cost him nearly a hundred yards,' muttered Gimlet, who did not trouble to return the fire.

The chase continued. Cub was breathing heavily. Breasting each slope, sweat poured down his face. Gimlet maintained a steady pace and appeared to suffer no distress. Slowly but surely the gap between pursued and pursuers shortened, but when they came in sight of the Lodge Slim still had a lead of a hundred yards. Several times he had stumbled, and it seemed to Cub that his endurance must be giving out; but at the sight of his goal so close he put on a spurt.

Gimlet shouted to Cub, 'This is it! Come on.' He tore on as though the race had only just started.

Slim was swaying now as he ran. It was clear to Cub that he was almost finished, but he nearly kept his lead. Reaching the nearest wall he turned, and leaning on it with one hand emptied his pistol at his pursuers. The bullets whistled close but did no damage. Gimlet ran on. Cub, putting every ounce of strength into a final effort, caught up with him. Slim disappeared round an angle of the wall. Ten seconds later came the sound Cub expected to hear. It was the whirr of a starter. An engine came to life. Gears clashed. When Gimlet and Cub burst round the corner the Buick was just moving. Gimlet made a dash for it; but the car was gathering speed, and he just failed to reach it. The Buick's horn wailed sardonically.

'He's done us, after all,' gasped Cub.

Gimlet, realising the futility of pursuit, had pulled up. 'Looks like it,' he said calmly. Then he stiffened. 'No! By gad! Look!'

The accident that followed occurred, as do most accidents, in a flash. Slim was hardly to be blamed. The last thing he could have expected at such a place, and at such an hour, was another vehicle. Yet, just as he reached the first bend in the road, travelling at high speed, another car swung into sight, coming towards the Lodge. The same applied to the driver of the other car, of course. Both drivers were on the crown of the road. The oncoming car, if anything, was a trifle on its wrong side. Slim, going too fast to stop, and seeing that he had no chance of passing on his right side, tried to get through on the other. But the road was too narrow.

For a brief instant it looked as if he might succeed; the Buick appeared to do no more than graze the other car in passing; but this, at the speed it was travelling, was enough to be fatal. The Buick tipped up on two wheels. For a few yards it ran thus, on the point of balance. Then it went over. There was a crash. For a split second it seemed to hang poised, its wheels spinning, on the brink of the steep bank that ran down to the river. Then, with a sort of horrible deliberation, it rolled over and disappeared from sight. It could be heard bumping and banging as it rolled over and over towards the rocky bed of the river far below. There was a final crash, then silence.

The other car had by this time stopped. The doors were flung open. Four men jumped out and hastened to the spot where the Buick had gone over. They were policemen. One wore three silver stripes on his arm. A constable turned and, looking up the road, saw Gimlet and Cub standing there. He touched the sergeant on the arm and pointed.

'I had an idea that policeman would come back,' said Gimlet softly. He walked forward to meet the sergeant.

'Are you coming quietly?' greeted the sergeant sternly, as he came within speaking distance.

Gimlet smiled faintly. 'You'll never have two more passive prisoners, sergeant,' he said evenly.

One of the constables followed the sergeant. Cub recognised the officer who had called at the hotel. The other two started scrambling down the bank in the wake of the wrecked car. The sergeant dangled a pair of handcuffs.

'You won't need those,' said Gimlet.

The sergeant hesitated. 'We'll see.' He pocketed the handcuffs and took out a notebook. 'Name?' he questioned.

'King. Captain Lorrington King.'

The sergeant looked suspicious. 'This is no time for joking.'

'That's the name he gave me last night,' put in the constable.

'Are you telling the truth?' challenged the sergeant, still suspicious.

'Every word of it,' answered Gimlet.

'What are you doing here?'

Gimlet raised his eyebrows. 'Is there any law to stop a man living on his own property, in his own house?'

The sergeant seemed puzzled. 'I've never seen you before.'

Gimlet smiled. 'Probably because I've never been here before. I've never seen you, for that matter.'

'What's been going on here?'

'You'd never guess,' replied Gimlet.

'Who was the man who went over that bank? A friend of yours?'

'Not exactly, sergeant. His name is Delano – commonly called Slim. He's a notorious American gunman and racketeer.'

'What was *he* doing here?'

'Distilling whisky – illicit spirit, of course.'

The sergeant started. His lips opened. 'He *what...?*'

'It's chilly standing here,' complained Gimlet. 'Suppose we go inside and I'll tell you all about it. It's a longish story, but I think you'll find it quite entertaining. Incidentally, I've some prisoners in the cellar – as nice a bunch of crooks as you've ever seen under one roof. I believe you've been looking for one of them for quite a long time. His name's Burke. With another fellow, he shot one of your men near Aberdeen some years ago. I'm sorry to say I've also got some casualties. You'll need more men than you've got here. You'd better send one of your fellows for help. He'd better bring an ambulance and a doctor.'

'Where are these casualties?' asked the sergeant, as they walked on towards the house.

'Away up the glen, in an old distillery. I've two men taking care of them.'

The constables who had been down the bank now returned. They were pale. 'Dead as mutton,' said one. 'Smashed to pulp. The car's half in the river. It'll take a crane to get it out.'

'Perhaps it's as well,' opined Gimlet quietly. 'It may save a lot of complications.'

The sergeant ordered one of his men to take the car and fetch the help that Gimlet had advised. This done, they went into the house.

'Personally, I could do with a cup of tea,' remarked Gimlet.

The sergeant whistled softly when he saw the bomb-shattered kitchen. 'My word! What's happened here, sir?' he asked in amazement.

'Slim didn't like the idea of us living here, so he tried to move us with a little arrangement of his own,' returned Gimlet casually. 'Naturally, we had to defend ourselves – that is, I and my staff. In the final argument some of Slim's men got hurt.'

The policemen righted the table. The sergeant rested his notebook on it and pulled up a chair. 'Perhaps you'd care to make a full statement, sir?' he suggested.

'Of course,' agreed Gimlet. And for the next half-hour, while Cub made tea, he narrated the events that had occurred since his arrival at Glencarglas. More than once Cub had to turn away to hide a smile at the expression on the sergeant's face.

'Are these other prisoners still in the cellar?' asked the sergeant.

'I should think it's more than likely,' replied Gimlet. 'Commandos have special training in tying knots that won't come undone. I'd leave them where they are till you get assistance. They're an ugly lot.'

'As you say, sir.'

Gimlet finished his tale. At the end he signed his name at the foot of the page in the sergeant's notebook.

'There's one thing this does explain, sir,' said the sergeant. 'For months London has been flooded with blackmarket whisky – pretty raw stuff, too, from all accounts. The police couldn't trace the source of it. Who'd have thought it was right here, under my nose?'

'Who indeed?' said Gimlet smoothly. 'You'd better get in touch with London as soon as possible and ask them to have a look at this alleged vinegar outfit. I fancy the Metropolitan Police will get a bit of a shock when they see the sort of vinegar these people are bottling.'

'I'll do that right away, sir,' asserted the sergeant. 'What about this man of yours down in Devonshire – Singer?'

'You'd better have him picked up at the same time,' suggested Gimlet.

'Very good, sir.'

Soon after this two police cars arrived, with a motor ambulance. From the cars dismounted eight policemen, under an inspector, who read through the sergeant's report.

'You've been having what you might call an exciting time, sir,' he observed as he put the book down. 'Not a very nice welcome to Scotland; but if you'll give us another chance, I think we can do better than that.

We shall want you at the enquiry, I'm afraid. I'll let you know when and where it is to be held. The coroner may ask some pointed questions about the shooting and the car accident – but you can leave it to the police to handle that.'

'Thank you, Inspector,' returned Gimlet. 'I'm sorry the affair came to a show-down before we could bring in the police, but that's the way it fell out. You'd better send some men to the distillery. My fellows there will think I've forgotten all about them. You'll need stretchers. You have only to follow the tracks in the snow and they'll take you right to the spot.'

The inspector went off with his men.

It was three hours before they returned with the prisoners. Some were able to walk. Others were carried on stretchers. Copper and Trapper arrived on ponies, leading another. They said they had found them in a stable. They had brought them along, as there would now be no one to take care of them; moreover, the inspector wanted impressions of their fake hoofs for evidence.

'I hope you've got some grub going?' said Copper. ''Strewth! I'm near famished.'

'What did you find at the distillery, Inspector?' asked Gimlet.

'I'd call it a very interesting exhibit,' was the answer. 'If you don't mind, I'd like to have some photos taken of it for the jury to see. Not so many men there as I thought. We could only find six – three of them well plastered with buckshot. The man they call Tiny and a negro won't give anybody trouble for some time to come.'

'Not many men to run a place that size?' suggested Gimlet.

'It doesn't take many hands to run a distillery,' stated the inspector. 'They were only working one still, but even that would turn out a good many gallons of spirit. It might have gone on for years if you hadn't turned up. They had everything handy – water in the burn, peat for the fire, and barley from the braes. As a matter of fact, sir,' went on the inspector confidentially, 'we haven't been happy about the Glencarglas Arms for some time. That fellow who calls himself Smith had been there too long. Of course, we had no proof of any funny business, so there was nothing we could do. But my man Ross, who does that beat, has been keeping an eye on the place. That's why he looked in last night. When he made his report at the station, I sent the sergeant along to have a look round. Finding the place empty and locked up and tyre marks leading up the glen, he came along to see if all was well at the Lodge. He didn't expect to find anything like this though.'

'I'll bet he didn't,' put in Copper softly, winking at Cub. 'Neither did we.'

'By the way, we'd better have those fellows up from the cellar,' decided the inspector. 'Fancy Burke being here all the time. Well, well!'

The four prisoners were fetched from the cellar, in handcuffs. They were a sorry-looking lot. They were now at war with each other, for Smith, the bounce gone out of him, had announced that he was ready to turn King's Evidence.

'You'll all get a chance to do all the talking you want at the station,' the inspector told them grimly. To Gimlet he added, 'We shall be up here on and off for some time, I'm afraid, sir. The Excise people will want to see the distillery and dismantle it. The press will be here, too, no doubt, with photographers. It'll be quite a big story when the newspapers get hold of it.'

'I was afraid of that,' murmured Gimlet. 'I think we'd better clear out until the excitement dies down.'

'You'll have to leave me your address, sir, of course,' said the inspector.

'Are you going straight home to Lorrington, sir?' asked Cub.

'Not necessarily,' returned Gimlet. 'I seem to remember something about a party at the Ritz, when I was absent from parade. I don't see any reason why we shouldn't try again. How about it, you fellows?'

'Suits me fine,' answered Cub.

Copper looked at Trapper. 'Suits us down ter the ground, I should say. What say you, Trapper, old pal? Am I right?'

Trapper clicked his tongue. '*Tch*! Are you right? *I'll* say you're right,' he agreed with enthusiasm.

GIMLET MOPS UP

Gimlet arrived on the scene as Cub was taking aim.

CHAPTER ONE

An Unofficial Rendezvous

According to contemporary accounts, to own a house a century ago
in Brummel Square, London, W.1., was a thing to boast of. But
a century is a hundred years, and in that time many things change. In
Brummel Square they did not change for the better. The decline of the
Square as a place of residence began when the Great Northern Railway
track was laid through the gardens on the east side. By the end of the
Victorian Era its atmosphere of decorous affluence had faded, like the
paint on its doors and windows, and the railings that penned in – as if
they were in danger of straying – the group of sun-starved lime trees that
occupied the central area.

One by one, by death or design, the proud householders had been called
away, leaving their rooms to be adapted to the requirements of small hotels
and boarding establishments. The brief period of prosperity that followed
was brought to an abrupt end by the blitz of 1940. Not every house was
destroyed, of course, but those not demolished were sadly scarred. By the
autumn of 1946 the damage had still not been repaired, so that even on the
brightest of days the Square presented a melancholy spectacle. In the bleak
gloom of a November evening, with a chill damp wind moaning through
the gaunt skeletons of the once happy homes, it seemed that the cold hand
of death still lingered – at least, so thought Nigel Peters as, for the first
time in his life, he surveyed its mutilated, fire-charred dwellings from the
rubble-bounded end of what had once been the Stratton Street entrance.

Nigel, better known as 'Cub' in No. 9 Troop, Combined Operations,
(the celebrated King's 'Kittens') was not alone. With him were two other
members of the once redoubtable unit, now disbanded: Corporal 'Copper'

485

Colson, and ex-trooper, 'Trapper' Troublay. The nicknames, as is so often the case in the army, were appropriate, for until the war had caused him to change his blue uniform for khaki, Copper had in fact been a London policeman; and Trapper, a French Canadian, before stories of Nazi atrocities had brought him from the back-woods wherein he had spent his early years, had been a trapper.

In appearance the three comrades had nothing in common. Copper, who had started life as a pickpocket in the East End,* as a man stood six foot two inches in his socks. His composition of bone and muscle, backed by a fast-working Cockney wit, had enabled him to create a record by winning the City Police Heavyweight Trophy three years in succession. His fresh-complexioned face normally wore an expression of naïve simplicity. This, however, was no guide to his behaviour in battle.

Trapper Troublay, lean, dapper, swarthy, was more French than British, a fact that became evident when he spoke, for although he had the usual trans-Atlantic drawl he had a habit of falling back on French expletives when his English failed him, as it sometimes did in moments of excitement or deep feeling. A wisp of black moustache decorated his upper lip – the surviving hairs, he once explained, of a beard he had tried to grow to hide a scar which had been the parting gift of a grizzly after a difference of opinion on the important matter of life or death. His favourite weapons, also survivors of his trapping days, were a small bow and arrow and a business-like-looking Indian skinning knife; and with these he was so singularly adept that his C.O., after one demonstration, had raised no objection to their inclusion in his war kit. Apart from these unorthodox weapons it must be made clear that he was no ordinary performer with rifle or revolver, as was only to be expected of one who had used both weapons constantly as a means of gaining a livelihood. From the same Indians who had given him the knife he had picked up a trick of grunting and clicking his tongue in moments of emotion, presumably to save words.

Cub Peters was several years younger than the comrades to whom he was attached by the battle-forged bonds of war, for he had gone straight from school to Europe at the time when death and destruction were the

* See 'King of the Commandos'.

486

orders of the day. He had grown into a lean, loose-limbed lad, although what he had seen in Occupied France had left its mark upon his face, ageing it beyond his years. He had not settled down to the routine of civil life for the simple reason that, like many others, he found it impossible to do so. When one is young the habits of four years are not easily discarded.

He stopped when he came to the Square and surveyed the ruins dispassionately. He had seen plenty of ruins in his time. 'Gimlet said number ten,' he remarked. 'As I can see only five houses standing our objective shouldn't be hard to find.'

'Nine o'clock was to be zero hour,' observed Copper. 'It must be close on that now. Let's keep movin'. Where Gimlet is concerned you might as well be an hour late as sixty blinkin' seconds. Besides, I want ter know what all this is about. Blimey, what a joint. They must 'ave copped a fair packet 'ere. What's Gimlet doin' in a place like this? That's what beats me.'

'Tch,' clicked Trapper. 'Let's find out.'

They walked on to the houses that were still more or less intact. Tarnished brass figures on a door told them when they had reached their destination. White letters on a cracked fanlight proclaimed that the establishment was, or had been, the Hotel Belvedere. Mounting two dirty steps Cub rang the bell.

The door was opened instantly by a man, a civilian, none of them had ever seen before; but there was something in his manner, in his bearing, that caused Copper to give him a second glance before nudging Cub with an elbow, with a whispered, 'Plain-clothes man. Spot 'em every time.'

'We've an appointment with Captain King,' announced Cub.

'Captain King is here,' answered the man. 'You must be the party he's expecting. Come in.'

They entered. The door was not only closed behind them, but locked, Cub observed. The janitor turned to an inner door, knocked, and pushed it open. 'Here's your men, sir,' he announced to someone inside.

Stepping forward Cub saw his late commanding officer, Captain Lorrington King, D.S.O., M.C., known affectionately to the troops under his command as 'Gimlet.' He was standing with his back to a fire that gave at once an atmosphere of warmth and comfort to a shabbily furnished room. The main feature was a large dining-table round which chairs had been placed as if for a committee meeting.

'Come in, you fellows,' invited Gimlet, offering a hand to all three in turn. 'Glad to see you looking so fit.'

'What's cookin', sir?' inquired Copper, with the easy yet respectful familiarity that comes of long association in dangerous places.

Gimlet selected a cigarette from a gold case. 'I know no more about it than you do,' he replied.

'We got our orders to be here from you, sir, so here we are,' said Copper. 'I mean, where did your orders come from if I may ask? After our jaunt in Scotland* I thought you said you was goin' back home a foxhuntin'?'

'That was my idea,' admitted Gimlet, 'but it happens that I'm still on Reserve, so when I received orders to report here tonight, I came. I was asked to bring you with me if you were available. That fact, considered in conjunction with the name of the officer who issued the order, leads me to suspect that as far as we are concerned the war is not yet over. My instructions came from the War Office. They were signed by General Sir Saxon Craig, late Assistant Director of Military Intelligence – now, he tells me in his letter, Chief Liaison Officer between the War Office and Scotland Yard.'

'Numero Neuf,' breathed Cub.

Gimlet nodded. 'That was the name by which he was known to the French Underground movement, and to us when we were mixed up with its**. Why he has asked us to come here, instead of going to the War Office or Police Headquarters, I don't understand, but doubtless he had a good reason for it. We shall soon know. He's not the sort of officer to keep us waiting. By the way, corporal, see about getting your hair cut. It's too long.'

'Blimey, sir, I 'ad it cut yesterday,' protested Copper.

'Then get it cut again by someone who knows how to handle scissors.'

Further conversation of an intimate nature was prevented by the entrance of a man who, like themselves, was dressed in civilian clothes. Cub recognised him at once, for they had met during the war, in France. It was General Sir Saxon Craig, once known in the enemy-occupied countries of Europe as Numero Neuf – otherwise Number Nine. Regarding him

* See 'Gimlet Comes Home'
** See 'Gimlet Goes Again'.

anew, Cub found it hard to believe that behind the mild, commonplace face, was one of the shrewdest brains of the British war-time Intelligence Service. It was clean shaven, with little about it to merit description. It was neither fat nor thin, nor was there an outstanding feature. Slightly bald in front, wearing spectacles, the General looked more like a prosperous tradesman than a spy hunter of international renown. But his manner, as he invited them to be seated, was brisk, alert.

'Make yourselves comfortable,' he requested. 'Smoke if you like. I shall be as brief as possible, but we may be some little time.' As he spoke he pulled out the chair at the head of the table, sat down, and opening a portfolio selected some papers.

'Now,' he continued, 'first of all let me make clear certain things that must to you seem to call for explanation – why you were sent for, and why such a place as Brummel Square should be chosen for the rendezvous when, as Liaison Officer between M.I.5. and the C.I.D., I have quarters at both the War Office and Scotland Yard. Both departments, and indeed, the Government, are faced by a problem, a threat, of considerable gravity. To me has been given the questionable privilege of solving it. It is not one for which any existing government organization is really qualified to deal, unless – and this is my own idea – it turns out to be a commando job. That is to say, for men with active commando experience. As far as I can see at present they alone have the necessary qualifications to deal with circumstances that may arise. That is why I sent for Captain King, and asked him to bring with him those members of his unit whom I met in somewhat peculiar conditions in France a year or two ago.' The General smiled faintly at the recollection.

'I am going to ask you all to help me to solve our problem,' he continued. 'But in fairness I must warn you not to be hasty in your decision. First hear what I have to say. I arranged this meeting here rather than at the War Office or Scotland Yard because, for reasons which will presently become apparent, the less we associate with either place the better. In short, we are out on our own – I hope. I say I hope, because the men against whom we are opposed may have a spy system of their own, so they may know that I am the individual who has been selected to destroy them. If they do know that, then I am already in danger, and so are you. However, I hope that here we shall remain undisturbed for at least a little while. Of course, being here doesn't mean that we are cut off from official support. On the contrary, the entire resources of the fighting services, and the national police organization, are at our disposal should we require them. That alone will give you an idea of the seriousness with which the heads of the State regard the menace, which, for your private ears, I will now reveal.' The General leaned forward and dropped his voice a trifle.

'You will have heard, no doubt, of the Nazi Underground Movement, the members of which call themselves Werewolves. It did not turn out to be the vast national secret army the Nazi leaders hoped for. Even in Germany itself, where the organization first operated, the majority of members were lukewarm and soon fell away; but there remained a kernel, an inner core of diehards, a murder gang which, supported by hidden funds, was powerful enough to spread its tentacles into the liberated countries. Who is at the head of it we don't know. We don't even know if the thing is one cohesive unit or a number of isolated bands, some slaying out of sheer revenge, others using the Werewolf organization to cover private criminal enterprises. Either way the thing is a formidable outfit, and one which, since the Werewolves have now launched an attack on this country, we have got to tackle. How many of them are here we don't know. How they got here we don't know. But we do know this. They are here and those who have arrived are, beyond all shadow of doubt, the worst possible type.' The General looked slowly round the table before he resumed.

'This is no common affair of gangsterism such as was seen in the United States in prohibition days. It is something infinitely more deadly. The American gangster was concerned primarily with making money and killed only in the furtherance of that object or in self defence. The men with whom we have to deal are not concerned with money. They kill for the sake of killing, inspired by such a hatred as is hard for a normal balanced brain to comprehend. They are, in fact, the ultimate product of Nazism. If the average Nazi is a fanatic, a man from whom the virtues and all humane emotions have been eliminated, how much worse, we may ask ourselves, are the high priests of this pernicious creed? – for that is what the surviving Werewolf leaders are.

'You will be wondering why these men have come here. That is soon answered, for they have told us. The information was broadcast from a secret radio station somewhere in Germany three weeks ago. These men have come here to kill. As you know, during the war the Allies compiled a list of war criminals, setting down the names of those Nazis who had committed atrocities, with the object of punishing them should they after a fair trial be found guilty. Certain Nazi leaders, in their rage and hate, are now claiming to do the same thing, out of revenge. They have compiled a list of selected victims – not men who have committed atrocities, mark you, but British subjects who played a major part in winning the war. Rightly or wrongly, possibly because we stemmed their victorious advance, the Nazis hold Britain responsible for their downfall. Now, as I say, they are out for vengeance. They have turned to assassination, and are attempting to justify their crimes by going through a form of mock trial. The victim, having been condemned to death – a foregone conclusion – is then seized and executed, by hanging, shooting, or decapitation, in a pseudo-official manner.

'The first intimation we had of this was, as I said just now, a broadcast by a secret Nazi radio station. This was followed by a broadcast from this country, from what we suspect was a mobile unit. Within the next ten days a number of people in this country received what purported to be a death warrant. How many of these sinister documents were sent out we don't know. Some of the recipients may not have taken the threat seriously. A few did, and got in touch with Scotland Yard. During the following week we had ample proof that the threat was no idle hoax. First, Sir Eric Gurney, one of our leading Intelligence Officers, was found hanged in Hyde Park. There were indications that a car had been driven under the tree on which his body was found, and a rope made fast to a bough. A noose was then passed round Sir Eric's neck and the car was driven away leaving him hanging. Captain Martin Winhope, V.C., of the Special Air Service, was the next victim. His body was found, riddled with bullets, at the rear of his own West End club. To both bodies was attached a card setting out, under the Nazi swastika insignia, the alleged crimes for which these officers had been condemned to death.' Again the General paused and glanced round at the faces of his listeners.

'There is no doubt that this terrorism will be continued,' he went on. 'Clearly, we shall have to do something about it, and without loss of time, for any day may bring us a fresh tragedy. Remember, not only are these Werewolves the enemies of those they intend to kill, they are the enemies of all decent society, and as such they must be dealt with. They call themselves Werewolves, so on their own admission they are inhuman creatures. There is only one way to deal with a blood-crazy wolf, and that is shoot it, for such a beast is beyond redemption. I am going to ask you to find the lair of these monsters, and having found it, drag them out one by one and kill them. It is a terrible thing for me to have to say that, because it would seem to put me on the same low level as the Nazis; but what is the alternative? Take them alive by all means if you can, and we will give them a fair trial, for that is our way of doing things; but a cornered wolf is a dangerous animal, and to attempt to take it alive may involve risks not justified by the circumstances. One cannot apply justice to a wild beast. Moreover, in this case the Home Office takes the view that these Werewolves, by announcing a policy of premeditated murder which they have already put into practice, have condemned themselves. Our business, therefore, is to destroy them, as they have destroyed others, and will, if we do not prevent it, destroy still more. Remember, it does not necessarily follow that these creatures will wear the appearance of wolves. It is more likely that they will be too crafty for that. There is an old fable about a wolf in sheep's clothing. These wolves may play the same trick – or some of them may. Indeed, we must expect that. Some may have been in this country right through the war, for it would be vainglorious to boast that we had caught every enemy agent planted here by the Wilhelmstrasse. No doubt the clever ones slipped through our counter-espionage net. They may still be here, with well-established hide-outs which the Werewolves may now be using as their dens. They must be found. Naturally, you will say how?'

'From which I take it that so far you have no clue as to who these Nazis are, or where they are?' murmured Gimlet.

'That, I regret to say, is the case,' answered the General. 'As to *who* they are – well, we might guess at some of them. We are aware that certain Nazi war criminals, knowing what their fate would be if they were caught, joined the Werewolf organization to carry on the war against Britain in their own way. So far these men have eluded us.' The General looked down at one of the documents he had taken from the portfolio. 'For example: there is Hugo Stresser, late Commandant of the Growsky murder camp – the man who on one occasion burnt to death in a barn more than six hundred internees; there is Rudolf von Pless, a savage who ordered the shooting of forty-seven British airmen prisoners of war for attempting to escape; there is Lother Eindhofen, a group commander of the S.S. who was responsible for many atrocities in Occupied France; there is Karl von Runtz, one of Himmler's pet torturers, and Otto Vossmayer, Under-Commissioner of Police in Austria, responsible for the deaths of hundreds of anti-Nazi Austrians. He speaks English fluently, having lived in this country and America. These are some of the Nazi criminals who have disappeared. In the chaos that followed the German collapse escape was not difficult. They had ample time to make plans. Together they would form about the worst gang of thugs ever brought together. They may be over here but that is surmise. Anyway, all of them hate us to the limit of mania.'

'Have you photographs of these men?' asked Gimlet.

'Fortunately, yes. I will show them to you later on, although it must not be overlooked that they may have adopted disguises. As to where they are, they may be anywhere between Lands End and John O'Groats – that is, if in fact they are in this country. So far we have had little time to get on their track. I must tell you that when this matter first arose a meeting of all responsible authorities took place in Whitehall. The first question was how to tackle the problem, for it was no ordinary one. Was it a matter for the War Office or the police? As you may know, before the war police methods in Europe differed considerably. In Germany, for instance, in the case of a major crime the entire police force was set to work like an enormous machine to find the criminal. France, relying on individual effort, detailed one or two highly trained detectives who worked independently. In this country we chose to compromise. A C.I.D. man was usually given the assignment with power to employ the entire police force if necessary. But the case now before us seems to call for a military operation rather than normal police procedure. We don't know how many men we are up against, but they will certainly be armed, probably with the latest thing in weapons. For that reason I decided to make the matter a military one – at least in the first instance. Turning over in my mind the men most able to deal with such a situation as this, naturally, knowing something of what you did in Occupied France I thought of you. Now you know why you are here. For the purpose of this operation, if you undertake it, you will be something between soldiers and policemen – shall we say, something in the nature of the G-men who dealt so effectively with the booze racketeers in America.'

'Have you a list of the people who have so far received death warrants?' asked Gimlet.

'I expected that question,' replied the General. 'Yes, we have a list. It may not be complete. Naturally, each man has been put under police protection, but that may not save them. The Werewolves will anticipate such a move on our part and act accordingly. Even if we provided each selected victim with a personal bodyguard it might not be enough. In any case, the average Briton resents having to live, sleep, eat and play, surrounded by armed men. With regard to possible candidates for death who so far have not made contact with us, you may say, why don't we issue a public warning? We shall have to do that, of course, if things get really bad, but the Government is anxious to avoid such a step if it is possible, for these reasons. First, such publicity would flatter not only the murderers, but a large part of the German population still smarting under the sting of defeat. The Werewolves would become national heroes and the organization would tend to grow. Secondly, the thing might be copied by hooligan elements in this country, who would commit crimes and make them look like the work of the Werewolves. As I have already observed, the Nazis are trying to give these proceedings some sort of legal status. The selected victims are tried, in some cases, in their absence. The findings of the alleged court – always the death sentence, of course, are sent to the accused by post. The condemned man is not murdered in his house, in the street, or at his place of business. He is abducted by his executioners and taken to some chosen place where, in a pseudo-official manner, the sentence is carried out. We are hoping that more of the men who have received death certificates will come to us, but without broadcasting a warning, or issuing a notice in the press, it is hard to know how to get in touch with them.'

Gimlet smiled curiously. 'I can tell you one of them,' he announced.

The General looked surprised. 'You can?'

Gimlet nodded.

'And who is the victim in this case?'

Gimlet put his hand in his pocket and took out a folded sheet of paper. There was dead silence in the room as he laid it out flat. 'The name on this particular chit is my own,' he said evenly. 'It came by yesterday morning's post. From it I gather that I was sentenced to death on Thursday last by a Werewolf military tribunal for the crime of espionage and murder within the Reich over a period of years. In particular, I am indicted for the killing of that bounder von Roth, at Chateaudun*, and a Gestapo agent named Bussemann, near Paris.' With a quiet laugh Gimlet tossed the paper on the table.

'This is no laughing matter,' asserted the General.

'It all depends on who laughs last,' returned Gimlet drily.

The General considered him pensively over his glasses. 'I fear that you still tend to underestimate the desperate nature of our undertaking,' said he, critically. 'I will endeavour to put the thing in terms that cannot be misunderstood. The enemy against who we are opposed is shrewd, calculating, resourceful, efficient, and is possessed – obsessed, if you like – with the fearlessness of a fanatic. He will be supported by all the money he needs, and, there is reason to suppose, every hellish device that modern science and human ingenuity can invent. He is not likely to walk about with anything as conspicuous as a Tommy-gun under his arm. We must be prepared for gas, drugs, new explosives, new weapons the existence of which we do not even suspect, and the lethal instruments which were being developed by the best brains in Germany when Hitler fell. If you accept this assignment, every step that you take may be your last. The sugar that you put in your coffee may contain a deadly poison. A cigarette may explode in your face. The man next to you in a tram or bus may carry in his sleeve a needle loaded with bacteria. These are the methods the Gestapo adored. Make no mistake; if once these Werewolves suspect that you are on their trail they will wipe you out – or try to – with no more concern than a housemaid swatting a fly. Should they capture you alive they may employ unspeakable tortures to make you speak. From liberated prisoners we have

* See 'King of the Commandos'.

learned that a well-trained Nazi can make medieval torments look like juvenile pastimes. Nazi cruelty knows no limits. It is normal procedure. I know this must all sound highly coloured and melodramatic, but unfortunately it is the simple truth, and it must be faced at the outset. I trust I have made myself clear?'

'Perfectly,' answered Gimlet.

The telephone on a side table shrilled its summons. The General picked it up, listened for a few seconds, and with a crisp, 'I see, thanks,' replaced the receiver.

'That was Scotland Yard,' he announced. 'The body of Major Hugh Beverley, who was at one time officer-in-charge of prisoner-of-war inter-rogation, has just been found, decapitated, in the garden of his Surrey home.' The General's eyes found Gimlet's face. 'He, too, received his death warrant by yesterday morning's post,' he concluded softly.

The brief interval of silence that followed this tragic statement was again broken by the General. He looked slowly round the table. 'Well, how do you feel about helping me to find these fiends?'

'I didn't know there was any question about it,' replied Gimlet. 'I think that goes for all present.'

There was a murmur of assent.

'There's your answer, sir,' Gimlet told the General. 'We are ready to start as soon as you like.'

'Tomorrow?'

'Certainly.'

'Where are you lodging?'

'At the Europa, in Piccadilly.'

'I see,' murmured the General. 'You can't go on living at an hotel, of course. In the first place it would be inconvenient, and in the second, dangerous. With all due respect to big hotels, their very size, the numbers of their staffs and the nature of their clients, make them a regular hunting ground for spies. I had no idea that you were a marked man when I wrote to you. I hope you weren't followed here.'

'I think that's unlikely,' opined Gimlet. 'I may have been followed from Devonshire to the hotel; there was no way of avoiding that; but in view of the engaging document I received from the Werewolves – which I took seriously, by the way – I left the hotel by the somewhat irregular course of taking the fire escape from the staff quarters to the rear premises.'

'Good,' acknowledged the General. 'Very well. For the most part I shall be here, at what we may call administrative headquarters. I can tell you now that I have been to some trouble in their preparation. This whole block of buildings has been taken over by us. There is more than one entrance, and exit, as I will show you presently. All are guarded by reliable men from the Yard. And in case you should wonder why I selected such an insalubrious area as Brummel Square it was because the place was admirably suited to our requirements. There is little traffic, and a stranger prowling about would quickly be observed. No one can approach without being seen or heard. I have mustered everything that we shall be likely to require – among other things an armoury, radio and transport. Incidentally, assuming that you are unarmed, I think you had better each put an automatic in your pocket before you leave here. You will have to keep in close touch with me, so in the morning I should like you to get your kits together and move in here. I'll have quarters prepared for you. We'll have another talk tomorrow and then get down to business.' The General paused, and taking an envelope from his pocket spilled four small green cards on the table. 'I have also had these prepared,' he went on. 'They are police passes – not ordinary ones, but extra specials. They will take you anywhere – into Buckingham Palace, if you wish. They are rarely issued, so take care of them; on no account must they be allowed to fall into the hands of the enemy. I have issued them to you because you may need them urgently. Any policeman will recognise one of these cards and without question give you all the assistance in his power. Finally, I have arranged for my telephone number to be an easy one to commit to memory. It's the same as the calibre of the service rifle – Central, 303. It's a priority number, so you can get me instantly, day or night. Avoid names on the 'phone. You can use your nicknames. I shall use mine. I have tried to think of everything, but I may have forgotten something; if any of you have a suggestion to make I shall be pleased to consider it. For the rest, I do not intend to issue orders to you. Work how you wish. I shall be here to act on your advice and to provide you with anything you may need. That's all for now. I'll just show you round; then we'll adjourn until tomorrow.'

CHAPTER TWO

Hotel Europa

The precautions taken by the General when the party left, struck Cub as being somewhat overdone. First, the man who had been on front door duty called up, on an inter-house telephone, an observation post on the top floor of the building. On the report 'all clear' being received, the party left, two at a time, at intervals of five minutes.

The exit was not made through the front door, but via a series of cellars which terminated in an empty static water tank, a survival of the blitz period, half buried under rubble at the end of the block. Here a second doorkeeper was on duty. He was equipped with a sound detector so that no one could approach over the fallen masonry without being heard. He unlocked a metal door, like that of a bank strong-room, which gave access to the open air beneath the fire-distorted girders of a gutted house.

The password, Britannia, would, the General said, gain them admittance by the same door at any hour. Cub perceived the wisdom of all this, although in the absence of any apparent danger it seemed theatrical and unreal. He was the last to leave. Climbing over the rubble to the pavement, he and Gimlet went on to the corner of Stratton Street where, by arrangement, they found the others waiting for them. A cruising taxi was picked up at the far end of the street and the driver instructed to take them to the Hotel Europa.

Little was said until the vehicle turned into Piccadilly, when Gimlet remarked: 'It's just occurred to me that we might do better than trooping into my quarters together. What I mean is, I received my chit from the Werewolves by the same post as Major Beverley. In his case action was so quickly taken that I am bound to suppose that my turn will come at any time. Admittedly, the death notice was addressed to my place in Devonshire, but it seems likely I was being watched even there, in which case the enemy would follow me to London. That being so, they would know that I am staying at the Europa. I assume, therefore, that the hotel is under observation. I don't want to scare the watchers by appearing to have a bodyguard, so I'll go in alone. The number of my private suit is thirty. It's on the first floor. You fellows follow on and join me there. Keep your eyes open. I'm inclined to agree with the General; this business is no joke, and it would be silly, having survived the war, to be bumped off on one's own doorstep. This will do – I'll drop you here. As I go in I'll warn the hall-porter that I'm expecting guests. He'll have you shown to my quarters. He's safe enough; I've known him for years; but we shall have to treat strangers with suspicion.'

Gimlet stopped the car some fifty yards short of the hotel and went on alone.

As the others walked quickly along the pavement, Copper observed: 'S'welp me! We've played this game in some queer places, but I never expected to do it in the old home town, and that's a fact.'

They saw Gimlet dismount and pay off the cab. Pedestrians and taxis were passing in both directions, but there was nothing to indicate that any of them had an interest in the man who had just entered the big hotel.

The hall-porter showed no surprise when the inquiry was made for suite thirty. He called a page boy who, acting as guide, led the way to the suite and left them there. The door was ajar. Gimlet evidently heard them arrive for he called to them to come in.

'Did you notice anything like a wolf on the prowl?' he asked lightly, as they entered the private sitting room and closed the door behind them.

'Not a sign, sir,' answered Copper. 'Did you?'

'I thought I caught a slight taint,' replied Gimlet slowly, and at the same time smiling curiously. 'I fancy there's one not far away.' As he spoke he opened an inner door which gave access to the bedroom. For a few seconds he surveyed the room without speaking; he inspected the wardrobe and glanced under the bed.

'Can you *still* smell that wolf, sir?' asked Copper, frowning heavily.

'Very faintly,' returned Gimlet. 'Someone has been in these rooms since I went out. As a simple precaution, when I left I stuck a narrow strip of Cellophane across the crack of the bedroom door, and another piece on the outer door; both pieces have been broken. It may have been a chambermaid, of course,' he added, as they returned to the sitting room. 'I locked the outer door, but the maid would have a master key. Sit down. Let's have some coffee and talk this thing over.' He pressed the bell.

It was answered by a chambermaid. Gimlet ordered coffee. 'By the way,' he remarked, as the girl was leaving the room, 'has anyone been in here since I went out?'

'Only me, sir,' was the ready answer. 'I put your bag in.'

'Ah! My bag,' murmured Gimlet.

'Yes, sir – the little brown attaché case.'

'Quite so. How did it arrive?'

'I think it came by taxi, sir. A porter from the reception office brought it up to me and I put it inside.'

'Where did you put it?'

'He said it was to go in a safe place, so I put it in the long drawer at the bottom of the wardrobe.'

'I see.' Gimlet thought for a moment. 'Will you ask the porter who brought it up to come and have a word with me?'

'Certainly, sir.' The girl departed.

'The smell of that wolf becomes more distinct,' remarked Gimlet quietly, as he returned to the bedroom. He opened the wardrobe and pulled out the bottom drawer. In it lay an attaché case. He regarded it suspiciously without touching it. 'No doubt you have realised that this bag isn't mine?' he said softly to the others.

'It's got your name on it, sir,' Copper pointed out.

'That still doesn't make it mine,' answered Gimlet drily. 'Anyone can paint a name on a case.'

A knock on the sitting-room door took them back to that apartment. It was the chambermaid again. 'It's a funny thing, but I can't find that porter, sir,' she announced in a puzzled voice. 'The reception clerk has no record of a case coming for you. I don't understand it.'

'Never mind,' returned Gimlet casually.

'But the porter said the bag was for Captain Lorrington King – I remember that distinctly. I trust there's nothing wrong, sir?'

'Nothing at all,' asserted Gimlet. 'You did quite right. I rather gather from what you say that you have never seen this particular porter before?'

'No, sir. But they're always chopping and changing.'

'Do you remember what this fellow looked like?'

'I can only say he seemed a young chap. I didn't pay much attention to him,' admitted the maid frankly.

'I see. Never mind. That's all.'

The chambermaid went out, closing the door behind her.

'I begin to get a whiff of that wolf you spoke about just now, sir,' said Copper shrewdly. 'I reckon there's a bomb in that bag.'

'I doubt it,' replied Gimlet. 'But it seems pretty certain that the enemy has started operations. I can think of no other explanation that would account for the arrival of this mysterious case, which certainly isn't mine, although it bears my name. The chambermaid is above suspicion. I've often seen her here. She was telling the truth. The porter is the fake.'

'What I'd like to know is, what's in that bag?' muttered Copper.

'So would I,' admitted Gimlet. 'It won't be a bomb. That isn't their way of doing things – unless they've departed from their usual procedure. They aim to take their victim alive, presumably to let him know why he's being killed. Call it a form of mental torture. They'd get no satisfaction from blowing a man to pieces with a bomb.'

'Why not open the bag and 'ave a look inside?' suggested Copper practically.

'I'm tempted to do that,' confessed Gimlet, 'but if we did it might upset their plan. Things are going so well that I hesitate to risk spoiling them. I thought we should have to go out hunting for those fellows; instead, it seems that they are hunting for us. That should save us a lot of trouble. They've started by planting a case on us. That means something is going to happen here, probably tonight. The question is what? The easiest way to find out is to wait and see. If, as I say, something is going to happen here, the Nazis, with their thoroughness in matters of detail, will have it nicely timed. Meanwhile, the place will be watched, in case I should go out. Corporal, you know your way round. I suggest you make a reconnaissance outside. Be careful. It's vital that the enemy should think I'm alone here.'

At this juncture the chambermaid brought the coffee. She set it on the table and withdrew. Copper followed her out, closing the door behind him.

'Let's have another look at the attaché case,' suggested Gimlet.

They went back to the bedroom. Handling the piece of luggage carefully Gimlet examined it. There was little to see. The case was a second-hand one on which the name had recently been painted. There was a small hole in one corner, as if the leather had been punctured by careless handling. Gimlet laid an ear to it. 'It ticks,' he reported quietly. 'That means a clock-work device of some sort.' Still handling the case gently he tried to open it, but it was locked and none of his keys would fit. 'We'd better not try using force,' he remarked, replacing the case.

A minute or two later Copper came back. 'There's only one thing, sir,' he reported. 'There's a taxi a bit along the other side of the road. I noticed it there when we came in. I've just had a closer look at it. There's two men in it besides the driver. One of them seems to be wearing what looks like a porter's uniform. Smells fishy. If the cab was waiting for somebody it'd be empty, except for the driver. Does your window overlook the street, sir?'

Gimlet said it did.

Copper switched off the light and drawing the curtain aside, looked out. 'It's still there,' he announced. Releasing the curtain he switched on the light again.

'They may be body snatchers,' opined Gimlet.

Cub raised his eyebrows. 'Body snatchers?'

Gimlet shrugged. 'They want me alive, I imagine, in order to carry out their execution ritual. It would require at least two men to carry me. The driver would have to stay with the cab. Did you take its number, corporal?'

'Yes, sir. If it is the enemy I'm wondering how they got hold of the cab.'

'They might have stolen it from a rank.'

Copper shook his head doubtfully. 'Not likely. If a cab was pinched every bobby in London would be on the lookout for it in five minutes. It would have been spotted before this.'

'You're sure it's a pukka taxi?'

'Absolutely. No fake about it. Of course, they might 'ave got 'old of an old cab from the scrap heap and done it up.'

'I suppose so.' Gimlet thought for a moment, and then went on. 'When in doubt, it's a good thing to try to see through the enemy's eyes. The first thing to remember is, the enemy wants me alive. Naturally, they would work out what my movements are most likely to be. In London few people in hotels settle down before midnight. Let us say, then, that nothing is likely to happen until that time. Anything can happen afterwards. Very well. Clearly, it would be next to impossible for the enemy to take me out of this hotel and across the street to the cab if I was conscious, because the noise I should make would certainly attract attention. So we may safely assume that when I am removed from this room I shall be – well, if not actually unconscious, in a condition which would make me powerless to resist. I shall certainly be escorted out. As the hour is getting late it is unlikely that I shall go out again tonight, so it follows that the enemy will have to come here for me. It will be interesting to see how they propose to get me out without attracting attention. They must have a reasonable plan or they wouldn't attempt it. What they may not know is, first, that I am not here alone, and secondly, that I shall be waiting for them.'

'So all we have to do is bash 'em when they come,' suggested Copper cheerfully.

Gimlet looked pained. 'Oh no. Nothing so primitive as that.'

'But this is our chance to grab a brace of Werewolves – maybe three,' asserted Copper, looking disappointed.

'What good would that do?' demanded Gimlet.

'There would be two skunks less in the world, anyhow,' declared Copper.

'That may be, but we should destroy our only link between the enemy and his headquarters,' argued Gimlet. 'These fellows will probably be junior operatives. We've got to get at the head man. The ideal thing would be to let these fellows think they have got what they came for, so that we shall know where they go when they have done the job. I'm inclined to let their plan work – up to a point.'

Trapper clicked his tongue. 'I get it,' he grunted.

'D'you mean you're planning to let them carry you out?' asked Cub, incredulously.

'I'm toying with the idea,' admitted Gimlet. 'You'll be watching, of course.'

Copper shook his head. 'I don't like it,' he averred bluntly. 'It's too risky. We might lose sight of you, and that's easy enough in London – don't I know it. Next time we see you you'd be on a slate slab in the mortuary. No, I don't like it. We're dealing with wolves, not rabbits.'

'Perhaps there is a better way,' concurred Gimlet. 'We could wait here until the enemy shows his hand, anyway. We should at least get a sight of them. We ought to be able to grab them.'

'And make them talk,' suggested Copper.

'They wouldn't talk – they're Nazis.'

'*Sacré*! I know a trick, an Indian showed it to me, that makes dead men talk,' asserted Trapper earnestly.

'I've told you before, Trapper, I bar torture,' said Gimlet curtly.

'Pity,' breathed Trapper, shaking his head. 'It saves time and trouble.'

'If we caught them we should hand them over to the General for interrogation,' decided Gimlet. 'Before doing that, however, you, corporal, and Trapper, could put on their hats and coats and escort me to the cab, which would then – we hope – drive on to its destination, where the enemy would find he'd caught a tartar. Cub could follow in another car to check up in case of accidents.' Gimlet glanced at his watch. 'It's a quarter past eleven,' he announced. 'Let's start to get organised.'

'They'll expect to find you in bed,' Cub pointed out.

'I shall be in bed,' answered Gimlet.

'What – with your clothes off?' inquired Copper in a voice of astonishment.

'No, with my clothes on,' returned Gimlet evenly.

'Won't they think that's a bit odd?' queried Cub.

'I shall pull my pyjamas on over my clothes,' said Gimlet. 'We shall have to lock the outer door, of course. If we failed to do that it would look suspicious. Having put the lights out I shall get into bed, leaving the door between the sitting-room and the bedroom open. You will take up positions where you can't be seen. All we shall have to do is then wait.

When I give the signal Cub will switch on the lights and we'll grab every one in these rooms. No shooting – we don't want more noise than can be prevented. By acting quickly we ought to be able to stop the enemy from using his weapons – whatever they may be.'

'Then you're going to leave the attaché case where it is?' queried Cub.

'Oh no,' answered Gimlet. 'Ask yourself – why did they put it here? It wasn't for fun. When they come they'll expect to find me unconscious. What is going to make me unconscious? Obviously the medium is in the attaché case. What is it most likely to be? Again the answer shouldn't be hard to find. Gas. Gas is a Nazi speciality. Don't forget the little hole in the attaché case. I'd risk a wager that the little case contains gas, with an arrangement to set it off about midnight or soon after. I may be wrong, but I'm not prepared to take the risk. We should not justify the General's confidence if we fell for such a trick.'

'But what can we do with the case?' asked Cub.

Gimlet thought for a moment. 'It won't do to go out again, and we daren't risk gassing other people in the hotel. I'll put it in the chimney,' he decided. 'It should be safe there. The draught will carry the gas up and out of the way.'

Handling it carefully he took the attaché case, and carrying it to the large old-fashioned fireplace lodged it just above the bars, with the escape hole at the upper end. 'That ought to do it,' he observed. 'But come on – it's twelve o'clock. We'd better see about getting into our action stations.'

Night Watch

Almost imperceptibly the muffled murmur of traffic in Piccadilly began to subside. Periods of quiet became more frequent and more clearly defined. The buses stopped running. To those in suite thirty the hum of an occasional passing taxi came faintly, a sound remote and detached.

Gimlet, with pyjamas over grey flannel trousers and a sweater, was in bed. The others could not see him because they were in the sitting-room and the bed was out of line with the door. In any case, all lights had been switched off, although a feeble glow from street lamps filtered through the bedroom window, the blinds of which had not been drawn. The door leading into the corridor outside had been locked, for to leave it unlocked, Gimlet had opined, would look suspicious. Copper had taken up a standing position behind the heavy curtain that covered the sitting-room window, a position from which, as the window overlooked the street, he could watch the suspicious taxi. Cub, with Trapper beside him, reclined in comparative comfort behind the settee, half supported by cushions removed from that piece of furniture.

In these positions they had waited, without incident, for half an hour. Occasionally footsteps padded softly on the carpeted corridor beyond the door, and on each such occasion Cub's nerves tingled with anticipation; but so far the footsteps had always passed on, presumably being those of other guests retiring to their rooms for the night. Once a woman laughed, a harmless and natural expression, but one so out of character with the circumstances behind the closed door that Cub frowned. As time wore on, however, such sounds became less frequent. The whirr of a distant lift and the faint clang of its gates, almost constant earlier in the evening, became intermittent, the intervals of silence lengthening as fewer guests remained to go to their beds.

Waiting is always tedious. Cub yawned. The atmosphere seemed oppressive, unduly so, even making allowance for the fact that the windows had been closed to deaden the street noises. He yawned again, wiping a hand across his forehead on which tiny beads of perspiration had formed, and then settling himself more comfortably on an elbow. He could not understand why he was so tired. Thinking became an effort. He could have fallen asleep easily. Presently he did in fact catch himself nodding. This did not worry him overmuch.

The others, he reflected drowsily, would wake him when the vigil ended. He heard Copper say, in a low voice: 'The taxi's moving; it's coming over to our side; it's creeping along the curb; it's stopped about ten yards down.' The voice seemed strangely distant.

It seemed to Cub that his hearing had become defective. Pondering in a detached sort of way on this peculiar occurrence he decided that the curtain behind which Copper stood must have muffled the sound.

When, presently, his ears began to sing, he became faintly alarmed. There was something wrong with his hearing. Not only with his hearing. He became aware of a peculiar sense of unreality, of detachment from the scene, as if he were a spectator rather than an actor in it. A sudden fear struck him that he was going to be ill. He decided to consult Trapper, and raised himself a trifle. The movement required effort, for his limbs were like lead. 'Open – a – window – Trapper,' he said dully, haltingly. His voice sounded far away. Trapper did not answer.

Copper spoke. 'What was that you said, Cub?' he asked, moving aside the curtain.

Cub tried to reply, but could not. He tried desperately. Darkness was closing in on him. Fear, a sudden fear of something he could not understand, took him by the throat. It partly restored him and spurred him to a tremendous effort. Clutching the back of the settee behind which he had been reclining he strove to drag himself up; but his strength seemed to run out of his fingertips and he slid back.

''Ere, come on, what's up with you?' demanded Copper.

In a vague sort of way Cub saw the curtain move, saw Copper's tall form move forward. It bent over him.

'What's wrong with you?' inquired Copper again. 'What's the big idea of going ter sleep ...' He took Trapper by the jacket, lifted him a little, then released his hold. Trapper's body flopped back to the floor with a sullen thud. Copper caught his breath sharply and then moved swiftly. There was a swish of curtains. A window scraped. Cool air flooded into the room. Copper snatched up the hearth rug and swung it round his head like a great fan.

The effect on Cub was almost instantaneous. Consciousness returned. He moved, slowly, like one awaking from a deep sleep. His head began to clear. He felt Trapper stir.

'We've been – doped,' gasped Cub.

'Doped my foot,' snarled Copper savagely. 'We've bin gassed. It must 'ave bin that blindin' case.'

'Gimlet. What about Gimlet?' said Cub.

Copper strode into the bedroom. A moment later his voice came through the gloom. 'Gimlet's out for the count.' He reappeared with the attaché case in his hand. He went straight to the door, opened it and disappeared. He was back in a couple of minutes, without it.

'What did you do with it?' asked Cub, rising. 'Don't gas the whole hotel.'

'I shoved it in a wash place just along,' answered Copper. 'I'll attend to it properly as soon as we've got things squared up here.'

Trapper was now also on his feet, a hand to his forehead, swaying gently. '*Sacré nom*! What happens?' he asked in a bewildered voice.

Cub's faculties were returning fast. 'We were being gassed,' he replied. 'But for Copper we should have had it. He must have got away with it because he was standing up, near the window. Let's see about Gimlet.'

It took only five minutes to bring Gimlet round, but several more were required to restore him to full consciousness. Brisk work with towels, with doors and windows open, cleared the room of gas.

Gimlet shook his head. 'By gad! We nearly bought it that time,' he muttered. 'I don't understand it. There should have been plenty of draught ...' He knelt in front of the fireplace and thrust an arm up the chimney. There was a dull metallic thud. When the arm was withdrawn the knuckles were black with soot. 'Would you believe that?' he breathed. 'One can't think of everything.'

'What is it – I don't understand?' murmured Cub.

'I suppose I should have remembered that nearly all these old-fashioned grates have a hinged flap that closes the chimney to prevent draughts when the fireplace is not in use. This flap is closed. The gas couldn't get up the chimney. We might as well have left the attaché case on the floor. But we'll talk about it later. Where's the case now, Copper?'

'I've put it where it won't do no harm fer a bit,' answered Copper.

'All right. Close the windows and we'll get back into position. The clockwork device must have been set to release the gas at twelve-thirty, or thereabouts, and the enemy must know exactly how long the stuff takes to operate. They'll be here any minute now.'

Cub returned to his position. The others did the same, and a hush, an expectant one now, settled on the apartment. The dragging minutes resumed their interrupted progress.

A distant clock had just struck one when the enemy gave the first intimation of his arrival. Had the silence not been profound the sound would not have been audible. It was no more than a faint scratching at the door, as if a key, or an instrument, had been inserted in the lock. Trapper nudged Cub, although the warning was unnecessary. Came another sound, this time a gentle click, and Cub knew that the lock had been turned. His eyes were on the door, just discernible in the dim light. It was pushed open, noiselessly, slowly, but deliberately. A figure appeared, vague, sinister, making no more noise than a shadow. It moved two paces into the room and stopped. Cub stiffened, his mouth drying, as his eyes probed, and probed again, the sombre light, trying to make a human outline of the head and shoulders of the visitor. The head in particular appeared to be distorted.

The figure moved again, so that it revealed a silhouette in profile. Then Cub understood. The figure was that of a man, but the head, with pointed muzzle and short erect ears, was that of a wolf. The apparition advanced, and such was its stealth that it appeared to float rather than walk. It halted again. A second figure materialized in the gloom behind it. The door closed.

A white beam from a small torch stabbed the darkness. The wedge of light moved furtively across the furniture to stop at the bedroom door. Soundlessly the figures advanced again towards the door, to disappear from sight.

With his heart palpitating uncomfortably, for there was something uncanny, unreal, something evil about the whole business, Cub rose from his place of concealment and edged towards the electric light switch. His fingers found and rested lightly on the tiny knob. His eyes never left the bedroom door, and presently, as he watched, a confused mass, moving slowly, filled the opening. He made it out to be Gimlet, with a Werewolf on either side supporting him. Copper was still behind his curtain. Of Trapper there was no sign.

For perhaps ten seconds the scene remained thus, vague, sinister, sluggish in movement; but in that time the picture was engraved indelibly in Cub's brain. Then, on the instant, several things happened simultaneously. The silence was shattered; the spell was broken and the picture leapt to spasmodic life.

Gimlet's voice cut through the gloom with the crisp decisiveness of a whip-lash. He said only two words. 'Get 'em.' And as he spoke he moved swiftly. Cub flicked on the light, locked the door on the inside and-slipped the key in his pocket. By that time Copper had stepped from behind the curtain. Trapper sprang up from the settee and vaulted it with feline speed and grace.

Coincidental with the light flashing on, the three central figures had broken apart, but not very far, for, as the light revealed, Gimlet's arms had closed round the furry necks on either side of him. The two Werewolves struggled convulsively and did, in fact, succeed in breaking away; but by that time Copper was upon them. With one blow he halved the opposition. His right fist swung up in a slashing uppercut that would have made a bull stagger. It took the nearest Werewolf under the pointed muzzle, lifted the creature off its feet and hurled it with a crash against the wall where it subsided like an empty sack. Both Gimlet and Trapper were grappling with the other Nazi whose mask had been torn off in the struggle. Copper's big hand reached out. With a deliberation that fascinated Cub to watch, he grasped the Nazi by the throat and stood him firmly on his feet. His left fist jabbed viciously into the pit of the German's stomach. With a convulsive gasp the man's body closed like a jack-knife. Copper's right swung up to meet the face coming down. The body spun into a corner and lay still.

Copper brushed his hands together as if they had been made unclean by the contact. He looked down dispassionately at the fallen man. 'That ought ter learn 'em,' he observed calmly. 'Blimey! What a set-up. What do they reckon this is – Guy Fawkes' Day?'

Gimlet picked up the mask that had been torn from its wearer and examined it curiously. It was a hideous thing, even in the light, with bared fangs and a lolling red tongue. 'Very pretty,' he remarked cynically. 'It had a dual purpose. Apart from anything else it's a gas mask.' With a sneer of disgust he tossed the mask into the nearest chair.

Copper looked amazed. 'Did they reckon that thing was going to scare us?'

'Probably,' returned Gimlet. 'I don't mind admitting that I got a nasty jolt when I opened my eyes and saw these monsters gazing down at me. Let's have a look at what we've caught.'

The two unconscious men were stretched out side by side on the floor. The second gas mask was removed and the face thus revealed. Both were young men – neither more than twenty, Cub judged. One wore a grey suit, the other a dark blue porter's uniform – evidently the man who had delivered the attaché case.

'Go through their pockets and truss them before they come round,' ordered Gimlet. 'Better carry them into the bedroom, in case some member of the hotel staff should come along.'

With the blind-cord the two Werewolves were tied up securely, commando fashion, and carried into the next room. While this was being done Gimlet telephoned the General at headquarters. There was a brief delay, for, as was to be expected, the General was in bed. However, he was soon at the instrument.

'This is King speaking, from the Europa,' Gimlet told him, speaking quickly. 'We've just picked up a couple of stray wolves, out for blood. You had better take care of them, so will you send round and collect the bodies? Yes, right away ... room thirty, on the first floor. Be as quick as you can because things are still on the move. We may need a spare car. Yes, we'll wait. Right-ho, sir.' Gimlet hung up.

In the brief intervals of silence that followed these words there came a sound, a sound so slight that had Cub's nerves not been screwed up he might not have noticed it. It came from the door. Switching his eyes in that direction he thought he saw the handle move slightly. He was not sure. Silence, a silence brittle with sudden tension, returned.

Gimlet had evidently heard the sound for he laid a finger on his lips. They all stared at the door. Then Gimlet took a pace forward, holding out a hand to Cub for the key. As he moved there came another sound. This time it was a knock. Not the bold confident knock of a visitor with a definite purpose, but rather, a gentle tap.

Gimlet advanced, inserted the key noiselessly, turned it and opened the door.

CHAPTER FOUR

A Chase and a Crash

A man stood on the threshold; a man loosely clad in a dark red silk dressing gown. Cub, who could see his face distinctly, judged him to be in the early fifties. He was shortish, heavily built without being fat, bald in front and wore an iron-grey close-trimmed beard. His expression was one of apologetic concern. When he spoke he expressed himself fluently, although with a curious, slight, trans-Atlantic accent.

'Sorry to trouble you at this late hour, but I have a very devil of a head-ache just come on,' he announced, after an almost imperceptible pause. 'Have you by any chance got a couple of aspirins? My room is next door,' he added by way of explanation. The man sniffed, twisting his nose, as if he had a cold coming.

'Sorry I can't help you, but I don't use them,' answered Gimlet evenly.

The visitor smiled wanly. 'Thank you. In that case I shall have to ring for the night porter and send him out for some. Sorry to have troubled you. Goodnight.' He turned away.

'Don't mention it,' murmured Gimlet, and closed the door. The instant this was done he turned to face the others. For a moment he stared at them with a queer expression on his face. 'You heard that?' he breathed. 'Unless my imagination is fooling me that inquiry had a phoney ring about it. It's hardly the time to knock up a complete stranger and ask for aspirins. Did you notice the pause before he spoke? He gave me the impression of finding something he didn't expect; he recovered quickly and trotted out the aspirin story; but it took him half a second to think of that excuse. I could almost swear he tried our door before he knocked. I have an uncomfortable feeling that our two Werewolves were not alone in

513

the hotel. There's another down in the street. Cub, slip down and take up a position near that taxi. You may see something. Watch your step. These wolves have teeth with venom in them.'

With a wave of understanding Cub departed. Outside the sitting room he paused instinctively to glance up and down the heavily-carpeted corridor; and in that moment he thought he heard a door close softly. As there was some twenty doors along the corridor there was nothing particularly significant in this; it might have been any one of the doors; but in the circumstances, to Cub at that moment any sound would have been suspicious. Hardly knowing why, he slipped into a convenient housemaid's pantry, and there he stood, listening, expectant. All he could hear was an indistinct murmur of voices in Gimlet's apartment.

He waited for perhaps a minute. Nothing happened. He was about to move on when the door of room thirty-one, the room next to Gimlet's, opened, and the head of the man who had asked for aspirins was thrust out. He, too, took a swift glance up and down the corridor; then three swift steps took him to the door of room thirty.

He no longer wore the dressing gown, but was fully dressed in a dark lounge suit. For about half a minute he stood outside Gimlet's door, listening. This apparently was sufficient for his purpose, for moving quickly and noiselessly he returned to his own room, the door of which he had left ajar. In order to enter he had to push it wide open, and in the brief interval of time occupied by this minor operation Cub observed, inside the room, a conspicuous object. It was a trunk; a big, old-fashioned receptacle made of stiffened fabric, painted black.

There is nothing remarkable about a trunk in a hotel bedroom; it is in fact the rule rather than the exception, and at the time it merely struck Cub as odd that such an unwieldy piece of luggage should be parked in the middle of the floor instead of against the wall, where one would expect it to be and where it would be out of the way. Cub was to remember this later. He was in a quandary. His duty lay outside, with the taxi under observation, for those were Gimlet's orders.

In view of what he had just witnessed he was tempted to continue watching room thirty-one, or at least warn Gimlet of the suspicious behaviour of the man next door. However, after a moment's reflection he decided that obedience to orders must overrule personal inclinations so he hastened down to the street.

The taxi was still there. As he sauntered past it he observed that the driver was in a curious position.

He was still in his seat, but he was bending forward and at the same time staring upward slightly to the left. It was at once evident to Cub that the man was watching the front upper windows of the hotel. Nothing else could account for such a posture. So as soon as he was behind the cab he looked up over his shoulder to see what it was that engaged the driver's attention. He was just in time to see a tiny red light flash three times from one of the windows on the first floor. That this was in the nature of a signal was at once apparent, for the driver settled back in his seat and put his engine into gear.

Who had made the signal did not for the moment matter, but it was evidently a warning and the taxi driver was acting on it. He was moving off. This, reasoned Cub swiftly, meant that Gimlet's plan of impersonation in order to track the vehicle to its destination had miscarried. Neither he nor Copper nor Trapper had appeared. Copper, from his position at the sitting-room window might have seen the taxi start to move, but he would know nothing of the red light.

By the time these thoughts had flashed through Cub's brain the taxi was gliding away. After turning in a tight circle it headed in the direction of Piccadilly Circus.

At this critical stage of the proceedings, when it seemed certain that the taxi would fade out of the picture, by what Cub imagined at the time to be a stroke of luck, two cars pulled up near the hotel entrance. From the rear one a man alighted and walked briskly towards the hotel. Cub, concerned only with keeping the taxi in sight, made a bee-line for the vacated vehicle. There was no time for explanations. The owner of the car turned as Cub settled himself in the driving seat and slammed the door; he gave a cry of alarm and ran back; but he was too late. Cub was on the move. And it must be admitted that having turned in the wake of the taxi, now a hundred yards distant, he gave no further thought to the man whose place he had so brazenly usurped. Putting his foot down on the accelerator he closed up a little on his quarry which, he did not fail to notice, was travelling faster than might be expected of a taxi plying for hire.

The pursuit that followed was never a chase. The taxi went on at a steady thirty miles an hour with Cub varying his distance behind from forty to sixty yards. His problem was how to be sure of maintaining contact without making it obvious to the taxi driver that he was being followed.

If he dropped too far behind he might be cut off by traffic lights, or by a policeman on point duty. If he got too near and remained in that position the driver could hardly fail to notice him. However, none of these things happened. The taxi went on, crossed Trafalgar Square, cruised down Whitehall and at the bottom turned left along the Embankment. Here it increased speed and was soon at the approaches of the East End.

Just where they were when the pursuit ended abruptly Cub did not know at the time, except that he was in the district of Limehouse. He was sailing along, quite content, with his quarry in plain view. As he admitted later, the thought that he himself might be followed did not occur to him; yet such must have been the case. The first intimation he had of it was when a big dark-painted car, travelling in the same direction, overtook him, turned in towards the curb and forced him into the gutter.

The thing happened so quickly that his first thought, not an unnatural one, was that he was the victim of an accident due to the atrocious driving of the man in the overtaking car; but when the car persisted in its pull to the left, forcing him on to the pavement, he realised with a shock that this was no mischance. It was being deliberately staged. Of course he jammed on his brakes, which was all he could do; but it was too late. A street lamp standard loomed up. There was no way of avoiding it. His radiator rammed it with a crash that flung him forward against the instrument panel. Luckily the car did not turn over. There was another crash, mingled with the tinkle of shattered glass, as the street lamp fell across the pavement. The car that had caused the damage did not stop.

Slightly dazed, muttering incoherently with rage and mortification, Cub scrambled out of the wrecked car, by which time the vehicle that had caused the mischief was thirty yards away, accelerating. But he could still see the registration plate. MAL747, he read, and repeated the number thrice to commit it to memory. There was nothing more he could do. One or two pedestrians appeared, then the inevitable policeman, calm and unhurried. He took out his notebook and approached Cub with the imperturbable confidence of a metropolitan guardian of the law. But before he could start asking questions another car drew up. Out of it, to Cub's infinite astonishment, stepped Gimlet.

'How did it happen?' inquired Gimlet curtly.

Cub told him.

'How long ago was this?'

'Two or three minutes.'

Gimlet shrugged. 'Then it's no use going on. The car and the taxi will have a lead of a mile or more. They could be anywhere by now. We may as well go back.'

By this time Copper and Trapper had joined Gimlet and the policeman had confronted the party. The authority of Gimlet's green police pass was instantly apparent when he produced it. The constable's manner changed to one of respectful obedience. What could he do, he asked. Gimlet told him to take charge of the wrecked car pending further instructions and left it at that. The policeman did not question the order. Then they all got into the undamaged car and headed back for the West End.

As they travelled, at Gimlet's request Cub narrated precisely what had happened since he left the hotel. He then learned with surprise that the car he had purloined was, in fact, a police car, on the strength of General Craig. Of the two cars that had driven up just as the taxi left the hotel one contained the General and two plain-clothes policemen of his staff, who, as requested, had come to collect the prisoners. The other car, the one Cub had 'borrowed', was the spare transport that Gimlet had asked for.

It turned out that Copper had seen quite a lot from the window. He had seen the taxi drive off, although knowing nothing about the red danger signal he did not know why. He had seen Cub grab the vacated car and had reported this to Gimlet, with the result that they had hurried down the stairs and followed in the General's car, leaving the General to take care of the prisoners. Gimlet had had bad luck near London Bridge, being twice held up by horse-drawn lorries, otherwise he would have overtaken Cub earlier. As it was he had lost him, and was hunting for him without any real hope of success when he had come upon the crash.

Cub drove after the taxi at top speed.

'In view of what you saw it seems practically certain that the fellow who has the room next to mine in the hotel is one of the Werewolf pack, even if he isn't actually one of the operatives,' remarked Gimlet as they turned into Piccadilly. 'It must have been he who signalled to the taxi to pull out. We'll inquire about him when we get back.'

'It was hard to tell from the street which was our window, consequently I couldn't locate the signal,' explained Cub.

'We'll talk the thing over when we get inside,' asserted Gimlet, as they slowed down at the hotel entrance. 'I imagine the General will still be here, waiting to learn what all this is about. Just a minute.' He walked over to the reception office. He was soon back. When he returned he murmured: 'Our interesting friend is Professor Wenson – at least, that's the name he has registered under. We'll call on him presently.'

As Gimlet had predicted, the General was waiting, with his police assistants from headquarters. The two Werewolves, no longer figures of fear now they were stripped of their masks, lay on the floor, half covered by a blanket from the bed. They lay very still. Indeed, they lay so still that Gimlet stared hard at them before turning questioning eyes to the General.

'Have you had a word with them?' he asked.

The General shook his head. 'They didn't give me a chance.'

'What do you mean by that?' asked Gimlet tersely, still staring.

'They're dead.'

'Dead?'

'That's what I said. They killed themselves.'

'How?'

'Poison. The divisional doctor has seen them. Each has a loose tooth in his head. The doctor is of opinion that the tooth could be unscrewed with the tongue and poison thus released. It should give you an idea of what we are up against. Succeed or die is the Werewolf creed. The blood-waggon is on its way to take them to the mortuary.'

'You've searched them, I suppose?'

'Thoroughly.'

'Find anything?'

'Only these.' The General held out two curious squat objects.

'What are they?'

'Gas pistols. They were ready for emergencies. Each carried one under his coat, concealed under the left armpit. I haven't seen this type before. I'll get our expert at the Yard to make a report on them, but we can be quite sure that they are deadly. Apart from the pistols they carried nothing. And when I say nothing I mean nothing. There isn't a mark of any sort on their clothes.'

Gimlet nodded. 'All right, let's deal with the living. I have reason to suppose that the man next door – he calls himself Professor Wenson – is associated with the wolf-pack. I'm going in to have a word with him right away.' He described the man's suspicious behaviour, mentioning the red danger signal and the trunk.

Cub stepped into the conversation. He addressed Gimlet. 'I think I know what the trunk was for,' he said. 'It's just occurred to me. I fancy it explains how you were to be carried out of the hotel. That trunk was plenty big enough to hold a body.'

Gimlet drew a deep breath. 'By gad! You've hit it.' He looked at the General. 'It's time we called on this gentleman.'

'I agree,' said the General.

Without further parley the party went outside and walked along the corridor until they stood outside room thirty-one. The door was ajar. Someone was moving about inside. Gimlet pushed the door wide open. A night-porter, who appeared to be tidying up the room, swung round.

'It's all right. We were looking for Professor Wenson,' stated Gimlet.

'He's just checked out, sir,' answered the man.

Gimlet frowned. 'How long ago?'

'About twenty minutes.'

'Funny time to check out of an hotel, isn't it?'

'That's what I thought.'

'And he took his luggage with him, I see.'

'Yes, sir. I got him a taxi and carried his stuff down.'

'One of his pieces of luggage was a trunk, I believe?'

'That's right, sir.'

'Was it very heavy?'

'It weighed next to nothing, sir. I fancy it must have been empty.'

'Did you know he was leaving tonight?'

'No, sir, but I believe he took the room by the day.'

'I see. We're from the police department. How long have you worked at this hotel?'

The man looked concerned. 'Twelve years, sir.'

'That's good enough. Say nothing about this to anybody. We'll speak to the manager in the morning.'

'Very good, sir.'

'Are you going to search the room?' the General asked Gimlet.

'Waste of time,' answered Gimlet curtly. 'A man engaged on the job he was on would take care to leave nothing behind.' He led the way back to suite thirty, and after they had entered, closed the door. 'So the bird has flown?' he muttered. 'That, I suppose, was only to be expected.'

'We'll find him, don't worry,' asserted the General. 'I'll have Professor Wenson checked up. We've got a fair description of him. And I'll get the Yard on the track of those two cars right away – the taxi and the private car, MAL747.'

'They'll have changed the number plate by now,' muttered Copper.

'But the plate will still be in existence,' averred the General quietly. 'I don't think we can do any more until we've had some sleep. You fellows might as well move round to Brummel Square right away. Your quarters are ready and it's a good opportunity to get round.'

At this juncture a police ambulance arrived and collected the bodies. The General and his men departed. Gimlet began packing his suitcase.

'Go and get your kits and take them round to Brummel Square,' he ordered. 'I'll see you in the morning.'

Copper saluted automatically, although he was in civilian clothes. 'Aye, aye, sir,' he acknowledged.

CHAPTER FIVE

Council of War

Nine o'clock the following morning found the conference in progress
at the Brummel Square headquarters. The General was speaking.

'We've checked up on Wenson,' said he. 'There is no such person. That
is, the particulars he gave on his hotel registration form are fictitious. I
suppose that was only to be expected if, as there is reason to suppose, he
was the organizer of last night's affair at the Europa. As a result of that
the situation has changed somewhat. The head of the Werewolf pack in
this country will know by now that the plan miscarried, and why. He will
know that a trap was laid and succeeded so far as to destroy two of his
men – not that it will matter much to him because one imagines he will
have ample reserves to replace them. He will know that the police are now
seriously on the trail, which means, in turn, that the Werewolves will exercise even more caution in their operations.' The General paused.

'The question arises, what to do next? Unlike a normal crime, when
the criminal is content to escape, in this case there is no fugitive.' The
General looked at Gimlet. 'What I mean is, it is not to be expected that
the attempt on your life will be abandoned. Thus, the curious situation
arises, while you are hunting the wolves, the wolves will be hunting you.
The side that finds the other first will have a big advantage – perhaps a
vital one. Our problem is, and will continue to be, how to catch the king
wolf. Killing members of his pack may irritate him, but will not seriously
affect his programme. As I said just now, there will be no lack of recruits.
We are therefore confronted – I might say handicapped – by the task of
having to undertake two jobs at the same time. Not only must we wipe
out the entire Werewolf brood, but we must, if it is humanly possible,

prevent them from continuing their programme of murder.' Again the General paused.

'The next point is, what clues, what information have we to work on? Very little. We have examined the police car that collided with the lamp post.' The General glanced at Cub. 'The car that did the mischief was marked, if not damaged. Its colour was dark green, for it left some of its paint on the police car when it grazed it in passing. I have men out looking for it, also the taxi. Just where they were heading for we don't know, beyond the fact that they were making for the East End; but the East End embraces an enormous area so that doesn't help us much.' Again the General turned his eyes on Gimlet. 'Have you any ideas about how you would like to proceed?'

Gimlet pondered the question. 'It seems to me that we have two schemes, two methods, open to us,' he answered slowly. 'The first is to allow my movements to become known to the gang so that they will lie in wait for me, and, I hope, find that they have caught a tartar. I will deal with that project in more detail should the need arise. The alternative is to discover, and mount guard over, the next victim selected for death, with the object of both frustrating the attack and following the operatives to their head-quarters – not an easy matter, I admit. However, on my own responsibility I have made a start in this direction. I am assuming that after last night's affair the Werewolves will exercise even more cunning than hitherto, but they are bound to go on with their dirty work, otherwise their object will have failed and interest in the Nazi homeland will start to flag. That wouldn't suit them, you may be sure.' Gimlet lit a cigarette.

'Early this morning I compiled a short list of probable candidates for Nazi vengeance, and I got in touch, by telephone, with some of them. At the third attempt I found what I was looking for. Freddy Ashton – Captain the Honourable Frederick Ashton to most people – was a star turn in the Intelligence Service during the war. Posing as a Frenchman, in Occupied Normandy he kept a pub by the name of the *Cheval Noir*. He did some wonderful work, getting a lot of people out of trouble – including ourselves on one occasion – and bumping off several important Nazis at the same time.' Gimlet smiled faintly at the recollection[*].

* See 'King of the Commandos'.

'By this morning's post Freddie received his death ticket. Actually, it's lucky I rang him up, because as one would expect, he was inclined to take the thing as a joke. He takes most things as a joke. Naturally, I disillusioned him, warning him to watch his step. The snag is – again as one would expect – he wants to go wolf hunting. I managed to persuade him to do nothing until we make personal contact with him. He lives at Wongerford Manor, in Sussex. Now then: it so happens that there is this morning a meet of foxhounds, of which he is the Master, on the village green. He will, of course, turn out. I tried my utmost to persuade him to make excuses and stay at home, but he wouldn't hear of it. Nothing, I fear, not all the wolves in Europe, will prevent Freddie from hunting if there is a fox to be found.'

'He may finish by being hunted himself,' put in the General drily.

'That is precisely what I told him, and why I propose running down to Wongerford this morning, to keep an eye on things. Of course, it doesn't necessarily follow that the wolves will try anything in broad daylight – so far they have worked in the dark; but they might, and as the field becomes scattered there would be opportunities.'

'The Werewolves will know all about the hunt, you may be sure,' asserted the General. 'I imagine they learn as much as possible about the movements of their victims before they strike at them. It might well be that they sent the death warrant to coincide with the meet of foxhounds at Wongerford.'

Gimlet nodded. 'That's why I think we had better go down.'

'Even so, if he rides as straight as his reputation suggests, you'll have a job to keep in touch with him.'

Gimlet smiled faintly. 'You may have noticed that I am wearing riding breeches myself. I'm hoping to pick up a mount.' He looked at his watch. 'If we're going to be in time we had better be moving. The meet is timed for eleven o'clock.'

'All right,' confirmed the General. 'Meanwhile I'll get busy at this end. You have no idea, of course, when you will be back?'

'If nothing happens during the day, we may hang on at Wongerford for the night,' said Gimlet.

The General nodded. 'Very well. Be careful. If the wolves spot you, assuming they know you by sight, they may decide to have another go at you.'

'I'll bear it in mind,' promised Gimlet. He got up. 'Come on, you fellows, let's move along.' He smiled. 'This seems to be a case where we run with the fox and hunt with the hounds.'

CHAPTER SIX

In at the Death

It was ten minutes to eleven when Gimlet's car threaded its way through the miscellaneous assortment of humanity that had converged on Wongerford Green to watch a scene that seems never to lose its fascination.

It was apparent at a glance that the meet was a popular one. The weather was as perfect as a late autumn day can be and everyone within walking or cycling distance had evidently taken the day off to watch the sport – or at any rate, the start of it. A big field had turned out and there were a good many motor cars – too many, Gimlet observed, as he wound a tortuous course between them in order to get in sight of the hounds.

'Freddie's all right so far, anyway,' he remarked, as he brought the car to a standstill. 'There he is, over there, in pink, on the chestnut mare. I'll bet that lady can travel. Whoever hopes to keep up with her will have to ride, and ride hard. I'm afraid it isn't much use trying to pick out any wolves in this mob. We shall have to see how we go.'

'Are you going to speak to Captain Ashton, to let him know you're about?' inquired Cub.

'No,' answered Gimlet. 'He may spot me, in which case he'll know; but I'm hoping he won't. If he did he'd want me to ride with him, and that would defeat my object. Stay where you are while I make some inquiries. By the way, you fellows, would any of you like to ride, if I can get mounts?'

Copper's answer was prompt. 'Not fer me,' he said warmly. 'I'm safer on me own legs.'

Trapper clicked his tongue. 'I've ridden a packhorse,' he observed dubiously.

'That won't help you much in the hunting field,' Gimlet told him. 'You'd better stay in the car with Copper. How about you, Cub?'

'I'd like to ride if it can be arranged,' replied Cub. 'My father made me start riding almost as soon as I could walk.'

'I'll have a word with Tom Lench, Freddie's huntsman,' promised Gimlet as he moved off. 'He knows me. He was Freddie's batman in the war. He may let me have his spare horse.'

The others watched him approach the huntsman who smiled a greeting and touched his cap respectfully as he leaned down from the saddle to hear what Gimlet had to say. There was a brief conversation and they disappeared together behind the throng. When, five minutes later, they reappeared, Gimlet was mounted on a tall, upstanding grey horse, leading a small but racy looking black mare. Tom Lench returned to his hounds. Gimlet came straight on to the car. He beckoned to Cub. 'Come on,' he said sharply. 'Up you get. Hounds are about to move off.'

While Cub was adjusting his stirrup leathers Gimlet spoke to the others. 'You'll have to follow the field as well as you can,' he ordered. 'We're going to draw the Gorse first – it's about half a mile down the road. There are plenty of roads – too many in fact – so you should be able to keep somewhere near us. If you can keep in touch with hounds you'll never be far away from Captain Ashton; he's the man you've got to watch. He's unmistakable in pink, on that mare. If you lose us come back here.'

'Aye-aye, sir,' answered Copper.

Further conversation was made difficult by a general movement of the crowd. The voice of the huntsman could be heard above the babble. 'Hounds, gentleman, please.'

The field, a long crocodile of pedestrians, cyclists and cars, followed the hounds down the road. Cub, caught in the press, moved with it. From time to time he could see their car but he had no chance to speak to Trapper, or to Copper, who was driving. In fact, not until hounds were put into the four-acre copse of undergrowth called the Gorse did he get an opportunity to speak to Gimlet. Then it was Gimlet who did the talking.

'Never mind the fox,' he said curtly. 'Our job is to watch Freddie. Keep as close as you can behind me. If you lose me, or if I should take a toss, don't wait. Follow Freddie. If anything happens – and anything can happen in this crowd – you'll have to act as you think best.'

'Okay, sir,' acknowledged Cub, holding with difficulty his mount, now crab-walking in her impatience to be away. He wanted to say something else, for out of the corner of his eye he had noticed a large dark green saloon car among those crawling along the nearby road to watch the proceedings; but at that precise moment somewhere in the near distance a huntsman wound his horn and a voice wailed. 'Gone – away.' That was enough for the little black mare. She reared, and when Cub next saw Gimlet he was fifty yards away.

The next few minutes, before the field settled down, were minutes of confusion in which he nearly knocked down an elderly parson whose enthusiasm had clearly exceeded his discretion. Cub's mount was almost unmanageable in her excitement, but as she knew the game and followed the field no harm was done beyond the fact that he was now some distance from the road so had no further chance to look at the green car.

The first fence, an ugly 'bullfinch', thinned the crowd considerably, most of the riders making for the nearest gate. Of those who tried to take the fence some were left because their mounts refused. Others fell. Cub nearly came down himself. The black took the fence gamely enough, but it was almost beyond her and she stumbled on landing. Cub was pitched on to her neck but hung on, and with a gasp of relief got back into the saddle. Before him stretched a rolling pasture beyond which was a belt of trees into which hounds were just disappearing. There were not more than a dozen riders in front of him. He made out Freddie, with Tom Lench close behind, followed by Gimlet, riding smoothly.

As far as the circumstances permitted Cub scanned the others, but as was to be expected, they were all strangers to him and he gathered no useful information from his inspection. Some were in hunting pink, obviously members of the hunt. He noticed a woman, bowler hatted and veiled riding astride a good-looking bay, and riding well.

Without losing its order the field went on through the belt of trees to a main road on the far side, clearly indicated by a thick collection of telegraph wires that accompanied it.

Here a farm hand had sensibly opened a gate, so the field went on across the road without casualties. In crossing, out of the tail of his eye, Cub noticed some cars, one of which he thought was their own; but there was no time to confirm this. A broad sweep of stubble lay ahead. Freddie was well on his way across it, followed by several riders, now strung out. Gimlet was still there, as was Tom Lench. Hounds could not be seen, but they were evidently on a high scent for their voices could be heard, indicating the direction of the run. Cub saw Gimlet look round and assumed he was looking for him, so he sat down to ride in the hope of catching him; he did, in fact, succeed in closing the distance somewhat, but nothing more.

A field of roots, another stubble, and Cub glimpsed hounds swinging round in a wide curve as if the fox might be trying to make back for the Gorse. Two riders came down at the next fence, a 'cut and laid' with a ditch on the far side. Cub's mare made no trouble over it, however, and when things had settled down again he could see only five people in front of him – Freddie, Lench, Gimlet, an elderly man in pink who had lost his hat, and the woman he had previously noticed, in that order, an order that was maintained for the next two or three miles, by which time the woman had nearly caught up with the hatless man.

Without being particularly concerned, it struck Cub that the woman was riding unnecessarily hard on the heels of the old gentleman. With the whole field at her disposal there seemed to be no need for it. The thought struck him that she might be a friend, or relative. But when, for no apparent reason that Cub could see, the old man fell with a fearful crash, he thought otherwise; for the woman without even a glance behind her, rode on. As Cub passed the old man was lying flat on his back; fortunately he had fallen clear, but his mount was galloping away and he was out of courtesy tempted to go after it; or at least stop to see how badly the old man was hurt.

For a moment he hesitated in indecision, and at that moment, for the first time, it struck him that what he had seen had not been an accident. Remembering the green car he had an increasing desire to speak to Gimlet, to tell him of what he had seen. A yokel running across the field helped him make up his mind, so he rode on, determined if possible to catch up with Gimlet, leaving the yokel to take care of the fallen man.

A minute later another strange thing happened. With a swift thunder of hooves a rider overtook him. Wearing ordinary riding kit he was mounted on a raking light chestnut that seemed extraordinarily fresh. Cub caught a glimpse of a young, pale, tight-lipped face, as the newcomer tore on without taking the slightest notice of him. Again Cub stared at the horse. Unlike his mare, which was in a lather, it was not even sweating. He could only conclude that the rider had just joined in the hunt.

How and from where he had so suddenly appeared he could not imagine, and the uneasy feeling of which he had previously been aware, struck him with renewed force. He looked at the man again, although by this time he could only see his back. The fellow, he noticed, had a stiff, military seat, and carried something like a small satchel slung over his shoulder. Apart from that Cub learned nothing. He could not recall seeing the man or the horse at the meet.

The man caught up with the woman rider and then steadied his pace, so that the two rode almost side by side.

Filled now with definite misgivings Cub called on his mare for a final effort in the hope of overtaking Gimlet, but he could get no nearer than fifty yards. Gimlet still turned occasionally and must have seen him, as he must also have seen the man and woman close behind him; but he in turn was obviously trying to keep in touch with Freddie, so he let the grey have its head, apparently content with things as they were.

At this juncture there came a change in the situation, and for this reynard was responsible. Hounds, in full cry, appeared suddenly in a dip on Cub's left. Fifty yards ahead of the leader ran a very tired fox, his brush trailing, caked with mud. It was clear that he was nearly all in, and with the cunning of his kind he obviously intended back-tracking his own scent to the Gorse, or to the belt of trees through which the hunt had passed earlier. A hundred yards behind the hounds came Freddie, yoicking, following as fast as a weary horse could carry him. Behind came Gimlet. Of Lench there was no sign.

Now what Cub could see was also observed by the woman and her male companion – for the two were unmistakably riding together; and they lost no time in taking advantage of a situation that might have been created for their benefit.

Wheeling their mounts they cut off a wide turn by riding straight down the sloping ground into the dip, towards the strung-out pack and the two riders behind. This, of course, was the obvious thing for them to do if they wanted to be in at the death, which clearly could not long be delayed. Cub did likewise, although he was now more concerned with the riders than with the fox. He noticed that the man and woman were not looking at the fox, or hounds, as might have been expected in the circumstances; they were looking at Freddie, and even making allowances for his imagination, it struck him that they were riding with a more definite purpose than the position warranted.

They would be in at the death, anyway, now, and as they were going there seemed to be some risk of their committing the unpardonable sin of over-riding hounds. Freddie evidently thought so too, for looking up at them he shouted and made a warning gesture. It had no effect.

The fox reached the covert for which he was making with the leading hound snapping at his heels. The rest piled in, and it was somewhere inside the belt of trees, or on the road just beyond, judging from the sounds, that hounds killed their fox. In this proceeding Cub was not interested, for thereafter things happened, and they happened quickly. This was the order of them.

Freddie arrived at the edge of the timber and reined in, as he was bound to, the undergrowth being thick. He glanced behind him, perhaps to see who had survived the run, or more probably to look for Tom Lench. Gimlet was at this time the best part of a hundred yards away. He had pulled up to a trot and the reason was at once apparent. His horse had gone dead lame.

The woman and her male companion rode straight for Freddie, who crop in hand, was about to enter the trees, on foot. The man, Cub noted with astonishment, was talking, or rather shouting, into an instrument like a small telephone receiver which he held in his hand. A cable connected it with the satchel. Cub, also riding on, realised instantly that the instrument could be only one thing – a mobile radio unit. The man finished speaking and thrust the microphone back into his jacket. His hand flashed to his pocket and came up holding a squat black object. Reaching Freddie, he was taking deliberate aim when Freddie turned, and seeing what was happening, ducked. He was too late, or so it seemed. There was a dull report, a sort of vicious *whoof*, and Freddie went over backwards as though he had been punched on the jaw. The woman, who had gone round behind him, dismounted.

Now, all this had occurred in three seconds of time, and, of course, Cub was no longer in doubt as to what was afoot. Without a moment's hesitation he rode straight at the man who had fired the shot and knocked him flying with his foot, unseating himself in the process. His horse jumped over Freddie's motionless body and galloped away. Picking himself up, he flung himself aside as he saw the woman taking aim at him with a short, fat pistol similar to the ones they had found on the Werewolves at the Europa. Again came the vicious *whoof*. A blast of wind spun him off his feet. Without getting up he groped for his thirty-eight and fired back; but he was in an awkward position and the shot missed its mark. It grazed the woman's horse, however, which reared, throwing its rider. She got up, still holding her pistol, and took aim at Cub; but before she could fire a shot rang out and she staggered, calling out something which Cub did not catch, speaking presumably to the man. The voice gave Cub a shock. It was deep and hard, clearly a male voice, and for the first time he realised that the dress was a disguise.

Both Werewolves ran into the wood. Gimlet arrived an instant later.

He hesitated, his pistol covering sounds of crashing undergrowth which indicated the direction taken by the fugitives.

Thus the situation remained, like a screen play suddenly arrested, for perhaps five seconds. Then Gimlet said tersely: 'Are you all right, Cub?'

Cub answered. 'Yes.'

Gimlet's eyes probed the bushes. 'Watch out. We're vulnerable here in the open. Cover me while I get Freddie into the trees.'

Cub stood guard, pistol at the ready, while Gimlet picked up the unconscious Freddie and carried him to a safer place. Said Gimlet: 'I don't know what hit him but he seems to be in a bad way. We'd better get him to a doctor. Let's carry him to the road – we may pick up a car.'

Not without difficulty they carried Freddie some fifty yards or so to the road where they laid him on the grass verge. And precisely at that moment a car came tearing round the nearest bend. Cub caught his breath, for its colour was dark green. In a flash he understood. The mounted Werewolves had been in radio communication with the car all the time and had called it to the spot.

'Look out!' he warned crisply. 'Here comes trouble.'

The car came on, slowing down. But before it reached the spot where

Freddie lay on the grass there was a shout, and the man in riding kit, without his pseudo-female attendant, burst out of the trees, an arm raised in a peremptory stop signal. The car slowed to a standstill, picked him up and came on again, by which time Gimlet and Cub, perceiving that the enemy had received reinforcements, had slithered into the ditch that skirted the road, dragging Freddie with them. How many men there were in the green car Cub could not see, but there were at least two, not counting the man they had just picked up.

As the car drew level, travelling dead slow, Cub took aim at the man nearest to him. The face seemed vaguely familiar. He fired, hoping to reduce the opposition by one, at any rate; but all that happened was a small white spot that appeared on the glass, and he realised with disgust that the glass was bullet proof. Gimlet had also fired with like result. He, too, must have perceived what they were up against, for he muttered a warning against wasting ammunition.

How the business would have ended had not a new factor appeared on the scene is a matter for speculation. The new factor was another car, their own, which, travelling at suicidal speed, now came tearing round the bend from which the green car had appeared. It turned out later that Copper had heard the shots – hence his haste.

Whether the occupants of the green car knew or suspected that they were being followed, or whether it was decided that there was nothing more they could do – which in fact they could not without getting out of the car, which would have been a dangerous undertaking, as they must have realised – was not known to those in the ditch. Somebody must have been on the lookout, however, for as the police car came to a skidding stop the green car shot forward, and accelerating swiftly sped on down the road. Out of the police car tumbled Copper and Trapper, pistols in their hands.

'Follow that car!' shouted Gimlet. Then he appeared to remember something and changed his mind. 'No! Wait! We've got a casualty on our hands. Captain Ashton has been hurt. We shall have to get him home and send for a doctor.'

Copper turned hostile eyes after the retreating car. 'Seems a pity to let 'em get away,' he muttered.

'Can't help it,' said Gimlet shortly. 'Freddie must come first. We can't leave him here.' He made a quick examination of the unconscious man, but could find no wound. 'It may be gas or it may be sheer concussion,' he decided. 'We'll get him home. Keep your eyes skinned – there's a female wolf about somewhere.'

'It isn't a woman, it's a man,' put in Cub. 'At least, if it's a woman she's got a man's voice.'

'That doesn't surprise me,' returned Gimlet.

With Trapper keeping guard they lifted Freddie into the car, by which time, of course, the green car had been out of sight for some minutes.

'Lucky you turned up when you did,' said Gimlet to Copper during the operation.

'I wouldn't say it was altogether luck, sir,' answered Copper. 'After we lost touch with you we spotted the green car. It was following the hunt, too, and when I sees a graze on the paintwork I sez to Trapper "My gawd! There's *our* fox." So we followed it, not knowing what it was goin' ter bring us to, but having a rough idea. That's all there was to it.'

'I see,' murmured Gimlet.

Tom Lench appeared, an expression of bewilderment on his face. 'What's happened, sir?' he inquired. 'My horse put his foot in a rabbit hole, the darned old fool, so I got a bit behind.'

'There's been an accident,' replied Gimlet. 'Captain Freddie has taken a nasty toss. We're getting him home. You'd better look after hounds.'

'Very good sir.'

Gimlet turned to Copper. 'Get a move on,' he ordered. 'Make for Wongerford Manor, but stop at the first house that looks as if it might have a telephone.'

'Aye, aye, sir,' acknowledged Copper.

'What about the wolf in the wood?' reminded Cub.

Gimlet hesitated. 'We'll attend to that later,' he resolved. 'Never follow a wounded beast into cover – it's asking for trouble. We've other things to do; we've only one car and we had better keep together. We may come back later. Go ahead, Copper.'

The car shot forward.

CHAPTER SEVEN

The General Takes a Hand

The car took the road towards Wongerford and ran on for perhaps half
a mile when Copper slowed down in front of a modern house of some
size standing in its own grounds not far from the highway. 'How about
this, sir?' he questioned. 'They're on the 'phone. I can see the wires.'

'Fine,' answered Gimlet, getting out. 'Wait for me.' He hurried up the
short drive.

During his absence of a few minutes the others tried without success to
restore the injured man to consciousness, at the same time discussing in
low tones the events of the morning. When Gimlet came back, he merely
said: 'I've spoken to the General, and to the butler at Wongerford Manor.
The hunt doctor is at the manor now. Get a move on, Copper.'

They went on to the Manor, a matter of just on two miles, where
Captain Ashton was handed over to the doctor, and the house servants,
who carried him to his bed. The visitors then waited in the library for
the doctor's diagnosis. After about a quarter of an hour he appeared, and
with a puzzled expression on his face asked Gimlet to describe just what
had happened. This information Gimlet could not, of course, withhold, so
taking the medico into his confidence he told him as much as he thought
would be helpful. Having heard this the doctor went off again, this time
for an hour. Then he returned.

'I've done all I can,' he reported. 'He seems fairly comfortable, certainly
better than he was, which leads me to hope that the trouble is not serious.
There are symptoms of shock, but I suspect he was brought to uncon-
sciousness by an anaesthetic of some sort being forced into his lungs under
pressure – perhaps by a weapon designed for that purpose.'

'A gas pistol might have that effect,' opined Gimlet.

'Quite so. I understand that the intention was not to kill him, but to make him unconscious in order that he might be carried off without offering resistance. If that is correct we may assume that the effects of the gas will soon wear off, leaving him in a condition comparable with that of a patient coming round from an anaesthetic. Different constitutions react differently, so it may be a matter of hours or days before he is quite normal. The time factor would depend on the potency of the gas used. I shall stay with him for the time being. He will be safe in my hands.'

'In that case we'll go along to the village inn for a bite of lunch and come back later to see how he is,' said Gimlet, picking up his cap.

'Very well,' agreed the doctor.

'Don't leave him or you may find you have a dead man on your hands after all,' warned Gimlet seriously.

'Don't worry about that,' the doctor assured him.

Leaving the Manor, Gimlet took the others to the village, where, at the Three Bells tavern he arranged for a late lunch to be served in a small private sitting room.

A simple but satisfying meal had just been concluded when the door opened and – to Cub's unbounded astonishment – the General entered, carrying a small but obviously heavy leather case which, after a nod of greeting, he put on the sideboard before opening it to reveal a compact radio unit. Having set the dials at what was clearly a fine adjustment he left the instrument and joined the others at the table.

'Things are going well,' he stated crisply, without preamble, looking at Gimlet. 'We've picked up the green car.'

'Strewth! That was quick work,' breathed Copper.

'Where is it?' asked Gimlet.

'It's on its way again,' asserted the General. 'We let it go.'

'Let it go?' gasped Copper.

'Don't interrupt, Corporal,' adjured Gimlet.

'I'll tell you exactly what I've done as a result of the information you gave me over the telephone this morning,' continued the General, still addressing Gimlet. 'I've put a cordon of picked men round the area in which the wounded wolf is assumed to have taken cover. They should see that he doesn't slink out and at the same time take care of any others who try to get in to his assistance. More important than that, though, is the car. I had all roads trapped that lead north from this area with the result that the green car was stopped by a barrier at Bletchworth. There's no doubt about it being the car we are interested in; your bullet marks were on the window. There were four men in it.' The General smiled faintly. 'The police were very nice to them, explaining that they had been stopped in connection with a smash and grab raid at Portsmouth. That put their minds at rest, or so we may assume, for on that charge they were most certainly innocent as there had been no such raid. They were therefore quite pleasant about it – said they quite understood – and gave us no trouble. After a delay they were allowed to go, with apologies from the police for their having been troubled. The guilty car, the police explained, had been picked up elsewhere. In the interval, however, while they were waiting, I got through on the 'phone to the new Special Air Police Department at Scotland Yard. It's under the direction of an ex-Air Force officer named Bigglesworth, whom I believe you know. Bigglesworth happened to be out, but I spoke to one of his assistants, a lad named Hebblethwaite, known unofficially as "Ginger", but officially as Number Four S.A.P. He grasped the situation right away. He is now in the air watching the car, which he should have no difficulty in following because while the wolves were being detained – out of sight of the car, of course – a large white circle was on my instructions whitewashed on the roof of the car. As the roof of a car is normally above eye level, as it is in this case, it is unlikely that the occupants will be aware of the mark for at least some time. The first rain will wash it off, so they may never know anything about it. It is to be hoped that they do not discover it, otherwise they may guess its purpose and our efforts will prove fruitless. Hebblethwaite's job is to watch the car from the air and by radio keep me informed of its movements. He should be coming through any minute now. Unless anything unforeseen occurs he should be able to watch the car to its destination, which is the information we so badly need. It may not be easy for Hebblethwaite to keep track of the car in London, which I imagine is its probable destination. Indeed, in the ordinary way it would hardly be possible on account of the volume of traffic; but today is Saturday, and on Saturday afternoon traffic in the City thins out considerably, as you know. We can only hope …'

At this juncture a voice from the radio broke into the conversation. 'Number Four, S.A.P. calling. Number Four. S.A.P. calling. Can you hear me Number Nine – can you hear me. Over to you … over to you.'

The General was already at the instrument, his mouth near the microphone. 'Number Nine here – Number Nine here. Go ahead S.A.P. Transmission good. Go ahead S.A.P. Over to you.'

The voice of the air constable came through again. 'Car under observation heading north on road N.3., approaching Caterham valley. Repeat. Car heading north on road N.3., approaching Caterham valley. Now passing Blindley Heath. Stand by.'

The General quickly unfolded a map and indicated a spot with the point of a pencil. 'Here we are,' he said.

Again the voice came over the air. 'Car still heading north on N.3. Approaching Purley. Weather deteriorating. Met. reports cold front coming down from north. Have you anything to say? Over.'

The General answered: 'Thanks, S.A.P. Go ahead. Keep car in sight as long as possible. Over.'

And so it went on for the next twenty minutes by which time the objective car was crossing Vauxhall Bridge. The weather continued steadily to deteriorate, and when such reports were received the General shook his head sadly. 'The only thing that could defeat us was the weather,' he muttered irritably.

Again came the voice from the air. 'Weather bad. Visibility poor and getting worse. Rain coming from the north. Give me your instructions please. Over.'

The General answered. 'Hang on as long as you can. S.A.P. Fly as low as you like. Forget regulations against low flying over the Metropolitan Area.'

'Okay, Number Nine,' replied the pilot. 'Car now moving eastward. Car moving eastward. Raining now.'

Another ten minutes passed slowly with occasional comments from the air. By the end of that time the weather had closed down, making observation increasingly difficult, particularly as the tell-tale white circle was being erased by the rain. The car was still heading east, the General following its position on the map.

The end came suddenly. 'Hello, Number Nine. Car stopped. Car stopped. Name of street unknown, but pinpointed on my map. One man getting out. Car moving on again.' There was a short interval, then: 'Sorry, Number Nine. Now in heavy rain. Visibility zero. Car last seen heading north-east. I am going home – I am going home. Over.'

'Thanks, S.A.P.,' answered the General. 'Will see you later about stopping place of the car, and its last known position. Am switching off now. Goodbye.' The instrument clicked and fell silent.

The General turned to Gimlet. 'Well, that might have been better and it might have been worse,' he remarked philosophically. 'S.A.P. should be able to tell us where the man got out. That may mean something or it may lead to nothing. We shall see. There's a great future in the Special Air Police. When Bigglesworth gets the thing properly organized, crooks are going to find it much harder to get away with it. That's all we can do for the moment. What would you like to do next?'

'I'd like to have a look at this place where the car dropped one of its passengers, but there are other things I must do here first,' answered Gimlet. 'There's a wounded Werewolf to be picked up and I must have a word with Freddie Ashton, if he's conscious.'

'Very well. You hang on here for a bit. I'll see Hebblethwaite and collect all available information about the car,' offered the General. 'I don't think the wounded wolf will get away; I've a pretty strong cordon round the area.'

'That may be the best way of handling things,' Gimlet concurred. 'You go back to town. We'll stay here until we have things cleaned up, then we'll join you at headquarters – bringing with us, I hope, a live Werewolf.'

'You'd better take steps to see that no further harm comes to Ashton,' instructed the General. 'Now that he has had a sample of what the Werewolves can hand out he may agree to lie low for a bit. If he goes barging about on his own they'll get him as sure as fate. Impress that on him.'

'I'll do my best,' promised Gimlet.

The General stayed for a cup of tea. Then the party broke up, the General starting back for London, and Gimlet's party, in the police car, returning to the Manor, where, to their relief, they learned that Captain Ashton had regained consciousness, and although he was still in bed appeared to be little the worse for his adventure.

Gimlet saw him alone in his room while the others waited in the library. When he returned he was able to report that Captain Ashton had agreed to move right away, under cover of darkness, to the house of his brother in Chelsea – this on the understanding that he would be allowed to have a 'crack at the wolves' should the opportunity offer.

'Let's get along to see what the police are doing about this stray wolf,' concluded Gimlet. 'The Nazis are a cold-blooded lot, so the king wolf may decide to abandon him. On the other hand, if he's a useful member of the gang, he may attempt a rescue.'

They went out to the car.

Night drew its sombre veil across the landscape as the car cruised slowly back over its tracks to the scene of the attempted abduction. The air was mild; the rain had passed; a full moon glowed mistily through a high cloud layer, with an occasional star blinking through the gaps.

The police cordon of whom the General had spoken was soon in evidence. While still half a mile from the wood a red light sprang suddenly to light in the middle of the road, and as the car slowed to a standstill two shadowy figures closed in on it. Cub could just make out a third standing in the background, with what looked like an automatic rifle levelled. Copper evidently noticed it too, for he breathed, 'Strewth! They ain't takin' no chances of bein' hit. Don't blame 'em either. I'd do the same. What say you. Trapper, old pal? Am I right?'

'*Tch*! Every time,' agreed Trapper.

Gimlet opened the door on his side, whereupon a voice of authority ordered, 'Stay where you are. This is the police. Who are you and where are you bound for?'

Gimlet revealed his identity, showing his special pass, which had the desired effect. 'Any news?' he inquired.

'Nothing so far, sir,' answered the police officer. 'We're gradually closing in, but the chief's orders were to cover every inch of ground and that takes time. The cordon is still best part of a mile across with the wood about in the middle. We've sent for a couple of bloodhounds. They're on the way. They should liven things up a bit.'

'In that case we'll wait for a while and see the finish,' returned Gimlet. 'Where can I park my car out of the way?'

'There's an old cart track a bit along the left,' replied the officer. 'It ought to be all right there.'

The car was parked and locked, Gimlet putting the key in his pocket. Leaving the police, the party then moved quietly to a spot at the corner of the wood, one that commanded a wide view of the open country beyond. For the most part it comprised broad rolling fields with very little cover. At one point the moonlight glistened faintly on a long, if rather narrow, sheet of water. This, Gimlet told the others, was an artificial lake, brought about by the damming of a brook at the lower end, the object being to provide Captain Ashton, who owned the property, with his own trout fishing.

'Not much risk of the wolf breaking out that way,' observed Copper.

Gimlet agreed.

Trapper spoke. He had been regarding the wood thoughtfully, and now put forward the suggestion that he should enter it, find the wolf, and either kill it or bring it out alive. He supported this request by pointing out that he had tracked plenty of wolves in his time.

But Gimlet would not hear of it. He said he did not doubt Trapper's ability as a scout, for this had been demonstrated often enough; but his entrance into the wood at that juncture would complicate things for the police, who might easily shoot him in mistake for their quarry.

Time wore on. Nothing happened for about an hour. Then an excited canine bay, quickly silenced by a sharp word of command, came from somewhere in the direction of the road.

'That means the bloodhounds have arrived,' murmured Gimlet. 'We shouldn't be long now.'

Hardly had the words left his lips when, from the inky recesses of the trees, there arose a long-drawn howl, so sinister, so horrible, that Cub experienced a tingling sensation at the nape of the neck.

'That's our wolf howling,' muttered Copper.

'Why should it howl?' demanded Gimlet.

Trapper shrugged. 'Why it should howl I do not know, but it is the howl of a wounded wolf calling to its mate. I have heard it before.'

'Calling to its mate? You mean – a wolf makes a noise like that when it calls for help?'

'So the Indians used to say,' replied Trapper carelessly.

'Then it may mean that our wolf heard the bay of that hound and is calling urgently for help,' suggested Gimlet. 'It might easily be a signal, and come to think of it, the fellow may have a portable radio,' he added.

'Could be,' agreed Trapper.

'Seems likely he's expecting help or he'd do better to keep his mouth shut,' reasoned Copper.

Silence fell again. A few minutes passed. Then came another sound, but this time one so common that no one remarked on it. It was the purr of an aircraft, distant, but coming nearer. Cub glanced in the direction of the sound but could see nothing. He made a casual remark about the machine not carrying navigation lights, but apart from that no comment was made. It was not until the drone ended abruptly that anything further was said about it. Then Gimlet said: 'What does that fellow think he's doing? I hope he isn't in trouble.'

No one answered. The truth was, as was afterwards admitted, it did not occur to any one of them that the aircraft had any connection with their own affairs.

It was not until a soft whine overhead suggested that the aircraft might be circling preparatory to landing that the first glimmerings of a suspicion entered Cub's head. Looking at Gimlet questioningly, he said sharply, 'That machine's coming down.'

'As long as he don't land on us, that's 'is worry,' asserted Copper dispassionately. 'He's got plenty of fields to choose from.'

'Yes, now you come to mention it, he has,' said Gimlet in a curious voice. 'By gad! I wonder ...'

What it was that he wondered was never revealed, although it did not take Cub long to guess; for at that moment there was a diversion of such significance that the conversation broke off short. There was a crashing in the undergrowth, and from out of the trees, a hundred yards from where the party stood watching, burst a man holding with difficulty on leash a couple of straining bloodhounds. Three figures, presumably policemen, followed close behind.

'*Sacré*! Those hounds are on a hot scent,' declared Trapper straining his eyes.

'Queer – they seem to be making for the water,' observed Gimlet in a puzzled voice. 'Surely our man wouldn't go that way.' He started forward at a run and the others did the same.

The aircraft now came into the picture. It was Cub who spotted it first and his voice rose in his excitement, for, suddenly he understood. 'Look!' he cried. 'The machine. It's down – on the lake. Watch out.'

Gimlet pulled up dead, stared for a moment and then went on. 'I should have thought of it,' he muttered in a hard voice.

His words were half drowned in the bellow of an aero engine as the machine, without finishing its run, opened up and swung in a smother of foam, sending white ripples racing towards the rushes that fringed the shelving bank. From these rushes a man's form now arose and floundered through the water towards the aircraft.

There was a shout from the police as their quarry broke cover. The hounds bayed furiously. Gimlet increased his pace to a sprint, as did the others, although it was evident that they were going to be too late; they still had fifty yards to cover and the fugitive was already being helped aboard the machine. Shots rang out as one of the policemen pulled up and opened fire; but the light was tricky and the range long, and as far as Cub could see the shots had no effect. There was no answering fire from the aircraft, but suddenly the air was filled with a curious whistling noise which Cub could not understand until from several points along the bank there arose grey clouds of what looked like steam. The clouds spread and merged swiftly until they formed an almost continuous curtain.

'Smoke screen, eh?' panted Copper.

'Steady!' shouted Gimlet suddenly. 'Stop! 'Ware gas! Keep back everyone.' He shouted an urgent warning to the police who were some twenty or thirty yards farther along the bank. In any case, it was obviously no use going on, for the aircraft was again on the move, racing away at ever increasing speed across the ruffled surface of the lake. Backing away from the spreading grey clouds those ashore could only stand impotent while the aircraft took off, to disappear almost at once in the night sky.

'Watch out,' shouted Cub, 'the plane's coming down.'

'So he got away after all,' said Gimlet bitterly. 'Well, we have at least learned this much. The enemy has aircraft at his disposal. We'll bear it in mind.'

The police came up. 'Sorry, sir,' said one. 'We weren't reckoning on an airplane.'

'Neither was I,' admitted Gimlet frankly. 'I'm afraid we're a bit old-fashioned. We shall have to buck our ideas up. Well, we might as well pack up and go home. I'll go and report to the General that our wolf suddenly sprouted wings. Keep clear of that gas – it can't be anything else. I imagine it will soon disperse.'

For a moment or two they stood watching the sinister clouds weaving and spreading until they lost themselves in the air. Then, with a brief, 'Goodnight, sir,' the police withdrew. Gimlet turned and strode towards the track where they had left the car.

CHAPTER EIGHT

On the Trail

It was eleven o'clock when Gimlet and his party reached headquarters. The General was waiting for them. He knew about the escape of the Werewolf, for the information had been passed on to him by Scotland Yard, so it only remained for Gimlet to give him the details.

'It boils down to this,' he concluded. 'We know that the wolves are using at least one aircraft. The machine we saw had a flying-boat hull, but it may have been an amphibian. It might have suited the pilot to come down on the lake. The machine is probably the link between this country and Germany. If it is, then that disposes of the transportation problem. But whatever type of aircraft it may be it must have a base, a landing ground and, perhaps, a refuelling station, over this side. We ought to be able to find it. The Special Air Police may be able to help us there. You might speak to Bigglesworth about it. Which reminds me – have you seen Hebblethwaite? I'm anxious to hear about this place where the car stopped and dropped one of its occupants.'

'Yes, I've seen young Hebblethwaite,' answered the General. 'I saw him at the Yard and brought back with me a copy of the map with the spot pinpointed. It's on the left-hand side, half way down a side street leading off the Whitechapel Road. Hebblethwaite, with commendable initiative, took a photograph. I understand Bigglesworth has had all police aircraft fitted with cameras. The picture is not very clear, owing to the weather, but it shows a car stationary outside a building which from the size and shape of its roof is larger than any private house in that district. It may be a store, a garage, or possibly a small cinema. Anyway, it shouldn't be hard to find. I haven't been to the place. There was no desperate hurry. I decided to wait for you to come back. You may prefer to make your own reconnaissance.'

'I'd certainly like to cast an eye over the place,' returned Gimlet. 'I think we'll have a quick cup of tea and slip down right away. That will save time tomorrow, and I've none to waste. I happen to be President of the Lorrington Cottage Garden Society, and they're expecting me down on Monday to judge the exhibits, and, in the evening, distribute the prizes at the village hall. Of course, I could get out of it, but this is the first post-war meeting, and as many of the competitors are my own tenants I don't like letting them down. I could catch the night train up and be back here on Tuesday morning. So if it's all right with you I'll leave my plans as they are – for the time being, at any rate.'

'You're not forgetting that you're a wanted man yourself?' put in the General.

Gimlet smiled. 'No, I'm not forgetting.'

'The wolves may have a go at you at Lorrington.'

'I think that's hardly likely.'

'Everything so far shows that they know all about the movements of their selected victims. They will know about the flower show.'

Gimlet shrugged. 'They may. But I shall be with a crowd of people all the time.'

'I'd rather somebody went with you. Two are harder to deal with than one.'

'I can take one of my fellows.'

'All right. You know what you're doing.'

Gimlet nodded. 'I'll have a look at this Whitechapel place before I go. In fact, I'll slip down right away. If a further reconnaissance is indicated, or if I decide to keep the place under observation, two of my fellows can take care of it while I'm down in Devon.'

'As you wish,' agreed the General. 'Let's go through to the mess and have a cup of tea. I've had a busy day and I'm tired, so I shall go to bed; but you can always get me if you need me.'

They went through to the room that had been fitted up as a canteen.

Three-quarters of an hour later the car was gliding down the Whitechapel Road. There was practically no traffic and only a few pedestrians remained in the streets, for the usual damp November mist hung over the City like a pall.

'This must be the turning – the next one on the right,' observed Gimlet, who was driving. 'It might not be wise to take the car any nearer. I don't think there's any point in us all trooping along,' he continued, after bringing the car to a stop against the curb. 'There shouldn't be any trouble. I'll stroll along with Cub and give the place the once-over from the outside. Copper, you can follow us and stand at the corner. You may not be able to see us all the time, but you should hear if anything unexpected happens. Trapper will remain in the car.'

Followed by Cub, Gimlet got out, and leaving the others turned down the street that held the object of the expedition. Being dark, all that could be seen clearly were those areas of road, pavement, and house that came within the radius of the old-fashioned street lamps. What these revealed was a scene typical of Victorian slum districts. Most of the houses were miserable little shops of miscellaneous character, drab, squalid, paint dilapidated and blinds awry. Some of the windows were boarded up, apparently victims of the London blitz. It was evident that the street had once been a narrow thoroughfare between cheap little houses of uniform plan, built in a continuous row, the sort of thing that may be found in almost any London parish.

There was no difficulty in finding the objective for there was only one structure that differed from the rest. It stood back a little way, behind railings. As they drew level with it Gimlet slowed down a trifle, but did not stop. He expressed surprise by a soft, 'Ah-huh.'

Cub also was surprised; so surprised, in fact, that for a moment he felt sure they were making a mistake; but there was no other building of any size for as far as he could see, so he quickly realised that however remarkable it seemed, the building must be the one they sought. It was not a store, or a garage, or a cinema, as the General had surmised. It was a small church, or chapel, or at any rate, a place of worship. This was at once made evident by the shape of the door and windows. The building was new, or comparatively so, for the bricks were still more or less red. Over the door appeared a notice. In passing, Cub could just make out the words, painted in white letters on a black board, TABERNACLE OF ST. BARNABY IN THE EAST. To what religious denomination it was devoted he could not even hazard a guess, but there it was – a church.

Gimlet walked on a little way and stopped in a shadow. 'Well,' he breathed, 'what do you make of that?'

'Nothing,' answered Cub frankly, without hesitation. 'Of course, the fact that the man got out here doesn't necessarily mean that he was going to church,' he opined. 'He might simply have chosen this spot to alight.'

Gimlet admitted the possibility of this. 'Let's go back,' he decided. 'We'll take it more slowly this time.'

They strolled back. All was still, dark and silent, outside the church. Gimlet stopped in front of a small notice board carved in the usual Gothic style affected by religious buildings. On it was pinned a small square of paper. His torch flashed on and made it possible to read a brief notice to the effect that there would be a special service at noon on the following day, Sunday, when the preacher would be Brother Geraldus. All were invited. All would be made welcome. The light switched off, but Gimlet did not move.

'Funny,' he said in a normal voice. 'I never noticed before that there was a church here.' Then he added quickly, under his breath: 'Is there any way round these railings?'

Cub did not answer. As his eyes had become accustomed to the gloom he had observed something that had previously escaped his notice. Hunched in the scant shelter provided by a shallow porch was a dark heap, a large bundle of what looked like rags. It was surmounted by a small round object, light in colour, and this, he now realised with a shock, was a human face. At least, he thought so. He wasn't certain. Nudging Gimlet he pointed. Gimlet stared for perhaps five seconds; then his torch switched on, and the beam threw into relief the crouching figure of the lowest form of tramp, ragged, dirty, half buried in an ancient greatcoat.

'Are you all right there?' asked Gimlet.

The answer came back in a bad-tempered growl. 'Why shouldn't I be? Why can't you let a man sleep?'

'Sorry,' returned Gimlet carelessly, and strolled on. But before reaching the corner he stopped again and drew Cub into a doorway. 'I've got a feeling there's something going on here,' he breathed. 'That fellow may have been a genuine tramp, or he may have been a sentry. If he was a sentry, as we seemed curious, the chances are he'll watch us. Keep still.'

They waited for perhaps five minutes, but they saw no sign of the tramp; and Gimlet had just stirred preparatory to moving on when a car, travelling quickly, came round the corner. With a squeak of brakes it pulled up in front of the church.

'Now what?' murmured Gimlet, bending forward to watch.

One man got out of the car, carrying a small black bag, and disappeared into the church entrance. When some five minutes had passed and he did not reappear, Gimlet said quietly: 'Stand fast.' He glided away along the path.

He was gone only for two or three minutes. When he came back, he said: 'There's no one in the car. I've got its number. We'll hang on for a little while to see what happens.'

They had to wait for nearly half an hour. Then the man, still carrying his little black bag, emerged, entered the car and drove away.

'I should say that's all for tonight,' murmured Gimlet. 'Let's go back to headquarters.'

They walked down the street. Copper joined them at the corner. 'You've bin a long time. I was just comin' lookin' for you,' he complained.

In the car there was a brief debate. 'Whether the place has anything to do with our business remains to be seen,' said Gimlet. 'We'll have a look inside that church sometime – but not tonight.'

'Why not tomorrow?' suggested Cub. 'There's a service at noon. It sounds like a ready-made chance.'

'I shall be on my way to Lorrington,' reminded Gimlet. 'I shall have to get the morning train down from Paddington if I'm to do my job on Monday.'

'I could attend the service and tell you all about it when you get back,' offered Cub.

'It's an idea,' admitted Gimlet. 'Be careful. If the place is what it pretends to be, all so well and good; but if it's what I suspect it might be it could easily be a death trap.'

'Copper and Trapper could keep an eye on things even if they didn't come to the service,' persisted Cub.

'I promised the General that I'd take one of you with me to Devon. Trapper had better come. Copper could stay here with you. I'll turn it over in my mind,' promised Gimlet, as he started the car.

Arriving back at Brummel Square they found that the General had not gone to bed after all. Gimlet told him what had transpired. When the number of the car was mentioned he reached for the telephone, asked the operator for Scotland Yard and put through an inquiry.

'If the number plate on that car is genuine we shall soon know who it belongs to,' he said, as he replaced the receiver. 'The black bag suggests that the man might have been a doctor or a lawyer, although I must admit that it was hardly the hour one would expect a professional man to visit a church.'

'I was thinking the same thing,' replied Gimlet. 'There might be one explanation. The rescued Werewolf was wounded, and would almost certainly be in need of medical attention. He might have been dropped off at the church. If we follow that line of thought we may discover that the church is a sort of Werewolf hospital, or a base where medical attention is available. It might even be the London headquarters of the gang.'

'More likely a meeting place – a church would serve that purpose admirably,' opined the General. 'Had it been the general headquarters surely all the Werewolves would have got out there? And there is the car to consider. It must be garaged somewhere. We should have to be sure of our ground before we dare make anything like a raid on a place of worship.'

'Cub is going to attend the service there tomorrow morning,' stated Gimlet. 'He may learn something.' He then explained his plan for taking Trapper with him to Lorrington, leaving Copper to watch events in the Whitechapel Road.

To this the General agreed.

At this point the telephone rang. The call was from Scotland Yard. The General took the message.

'Hm. I wasn't far wrong after all,' he remarked as he hung up. 'The car belongs to a Doctor Guthram Paul, a practitioner in the Mile End Road.'

'British subject?' queried Gimlet.

'Apparently,' answered the General. 'But that is nothing to go on. Too many enemy agents in this country carry British nationality papers. We'll keep an eye on this particular gentleman – it shouldn't take us long to find out who his patients are in Whitechapel.' He got up. 'Well, it's getting late. We'd better see about some sleep,' he concluded. 'We'll discuss the matter further in the morning.'

CHAPTER NINE

Cub Goes to Church

Eleven-fifty the following morning found Cub, feeling unusually respectable in a navy blue suit, walking down the Whitechapel Road on his way to attend divine service at the Chapel of St. Barnaby in the East. Behind, at a reasonable distance, strolled Copper, who had undertaken to see that Cub emerged safely from the church when the service was over. Trapper had gone with Gimlet to Lorrington, whither the others were to follow late in the day if they felt inclined, or should they have any urgent information to impart.

Cub's paramount sensation as he turned into the narrow street was curiosity. With Copper standing by, and the entire Metropolitan police force available should it be required, he felt that he had no cause to be afraid or even nervous of the outcome of his adventure. Nothing, he thought, could have looked more innocent, more mundane, more devoid of anything sinister than the little brick church, at the door of which two men in black clothes were engaged in conversation.

Just short of the entrance a middle-aged man stood leaning against the door post of a tawdry newsagent's shop, scanning a newspaper. Coatless, hatless, collarless and unshaven, it was evident that he was the proprietor of the establishment. He threw a casual glance at Cub as he passed.

'So they've got a new recruit, eh?' he observed, half jocularly, with a strong Cockney accent.

Cub pulled up. 'Who's got a recruit for what?'

The newsagent jabbed a thumb towards the church. 'That's where you're going, I'll bet.'

Cub admitted this was correct.

'I've got to know most of 'em, but you're a new 'un to me,' stated the man.

Cub became interested. 'I see. You watch the people who go to church every Sunday, eh?'

'Not *every* Sunday. The church ain't open every Sunday.'

Cub raised his eyebrows. 'Is that so? How often is it open?'

'Oh, every now and again, when they feel like psalm singin', I suppose.'

'Then how do people know when they may come to the church?'

'The fellow who runs the joint puts a notice in the paper.'

Cub became even more interested. 'Do I understand that the church only opens occasionally and advertises the doings?'

'That's right. Funny bloomin' show I calls it. They must be a queer lot.'

Cub nodded. 'As you say, they must be a queer lot. In what paper does this advertisement appear?'

'On a Saturday, in the *Evening Herald*.'

'I see. And there was an advertisement yesterday, I suppose?'

'That's right. Here, I'll show it to you if you don't believe me,' went on the Cockney tartly, as if he resented his information being doubted. He went into the shop and returned unfolding a newspaper. 'There you are. There it is,' he declared, stabbing the paper with a blunt finger. 'Of course, they put a notice outside the church as well.'

Cub read the advertisement, which was framed in general terms under the heading of 'Brotherhood of St. Barnaby in the East'. 'Can I keep this paper?' he asked.

'You're welcome, I've done with it,' was the ready answer.

Cub folded the paper and put it in his pocket. For a moment he hesitated. Copper, he observed, was standing at the corner. 'Well, I only happened to notice the place by chance,' he remarked carelessly. 'Having nothing better to do I thought I'd take a look inside....'

At this juncture the conversation was interrupted by the arrival of another man, apparently a friend of the newsagent. The two greeted each other cheerfully and retired together into the house. Deep in thought Cub walked on to the church.

As he turned from the pavement to the entrance a man in a black suit was about to close the door. Seeing Cub coming, he paused long enough for him to enter, regarding him the while with a steady, appraising glance, natural, perhaps, in the circumstances. At least, Cub thought so. But he experienced a twinge of uneasiness as he heard the door being closed behind him. It reminded him that he had crossed the threshold from the security of the public street into – well, he did not know what.

The first thing he noticed was a curious smell – curious only because of where it occurred. It was faint but unmistakable. He recognised it for iodoform. Then he remembered the doctor and the remarks that had been made at headquarters overnight. The supposition that the doctor had called at the church to attend a patient was practically confirmed. There was less time to dwell on this than he would have wished, for the service, apparently, was about to begin. The congregation were standing.

It was a very small gathering and it took him only a moment to count the members of the congregation. It comprised eleven men. No women were present. No one took any notice of him as he tip-toed into one of the rear pews, but he observed that the verger – or the man who had been on door duty – did not leave his post. He wondered what would happen if he tried to leave, but it was not the moment, he decided, to put the experiment to practical test.

The minister entered and took his place at something that was half way between a reading desk and a pulpit. He was an elderly man dressed in an ordinary dark suit without anything in the nature of vest-ments. His eyes roved over his flock. It struck Cub that they rested on him rather longer than on the others, although this again was natural, since he was a stranger and the others were probably known to him. Cub stared back, and as he did so a feeling came over him that he had seen the man before somewhere. When he spoke he became more than ever convinced that this was so, that he had heard the voice in entirely different circumstances; but search his memory as he would he could not recall the occasion.

'Let us pray,' ordered the preacher.

The congregation knelt. Cub did likewise.

After that the service proceeded in a manner that was normal enough although the ritual was a strange mixture of spiritual and temporal exhortations. He did not know quite what to make of it. He appreciated, of course, that if the church was a genuine place of worship the service would be strange, because the worshippers were not of an orthodox sect; but he could not shake off a feeling that what he was watching was insincere; that it was an act put on for a particular purpose – possibly for his benefit. Several times the preacher hesitated as if he was at a loss for words, or was not certain of the procedure; and the congregation was sometimes slow with its responses, as if for the same reason. And when, after about twenty minutes of this, the service ended abruptly, Cub became increasingly convinced that the whole thing was a sham; that the service would have been different had he not been there. An atmosphere, a sort of tension, had become perceptible.

As the minister rose after the final prayer – a curious extemporaneous speech which, as far as Cub could make out, meant nothing – one of the congregation left his place and made a collection in a small black bag. This was usual enough and Cub thought nothing of it until he noticed that one of the worshippers furtively dropped into the bag a small folded piece of paper. When, presently, another did the same, Cub's suspicions were again aroused. That these little pieces of folded paper were treasury notes he could not believe. None of those present looked particularly affluent. Had one put in a note it would have been remarkable, he thought, but that two should do so was straining credulity too far. When his own turn came he dropped in a shilling. It clinked, he noticed, when it fell, so apparently some coins had been put in.

The preacher retired and most of the members of the congregation moved towards the door which, to Cub's relief, was opened to permit them to leave. Cub would have gone too, but when he left his pew he found his way barred. It might have been accidental, but two members of the congregation occupied the gangway. And they did not move aside.

The verger came forward. 'Our preacher would like to have a word with you,' he said softly. His lips smiled, but there was no humour in his eyes.

'What about?' inquired Cub evenly, but fully aware that if things were not what they appeared to be this was going to be the show-down.

'You are a stranger in our midst,' explained the verger in a flat voice.

'Our minister makes it a rule to ask strangers if they enjoyed the service and if they would care to join the Brotherhood.'

Cub was thinking fast. His eyes went to the door hoping to see Copper outside; instead, he saw that with the exception of three men the congregation had gone. Two were standing by him; the other was closing the door from the inside. 'I'd like to think it over,' averred Cub.

'But it would be discourteous not to speak to the preacher,' chided the verger gently. 'Come, he is waiting.'

The other two men were watching with cold dispassionate eyes. Again it might have been accidental, but one of them put a hand into his pocket.

'Very well,' agreed Cub, who now saw clearly that he was in no case to argue.

'This way, please.'

Cub was no longer in doubt. The procession that moved down the aisle was by its very nature a threat. The verger led the way. Cub followed. Close behind came the two members of the congregation.

Reaching the vestry, or what in the ordinary way Cub would have called the vestry, the verger tapped on the door.

A voice called, 'Come in.'

The verger pushed the door open and by a wave of his hand invited Cub to enter.

The minister was waiting, seated at a low writing table. As he glanced up he sniffed, screwing his nose sideways, and the movement, slight though it was, acted as a spur to Cub's memory. With a sudden tightening of the heart-strings he remembered where he had seen the man before. It was at the Hotel Europa. The man was Wenson.

There was something different about his general appearance suggesting that either then or now he had affected some simple form of disguise, but Cub knew that he was not mistaken. He hoped fervently that nothing in his own manner had revealed that identification had been established. On the other hand, had Wenson recognised him? Neither by word nor deed was it suggested that he had, although this could not be accepted as proof. After all, thought Cub swiftly, although he had seen Wenson when the man had come to Gimlet's room at the Europa, Wenson may not have seen him, or noticed him, for his eyes had naturally been on Gimlet, who had opened the door.

Surmise was cut short by a remark from Wenson. 'I hope you enjoyed our little service,' he said smoothly.

Cub shrugged. 'It was all right,' he answered casually, seeing no reason to pretend an enthusiasm which he did not feel.

'What brought you to our little church?' Wenson still spoke quietly, but his eyes were on Cub's face, and they were hard, suspicious.

'I happened to be passing. I saw the notice on the board about the service so I thought I'd come in.'

'You are interested in religion, eh?'

'Not particularly.'

'So!' Wenson's voice took on a slightly harder quality. 'And now suppose you tell us the real reason why you came?'

Cub affected surprise. 'Is this usually how you talk to new members of your church?'

'Who sent you here?' demanded Wenson.

'I came entirely on my own account,' returned Cub, truthfully enough.

'Very well. We shall accept you into our Brotherhood,' decided Wenson.

'I have no objection,' replied Cub. 'What does it involve exactly?'

'In the first place it involves a little ceremony of initiation.'

'What sort of ceremony?' asked Cub slowly. Out of the corners of his eyes he could see the men who had remained behind edging closer to him.

'It is a sort of confirmation. We call it the Spirit of Truth.'

'Would you mind being a little more explicit?'

'Not in the least. Quite recently, as you may have heard, some very remarkable drugs have been discovered, and they can be made to serve very useful purposes. There is one which, when injected into a human body, makes that person a simple subject for interrogation. In other words, the answers that he gives are truthful. He cannot lie. It is reasonable that before adopting you we should like to know something of your past life. You may have made mistakes, committed indiscretions which, naturally, you would wish to conceal. We shall remove the risk of such temptation. There is no need for you to be afraid. We have a doctor present. He will apply the necessary treatment.'

The word 'doctor' came as another shock to Cub. Remembering the man with the black bag he did not doubt the truth of Wenson's statement. 'I shall not, of course, submit to any treatment,' he declared.

'My dear boy,' murmured Wenson blandly. 'I do not think you are in a position to refuse our little request. You came here entirely of your own accord, remember. Refusal on your part would suggest that your true motives are open to suspicion. If you have told the truth you have nothing to fear.' Wenson turned to a man who was standing a little apart. 'Please proceed, doctor,' he ordered.

Cub, of course, had everything to fear; and he had an increasing feeling that Wenson knew it, or suspected it. He was in a trap and it was not easy to see how he could get out of it. These people would do as they had threatened. He had heard of the drug such as Wenson had described. They would not hesitate to use it; of that he had no doubt at all. They would do anything to achieve their purpose. If he struggled he would be more likely to hurt himself than the four men who stood about him. His pistol was in his pocket. But these men would also be armed. He might shoot one of them, or even two, but he could not reasonably hope to kill four men before he himself was brought down. Apart from that he was by no means sure that the circumstances justified wholesale homicide.

Hands closed over his arms. Instinctively he began to struggle to free himself, even though in his heart he knew that such efforts would be futile. The doctor, ignoring the commotion, had put a bottle on the desk and was calmly sterilizing a hypodermic needle.

At this critical juncture the door was burst open with some violence, and Copper strode in. 'What goes on here?' he demanded.

Silence fell. Movement stopped. Wenson glared. 'Who are you?' he demanded harshly.

'What's that got to do with you?' flared Copper. 'A pal of mine came into your lousy tabernacle and he didn't come out, so I came in to see why. What's all the fuss about?'

It was, Cub perceived, a curious state of affairs. Wenson did nothing, perhaps because he did not know how to meet a circumstance for which he had made no provision. The others, not daring to act on their own initiative, waited for a signal from their chief. The signal did not come.

'They were proposing to initiate me into their Brotherhood,' Cub explained to Copper.

'Pah! Don't make me laugh,' sneered Copper. 'You told me you were coming with me to Hampstead Heath. What are you messing about here for? If I hadn't happened to see you drift into the church I shouldn't have known where you were. Come on, we ain't got no time ter lose if we're a'goin'.'

For a moment the situation hung in the balance. Wenson, Cub could see, had been taken in by Copper's off-hand manner. Or if he was not entirely taken in he was in doubt. In any case, now, a fight would be a different matter from what it would have been before Copper arrived.

In the end Wenson did nothing. Accepting defeat he put the best possible face on it. 'Very well,' he said in a hard voice. 'This is disgraceful behaviour on a Sunday morning.'

'You asked for it,' returned Copper carelessly. 'Come on, kid, let's get cracking.'

Cub backed out of the room. Copper followed, and with a swift movement slammed the door behind him. Together, keeping close watch behind them, they strode down the aisle, opened the door and went out into the street.

'Phew!' gasped Cub, 'You were just about in time.'

'You're telling me!'

'That bunch had got me where they wanted me.'

'That's what I reckoned when you didn't come out.'

'How did you get in?'

'Through a window – no trouble at all.'

'It's a Werewolf nest all right. That fellow on the desk was Wenson, the man we saw at the Europa.'

'I've got eyes, ain't I?'

'The question is,' murmured Cub as they strode on down the street to where they had left the car, 'what will Wenson do now?'

'Search me.'

'He's be reluctant to abandon his headquarters while he thinks there is a chance that we were a genuine pair of casuals. You put on a great act. I don't think he recognised us.'

'No?'

'In that case he may hang on for a bit to see what happens.'

'That'd suit us.'

'They've got a sick man there – that wounded Werewolf, I imagine. The place stinks of iodoform. The doctor is there, too.'

'So I saw. I spotted his car higher up the street after you'd gone in. That in itself was enough to make me anxious.'

They got into the car.

'Well, what are we goin' ter do?' demanded Copper.

Cub thought hard. 'We can do one of two things,' he decided. 'We could ring the General and ask him to tell the police to raid the place. The only thing about that is, the raid would take a little while to organize. If Wenson does take fright, by that time he would have bolted and we should simply show our hand for nothing. The raid would do more harm than good, because we should lose touch with the enemy. Even if we got Wenson I'm not sure that we should have done anything very clever. He isn't the head man. He isn't big enough. He's no more than a section leader. It's the king-pin Gimlet's after. The only other thing we can do is to head for Lorrington, tell Gimlet what has happened, and leave the decision to him.'

'That sounds more like it ter me,' said Copper, nodding.

'On second thoughts, there is a middle course,' resumed Cub pensively.

'I'm listening.'

'We could keep an eye on the chapel for a bit in the hope of finding out definitely what happens. After all, it won't be much use going to Gimlet not knowing whether the church has been abandoned or not. The first thing he'll want to know is whether the wolves are still there or if they've pulled out. If they go we might with luck keep track of them.'

'That's better,' agreed Copper. 'We ain't in no hurry. The flower show ain't till termorrow.'

'Okay, then, we'll do that. Move the car along to the end of the street so that we can watch the church.'

The car was moved so that a window commanded a view up the street in which the chapel was situated.

'The doctor's car is still there, anyway,' observed Copper. 'That's it, on the right, about a hundred yards up. Just a mo', though. I wonder if there's a back entrance to the chapel. If there is they might slip out without us spotting them. You stay here while I go and find out.'

Copper was away about ten minutes. He returned with the information that there was a way out to the rear, although it was only a narrow path.

'Could a car get through it?' asked Cub.

'No – why?'

'Because if they go they'll have to use a car,' Cub pointed out. 'They've got a wounded man on their hands, don't forget. The wound will have stiffened by now, particularly if that doctor has had to take a bullet out of the fellow Gimlet hit.'

'Aye, that's right enough.'

An hour passed. Nothing happened. Cub began to fidget. For one thing, he was getting hungry. 'I'll tell you what,' he suggested. 'I think we ought to let the General know how things are going. I'll slip along to a call box and 'phone him. Then I'll have a bite to eat at a café and come back.'

'Okay. Bring me a sandwich and a packet of gaspers.'

Cub went off, made his report to the General who confirmed that they had done the right thing in keeping the chapel under observation, had a snack at a coffee shop and returned to the car with Copper's sandwiches and cigarettes. He was away about an hour.

Copper had only one item of news. The doctor had gone off in his car, alone.

'Fine. I take that to mean that the others have decided to stay,' said Cub. 'Had they been going to pull out I reckon the doctor would have had to take his patient with him. We'll go on watching for a bit.'

To pass the time Cub narrated in detail what had happened in the chapel from the time of his entry. He also told him what the newsagent had said and showed him the advertisement in the paper, which he still had in his pocket. 'It looks as if it all boils down to this,' he concluded. 'The chapel is a Werewolf depot, although I do not think it is the general headquarters. It was probably a spy hang-out during the war. When the day comes that we raid the place we shall find radio there. The church service is, of course, sheer bunkum. When a service is advertised the spies who have anything to report come in. The information is dropped into the offertory bag – all very simple. The doctor was in this country during the war. We may assume, I think, that he was a spy. Now, whether he likes it or not, he's in the Werewolf racket. If the chapel is, in fact, equipped as a spy depot, one can understand that Wenson would be reluctant to lose it.'

The afternoon wore on. The short November day began to close in.

'We shan't be able to watch from here much longer,' Copper pointed out.

The truth of this was evident. 'If they haven't gone by now then we can pretty well take it for certain that Wenson's decided to stay,' averred Cub.

'They may have slipped out down that back way,' said Copper anxiously.

'I could soon settle that,' answered Cub.

'How?'

'By knocking on the door.'

Copper started. 'Are you nuts?'

Cub smiled. 'No. I could just go along and say that I was sorry about the rumpus this morning. Apart from giving us the information we want that would do good because it would help to settle any uneasiness that Wenson may feel. I mean, it should help to convince him that my visit this morning was all straight and above board. He was suspicious of me – but then, in his line of business he would be suspicious of any stranger. I'll drift along.'

'Don't you go inside,' ordered Copper crisply.

Cub laughed. 'I'm not likely to.'

He strode quickly up the street to the chapel, stopped at the door and knocked. There was a short delay in which, he thought – he wasn't sure – that someone was inspecting him from a window. Then the door was opened by Wenson himself.

'Well, now what is it?' he asked sharply.

'I just called in passing, sir, to apologise for my friend's rowdy behaviour this morning,' said Cub meekly. 'He's got a silly idea that I can't take care of myself. Perhaps I was wrong to keep him waiting. I'm sorry about the whole business.'

Wenson drew a deep breath that might have been relief. 'That's all right,' he replied. 'I understand. It was courteous of you to call. Won't you come in?'

'Not now, thanks; I've got to get home,' answered Cub evenly. 'Maybe I'll come to the service another day, when I'm on my own.'

'Do,' invited Wenson. 'You will be welcome.'

Cub backed away. 'Goodnight, sir.'

'Goodnight.'

The door closed.

Whistling, Cub walked back to the car. 'It's okay,' he told Copper. 'Wenson's still there, which means he must be staying. At least, he raised no objection when I said I'd attend another service later on.'

'I'll bet he didn't,' growled Copper. 'When I saw you talking to him at the door I broke into a sweat. I wouldn't trust that murdering rat inside the length of a barge pole of me.'

'Neither would I,' returned Cub cheerfully.

'Well, what do we do now?'

'I think for a start we ought to go back to headquarters for a word with the General,' decided Cub. 'Then we'll have a night's rest. In the morning we'll run down to Lorrington to see how the others are getting on.'

'Suits me,' agreed Copper.

CHAPTER TEN

What Happened at Lorrington

In spite of an early start, it was four o'clock when, the following evening, in deep twilight Copper brought the car to a skidding stop at the front entrance of Lorrington Hall. Iced roads had caused the delay. Cub pulled the bell, only to learn that Gimlet and Trapper were then at the prize-giving in the village hall. They hastened on. Leaving the car in the street, where several others were parked, they made their way into the hall.

It was full; packed to suffocation. Clearly, the annual prize-giving was an event not to be missed. Not without difficulty Copper and Cub found standing room at the back.

When their eyes had become accustomed to the bright electric light, through a cloud of slowly rising tobacco smoke, Cub could just make out Gimlet on the stage, the central figure of a line of people of both sexes, seated in chairs. Cub's eyes roved over the scene. Trapper he could not see, but assumed that he was sitting somewhere in front. For the rest, the gathering was, as might have been expected, almost entirely composed of farmers and farm hands, with a sprinkling of artisans who, apparently, were gardening enthusiasts.

'I don't think Gimlet can get far wrong here,' said Copper to Cub in a low voice. He was also surveying the picture.

'If the Werewolves know about this, they might try to get him between here and the Hall, when he goes home,' opined Cub thoughtfully.

'Not if Trapper is with him,' declared Copper confidently. 'I'll bet Trapper has got a finger on the trigger all the time.'

At that moment Gimlet rose to speak. He was given a boisterous greeting, with hand clapping and cheering.

Copper glanced at Cub and winked. 'Sounds as if the Skipper's kind of popular in his little home town. Am I right?'

Cub smiled. 'You certainly are.'

'No use tryin' ter talk to 'im till the speech-makin's over, I reckon.'

'No, we shall have to wait.'

'I hope he ain't goin' ter be long, that's all. 'E's got more important business to attend to.'

Gimlet, who had waited for the welcome he was receiving to subside, raised a hand. Silence fell. Nothing happened. The silence became embarrassing. Twice Gimlet opened his mouth to speak, but no sound came.

Copper stared, frowning. 'What's the matter with 'im?' he asked sharply, in a hoarse whisper.

By what was obviously an effort, Gimlet managed to get out the words, 'Ladies … and … gentlemen …' His voice trailed away, and he swayed suddenly.

'There's somethin' wrong 'ere,' rasped Copper.

'You're telling me,' returned Cub tersely.

Before either of them could speak again the lights went out.

There was a brief silence; then the audience reacted as it usually does in such circumstances. There came a buzz of conversation that mounted to something like disorder. Some people laughed, as if the thing were a joke. Some tried to get out. Others shouted, 'Sit still!' A few of the men struck matches. Others held up lighted petrol lighters, although the light they gave was futile.

Cub's first thought was, naturally, that the lights had fused; that the thing was a simple accident. But hard on the heels of this sprang a doubt, a doubt which grew to apprehension. It gave him a sinking feeling in the stomach. Was it an accident? Accident or not, it was a contingency that had not been foreseen, and it was in a fever of impatience that he waited for the lights to go on again. His eyes tried to probe the gloom, but except in the limited areas of light given by the petrol lighters and matches it was impossible to see what was going on. The stage was in total darkness. He had a feeling that he ought to do something, but it was hard to know what could be done. It was obviously too early to give way to anything like panic.

'I don't like this,' he told Copper tersely.

Copper grabbed him by the arm. 'Hang on to me,' he ordered. 'If once we get separated in this mob we shall never get together again. It might be a pukka accident.'

'And it might not,' answered Cub anxiously. 'Let's try to reach the stage.'

This was easier said than done, but Copper, heedless of expostulations, ploughed a way down a side gangway. Cub, by keeping close behind him, as a tug hangs in the wake of a big liner, found the going fairly easy. This went on for about five minutes, by which time he judged that they were somewhere near the front row.

Suddenly Copper shouted. 'Trapper! Trapper, where are you?'

The lights, as suddenly as they had been extinguished, came on again. The first person Cub recognised was Trapper. He was on the stage, one hand in a side pocket, looking about him. But Gimlet was not there. His chair was vacant.

Copper vaulted on to the stage. He caught Trapper by the arm. 'Where is he?' he rapped out.

'He's gone,' snapped Trapper. 'Who would think—'

'Which is the quickest way out of this place?' broke in Cub, who realised that they could do no good in the hall.

'This way.' Trapper pointed to a stage exit. 'That's the way we came in.'

'Then let's get out of this,' said Copper grimly.

A nervous-looking curate tried to bar their way, but Copper thrust him aside. 'Sorry, mate, but I'm in a hurry,' he flung back over his shoulder.

Half-a-dozen strides and they were in the open air. There, after the babble inside, things were comparatively quiet.

'Gimlet!' called Copper sharply.

There was no answer.

'They've got him,' declared Cub. 'He wouldn't have left the hall voluntarily.'

'Where do we start looking?' muttered Copper. He asked the question hopelessly, for night had now fallen. To make things worse, they did not know their way about. 'Gimlet!' shouted Copper again.

The only answer was the sharp purr of an engine as a car, apparently in the street, was started up.

'After that car!' cried Copper, and started running towards it.

He was too late. A big touring car slipped out of the rank and accelerating swiftly sped up the road. Cub tried to see the number plate, but could not, for the rear light was dim and the plate was smothered with mud.

'*Sacré*! I'd say he's in that car,' asserted Trapper.

'The trouble is, we ain't sure of it,' returned Copper. He looked at Cub helplessly. 'Well, what are we going to do?'

Cub thought for a few moments and then made up his mind. 'We'll have a look inside the hall. If he isn't there, we can assume that he has been taken away by force. If he was taken by force then obviously the Werewolves are responsible. They'll murder him unless we prevent it. I should say Trapper is right; he was in that car that just went off.'

'We might overtake it,' said Copper quickly.

'Yes, we might,' agreed Cub. 'But if they realise that they are being followed they'll probably kill the skipper and chuck him out. Once having got him in their hands they won't let him go alive. That's the snag. If it comes to a show-down the first thing they'll do is kill Gimlet. Our best chance, as far as I can see, is to try to track the car to its destination and do something then. Of course, we can't track the car literally. We can only guess where it has gone. As it started up the west road it had probably gone to London. The only Werewolf depot that we know of in London is the chapel. We might try it. If he isn't there, we're sunk. There is just a hope that they may have taken him there. He isn't here, that's certain, so it's no use staying. We might as well tell the parson, or whoever is in charge of things inside, that Gimlet won't be coming back. We needn't go into explanations.'

Cub spoke quietly and calmly, but his brain was racing. He felt sick inside, for he realised that of all the tight corners that Gimlet had been in, he was now in the tightest. The chances of it happening were always on the boards. Reasonable precautions had been taken. They had failed. That's all there was to it. No one was to blame. The thing might have happened anywhere at any time. In his heart he had no hope of seeing Gimlet again, alive, but to save his sanity he felt that they must do something. 'I'll go and let the parson know that Gimlet won't be back,' he said dully. 'Then we'll hit the road for London.'

Gimlet was not in the hall. His disappearance had created a sensation. No one knew why he had gone, the parson said. Cub did not enlighten him. He merely explained that Gimlet had been called away on duty and would not be coming back. They would have to conclude the show without him. Then he hastened to the car where the others were waiting, Copper at the wheel, the engine running. 'Okay – step on it,' he said quietly. 'Make for Brummel Square first. We shall have to let the General know what has happened – not that he'll be surprised, I fancy.'

CHAPTER ELEVEN

Back to Town

The car ran straight to headquarters, arriving in the early hours of the morning. The General was, of course, in bed. Cub aroused him and told him of what had happened.

The General's instant and rather obvious plan was to throw a police cordon round the chapel and then send in a special squad to clean the whole place up.

To this, with due respect, Cub objected, on the grounds that it would involve delay when every minute was precious. The Werewolves, he declared, might even at that moment be putting Gimlet to death. Again, an official police raid could not be made without a certain amount of noise. Whether Gimlet was on the chapel premises or not this would alarm the Werewolves who were there. They might still escape. It was hardly likely, he asserted, that they had failed to make provision for such a contingency.

'What do you suggest, then?' asked the General, quickly getting into his clothes.

'I suggest, sir, that you proceed with your plans for raiding the place, but give us time to do what we can, first. We'll go straight on down and try to find a way in without creating any disturbance. Copper – that is, Corporal Colson – is an expert at getting into a place. If he can't find a way into the chapel, I shall be surprised.'

'I see. The main thing is, you want to be inside the chapel building before we arrive?'

'That's right, sir. Your men can stand fast while all remains quiet; but should anything like a rough house start they had better come right in and mop the place up.'

To this the General agreed. 'Have you got everything you're likely to require?' he asked.

'We've got guns and torches – they should be enough, sir,' replied Cub.

He returned to the car where he found the others waiting with irritable impatience.

'Here, come on; what's all the jawing about?' muttered Copper. 'What about it?'

'Push along to the chapel. I'll give you the set-up as we go,' answered Cub.

In twenty minutes, without incident, Copper brought the car to a stop in the Whitechapel Road just short of the turning in which the chapel was situated. Apart from an occasional pedestrian the street at that hour was deserted. It was still dark although dawn was not far off. Leaving the car as it stood they all walked on through the gloom towards the objective.

'Even if Gimlet ain't 'ere I'll bet that rat Wenson and his thugs will know where he's bin taken to,' said Copper in a low voice.

'He wouldn't be likely to tell us,' Cub pointed out.

'Is that so?' breathed Copper grimly. 'Wenson will answer my questions or I'll twist his wolf's head off 'is shoulders with my bare 'ands – and I ain't kiddin'.'

There was no sign of life as they approached the chapel, but Cub, remembering the tramp in the porch suspected by Gimlet of being a sentry, asked the others to stand fast for a moment while he went on alone. Advancing cautiously on tip-toe, making no more noise than a shadow, he peered through the railings. The tramp was there; at least, there was a dark motionless heap, which told Cub what he wanted to know. Backing away he conveyed the information to the others.

'Leave 'im ter me,' breathed Copper.

'No noise,' warned Cub.

'There won't be no noise, mate,' murmured Copper meaningly.

They moved on, slowly, silently, Copper now leading. The progress was maintained until the railings were reached. Copper stopped and drew a deep breath. When he moved again it was with such speed that even Cub, prepared for something of the sort, was startled. One vault took Copper over the railings. There was a scuffle and a sharp intake of breath, cut short by a double thump.

Copper reappeared. 'Okay,' he said softly. 'He's sleepin' as peacefully as a baby – and 'e'll stay asleep for a little while, I reckon.'

The others joined him within the precincts of the chapel. The tramp lay in a huddled heap in a corner of the porch.

'Which way now?' asked Copper.

'I think we ought to give the place the once-over from the outside to see if any lights are showing,' whispered Cub. 'If there aren't any you might try getting through the window you used on Sunday.'

'Suits me,' agreed Copper.

'What about this guy?' inquired Trapper, indicating the unconscious sentry.

'I swiped 'im pretty hard,' answered Copper. ''E should be all right for half an hour or so if I know anything about it.'

'The police can pick him up when they come,' put in Cub. 'We're wasting time. Let's look round.'

A cautious reconnaissance of the chapel premises revealed no signs of activity. Not a light showed anywhere.

'Come on, let's get into the joint,' growled Copper impatiently.

Groping his way along a narrow alley he stopped under the window which, he said, was the one he had used on the previous occasion. Entry then had been affected by the simple method of using the blade of his knife to turn the hasp. He tried the same method now; but he did not succeed in opening the window. Instead, he dropped back to inform the others that he was a fool to suppose that the same trick would work twice. Counter-measures had been taken. They took the form of a wedge to prevent the hasp from being turned, and iron bars arranged horizontally across the window frame. 'We'd need a hacksaw to cut a way in and we didn't bring one with us,' he lamented. 'No use wasting time fetching one. We shall have to find another way in. If there ain't one it'll be the first time I've bin beat.'

They tried the front door of the church, not expecting to find it open. Their expectations proved correct. It was locked.

'No use,' muttered Copper, feeling the heavy timber. 'It'd take axes ter knock a 'ole through that, and even then it wouldn't be no easy job.'

'It would also make a certain amount of noise,' Cub pointed out sarcastically.

'Let's try round the back,' suggested Copper.

It was soon discovered that as the one window had been treated, so had the others. As each in turn was tried it was found to be barred.

'Okay, don't worry.' murmured Copper. 'I'll bet there's one they've forgot. It'll be either the pantry or the lavatory. People usually make the mistake of thinkin' they're too small fer a man ter get through. It's easy. You'll see.'

He was right. A small window had been left out of the general scheme. It was so small that Cub looked at it doubtfully. Then he tried to climb through, head first.

Copper pulled him back. 'Not that way – silly,' he growled. 'You'll get your shoulders stuck. Catch hold of the sill with your 'and and pull yourself through feet first.'

Cub tried the new method and to his surprise, after some slight wriggling, found that he could slide through, landing, of course, on his feet instead of his head, as would have been the case had he succeeded in his own method. Switching on his torch he found himself in a small pantry. This told him that he was in the living quarters attached to the chapel. Again he caught the whiff of iodoform. He tried the door. It was unlocked and gave access to a passage. The silence was of a tomb. He took pains not to break it. Advancing with infinite care he found the back door. It was locked and bolted. Still taking the greatest possible care not to make the slightest noise, he unfastened the door. Copper and Trapper stepped in. Trapper closing the door behind him.

'Where are we?' whispered Copper.

'We're in the house attached to the back of the chapel – Wenson's living quarters, I imagine,' answered Cub.

'Let's explore.'

'All right. Hark!' Cub did no more than breathe the last word.

Somewhere at no great distance a door had opened and closed. For the two or three seconds it was open a faint murmur of conversation could be heard. This was cut off by the closing of the door.

'They're still here, anyway,' whispered Copper. 'Let's look round. Cub, you're lightest on yer feet – you go first. I shall be close behind if you bump into trouble. Use yer torch, but switch it off if you hear anyone amovin'.'

In silent procession they made their way along the corridor and presently came to a door on the left. Very slowly Cub turned the handle and opened it, first an inch, then more. It was the vestry, the scene of his encounter with Wenson and the doctor. The room was unoccupied. A door at the far side, he knew, gave access to the church. He glanced into it, but all was in darkness.

'We shall 'ave ter get a move on; it'll start ter get daylight in less than no time,' whispered Copper.

Proceeding, they had only taken a pace or two when Cub halted again. He looked at the others, raising his eyebrows. Speech was unnecessary. Near at hand two people were engaged in conversation. The voices came from behind the next door on the right. Cub jerked a thumb. 'In there,' he breathed.

Even as the words left his lips a hand was laid on the door handle from the far side. His torch was out instantly, but it made no difference. The door of the room swung open and the corridor was flooded with light.

What followed occurred faster than it can be told. The man who had opened the door was the doctor – Doctor Guthram Paul. Cub recognised him instantly. The doctor was still talking when he opened the door, but when he saw the invaders in the corridor the words died on his lips. For a split second, while the reek of iodoform flooded out of the room, no one moved; then the doctor, with a single action, slammed the door; but not before Cub had caught a glimpse of the interior of the room. He did not see much, but what he saw was significant. A man, obviously the patient with whom the doctor had been talking, was lying on a small bed of the 'camp' type. From behind the closed door came a shout of alarm.

'Get going, Copper,' rapped out Cub. 'It's our only chance now.'

Copper needed no second invitation. Now that they were discovered the need for stealth had gone. Putting his foot against the lock he sent the door crashing inwards, the lock torn from the woodwork. His war experience made him side-step automatically as the door went in; and it was as well that he did so, for a pistol crashed. The bullet crossed the corridor to bury itself with a vicious thud in the wall. The lights went out, but Trapper was already shooting. Cub could see the sparks streaming from the muzzle of his gun to end at a stumbling figure. He switched on his torch, and by that time the doctor was on the floor. The patient was no longer in the bed. The clothes had been flung off, and the man might have made his escape had he not in his haste caught the tail of his pyjama jacket in the door by which he was leaving the room. Foolishly, as it fell out, he opened the door again to release himself. He would have done better to discard his jacket. With a bound Copper had crossed the room. Reaching out he caught the fugitive by the back of his pyjamas, dragged him back and flung him on the bed, where he lay panting.

'Never mind him,' said Cub tersely. 'There must be others. It's Gimlet we want.'

There was only one way to go, and that was through the door by which the sick man tried to leave. It opened into a corridor. Down this Copper sped to fling open a door at the far end. Cub was hard on his heels, but he now stopped short, astonished at the sight that met his gaze.

Before them was a long low room which, since it ran under the chapel, was actually a cellar, but a cellar much larger than a genuine place of worship could have demanded for any proper purpose. The walls, Cub noted at a glance, were of concrete. But for the furnishings the place might have been a public air raid shelter; and, Cub thought, during the war it might well have been used for such a purpose by those who frequented the chapel. The furnishings were curious. They reminded Cub of a courtroom. So much he observed in one sweep of the eyes. At the same time he noted subconsciously that the atmosphere was warm. This, and a faint aroma of tobacco smoke gave the impression that the place had recently been occupied. However, there was no time for attention to details, for with a shout Copper was on the move again, fairly leaping across the seating accommodation towards an aperture in the wall that had just started to close. This aperture was, in fact, a sliding door, the moving part being to all appearances concrete as solid as the walls. Seeing that he would not reach it in time to prevent its closure Copper snatched up a heavy chair and flung it into the gap. The door crushed it slightly, then stopped, from which it was evident that the machinery operating the device was of no great strength.

'Watch your step!' cried Cub in a warning voice, as Copper, ignoring risks of which he must have been aware, went on towards the opening.

Copper, growling a remark which Cub did not catch, raced on. Revolver in hand he jumped over the chair into the darkness beyond. Cub held his breath, fully expecting shots, but none came.

Trapper now joined Cub. 'I've tied that guy to the bed,' he announced. 'Where's Copper?'

Cub pointed.

'Let's go,' snapped Trapper.

Cub jumped over the chair. His torch revealed a narrow subway. The walls were of brick and obviously of fairly recent construction. Somewhere ahead, at a distance impossible to judge, a nebulous area of light was dancing. Cub made it out to be someone running in front of him, holding a torch, presumably Copper; it struck him as a most dangerous thing to do, but it was obviously impossible to proceed without a light of some sort. A pistol shot crashed, another, and another, and bullets came slithering and scuttering as they ricocheted from floor to walls along the tunnel. After that the only sound was the echoing thud of running feet. It was a weird, unreal effect, and Cub was not sorry when he came upon Copper standing at a point, a junction, where the tunnel ran into a subway of greater size. Here the brickwork was much older, besides being in a foul condition, and for a moment Cub wondered what they had struck. A ledge, a sort of catwalk about two feet wide running along one side of the tunnel, gave him a clue. He recalled seeing a picture of such a place in one of the illustrated magazines.

'This is one of the old London sewers,' he told the others.

Copper answered that he already knew that. What worried him was, he could turn to left or right, and he was uncertain which way to go.

Trapper answered the question. After examining the ledge closely in the light of his torch he pointed to the right. 'That's the way they went,' he declared, and the pursuit was resumed as fast as circumstances would permit.

Cub, being lightest on his feet, took the lead. A sound of splintering woodwork some distance ahead spurred him on, and before he had gone far, grey light, light that could only be daylight, appeared at no great distance. As he drew near he saw that it came from a large jagged hole, as if the end of the tunnel had been boarded over and someone had smashed a way through it. Figures could be seen silhouetted against the light. There appeared to be several. He put on a spurt, and a moment later all lesser sounds were drowned in the throbbing roar of a powerful engine. Out of the corners of his eyes he noticed that the floor of the sewer, below him and on the left, was now a turgid stream of water along which surged sinister ripples. It did not require much imagination to guess the cause. The engine that he could hear was the power unit of a boat of some sort.

With his attention now focussed on the figures that loomed darkly against the eerie light, Cub tore on. Sometimes the figures were a confused blur; at other times they seemed to open and close as they sank down into what he soon made out to be a boat. Then one of the figures detached itself from the rest. There was a shout. An arm was raised. It fell, and as it fell the detached figure recoiled and disappeared. There was a loud splash. Instantly the roar of the engine became deafening; then, as suddenly, it began to recede.

Panting, Cub arrived at the end of the tunnel just in time to see a motor boat in which several figures were hunched, fade into a pea-soup fog that hung low over the sullen waters of a large river which could only be the Thames. He perceived that dawn had broken, but he wasted no time in contemplation of it. Sick with disappointment he climbed through a large advertisement hoarding facing the river, and stared about him. There was nothing he could do. There was no way to left or right. Water lapped at his feet. Remembering the splash he had heard he looked down at the water, not really expecting to see anything; but as he stared there was a swirl, and for a second a pallid face broke the surface. Shouting to the others who now ran up behind him he threw off his jacket and jumped in. Not knowing the depth of the water he dare not risk a dive. The sudden immersion nearly paralysed him, but groping about he found what he sought. His fingers closed in the material of a garment and he came up dragging a body with him. It was heavy, so heavy that alone he could not have got it out; but Copper, seeing his plight, helped him. Gasping, dripping water, Cub got to his knees to see Gimlet trying to do the same thing. Copper and Trapper were helping him.

Gimlet was conscious, but seemed half dazed. He was in a dreadful state. There was mud on his clothes and blood on the side of his face. His collar had been wrenched back to front and his hands had been fastened

Cub arrived just in time to see the motor boat disappear into the fog.

behind him with a piece of cord. This Copper lost no time in removing. Trapper gave Gimlet a handkerchief to wipe his face. Situated as they were there was nothing more they could do.

It was a minute or two before Gimlet could speak. Then he said, 'Which way did they go?'

Cub pointed. 'They got away in a motor boat.'

Gimlet wrung the water from his hair and eyes. 'No use worrying about it. They had everything set for a getaway. I'm lucky to be here. Br-r-r – it's cold. Let's get out of this.'

'What about your face, sir?' asked Copper. 'Someone hit you pretty hard.'

Gimlet stood up. 'It's nothing serious. Wenson tried to crown me with the butt of his pistol. I'll tell you about it later. There's nothing we can do here. Let's go home and get into some dry clothes. The police will never find that boat in this fog.'

They set off up the tunnel. Before they had gone far, lights appeared, and the sound of running footsteps could be heard. But the newcomers turned out to be a police sergeant and some constables. The sergeant challenged, but when he realised who they were he came on.

Gimlet told him that he need not go any farther, and why. As they walked back up the tunnel the sergeant informed them that the General was in the chapel. He went on to say that the cordon was just being formed when shots inside the chapel buildings had caused the General to give the order to break in. The police were now in occupation.

Reaching the underground chamber the first person they saw was the General, who, upon their arrival, greeted them with a cry of relief. 'I was afraid they'd got you!' he exclaimed, speaking to Gimlet. Then, when he saw the condition they were in he suggested that they should go straight on to headquarters for a bath and a change of clothes. He would join them there as soon as he had made the arrangements called for by the situation.

Gimlet gave him a brief account of what had happened, after which, in a police car, they went on to Brummel Square.

CHAPTER TWELVE

A Wolf Comes Back

Some three hours later, after a hot bath, an overdue meal and a change of clothes, in the presence of the General notes were compared and Gimlet was able to tell the others how he had fallen into the hands of the enemy, and what had happened afterwards – not, as he explained, that there was very much to tell.

The trouble really began, he revealed, when he had taken his seat on the platform of the village hall at Lorrington. When he sat down in his chair he was conscious of a sharp pain, a prick, and looking for the reason he discovered a drawing pin. He thought little of it at the time. He certainly did not connect it with the Werewolves. He took it to be a mischievous prank on the part of someone with a warped sense of humour, or else it had been left there, carelessly, by the people who had decorated the hall for the occasion. In the light of subsequent events he had realised that it had been deliberately planted there. The chair provided for him, as President, was in the middle; moreover, it was the largest, so there could be no mistake as to where he would sit. The point of the pin, asserted Gimlet, must have been treated with some sort of drug or poison, although there was no indication of that at the time.

'I imagine it would be one like this,' put in the General, taking a match-box from his pocket and shaking out of it a number of squat, rather fat drawing pins.

'Exactly,' agreed Gimlet quickly. 'Where did you get those?'

'I found them at the chapel – to say nothing of some other interesting lethal devices,' returned the General. 'Watch.' Picking up a pencil he pressed gently on the point of the pin. It sank slightly and two drops of liquid oozed out. 'It works rather on the lines of a snake's poison fangs – simple but effective,' murmured the General. 'I imagine they could be used either for poison or dope, as the case demanded. But carry on.'

'In my case it must have been dope,' resumed Gimlet. 'I remember feeling drowsy, but it was not until I stood up to speak that I realised that something was seriously wrong, and then it was too late to do anything about it. I recollect the lights going out, and that's all. I must have lost consciousness. When I came round I was in the chapel, although I did not know it at the time.'

He went on to describe how the doctor, who was one of several people present, was just putting away a hypodermic syringe, having injected him with an antidote for the drug. At any rate, his faculties quickly returned. When it was seen that he was fully conscious he was taken to an imitation courtroom where a mock trial was staged, with a masked man playing the part of judge. Wenson was there. He acted as the prosecuting counsel, reading a list of alleged crimes. There was no question of putting up any sort of resistance, explained Gimlet, because his hands were tied behind his back. Moreover, he was guarded by two men who wore the wolf headdress of the organization.

Suddenly, he continued, there was a good deal of noise overhead, and soon afterwards the proceedings were interrupted when a man burst into the room to say that the police were upstairs. The result was a panic flight in which he hoped he might be overlooked and left behind. In this he was disappointed. He was grabbed by his guards and taken along the escape tunnel which now appeared. Wenson seemed determined that he should go with them, and that undoubtedly would have happened had not two factors combined to prevent it. The first was the speed of the pursuit, which gave Wenson no time to get the retreat properly organized; the second, said Gimlet, smiling at the recollection, was his own behaviour. Perceiving that he was doomed and so had nothing more to lose, he refused to walk, which meant that his guards had to half carry, half drag him along. This not only slowed down the escape, but kept the retreat in a state of pande-monium. Gimlet smiled again as he described how, on reaching the boat, he had kicked out at everyone who came within reach. This also helped to make the arrangements for departure run less smoothly.

Here the General put in another word. 'What I can't understand is why they didn't shoot you out of hand.'

'Some of them were most anxious to,' replied Gimlet. 'But you know what the average German is for implicit obedience to orders – not so much as a matter of willing discipline as because he is scared stiff of the people over him. Apparently Wenson's orders were to get me alive, and to give the devil his due he tried his utmost to do that. Had he not been cluttered up with me the whole bunch could have got away quite comfortably; as it was, there seemed to be a fair chance that if I continued throwing my weight about I might sink the ship – literally. Finally, as the business was getting urgent – we could hear someone running up the tunnel – even Wenson lost his temper and made a swipe at me with the butt of his pistol. I ducked, but I was not quite fast enough, with the result that instead of the pistol landing on my skull it caught me on the side of the face and knocked me into the drink.'

'I saw that happen,' declared Cub.

'That's all there was to it,' concluded Gimlet. 'Either they hadn't time to finish me off or else they assumed that I had gone to the bottom for good; anyway, they left me to it. I should have gone to the bottom, too, if you fellows hadn't turned up because with my hands tied I couldn't swim. All I could do was hold my breath and kick out with my legs – and I couldn't have gone on doing that for long.'

Cub then took up the story, giving Gimlet an account of all that had happened since he departed for Lorrington.

The General concluded the debate by describing how, in accordance with Cub's plan, he was throwing a cordon round the chapel when the noise of shooting inside took them in with a rush. There was no opposition. Three casualties were picked up – an unconscious tramp, the Nazi who Trapper had tied to the bed, and the doctor. All were now dead. The tramp had come round and had been shot dead resisting arrest. The doctor had died of gunshot wounds on the way to hospital – presumably the shots that had been fired when Copper burst into the sickroom – and the Nazi had killed himself by poison in the same manner as those in the Hotel Europa. 'In future we shall have to try to remember to unscrew these false teeth they carry,' observed the General drily.

'I put the River Police on to search for the motor boat right away, but they haven't a hope while this infernal fog persists,' he continued. 'We don't even know which way the boat went, upstream or down. The Wolves may have another bolt-hole somewhere, like the one through which they escaped. They might have a hiding place on one of the hundreds of ships of one sort and another in the dock area. To start and search every one, every warehouse and every wharf, isn't a practicable proposition. However, we can rely on the River Police to do everything possible. By the way, the casualties were taken to the mortuary. I put a man from the Yard on the job of going through their clothes to see if there was anything of interest, anything in the nature of a clue to where the others might be going. There was nothing, although after our experience with the two Wolves at the Europa that didn't surprise me. Nazi security precautions were always like iron, so it is only reasonable to expect it from these fellows. The only remaining hope was the doctor's house. I went there myself. There was nothing there, either. The man was unmarried – lived with a housekeeper. She's a German of the sullen sort. She says she knows nothing – which may be true. Anyway, she won't speak. The doctor seems to have been running a genuine practice; his books prove that. He may have been forced into this Werewolf business quite recently, and was then only called upon when he was needed. Anyhow, the point is, up to the moment we've found nothing there likely to help us. I've still got a man searching.'

'What's happening at the chapel?' asked Gimlet.

'I've got two of the best men from the Yard going through the place with a fine comb,' answered the General. 'If you feel up to it I was going to suggest that we went back to see if the search has produced results.'

'I hope it has, or we're going to lose a lot of time trying to pick up the trail again,' said Gimlet. 'We've lost the one we were on, that's certain. The chapel, as a wolf den, is finished. As things fell out that couldn't be prevented, but it's a pity.'

'The Wolves will have to show their tracks somewhere pretty soon,' asserted the General.

'Yes, and when they do it will be to kill somebody,' returned Gimlet bitterly. 'Well, we'll do what we can. I'm still of opinion that the chapel was not the general headquarters of the gang in this country. It may have been the London hide-out, but Wenson was in charge there and he didn't strike me as being the big noise of the entire organization. In fact, I'm sure he wasn't, from the way he dealt with me. He was acting under orders. We know that the Wolves have an aircraft and unless I've missed my guess the King Wolf won't be far away from its base. It seems likely that he would have to go to Germany from time to time, and the only way he could do that would be by air.'

'I think you're right,' agreed the General. 'Apart from going to Germany it is my experience that the head man of any crooked show places himself in the best position to get clear should the need arise. But let's go down to the chapel to see if anything has turned up to give us a fresh scent. That building has been in use for some time, so we've got a fair chance.'

Cub stepped into the conversation. 'Talking of picking up a fresh scent, sir, reminds me of the hunt,' he said. 'Would it be worth while trying to find out how those two Wolves who went hunting managed to get horses? They could hardly have brought them from Germany.'

'I went into that right away,' answered the General. 'Obviously it was an angle not to be overlooked. The horses were hired from a local livery stable, by two strangers. They paid a deposit – which incidentally has been forfeited – and they haven't been seen since. The horses were found wandering about by a farm hand who recognised them and took them back to their stable. But let's get along to the chapel.'

On arrival it was at once evident that the two expert searchers from the Yard had done their job well. The contents of every drawer, cupboard and receptacle, had been collected, neatly arranged and numbered. The walls and floors had been probed for secret hiding places. The result was that a considerable amount of material had been accumulated, much of it of course, being wearing apparel which the Werewolves in the haste of their departure had not had time to pack. There was, in fact, so much stuff that time would be needed to go through it all. Evidence of Werewolf activity was there in plenty. There were weapons of many sorts, bottles and jars of chemicals, grenades, metal gas containers, garotting ropes, daggers – a miscellaneous collection that was not without interest although it served no useful purpose. As the General remarked, it was all stuff that could be replaced easily by the Wolves. In a cupboard had been found a number of the wolfish masks such as had first been seen at the Europa; some were fitted with gas filters, others not. Perhaps the most gruesome discovery was an axe, stated by the General to be a German execution axe, the purpose of which was known to them, although they did not discuss it.

The General, with the help of the men from the Yard, went over everything in turn, while the others watched, satisfied to leave the examination in the hands of men specially trained in the work. This occupied some time, and Cub, getting bored, went for a stroll round. Presently he found himself in the chapel. It was just as he had last seen it. Finding nothing of interest there he walked on to one of the windows that overlooked the street. There was only one person in sight – the Cockney newsagent with whom he had held a conversation on the occasion of his first visit. He was sweeping the pavement in front of his shop. After watching him for a moment it occurred to Cub that the man might be able to tell him something, for he recalled that he had made a remark about knowing most of the regular congregation by sight. Not with any great confidence, but feeling that he might as well be doing something, he unfastened the front door and stepped out.

The newsagent recognised him instantly, and greeted him with a wave. 'What cheer!' he cried, pausing in his sweeping. 'You must 'ave got it bad, mate.'

'Got what bad?' inquired Cub, sauntering along to the man.

'Why, the religious bug. Today ain't Sunday.'

'What of it?'

'Oh, nothin'. I jest wondered if you'd got a special prayer meetin' on or somethin'.'

'What gave you that idea?'

'Well, first I see one o' the regular churchgoers moochin' round, then I see you come out. I thought maybe there was something goin' on.'

Cub's manner changed as the significance of these words dawned on him. 'What's that? You saw one of the regular congregation?'

'Yus.'

'Where?'

''E was 'ere a minute ago. I think I saw 'im go round the back.'

'Ah,' breathed Cub. 'I'll go and find him.' By an effort he kept his voice normal, for if what the man had said was true there seemed to be more than a possibility that those inside were in danger. There was, he reasoned, a chance that the Wolf might be merely a scout, sent round to find out what was happening at the chapel; but even so, in that case there would be no need for him to approach so near. The police car outside would tell him all that he needed to know.

As soon as he was inside the building Cub quickened his steps. The thought in his mind was, should he try to find the Wolf or first warn the others that there was one about? He decided on the latter course, and hastened on towards the door of the vestry, through which he passed to reach the chapel. Reaching it he pulled up short. The door was shut. He was sure that he had left it open. None of the others would be likely to close it. Who, then...? A sudden awareness of danger prompted him to draw his pistol. Taking a step forward on tip-toe, with the greatest possible caution he turned the door handle. To his great relief the door yielded to his pressure and he peeped inside.

One glance confirmed what he half suspected. A man, a young man who was a complete stranger to him, was there. Fortunately his back was towards him. He was working at feverish speed, cutting with a knife a small circle out of the wallpaper; and this he did so easily that there was evidently a hollow behind it. This was proved when an instant later the man impatiently ripped aside the paper to disclose a piece of apparatus, rather like the plunger of a fire extinguisher. With a gasp of satisfaction he thrust the knife into his pocket and reached for the plunger.

Now all this had happened in two seconds of time, but it was plenty long enough to give Cub an idea of what was going on. He had not stood still. He had the man covered, and consequently had ample reason to suppose that he had the situation under control. His voice cut across the room like the lash of a whip. 'Don't move. Get your hands up!'

At the sound the man started violently and looked over his shoulder. He saw Cub at once, of course, but his reactions were not in the least what Cub expected. Instead of being nonplussed, or reaching for a weapon, he let out a yell of triumph, and before Cub could pull trigger, with a swift jerk he thrust the plunger home.

Cub's pistol spat, and although the bullet found its mark it was too late to prevent the movement. What had happened, just what the Wolf had done, he did not know, but the unmistakable triumph in the man's voice boded trouble, if nothing worse. Indeed, the expression of triumphant success still frozen on the Wolf's face as he slid slowly down the wall to collapse in a heap on the floor, terrified him. There was something almost inhuman about it.

A flying leap took him across the room. He flung open the opposite door to come face to face with the others, looking startled, on their way to ascertain the reason for the shot.

'Get out!' shouted Cub. 'Don't ask questions – get out!'

Without further explanation he tore through the building, out of the back door and down the alley as fast as his legs would take him. Not until he reached what he considered a safe distance did he pull up and turn, to see the others coming along with expressions of bewilderment on their faces. The two official searchers followed slowly.

'Run!' yelled Cub.

'What's all this about?' snapped Gimlet.

Feeling rather foolish as nothing had happened, Cub pointed at the chapel. 'There's a Wolf in there.'

Gimlet stopped. 'Then what—?' he began. He got no further. A sheet of flame and smoke leapt skyward, and an instant later they were all flung to the ground by a tremendous explosion and a wave of blast that lifted them off their feet. They lay still with their hands clasped over the backs of their heads while debris rained down. As the clash and clatter died away Cub looked up to see a great pile of rubble where the chapel had been. The others, of course, were also looking at it, but several seconds elapsed before anyone spoke.

Then it was Copper who ejaculated. 'Phew! Swipe me with a blanket! What a wowser.'

They all got to their feet – the General holding a pair of flying boots. From all sides came shouts of alarm. A police whistle shrilled.

Gimlet looked at Cub. 'What was it?' he asked,

Cub told him what he had seen, and done. 'I had a feeling that something of the sort was going to happen,' he concluded. 'There must have been a delayed action fuse in the bomb to give the Wolf a chance to get out – which he would have done I suppose, if my bullet hadn't stopped him. He's inside under the wreckage. I hadn't time to think of getting him out – I was in too much of a hurry to get out myself.'

The General looked at Gimlet and shrugged. 'I suppose we should have taken precautions against such a thing happening,' he said wearily. 'But there, it isn't easy to think of everything when you are dealing with madmen. Let's get back to headquarters. We can leave the local police to deal with this mess. I have at least saved the boots. Luckily I had them in my hand at the time.'

Just what the General meant by this was not clear to Cub, but he understood later.

The police car, which had been standing by the front door, was, of course, a complete wreck, but they hired a taxi which, under the General's instructions, took them, not to Brummel Square as Cub expected, but to Scotland Yard. Asking the others to wait the General went inside, taking the flying boots with him. He was away about five minutes. When he returned it was without the boots, but he made no reference to them. The taxi went on to Brummel Square.

CHAPTER THIRTEEN

Dead Men's Boots

After lunch, as they sat over their coffee discussing the situation that had arisen, Cub's curiosity regarding the flying boots was satisfied. He had a feeling that the General was waiting for something, and because of the reference to the boots at the time of the explosion he suspected that it had some connection with them, although he could not imagine what.

The telephone rang. The General answered it and had a long conversation with someone, although the person at the other end did most of the talking. The General's comments were confined to an occasional 'Yes ... quite so,' Having rung off he returned to his seat.

With a ghost of a smile hovering about his lips he said: 'I shall now have to let you into one of our little backstage secrets. We have quite a number of departments at the Yard about which the public knows nothing, departments where the latest scientific knowledge is applied to the detection of crime. One such department would, I think, win the warm approval of that redoubtable sleuth, Mr Sherlock Holmes, who, you may remember, had a wonderful eye for detail. He could tell, or he pretended to be able to tell, where a man came from by the colour of the mud on his boots. But that was before the era of fast transport. Nowadays, with travel made easy, colour is hardly enough. We prefer to rely on chemical analysis. Just before the explosion occurred in the chapel I was pleased to come across a pair of flying boots. It was not so much the boots that pleased me as the fact that there was a good quantity of mud on them. This was the most promising clue I had struck. It was interesting to note in the first place that the man who had used them, whom we must presume was an air pilot, found it necessary to operate from a small airfield – or from a place that was not, in fact, a regulation airfield. Most modern airfields are provided not only with a concrete or macadam apron in front of the hangars, but with concrete runways, for which reason pilots, air crews and passengers, are able to keep their footwear reasonably clean. The pilot in this case, however, had obviously been walking about a very muddy field. That was the first clue – a slender one, of course, because mud alone could not have given us even an inkling of the locality of this particular field.' The General sipped his coffee.

'In the department of the Yard to which I referred a moment ago there are filed several thousand analyses covering every type of soil found in Great Britain. This has enabled the officer in charge of the department, who just rang me up, to state definitely that the mud on the boots is peculiar to the eastern side of the county of Norfolk. He can be even more specific than that. The mud was picked up on the edge of one of the lakes, known locally as broads, or from one of the canals that sometimes connect them.'

'How did he work that out?' asked Gimlet.

'Had the mud been picked up from agricultural land – that is, arable land – analysis would reveal traces of organic or chemical manure, which in fact, it does not. Had the man been walking over grass land the question would not have arisen, because the boots could hardly have picked up so much mud. The mud on the boots is river mud. A further proof of that is, the mud contains only one sort of seed – stinging nettles. All earth contains a certain number of seeds, mostly grasses. But in damp earth they either grow or they rot – all except stinging nettle seeds. The seeds of the nettle will last under water for twenty years or more, which is why, when a river has been dredged, you will always find a good crop of nettles springing up on the bank. So the fact that the mud on the boots carries a number of stinging nettle seeds suggests, if it does not actually prove, that the wearer picked up the mud on the banks of a recently dredged waterway.'

'That fits in with what we already know,' asserted Gimlet. 'I'm thinking of the type of aircraft we know the Wolves are using. A flying-boat or amphibian could land easily on one of the Norfolk Broads, which, when you come to think about it, are one of the few places where such an aircraft could land, outside marine airports. Moreover, some of the broads are very lonely, certainly at this time of the year. Another point worth taking into consideration too, is the fact that Norfolk is on the east coast, the most convenient point for flying to and from Germany.'

'Quite so.' The General sat back in his chair. 'Well, gentlemen, there you are. I think you will agree that the Norfolk Broads should be given the once-over. It does not necessarily follow, of course, that the Wolves have made their headquarters there; but if we can locate the enemy's air base we might get a line on it.'

'The only snag about that I can see is this: it's going to take some time to cover all that ground,' observed Gimlet.

'We can save a lot of time by using aircraft ourselves,' the General pointed out. 'I wasn't thinking of exploring Norfolk on foot. We needn't take to the air to do it. We can leave that to the Special Air Police, who have already helped us, and I am sure will be pleased to do so again. I'm all in favour of using up-to-date methods, particularly as the enemy is doing that. We must not forget too, that it takes a trained eye to pick out from the air objects on the ground.'

'Even if the Air Police had to reconnoitre the whole of the Broads area it wouldn't take them very long,' put in Cub. 'They carry cameras. They could photograph all likely spots, anything that might indicate an aircraft landing station.'

'Exactly,' agreed the General. 'That is obviously the most expeditious way of setting about it. If everyone is agreed, I'll ring up Bigglesworth, who is in charge of the air squad, to see what he can do about it.'

The General went to the telephone, put through the call on the private wire and had a long conversation. When he came back he said: 'That's fixed. Biggles – that's what they call him – doesn't let grass grow under his tyres, so to speak, when he takes on a job. He's putting four machines in the air right away; in fact, he says he'll go out himself. Visibility is good along the east coast so each machine will take on a zone and photograph any likely spots. He'll have the photographs developed right away and bring the prints round this evening. That seems to be all we can do for the moment. You fellows had better get in a few hours rest while the opportunity offers. You can't go on without sleep. If Bigglesworth should happen to spot anything you may have a busy time ahead of you. We must keep going if it is humanly possible, to prevent these fiends from resuming their programme of murder in their own time.'

This was agreed and the meeting adjourned.

Cub went to his room. He needed no rocking. Throwing off his jacket he fell on his bed and slept like a log for four hours, although he disputed the time hotly when, after what seemed like ten minutes he was awakened by Copper to be told that it was nearly six o'clock and that Sergeant Bigglesworth of the Air Police was below with a batch of photos.

Cub lost no time in getting into his jacket and joining the others in the conference room. Photographs, still damp, were lying all over the table, and the Chief of the Air Police, with a large magnifying glass in his hand, was talking about them. As Cub joined the party he smiled a greeting and went on with what he was saying.

'On the whole the reconnaissance would appear to be rather disappointing; but then, we could hardly expect these people to be so foolish, so ill-advised, as to litter the area with obvious signs of their presence. We were able to save a lot of time by ignoring the larger broads which, as they are overlooked by roads, hotels and houses, would hardly suit their purpose. As far as the lesser-known sheets of water are concerned we pinpointed three places, one of which might turn out to be what you are looking for. The one which looks most promising came into Hebblethwaite's zone. He called me on his radio to look at it, which I did. I daren't go too low for fear of alarming the Wolves if they were there, but I had a good look and took several photos, both vertical and oblique, from different angles. Of course, there was no aircraft on view, but we could hardly expect that. Here are the prints. This particular piece of water is known locally as Grimston Broad. For reference purposes I have called it Objective A.' Biggles picked up half a dozen enlarged photographs and arranged them in line on the table.

Taking a magnifying glass the General examined each one in turn. 'There doesn't seem to be much here,' he observed in a voice that held a suspicion of disappointment.

'Actually, there is more than you might suppose,' returned Biggles. 'Suppose I read the picture for you as I see it.'

'Please do,' invited the General.

'The first thing that might strike you is, the actual water area seems to be on the small side,' began Biggles. 'So it is, but the shape is important. As you can see, the water is in the shape of a letter T. Admittedly, the two arms are narrow, but arranged as they are they could enable a pilot to take off no matter in what direction the wind was blowing. In other words you can take it from me that an efficient pilot, in normal weather conditions, could put a marine aircraft down on that water and take it off again. The very fact that by reason of its shape no one in the ordinary way would imagine an aircraft landing on it, would all be in favour of these Nazis if, in fact, they are using it. The next point is this. It is just about as lonely a spot as you could find in England. There isn't a house within four miles. The nearest village is Reedsholm, and that's a good five miles away.'

The General pointed with his pencil to a small black mark not far from the water. 'What's this thing?' he inquired.

'I'm just coming to that,' answered Biggles. 'The nearest road, a second class road, is nearly three miles away, although from it there is what appears to be an overgrown track, originally an accommodation road, no doubt, leading to the building you just put your finger on. That is a windmill. As you probably know, windmills are a common feature in Norfolk. In passing I might mention – although it hasn't much bearing on our case – that the land near the windmill was once under cultivation. If you examine the photograph closely you can just see faint lines marking out what seem to be squares. Originally those lines were dykes. Apparently the land didn't pay for farming, or it may have been ruined by flood water – but we needn't bother about that.' Biggles lit a cigarette.

'Originally, too, I suspect that Grimston Broad was connected by a waterway to the River Yare,' he continued. 'You can see the line of rushes following the old river bed – or it may have been a canal. That interests us because it means that the windmill could, if it wished, employ water transport, and that is borne out by what seems to be the remains of a large boathouse – here.' Biggles pointed to a dark spot at the extreme end of the broad, where the water approached nearest to the windmill. 'The place is a ruin, or it appears to be,' he went on. 'I looked at it very closely. It appears small in the photo, but when it was in order it could have accommodated a barge; and even now, assuming that it isn't an absolute ruin, it could easily accommodate an aircraft of the folding-wing type.'

'Aren't you drawing rather a long bow?' queried the General dubiously. 'I mean, aren't you rather trying to make the place fit what we would like it to be?'

Biggles smiled. 'Possibly. But I'm only telling you what I see; and that is supported by my final observation, which is this. On the face of it, these buildings – the windmill and the boathouse – haven't been used for years. As a matter of fact, they are both in use now, or they were until recently. There is no actual track leading from the windmill to the boathouse. Doubtless there was one years ago, but it is now overgrown with long grass; but from topsides long grass can tell quite a story. For instance, I can tell you that the grass was disturbed as recently as this morning. It was wet early on, and foggy, you remember? Fog or mist leaves grass loaded with water. If you disturb the grass the water falls off, so that from the air it shows up as a different colour. You can often see that on the grounds if you walk across a field of wet grass; from the air one sees an unmistakable track. This morning somebody walked from that windmill to the boathouse, or *vice versa*. My final point is, perhaps, the most important. There is, in that old boathouse, a piece of machinery of some sort. For a distance of thirty or forty yards in front of it the water is of a slightly different shade to the rest. That is caused by oil on the water. If there is oil there then we may take it that a machine of some sort isn't far away.'

'Ah,' breathed the General, 'That makes a difference. It begins to look as if this might be the place we're looking for.'

'It's the most likely place I could find in the short time at my disposal,' replied Biggles.

'You didn't see anybody moving about near the windmill?'

'Had I done so I should have dismissed the place from my mind instantly,' answered Biggles, smiling faintly. 'Wolves don't walk about in the open when hunters are on the trail.'

'True enough,' agreed the General. 'Then you saw no sign of life at all?'

'None, which again is a factor on our side,' returned Biggles. 'I am taking the expression "signs of life" literally. On or around most of the broads you will see a certain amount of wild life, particularly birds. The fact that there was not a single bird, not even a gull, near the windmill or the boathouse, supports my argument that someone is there, or has been there. Whoever it was disturbed the birds. It is quite possible that someone was moving about right up to the time of my arrival; but as soon as he heard aircraft approaching he would take cover, naturally – or we can assume he would if he was up to no good. If the windmill was occupied by a miller it would seem reasonable to suppose that the sails would be revolving, as there was quite a fair breeze; but they were not. The place looked abandoned, but in my opinion someone is there, or had been there this morning. I needn't remind you that during the war a lot of places looked abandoned when, in fact, they were far from it. Well, sir, there it is. I think that's all I have to say.'

'In your opinion, this place is worth exploring?'

'Definitely. If you like I'll keep an eye on the place from the air for a day or two, but it doesn't necessarily follow that I should get results because even if the Wolves are there they would be most unlikely to show themselves. In all probability they operate only after dark.'

'In view of what has happened during the past twenty-four hours I imagine the Wolves must be pretty busy,' murmured the General. He thought for a moment. 'I'll tell you what I think is the best plan, Bigglesworth. I'll get Captain King to go and have a look round this place right away. It shouldn't take him long to ascertain if there is anyone there or not. If we find we are on a false scent I'll get in touch with you in the morning and you can resume the reconnaissance. If we tackle every possible place in turn sooner or later we ought to find what we're looking for. Naturally, we will start at Objective A, as it is the most promising.'

Biggles got up. 'I think that's your best line, sir. I'll leave the photographs with you. You can study them, and so get the lay-out of the place at your fingertips before you start operations. I may fly over to have a look round as soon as it gets daylight, otherwise I won't take any further action until I hear from you.'

'Very well – we'll leave it at that,' agreed the General. 'Thanks, Bigglesworth, I'm much obliged for your co-operation.'

'That's what we're here for, sir,' returned Biggles, taking his departure.

As soon as the door had closed behind him the General turned to Gimlet. 'Well, how do you feel about having a look at this place?' he suggested.

'I think the sooner I'm on my way the better.'

'Good. I'd better stay here where you can get in touch with me should it become necessary. If you need anything, let me know.'

'We'll see how it pans out,' asserted Gimlet.

The General looked at his watch. 'The time is now seven o'clock. By taking one of the fast cars you ought to be on the spot somewhere about ten.'

'Unless anything goes wrong, or if we draw a blank, we ought to be back by daybreak,' said Gimlet. 'If the Wolves *are* there – well, if we do nothing else we'll stir the devils up and keep them on the move. What do you say, corporal?'

Copper grinned. 'Every time a coconut, sir.'

Gimlet rose. 'All right. We'll see about putting our stuff together.'

'Just one last reminder,' said the General quietly. 'There is no need for me to tell you what you are taking on. If you *should* run into a pack of Wolves don't hesitate to use your guns. Regard the operation as a military one rather than a police job. I'll go so far as to suggest that you imagine the war is still on, and that your task, as commandos, is to take a Nazi military post. Whatever happens you can rely on my support. Any Wolves you find will not submit to arrest, you may be sure of that. They will do their utmost to kill you. Failing that – as we have seen – they will kill themselves. If you can take prisoners without incurring unnecessary risks – well, do so; but in a business of this sort, my policy would be to shoot first and ask questions afterwards. In the interests of those fellows who have been sentenced to death for doing their duty – indeed, in the interests of society – these fanatics must be wiped out, and I don't care how you do it. Nothing could be too bad for them. Already they have blood on their hands. See that they don't get more. That's all. Good luck.'

'They'll get from me what they gave other people,' declared Gimlet grimly.

'That goes for me, too – my oath it does,' muttered Copper.

'All right,' concluded Gimlet. 'Now we've got that clear, let's move off.'

CHAPTER FOURTEEN

'Like Old Times'

It was shortly after ten when the police car cruised quietly into the hamlet of Reedsholm. A few lights showed but for the most part the villagers had evidently retired for the night. Gimlet, who was driving, did not stop, but taking the secondary road pointed out by Biggles, went on with dimmed lights through a flat, dreary landscape, for another mile before slowing down to walking speed.

'We're getting near enough,' he remarked. 'Better not get too close. Keep your eyes open for somewhere to park the car – either side, doesn't matter which, but we must put it out of sight if we can.'

A good parking place was not easy to find, for the country was open, and being windswept could boast of few trees; but after going on for half a mile or so Cub spotted what Gimlet presently agreed was an ideal place. A farm track branched off from the road, and a short distance from it plunged through a thicket of stunted birches and gorse. In the middle of this the car was stopped and they got out. Short of anyone actually walking down the track, an unlikely occurrence at that time of night, the presence of the car would not be suspected.

Looking round as he stepped out Cub decided that the night was well suited to their purpose. A young moon and occasional clusters of stars played hide and seek behind a high layer of cirrus cloud that was drifting up slowly from the west, so that while it was dark there would be just sufficient light to enable them to find their objective without the aid of flash lamps.

As far as the landscape was concerned, nothing more dreary and depressing could be imagined, thought Cub, as he gazed around. The country was practically flat, without a conspicuous landmark of any kind. On one side of the road it appeared to be mostly gorse and heather, with an occasional silver birch, stunted and twisted by the wind. To the left, the direction they would have to take, the land fell away slowly to a wilderness of marsh, a vast area of coarse grass broken only by growths of bullrushes, with here and there small pools of water, the result of recent rain, lying pale and stark under the moon. Every hollow, no matter how small, was draped in dank mist. Not a light showed. Not a sound broke the sullen silence. A more melancholy spectacle could not have been visualised, decided Cub, as he turned away to help with the equipment.

'Blimey! This is like old times,' murmured Copper softly, as he fingered a Sten gun affectionately. 'Do you think we shall need this, sir?'

'We'll take it to be on the safe side,' answered Gimlet. 'You haven't forgotten how to handle one, I hope?' he added slyly.

'There are some things you don't ever forget, sir, and this is one of 'em,' answered Copper simply. 'What say you, Trapper, old pal? Am I right?'

'*Tch*! Every time,' agreed Trapper.

'Are you goin' ter take yer bow-and-arrer?'

'It may come in useful,' asserted Trapper softly.

'Better take a rifle as well,' ordered Gimlet. 'What about you, Cub?'

'I think I shall be able to hold my own with my thirty-eight,' replied Cub.

'All right; then as you haven't much to carry, you can hump these along,' requested Gimlet, passing a small but heavy bag.

'What's in here, sir?' inquired Cub.

'Grenades,' returned Gimlet. 'I thought we'd better have a few with us in case we have to do any winkling. It's always a good thing to have any tools you are likely to want with you – one doesn't always have time to go home and fetch them.'

In a few minutes they were ready to march. Gimlet locked the doors of the car and made an unhurried survey of the landscape. Then he looked at his watch. 'The time is now ten-thirty,' he announced. 'We have an hour's march in front of us. I daren't risk taking the car any nearer in case the enemy has scouts out, and over these damp marshes sound travels a long way on a still night. It's an even chance that the whole thing may turn out to be a flop, but it's better not to look at it that way. Bigglesworth knows what he's talking about, so we'll behave as if we knew for certain that the enemy is in force at the objective. In fact, we'll act as though we were in Germany with the war still on. No noise, and no more talking than is necessary, and then speak in whispers. If we draw blank – well, we shall have a good laugh about it. If we are on the right track there'll be nothing to laugh about. Our best chance will be to spring a surprise, and then hit hard and fast. All right. If we're all ready let's move along. The idea is to keep parallel with the road until we strike the track that leads to the windmill. If we tried marching on a compass course across this marsh we might find ourselves bogged. Let's go.'

In single file and in silence, with Gimlet leading, the party set off. Cub took second place and Copper brought up the rear.

More than once during the march that followed Cub found it hard to convince himself that this was really happening. Everything conspired to make it seem like a dream – the gloom, the silence, the lack of colour, the vague outlines of the landscape and the apparent lack of anything solid. Together these created an atmosphere of unreality not easy to dispel.

More difficult still did he find it to believe that this was happening in England. It was something that belonged to the past, to the period known as the War, a curious interlude in his life that was already becoming a memory. It was as though he was in some strange way living something over again, something that had already happened – which in a way was true, for he had made several such marches, with the same companions and in similar circumstances.

Instinctively nerves became keyed up, each one super-sensitive, ready on the slightest provocation to play tricks with the imagination. Commonplace features that occurred by the wayside, features that would pass unnoticed or ignored in the broad light of day, became distorted, became objects of suspicion, of apprehension and of fear. A tuft of gorse became a crouching man, and the rustle of bullrushes, moved by an imperceptible breath of air, became the swish of enemy feet advancing through long grass.

It was an eerie sensation too, this marching, marching, marching, moving over the ground without seeming to get anywhere – for one aspect of the landscape was as another – towards an objective which, still unseen, lurked somewhere in the mysterious distance ahead. It seemed hours before Gimlet held his right hand high and the party came to a halt.

Turning left Gimlet gazed steadily for some time, and then pointed to what appeared to be a long strip of grey material lying across the marsh, perhaps a quarter of a mile away. 'That's Grimston Broad,' he whispered. 'The windmill is a trifle to the right. We should soon see it against the sky. We'll have a look at the boathouse first. That may tell us something. I think we might try a straight march now. If we strike a wet patch we shall have to make a detour. Keep your eyes skinned.'

Copper was staring into the gloom. 'There's no light at the windmill or we should see it.'

'If they're there they'll have the place blacked-out for fear of attracting attention,' returned Gimlet. 'Let's move on. Open out a bit – say, to intervals of ten yards.'

The march was resumed, in the same order, with even more caution, Gimlet stopping frequently to survey the landscape, crouching when the moon sailed clear of the clouds. Cub also examined the ground around methodically, but could not make out a movement of any sort. In the heart of the lonely waste the silence seemed even more intense, and such sounds as were audible from time to time were so out of place, and so distant, that they might have belonged to another world. Once it was a church clock striking the hour of eleven, and, shortly afterwards, the whistle of a locomotive.

Before they had gone very far the gaunt sails of the windmill slowly took shape against the sky, like black arms upflung in a sinister 'stop' signal. The actual boathouse could not be seen because a straggling clump of osiers, near which it was situated, intervened. Making no more noise than shadows, the party moved nearer and ever nearer to it, and it was during a halt, when they were no more than a hundred yards away, that a minor incident occurred which, for uncanny effect, surpassed anything in Cub's experience.

It began when the silence was stabbed by a sound that can best be described as a *honk-honk*. Cub thought it was a motor car sounding its horn, and he went flat, as did the others. Peering over the fringe of grasses in front of his face he stared in the direction of the sound, expecting to see a vehicle. He could see nothing, yet a moment later the sound came again, closer this time, a single *honk*. This time it came from somewhere in the air.

Listening with every nerve strained and muscles tense, Cub soon became aware of another sound, a musical swishing hum that rose and fell with machine-like regularity. It seemed to approach so quickly, and was now so close, that instinctively he ducked; and then, as he realised suddenly what it was, his nerves relaxed and drama came near to comedy. Suddenly out of the tenuous mist, to swing overhead not twenty feet above, appeared a skein of geese flying in perfect V formation. As the flight passed over the leader let out another *honk-honk*, and after the utter silence the sound was so loud and so incongruous that Cub could have laughed. The weird noise receded swiftly and the birds were soon lost to sight.

Gimlet raised himself and gave the advance signal.

The next five minutes would be, Cub knew, the critical time. If a sentry was on the watch, or should there be anything in the nature of an automatic alarm signal set, it was now that their presence would be discovered.

Time seemed to stand still. The forward movement became slower and slower. Gimlet, who was ten yards ahead of Cub, sometimes stopped and spent a full minute staring at the boathouse, which could now be seen, not clearly, but rather as a confused dark mass with its outline broken up by straggling osiers. At a distance of perhaps a dozen paces Gimlet signalled to the others to join him.

When the party had mustered he breathed: 'I'm going on alone now. I can't hear anything, and there are no lights that I can see, but it wouldn't be safe to take too much for granted. Cub, you'll stay here. Trapper will stay with you. Copper, find yourself a position out of sight between the boathouse and the windmill. If anyone is here, and bolts, that's the way he'll go. Stop him, but avoid shooting if possible. The more silently we work now the better chance we shall have. If trouble starts in the boat-house you'd better come in. If all remains quiet stay where you are till I come back. Is that clear?'

'Clear enough, sir,' whispered Copper.

Without speaking again Gimlet moved like a wraith towards the boat-house. Cub was able to watch him for a minute, then the shadow merged into the dark silhouette of the building. His heart began to beat faster now, as it always did on such occasions. He was very conscious of it, but there was no way of steadying it. Each tiny sound, magnified out of all proportion by the situation, reacted on it as on a delicate instrument. There was nothing unusual about this, of course. Suspense is always a greater strain than action.

Ten minutes passed – it seemed much longer – and then he saw Gimlet coming back. He was walking upright so he knew there was no immediate cause for concern. Indeed, an unpleasant feeling of disappointment, that they had drawn a blank, that this was all a wasted effort, surged through him. This emotion was soon corrected, however.

'Fetch Copper,' commanded Gimlet curtly, as he came up.

In a minute Cub had carried out the order, and Gimlet led the party into the osiers. 'Now listen carefully,' he said softly. 'I think we're on the right track. There's nothing in the boathouse, but it has been in use quite recently. It has a feeling, a smell, as if people were in there not long ago. It isn't a ruin. It may have been one some time ago, and it still looks like one from the outside, but the inside has been repaired and it is now snug and watertight – and light-proof. The water – that is, the lake – comes right in, and there are recent footsteps in the mud on either side. There's a big store of oil and petrol, which may be aviation spirit – I don't know. The place is being used either for a motor boat or an aircraft – at least, I can't see how it can be anything else. There's an entrance on the landward side but the door's locked. The gable end over-hanging the lake is open and I was able to get in by wading. There's nobody there at the moment.'

'Then it's no go, sir,' muttered Copper.

'Not so far as this place is concerned. Whatever type of vehicle is using the place it isn't there now, and without any idea of how long it is going to be away I don't think it would be advisable to sit here and wait for it to come back. We'll try the windmill.'

Cub, who happened to be gazing in the direction of the building, stiffened suddenly. '*Ssh!*' he breathed, catching Gimlet by the arm to add weight to his warning.

They all stood motionless for several seconds. Then, as nothing happened, Gimlet said quietly: 'What was it? Did you think you saw something?'

'I saw a flash of light,' answered Cub. 'It may have been a window or it may have been a door opening. I couldn't have been mistaken. There's somebody there.'

'Stand fast,' breathed Gimlet.

They heard a man approaching before they saw him. He stumbled over something and cursed. An electric torch showed for a moment before being switched off again. Then a dark figure separated itself from the black mass of the windmill and the matter was no longer in doubt. A man was coming down to the boathouse. Before he reached it he stopped and looked back. The reason became apparent when a second figure appeared, hurrying, following the same track. He overtook the first man and they continued together. Even more important than their appearance was the fact that they spoke in low tones, and the language they used was not English. It was German. Cub recognised the sound of it although he was not able to distinguish the actual words. Hardly daring to breathe he waited to see what Gimlet would do.

Gimlet did nothing. He might have been a block of stone for all the movement he made.

The two men reached the landward side of the boathouse. A key scraped in a lock. A chain clinked. A door rasped as it was pushed open and the men disappeared from sight.

'We could have grabbed those two,' breathed Copper.

'We shall get them with less noise where they are,' averred Gimlet. 'Before I start knocking people about I want to be sure that they're the people we're after.'

'They were talking German,' said Cub softly.

'So I heard. But they might be a couple of German prisoners, posted here for land work, sent out by a farmer to do some job or other. There are plenty of German prisoners about.'

'I'd forgotten that,' confessed Cub.

'We shall soon tell from their conversation what they are,' asserted Gimlet. 'If we decide to nail them we shall handle them better where they are than outside. They didn't lock the door behind them or we should have heard it. Let's go and see if we can find out what they're doing; that will be the guide to our future actions. Quietly.'

This conversation had, of course, been carried on in voices so low that only those for whom they were intended could hear them.

Gimlet moved forward and the others followed. From a distance of five yards they learned all they wanted to know for the men, behaving as though they were sure they had nothing to fear, made plenty of noise and spoke in ordinary voices as they went about whatever task they had come to do. The language was German, which was as well known to Cub as his own tongue.

Said one, with a short laugh: 'I'd rather be here in the middle of these damned Englanders than sitting at home being told what I can do by the swines, even if there is a risk.'

'There is no risk here,' replied the other. 'For us this is the safest place in the world. Why should anyone come here? I only wish the Fuehrer was here to see how his Wolves still sharpen their teeth on English bones.'

The conversation was continued on these lines, until Gimlet, who could also speak German, nudged Cub, and laying a finger on his lips moved slowly towards the door.

At this moment a new sound was borne on a slant of wind to Cub's ears. It was not loud, but it was significant. It was the whine of a gliding aircraft, surprisingly close. Apparently the sound was also heard by the two men inside, for one of them said sharply. 'So! Here they come. Get the lights on, Karl.'

There was a swift movement inside the boathouse, and a split second later the reeds that lined both sides of the lake were illuminated by a pale, ghostly light. Cub knew enough of aviation to realise that these were boundary lights that had been switched on to mark the landing area.

Gimlet evidently realised it too, for he swung round and whispered tersely: 'That machine's coming here. We've got to get these two before it lands. Trapper, stand fast to stop either of them getting back to the windmill. Corporal, you take the water entrance, and get them if they try to bolt out that way. Come on, Cub.'

Gimlet moved swiftly towards the door.

Overhead a shrill whine announced that the aircraft was nearly down.

CHAPTER FIFTEEN

Objective A

Cub's paramount sensation as he stepped forward with Gimlet was one of curiosity to see what the men inside were doing. Of course, he experienced that tingling sensation that usually precedes an offensive action, but this feeling only had the effect of putting him on his toes, as the saying is. He had left the bag of bombs in the grass because this was obviously an occasion when they would not be needed, but he had his thirty-eight in his hand, not so much because he intended using it – unless he was compelled to do so in self-defence – as because it gave him confidence.

They reached the door. It was ajar. Gimlet gave it a gentle touch with his foot and the scene inside was revealed, in the light of a small electric lamp, as clearly as a picture thrown on a screen.

One of the men, the nearer, was bending down doing something to a rope. The other was standing at the far end of the building gazing up into the sky, apparently watching for the aircraft to appear. It was this man who saw them first. He may have heard a sound, or caught a movement out of the corner of his eyes; or perhaps it was sheer instinct that made him swing round suddenly; but turn he did, and at once saw Gimlet, who was already inside and still advancing.

The man's reaction was the natural one. He let out a sharp cry of alarm and his hand flashed to his pocket. From this moment things happened faster than they can be described.

On hearing the cry, the man with the rope looked up. How much he saw is questionable, for the next instant he went flying backwards as Gimlet's foot came in contact with his chest. Gimlet did not stop. He took two jumps forward, side-stepped, and hurled his revolver into the face of the second man, who by this time had drawn a pistol although he had not had time to raise it. Gimlet's revolver found its mark and sent the man reeling. The Nazi's pistol exploded with a dull *whoof*. The charge, whatever it was, struck the ground, sending mud flying in all directions. Before he could use it again a tall figure loomed up behind him. There was a thump, a gasping intake of breath, and the Wolf collapsed like an empty sack.

Cub only saw this in a detached sort of way, because his attention was occupied by the man Gimlet had kicked over. He was not badly hurt, it seemed; but taken entirely by surprise his actions were defensive rather than offensive. He had fallen on the muddy bank with his legs in the water; he tried to get up, at the same time scrambling away from Cub, who made a rush at him. Cub's haste was his undoing. He, too, slipped on the mud, and sprawled flat on the man already there.

The result was a wrestling bout which lasted for perhaps ten seconds, at the end of which time Gimlet took a hand in the affair. Cub did not see exactly what happened, but feeling his opponent go limp he scrambled quickly to his feet to see Gimlet bending over him.

There was no time for explanations, nor even for an examination of the field of conflict, for Copper in a hoarse whisper announced that the aircraft was down on the water. Actually, Cub was aware of this, for he had heard the swish of the keel and the surge of water as the machine landed.

Gimlet gave his orders. He called Trapper. Then he said, 'Get those fellows trussed up. Put something in their mouths to keep them quiet in case they come round, then dump them in the osiers. Make it snappy. We've only got two minutes.' Having said this Gimlet strode to the end of the boathouse that overlooked the lake. Cub followed him to see the machine only forty yards away, surging slowly under short bursts of throttle towards the place where they stood.

Noticing Cub beside him, Gimlet told him sharply to take up a position at the other door and watch the direction of the windmill. The wisdom of this was evident, as Cub perceived. It was not the moment for they themselves to be surprised by an attack from the rear. He took up his stand, while Copper and Trapper, having tied up their men, dragged them with scant ceremony into the osiers, where they left them.

By the time this was done a voice was hailing from the aircraft, and it was evident that the affair, far from being finished, had barely begun.

As far as Cub was concerned two things were conspicuously clear. The first was that they were now definitely committed to the undertaking, no matter how long the odds were against them. Whether they liked it or not they would have to go on. The second was that the two men who had come down from the windmill had known about the arrival of the aircraft. Their job was to handle it and bring it to its mooring. Much depended now on how many people there were in the machine, passengers and crew. However, there was no time to indulge in speculation on this point.

Gimlet gave his orders as quickly as the circumstances demanded. Copper and Trapper were instructed to take cover inside the boathouse; they were to watch events, and provide assistance if and where it was most needed.

'They'll know we're not part of their organization as soon as they clap eyes on us,' said Cub.

'I'm well aware of it,' answered Gimlet. 'All we can do is keep in the shadow as far as possible so they don't get a clear view of us until they're all out, by which time we shall be able to see what we're up against. There may be only one man – the pilot. If so, it should be easy.'

Cub said nothing, but he was thinking fast. From the size of the machine, a flying-boat, it could quite easily hold half a dozen people, and if that turned out to be so, the scrimmage that would inevitably occur in the boathouse was going to be a grim business, particularly if shots were fired. It would be difficult, if not impossible, to distinguish friend from foe, and both parties might well cause casualties on its own side. However, there was no time to take measures to prevent this. There was no time to do anything, for the machine, still moving slowly, had reached the boat-house.

A cockpit cover scraped as it was thrown back. The pilot stood up. Cub, standing well back in shadow, could see his silhouette against the sky.

'Are you there, Karl?' called a voice, speaking in German.

'*Ja*,' answered Cub.

'Then why don't you show a light, you fool?' demanded the pilot irritably. 'You know who I've got on board. Let's have a little efficiency.'

So the pilot was not alone, thought Cub swiftly, as he switched on his torch and directed the beam full on the pilot more with the intention of dazzling him than for any other reason.

'Be careful where you're flashing that light,' protested the pilot, who seemed a bad-tempered fellow. 'Catch!' A rope swished through the air and hit Cub in the face. However, he caught hold of it, took in the slack and drew the aircraft in. By this time Gimlet had also switched on his torch, so that while those inside the boathouse were in black shadow the aircraft was bathed in light. This, of course, was a tremendous advantage to those behind the torches.

'Haul away,' ordered the pilot. 'What are you waiting for?'

Cub had to put his pistol in a pocket in order to use both hands on the rope. Gimlet came to his assistance and they backed to the far end of the boathouse dragging the machine with them.

'All right, that's enough,' said the pilot curtly, and without giving any warning of his intention, jumped down, landing almost on top of Cub, so that when he looked up their faces were less than a yard apart. For a spilt second they both stood still, the Nazi and Cub, staring at each other. Cub saw suspicion then fear leap into the Werewolf's eyes. His lips parted and he sprang back, his hand going to his pocket. He may have forgotten that there was another man in the boathouse. At any rate he did not see him, for Gimlet, who had taken a swift pace forward, brought his revolver down on the helmeted head and the man collapsed without a sound.

'Get him out of the way,' said Gimlet in a low, tense voice, and without waiting to see the order obeyed strode to the cabin door and opened it.

Copper darted forward, picked up the unconscious man and carried him out of sight.

With what interest Cub watched the cabin door can be better imagined than described. He stared, fascinated, wondering what was going to happen next. In particular he wondered what Gimlet would do, and what he was expected to do. No order had been given, nor could be given. It was one of those occasions when every member of the party would have to act on his own initiative.

Gimlet held the door wide open and stood behind it. At first Cub thought this was a curious thing to do, but then he saw the reason for it.

Gimlet wanted to ascertain the numerical strength of the enemy before he tackled him; and just what form the attack would take would depend on the number of men they had to deal with. He turned the beam of his torch on the muddy bank so that those inside could see where to put their feet.

A man stepped out of the aircraft – a youngish man. In his left hand he carried a black portfolio. Having alighted he turned and held out a hand to someone inside. A second figure stepped out – this time a heavily-built man in a fur coat.

'Two,' counted Cub, praying fervently that there would be no more.

Another man jumped out – again a young man.

'Three.' The number registered itself on Cub's brain. He was holding his breath under the strain of watching the drama unfold.

To the third man, yet another one inside handed out two suitcases.

As the fourth figure emerged, to Cub's unbounded relief he closed the door behind him, indicating that he was the last.

All four passengers were standing where they had alighted, like four sheep waiting for a shepherd to guide them. It was clear that they had no suspicion of anything wrong. Said the man in the fur coat, speaking in a deep commanding voice: 'Where is the pilot? What is he doing? Why does he leave us standing here?'

Gimlet answered the question. Speaking from behind them he spoke in German, and there was a brittle quality in his voice that made Cub's nerves jump.

'Everyone will raise his hands above his head and stand quite still,' ordered Gimlet.

The words were received with a sort of shocked silence. None of the men moved. It was almost as if their brains had failed to comprehend the order. The only sound was a soft squelch of mud as Cub, pistol in hand, walked two paces nearer. The beam of his torch, held in his left hand, threw the picture into sharp relief.

'Any man who has not raised his hands in three seconds will be assumed to be resisting arrest, and will be shot forthwith,' went on Gimlet relentlessly.

Very slowly one man raised his hands. Another followed, and after a short interval, another. Only the man in the fur coat had not moved.

'Is this a military force?' he inquired.

'It is,' answered Gimlet.

'Then in the event of surrender I shall be entitled to the privileges of a prisoner of war?'

'There is no war apart from the one you have thought fit to wage,' returned Gimlet grimly. 'You are entitled to nothing.'

Cub drew a deep breath. Things were, he thought, going well. And they may have continued to go well had there not at this juncture been an interruption. From somewhere not far away there was a scuffle and a cry of alarm, cut off short. Cub learned subsequently that a man had come down from the windmill, possibly to greet the new arrivals. Copper, who was watching, saw him coming, waited for him and knocked him down, although unfortunately he did not succeed in doing this without a certain amount of noise. Considering everything the noise was negligible, but it was enough to be heard by those inside the boathouse. As far as the prisoners were concerned it seemed to break a spell. Perhaps they thought that assistance was at hand. Be that as it may, as if actuated by a single brain the group broke apart and each man made a dash for liberty.

Gimlet's gun roared twice. Sparks streamed, smoke swirled. There was the vicious *whoof* of a gas pistol. Mud spattered. A lump struck Cub in the face, causing him to wince and drop his torch. A dark figure loomed up in front of him, an arm swinging as if to strike. Cub fired from the hip and the figure sprawled forward, knocking him down. In the flash of his pistol he caught a fleeting glimpse of someone jumping into the aircraft. As he scrambled up there was a splash, and another splash, followed by the thud of running feet. Came a shout, a shot, and the vibrant twang of Trapper's bow.

Gimlet appeared, dripping water. Dashing past Cub he went on to the door. Cub followed. Trapper appeared.

'Did you get him?' Gimlet fired the question.

'Okay, sir – he's down,' answered Trapper dispassionately.

Gimlet swung round, sweeping the floor of the boathouse with his torch. Two figures lay sprawled on the mud. He picked up the black portfolio that lay near one of them. 'There's another one somewhere,' he said sharply.

'He's in the machine,' informed Cub, remembering what he had seen. They all looked at the aircraft.

'Look out! Down!' snapped Gimlet, and they flung themselves flat.

They were only just in time. A machine-gun roared, making a terrible noise in the confined space, and a stream of bullets swept over them. A pile of petrol cans at the back of the boathouse came down with a crash. Cub could see the weapon that caused the mischief projecting from a cabin window. He fired at it without effect. Then Copper's Sten gun came into action, tearing wood, fabric and strips of metal from the side of the machine.

Cub was already half way to his feet, for he had seen what was about to happen. A stench of petrol filled his nostrils. Blue flames danced in the air as the vapour, ignited by the flash of Copper's gun, took fire.

There was a wild rush for the door. Again they were only just in time, for hardly were they outside when there was a dull explosion, and in another second the boathouse was a blazing furnace.

Copper moved towards it.

'What are you going to do?' demanded Gimlet.

'Get those fellows out.'

'Stay where you are. No one could go into that hell and live.'

This was obviously true, for they had to back farther and farther away from the fierce heat.

'It's no use wasting time here,' said Gimlet curtly. 'The cat's out of the bag. The windmill must be buzzing. Let's see what's happening there. Cub, fetch the bombs. We're likely to need them now.'

Cub ran to the osiers and returned with the bag.

'Open order, and swing away to the right so that we haven't the light of the fire behind us,' commanded Gimlet. 'Keep going until we run into opposition, then take cover. Shoot at anyone you see. The only people here beside ourselves are Wolves and that windmill is the den.'

As a matter of detail, in this statement Gimlet was not entirely correct, as was made evident when a voice, rich with honest Norfolk brogue, suddenly shouted, 'What do you fellers think you're a doin' of, eh? Come on, I want you, and you'd better come quiet like.'

Out of the smoke that was drifting across the landscape stepped a policeman, evidently the local constable.

They rushed out of the boathouse just before it blew up.

Cub smiled, for anything more utterly incongruous could hardly be imagined. What amused Cub was the police officer's calm self-assurance as, single-handed and unarmed, he stepped forward to arrest four men.

'Well, strike Old Riley!' cried Copper delightedly. 'I'll take my oath that couldn't happen nowhere else but in this country.' To the constable he said: 'What do you reckon you're goin' ter do, old cock?'

'What's a-goin' on 'ere?' demanded the constable, taking out his note-book.

'You won't want that,' Gimlet told him. Speaking quickly, in a few words he told the constable what was happening and showed his special police authority. Noting a double row of medal ribbons on the blue tunic he asked the policeman if he would help them with the operation.

'Have you got a spare rifle, sir?' asked the constable simply.

'He can have mine,' offered Trapper. 'My two six-guns and the bow will be enough for me.'

The policeman took the rifle.

Gimlet turned towards the windmill. 'Let's get 'em out,' he ordered. 'Keep your heads down. Come on.' He set off at a run.

CHAPTER SIXTEEN

Operation Complete

A s the party, now increased to five, swung out of the line of the fire
and then advanced on the final objective, it became apparent that the
windmill was occupied and that those within had observed the fate of the
boathouse.

Apart from the noise of the shots this could hardly be otherwise, for the
whole area was bathed in a lurid glow, so that even the ancient arms of
the windmill became fingers of fire. Nevertheless, thought Cub, it seemed
unlikely that those in the windmill could know just how all this had come
about, and what was even more satisfactory, they had lost their aircraft, so
that should anyone succeed in getting away from the mill he would have
no means of leaving the country.

As they approached the mill a small group of people could be seen
standing outside; indeed, one or two actually started towards the fire; but
they retired hastily when they saw strangers approaching. Then they all
disappeared from sight – presumably into the mill.

Gimlet now veered off to the right. His object in this, he told Cub who
was nearest, was to cut across the old track leading to the road, in case
there was any sort of motor vehicle at the mill. He did not think there was;
at any rate, if the Wolves possessed a car it had been very little used, or
wheel marks would have been observed by the pilots who had made the
reconnaissance. Anyway, he was taking no chances. As they reached the
track a missile of some sort thudded into the ground not far from Cub.
Gimlet heard it and brought the party to a halt, telling them to keep flat
but not to bunch together.

'There's too much light,' he averred. 'If we try to get any closer we shall be seen, and once they locate us they'll do something about it. Watch out for gas; if you notice anything that looks or smells like it, let me know. We shall be able to move nearer when that confounded fire dies down a bit. Copper, get a little over to the left; Trapper, work a bit to the right, to cover the rear of the building in case anyone tries to bolt from the far side.'

With these arrangements made the party rested, waiting for the flames of the burning boathouse to subside. Already they were not so fierce as they had been, for the structure of the actual boathouse was already consumed; what light remained was mostly caused by burning oil and petrol that floated on the surface of the water. This did not last long, although occasionally a group of dry reeds, touched by the creeping flames, burst into a minor fire, to illuminate the scene for a moment with disconcerting clarity. Watching the mill, more than once Cub thought he saw a movement in the upper part, but not being sure he did not waste ammunition. In the ordinary way, he thought, the operation of taking the mill would have presented no great difficulty, but having seen something of Werewolf methods he was afraid they might have some secret weapon which would take effect before they were aware of it. There was, too, a risk of gas, but he perceived that the employment of this would not be easy on account of the gentle breeze that sometimes stirred the grass. Either by accident, or design on Gimlet's part, they were on the upwind side of the mill, and any gas released would drift away from them.

By the end of a quarter of an hour the fire had so far died away that what little light remained was unimportant. Gimlet called Cub to him, and having told him to keep handy in case he needed the grenades, passed the order to advance.

'What do you think they're doing in there?' Cub asked him.

'I should say they're trying to make out how many there are of us here before they decide whether to bolt or fight it out,' answered Gimlet. 'They must know they've lost the aircraft. Whether or not they have any other mechanical transport remains to be seen.'

'Hello – what's happening now?' asked Cub suddenly, as smoke, increasing in volume, appeared from the lower part of the mill to drift away before the breeze. 'Can they have set the place on fire?'

'More likely they're burning secret documents or something of the sort,' replied Gimlet. 'Unless … unless they're putting up a smoke screen to cover a get-away,' he added quickly. He called urgently to Copper and ordered him to move nearer to the smoke and open fire if he saw a movement.

They waited for Copper to crawl forward to his new position; and hardly was he in place when through a thin film of smoke Cub saw a car, or a vehicle of some sort, back away from an outbuilding, turn, and then move off, travelling down the line of smoke. He shouted a warning to Copper, but he needn't have bothered. Apparently Copper had seen what Cub had seen, for he made a dash forward to a fresh position from which he could enfilade the smoke trail. The moment he stopped, his Sten gun began its vicious chatter, firing short bursts, the tracer bullets with which it was loaded cutting a white line from the muzzle into the smoke. He made another dash forward and fired again. This time the effect was apparent. A car, swaying drunkenly, appeared from the smoke, and running off the old track which it had been following, sank axle deep into the soft ground of the marsh. Copper gave it another burst, raking it from front to rear, although there was no sign of life in it. At any rate, no one attempted to get out.

'That's the green car!' called Cub, recognising the vehicle by the shape of the body.

'Aye, and I reckon I've scratched a bit more of the paint off it,' returned Copper.

Gimlet spoke to them. 'Start moving towards the mill. Keep low. Fire at anything you see moving.'

The attack advanced slowly, converging on the objective. Once Copper's gun stuttered a brisk burst. There was a tinkle of splintering glass. 'You keep your 'ead inside, chum,' he advised some person unseen by Cub.

At a distance of about forty yards Gimlet stopped again. Cub wondered what he would do. He also wondered what the people in the mill were doing; he felt they ought to be doing something, although the difficulties of defence were evident. The attackers could see their objective owing to its bulk, but those inside the mill could not see the attacking force in the darkness. Therefore, any shooting that they did would be guess work. It may be that they thought they could hold the building until daylight, when, of course, the advantage would swing round to their side, for they would then be under cover while the attacking force would find itself in the open, in full view.

Gimlet started crawling forward again and Cub kept near him. An occasional shot was now being fired from the windmill, but Gimlet gave orders that the fire was not to be returned because the flash of weapons would reveal their positions. What disturbed Cub more than the reports of gunshots was the occasional *whoof* of a gas pistol. But either these weapons were non-effective at long range or else they were entirely local in their effect, for no results could be observed.

'Pass me the bombs, Cub,' ordered Gimlet. 'I'm getting chilly. We'll make an end of this business.'

Taking the bag containing the bombs Gimlet selected two grenades – one a 'sixty-nine' concussion bomb, and the other an incendiary. 'You stay where you are, but cover me if anything starts,' he told the others. Then, cupping his hands round his mouth, he shouted: 'Hi! You, in the mill! I'll give you five minutes to come out with your hands on your heads!'

There was no answer – unless a single shot fired blindly from the upper part of the mill could be called an answer.

Gimlet waited five minutes by his watch – a weird, uneasy period. At least, so thought Cub, to whom the whole thing still wore an atmosphere of unreality.

'Time's up!' shouted Gimlet. 'You've had your chance!'

Before he could move, a door in the windmill was flung open, leaving a bright rectangle of yellow light. Against it a man could be seen running, crouching as he ran. One man at least had had enough, thought Cub. However, he did not get far. Several shots were fired from the mill in quick succession and the deserter fell. He did not get up.

When Cub looked back for Gimlet he was no longer there. Again came a period of waiting, of suspense, of brooding, sinister silence. A few minutes passed. Then the hush was broken by a crash of glass, followed an instant later by an explosion, muffled, but violent.

'That was Gimlet tossing in a pineapple,' Copper told Cub dispassion-ately.

A few seconds passed; then came another explosion, this time not so loud. A white incandescent glare lit up the inside of the mill, showing unsuspected cracks in the woodwork. It grew brighter and brighter as the incendiary bomb flared up. It took on a yellow tinge, the yellow turned to orange, and then to dull red. A mighty cloud of smoke began to drift away from the mill.

Copper crawled closer to Cub. 'Looks like 'e's done it,' he observed without emotion. 'She's on fire. That old wood'll burn like straw. I'd say the Wolves 'ave 'ad it. Any that didn't get knocked out by the concussion of that sixty-nine will look like kippers in about five minutes – unless they bolt. You can't stay in the smoke of a phosphorous bomb and stay alive. Don't I know it!'

A man dashed out of the building, bending low, his figure cast into bold relief by the brightly illuminated smoke. A revolver crashed a single shot. The man fell.

'That's one for Trapper,' said Copper evenly. 'Well, they asked for it, the skunks. Who did they reckon they were, comin' over 'ere knocking our fellers blocks off? Let's get a bit nearer. Ah! No you don't.' Copper's final remark was addressed to two more figures that sought safety in flight. His gun stammered its dreadful message. The figures spun, fell, and lay still.

The windmill was now well and truly alight, a terrible spectacle with the flames leaping skyward and the woodwork crackling like dry kindling. It turned night into day. A man jumped from one of the top windows and landed on the outbuildings with a fearful crash.

'I reckon 'e won't need no doctor,' remarked Copper.

'Don't be so callous,' chided Cub, who, now that the battle was won, could not help feeling a passing qualm for the losers.

'Callous!' cried Copper indignantly. 'I like that. You 'eard what Gimlet said? What's the use of strokin' a mad wolf?'

Cub could see Gimlet kneeling on the grass not far away so he went on and joined him. Trapper was a little to the right, crouching low so that he could see under the cloud of slowly drifting smoke in case a Wolf should attempt to use it for cover. The constable was a short distance to the left, rifle at the ready.

From a distance of thirty yards they stood and watched the end. It would not have been safe to go nearer, for explosions occurred from time to time inside the doomed building, throwing clouds of burning splinters high into the air.

'They must 'ave 'ad a fair store of bombs and ammunition in there,' remarked Copper. 'There can't be anybody left alive.'

'I fancy my first bomb must have knocked out anybody on the ground floor,' opined Gimlet.

Together they stood and watched the end. As Gimlet said, there was nothing else to do. After about five minutes Copper let out a shout and pointed down the track. Looking in that direction the others saw a strange procession approaching.

'What on earth's all this!' exclaimed Gimlet wonderingly.

'Looks like the N.F.S.,' answered Copper. 'Trust the fire brigade to turn up. What a hope they've got. Someone must have spotted the fire from the village.'

They walked over to the new arrivals. Gimlet did not interfere when the firemen ran a hose down to the lake.

'They'll be able to get in a bit of practice, anyway,' observed Copper cheerfully. 'What do we do next, sir?'

Gimlet pocketed his revolver. 'I think we might as well go home and let the General know what has happened,' he replied. 'There's nothing more we can do here, and I'm beginning to feel as if I could do with a few hours in bed. The constable can take charge of things until the General arrives to clear everything up. I imagine he'll come along as soon as he hears about it. Well, there is this. Quite a lot of fellows with death warrants in their pockets will be able to breathe more freely now.'

Gimlet called the constable and thanked him for his support; he told him to say nothing about what he had seen, and invited him to take charge until the security police arrived from London.

This the constable promised to do.

Leaving him standing there, a lone guardian of the law, they walked slowly back to the car. Little was said. There was not, after all, very much to say.

The destruction by fire of the Grimston mill, and the extermination of the enemy fanatics that occupied it, was the end of the Werewolf attempt to create a reign of terror in Britain, as had been done elsewhere in Europe. Not a word of the story appeared in the newspapers, the authorities deciding that it was better to leave the promoters of the organization in Germany to guess the fate of their accomplices.

As far as is known there were no survivors. From certain remains found, and documents in the portfolio which Gimlet had picked up in the boat-house, it seemed that the General's early remarks about the identity of the big Nazis behind the conspiracy were nearer to the truth than he may have supposed at the time. No fewer than four of the men who died in the boat-house, or in the mill, were on the list of Nazi war criminals. Apparently they thought that they were safer in Britain than in their own country, where the search for them was being prosecuted with greater diligence. One of these was Wenson, or, to give him his proper name, the notorious Hugo Stresser. The man in the fur coat was another of those mentioned by the General. This was Karl von Runtz, and it was to him that the portfolio belonged. There was reason to suppose that he was the head man of the movement, or as Copper would say, the King Wolf. From papers found in the portfolio it seemed probable that he had come over to straighten things out following the confusion caused by the raid on the London headquar-ters. If this was so, then he had reached Britain just in time to be caught in the round-up, in much the same way that Wenson had fled from London, only to perish in the flames of the old Norfolk mill.

That is as much as Gimlet and his comrades were told at the time, beyond the fact that the contents of the portfolio enabled the police of certain liber-ated countries to do a little cleaning up on their own account, rumours of which trickled through from time to time to Lorrington Hall, where the comrades were enjoying a well-earned rest, made all the more pleasant by a useful cheque received from the Home Office for 'services rendered.'

'Just what do you reckon they mean by services rendered?' inquired Copper, as he carefully folded his share and put it in his wallet. 'I don't remember rendering anything. I did the job I was asked to do and a cove can't do more than that. Am I right, Trapper?'

'*Tch*! Every time,' agreed Trapper.

'That's probably what they mean,' said Cub smiling.